Caladwo Sprigo
mey 1981

THE BOOK OF
EBENEZER LE PAGE

THE BOOK OF
EBENEZER LE PAGE

by G. B. Edwards

Introduction by John Fowles

Alfred A. Knopf   *New York*   1981

THIS IS A BORZOI BOOK
PUBLISHED BY ALFRED A. KNOPF, INC.

Library of Congress Cataloguing in Publication Data

Edwards, G B   The book of Ebenezer Le Page.

  I. Title.
PR6055.D87B6   1981   823'.914   80–2719
ISBN 0–394–51651–6

Manufactured in the United States of America

FIRST AMERICAN EDITION

Local names are used in this book; but, apart from
some topographical features and a few peripheral
figures who play no very active part in the story, are
not to be identified with places or persons of those
names, or any others, existing on the Island of
Guernsey at any time.

A note on spoken and written Guernsey English and
a Glossary of the French patois of Guernsey appear
on pages 395 and 399.

For Edward and Lisa Chaney

SARNIA CHÉRIE

Sarnia, dear Homeland, Gem of the sea,
Island of Beauty, my heart longs for Thee,
Thy voice calls me ever in waking, or sleep,
Till my Soul cries with anguish, my eyes ache to weep.
In fancy I see Thee again as of yore,
Thy verdure clad hills, and Thy wave beaten shore,
Thy rock sheltered bays, ah; of all Thou art best,
I'm returning to greet Thee, Dear Island of Rest.

I left Thee in anger, I knew not Thy worth,
Journeyed afar, to the ends of the earth,
Was told of far countries, the heaven of the hold,
Where the soil gave up diamonds, silver and gold.
The sun always shone, and 'Race' took no part,
But Thy cry always reached me, its pain wrenched my heart,
So I'm coming home, Thou of all art the best,
Returning to greet Thee, Dear Island of Rest.

Chorus

Sarnia Chérie, Gem of the sea,
Home of my childhood, my heart longs for Thee,
Thy voice calls me ever, forget Thee I'll never,
Island of Beauty, Sarnia Chérie.

G.A. Deighton

INTRODUCTION

by John Fowles

There may have been stranger recent literary events than the book you are about to read, but I rather doubt it. It is first of all posthumous, since the author, born a year older than the century, died in 1976. Then it is an only novel, seemingly not begun until he was in his late sixties. Even without those oddities, its voice and method are so unusual that it belongs nowhere on our conventional literary maps. Such a writer might at least have enjoyed the thought of a little personal publicity beyond the grave? Not at all: he made very sure before he died that any future biographer would have an exceedingly hard time of it. Mr Edward Chaney has kindly let me see a series of letters Gerald Edwards wrote to him in his last years. They tell us a good deal of the psychology and character of the man, and even something of his family background; but of his own history, next to nothing.

So far as we know it was not until 1974 that Edwards made (through Mr Chaney, to whom he gave the copyright) any attempt to have *The Book of Ebenezer Le Page* published. He bore the rejections it then received with an at least outward patient obstinacy. He more than once likened his stubbornness to that of a donkey; but this was a wise and well-read donkey, a very long way from being the innocent that a surface view of his book might suggest. He knew very well that it no more fitted contemporary literary taste (what in one of his letters he called 'helicopter thinking', judging everything 'from a superior height') than a furzebush does a greenhouse. If I cannot think much of the judgement of the various eminent London publishers who turned the typescript down in the mid 1970s, at least I can understand why they all seem to have had trouble explaining the rejection. What had landed in their nets was a very strange fish – and one, I suspect, that on a quick reading it was only too easy to place in a wrong literary species, that of the provincial novel.

I think myself that it is no more properly classifiable so than Flora Thompson's famous trilogy, *Lark Rise to Candleford*. Of course any book whose ground is the close observation of a small community risks this damning label of 'provincial'. Yet even if Edwards' account of the life and times of one Channel Islander had to be thus valued, it would still seem to me a remarkable achievement. If Guernsey feels that it has, since Victor Hugo's famous fifteen years of exile there, been rather left out in the literary cold, it need worry no more. It now has a portrait and memorial that must surely become a classic of the island.

But what Edwards does, as readers will soon realize, is to extend the empire of the book well beyond the confines of one particular island. All small islands conform their inhabitants in markedly similar ways, both socially and psychologically. On the credit side there is the fierce independence, the toughness of spirit, the patience and courage, the ability to cope and make do; on the debit, the dourness, the incest, the backwardness, the suspicion of non-islanders ... all that we mean by insularity. None of these qualities and defects is special to islands. One might argue that the 'island syndrome' occurs with increasing frequency in many of our embattled inner cities, and very much in the context of what finally becomes the major theme of this book – that is, the impact of new values on old ones, of ineluctable social evolution on individual man.

Edwards' own view is made very clear through his fictional *alter ego*. For him the new values – in local terms, all that has turned Guernsey into tourist resort and international tax haven – are anathema. They have destroyed nearly everything on the island – and by implication everywhere else – that he cherished and celebrates so well and elegiacally, beneath the plain language, in the first half of the novel. Whether Edwards was right or wrong to see more ashes than hope in progress is not, I think, what matters. What does is to have such a richly human account of what it felt like to live through the period of the book, from about 1890 to 1970.

We are still too close to it to realize what an astounding and unprecedented change, unprecedented both in its extent and its speed, has taken place in the psyche of Western mankind during those eighty years. In very many ways, and certainly for the working-class majority, the late 19th century remained closer to the 17th than to our own. It is only the very old now who can fully understand this: what it means to have known, in the one lifespan, both a time when city streets were full of horses, the car not yet invented, and a time when man stood on the moon; or even more incomprehensibly, both a time when even the most terrible weapons could kill a few hundred at most, and a time when their power risks entire cities – and their aftermath, whole countries.

It is almost as if in those same eighty years we left the old planet and found a new; and we are all, however brashly contemporary, however much we take modern technology for granted, still victims of that profound cultural shock. One symptom of it is the recurrent recrudescence of conservatism (and in far more than politics) in the second half of this century. We have at least realized we made a very clumsy landing on our new planet, and also left a number of things behind on the old that we might have done better to bring with us – qualities very close to that list of traditional island virtues I mentioned just now.

This inability to forget the old, this querulousness over the new, is what makes Ebenezer Le Page such a convincing portrayal of a much more universal mentality than the matter of the book might at first sight suggest. Edwards himself recognized this when he wrote that Ebenezer 'expresses from the inside out the effects of world events'. His novel is really far more about the impress of recent human history on one fallible but always honest individual than about Guernsey and its traditional manners and mores, fascinating and amusing though those often are to read.

The ubiquitous contempt for England and the English (and outsiders in general, even the sister Channel Island of Jersey) must similarly be taken in a metaphorical way. The encroachment is of infinitely more than ugly holiday bungalows and tourist dross, of greedy entrepreneurs and tax-evaders; it is essentially upon the individual mind, and therefore upon individual freedom. To those who want a homogenized world (because such worlds are easier to manipulate) Ebenezer is an eternal thorn in the side. He may seem an exceedingly unfashionable reactionary about a number of things, including woman. But his saving grace is that he is equally reactionary about anything that tries to occupy, as the Nazis did Guernsey in the last war, the island of the self. He is much more against than he is ever for, and that kind of againstness, or bloody-mindedness, however irritating it may be in some circumstances, is a very precious human (and evolutionary) commodity. Provincialism is not merely lacking city taste in arts and manners; it is also an increasingly vital antidote to all would-be central tyrannies. To give such a convincing illustration of this ubiquitous contradiction, this eternal suspicion at the less articulate base of society, is one of Edwards' major achievements.

Another seems to me a technical one, and that is the creation of such an intensely colloquial speech, with its piquant French undertones, for his hero. Even more remarkable is his almost total reliance on it – how he manages, despite the general absence of normal linear narrative, despite the way characters meander almost haphazardly in and out of his pages, despite the minute stitch of social detail, to carry us through with him, at times to the point where we no longer care how inconsequential or digressive the story becomes, as long as that voice is still speaking. I can think of very few novels where this extremely difficult device, of the prolonged reminiscence, is worked so well.

Edwards' choice of it was quite deliberate. He spoke several times of the 'circular form' of the book, of its 'indirection'. On another occasion he said 'Writing has for me, I think, always to be done obliquely ... it feels to me phony when I'm not allowing an incubus to speak in a circumstantial context'. He also revealed that 'the beginning and the end were conceived simultaneously ... the book grew out of the pivotal image of the gold under the apple-tree'. That may have been true thematically; but the literary gold was buried in the voice of the incubus. We may note too that Edwards always thought of the patois as his native language. His deep regard for Joseph Conrad was not purely literary. Here was another exile forced to write in an 'acquired' English.

Two other things must be said. One is that Edwards never received expert editorial advice. This is most noticeable at the very end, where one senses that he begins to identify too closely with Ebenezer, and surrenders to a common impulse among novelists: the wish to reward his surrogate, or hero, with a distinctly sentimental ending. This was pointed out to him, but he refused to change his text. He wrote that the aged Ebenezer 'sees in a romantic glow. I don't; and the reader should not'. Perhaps here the 'Guernsey donkey' was sticking his heels in a shade too firmly; but even a professional editor might have had some difficulty in persuading him to wear less final heart on his sleeve. Mr Chaney once sent Edwards a copy of Wyndham Lewis's *The Lion and The Fox*, and the judgement in return showed no mercy. After condemning Lewis for his slipshod scholarship and 'his rasping, harsh, abusive manner', Edwards went on: 'It all adds up to no more than a chaos of logical positivist deductions, heartless and intellectual ... "romantic" is not a dirty word, you know.'

The second thing to be said is that the present book was to form the first part of a trilogy. The second and third were to be called *Le Boud'lo: the Book of Philip le Moigne* and *La Gran'-mère du Chimquière: the Book of Jean le Féniant*.* Edwards left enough hints in his letters to make it plain that he saw the first part as something of a humorous contrast to the other two. Readers may be interested to know that Neville Falla, the cause of much of the final sentimentality here, was in fact earmarked for an early death in the second part, and that its tone was to be much more tragic than comic. Edwards himself remarked wrily of it: 'I will certainly thereby graduate out of the charm school.'

But the main virtues sit to a rare extent in each page, each episode, each character, in the waywardness of memory, in the accuracy and strength of evocation within the strictly imposed linguistic means. What Edwards was aiming for is expressed in a passage of the same letter in which he

---

* Literally, 'The Puppet: the Book of Philip the Amputated' and 'The Grandmother of the Cemetery: the Book of John the Sluggard'. Edwards' full title for the present book was *Sarnia Chérie: the Book of Ebenezer Le Page*, in symmetry with the other two. The first phrase has been dropped in this edition because of the unfortunate connotations of *chérie* to English ears and the general ignorance of Sarnia – the Latin name for Guernsey. The phrase was not of Edward's invention. 'Sarnia Chérie,' beloved Guernsey, is the island's private anthem. There is incidentally a short essay by Edwards on the patois of Guernsey at the end of the book, to which I have added a glossary of the more difficult words in the text.

damns Wyndham Lewis. He praises Conrad by contrast for remaining 'within a human and material continuum; but masterfully with controlled passion and exquisite tenderness'. It was clearly this sort of quality that he found so lacking in an age of helicopter thinking and that also helped explain for him why his own book found so little sympathy among publishers' readers. Elsewhere he defined its purpose as 'humanizing'; and to that end, he realized that it had to risk things that no trend-conscious novelist today would care to risk his reputation on, just as in some ways it had to stay resolutely old-fashioned and simple-tongued. But that is precisely what I like most about it. It seems to me, beyond all its more obvious achievements and attractions, beyond its occasional lapses into cantankerousness and sentimentality, an act of courage; and of a kind that can never be old-fashioned if the novel, and the free society of which it is still the deepest artistic expression, are to survive.

*

'The mere thought of having a public image appals me.' 'I would not willingly supply the public with any autobiographical data whatever.' 'I'd rather be a hermit-crab than live *en famille*.' 'By the way I've got rid of all fragments, correspondence and records (except for those essential for my official survival).' So Gerald Edwards wrote in various letters to Edward Chaney; the last quotation comes from one written six months before he died. Mrs Joan Snell, with whom Edwards stayed in the final five years of his life and who has kindly relented a little over one of his last instructions to her (that she should stand 'like a dragon' in the path of any future researcher), tells me the holocaust was total: only his birth certificate and – touchingly, as will shortly be seen – a photograph of his mother were spared. Nor was this an isolated act of self-destruction.

Gerald Basil Edwards was born on July 8, 1899. He gave an account of his family past in a letter to Edward Chaney, and it is worth citing at some length. Dalwood, a small village near Axminster in East Devon, was long blessed or notorious locally (depending on one's religious viewpoint) for being a breeding-ground of dissenters.

'The earliest ancestor I know of on my father's side was Zackariah Edwards of Dalwood, Devon, who married a gipsy and begat a brood of stalwart sons, who migrated to every quarter of the globe. He was my great-grandfather. My grandfather, Tom, married one Mary Organ of Honiton and migrated to Guernsey at the age of 19 for the "stone-rush", when the quarries of the north were opened. It was a hard life. My father, the eldest son, also Tom, was born on Guernsey, but at twelve ran away from his strap-wielding father and his mother, who had a bosom of iron, to the softer usages of sailing ships. He sailed and "saw the world" until he came home and married at the age of 26. He wouldn't have come home then, except that he never overcame his tendency to sea-sickness. He worked for his father, who was by now a quarry-owner, and in due course inherited the quarry and the house, Sous les Hougues, where I was born. I was the only child of his second marriage ... my mother died in 1924. A couple of years later he married the housekeeper and sold up to disinherit me, buying another property which he could legally leave her. Hence my exile. (It won't make sense to you; but it's Guernsey law.) He was a very tough man, my father: with a very tender core. He was passionately attached to Guernsey and refused to leave before the Occupation. He lived for more than a year after the Liberation and must have been well over ninety when he died. I have to be vague on this, for it was not considered decent for a Guernsey child to know the precise age of its parents. I was only truly in touch with him on one occasion; and that was in 1938, the year of the Munich Crisis, when I visited him at Les Rosiers, where he ran a small growing concern, the quarry being worked out. He was rather humiliated, though over 80, by being reduced to so effete an occupation. He regarded quarrying granite as the only work fit for a man.

'My mother was a Mauger. I cannot claim she was pure Guernsey, for the purest Guernsey are Neolithic ...

'My boyhood, adolescence and young manhood was an increasingly intense fight to the death against my mother; and indeed all my relationships with women have been a fight to the death. I survive, but in grief; for I have sympathy with what I fight against, and sorrow at the necessity. That should make clear to you my disorientation from Lawrence, with whom in other ways I have much in common ... underneath I am steel against the female will. I do not mean the feminine nature. D. H. submitted. To my mind, his is the saddest story. The White Peacock becomes the flaming uterus of Lady C. They are the same. The Phoenix is swamped.'

I should add that in fact very few names could be purer Guernsey than Mauger; it goes back to Norman times. Edwards must have savoured the possibility of descent from the first member of the clan, who is said to have been banished to the island by William the Conqueror for having had the temerity to suggest that no good would come of adding the perfidious English to his subject peoples.

In 1909 Edwards won a scholarship from the Hautes Capelles primary to the States Intermediate School, now the boys' grammar-school of the island. In 1914 he was made a pupil-teacher at Vauvert School, St Peterport. A contemporary remembers how Edwards was 'a real loner, an odd sort of character who never had any friends'. In 1917 he joined the Royal Guernsey Light Infantry. He never saw active service, but ended in Portsmouth as a sergeant instructor of gunnery. Between 1919 and 1923 he was at Bristol University, but neither subject nor degree can be traced. It seems from the above letter that he placed himself in permanent exile from Guernsey about 1926. In this period he worked for the university settlement of Toynbee Hall in London and also joined the Workers' Educational Association as a lecturer in English literature and drama. He apparently also had a spell with the Bolton Repertory Company, and wrote plays for them. At some point he got to know Middleton Murry, and through him met Frieda Lawrence. That manifestation of 'the female will' he recalled frequently to Edward Chaney, with a predictable blend of fascination and repulsion. He told Mrs Snell that he had also known Tagore and Annie Besant quite well.

By 1930 he was married. A survived document of that year reveals that he was living in Hornsey; and he gave his profession as 'author'. The marriage was not a success, and he seems to have gone abroad to Holland and Switzerland in the early 1930s to try to earn his living by his pen – articles and poetry, as well as plays. He told Mrs Snell that he destroyed much of his best work, including 'a very good play'. Like many, perhaps all, writers he remained a manic-depressive about his work throughout his life.

His marriage finally broke down about 1933. One of its four children tells me that her father disappeared entirely from her life between that date and 1967, and the gap had become too great by the time the relationship was renewed to be very successfully bridged. Even to her, very little was ever said of the past. Where or how Edwards spent the next years (the Toynbee Hall records were severely war-damaged) is not known; but during the Second World War he worked in an employment exchange and he seemingly remained a civil servant (in 1955 he was living in Balham) until retirement in 1960.

The storm-petrel then went to 'live rough' in Wales for a year; from 1961, he spent three years in Penzance; from 1964, three years in Plymouth; and in 1967 moved on to Weymouth. In that latter year he told his daughter that the first draft of this book was completed, and the second part, *Le Boud'lo*, half done. He also spoke of returning to Guernsey 'to die', but one may guess that the high cost of living – and property – on the island made that impossible for a man of his limited means; and perhaps added a bitterness to both his book and his exile. That his sense of the latter remained very real can be deduced from the move to Weymouth – the nearest place one can be to Guernsey on the English mainland.

In 1970 he became Mrs Snell's lodger in 'the small room of a large house' at Upwey, just outside Weymouth. Mrs Cynthia Mooney, a Guernsey woman herself, remembers the room as 'like that of a monk'. It was 'very tidy, terribly tidy'. Edwards himself wrote in 1972 that 'I live from day to day, at the edge of living'. But the general impresssion given from his letters to Mr Chaney is not of crabbed misery, but of a kind of tart serenity of soul, an acceptance of ascetic outsiderdom. The tartness – 'My dislike of Heath, like my aversion to television, is almost pathological' – did not spare anything or anyone surrendered to what Edwards saw as false values; on the other hand his affection, when it was given, was unmistakably sincere and unstinting. One can assume that the very similar combination of traits in Ebenezer was closely autobiographical.

The vital new encounter for him in this last period was undoubtedly with Edward Chaney and his wife. Their sympathetic encouragement made him entirely re-write this book, a task he undertook in 1973 and 1974. He continued revising it until the end. Mr Chaney thinks there were never more than brief drafts for the rest of the intended trilogy; and most of those Edwards seems to have destroyed before he died. Once or twice he showed a restlessness, a need to escape Weymouth (and a truly remarkable willingness in a man of his age to travel light); but these fugues to the Scillies and the Orkneys ended back in Upwey. The letters show an impressive blend of honesty and self-humour, besides a frequent Orwellian excellence of plain English prose. They would do very well as a contemporary appendix to the Grub Street side of Dr Johnson's *Lives of the English Poets*, and I hope that one day Mr Chaney will consider publishing parts of them.

Joan Snell sums up her recollections of him thus: 'He was a man of dynamic character, yet full of feeling and sympathy. Proud but humble, he had a superb memory. He could remember conversations of fifty or sixty years before, word for word. He hated machines, modern technology, he thought they had brought so many bad things into the world. He needed nothing, and lived on a small pension. All he possessed could be packed in a small suitcase. He was charming and endearing; he was despairing and moody. A man of heights; and of deepest, blackest depths. I cannot do him justice in a short comment. All I can say is that it was a great privilege to have known him.'

Gerald Edwards died after a heart attack, in his small room near Weymouth, on December 29, 1976. His ashes were scattered at sea. I should like to think that some at least were washed up among the *vraic* and granite of his long-lost native shore.

John Fowles, 1980

The Property of Neville Falla

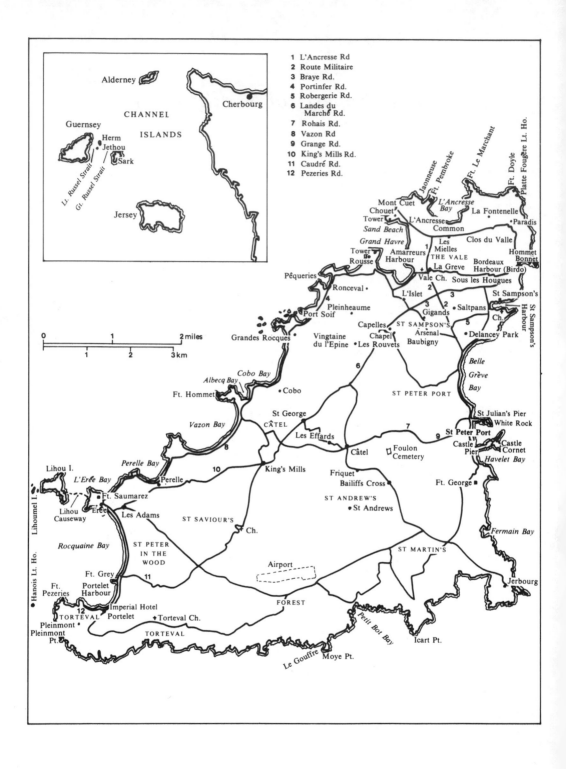

1 L'Ancresse Rd
2 Route Militaire
3 Braye Rd.
4 Portinfer Rd.
5 Robergerie Rd.
6 Landes du Marché Rd.
7 Rohais Rd.
8 Vazon Rd
9 Grange Rd.
10 King's Mills Rd.
11 Caudré Rd.
12 Pezeries Rd.

Alderney

Cherbourg

CHANNEL
ISLANDS

Guernsey
Herm
Jethou
Sark

Lt. Russel Strait
Gt. Russel Strait

Jersey

Jaonneuse
Ft. Pembroke
Ft. Le Marchant
Ft. Doyle
Platte Fougère Lt. Ho.

Mont Cuet
Chouet
Tower
L'Ancresse Bay
L'Ancresse
Common
La Fontenelle
Paradis
Sand Beach
Grand Havre
Les Mielles
Clos du Valle
Hommet
Bonnet
Tower
Rousse
Amarreurs
Harbour
THE VALE
La Greve
Bordeaux
Harbour (Birdo)

Pêqueries
Ronceval
Vale Ch.
Sous les Hougues
L'Islet
St Sampson's
Port Soif
Pleinheaume
Gigands
Saltpans
St Sampson's Harbour
Grandes Rocques
Vingtaine
du l'Epine
Capelles
Chapel
Les Rouvets
St SAMPSON'S
Arsenal
Baubigny
Delancey Park

Cobo Bay
Albecq Bay
Ft. Hommet
Cobo
Belle
Grève
Bay
St PETER PORT

Vazon Bay
St George
CÂTEL
Les Effards
St Julian's Pier
White Rock

0   1   2 miles
1   2   3 km

Lihou I.
L'Erée Bay
Ft. Saumarez
Perelle Bay
Perelle
Les Adams
Erée
10
King's Mills
Câtel
Foulon
Cemetery
7
9
St Peter Port
Castle
Pier
Castle
Cornet
Havelet Bay
Ft. George
Friquet
Bailiffs Cross
St ANDREW'S
St Andrews

Lihoumel I.
Lihou
Causeway
ST SAVIOUR'S
Ch.
ST PETER
IN THE
WOOD
Fermain Bay

Hanois Lt. Ho.
Rocquaine Bay
Ft. Grey
11
Portelet Harbour
Airport
ST MARTIN'S
Jerbourg

Ft.
Pezeries
12
TORTEVAL
Imperial Hotel
Portelet
Torteval Ch.
FOREST
Pleinmont
Pleinmont
Pt.
TORTEVAL
Petit Bot Bay
Icart Pt.
Le Gouffre
Moye Pt.

PART ONE

1

Guernsey, Guernesey, Garnsai, Sarnia: so they say. Well, I don't know, I'm sure. The older I get and the more I learn, the more I know I don't know nothing, me. I am the oldest on the island, I think. Liza Quéripel from Pleinmont say she is older; but I reckon she is putting it on. When she was a young woman, she used to have a birthday once every two or three years; but for years now she have been having two or three a year. To tell you the truth, I don't know how old I am. My mother put it down on the front page of the big Bible; but she put down the day and the month, and forgot to put down the year. I suppose I could find out if I went to the Greffe; but I am not going to bother about that now.

My father was killed in the Boer War. He went off and joined the Irish Brigade and fought for the Boers. His name is with the others who died for their country on the monument was put up in St Julien's Avenue and unveiled by the Duke of Connaught. I remember that day well, because me and Jim Mahy, my chum, went to Town to see it unveiled. It was drizzling in the morning and, by the evening, the rain was coming down in dollops. It put out the Chinese lanterns was all the way along Glatney and the fairy lights right to the end of the White Rock. There was an illuminated barge in the Pool, where the Band of the Militia was going to play; but it was a wreck. I thought it was going to be lovely to hear music coming over the water. They tried their best; but they had to give up. The Duke of Connaught was all right, him: he was indoors out of the rain, eating and drinking.

I was a young man already when my father died; yet I can't see his face now, what he looked like. I have seen his photo in the Family Album, of when he was a young man. He was wearing a braided jacket and trousers wide at the bottom; and he had a thick moustache and his hair done in a curl across his forehead. He looked as if he got a spice of the devil in him. I don't know how he came to marry my mother. She was a good woman. She read the Bible day and night and, towards the end, when she got so big she couldn't move, she did hardly anything else.

She had been a handsome woman in her time, going by her photo of before she was married. She had straight black hair parted in the middle and done in a chignon at the back of her neck; and was in a black dress from under her chin to the tips of her toes, and wore a bustle. When she was a widow, she wore a black crêpe veil over her face for a year; and then went into half mourning and put a mauve flower in her bonnet. I never heard her speak of my father as 'Alf', or 'Alfred', or 'my husband'; but only as 'the father of Ebenezer and Tabitha': me and my sister. When she said anything to me my father had said, it was always 'according to your father'; and the way she said it made me think he was something I had done wrong. The only time I ever heard her speak of 'my husband' was once when she said to me, 'Your father was my husband in the flesh: he was not of the Household of Faith.'

The trouble was he was Church and she was Chapel. She didn't mind being married Church. As she said, 'After all, marriage is only for a few years'; but she made him promise that if she was the first to go, he would see to it she was buried Chapel. She didn't want there to be any mistake later on. For some reason, she turned against the Wesleyans soon after she was married, and joined the Brethren. There was two lots of Brethren: the Open Brethren and the Closed Brethren. She joined the Open first; but they sang the hymns with a harmonium, and she said that was sinful because the first musical instrument was made by Jubal, who was of the offspring of Cain. So she changed over to the Closed. They sang the hymns only from their hearts and prayed and read the Bible and preached and broke bread. She said theirs was the pure milk of the Word.

There wasn't no rows in our house, mind you. My father didn't come home drunk and swear and knock my mother about like Dan Ferbrache and Amy from Sandy Hook. There was very few words spoken in our house. My mother would say 'Will you do that?' and my father would say 'Yes'; or my father would say 'Can I do this?' and my mother would say 'No'. He was only home to eat his supper and go to bed; except for Saturday afternoons and Sundays. He worked for old Tom Mauger from Sous les Hougues in the Queen's quarry from seven in the morning to six at night, and took his dinner with him in a tin, and a can of tea he kept warm by the stove in the tool-house. He was a good quarryman. In the summer, when he worked a quarter overtime, he would come home of a Friday night with as much as twenty-five bob in his pocket. We wasn't poor, you know: we didn't go without and always managed to save.

I used to go to work with my father some days: that is, before I was big enough to go to school. I liked going to the quarry with my father. He would sit me on the horse in the horse-box and I would go right down into the pit. When the gun went dinner-time, I had to climb the ladder up the side, because the horse ate from his nose-bag and didn't come up for dinner. My father would be behind me on the ladder shouting 'Va t'en, fényion! Va t'en, donc!' I wasn't afraid. I knew if I was to fall, he would catch me. The dinner-hour I'd sit in the tool-house with the men and have a sip of his tea and a bite of his dinner; then he would take me down to St Sampson's to see the ships. St Sampson's Harbour was full of sailing ships those days, and there would be three or four anchored in the Roads outside, waiting to come in. I couldn't make up my mind if I wanted to work down the quarry, or go to sea when I grew up; but sail was fast giving way to steam, and when it was nearly all steam-boats in St Sampson's Harbour I didn't have the same feeling for going to sea.

In the afternoon he would leave me with Fred Tucker, the crane-driver. I liked being with Fred Tucker in the cabin of the crane. He would let me pull the lever that started the machinery to go. 'Look, you're bringing up a load!' he'd say; and when it came up out of the quarry, he would swing the jib round and lower the cart until the wheels touched the ground. There would be a horse and driver waiting to take it to Mowlem's cracking-machine on the North Side. The North was busy those days with the humming of the cracking-machines and the rumbling of the iron tyres of the heavy carts on the roads. When the time came to knock off, I was dog-tired and could hardly put one foot in front of the other. My father had to carry me on his shoulders most of the way home.

Saturdays he came home for dinner at one o'clock and, in the afternoon, worked in the back garden; or went out fishing in our boat. I liked going out fishing in the boat with my father. He let me pull the rudder. 'If you pull that way, the boat will go this way,' he'd say, 'if you pull this way, the boat will go that.' I got the idea. After tea, he would wash himself all over in front of the fire, while my mother got me and my sister ready in the other room to go to Town. He would have the pony harnessed and the trap waiting by the time my mother was satisfied us two was fit to be seen. It was a high trap with thin wheels and a narrow seat; and my father used to sit at one end and my mother at the other and me in the middle with my sister at my feet. It was a heavy load for poor old Jack.

On Sundays my father wasn't allowed to work out-of-doors, but had to sit by the grate and watch the potatoes didn't boil dry and the meat didn't burn in the oven, while my mother and Tabitha was gone to Morning Service. Once he forgot and didn't take the potatoes off; and that was the only time I ever saw my mother lose her temper. Other times, if he did wrong, she would give a big sigh; but that was all. This time she went for him and told him she couldn't trust him out of her sight. It was his fault really. He would forget everything else in the world once he got his head stuck in his old newspaper. It was a pink paper called the *Police Budget*, which he used to buy from Tozer in Smith Street on the Saturday night; and it had pictures in it of all the murders they do in England: women with their throats cut and blood all over the bed! It was always a heavy dinner Sundays and, if my father could have had his way, he would have had a nap after; but my mother made him change into his best clothes and sit on the sofa in the front room, in case any of our relations came to tea. I don't like to think of my father those Sunday afternoons. I like to think of him in the quarry, where he was respected by the men and might have become a foreman, if he had lived.

La Tabby, as we called my sister, was put to bed early of a Sunday evening, and my mother went to Evening Service on her own. As soon as she was out of the front gate, my father would say, 'Come along, son: let's go mitchin'!' and we'd go out to the shed at the back and take the lamp, if it was dark. He kept his chisels and hammers and saw out there; and wood and glue and string. It was those Sunday nights he taught me how to make kites. I always had the best kite of any of the boys who flew kites on L'Ancresse Common; and everybody knew it was mine, because it was covered with the pink paper of the *Police Budget* and all the women with their throats cut went up flying in the sky. When my mother came in, we would both be back indoors sitting like two angels, one each side the fire.

He had been all over the world, my father. He didn't have any schooling to speak of, but knocked round with the Noyon and the Corbet boys of Birdo in the pilot boats; and at the age of twelve he went to sea. He rose from cabin boy to second mate, and yet he came back and settled down in Guernsey. It is true he had a nice little house to come to, when his father died; but it wasn't only that. I have seen the same happen to dozens of Guernsey boys. They're just busting to get away from the island; and, when they do get away, they're breaking their hearts to come back. That's why I have never left Guernsey, me. I knew I would only end up where I begun.

It was funny my father going off to fight in a war when he didn't have to; but he had some funny ideas in his head. He wasn't against the English; but he thought they was wrong to be against the Irish and the Boers. Of course, he didn't talk about such things to my mother; but I heard him talking it over with his young brother, my Uncle Willie. My father thought the world of his young brother. Willie was a great sportsman and won the championship cup three years running at the Cycling Track. His Photo was in Bucktrout's window down High Street, standing by his penny-farthing bicycle, which was nearly as high as him, with the big silver cup at his feet. He laughed at my father for bothering about what was going to happen to the Boers. 'Look after Number One, Alf,' he said, 'and let the world manage its own affairs.'

He didn't manage his own affairs very well, my Uncle Willie. He was gardener for Mr Roger de Lisle from the Grange and a friend of the son and lived in the house: then if he didn't let himself be dragged into getting engaged to a girl Le Couture from St Martin's. The evening before the wedding he said he was going to shoot rabbits on Jerbourg. When long after dark he didn't come back, young de Lisle went to look for him and found him shot dead through the head. It was decided at the inquest it was an accident; but everybody knew he had done it on purpose. He was used to handling a gun from a boy, and had won prizes at Bisley. I knew why he had done it, the poor chap. He did the brave thing. After waiting a year, the Le Couture girl married old Cohu from Les Petites Caches for his second wife and he left her well off.

I will say for my mother she was not vainglorious for the things of this world; but there was one thing she was proud of. I often heard her say to people 'When I marry, I do not change my name, me.' It was true. She was a Le Page and my father was a Le Page; but, as she said, he was no relation. He was a Le Page from the Clos-du-Valle and his people all had to do with the sea. His great-grandfather, Captain Alf Le Page, was Master of the schooner *Daisy*; and Captain Alf Le Page's brother, Dick, was the famous Richard Le Page who served under Admiral Lord de Saumarez and got killed at the Battle of the Nile. When the quarries was opened in the North, there was good money to be made; and my grandfather, who was no higher than a cook aboard ship, gave up going to sea and worked in the Chouey quarry. He can't have done too bad. It was him built Les Moulins, where I have lived all my life. It is built of solid, blue Guernsey granite and will last for ever. It ought to, too. It cost a hundred pounds; and that's a lot of money.

There was plenty of talk about a great-uncle of mine, the brother of my grandfather. He came home from sea with a woman who called herself Bella Devine. Nobody knew who she was, or where she come from. She preached in the Seaman's Bethel on the Banks; and they lived in the dirtiest of a row of dirty old cottages by the Vale Church. He used to pick up the horse-droppings by the gate of L'Ancresse Common in a gelignite box on two wheels to put on his garden. I wasn't supposed to know he was a relation; but when I saw him, I used to say 'Hullo, Uncle!'

There was nobody people could talk about much in my mother's family; unless it was her brother. She was of the Le Pages from the Câtel, who was pretty well-to-do growers and farmers; though some of them did a bit of fishing as well. Anyhow, they was thought of as good people and well spoken-of. Her father was Nicholas Le Page of Les Sablons, Cobo; who was the son of Eliazar Le Page; who was the son of Obadiah Le Page; who was the son of Thomas Le Page, who was converted to Christianity by John Wesley, when he landed on Guernsey. Les Sablons wasn't as good a house as ours. It was built of bricks and mortar and whitewashed, and had rooms only one side of the front door; but it had a room upstairs with a dormer window, and a room in the wing. It is there to this day; but I don't know who live in it now.

Nicholas Le Page, my grandfather, was a local preacher and dropped dead from a stroke in the pulpit of the Capelles Chapel. I don't remember him. My grandmother was a widow as long as I can remember. She was a tiny little woman and wore big sabots and a big scoop. I liked my little grandmother. She went to Chapel regular, but you would never have thought she was religious: she would do anything for anybody, it didn't matter who they was. She was dying of cancer and when I went along to see how she was, she would reach up and pick me a fig off the fig-tree because she knew I liked figs, although it hurt her to do it. I especially liked to go the day she was making bread. I would help her to cut the furze, and watch her set fire to it in the oven in the wall. She always put a small loaf on a hot stone only for me; so I could have one all to myself. She didn't speak the English, and could only read the Bible in French. My mother spoke the English a little, and the big Bible was in English.

My mother was the eldest of the family. After her came two or three who died, and then my Uncle Nathaniel, or Nat, as he was called. I liked my Uncle Nat. He was gay and good-looking and spent his time fishing and drinking and playing cards with the boys round Albecq and Vazon, and chasing after the girls. He had no respect for his father. One day, the Reverend Dumond, Pastor of the Capelles Chapel, knocked on the front door and, when Nat opened it, asked where his father was. He answered, 'Aw, he's round the back in the pigsty: he's the one with the hat on.' When my mother told me that terrible story, I forgot myself and bust out laughing; yet I would never have said that about my own father, because he wasn't a pig.

After my Uncle Nat came twins, who died, and then the two younger sisters, Priscille and Henriette, or La Prissy and La Hetty, as they was called. There was five years between them and they married the eldest and the youngest of the Martel boys, sons of Harold Martel of Ronceval, the builder. The Martels of Ronceval was quite well-to-do: but the older one, Harold, married the younger sister, Hetty, who was years younger than him; and the younger one, Percy, married the older sister, Prissy, who was years older than him. It wasn't at all the way I would have arranged it, if it had been me.

The most terrible thing was what happened to my Uncle Nat. He wasn't forty yet when he lost his strength and went funny in the head; though there was some people with bad tongues who said it was only because he was too lazy to work. He would lie on the green-bed all day long sewing pictures of boats on canvas with coloured wools. They was pictures of wild mad boats on wild mad seas, and came to his sisters when he died. There is one on the wall in front of me at this moment; and sometimes I think it is better than a real boat on a real sea.

I had a load of great-aunts; but the only one who had anything to leave was my great-aunt Sarah. She was my mother's aunt, her father's sister;

and they said she was mad too. She lived in a big house among a lot of trees at the Hougue Chaunée, and had a paid companion to look after her. It was a great worry in the family for years who she was going to leave her money to. My mother took me and Tabitha to show to her; and La Prissy and La Hetty took theirs, though La Hetty's wasn't much to show. My mother explained to us before we went that it was not for her sake she was taking us, but for ours: so as we might have that which was needful in this world and be beholden to no man. My great-aunt was wrapped up in a shawl and looked like an old bird, sitting in her chair by the fire. All Tabitha could say was 'Ooo!' and look at her with big eyes. I didn't say a word because my mother had told me I mustn't open my mouth, or I would be sure to say the wrong thing.

Anyhow, my great-aunt gave orders that all her money was to be given to her in pound notes, so as she could burn it; because none of her relations was worth leaving it to. That was when the de Garis girl, who was her paid companion, was clever. She gave her pieces of paper cut to the size of pound notes; and my great-aunt would sit for hours throwing them one by one on the fire, and laughing and laughing at the thought of all the money going up in smoke her nieces and their brats wasn't going to have. That's why they said she was mad; but I think she knew what she was doing as well as I do. When she died and was buried and the will was read, it turned out she had left everything to the Presbyterian minister.

It say in the Bible 'Look unto the rock whence ye are hewn, and to the hole of the pit whence ye are digged.' Well, those people are the rock whence I was hewn, and the hole of the pit whence I was digged. I haven't said nothing about my cousins, and the cousins of my cousins; but then half the island is my cousins, and the cousins of my cousins.

2

I had a good education, me. I went to the Vale School for Boys until I was twelve. I can see the old schoolroom yet: the broken-down desks and the worn-out forms with knots in that got stuck into your backside and the picture of the old Queen on the wall and of Jesus Christ walking on the water and the jam-jar of tadpoles on the windowsill. The Headmaster was Mess Henri Falla from La Moye. He taught us Scripture first lesson in the morning; and Reading, Writing and Arithmetic later in the day. The Scripture didn't count. All we had to do was to sit still and listen, and it went in one ear and out the other; but Reading, Writing and Arithmetic we had to learn. Mess Falla was a good schoolmaster: he taught with the stick in his hand. If I said '2 and 2 is 5', he would shout 'Come out, Le Page E!' There was Le Page A, B, C, D, E, F, and G in the school. I was Le Page E. 'Bend over! Touch your toes!' he would say: '2 and 2 is 4!' Whack! Whack! Whack! 'That'll learn you!' It did, you know. He didn't do it to hurt.

Miss Emily Tostevin did, though. She had a down on me. I don't know what for, I'm sure; because I never said a word. I would just sit with my arms folded and look at her. She said I was cheeky. 'Come out in front for impudence, Ebenezer Le Page,' she'd say. I would go out in front: bend over, touch my toes. She thought that was rude. 'Stand up!' she'd say. 'Hold out your hand: your LEFT hand!' She would only hit boys on their left hand, or, after, they made out they couldn't write. She didn't use a cane, but the edge of a ruler; and, golly, she knew how to hurt with it, too! I learnt the trick of holding my hand out sideways and lowering it the same time as the ruler came down: then I would rub it hard under my arm-pit and wrinkle up my face as if I was going to cry, so as she wouldn't know it hadn't hurt much.

She taught us History, Geography and Nature Study. History was dates. I have forgotten most of it now, but I know it began in 55 B.C. when Julius Caesar landed in Britain; and I remember A.D. 1066, because that was the year we conquered England. Geography was the countries and capitals of Europe and the capes and bays of England. Some of the countries of Europe have changed since then, I think; but, as far as I know, the capes and bays of England are the same. Nature Study was the only thing I did right for Miss Tostevin. She gave me ten out of ten once for my composition on 'The Life of The Frog'.

I had to go to Sunday School as well. That was a nuisance. I would much rather have been flying my kite on the Common, or gone down on the beach; but I wasn't allowed to fly my kite on a Sunday, and if you went down on the beach, people said you was a heathen. There was one good thing about Sunday School; and that was there was nothing you had to learn. They made you sing hymns: 'Onward, Christian soldiers!' or 'Fight the good fight with all thy might!' or 'Trust-and-obey-there-is-no-other way-to-be-happy-in-Jesus-but-to-trust-and-obey', while they took up a collection for Foreign Missions. My father used to give me a penny for that; and I always put it in the box. I was honest. The Headmaster, he was called the Superintendent, prayed and read a chapter from the Bible; and then there was Announcements, but I never listened to those. After that came the Lesson. The boys was sorted out, a dozen or more in a class according to their ages; and each class sat on forms making three sides of a square. The Sunday School teacher sat on a chair in the open side and told the class a story with a moral.

I got into bad trouble at Sunday School. There was boys and girls in the same room in that school, the boys on one side and the girls on the other; and down the middle of the room the boys' classes and the girls' classes was back to back. A Mr Johns from on the Bridge was our teacher, I remember; and he had a long straggly moustache, and when he spoke he spat. I had to sit right back so as not to have a shower of his spit all over me. It happened on that Sunday I was sitting back to back with Marie Le Noury. I thought she was lovely. She was wearing a tight blue velvet frock and was well developed for a girl and had rosy cheeks and sly black eyes; and when I looked round, she looked round and smiled at me with those sly black eyes. I thought I would write her a little note. I had a stub of pencil in my pocket and tore a page out the back of my hymn-book and wrote, 'Je t'aime, Marie.' I dug her in the ribs and she took the note and the pencil. I thought she would write back 'Je t'aime, Ebenezer', but instead I heard her saying, 'Look, Miss Collas, what one of the boys has given to me!'

Her teacher was a Miss Collas from The Hermitage. She was an old maid and I am not surprised. She looked as if she had been brought up on the vinegar bottle. Mr Johns stopped telling his story with a moral and all the other classes stopped listening to their teachers. 'Who gave you this?' said Miss Collas. 'Him!' said Marie and turned round and pointed to me. My heart broke. Miss Collas was holding my poor little love-letter with the tips of her fingers, as if it was too dirty to touch. 'Disgusting!' she said and got up and put it under the nose of the Superintendent, old Peter Le Maître. 'One of your boys is interfering with my girls,' she said. Old Peter Le Maître was a big man with a big face and big spectacles, and sat at a high desk at the top end of the room. 'Who wrote this?' he said. 'Ebenezer Le Page!' screamed all the girls. 'Come here, Ebenezer Le Page!' said old Peter. I went and stood in front of his high desk. He looked at me over the top of his spectacles; and he looked at my note through his spectacles; and looked at me again over the top of his spectacles. 'Is this what you come to Sunday School for?' he said. 'I don't know, sir,' I said. 'Go and stand in the porch!' he said. I went out to the porch with my tail between my legs; and then I said to myself, me: 'Bugger you, old Peter Le Maître!' and put on my cap and walked out.

I never looked at Marie Le Noury again. She married Reg Symes, an English chap in the Artillery stationed at Castle Cornet. He was a great boy with the Indian clubs and used to give displays at military concerts; but he came out of the Army to please her and opened a little shop in the Commercial Arcade for mending clocks andwatches. He worshipped the ground she walked on. When she got to middle age she left him and went to live with her married daughter in England; and he put his head in the gas oven and was found dead in the morning. I was lucky, really.

I went home round Birdo, so as not to be back too soon. There was an old man sitting on a rock with a spy-glass. I wondered what it was he was looking at; and then I noticed a young chap and a girl had managed to get themselves cut off by the tide on the Hommet and was curled up together on the grass. I couldn't see what they was doing; but the old man could see, him. I thought it was funny way for an old man to pass his Sunday afternoon. I went round by the Vale Mill; but the big vanes wasn't turning. The cows was chewing the cud in the field. When I got indoors, my father asked me what the golden text was for that Sunday. He always asked me what the golden text was to make sure I hadn't played truant. I told him. 'Love thy neighbour as thyself.' He said, 'Well, if you do that, son, you can't go far wrong.' I had my doubts about that.

I didn't go to Sunday School again. I left the house the same time as if I was going and took the penny my father gave me for the Foreign Missions. I was sorry to have to steal that penny from my father; but what else could I do? I went and sat on the gate of L'Ancresse Common by the Vale Church with the boys from round there. In those days there was hundreds of sheep loose on the Common and the gate had to be kept shut, or they would have strayed all over the Parish. It was a nuisance for the gentry who wanted to drive across the Common in their carriages. They had to get down and open the gate and get back up and drive through and get down again and close the gate behind them. The boys was good. They would open the gate when they saw a carriage coming and close the gate behind it: then run after the carriage, calling out 'Apenny, please! Apenny, please!'

Sunday afternoons was a good time for making money on the gate; because the Townies, who was all gentry on Sundays, liked to drive out to

L'Ancresse Common in their carriages to look at the sheep. I will say some of them was honest and would throw a halfpenny, and there'd be a run and a fight for it; but there are always some mean people in the world. The gentleman would pull a handful of change out of his pocket and say, 'Sorry, haven't got a halfpenny. Have you, my dear?' The lady would rummage in her handbag and say, 'I am afraid I haven't, darling.' By that time we'd have run after the carriage nearly to the Druid's Altar. Goodness, a penny would have done!

I had to keep my eyes skinned for some boy who had been to Sunday School, so as I would know what the golden text was for that Sunday. I usually managed to nab Bill Rihoy, who lived at L'Islet; but I don't think he always remembered it right. Once he told me it was 'An eye for an eye and a tooth for a tooth.' When I repeated it to my father, he said, 'Well, if that's what they teach you in Sunday School, soon there won't be many of us with any eyes, or any teeth, left.' As I have said before, he got some funny ideas in his head, my father.

I put the money I made in my money-box. I didn't tell a soul: not even my sister. It wasn't she was a tell-tale. She was the most honest and straightforward girl and woman I have known in my whole life. She was so honest and straightforward you had to be careful what you said to her. The first thing I remember in this world is putting a penny in my money-box. I can't have been more than three or four. I earnt it for picking slugs off the cabbages. My father would give me a penny for twelve slugs and drown them. It was good money, when you come to think of it. My father was good that way. He believed in paying for everything and paying on the dot. From the time I was ten I earnt extra money cracking stones. My father knew Bert Le Feuvre, the foreman of Griffith's yard, and there was a little heap of spawls waiting ready every night in summer after school for me to crack. I was paid a shilling a week for that and my father let me keep it.

I knew to a penny how much I got in my money-box. When I had ten pennies I'd shake them out and change them for a franc. I kept a lookout for English pennies because I could get thirteen Guernsey pennies for twelve of those. I was only a boy at school yet when I had over a pound in my money-box. On the Ash Wednesday, when we had holiday from school, I trotted into Town on my own and walked into the Old Bank and plonked down on the counter twenty-one Guernsey shillings in pennies and halfpennies and fippennies and francs. The chap behind the counter looked over at me and counted my money and pushed me across a sovereign. I had a golden sovereign in my money-box. I was rich!

I suppose I would have gone to work in the quarries and perhaps done well, if something awful hadn't happened at the Queen's quarry. Young Emile Thoumine was killed in the pit. He was only nineteen and hadn't been married three months. It was said the blasting must have loosened the side of the quarry, or water trickling down. Anyhow, a great block of granite came toppling over without warning and crushed him. I had never seen my father so upset as when he came in that evening. He was early because old Tom Mauger was with the doctor bringing up in the horse-box what was left of poor Emile; and he had asked my father to go in the trap and break the news to the young wife. They lived in Town. When my father told my mother what had happened, she said, 'What did he belong to?' She meant was he Church, or Chapel, or what; so as she would know where he was going to. I saw my father clench his fists; and I think, if she had been a man, he would have knocked her down. 'The man is dead!' he said. 'Come with me, son!'

I was pleased and excited to be going with my father in the trap. It was beginning to get dark and, while he was harnessing the pony, I lit the big candles in the lamps. It was rough along the front and the sea was coming across the road by the gas-works and over the Salerie Corner. The house was in the Canichers. It was too narrow for the trap to go up and my father tied Jack to the lamp-post at the corner and told me to stop there and mind him. I felt very sad left there all by myself and talked to Jack. I remember the flickering gas-light and the round shadows on the road and a big old tree dropping leaves and the wind blowing them about. My father wasn't long gone. When he came back all he said was, 'She is with her mother.'

When we got home and was having our supper, my father said to my mother, 'Our boy is not going to work in the quarries.' 'What, then?' said my mother. 'We must find something better for him to do than that,' he said. I don't know if it was better, I don't think it was; but when I left school he got me a job in Dorey's Vineries. They was still growing grapes, but trying out tomatoes under the vines. I thought tomatoes was a funny sort of fruit. I didn't like the taste much. I liked the grapes, though. It turned out there was a better sale in England for the tomatoes and in the end the greenhouses grew nothing else.

I had to do what my father said; but, when he'd gone, I used to chuck it sometimes and go fishing for a spell. I was happier working out-of-doors and in a boat; but you can't trust the sea, and the fishes get ideas into their heads and sometimes they are where they ought to be and sometimes they are not. The tomatoes are always there, so back I would go; but, golly, it was hot in those greenhouses! Ah well, I was born to trouble as the sparks fly upwards. I earned my bread by the sweat of my brow.

3

I mustn't complain. I have never had a day's sickness in my life. I put that down to the good food my mother made me eat. Now that I have seen how the English eat, I wonder how it is they keep alive at all. I always had a big breakfast at seven, a big dinner at twelve, and a big tea at six, or just after. At work I'd have a lunch in the morning at half-past nine, and a lunch in the afternoon at half-past three; and we always had a supper at half-past nine at night, before we went to bed. Our food didn't come out of tins, either. The only thing we ate out of a tin was red salmon of a Sunday afternoon, if anybody we didn't expect came to tea. There was a rack over the table on which there was always the salted side of a pig. It was from one of our own pigs we'd killed; and, if we ate a fowl, it was one of our own fowls.

My mother believed in me eating plenty of beef. She bought it from Webb, the butcher, on the Bridge; and it had to be Guernsey beef. She said the white fat of the English beef made her feel sick. When she came home with a steak, it was a steak; and an inch thick. She bought mutton for sometimes, the best cut of the leg; and fresh pork from old Piggy Wright, the pork butcher. Fish she was very particular about. It had to be fresh from the boat. She wouldn't cook a mackerel unless it had its tail up. I liked the long-nose better. The English are funny about the long-nose; or orfi, as we call it. They say it is poison because it got green bones. Well, I've eaten orfi all my life and I'm still alive. The fish I liked best was conger. My mother would buy the thickest part and stuff it like a fowl and bake it. It was so good you would never have thought it was fish.

My father had crab-pots out and we had plenty of crabs; and sold some. It was the lobsters we sold most of. They are for the English, those; and the gentry. You can't trust a lobster. He's often half empty. A crawfish is always as full as an egg; but then he have coarser flesh and, of course, no claws. We used to have a chancre for supper of a Saturday night when we came home from Town. It was cooked on the Friday in the copper in the wash-house. It gave a scream when it was dropped in the hot water; but my father was funny about that and wouldn't let my mother put it in cold water and bring it to the boil. He said it suffered. If it was dropped in boiling water, it died outright. It was one of the few things my mother had to do as she was told. She didn't like having to cook it that way, because sometimes the claws came off from the shock and the water got in. The crab I like best, me, is the spider crab. I like to see him on the table in a dish: round and with his legs out like a spider, and knobs and spikes sticking up on his back. I used to catch lady-crabs in the pools and under the rocks. I don't know why they are called lady-crabs. They are male and female like all the other creatures in the world. They have a crown on their back and people say it's because they belong to the Queen; but I suppose everything belong to the Queen really. I used to catch them for Tabby. She liked them. I liked them all right, but they're so small they take an hour to pick; and there's not much to eat when you've done it.

The food I like best of all foods is ormers; but you can't always get them. My father used to take me with him ormering. It was always at the spring tide when the sea was right down; and you had to go in up to your knees to get to them. If it was at night and fine weather, there would be a big moon shining on the rocks and on the wet sand and on the water. My father went further out than me and got more; but the ones near to he left for me. I'd have a hook and a bucket and he'd lift a big stone for me to see; and there would be the black creature sticking to it underneath. I daren't breathe for fear he would know and clamp down, for then a stick of gelignite wouldn't get him off. I'd make one sudden grab with my hook and have him in my bucket. He's a funny creature when you see him close to. He have holes in the shell on his back, but I don't know what for.

My mother knew how to cook ormers. When she had cut the part you eat out of the shell, she would scrub the black edges with a scrubbing brush until they was perfectly clean; and that took some doing. Then she would put them between two towels and beat them with a flat iron for half an hour, or more. They are hard as leather, but she'd roll up her sleeves; and she had muscles on her arms, my mother. That was when she was happy. She'd be singing hymns all the time and you could hear her all over the house. When they was properly broke up and soft, she'd fry them over the fire in the iron frying-pan; and then stew them in the oven to finish up with. Some people stew them with onions, but my mother didn't believe in that. She said it take the taste away and spoil the gravy. She liked them with just boiled potatoes.

When there was a lot to be had, she would pickle some. They was four-pence a dozen, if you bought them; but they was worth it. After they had been scrubbed and beaten, they was boiled for a long time; and then pickled in the best vinegar with bay leaves in an airtight jar. We didn't have no bay leaves in our garden; so I had to go and steal some from Mr Dorey of Oatlands. He had a bay tree with leaves hanging over the road. Mr Dorey would have given us as many bay leaves as we wanted, if we'd asked him: but my mother wouldn't let me. She was proud, my mother. She would

rather steal than beg; and I'm the same. The jar was kept on the shelf with
the pots of jam; and sometimes I'd be given a pickled ormer for my tea with
bread and butter, when I came home from school.

I can't say what ormers taste like. They are not like fish, flesh, or fowl.
They are like no other food on earth. I have heard of the nectar of the gods.
Or is it ambrosia they feed on? That must be ormers. Well, my poor old
mother is in heaven now, if she is anywhere at all. If they got any sense up
there, they will get her to cook them a meal of ormers. I can just see her
banging away at the old ormers with a flat iron and her sleeves rolled up and
singing 'Where is my wandering boy tonight?'

She was as fussy about butter as she was about meat. She wouldn't look
at the sickly white English butter. It had to be golden Guernsey. My
grandfather kept a cow, as he was working only round the corner and
could look after it; but there was no cow kept at Les Moulins in my time,
and I had to fetch our milk, butter, and curds from the Roussels of the
Grand Fort. My mother and Tabitha liked curds, but I didn't. Of course
there was no wine, beer, or spirits drunk in our house; but, for some
reason, there was always a barrel of cider. In the early days, it was made
from our own apples; but when most of the apple-trees had been cut down
to make room to build a greenhouse it was delivered from Randall's
Brewery in the Truchett. My mother wouldn't touch it; but my father
used to let me have a glass with my dinner Sundays. It goes without saying
my mother was against smoking. She said if men was meant to smoke they
would have been born with a chimney on the nose. It didn't make any difference to my father. He smoked cigarettes he rolled himself and black
twist in his pipe and a cigar at Christmas. I didn't smoke in the house until I
was a grown lad; but I smoked when I was a boy at the Vale School, of
course.

My little grandmother didn't mind my father smoking: she said she
liked the smell of smoke on a man. He got on well with his belle-mère, my
father. He would often go along on his own to see how she was, or take me
with him. 'Hello, ma mère!' he'd say and take her in his arms and kiss her
on the forehead. He was big and strong and she was very small and frail
against him. 'Ah, comment s'en va, mon Alfred?' she'd say. 'Pas trop mal,'
he'd say.

My mother thought more of her father than of her mother. She said he
was a man of God. She knew he had been misled and in error while he was a
Wesleyan, but she believed he had seen the Light when he was struck
down. Her sisters, my Aunt Prissy and my Aunt Hetty, was so much
younger than she was they hardly remembered their father, and thought
more of their mother: especially La Hetty, the youngest. When my grandmother died, La Hetty said she wanted to die too; and cried so much they
thought she was going mad.

I was to school yet when my little grandmother died. She didn't know anybody for seven days and seven nights. I think the doctor gave her some stuff at the end to ease the pain. She lay on her back breathing loud and they had to feed her with a feather. The three sisters and the husbands went every night; and people came from the Vale and St Sampson's and the Câtel, and even as far as from St Saviour's, to see her. They would go into the bedroom one by one on their tiptoes, and come out saying 'Ah, la pauvre Charlotte! la pauvre Charlotte! Ch'est la fin, enfin: ch'est la fin!' The last night the three sisters stopped all night and sat by the bed watching. The husbands went home to have a sleep, so as they would be able to go to work in the morning. I stopped with my mother. I was the only big boy there. My Cousin Horace, Aunt Prissy's first, was only three and was put to sleep in a cot in the little room. My Cousin Raymond, Aunt Hetty's boy, was there; but he wasn't born yet. I said I didn't want to go to sleep. I had never been allowed to stop up all night before. I wanted to sit and watch my granny die.

My mother wouldn't let me and made me go in the kitchen, and I sat with my Uncle Nat. The lamp was lit and there was a stuffed owl on the table, and lustre-ware jugs and willow-pattern plates on the dresser, and a china fowl to keep eggs in; and two china dogs on the mantelpiece. A big fire was burning on the hearth and a copper kettle boiling on the terpid, in case hot water was wanted. My uncle was sitting up on the green-bed wide awake. I don't think he knew what was going on. He was busy making the picture of a wonderful boat with a golden hull and curly gunnels and black masts curling aft and red sails like the combs of cockerels; and a big green wave was curling over it. I could hear my granny breathing with a rattle in her throat, and I began to pray, 'Please God, don't let my granny die! Please God, don't let my granny die! Please God, don't let my granny die! Please! Please! Please!' I fell asleep in my chair.

She was laid out by the time I woke up in the morning. My Aunt Prissy was a great one for laying out the dead; and she'd made sure beforehand everything was ready in the top drawer of the chest-of-drawers. On the day of the funeral I saw my granny in her coffin before it was screwed down. She was like wax. They said she had come to herself before she died and sat up in bed and called out. She had seen somebody. My Aunt Prissy said it was Nico, her husband, she saw; but my Aunt Hetty said it was SOMEBODY ELSE. My mother didn't say nothing.

She was given a grand funeral. It stretched from Cobo to Grand Havre. My Aunt Hetty didn't go because she couldn't stop crying; but my Aunt Prissy went, and my mother. The three husbands was pallbearers, and Mess Phineas Le Page from the Coutanchez, the écrivain. She was buried Chapel; but the cemetery was only over a wall from the Church. All the way along the road from Les Sablons to the Vale there wasn't a house that didn't have its blinds down. I was wearing a black suit. My Aunt Prissy cried at the grave, and my mother put a handkerchief to her eyes. I didn't cry. After the funeral, the Reverend Dumond came back to Les Sablons to have tea with the mourners and near relations. It was only bread and butter and cheese and Guernsey biscuits, but there was enough for everybody to have a good feed. When he had gone, the will was read.

Mess Phineas Le Page read it. It was in a tin box on the side table in the kitchen, where my grandmother kept the tickets she was given each month from the Capelles Chapel to show she was saved. It was as everybody expected. My Uncle Nat was to have the house and furniture until he died, and a quarter of the money. My grandmother had quite a nice little nest-egg in the pied-du-cauche. Her clothes was to be divided among the three daughters. The sharing was done in the bedroom where she died. They sat on the floor and cast lots. My Uncle Nat was out of it; but he understood enough to fish up a couple of dice out of his pocket for Mess Phineas Le Page to rattle in his tall hat.

It worked out quite peaceful to begin with. My Aunt Prissy won the sabots and my Aunt Hetty the scoop and my mother the widow's veil. The best bonnet went to Prissy, who said it was too old for her; and the second best to Hetty, who said she was only glad to have anything that had belonged to her mother. The best blouse went to my mother, who said it was too small for her and gave it to Prissy, who was thin. There was three bundles of underclothes; but they was wrapped up in brown paper, so as the men wouldn't see. They went one to each. There was only the wedding-dress left. It was a lovely dress of white corded silk and had been kept in the bottom drawer of the chest-of-drawers with camphor and between tissue paper for fifty years. It went to Prissy. Then there was the most terrible schemozzle. My Aunt Hetty said her mother had always promised the wedding-dress to her, for when she had a daughter. My Aunt Prissy said it was hers now by the will of God; and she wasn't going to part with it for anybody. My Aunt Hetty screamed, 'Mais je te grimerai, donc!' and clawed at my Aunt Prissy's hair. My Aunt Prissy screamed, 'Ah, tu fichu petite volresse, té!' and tried to scratch my Aunt Hetty's eyes out. The two husbands had to separate the two wives and hold them back like fighting cocks. My father didn't do nothing. Mess Phineas Le Page didn't know what to do. He kept on saying, 'Ah, mes pigeons! mes pauvres petites pigeons!' It was my mother who showed she had the wisdom of a Solomon.

She said she had better have the wedding-dress herself. If either of the others had it now, it would make bad blood in the family; especially as they lived next door to each other. The husbands said, 'Anything for peace!' My mother played fair. She offered to La Hetty the widow's veil and to La Prissy her bundle of underclothes. My Aunt Hetty said she didn't want the widow's veil, because when she was a widow she wasn't going to wear a veil. My Aunt Prissy said she'd have the bundle of underclothes: they would always do for rags and dusters.

It turned out for the best, in a way. My sister was married in the wedding-dress and looked lovely. La Prissy had a second, but it was a boy again when she wanted a girl; and, after Raymond, La Hetty couldn't have any more. The dress would have been wasted; and it wasn't so many years before my mother had to wear the widow's veil. Ah well, in the midst of life we are in death, as it say in the Bible.

4

My Uncle Nathaniel lived a few years after his mother died; but not many. There was a lot of talk about him living alone at Les Sablons. People said he ought to have been put away in the Country Hospital; but he could feed himself and do his business and mooch round the house. He didn't keep the place very clean, it is true, and his sisters went along now and again to give the house a good spring-clean. It was small thanks they got for it. 'It aint for the sake of your brother you come,' he said, 'it is for the sake of what the people say. What the people say is the Ten Commandments on this island. Fiche le can'!'

The fellows who had been his friends when he was in health brought him fish, if they had any to spare, and drink, which he paid for. They dug and planted the back garden for him, and the neighbours fetched his meat for him, and groceries. I suppose he had enough to eat, one way and the other. The front garden was a wilderness. The marigolds ran wild and big sunflowers on tall stalks looked down on you as you passed; and the hedge grew and grew until all you could see of Les Sablons from the road was the dormer window. It was like the forest around the Castle of Bluebeard. The neighbours, who was Domailles and cousins of the Domailles from the Hautes Capelles and so of a good family, came and complained to my mother and my aunts and said it was a disgrace. There was a council of war in our kitchen.

It was decided it couldn't go on any longer, something must be done about it; and the Reverend Dumond, who had managed to get himself dragged into it somehow, said it would be a good idea if the family was to call on my uncle in a body and 'appeal to his better feelings'. The husbands didn't have time, or couldn't be bothered; but the brigade of Le Page women and children, under the command of the Reverend Dumond, advanced in line of attack on the enemy camp. The children brought up the rear to appeal to my uncle's better feelings. Raymond was three or four, and holding on to his mother's hand; and Horace was seven or eight, and rough already and throwing stones; and his young brother, Cyril, was in the bassinette. Tabby, my sister, who'd just left school, had her hair up because she was going out to service. I was in long trousers. The good minister forced a way through the jungle and got to the front door. My uncle had a crowd of fellows in the house singing drunk; and he must have had his spies out, for they had piled the furniture against the front door and barricaded themselves in. The Reverend knocked and knocked, and tried the handle, and begged them to open in the Name of the Lord. He then commanded them to let him in if they feared damnation. They didn't. He had to beat a retreat. He said even the Grace of God was unavailing against the unrepentant sinner.

The drinking and singing went on for a week. The neighbours gathered outside and stood by the hedge and listened, while the big sunflowers looked down smiling. Then one morning all was quiet. The front door was open and my Uncle Nat's friends had vanished in the night. The good neighbours got worried and, to cut a long story short, he was found lying dead with not a stitch of clothing on him, or a rag on the bed. All the money had been spent and the friends had taken everything they could lay their hands on, except the pictures and ornaments, which they didn't want, and the heavy furniture they couldn't carry.

He was put away privily, as it say in the Bible. A hearse and two carriages: the three sisters in one and the three husbands in the other. He was buried with his mother, and was the last to be put in that grave because it was full. There was a share-out of the few things left; but there was no trouble. Nobody wanted the pictures; but nobody had the heart to burn them because he had made them with his own hands, stitch by stitch. La Hetty got the china fowl she wanted; and was happy. My Aunt Prissy said I could choose anything I liked, because I had grown to be such a fine strong boy. I chose the two china dogs on the mantelpiece. They are on my mantelpiece at this moment, listening with their long ears to every word I am writing down. I like my two china dogs. When I write down anything wicked, one of them look very serious; but the other one, he wink.

The only article of furniture that came to my mother was the grandfather clock. It was made by Naftel, his name is on the front; and it have only five or six wheels and a weight on a chain and a long pendulum with a big brass bob, yet it is never a minute wrong. I don't think I could live now, if I didn't hear the slow tick-tock, tick-tock of my grandfather clock. One night, only a few weeks ago, I forgot to wind it before I went to bed. I'm getting into the way of forgetting to do things, I don't know why. When it stopped in the night, I woke up. The place was dead.

Les Sablons was sold and the money divided among the sisters. I know there was a lot of fuss and bother about getting the money, because La Prissy and La Hetty wasn't speaking at the time and wouldn't meet together in the lawyer's office to sign the papers. When La Prissy and La Hetty was speaking, they went around together like a pair of Siamese twins and wore twin mushroom hats. When they wasn't speaking, they didn't know each other if they met face to face in the Pollet. When they was speaking, we never saw them at Les Moulins; but when they wasn't speaking, they came one at a time to tell everything to my mother. I have known my Aunt Prissy be talking to my mother in the kitchen when, lo and behold, my Aunt Hetty would be coming down the garden path to the front door. My mother would let Prissy out quick by the back door, before she let Hetty in by the front. She was good that way, my mother. She was all for peace in the family.

When my Aunt Prissy and my Aunt Hetty wasn't speaking, they blamed each other for everything. When they was speaking, they blamed everybody else. I have never known the rights and the wrongs of how they came to marry the Martel boys. That's the trouble of trying to write the true story of my relations; or of myself, for that matter. I don't know the beginning, or the end. Hetty didn't want to marry Harold Martel; I'm sure of that. It was not only that he was years older, but he had been married before. Hetty really wanted to marry Jack Bourgaize, who was her own age; but he was one of those boys who was mad to get away from Guernsey, and had gone to Australia to make his fortune. He had wanted her to go with him, but she wouldn't because she didn't want to leave her mother. It happened just then that Harold Martel was on the look-out for another wife; but, to be fair, I think he liked Hetty better than his first one. Hetty said she only went out with him for company, because Prissy was going out with Percy. Prissy said she only went out with Percy, because Hetty was going out with Harold. She didn't like Percy. He was soft. Nobody could say Harold was soft. He was a big surly-looking bloke with heavy shoulders and, as the eldest, used to having his own way. Anyhow, they all four found themselves engaged.

Then Jack Bourgaize wrote from Australia to say he'd got a smallholding. From his letter, it sounded as if the smallholding was as big as Guernsey, but all trees. He said he had made a clearing in it and built a shack; and he wanted Hetty to go out at once and marry him. Her mother said she must do what she wanted; but she went to ask advice of her Aunt Sarah, who she hoped was going to leave her some money. Her Aunt Sarah, who had never married, said, 'A bird in the hand is worth two in the bush, my girl.' Hetty married Harold Martel.

He already had a house at Pleinheaume, where he had lived with his first wife; but Hetty didn't want to live in the same house as that other woman and use the same things. Harold thought he might as well turn over a new leaf and start on a clean page. He sold the house at Pleinheaume and bought the ground to build another. Prissy said Percy must build one next to it, so as whatever was to happen, she and Hetty would always have each other.

The two brothers went into partnership. Everything was arranged for the best and turned out for the worst.

It's a wonder those two houses ever got built at all, there was so many quarrels. It wasn't the brothers. Percy was quite willing to give in to Harold; and Harold worked with Percy all right, so long as he was the boss. It was the sisters. There never was two sisters more different from each other than those two. Hetty wasn't stout yet, but she was short and roundish. She had a beautiful face really: squarish with strong bones and big sky-blue eyes and a lovely straight nose. If only that face had been on a body to match, she would have been one of the beauties of those days. Prissy wasn't a beauty. She was pretty with a small face, a small body and small bones; and, though she was five years older than Hetty, could pass for the same age. She had a tongue like a needle, and she knew exactly where to dig it in so it hurt; and Hetty was easy to hurt and easy to make happy. She was always either laughing or crying.

It was agreed between them that the houses must be exactly alike, since they was for two brothers marrying two sisters; but for everything Harold did to his, Percy was made to do something different by Prissy. Harold's idea of a house was four walls and enough windows and a door back and front and a roof on top. Percy had to do everything fancy. Harold wanted plain granite. Percy had to do dashing. Both houses finished up half dashing and half granite. Percy had to build a front porch. Harold had to build a front porch. Percy had to make the top windows with points like a chapel. Harold had to re-build the top storey to have windows with points like a chapel. Then Hetty got ideas of her own. She wanted bow windows downstairs; so as she would be able to sit behind the curtains and watch the people pass, without being seen. Percy had to put in bow windows. The last great row was over the names of the houses. La Hetty decided she would have hers called Wallaballoo. It was the name of the place where Jack Bourgaize had his smallholding in Australia. La Prissy came to tell my mother about it in a rage. 'What d'you think she's going to do now?' she said; and she told us. 'Have anybody ever heard of such a name for a house?' she said. 'The people will think she's mad! Well, if she's going to call hers Wallaballoo, I'm going to call ours Timbuctoo!' She did, too. There they are to this day, the two houses, in the meadow the other side of Braye-side with a high wall between them. There wasn't a high wall between them when they was built. It was a low hedge with an open gap to go from one to the other. Well, I have seen hells and hells lived through at Wallaballoo and Timbuctoo.

The Martels of Ronceval was Church and the two brothers was married at St Sampson's Church on the same day and went on the same boat to England and in the same train to London for their honeymoon. They all four put up at the Empress Hotel in Waterloo Road and went to the Zoo and the Crystal Palace and Madame Tussaud's and saw the Chamber of Horrors and the old Queen driving in her carriage out of Buckingham Palace. The sisters wasn't speaking when they came back; and the brothers wasn't allowed to speak either. There was a letter waiting for Hetty. She had written to Jack Bourgaize that she was getting married to Harold Martel, but it had crossed with a letter from him saying that, if she wouldn't go out to Australia, then he would sell his smallholding and come back and settle down in Guernsey and marry her. She cried for weeks and had to have the doctor. It was three or four years before Raymond was on the way; and when he was born she nearly died. Horace arrived before the first year was out.

I have never been able to understand how Horace came to be a Guernsey boy. He was a born American. He was showing off and making a big noise from the moment he poked his head out. Raymond was a quiet boy. Sometimes I think he was born too good for this world. He worshipped the big Horace from a child; and Horace was quite willing to have him following along behind like a little dog. That is, if La Hetty and La Prissy was speaking. Of course, if they wasn't speaking the boys wasn't supposed to speak either; but there was no keeping them apart.

They both went to the Secondary School in Brock Road. At first it was the Misses Cohu's School at the Albion Terrace Raymond went to, and Horace was sent to the Capelles School for Boys. Prissy said she didn't want him to grow up to be a girl. There was no fear of that. Raymond was ten when he went to the Secondary, but Horace stayed on at the Capelles until he was old enough to leave school altogether; and Prissy only sent him so that Hetty couldn't say Raymond had been to the Secondary and Horace hadn't. He was put in the same class as Raymond. Hetty said to Prissy, 'It isn't always the boys with the big legs got the big brains. Le Raymond will finish up working in a bank yet, you'll see!' Prissy said to Hetty, 'It isn't those who work in the bank got the money. It's those put the money in the bank got the money. Le Horace is going to make plenty, you'll see!' For six months after, Le Raymond and Le Horace had to go different ways to school. Horace would go along the Vale Road on his bike and Raymond would go round Baubigny on his; and they would meet at the Half-way. Raymond was a boy who didn't like to do the slightest thing wrong, yet he would break any rule to be with Horace.

Cyril, the baby, grew into the most beautiful child I have ever seen. He looked like an angel. He had long golden curls Prissy wouldn't have cut off; and she was for ever having his photo taken. She adored him. I am sure he was the only creature in the world she ever adored. Nobody, not even his mother, could adore Horace. The funny thing was that Cyril really took after his father. Percy had been a good-looking young chap with fair curly hair; and he was of a sweet nature until he married Prissy and turned nasty. When Cyril was five he got diphtheria and died. The sisters wasn't speaking at the time, but they came very close together then; and the whole family went to the funeral. He had a small grave to himself in St Sampson's cemetery; and a small tombstone, and on it: CYRIL MARTEL. AGED 5 YEARS, 3 MONTHS. Prissy wouldn't have any words put under.

5

The worst schemozzle between the two sisters was over the planchette. They was never properly friendly again after. It wasn't that they didn't speak. It was worse. I remember once I was talking to La Hetty by her gate and La Prissy came out from round the back of Timbuctoo, going to the shop. She went out of her way to speak. 'Ah, well I never, there you are, then!' she said. 'It is such a long time I haven't seen you, I was beginning to wonder if it was that you was laid up for life!' La Hetty laughed. 'Ah, but no, then: I'm fine, me!' she said. 'I was saying to Le Harold only this morning: "It's such a long time I haven't seen that Prissy, I wonder if it is she can be dead!"'

To tell you the truth, I would have liked to have had one of those things myself; but if I had brought one into the house, my mother would have said I was trafficking with the Devil. I was earning the money and was the man in the house; but there was some things I wouldn't do to hurt the feelings of my mother. I'd seen the planchettes on show in the window of Le Cheminant's toy-shop in the Commercial Arcade, when me and Jim was in Town one Saturday night. He said, 'Let's buy one each, eh?' but I explained to him about my mother and he said, 'Yes, that would never do.' He bought one for himself and said, 'You can try it to my house.' I was in and out of his house, as if it was my home and I always had supper there Saturday nights.

After supper he tried to make it work on a big piece of paper on the kitchen table. It was a funny thing, the planchette. It was a flat piece of wood made like a heart with a pencil through the point and two little wheels at the back of it for it to roll on. It said on the box that if you put your hand on it and asked it a question, it would write out the answer. Jim put his hand on it and said, 'Planchette, Planchette, is it going to be fine weather tomorrow?' He wanted to know because it was Sunday, and we was going for a ride on our bikes after dinner. It didn't move. Jim said, 'Well, I thought that was an easy one. It only had to write Yes, or No.' I said, 'I'm going to ask it something harder.' I put my hand on it and said, 'Planchette, Planchette, am I going to win the leg of mutton off the greasy pole?' The one thing I wanted to be able to say I had done was to have won the leg of mutton off the greasy pole at the Grand Havre Regatta.

'It moved!' said Jim. It did move, damme; and made a small mark on the paper: but you could hardly see it. 'It's the electric in you!' he said. I don't know if it was the electric in me; but I swear I didn't push it on purpose. Old Jim was always willing to give me best and I wouldn't have played a dirty trick like that on him. I said, 'Planchette, Planchette, is that all you can do? Are you really able to answer any questions? Say Yes, or No!' It didn't move at all. I said to Jim, 'A pity you throw away a shilling for nothing. I'll pay half,' but he wouldn't let me.

Of course Le Raymond had to have a planchette because Le Horace had a planchette; and Le Horace had to have a planchette because Le Raymond had a planchette. Le Raymond was unlucky like Jim. It wouldn't move at all for him; but for Horace it wrote out answers for every question he asked. La Prissy was cock-a-hoop and invited herself and Percy and Horace to Wallaballoo on the Sunday evening to show what wonders the planchette could do. She went so far as to say that Horace would do it with Raymond's planchette, just to show that everything was open and above board. Raymond tried again and nothing happened. 'Ah well,' said Prissy, 'it isn't everybody have got the gift.' It behaved wonderful for Horace that night. He asked it his name, and it wrote it out; he asked it his birthday, and it wrote it out; he asked it where he lived, and it wrote out his address long: Timbuctoo, Braye Road, St Sampson's, Guernsey, Channel Islands, British Isles, Europe, The World; and when he asked it if he was ever going to leave Guernsey, it wrote that he was going to America and make millions.

'There, you see!' said Prissy. 'The planchette know. Horace is going to be somebody. It isn't working in a bank he is going to be, and earning less than if he was working in the greenhouses and think he is one of the gentry because he is wearing a white collar and a tie.' 'The planchette write big,' said Hetty. 'That only go to show that it is the planchette who is writing, him; and not Horace,' said Prissy, 'because Horace, he write small.' 'It don't spell very well,' said Hetty, 'I've always thought the word millions have two l's, me.' 'Well, you can't expect a piece of wood to know everything,' said Prissy. 'It is not the planchette who do not know how to spell,' said Hetty, 'it is Le Horace who do not know how to spell. Do he think we are all fools that we cannot see him pushing it?' 'Well, if THAT is what you think!' said Prissy; and she got up on her two feet. I can just see her standing there with her thin lips together. 'After we have been sisters for so many years, I thought we was going to be sisters for the rest of our lives,' she said. 'Come Horace, come Percy: we are no relations!' and they both followed her out like sheep through the gap in the hedge to Timbuctoo.

My mother had to listen to the sad story a dozen times from the one and the other. I don't know why they came and told everything to my mother.

I never told my mother anything. She didn't say much. She would listen with her big white face and go on with her work. 'Ah, la, la,' she'd say, 'mais es-che comme chonna, donc? Es-che la véritai?' She didn't take sides. She only wanted to know the truth. Prissy said, 'Well, even if Horace did push it, Raymond could have pushed it too. He'll never get on in the world, that boy, if he don't learn how to push!' When Hetty's turn came, she said she was glad it had happened; for it meant that at last Horace wouldn't come bothering Raymond any more. From the time Raymond was a little boy the big Horace was always around the place, breaking his toys and climbing over the roofs of the sheds, and Raymond would try and follow and make holes in his trousers. 'It's all for the best,' she said.

She was wrong about Raymond. Unbeknown to her, they often came together of a Saturday afternoon for a bathe in the little bay under Les Moulins. That is a thing I would never have thought of doing, me: to wash myself all over in the sea. Once when Horace was undressing, I saw he got some bad marks on his back. I asked him how he got those marks. 'Oh, it's my old man with his belt,' he said and laughed. I'd have never thought Percy would do that with his soft ways. I took the two of them out in my boat with me a few times. Raymond wasn't much use, but he liked to sit looking at the sea and the rocks. 'It's nice here, eh Uncle?' he'd say, and smile. I was only his cousin really, but I was so much older he called me Uncle. I liked Raymond. He was weak and sickly when he was a child, but by the time he was twelve or thirteen, he was quite healthy and strong. He wasn't big built but had a well-made young body and an old-fashioned face with fairish hair and bright blue eyes that looked at you very straight. He was serious for a young boy, but had a nice smile and sometimes he'd wrinkle up his face laughing at something all to himself. He was no fool.

I suppose Horace was a good-looking boy: everybody said he was, but I couldn't see it myself. He was big built with heavy shoulders like his Uncle Harold, and he had thick black hair and very dark eyes and full lips and a mouthful of big white teeth he liked to show when he smiled; but when he smiled, you could bet your bottom dollar it was because he wanted to get round you for something. He started to throw his weight about the moment he got in the boat. He wanted to show me how clever he was and had no more idea than the man in the moon how to handle a sail. If I'd let him have his way, he'd have had us capsized in two shakes. 'Now you just sit where I tell you; and do what you're told!' I said to him. He was already bigger than me and looked quite surprised. He put on his smile; but I didn't smile back. 'I mean it!' I said. 'If you get yourself knocked overboard, who is going to fish you out? I won't.' I couldn't swim. He couldn't swim far. Raymond was a much better swimmer.

It was the only thing Raymond could do well as far as sports go. Horace played football for the Secondary School and was captain of the first team.

Raymond kicked a ball about in the second. I saw the school match against the High School once. The Secondary won, but more by luck than good management. Horace was no good as a footballer really. He played half back but was always getting off-side and would keep the ball to himself when he ought to have passed it to the forwards. He wasn't out for his team to win. All he wanted was to show everybody that Horace Martel was the best footballer on the field. I know perhaps I'm not being fair to Horace. Well, he's gone now. He was the way he was made.

Perhaps things would have turned out better for Raymond if it hadn't been for his mother; yet I don't like to throw the blame on Hetty altogether. She suffered. I know she did wrong. By rights, it was Jack Bourgaize who ought to have been Raymond's father; but then Raymond wouldn't have been Raymond. He was one of those who ought never to have been born; but, at that rate, I wonder how many of us ought to have been born?

At least, as far as Raymond was concerned, Hetty did everything she thought was for the best. It was a pity she didn't know her boy. I came to know much more about him than she ever did; but even now I can't pretend I understand Raymond. She gave him everything he wanted, or that she thought he wanted, or ought to want. He was well fed and clothed and cared for; he was given a good education; he was taught to play the piano, first by Miss Annette Cohu and then by Mr Pescott from the Vale Avenue, who was the best pianist on the island; and he always had plenty of money in his pocket, though he wasn't one to spend much. At least, he never had to worry where his next penny was coming from. Yet, if she had only known it, she kept him in a cage. I wish I could think he got out of that cage in the end; but, if so, it was not in this world, though perhaps he did die happy.

Nothing could have turned out more different from how she planned. In her mind she had it all arranged. Harold was years older than she was and was going to die first. The house and everything would be hers. Raymond would live with her until she died; and then the house and everything would be his. There might be a wife: she had thought of that. 'I don't want my Raymond to grow up to be a funny old bachelor like some people I know,' she said to me once. I wondered where the wife was coming from who would satisfy Hetty. She would have to come of a good family and have money and, of course, be a good-living girl and no gad-about; and she would have to be willing to live with her mother-in-law and give her first place. I didn't think there was a girl in Guernsey, or in the world for that matter, would have done. I remember Raymond telling me years later how when he lived at home, if his mother heard he had been seen as much as talking to a girl, she would kick up a dido. I am willing to bet they wasn't talking about nothing but books. He belonged to the Guille-Allès

Library, and you never saw him about without a book under his arm. I am not sure all that reading do a fellow much good. Me, I used to read the *Gazette*, and now I read the *Guernsey Evening Press*, and I have read *Robinson Crusoe*.

Raymond didn't go into a bank, after all. He could be very stubborn when he wanted to be. He said he didn't want anything to do with figures. It is true at the Secondary School he hadn't been all that good at sums. It was History and Literature he was good at. Anyhow, he got his own way and went as a clerk to the Greffe. He didn't earn much, but that didn't matter then; and he got to know about the Court and the States and the Advocates, and rummaged among the old papers that had to do with the past history of the island. Hetty was quite pleased, as it turned out. She could say 'My son is in the Greffe,' and it sounded as grand, if not grander, than 'My son is in a bank.'

He didn't do a thing to help his father. I don't think he ever sawed a plank of wood. He was the greatest disappointment to Harold. He had no children by his first marriage and had always wanted a son; but his idea of a son was somebody who would carry on with the business, when the time came for him to give up. He didn't grumble much and he wasn't rough with Raymond. He would shrug his shoulders and say, 'Well, he's his mother's boy, that one.' He always let Hetty have her way. Hetty didn't think any the more of him for that. I remember her saying to my mother: 'All I hope is that Raymond don't grow up to be like his father.' I didn't know why at the time. Nobody knows what goes on between a married couple inside the four walls of a house. I liked Harold, myself. There was nothing behind-hand about him.

Horace worked for his father when he left school. That is, when he wasn't hanging about on the Bridge with the boys. I doubt if he ever gave his father a full day's work. Raymond went around with him on his own, but openly now. I would often see them going off together of a Sunday afternoon with towels round their necks; and now and again Jim and me would run into them at Pleinmont, or Icart, or one of the bays. They would be lying on the rocks in the sun talking. It was then I noticed Horace was different with Raymond from how he was with his other pals. He was cock of the walk among the rougher boys and his word was law; but with Raymond he was almost humble and willing to listen to what he had to say.

By then the partnership between the two fathers was broken up, and the sisters was neighbours but no relations. The last job Harold and Percy did together was to build the wall between the two houses. Prissy said, 'I don't want strangers to see every time I go to the back, me.' Harold went on building plain, solid houses and, later on, greenhouses. Percy branched out and went in for moulded concrete pillars and ornamental railings and windows with spikes that had no use nor beauty. Then he employed a young chap from Town who had done a lot of work in the Foulon Cemetery and went in for grave-stones and crosses and vaults for the dead. His last craze was for having angels made to decorate the crosses. Raymond, who knew about such things, said they wasn't angels, but cherubs. I don't know the difference, myself. I used to see what was going on when I passed down the Braye. The board that used to stand in front between the two houses with the words MARTEL BROS. BUILDERS on it had been taken down. At the side of Wallaballoo was a board with the words H. MARTEL. BUILDER on it; and at the side of Timbuctoo was another with the words P. MARTEL. MONUMENTAL BUILDER.

It was a pity they wasn't in partnership; for together they would have made a fortune. They supplied everything needful. If you was going to live, you went to Wallaballoo; and if you was going to die, you went to Timbuctoo. There was some people who went to both at the same time, to get it all settled and done with. I remember Muriel Bisson, who was a distant cousin of mine and a pretty little thing. She married Frank Nicolle from the Saltpans; and they was like turtle-doves, those two, while they was courting. After they had been to Harold to arrange about having a house built, Muriel happened to see one of those crosses with angels, or cherubs, climbing up it in Percy's yard. 'Oh I'd love one of those for you, darling!' she said. 'All right, my sweet,' he said, 'get it!' It was ordered. I don't know if it was paid for. Anyhow, she died before they had been married a year. She was never strong. Prissy hoped he would put it on her grave and order another for himself; but he said, 'No, it'll do for the next.' Marriage is a terrible thing, when you come to think of it. Perhaps it's as well I've never married. Mind you, I've had it a few times under the hedge.

6

I thought a lot of myself when I was a young chap. I wasn't bad-looking
for a Guernsey boy. I was dark with a round museau of a face and thick lips
and a pug nose and high cheekbones and deep-set brown eyes and a bush of
black hair. I haven't got much of that black hair left now, and what there is
of it is white. I've still got enough teeth to eat with and I can hear all right
and have never had to put spectacles on my nose, though I have to look
through a magnifying glass to read the Births, Deaths and Marriages in the
Press, and I write big in this book so as to be able to see what I'm saying. I
didn't grow very tall and wished I was taller; but I had broad shoulders and
a good chest which I used to go round with stuck out like a pigeon. I was
given fine strong legs, but they was a trifle bandy even then, and have got
bandier and bandier the older I've got. I wish now I could straighten them
out a bit; but I can still get along on them all right. With a stick.

I was very particular about my clothes. At work I wore a guernsey, or a
singlet if it was too hot in the greenhouses; but when I sat on the galley wall
of a Sunday evening watching the girls pass, I was wearing my best. It was a
suit made of good blue serge with the jacket braided at the edge and the
trousers narrow at the top and wide at the bottom; and I wore a white shirt
with it and a starched white collar and a shiny silk tie. I stuck my cap sideways on the back of my head, and my hair was done in a curl across my
forehead. I had done it with the curling-tongs my father used to heat over
the fire to do his with; and, as soon as I could, I grew a moustache. I wasn't
sure about myself in a moustache. Sometimes I thought my face looked
better without, and would shave it off. Jim used to laugh at me over my
moustache. He didn't have one himself and would make out he didn't
know me when I grew it. 'Why, if it isn't old Ebby!' he'd say. 'I'd never
have known it was you, if you hadn't spoke.' When I cut it off, he would
again make out he didn't know me; until one day he said, 'If I was you, I
would let one side grow and cut the other off for good; and then everybody
would know who you are.' After that I cut both sides off for good; and
have never kept any hair on my face since. I still shave every morning with a
cut-throat razor; and sometimes my hand shake and I cut myself.

I didn't have a moustache the day I went to my Cousin Mary Ann's wedding; but I had a big flower in my button-hole. She was only a third cousin really, but she was a cousin both sides; and all the Le Pages and all the Martels was invited. I don't want to say anything against my Cousin Mary Ann, because in her old age she was one of my very best friends, and you didn't notice her looks as an old woman; but when she was young, she was downright ugly. She was short and squat with a coarse skin and a snout of a nose and a sulky mouth and a heavy jaw. La Prissy said she looked like a mule, but I don't know, because I have never seen a mule. She got married to the chap who must have been the best-looking young fellow on the island. He had a boyish face with crisp curly ginger hair parted in the middle and bright blue eyes and a skin as smooth as a girl's; and he was slim yet well-built, and so light on his feet he might have been an acrobat in a circus. It was said he didn't have a very good character, but I don't believe Eugene Le Canu was nearly as bad as he was painted. The girls was round him like flies round a jam-pot, and he had to do something to get rid of them. He came of a very mixed family: Guernsey and French and, I think, Jersey as well; and nobody quite knew which was the fathers and mothers of which. He was coachman for La Princesse Zubeska.

There was a mystery about La Princesse Zubeska. She had red hair like Eugene, but it was grey when she came to Guernsey. I don't know if she was a Russian princess, or a German princess, or what; but Eugene said she could speak French and was easy to wind round your little finger, if you let her think she was having her own way. La Prissy said she wasn't a princess at all, but a cook who had been left some money by her mistress and come to live in Guernsey where nobody would know who she was. If so, she must have been left quite a lot of money, because she had a lovely carriage and pair and covered herself in scent and when she passed you could smell her for a mile. I think myself she was a real princess; but perhaps not very high up as princesses go.

My Cousin Mary Ann had set her heart on a white wedding, but La Prissy said, 'Mon Dou, but you wouldn't have the cheek, you!' so the bridesmaids was in white, but she wore a blue dress cut loose and with a long train. In the wedding photo she was taken sitting down with the handsome Eugene standing behind her. Her father had given her a cottage in the Robergerie with a vergée of land and a greenhouse. He thought Eugene would be able to work in the greenhouse in the evenings; but it was in the evenings La Princesse wanted him to drive her all dressed up to visit the gentry in the Grange and Queen's Road. She left him very little time for his wife. She didn't go to the wedding, but she sent a present. It was a big bowl made of solid silver; and you could see it was old, it was brown at the bottom. La Prissy said she had bought it second-hand.

They was married in the afternoon; and there was a good meal at the house afterwards of cold fowl and ham and wedding cake, and plenty of everything to drink. For once my mother drank a small glass of wine when everybody stood up and drank the health of the happy couple. In the evening there was dancing in the packing shed. It was done up like for Christmas with paper chains and coloured lanterns; and the boys played the concertina for the dancing. I remember La Prissy danced with my Uncle Harold, and I heard her say to La Hetty after, 'Well, I will say this for you, my sister: it is a man you are married to.' My mother didn't dance, but tried to look as if she didn't think it was sinful. My father danced with Hetty. He couldn't dance, but just jumped about. He'd had a few drinks and was sweating, and I remember the smell of his sweat. My Cousin Mary Ann didn't dance, but sat in an armchair with her train arranged around her like a queen. Eugene danced with all the young girls.

I had no more idea of how to dance than my father, but I made out I did. Big Clara Fallaize said I would become a good dancer if I practised. She was three or four years older than me and a big jolly girl with fat legs; and every fellow knew she was easy. She had been one of the bridesmaids and had flowers in her hair. After she'd danced with me a few times, she said she was tired and wanted to go back in the house and have a rest. On the table in the front room was the ruins of the meal and a number of open bottles of different sorts of drink. I tried them all and she had some; and then pulled me down on the sofa. I mustn't put the blame on Big Clara and say I was backward, because I wasn't. It was the first chance I'd had of doing it properly and I wasn't going to miss it. All the same, if I am going to be honest, I must say I was disappointed. I thought it was going to be more than that. It was all right while it was happening because I forgot myself; but afterwards I expected something else. I didn't want her to smother me, but I did think she might have said something nice. All she said, when she had done up her clothes, was, 'Now I want to dance, me!'

She went back to the packing shed straight away, but told me to wait a little, so as the others wouldn't know we was together. I didn't mind because I was afraid it might show in my face. When I plucked up courage and went back, she was dancing with Eugene; and she danced with him most of the rest of the evening. When supper-time came she sat on his knee, and everybody laughed and thought it was a joke. I didn't dance any more. I wished Jim was there so I could talk to him; but he hadn't been invited because he wasn't a relation. I heard the dancing went on until three or four in the morning; but I walked home with my mother and father hours before that. 'Well, I wonder what's going to happen there,' my mother said. 'It won't be nothing good.'

The baby came in a few weeks and there was two more children after. My Cousin Mary Ann had to work the greenhouse herself, though her brother did come round a few times to help. Eugene was never home. The people said, I don't know if it was true, that while he was waiting for La

Princesse of an evening outside big houses in Town, he often had one girl or another in the carriage with him. The last baby wasn't born yet when La Princesse decided Guernsey wasn't grand enough for her and she was going to open up her Town House. It's only fair to Eugene to say he didn't want to go with her, but she said he was the only one of her servants she could trust. She promised she would pay him high enough wages for him to be able to send some to his wife every week. La Prissy said it was the chance of a lifetime: the old woman would leave him everything when she died. So off went Eugene to London with La Princesse. He wrote a few times to Mary Ann and sent money; but he said he wasn't satisfied with his job. The Town House turned out to be two shabby rooms in a hotel in Bloomsbury, and he had to sleep in the garret and eat with the servants of the hotel in the cellar. It also got about in Guernsey that La Princesse had to leave because she owed money right and left.

After six months my Cousin Mary Ann didn't hear any more. She wrote and wrote but got no answer. At last she thought she would write to La Princesse. Prissy helped her to write the letter. La Princesse answered on mauve paper that stank of scent and said that if Mrs Le Canu knew how to keep her husband under control he might be able to leave the maids alone. Then my Cousin Mary Ann wrote to Eugene himself: a letter full of tears saying she would forgive him for everything, if only he would come home. She didn't hear another word. A year or so later, Mr H. Le Marquand from on the Esplanade was in London on business and saw Eugene Le Canu driving a hansom cab down the Strand. I think to her dying day my Cousin Mary Ann hoped Eugene would turn up on her doorstep; but he never did.

I have known one happy marriage, and that was my sister's; and, if ever a girl deserved it, it was Tabitha. She was a good girl. I don't mean she was strait-laced, she was full of fun; but she wasn't loose, and was as loyal as only the best sort of fellow can be. She went out to service to the Priaulx from Le Courtil à Bas from the time she left school, and they thought the world of her and treated her as one of the family. The eldest son, Jack, wanted her to marry him, but she wouldn't. Her heart was set on Jean Batiste from Perelle. He was only a young fisherman and lived in a cottage smaller than ours. La Prissy said Tabitha was a born fool, seeing as Jack Priaulx would have Le Courtil à Bas when the old man died. 'That Jean Batiste got nothing,' said Prissy. 'He is nobody.' Tabitha said, 'He is Jean.'

I must give him his due and say he was a nice chap; and he was good to Tabitha. I reckon I was a bit jealous of Jean. Tabby had always trusted me and told me everything. I think she still trusted me; but her confidences was for Jean. My mother liked him all right when Tabitha brought him along to tea Sunday afternoons; but she didn't set much store by marrying and giving in marriage in this world. They was engaged for two years before they could get married. He was an only son and lived with his mother, who was an invalid; but when she saw he was going to be all right after she'd gone, she was willing to go. The wedding was at the Câtel Church and arranged from Le Courtil à Bas; and everything was given by Mrs Priaulx. They didn't go away for a honeymoon, but settled down right away in their little house at Perelle. It was a hard life for Tabitha. They had enough, but only enough. The ground is sandy round there and they couldn't grow much; and there was no protection against the south-west winds and, in rough weather, often the waves would go right over the house. Tabitha must have had some anxious times when Jean was out to sea and it was rough. 'I always knew he would come back to me,' she said.

Well, she had him for ten years. He had done his training in the Militia and when the war against the Kaiser came, he was among the first to go. He was killed in 1915. Tabby didn't make a fuss. I never saw her cry. She went back in service for the Priaulx and, when the old people died, she stayed on with Jack and his young wife, Annette Gaudion. It wasn't that she forgot Jean. The last thing she said to me before she died, and she was by no means an old woman, was 'I want to go to Jean now.'

It's strange they had no children. It wasn't because they didn't want any; and I find it hard to believe it was because they couldn't. I have often wondered about that. They say children are born because of the love the parents have for each other. I haven't noticed that myself. Perhaps the children are born because the love of the parents for each other is not perfect. Perhaps the children come into the world through a gap between the parents. I don't know. I do know that Jean and Tabitha was very close. It wasn't that they made a show of it, or said silly things to each other. They seemed to understand each other with very few words; and when they was together, there was a quietness around them.

I haven't got no children, that I know of; but that don't mean I've been a perfect lover. I haven't led any girl up the garden, either. When I took a girl out I soon let her know what it was I wanted. I kept my nose to the ground and, if there was nothing doing, I trotted off. All the same, I often think it is a pity one got to do such things. When old Jim used to come round for me to go out with him, he'd say, 'Es-che pour la royne, ou es-che pour la nanny-goat, eh?' If I said, 'Ch'est pour la royne,' we'd go to the Pictures. If I said, 'Ch'est pour la nanny-goat,' we'd go square-pushing. He didn't care which. I was the one for chasing the girls, he wasn't. The girls hung round him; but with most of them he was more like a big brother. If one got desperate, he was good-natured.

7

Jim. Jim Mahy. Jim Mahy, my chum. Nobody know where his dust and his bones lie, or exactly where he died, or how; but he is dead. If I don't put up a monument to Jim Mahy, who will? His children was too young to remember him and, anyway, left Guernsey long ago; and Phoebe is dead, such as she was, God forgive her! I wasn't such a good friend to him, either. I would give everything I have, and I have more than people think, for him to walk in the back door this minute and say, 'Wharro, Ebby!' and I would say, 'Wharro, Jim!'

It was over the football I met Jim. I liked the football, me. I played for the North for three years, the good old chocolate and blue; and the Rangers didn't get much of a look in those years, I can tell you. They never was much cop, anyhow; but then what could you expect from a lot of Townies? Jim didn't play for the North regular, but he was in the reserve and played a few matches. He had the weight, but not the speed. I was a boy at school yet the day I saw Jim the first time. I was playing for the Vale and he was playing for the Capelles Boys' on Delancey Park. I dribbled the ball right from under his nose and scored a goal. He tried to charge me, but I was too quick for him and he fell over. After the game, he said to me, 'Damme, you're quick on your feet, you!' I looked at him. 'A pity you fall over,' I said. I knew there and then I didn't want to play against him ever again: at football, or in any other way. I wanted to be always on his side.

Everybody liked Jim. The only person I ever knew who didn't was Liza Quéripel. She said he was a charmer. I don't know where she learnt that word. There was nothing put on about Jim. He wasn't like Horace, who showed you his teeth while his eyes was reckoning up what he could make out of you. Jim had big grey eyes and, when you said anything to him, he would look at you for a long time with his head on one side like a big dog; and when the smile came, it was in his eyes first and they'd wrinkle up at the corners; and then he would open his big mouth and laugh. 'Ça va!' he'd say.

He was a real farmer's boy, and slow; but he was nobody's fool. I don't think anybody could pull his leg really; though sometimes he let chaps think they did, rather than make bad feeling. He was big and clumsy and slouched along as if he had all the time in the world. If we was late for going anywhere, it was no use trying to get Jim to hurry. 'Aw, we can always go another day,' he'd say. I don't know why Liza didn't like him because even my mother did. Her serious old face would light up every time he came into the house; and my father said he was a fine strapping lad. As the years went on and we was still always going about together, my Aunt Prissy said, 'I will say for your friend, Jim Mahy, he come of a good family; but it's high time he began to think of looking for a wife.'

It's true Jim's people was much better off than us; but they never made me feel it. I was always made welcome. His father owned the farm and the cottages and vergées of land; though most of it have long since been sold, and there are bungalows built where Jim and me used to cross the meadow to stake the cows. The farm itself is a guest-house now and owned by I don't know who. It belonged to Jim's sister while she lived, and she haven't been dead for so long. I can't believe that if Jim was alive now he would be an old man. He was never old. The kitchen where I ate so many meals with him was three or four times the size of ours; and there was lovely copper pots and pans on the walls, and always a big fire blazing on the hearth. I will never feel warm and happy again as long as I live, the way I used to feel those Saturday nights when I was sitting in that kitchen having a good supper with Jim.

Jim's mother was a de Putron from St Martin's, and of a better family and better off than his father. A lot of people had to pay rentes to Mrs Mahy, though we didn't; and she had money in the bank and owned a house in St Martin's and another in St Saviour's. She could have lived without working, yet she was busy from morning to night; only somehow she always managed to make you feel she was a lady. As far as I know, farming those days didn't pay any better than it do now; but that didn't worry Jim's father. If there was a bad year, he knew he could depend on his wife's money to make it up. He always looked well-to-do and, when he was togged up to go to the Cattle Show, he looked as if he owned the island. It was Jim did the work.

Jim could have gone to Elizabeth College, if he had wanted to; but he wouldn't go. He only went to the Capelles. His one idea was to work on the farm. 'I don't have to go to Elizabeth College to learn how to milk a cow,' he said. His brothers, Wilfred and Gerald, went to the Secondary School, or the States Intermediate, as they preferred to call it; but they was younger than Jim and more spoilt by their mother, especially Gerald, the youngest. The sister, Lydia, who was next to Jim, was spoilt by her father. The darling Lydia must have everything she fancied and be brought up to do nothing at all. She had long white hands and wouldn't even help the girl in the dairy, for fear they got dirty. She passed her time reading love stories and playing the piano and painting flowers on satin. I had no patience with her. I would have given her a turn on the purain cart, if I'd had my way; but Jim waited on her hand and foot. 'After all, she's my sister,' he said.

I suppose some people would say she was beautiful. She was tall for a girl and thin and had a long pale face and big dreamy eyes and always looked as if she was going to cry. She floated about in a dress of pale grey or blue with a chiffon veil like a shawl over her shoulders, and had a very small waist with her skirt trailing to the ground; and she wore a rose in her bosom. She had a great romance in her life. It was talked about from one end of the island to the other. Myself, I don't believe Terence de Freis was real. He came out of a book. He was a big, strong chap and might have been a boxer, but he looked like a woman dressed up. I don't remember his face now. I know he had long black hair that curled over his coat collar and a big black moustache. It wasn't a natural moustache like my father's; or even mine, when I tried to grow one. It looked as if it had been grown in a greenhouse. I remember he carried a walking stick with a silver knob.

He said his father was a 'veterinary farrier'. I didn't know what that was, but it turned out he was a blacksmith at Bailiff's Cross. Terence himself worked in the office of Advocate Randall by the Court; but he was only a clerk. He just copied. He didn't know nothing. The great lovers would walk together to St Sampson's Church arm-in-arm every Sunday evening for everybody to see them; and after the service they would go to Town and walk to the end of the White Rock. The good people those days used to walk to the end of the White Rock after church so as the women could see each other's clothes. Jim and me would go sometimes, for a laugh. Lydia was too much lost in love to speak to her brother on the White Rock. She would be hanging on to the arm of the dear Terence and looking up into his face as if she was going to melt into him there and then in front of everybody. All the women was saying how beautiful she was; but I expect they said other things as well. La Prissy said, 'Who are they, those de Freis, for goodness sake? They haven't got the paper to wipe their backsides with! She will soon find out, that girl, when the poverty come in through the door, the love go out through the window.'

He left her. The reason was never made known. He went off to Canada, and the last we heard of him was he had joined the Rocky Mountain Police. Lydia went into a decline. She got whiter and whiter in the face and thinner and thinner, and lay all day long on the sofa by the fire in the front room reading books called The Princess Novelettes, which had pictures of loving couples just like her and Terence on the cover. Now and again she would put her hand on her bosom and cough; and sometimes she managed to spit. Everybody in the house waited on her; even the young Gerald, who was a wicked little bugger. Jim had to take his boots off and leave them on the mat before he went in the front room, because she couldn't bear to have rough men around her. I told him he was a fool. 'Ah well, it might be you, or me,' he said.

Sunday evenings she had to be driven to church in the dog-cart, and she would walk up the aisle between her mother and father, holding on to their arms. After church, she was driven to Town and, by some miracle, she had the strength to walk to the end of the White Rock. She didn't look at anybody, but everybody looked at her. 'Mais qu'elle a souffert! mais qu'elle a souffert!' the women said. I can remember seeing her myself, walking between her parents with a pale blue ostrich-feather boa draped over her shoulders and hanging down, and wearing a pale blue dress and long white gloves and a white hat. When Hetty saw her, she said, 'Ah, la pauvre Lydia! la pauvre Lydia! Chn'est pas pour longtemps.' Prissy said, 'Elle sera en vie quand nous sommes tous morts, tu verras!' She was right. Lydia was the last alive of Jim's people, and got everything that was left.

Going down the White Rock of a Sunday evening wasn't my idea of going to Town. It was going on the Albert Pier of a Bank Holiday. Nowadays it is offices and rows of motor cars; but in those days they used to have the Fair there. The Pier was like a carpet under your feet with confetti; and every fellow carried a teaser with a mop of strips of coloured paper on the end to tease the girls. There was swinging-boats that swung right over the water, and coconut shies where you could have three goes a penny. I nearly always knocked off two out of three. I was a good shot. Jim wasn't so good at the coconut shies, but there was a strong-man machine you had to hit with a heavy hammer, and, if you rang the bell, you got a coconut. Jim rang the bell every time. It was three tries a penny, the same as the other; but Jim used to give two of the coconuts back to the fellow, or he would have ruined him.

What I liked best was to go on the merry-go-round. Jim and me would sit on two horses side by side and gallop up and down and round and round, while the music of the steam-organ was playing 'Over the Waves'. I spent a lot of pennies on the merry-go-round. There was also stalls where you could win prizes, if you was lucky with numbers. I have never been one to go in for lotteries and games of chance. I like to know what I am going to get for my money. Jim would have a go; and once he won a lovely plush box with shells round the edge, and a picture of the Houses of Parliament on the cover. He took it home and gave it to his mother.

One Whitsun, I'm not sure which, I think it was the year after my father got killed, the Great Sequois came to Guernsey for the Fair. I thought from his name he was a Frenchman, but he didn't speak as if he was French; and a chap from off one of the colliers told me he was a Cockney. He was on a waggon with a brass band. Talk of electric in him: I bet the planchette would have written out answers to anything he asked! He cured the people of the rheumatics by just feeling their legs. Old Peter Boissel, who had walked on two sticks for years, climbed up the ladder into the waggon with the help of other people; and the next minute came dancing down, and waving his sticks above his head. It's true he was back on his sticks in a week, and doubled up; but Sequois had gone away by then. He also sold bottles of the Elixir of Life for a shilling. It was green. He said as long as you could drink it you would never die. I didn't buy a bottle, because I didn't think I needed it then; but I'm not so sure I wouldn't have, if it was now. I heard after that he got it from Cumber, the chemist, in Fountain Street, and it was out of the big green bottle over the shop window. It cost him a penny a gallon.

His great stunt was pulling out teeth without pain. He pulled out hundreds of teeth that night. The people was all mad to have their teeth out. They said he didn't hurt at all; but the brass band made such a row while he was doing it they couldn't hear themselves screaming. It happened poor old Jim had toothache that night. It was a big one at the back that hurt, he said. I said he was lucky: it had happened just at the right time. It was only sixpence a tooth. Up the ladder he went and paid the sixpence. He sat in the chair. The band played and Sequois pulled out the tooth. He put it in Jim's hand. There was nothing wrong with it. Jim knew there ought to have been a hole in it, because he had felt it with his tongue. 'Hi, you've pulled out the wrong one!' said Jim, 'it's the other side.' Back he was in the chair and his jaw open, and Sequois pulled out the other. It had a hole in it all right. 'I'm not going to pay you for this one,' said Jim. 'That's all right, boy!' said Sequois: 'Two for the price of one! Two for the price of one! Walk up, ladies and gents! Two for the price of one!' 'That's all very well,' said Jim, when he came down the steps, 'but it don't put the other one back.'

I only go to Town when I got to these days and I haven't been at night for years. It is dead compared to what it used to be. It used to be good of a Saturday night. The shops was open to nine or ten, and everybody was there, except the gentry, of course, who did their shopping in the morning. I remember one Saturday night especially. It must have been before Sequois because my father was alive. My mother had come to Town with him in the trap, and I was with Jim. She didn't bother about what I might be up to, as a rule, if I was out with Jim; but that night, when she saw us, she said, 'Now mind you boys don't go up Horn Street, or they'll throw rotten eggs at you.' I wondered how my mother could know about Horn Street.

It put ideas into our heads and we went down to the Green Shutters to have a look at the whores. There wasn't none of them on show. All the shutters was closed, so they was all busy; but Madame Hamon herself was standing in the door. She said, 'Bon soir, messieurs,' and we said, 'Bon soir, madame.' Then we went for a walk along Havelet and up Hauteville and came back the short cut down Horn Street. My mother and father was standing against the railings by the market, looking over at the fire-swallower and the cheap-jack and the Salvation Army down below; and the German Band was playing round the corner of the Commercial Arcade. We was following our noses to the French Halls for to buy hot chestnuts we could smell roasting, but my mother spotted us and called us over. 'Where have you two been?' she said. 'Aw, we've just come down Horn Street,' said Jim, 'but they didn't throw no rotten eggs at us.' My father doubled up laughing, and even my mother had to smile.

As a matter of fact, La Rue des Cornets was rough, but there wasn't many proper whores living there in those days. It wasn't until the Green Shutters was closed down by the States at the beginning of the First World War, so as the pure English boys who came over for their Army training wouldn't be led into temptation, that the whores went into private business in Cornet Street. They was very well behaved in public, I will say that for them. They used to sit quietly on the seats in the cemetery facing the Town Church and wait for customers. There was old tombstones all round against the walls and a lovely big tree growing in the middle. The road have been widened since then and part of what was the cemetery and all the tombstones have gone; and so have the old whores. St Peter Port is not St Peter Port without the old whores.

8

It's funny how when you remember you can't choose what it is you remember. Nowadays I forget things from one day to the next. Of things that have happened of late years, I forget even the people's names; yet I remember some things have happened fifty or sixty years ago, as if it was yesterday. I don't mean to say I don't get it mixed up sometimes.

I am not the only one. There's old Abe Robilliard from Rocquaine. He was only a boy when he used to bring stuff for his father to the Huts and I was there doing my time in the Militia. He had his golden wedding the other day. It was in the paper. He have had seventeen children, and fifteen are alive; and there are dozens of grandchildren and great-grandchildren, and over a hundred in the family. I ran into him in Town one Friday morning, and we had a drink in the Albion. A young chap came in and said, 'Hullo, Gran'pa!' He said, 'Hullo, sonny!' I said, 'I didn't know he was one of your grandchildren.' He said, 'I suppose he is. They all know me.' I said, 'Why, don't you know, then?' He said, 'Goodness, no: the wife do!' He remembered his own lot, though he didn't always know which came first; but when it came to grandchildren and great-granchildren, they was the ones who had to do the remembering. I'm like that; and I don't always remember which came first.

I like soldiering. I fancied myself in a red coat and a red stripe down my trousers. I was a good soldier. They made me a full sergeant and I enjoyed myself. Three weeks at the Huts each year was a change from the greenhouses. Jim didn't do so well; but all the fellows liked him. He wasn't cut out to be a soldier. He never looked smart. He looked better on the farm in his dirty boots and dung on his leggings and his shirt open at the neck and his old hat on the back of his head. They made him a lance-jack; but it was only because they wanted somebody tall at the end of the front rank to fix bayonets by. I was glad he was never in my platoon. I couldn't have brought myself to make him jump to it, as I did the others.

It must have been round about then we went to Jersey to see the Muratti. I don't know which year it was, but I know they hadn't been having it long. Football was getting more popular, and our Cycling Track was become a football ground. I wasn't all that struck on Beautiful Jersey, as they liked to call it; and I have never wanted to go again. I was glad it was us won. The Jerseys came down to the harbour after the match to see us off on the boat. It was loaded with people, what with the team and supporters. Jack Priaulx, who was the captain of our team, was standing high up on the deck, waving the cup about. It's true he'd had a few drinks and was perhaps looking too pleased with himself. One of the bright Jersey boys shouted out 'Guernsey donkeys!' The others laughed and we laughed too; but then a whole crowd of the sods started calling out 'Guernsey donkeys! Guernsey donkeys!' Our boys wasn't having that. They started shouting 'Crapauds! Crapauds! Jersey crapauds!' There would have been fights if we could have got ashore, but the gangway was up. As it was, the boat went out the harbour with the Jerseys on the quay shouting 'Guernsey donkeys! Guernsey donkeys!' and all of us bawling out 'Crapauds! Crapauds! Jersey crapauds!' and Jack waving the cup. They came over to Guernsey the next year and got it back. I am glad I am not a Jerseyman. I would rather be a black man than a Jerseyman. A black man is a black man but a Jerseyman is a Jerseyman.

Jim and me wasn't much more than kids when we got ourselves stranded on Lihou Island. I remember I'd only just got my first bike. It was an old bone-shaker and didn't have neither a free wheel, nor a three-speed gear, and went grinding up the hills; and Jim's wasn't much better. It was on our bikes we explored Guernsey; though the visitors nowadays have seen more of it than I have. There are plenty of parts I haven't been to; and places like Jerbourg and Petit Bôt and the Gouffre I haven't been to since I went with Jim. Though it was more often along the west coast we went for our rides because it was flat; and the day we went to Lihou we had been right to Pleinmont. There wasn't so many houses round there those days: only a farm here and there inland, and a few cottages by the sea, and the old Imperial Hotel. That day we went up by the side of the Imperial and along the top by the haunted house and then full-pelt down the zig-zag with our feet off the pedals. On the way back round Rocquaine, Jim said, 'Let's go on Lihou.'

It was Sunday and nearly evening by then. I said, 'We'll have to see first if the tide is down far enough.' When we got to L'Érée we turned up by Fort Saumarez, and there wasn't a soul about. The stone causeway for horses and carts to go vraicing wasn't covered by the sea yet. Jim said, 'It's all right, the sea is going down.' I said, 'The sea isn't going down, it's on the turn.' He said, 'Come on, I'll go by myself, if you won't.' I said, 'All right, I'll come,' and we dumped our bikes against a hedge and I went across with him. There wasn't much to see. There was a few old walls and a house with nobody living in it. There was some sort of big pans, I didn't know what they was for; but Jim said once upon a time they was used to boil vraic to make iodine. There was thousands of rabbits on the island. It didn't matter where you walked they popped out from under your feet. Jim wanted to go on Lihoumel, the smaller island at the other end, but the sea was in between. He was going to try and jump it, but I told him not to be a fool. 'The sea is coming up,' I said, 'we must get back quick.'

He was in no hurry, as usual. He wanted to see all there was to see. There was a good view of the Hanois Rocks and the lighthouse. While we was looking at it, the light came on; but it wasn't dark yet. By the time we got back to the L'Érée end again, the sea was over the causeway. He couldn't swim and nor could I, and to get back up to our waists in the water it was hopeless to try because the current is very strong there, and we would have only been swept out to sea. Jim said, 'Well, it looks as if this is going to be our home for the night.' I said, 'Yes, but what about our bikes?' He said, 'Aw, they'll be all right, nobody will pinch those.' I said, 'If we was to light a fire, somebody might see it and fetch us off in a boat.' He said, 'If we had any matches, we could light a fire; but I haven't got any. Have you?' I hadn't. It was before I smoked openly. I wasn't worried, though. I'd never felt so happy.

I wish I could remember what we said to each other that night. I know we sat down on the grass and talked more friendly than we ever had before. Jim was always open with me, and said anything that came into his head; but I wasn't so open with him, as a rule. That night I was. I could say anything to Jim. If I had done a murder, as it happens I have in a way, I could have told him; and he would have liked me just the same. It was quite dark and we was still talking. There was a few lights twinkling on the land from the farmhouses and the cottages, and the Hanois light was going on and off. The sky was pitch black but full of stars. There was millions and millions of them. Jim said, 'There are a lot of stars in the sky, eh?' I said, 'There are a lot of stars in the sky.'

'Now it's time for by-bys,' he said. He found a place out of the breeze behind a rock that had bracken growing against it, and we curled up together: him with his back to the rock, and me against him. 'The babes in the wood,' he said. 'I don't see no wood, me,' I said. 'Mustn't be so particular,' he said. I fell asleep with his arm around me. I woke up once in the night. He was awake as well. 'Are you cold?' he said. 'I'm as warm as toast,' I said. I was cold in front, but I didn't want to change places. 'Are you all right?' I said. 'Snug as a bug in a rug,' he said. It was broad daylight when we woke up again. I said, 'Goodness, I'm going to be late for work!' I had only just started working for Mr Dorey, and I didn't want to be late. I ran up to the top to see if our bikes were still there. They was where we'd left them; but the sea had gone down and was coming up again, and would soon be over the road back. Jim was stretching himself and yawning in his lazy way. 'If you don't buck up,' I said, 'we'll have to live here for ever.' 'I wouldn't mind,' he said. I had to grab hold of his big hand and drag him across, or he would be there yet.

When I got home and indoors, my father was gone to work, and my mother was cooking the breakfast for herself and the rest of us. 'Oh, it's you,' she said, 'I thought you'd run away to sea.' 'Jim and me got cut off on Lihou Island,' I said. Tabitha wasn't up yet, but she must have heard me. She came running out of the bedroom in her nightdress and threw her arms around my neck and kissed me. Ours wasn't a kissing family, and I was quite surprised. 'He's come home, he's come home!' she said. 'Now you go and get yourself dressed this minute, my girl!' said my mother. Tabitha was still going to school. I went into my little room and changed into my working clothes. I gobbled down my breakfast as quick as I could: I was late already. When I was going out the door, my mother said, 'Your father is going to tan you when he comes home.' It was at the back of my mind all day. He had never hit me in his life.

I was having my tea that evening when he came in. 'So you're back!' he said. 'Yes, Pop,' I said. 'Finish your tea,' he said. 'I'm finished,' I said. He said, 'Come in the wash-house.' I followed him out to the wash-house. He began to undo his belt. 'Where was you last night?' he said. I explained to him what had happened. 'D'you know you kept your mother awake half the night?' he said. I looked him in the eye. He couldn't look at me straight. 'I am sorry I kept you awake half the night, Pop,' I said, 'I didn't mean to.' He did up his belt. 'Please don't do that to me again, son!' he said. 'I won't,' I said.

Jim didn't get into trouble, either. I went down later to find out how he'd got on. 'Lumme, they didn't even miss me!' he said. 'They wouldn't have known I was out, if it hadn't been for Victor howling his head off.' Victor was a bull-pup Jim's father had bought him for his birthday. He was the apple of Jim's eye. He was ugly enough, goodness knows, and, when he got old, he was grumpy as well. Jim wouldn't be separated from him. If you saw Victor lying in the sun anywhere on the farm, you could be sure Jim wasn't far off. He would have had him to sleep on his bed, if his people had let him. As it was, Victor had to have a basket in the kitchen by the fire that never was let go out at night.

Victor was only a pup when poor old Jim was laid up. He got terrible pains in his inside. Dr Leale was sent for and came and said he had appendicitis, and must be cut open and have his appendix taken out. He said the King had had his taken out and was as right as rain. Jim was taken away to the Cottage Hospital, and Dr Benson did the operation. I was worried to death. His people went to see him after he came out from under the chloroform and said he was all right, but weak and pale. I didn't like to poke my nose in, because they was as worried as I was; but I did ask his mother if perhaps I could go and see him one day in the hospital. She said I could go on the Sunday afternoon, and she would make a gâche I could take to him. The hour for visitors was from three to four.

After dinner on the Sunday I went down to the Grands Gigands to get the gâche, and Jim's mother wrapped it in a towel. Victor was in his basket by the fire, looking as miserable as sin. 'I know what I'll do,' I said, 'I'll take Victor with me. He'll cheer Jim up.' 'You can't do that!' said his mother. 'Yes, I can,' I said. 'Lend me Jim's overcoat. He won't be seen underneath.' It was about four sizes too big for me, but it was a cold day and didn't look out of place. I put Victor's collar on him, and took the strap so I could hold on to him. He walked all the way there on his own four feet. I swear he knew where he was going. He pulled and pulled, and dragged me along, and I could hardly keep up with him going up the Rouge Rue.

When I got outside the hospital, I put him under the coat and made him snuggle down. He wanted to peep out, but I wouldn't let him. I didn't like the smell in the hospital; it made me feel sick. Jim had a nice little room to himself, and a nurse showed me in. He was surprised to see me, because they hadn't told him I was coming. I said, 'I've brought you a gâche from your mother,' and put it on the table by his bed. He wasn't looking very well, I thought. 'How are you?' I said. 'I'll have a mark,' he said. 'That don't matter, if you're all right,' I said. 'It isn't where it will show.' He said, 'You're wearing my coat.' I said, 'Yes, it's cold outside.' He said, 'You look like a sack of potatoes.' 'I've brought somebody to see you,' I said; and let Victor out on the bed.

Golly, it was worth it! I have never seen two such happy people. Victor was jumping up and licking old Jim, and Jim was hugging Victor, and the colour came back into his face. There was a scream from the nurse, and other nurses came running in. 'A dog, a dog!' they screamed: 'Who bring a dog in? It is not allowed to bring a dog in!' The head nurse, the Sister, came in. 'That dog must be put out at once!' she said. I said, 'Why?' 'It is against the rules,' she said. 'It is not against the rules,' I said. 'On the board down-stairs it say VISITORS. 3 to 4. He is a visitor.' She said, 'The Matron will murder me, if she finds out.' I said, 'She won't do anything of the sort: you are much too good to the patients.' I gave her a wink. 'Well, I know one patient I won't be good to, if I get him in here,' she said. 'For heaven's sake, keep it out of sight, when you go out of this room!' He lay quiet on the bed against Jim while we had a chat; and when I said good-bye I put him under my coat. Outside I put him down on the road and tried to make him walk home, but all he would do was try and pull me back again to the hospital. I had to carry him all the way to the Gigands.

The last time I saw Jim in this world, before he went back to the War, was outside Salem Chapel, where we stopped to say good-bye. He had come for tea to our house that Sunday afternoon. He didn't want to go, and I didn't want him to go; and we stood there like two mommets and there was nothing we could say. At last he said, 'Well, cheer-bye, then!' and I said, 'Best of luck!' and we shook hands. I watched him go down the road. All of a sudden he turned round and came right back and caught hold of me by the jacket. 'Remember the day you brought Victor to see me in the Cottage Hospital?' he said. 'There isn't another boy in the world would have thought of doing that!' and he went off laughing. 'À la prochaine!' he called out.

9

Jim is the only chap I have ever known who I can think nothing bad about. He never said or did a thing to hurt me; or anybody else, as far as I know. I've got mixed up with all sorts of people in my time. I haven't always been 'that funny old man who live by himself at Les Moulins'. For example, Horace and Raymond: I got to know quite a lot about those two. Horace I didn't really know much about before he went away; but I got to know much more about him when he came back. He went to America, after all. He didn't go because he wanted to, though. He went because he was pushed. He put Isobel Mansell in the family way and Percy said if that was all he could do, the only place for him was America.

Isobel Mansell was a very pretty girl. She worked in the Post Office on the Bridge and her father kept a grocery shop at the Longstore. Her mother was dead. Of course a Mansell from the Longstore wasn't good enough for Prissy, and Horace daren't bring her home. When her father found out what had happened, he came to see Percy and nearly killed him. He put all the blame on Percy for the soft way Horace had been brought up: as if it was poor Percy's fault! Horace couldn't be brought up. The only person who could ever do anything with Horace was Raymond. Bill Mansell said the great lout of a Horace wasn't fit to untie the shoe-laces of Isobel; and he wouldn't have him marry her, if he was the only boy in the world. Horace was quite willing to. I think Isobel Mansell was the only girl he ever really liked.

Nobody knew a word of this at the time, mind you. La Prissy said in a grand way to everybody that they had decided to send Horace to America, because there was no chance for a boy like him on a small island. I wouldn't know even now what really happened, if it wasn't for my Cousin Mary Ann. When I got friendly with her and used to go and visit her for a chat in her old age, I discovered she knew more of what had happened between the four walls of every house in the Parish of the Vale and the Parish of St Sampson's and the Parish of the Câtel than anybody else on the island. By rights, it was her who ought to have written this book.

When she was left with three children and no husband, all she had was her small house, and the garden and the greenhouse behind. Her father helped a little and her brother helped a little; but her father died and her brother got married, and that was that. I don't know how she would have managed if she hadn't been everybody's cousin. They was all sorry for her, of course; and always spoke of her as 'La pauvre Mary Ann'. I expect that's about as much as they'd have done, if it hadn't been that she always managed to find time to go round and help. She would do anything. She'd milk the cows, pack the flowers, pick up the potatoes, or do the dirty work in the house. As she was a relation, they didn't like to pay her; but they gave her clothes for herself and the children, and butter and eggs and a cut from the pig, and anything that was left over. You would see her trudging home along the lanes of an evening, bowed down from being loaded like a donkey with all the things she had been given. Her own garden was doing so well she could afford to pay a boy to look after the greenhouse.

My Cousin Mary Ann was a very wise woman. She said very few words and listened to every word that was said. 'Mais wai, mais non-nein' was all anybody could get out of her; but not a word that she heard did she ever forget. Her relations hardly noticed she was there and would say anything in front of her. After all, she was only 'La pauvre Mary Ann'. I don't know how it was, but she always happened to turn up when something bad was going to happen. I remember she turned up at Les Moulins the day my mother died; and yet my mother was no worse than she had been for months. If somebody was going to die, she was there. If an engagement was going to be broken off, she was there. If a scandal was brewing in the family, she was there. So, of course she turned up at Timbuctoo the morning Horace was going to America.

She was there when at the last minute he brought Isobel home for to show to his mother. When Prissy saw what a lovely girl she was, she took her in her arms and kissed her and cried and said, 'Ah, mais qu'elle est belle! Si j'aurai su! si j'aurai su!' Isobel was the very daughter she had always longed for; she could come and live in the house, she could be engaged to Horace and, when he had made his fortune in America, he could come back and marry her. It was all settled. Percy then took Horace in the van to the White Rock to catch the boat to Southampton; from where he was going to get on the liner for America.

When they had gone, La Prissy began to think about the baby that was coming. What would the people say? 'Ah, how they'll laugh! how they'll laugh!' she said. She was thinking of Hetty the other side of the high wall. So the lovely Isobel was kept shut up in the kitchen all day long like a prisoner, and poor Percy was ordered to go and talk things over with Bill Mansell, who was the last man on earth he wanted to talk things over with. Anyhow, it was arranged between them somehow, without Percy getting murdered, for Isobel to be packed off to Grandma in Alderney to have the baby. I don't know what they thought they was going to do with the baby when it arrived.

Grandma in Alderney was no relation; or, at least, only by marriage. She was the widow of old Harold Martel from Ronceval. She was English. That's why she was called Grandma, and not La Gran'mère. She had been married twice in England and had come to Guernsey when she was a widow for the second time for a rest-cure. Dick Stonelake, who married Harold's and Percy's sister, Lil, was a nephew of her second husband and, on the strength of that, she had invited herself to stay at Ronceval. Dick Stonelake and Lil lived at Ronceval with old Harold, who was then a widower. The merry widow wasn't a young woman, but she had a way with her; and old Harold was married to her before you could say Jack Robinson. The children wasn't all that pleased to have a step-mother; but she didn't push herself. In fact, she went out of her way to make things easy for them. She got round old Harold to buy a house in Alderney, where she lived with him until he died: which wasn't long. The house was then hers.

She kept on very friendly terms with the step-children. 'The children of all my dear husbands,' she said, 'are my own dear children as well.' She treated them all alike. When she went to England for a holiday, she stayed with each of her children and step-children in turn; and when she came to Guernsey, she stayed a week at Ronceval with Dick and Lil and a week at Timbuctoo and a week at Wallaballoo. She never gave more to one than to the other. I don't know that they would have minded much, if she had, judging from what they said about 'the old woman from Alderney' behind her back; but she had such a way with her that, while she was with them, they would use the silver tea-pot and bring out the best china and make as much fuss of her as if she was the Queen of England.

It was clever of Prissy to think of sending Isobel to Grandma in Alderney. Grandma could hardly refuse because she had had Raymond to stay with her one summer for a month when he wasn't well. It was wonderful how Prissy managed to do it without Hetty ever knowing. The morning Isobel was bundled in the van and taken to the harbour and put aboard the *Courier*, my Cousin Mary Ann was sent round to Wallaballoo to help Hetty and keep her busy indoors out of the way. Luckily, Harold was along the Braye Road working on a new house he was building for Tom Mauger, the son of old Tom Mauger my father worked for. They say 'Be sure your sins will find you out.' Well, that was a case when they didn't. The only person who knew was my Cousin Mary Ann; and she didn't tell a soul until she told me, and that was years after they was all dead and buried. It's funny, because I've got a secret too, but that secret even my Cousin Mary Ann didn't find out to her dying day.

She heard news of Isobel through Prissy from time to time. Isobel got on well with Grandma in Alderney. She was allowed to go where she wanted, and talk to who she liked; and Grandma was given to entertaining soldiers stationed at Fort Albert, because they was such nice boys and had no homes to go to. The baby was still-born. 'Ah well, everything turn out for the best!' said Prissy. 'When Horace come back, they can start all over again with clean sheets on the bed.' The next news was that Isobel was married to a sergeant in the Staffords, and living in the married quarters at Fort Albert. When the regiment left Alderney, she went with it to England. Prissy said, 'It only go to show what happen if you try to do the best you think for somebody. I will never be such a fool again, me!'

Hetty came to see my mother full of complaints against Prissy because Horace was gone away. She didn't know how Raymond was going to live without him. To make it worse, Horace hadn't even told Raymond he was going away, or as much as come to say good-bye to him. Raymond was off his food and couldn't sleep and was going about looking like a ghost. Then La Prissy came with her side of the story. She said Horace would have come to say good-bye to us, if he'd had the time; but he had to go away in a hurry, so as to be sure to get a good place on the liner. I happen to know he was made to travel steerage and given fifty pounds by his father and told never to show his nose in Guernsey again, or ask for more. Grandma from Alderney didn't come and stay in Guernsey again; though she had to pass through on the way to England, but put up at the Belle Vue Hotel in Town for the night. She was going to stay with a granddaughter in Hampshire, who had just got married. While she was there, she tripped over the root of a tree in the New Forest and broke her leg and died from the shock. The house in Alderney was sold and the money went to the granddaughter. The Martels got nothing.

There had been business going on with the lawyers for years over the house at Ronceval. Old Harold Martel was supposed to have given it to his son-in-law, Dick Stonelake, before he went to live with his new wife in Alderney. He can only have given it; because Dick Stonelake didn't have a penny of his own. He came over to Guernsey with the English company that put up pumps and what-not to get gold out of the sea at Vazon. If a Guernseyman had got such a crack-brained idea, every other Guernseyman would have said he was mad; but because it was a Mr Smith from London, they believed every word he said and gave him their money in hundreds to throw in the sea. He didn't get a penny of mine. Everybody on the island went to Vazon on Sunday afternoons in their traps and carriages to see the machine that was put up; and me and Jim went on our bikes. I heard they did get a little gold out of the sea, because there are a few specks of gold in the rocks around there; but they'd have had to pump up and boil away the whole of the English Channel to get enough to make a sovereign. The heads of the company vamoosed back to England, pumps and tanks and boilers and all; and with a lot of Guernsey people's money in their pockets.

Dick Stonelake wasn't one of the heads. He was only a workman helping to put up the pumps and tanks and boilers, so perhaps he didn't mean to rob the Guernsey people. Anyhow, he married Lilian Martel, and his part in the gold-rush was forgiven, if not forgotten. Old Harold had long before let his building business pass to young Harold and Percy; and, for his old age, had put up greenhouses and become a grower. Dick worked for his father-in-law, though he knew nothing about growing; and, when he was given the place, if he ever was, took over altogether. When the old man died, Harold said he had been cheated. The property at Ronceval ought to have come to him by rights, as the eldest son. He found a lawyer in Town to back him up; and Dick found another lawyer who said old Harold had every right to give away his property to who he liked while he was alive. They went at it hammer and tongs; but I don't think they ever meant to settle it, those two lawyers. There was old laws dug up and new laws made up, and appeals against the old laws and appeals against the new laws, and appeals against the appeals. In the end, all the money Harold might have got from his father's house went to pay the lawyers; and Dick had to borrow from the bank, or he would have gone bankrupt. Lawyers are rogues. I always say whatever you do in this life, keep away from doctors and lawyers, or you will end up dead and have nothing left.

It was Raymond who told me the story. He used to laugh about it. He called it the Hundred Years' War. 'What was that, then?' I said. He said England and France was once at war for a hundred years and Guernsey was in between, so got it from both sides. I didn't know that, me. I thought Guernsey had always been a peaceful little island. I learnt a lot from Raymond. After Horace was gone, he often came to have a chat with me. He missed Horace terrible. He said, 'I'd have gone with him, if he'd let me!' Horace didn't send him as much as a postcard. Prissy got letters and said he was going wonderful. He was working for a company rich enough to buy up the whole of Guernsey and not notice it. She didn't say what he was doing for that company, or how much of their money was going into his pocket. There was no mention of Raymond.

Raymond have puzzled me more than any other chap I have ever known. He was a serious boy and a good boy; yet sometimes he pulled people to pieces so much he quite frightened me. For instance, he said when he was living with Grandma in Alderney, she had pictures of her three husbands on the wall of the sitting-room. They was all enlarged photos of old men with piggy eyes and bushy beards; and she would come into the room and say, 'Whenever I come into this room, Raymond, your dear grandfather's eyes follow me everywhere,' and look from one picture to the other. Raymond said, 'I bet she didn't know which was which!' He was the same about religion. He went to St Sampson's Chapel regular, but sometimes I thought he didn't believe a word of it. He said Horace said it was all made up. That was the first I heard of Horace having any idea in his head except girls and his belly and swank. Horace didn't believe Jesus was conceived of the Virgin Mary by the Holy Ghost. He said there are plenty of virgins on Guernsey who conceive, but it is not by the Holy Ghost. Raymond was worried about Jesus Christ going up to heaven in a cloud. He said it was awful to think of the people in all the churches and chapels on the island praying to somebody who perhaps wasn't there: yet sometimes you have the feeling somebody is there, he said; and then everything is all right.

Once I thought Raymond was gone in the head when he was talking about Horace. 'Horace used to save me from sin,' he said. It was the last thing I could imagine Horace doing for anybody. Raymond said, 'I sin on my own. D'you know what I mean?' He was looking at me very straight and honest with those blue eyes of his. He was innocent, Raymond. 'I think I do,' I said. 'Who started you on that tack?' 'A boy at the Secondary,' he said. He didn't tell me who. I said, 'Well, don't worry: you'll soon go with a girl.' He said, 'It isn't a girl I think of while I'm doing it.' I didn't know what to say. He said, 'Horace didn't do it. I asked him. That's why when he was here I didn't either; or I couldn't have looked him in the face.'

I was glad one night on the way home from work when I saw Raymond talking at the corner at Baubigny to Christine Mahy from Ivy Lodge. She was a cousin of Jim's and I had met her a few times at his house. I can't say I liked her very much. I know people said she was a lovely-looking girl. She had the Mahy look and was not unlike Lydia, but not so tall and thin; and I couldn't see her going into a decline. She was a strong country girl, really, for all her pale face and high cheek-bones and big mysterious eyes. She had a lovely singing voice, and sang solos in the chapel choir; but she also had a sing-song holy way of speaking, as if she was saying her prayers. I didn't trust her. By then I had been with two or three besides Big Clara and was getting to know what girls was made of. I put Christine down as one of those who looked as if she was cool, but was hot. I had seen her out with the Renouf brothers and the Birds from St Sampson's; and they wasn't at all the sort of boys who would go out with the Virgin Mary. She was a pupil-teacher in St Sampson's Infants' School; and it was not long after I had seen her talking to Raymond that she went away to England to study for two years in a Training College. I ran into Fred Renouf one evening and said, 'I hear your friend, Christine Mahy, have gone to England.' 'Good riddance!' he said. 'Why, what's she like, then?' I said. 'Prick teaser,' he said.

When I saw Raymond again I mentioned I had seen him talking to Christine. 'For goodness sake, don't tell my mother!' he said. 'What d'you take me for?' I said. 'It's only platonic,' he said, 'we were talking about

Robert Browning.' 'Who's he?' I said. 'A poet,' he said. 'I wouldn't understand,' I said. 'I like Tennyson better,' he said: 'In Memoriam.' 'What's that mean?' I said. 'It's a poem he wrote in memory of his friend who died,' he said. I didn't think Hetty had much to fear from Christine Mahy. He said, 'God is love. That's true, isn't it?' I said, 'It say so in the Bible.' He said, 'Yes, but it's true, isn't it?' I said, 'I'm not a minister.' I didn't want to argue about religion. He said, 'If it isn't true, everybody who is alive ought to go down to the sea and drown themselves; because then there is no hope for anybody.' I said, 'Come on, let's go and see what's in the crab-pots.'

10

I am Church, me. I was christened Church and I will be buried Church; and, if I'd got married, I would have been married Church. I go in the Vale Church sometimes, when there is nobody there. I like the old place. I have lived all my days to the sound of the bells of the Vale Church, coming to me on the wind over the water. When I was a boy I used to hear them playing a hymn of a Sunday evening, and then the quick ding-dong, ding-dong, before the service began; and I would hear them practising of a Wednesday night. I have heard them ring out merry for weddings, and toll the big bell for funerals; but, even when they ring out for joy, they are sad, the bells of the Vale; and now I am old, when I hear them, I tremble.

The young people of nowadays can have no idea how much religion there was on the island, say sixty or seventy years ago. There was nothing else to go to. People didn't go on the beach much and picnics was only for Thursday afternoons early closing. There was no Pictures, or they was only just beginning; and the Radio and the T.V. hadn't yet been thought of, thank God! La Hetty had a phonograph. It was the first of those sort of things I heard. It was a machine with a roller that turned, and the music came out through a trumpet. I can remember it playing:

> Side by side in sunshine,
> Side by side in rain,
> Sharing each other's troubles,
> Bearing each other's pain.

La Hetty used to cry she thought it was so lovely.

Of course, people still go to church and chapel, but not as many as used to. I know one chapel that have been a Picture House, and then a garridge; and another is now the Labour Office in Town. There are people who would turn in their graves if they knew. Me and Jim went the round of most of the churches and chapels to see what was going on. There was plenty to choose from. I think every religion in the world, except the Mormons, must have come and built a place of worship in Guernsey at some time or another. I heard there was even two of those came over once;

but they was thrown into the harbour, because they believed in having three or four wives like in the Bible. I don't see why they should have been thrown in the harbour for that: there have been more than one Guernsey-man who have had three or four wives. It's true, perhaps they didn't always all live in the same house; but it come to the same thing.

Jim and me used to go to the Baptists when there was baptizings going on. There was two lots of Baptists. There was those who didn't think they was properly baptized unless they went right down into a tank of water, and those was the ones Jim and me used to like to go and see; and there was those who was satisfied if they had a few drops of water sprinkled on the forehead. Jim said, 'I had that done to me when I was a baby. I don't want to get wet again, me!' There was the Quakers we heard about; but we didn't go. There was only a few on the island and Mr Vaudin, the one I knew, was such a patient, kind, good man, I didn't want to be disrespect-ful. He said they didn't say or do anything arranged beforehand at their meetings, but just waited for the Spirit to move them. That wouldn't have done for me. If I had to wait for the Spirit and was honest, I would have to be dumb and wouldn't move for the rest of my life. There was also the Christian Scientists in Mount Row; and we went once. They had a woman for a Minister, and she told us that if you think you haven't got a pain, then you haven't got a pain; but I have always found I get the pain first and the thought after. Then there was the Wesleyans.

The Wesleyans was nearly Church. The difference was that in Church you said your prayers for yourself, according to the words was written in the book; and, in Chapel, the Minister said your prayers for you in his own words. The great attraction in Chapel was the sermon: people would follow what they thought was a good preacher from chapel to chapel, Sunday after Sunday. I have never liked the people who preach, me. They pray for themselves and preach to themselves, and do not know the good and the bad that is in the heart of Ebenezer Le Page. It wasn't to hear the sermon Jim and me went to the Wesleyans. It was for the Harvest Festival. It was as good as Church, if not better. Jim liked to see the fruit and the flowers and the vegetables and the big loaves. There was a lot of well-to-do people belonged to the Wesleyans; and they gave plenty. It was for the poor after. I have noticed if you belong to the Wesleyans and are in busi-ness, you get on well. The Lord look after His own.

One Sunday evening when we couldn't think where to go, I said to Jim, 'How about going to hear my great-aunt preach, eh?' He said, 'Goodness, I didn't know you have a great-aunt who preaches!' I said, 'Well, she is not my great-aunt, really. She live with my great-uncle.' He said, 'Then she is your great-aunt by marriage.' 'They're not married,' I said. 'Then she's your great-aunt in sin!' he said. 'Golly, let's go and hear her!'

It was a rough night, and at first I wasn't sure where the Seaman's Bethel was along the Banks. It was well back in a field by a quarry before you come to Richmond Corner: there are houses there now. I had seen it by day. It was only a tin hut and there was a board outside which said SEAMAN'S BETHEL. BRIGHT GOSPEL SERVICES. ALL WELCOME. They had already started when we got in and was standing up singing 'Eternal Father, strong to save'. The place was packed and we had to stand at the back. I had never seen such a congregation. It was all men. They was of every race and colour and nation, and young and old, and bald and curly and straight; and had come every one from off the ships in St Sampson's Harbour. They had wonderful faces. They wasn't in no Sunday best clothes, but in guernseys and old jackets and coloured mufflers and sea-boots, and holding their caps in their hands. The only light was a paraffin lamp hanging from the rafters; and, on a low platform at the other end, my great-aunt was conducting the service.

She was a finely built woman, but looked as if she hadn't washed for years, and was wearing a skin-tight black robe that was green with age. She had a crumpled old black hat on her head with what had once been an ostrich feather on it, but was now only a spike sticking up. She was leading the singing in a voice that shook the corrugated iron roof and rose above the voices of the seamen, who was singing like the roaring of the sea. My great-uncle in a reefer-jacket, and looking like an old sea-captain with his white beard flying, was putting his whole heart and soul into the wheezey old harmonium and bringing out the rage of the storm and the whistling of the wind in the shrouds, until I thought every minute the old harmonium was going to fall to pieces on the floor.

When they had sung the hymn, the seamen sat down on the forms and bent over with their faces in their caps, while my great-aunt prayed. I have never in my life heard anybody pray so good as my great-aunt. She didn't ask God for what she wanted: she told Him what He'd jolly well got to do. He'd got to look after every one of the boys now in His Presence as He looked after the birds of the air and the beasts of the field, and not let a hair of their heads perish. If He did that, she would praise His Name.

They all said Amen and sat up; and she read a piece from the Bible. It was the story of the stilling of the tempest on the Lake of Galilee; and every fellow listened with a face as set and serious as if he was in that boat and in that storm. Then they stood up and sang another hymn:

> Jesu, Lover of my soul,
> Let me to Thy bosom fly,
> While the nearer waters roll,
> While the tempest still is high.

I thought the collection was coming next, and got a penny ready; but there was no collection. Instead, the chaps sat down and made themselves as comfortable as they could on the hard seats. They knew what was coming.

I wish I could remember the sermon my great-aunt preached that night; but I laughed so much, it went clean out of my head. I remember the text. 'Strait is the gate and narrow is the way that leadeth to destruction; but wide is the gate and broad is the way that leadeth unto salvation.' I knew there was something like that in the Bible, but I thought at the time she'd got it the wrong way round. Or perhaps it was me who'd got it the wrong way round. She brought down the fire from heaven and frizzled and blistered the churches and the chapels of every denomination, even the Salvation Army. She was all for Jesus. He was the only Person ever lived on earth who had dared to stand up and say He loved sinners. 'I know you're all sinners, boys!' she said, and wagged a finger at them and winked: 'Jesus loves you. Who will give himself to Jesus?' 'I WILL!' It was a mighty shout from every man-jack there. 'Now let us refresh our spirits in the Lord,' she said.

I'd noticed my great-uncle had disappeared round the back. In he came with his eyes twinkling and every curly hair of his beard twinkling, and three or four bottles under each arm and a corkscrew in his hand. He uncorked a bottle and gave her a swig, and had one himself, and passed it round; and another and another: gin and brandy and cognac and rum and goodness knows what. 'For Christ's sake, let's get out of here!' I said to Jim. 'She knows who I am and will be dragging me in. If my poor old mother could see me now, she'd drop dead!' 'A pity,' said Jim, 'I thought we was going to have a free wet.'

He hung about outside to see the end of it, and I kept out of the light. My great-aunt brought the lamp to the door and held it above her head, so as the boys could see their way along the rough path; and when in twos and threes they staggered on to the road, she burst out singing 'God be with you till we meet again!' and her lovely ginny voice rang out like a trumpet and a bell and you could have heard it to the Town Church. The seamen went rolling along the Banks and up past the Grandes Maisons on the way back to their ships singing, singing 'God be with you till we meet again!' Jim and me was falling on each other laughing, and as drunk as they was. The sea was up against the galley wall and the waves was coming over and the spray was blowing in our faces, and there was a full moon and flying clouds and the sky was green between, and the moon sailing behind the clouds and out again, and we was singing too:

> God be with you till we meet again,
> Till we me-ee-eet . . . till we me-eet,
> Till we meet . . . at Je-ee-su's feet,
> Till we me-ee-eet . . . till we me-eet,
> God be with you till we meet again!

'Damme,' said Jim, 'that's a grand religion!'

I won the leg of mutton off the greasy pole. It's the one time in my life I have done what I really wanted to do. I only tried for it once; and I succeeded that once. Until then, every year I'd gone to the Grand Havre Regatta and watched it being done. Some years nobody really won it, but it was given to the one who got the furthest up. I didn't want that. I wanted to get right to the top and win it properly; or not at all.

The pole wasn't straight up and down: it was on the slant, but it was a steep slant and greased as smooth as glass, and was out over the water. Most of those who tried was like me and couldn't swim; but there was boats around to pick them up if they fell in. It's what most of them did. I had seen chaps try it all ways: hanging on by their hands, hanging on by their knees, rolling around it, wriggling along it and Edwin Gaudion from Les Salines, I remember, tried to push himself up feet first. He got plenty of laughs; but he didn't get the leg of mutton. The crowd always gathered round to watch those who had a go make fools of themselves; but the one who got the leg of mutton was the joker in the pack and the hero of the hour.

I had my hour. I was cheered another time when I played football for the Upton Park Cup on the Cycling Track and the North won; but that was for the others as well as me. When I heard the laughing and the shouting and was at the top of the greasy pole, I knew it was only for me. I was clever. I wasn't called Monkey Le Page for nothing. It was with the flat of my feet and my bandy legs I climbed the greasy pole. I started slow. 'Go on, go on, Monkey!' the boys called out: 'Are you asleep?' I wasn't asleep. I went up a bit and slipped back a bit; but I wasn't as far down as when I started. 'Are you going up, or coming down?' they called out. I was going up. I hung on with my hands and my knees like grim death. The pole got narrower towards the top and it was easier to brake with my arms and not slip back; and I twined my legs around the wider part. I didn't hurry, or even look how far I had to go yet; and when I saw the leg of mutton in front of my nose, it was like the crown of glory in the Bible.

I untied it and held it up; and it was then the shouting and the cheering began, and you could have heard it on L'Ancresse Common. 'Now mind, Ebenezer,' I said to myself, 'no swank!' I let myself slide down slow and steady, and kept a firm grip with my legs. I didn't want to fall in the sea at the last minute and get the meat wet. Jim was the first to thump me on the back. 'I knew he'd do it!' he said. 'I said so from the start, didn't I?' I gave him the leg of mutton to hold, while I slipped away and cleaned myself and got properly dressed. When I got back he was holding it as if it was a bunch of flowers, and all the fellows laughing. He was laughing too, and was as pleased as if he had won it himself. I had a few drinks and could have been rolling drunk, if I'd taken half what was offered me; but I wanted to see the final of the first class sailing. They had to go round the Moulinets and across to Chouey and back. The Renouf brothers won it; and they deserved to. I shook hands with them, but I wouldn't go back to the marquee for more drinking; or hang about after the girls. The fun was only just beginning, but I wanted to get home with my prize and give it to my mother. Jim came with me as far as Salem. 'That old planchette was a fool,' he said, 'it ought to have known it would be right if it said yes.'

When I got indoors my mother was laying my supper at one end of the table. 'Look, Mum!' I said: 'That's for you!' 'Where d'you get it from?' she said. 'I won it off the greasy pole,' I said. She looked it over and poked it with her finger. 'It'll do for our dinner Sunday,' she said, 'and we can have it cold Monday, and Tuesday for soup.' She took it and put it in the meat safe outside. She came back in and I sat and ate my supper. She was sitting at the other end of the table reading the big Bible, as she always did before she went to bed. It was then I wished my father was alive. He'd have said 'A.1., son! That's the ticket!'

11

I suppose I will have to say something about Liza Quéripel. If she knew I was writing this book, she would be dying to know what I am saying about her. It is not that she would care tuppence what I do say, so long as I say something. Well, I've got plenty to say about Liza Quéripel; though for two pins I'd leave her out just to punish her! I don't know how many years it is since I have seen her, but she must be quite an old woman by now. She is not as old as I am, of course, but she is well on the way to catching me up. Anyhow, there she is, living at Pleinmont in the same small cottage her mother and her wicked old grandmother lived before her. It is far enough away from Les Moulins, thank goodness, for us not to be able to fight any more. It isn't possible for two people to get further away from each other on this island and not fall off. Yet who would ever have thought Liza Quéripel would end up the way she have, when she could have married a lord?

Was I sixteen or seventeen the first time I saw her? About that. I didn't know who she was, or where she came from; but she was a girl you would have picked out from among a dozen. I was sitting on the galley wall at Cobo that Sunday evening with Jim and Jim Le Poidevin and Jim Machon, the three Jims, and Eddie Le Tissier from the Landes du Marché, watching the girls coming out from the Salvation Army. A row of them was passing arm-in-arm, all wearing light summer dresses down to their feet with tight little waists and coloured ribbons and small round hats perched on the front of their heads. The two Roussel girls from the Rouvet had their hair down yet and the youngest, I remember, had five black cork-screw curls hanging down her back. Muriel Bisson, my cousin who married Frank Nicolle, was another; and Ada Domaille, who was plain and never married. Liza was in the middle, as she always was when she was with a crowd of girls. I wonder if I would know her now, if I was to meet her in Town. I can see her yet as she was that Sunday evening with her small square chin and straight nose and her hair done up for show. She had lovely hair. It wasn't red and it wasn't gold, but in between; and she didn't have a flaw in her skin. It was smooth and rather pale, but it could flush really like a rose; and she had the mouth of an angel when she was pleased, and the

mouth of a she-devil when she was vexed. She was taller than the others
and they wasn't so much walking along as dancing, and their little feet was
coming out like mice from under their skirts and they was singing:

> There is a fountain filled with blood,
> filled with blood,
> filled with blood,
> There is a fountain filled with blood
> flows from Emmanuel's veins!

They knew they was being watched by us fellows on the galley wall. Ada
Domaille nodded and my Cousin Muriel smiled; but the Roussel girls was
shy and made out they didn't see us. Liza, as she would, looked us over one
by one from head to foot, as if we was fish on a slab in the fish-market she
didn't want to buy. I thought, you wait, my bitch! I'll show you yet I'm
not a fish! 'Who's the one in the middle?' I said. The fellows didn't know.
'She's a hot bit of stuff,' I said. 'She think a lot of herself,' said Jim.

It wasn't long after, I ran into Ada Domaille on the Bridge. She was
going to get some ointment from Burgess, the chemist, for old Mrs
Tourtel's bad legs. She was always doing things for other people, that girl.
'I didn't know you was Salvation Army,' I said. 'I'm not,' she said, 'but
Liza wanted to go and hear them crying for their sins.' 'Who is Liza?' I
said. 'Liza Quéripel,' she said, 'didn't you notice her?' 'I can't say I did,' I
said. 'She noticed you all right,' she said. 'She wanted to know who you are
and where you come from.' If I'd been talking to any other girl, I might
have said, 'I didn't notice Liza because I was looking at you,' but I didn't
have the heart to say that sort of thing to poor old Ada. 'If she was the one in
the middle,' I said, 'she is too stuck up for my liking.' 'She is not at all stuck
up,' said Ada. 'She can't help being so beautiful. She is a wonderful girl!' If
ever a girl had a good friend, it was Liza in Ada Domaille. She went on to
say that Liza wasn't happy at home and so had come to live with her and her
mother at the Marais to get away from the mess. There was a step-father
and a mother who drank and a brother who wasn't a brother and old Mère
Quéripel and a lodger she'd had living with her for fifty years; and they all
had to make do in two or three pokey rooms.

I had heard of Mère Quéripel from Pleinmont. Who on the island
hadn't heard of old Mère Quéripel? She was a witch. She gave powders
for those who wanted husbands, and powders for those who had husbands
they didn't want. La Prissy and La Hetty went to see her once, while Percy
and Harold was out watching a boxing match in St Julien's Hall. Horace
drove them in the buggy. I don't know what they went to ask her for; but
Percy and Harold didn't peg out. It's possible the old lodger was Liza's
grandfather, but she wasn't sure herself. She liked to think her grandfather

was an officer from the Fort, or a captain off one of the ships. Her idea was to go into good service in Town.

It was through Jack Domaille, Ada's brother, that Liza got her feet on the ladder. He was head groom in the stables at Castle Carey, and was thought the world of by the mistress. It was him arranged for Liza to see Lady Carey. The lady took an instant fancy to Liza and engaged her on the spot as a lady's maid; but Liza wasn't a lady's maid for long. She was friend and companion to the lady, and lived and ate with the family; and for many years she ruled the whole Carey household, as only Liza could do. Her grandfather may well have been an officer in the Army, or a ship's captain, for she was to the manner born. The Careys was real gentry, but dowdy and old-fashioned. Liza looked and dressed and behaved as if she belonged to the Blood Royal. 'If I had played my cards right,' she said to me once, 'I could have been Queen of England.' I don't know about Queen of England, but she did get to know King Edward VII. The trouble was that, for all her grand manner, she was also everything you might expect the wild granddaughter of a wicked old witch to be.

She hadn't been living long at Castle Carey when me and Jim spotted her in Town one Saturday night. She was with a young chap I knew at a glance must be English. He was a pale thin weed of a chap with a few fair hairs on his upper lip, and looked as if he had a nasty smell under his nose. He was well-dressed and carried a cane he kept on whacking against his leg. I thought he must be an officer in mufti. It turned out he was a Lieutenant Leslie Carstairs who was a guest at Castle Carey and on leave before going out to India. I nearly dropped dead with surprise when Liza called out, 'Hullo there, Ebenezer! How goes it?' as if she had known me all her life.

It was at the top of High Street and the Pollet and the bottom of Smith Street; and there was crowds of people going all ways, and everybody talking to everybody else and waving their hands about the way Guernsey people do when they talk. She stopped and introduced me. 'This is Ebenezer Le Page from Les Moulins,' she said. 'He belongs to one of the oldest families on the island.' 'Oh?' said Leslie and shook hands with me. I introduced him to Jim, and Jim said, 'Wharro!' and shook hands with him. Leslie had been holding Liza by the elbow with two fingers, as if she was so delicate she might break; but I noticed, after he had shaken hands with Jim, he kept on trying out his fingers to make sure they wasn't broken. Jim didn't know his strength.

I couldn't think what Liza went out with a bloke like that for. I wouldn't have, if I had been a girl. She said he wanted to see the native life. Well, I agree he wouldn't see much native life with the Careys. The gentry are the gentry, whether they're Guernsey or English. I didn't like the way he was looking at the natives, anyway. It was as if they was animals in a zoo. 'Amazin', amazin'!' he said. Liza asked me if I'd seen Ada lately. I said I'd met her once on the Bridge. 'She speaks very well of you,' she said. I thought bless old Ada! Leslie was edging to get away. 'Aren't we being rather con-spic-u-ous?' he said. She shrugged her shoulders, as if she had to obey him but didn't want to. 'I must go now,' she said. 'À bientôt!' 'When?' I said. I wasn't letting the chance slip. 'That's for you to say,' she said, and looked down as if she was shy; but I knew she was putting it on. 'How about Thursday?' I said. 'Half-past six at the Weighbridge.' 'I'm afraid it will have to be half-past seven,' she said, 'after dinner.' I thought that was a funny time of the day to be having dinner, me. 'All right,' I said, 'half-past seven, then. Mind you're there!' 'I may have to be a few minutes late,' she said.

Jim and me had a drink in the Crown before we went home. While we was drinking, he said in a dreamy sort of way, 'O dare to be a Daniel!' I said, 'What you drooling about now?' He said, 'I was only thinking about Daniel in the lion's den.' Anyhow, she wasn't late that Thursday for a wonder. I hadn't been waiting at the Weighbridge more than two minutes when she turned up. She was like a girl let out of school. I remember she was wearing a little sailor hat and a pink dress with puffed sleeves. She caught hold of me by the arm and said, 'Oh, it's nice to be going out! Where are we going?' I said I thought we'd go to the Terres. 'What's on there?' she said. 'Singing and dancing on the stage,' I said, 'and Living Pictures.' It was a big oblong tent in the gardens past Havelet, before you get to the tunnel. The Living Pictures was what I wanted to see. I hadn't seen any yet.

On the way she wanted to know everything about me: where I worked and what I did and if I had brothers and sisters and if my father and mother was alive. I told her straight out everything, and we was quite friendly. I think she liked me all right when she didn't forget she was a Guernsey girl, and try and be half English like the gentry. Mind you, I didn't look so bad that night. I was all spruced up in my best blue serge suit, and had a rose in my buttonhole. They was just going to begin at the Terres when we got there. The seats was sixpence and a shilling and one-and-six and a few rows in front at two shillings. Jim and me would have sat in the shilling, but I bought two one-and-six. The Living Picture was after the interval. A white sheet was let down from a roller in front of the stage, and the magic lantern was in the gangway. The lights was put out and all the girls giggled.

I wondered after, if perhaps Liza thought I was going to hold her hand in the dark; but I was too interested in the picture. It was an exciting picture. A fellow on a bike was being chased by a steam-roller. It went after him hell for leather along roads and down lanes and round corners, until the poor fellow fell off his bike from going so fast and the steam-roller ran right over him and flattened him out. You could see the shape of his body flat on the road. The driver of the steam-roller stopped and got down and had a look. He was quite worried. He scratched his head and didn't know what to do; and then he spotted the fellow's pump had fallen off his bike. He picked it up and fitted it in the fellow's ear and pumped him up. The fellow swelled out and jumped on his bike and rode off again as fast as before with the steamroller going full pelt after him. I laughed and laughed. 'I think that's silly!' said Liza. 'It isn't silly,' I said, 'it's funny. It's you that's silly!' After that everything I liked, she didn't; and everything she liked, I didn't. There was a fellow made me think of Terence de Freis. When the lights went up again, he sat by a table looking at a photo of a beautiful woman and sang to it:

> If those lips could only speak,
> And those eyes could only see,
> And those beautiful golden tresses
> Were there in realitee,
> Could I only take your hand
> As I did when you took my name,
> But it's only a beautiful picture
> In a beautiful golden frame!

Liza thought it was lovely. I said, 'He's a turd!'

I saw her back to Castle Carey, but we quarrelled all the way. I don't know what about. I tried to put my arm around her waist, but she wouldn't let me; and when I tried to kiss her, she said I wasn't the nice boy she had thought I was. She had to go in by a side door; but when we got there she stood in the porch, if you please, waiting to be kissed. I made out I didn't understand. 'Am I going to see you again?' she said. 'I don't know!' I said and walked home in a fury.

I went along to the Weighbridge the next Thursday at half-past seven in case she turned up; and, sure enough, after I had been waiting for a quarter of an hour, along she came. She said she just happened to be passing. I deserved that, so I took no notice. That night we strolled along the Castle Walk to the end of the breakwater. We got on better than the week before, but I nearly had a fight with her by the lighthouse. There was fellows sitting on the end of the pier fishing, and she wanted me to stop them because she said it was cruel. I'd have looked a fool! When I wouldn't, she was going to do it herself, and I had to stop her by force. I managed to turn her round and walk her back; and when she didn't see the fellows fishing, she forgot. I took her home up St Julien's Avenue and along Candie and across Cambridge Park. She let me put my arm around her waist and kiss her good-night. I asked her if she'd come to the Circus with me the next

Thursday. She said she'd be delighted to: I was so refreshing after the people she had to put up with at Castle Carey. I didn't know what she meant by that, quite.

I had been to the Circus several times with Jim. Sloan's Circus came to Guernsey every year for two months in the summer and pitched in a field by the Tram-shed. It was a green tent with a pole in the middle and slanting poles all round; and inside it was lit by rings of gas-jets. When you went in, it was like being in a jelly-bowl turned upside-down under the sea. It was sixpence to sit on the wooden steps at the back; and Jim and me always sat in the top row, so as not to have other people's knees sticking in our backs. It was a shilling to sit in the chairs down by the ring; and there was a special block of chairs with antimacassars for three shillings. I never saw nobody sitting there, except Dr de Jersey and his wife. They wasn't for people like us. I bought two tickets for the shilling seats down by the ring.

The first part of the programme Liza enjoyed as much as me. She was quite excited and gripped hold of me when the brass band struck up a Sousa march and the horses came galloping in. I had seen it all before, and it wasn't very good really. Mr Sloan had been a good horseback rider in his time, but now if he did Dick Turpin's Ride to York, he didn't have enough breath left when he got there to cry tears over the death of Black Bess. Mrs Sloan didn't do much. She sat sideways on Prince, who trotted round the ring and showed her off. She was on the heavy side and poor old Prince's back was hollow from her weight. I said I was sorry for old Prince and Liza said she was sorry too. Miss Sloan stood on the rump of Darling, her Arab steed, and jumped through a hoop held out by Shadow, the clown. I said she wasn't much cop. Liza thought the same. Shadow, the clown, had a white face and tried to be funny by being miserable. I didn't laugh. Liza didn't laugh either. The Shetland ponies made me laugh. The smallest always wanted to go round the wrong way. He was the one I liked. Liza said he was a pet.

The second half of the programme was Colonel Cody, instead of Dick Turpin's Ride to York. He was supposed to be a Red Indian; but I don't know if he was or not. He was bald on the top of his head, but had long hair hanging down his back. He was a wonderful shot. He could hit a sixpence while he was riding round the ring and turning a buncho on his horse. I don't think that interested Liza much. The next thing he did was to take out cataracts from the eye with his tongue. It was that upset Liza to start with. When I'd been with Jim the shilling seats was mostly taken up by families; but that night, because Cody was there, the fellows from the quarries who had cataracts on their eyes sat down in front. He went from one to the other, held open the eye-lid, licked the cataract off the naked eye, and showed them the skin on the back of his hand to prove he had done it. It wasn't a trick because my father used to do it for the fellows at work, only he wasn't as quick as Cody. Liza said it was filthy. I said a chap who had a cataract on his eye didn't care if it was filthy or not, if he got rid of the cataract. Besides, my father wasn't filthy.

Cody's great act was to mesmerise a woman he had brought over from Jersey. Some said she had been given stuff beforehand; but I don't think so. I noticed once she got behind the tent pole out of range of his eyes, and he swore at her to move. People said she lived with him and he knocked her about, so that she was afraid of him, and would do anything he said. Others said he had snakes in his lodgings at the Bouet, and had learnt how to do it from them. Anyhow, she fell down on the sawdust of the ring like a limp rag. Liza already wanted to jump in the ring and stop it, and I had to hang on to her. I don't think the woman suffered. Cody stuck a pin in her and she didn't bat an eyelid. He then picked her up in his arms and arranged her with her head on the edge of one chair and her feet on the edge of another. He did something to her muscles and she went stiff. He then put a board on her body, but it wasn't touching either of the chairs; and he got three cart-horse drivers to stand on the board. She didn't bend. In the excitement I let go of Liza, who was wriggling like an eel. She made one jump and was in the ring.

I didn't know where to put myself: I was so ashamed. She was cheered by half the crowd and boo'd by the other. All the circus people gathered round her and said the woman was perfectly all right and couldn't feel a thing. Liza wanted for her to be brought round there and then; but it was explained the woman had gone under expecting to be as if she was asleep until the Saturday night, and it would be dangerous and not for the good of the woman to bring her round before. Mr Sloan himself, who was then in a frock coat and had a big white shirt front, offered Liza two free tickets for the three-shilling seats for her to come and bring a friend with her to see it done. Liza snatched the tickets from his hand and tore them to shreds and threw the pieces in his face. 'Brutes! Brutes!' she said. 'Brutes of men! That poor woman! That poor woman!' and she walked out of the ring and out of the Circus with her head in the air, and everybody cheering and laughing. I let her go. I'm no Daniel, me.

12

Jim only laughed when I told him about Liza. He said he always knew when I had been out with Liza because I looked like Victor when he came back from one of his gallivants. Victor was a good and faithful dog and hardly ever left his master's heels; but every now and then he would go off after a bitch. He'd be gone for a week sometimes, and would be seen mooning along the lanes; but nobody would dare to try and bring him back. Then one morning, lo and behold, he'd be in his basket again. He would look grumpy and miserable, and have his fur torn; and, once, a hole in his ear and, another time, a bad wound on the top of his head. For days after, he would only crawl out and lie in the sun, saying to himself, 'Never again! Never again!'

I gave up all thought of Liza. I chased after Florrie Brehaut, who was learning to be a nurse. She liked the boys and was easy; and she knew a thing or two, that girl. I saw Liza in Town a few times, and once when I was out with Florrie. She was nearly always with a different bloke. The only one she went out with at all regular was Don Guille, the son of Jurat Guille; but even when she was with him, she would smile and wave to me, as if nothing had happened. Florrie didn't like her. I liked Florrie all right, but I was glad when she went to England. 'It's no good me writing, is it?' she said. 'It isn't much,' I said: 'I'm not one for writing letters.'

I spent a lot of my spare time on the farm with Jim. Of an evening, when I'd finished work and there wasn't much had to be done in our garden, I'd go down; and on Saturday afternoons. I liked farming better than working in the greenhouses. Jim said I would have made a good farmer. 'Better than you, anyway,' I said. The trouble with Jim was that he was soft about the animals. They wasn't just so much milk and butter and meat so far as he was concerned, but Rosie and Marie and Evangeline and Boney, the bull. It nearly broke Jim's heart when the young bullocks had to go off to the slaughterhouse. 'They haven't had half a life,' he'd say. When Timothy, the donkey, got so old he was of no use to anybody and was eating every other creature out of house and home, Jim's father said he would have to be put down. Jim turned on his father. 'All right,' he said, 'and when you get to be an old man, we'll have you put down by a humane killer and your carcase carried on a truck to the Tram-shed to be burnt.' Timothy lived on for many more years and got fatter and fatter, until one day he was found dead in a field from overeating. The creatures knew Jim's weakness. I could get the cows down the lane in five minutes. It used to take Jim half-an-hour and, even then, two or three would be wandering back to where they'd come from. He'd swear at them in all the colours of the rainbow; but they didn't take a blind bit of notice. 'Ah well, cows are cows,' he'd say.

Christmas I always spent at home with my mother; but Jim came to us for Boxing Day. Tabitha and Jean came for the New Year. They would arrive New Year's Eve and take my mother to Town with them, and come back with her to Les Moulins and stay the night. Those days New Year was kept up nearly as much as Christmas; and New Year's Eve in Town was nearly as good as Christmas Eve. I always went to Town with Jim New Year's Eve, and stayed the night at his place. After a good supper, we would lie awake in his big bed and wait to hear the New Year come in. When the whistles and the hooters started going down St Sampson's, and the sirens from the ships, he would wish me a happy New Year and I would wish him one too; and then we'd curl up together and go to sleep.

New Year's Day I helped to get ready for the party. The Mahys used to have a quiet Christmas with just the family; but New Year's Day they gave a big party. I remember one year Christine Mahy was there. She had done her time in College and was teaching in a school at Frimley in Surrey, but she was then home for the holidays. I asked her if she had seen anything of Raymond lately. He hadn't been round to see me for months, and I was beginning to wonder if something was the matter with him. 'Oh yes,' she said, 'I've been seeing quite a lot of Raymond.' His health was all right, it seemed, but he had decided he wanted to be a minister. I couldn't make that out at all. He was such a sincere boy, I'd have thought a minister was the last thing he would want to be.

La Hetty came to see my mother soon after to tell her all about it. The two of them was having tea and a chin-wag when I came in from work. La Hetty was half for it, and half against. At first she blamed Horace. She said Raymond only wanted to be a minister so as he could go away from Guernsey, because Horace had gone away from Guernsey. I was sure there was something more to it than that. She went on to say that Raymond had been converted. He had always gone to Chapel; but he had never 'come forward', as they say. Hetty was ashamed he had made a show of himself in front of everybody. She did say there hadn't been much talk. As a matter of fact, it was done quiet at St Sampson's. They didn't cry aloud their sins and throw themselves on their knees at the penitent form, as they did at the Salvation Army. They just stood up in an after-meeting where most of those present was already converted.

Hetty said Raymond now taught in the Sunday School and was out most nights of the week on something to do with Chapel. He helped with the Band of Hope and the Scouts and went to Mr Carrington's Bible Class. Mr Carrington was manager for John Leale on the Bridge, and Hetty was pleased Raymond was getting mixed up with the Leales and the Birds and the Doreys and the Johns and such people, who was all well-to-do and relations of each other in one way or another. 'After all,' she said, 'the Le Pages are as common as flies.' She wasn't as worried as I would have thought at the idea of him going away. She said she didn't know how she was going to bear it while he was away; but if when after he came out of College, he was sent to preach in a Chapel in England, she could sell up everything and go and live with him. She didn't say what was going to happen to Harold. I didn't know if Wallaballoo was her house, or his. I thought it was his. She said, 'There's nothing I'd like better than to go and live in a place where I'm not known, and where everybody don't know all my business.' I listened, but I didn't say nothing, except that I hoped Raymond hadn't forgotten he got a Cousin Ebenezer.

He came round the next evening. 'Hullo, stranger!' I said. He said he was sorry he hadn't been to see me before, but he'd been busy. It sounded all right; but he was different somehow. He didn't look at me straight. It was as if there was something he was ashamed of. I said I was just going down to my boat to mend a net, if he'd like to come with me. He said he'd come and he sat on the shingle watching me. La Petite Grève is only a small bay, but it's nice with the rocks and the noise of the sea, and only the sea and the rocks to look at. I was quite happy working with him sitting there saying nothing. I wasn't going to bring up religion, unless he did. At last he said, 'I suppose you think I am a hypocrite.'

I said, 'I reckon we're all hypocrites, one way or the other, if the truth was known.' He said, 'Jesus saves.' I didn't like to hear a boy talking like that. I said, 'It was brave of you to stand up for what you believe.' He said, 'It's true, you know. I've proved it.' I said, 'Well, I haven't. I'm not saved.' He said, 'I don't do it any more.' I wondered how that could be. Myself, since I was thirteen or fourteen, I hadn't managed to live without something having to happen sometimes. I said, 'Yes, but nature is nature. Something got to happen.' 'It doesn't happen to me now,' he said, 'except when I'm asleep, and, when I wake up, I repent.' I began to feel rather sick of Raymond. I liked him better when he was a sinner. I said, 'How long before you go to your college?' 'Years yet,' he said. 'I have exams to pass first.' 'You'll do that all right,' I said. He said, 'I really came to ask you to do the same.' 'How d'you mean?' I said. 'Make the Great Decision,' he said. 'I don't know,' I said. 'We'll see.'

My mother prepared some supper for us and sat reading her Bible while we ate it. I will say for my mother's lot they didn't go round trying to convert everybody. They knew they was right and it was other people's own look-out if they wasn't. Raymond started me thinking about Liza again. She was my idea of being saved. I didn't want to have to keep on chasing after this one and that one for what I could get. The chance came. It happened it was that year Jim and me went to the Coronation Fête at St Peter in the Wood. There was a Fête in each parish on a different Thursday for the Coronation of King George V, and we went to them all; but it was the one at St Peter in the Wood was the red-letter day for me, because it was there I tried to get down to brass tacks with Liza.

Before the free tea, which was what we went for, was a Grand Procession of farm waggons with chaps and girls in dressed up showing tableaux of the History of England. There was King Alfred burning the cakes and King Canute getting his feet wet and King John looking for the Crown Jewels in the Wash and King Richard murdering the Princes in the Tower and Queen Elizabeth sitting on her throne. Liza was Britannia. There was going to be three prizes given: first, second and third; and a lot of people thought Queen Elizabeth was going to win the first. Eva Robilliard was Queen Elizabeth. She was a very pretty girl and wore a lovely dress; but she was bowing and smiling and throwing kisses to everybody: not at all like a queen. Liza stood like a statue. She didn't move a muscle. Her lovely hair was down over her shoulders and she was wearing a long white robe with a golden girdle and golden sandals. She was standing on shingle with a conch shell at her feet. She rested one hand on a shield of the Union Jack done in flowers, and was holding a sort of fork thing in the other. She had a helmet on her head like you see in pictures of Britannia in books. She came on the last waggon and, when the crowds of people saw her, they cheered so loud the judges had no choice but to give her the first prize. I thought that's the girl for me!

Jim and me was with the three Bichard girls from La Croûte. Jim always said there was safety in numbers and thought three was a good number because you couldn't very well ask one to play gooseberry. The tea for everybody was spread on trestles set up on the grass at L'Érée, and each of us was given a Coronation mug. I have mine yet. When we was just going to begin, who should come along but Liza? She'd dropped the shield and the fork thing, but still had the fancy helmet on her head. She saw me and came over, all smiles. 'Fancy seeing you right out here!' she said. I said, 'I'm glad you got the first prize. I'd have given it to you myself.' She said, 'Is there room for me?' I said, 'Of course there's room for you!' and pushed up and made room on the form for her between me and Jim. I had never known Liza be so nice to everybody as she was that afternoon. She went into raptures over the Bichard girls because they had such lovely hair, though it was nothing like as lovely as hers. She said Jim looked the picture of health and ought to have gone in the Procession as Richard, Coeur de

Lion. After the tea there was going to be racing and games, but she said she couldn't go in for racing and games in her present dress. I said, 'How about coming for a stroll along the beach?' 'All right,' she said, 'then I can call in to my mother's house and change. I don't like being looked at by everybody.' I thought well, that's a lie to start with.

She gave me her hand to help her down over the rocks, and we walked across Rocquaine Bay towards Fort Grey. She asked me if I knew the story of how it was Fort Grey came to be haunted. I didn't. She said that hundreds of years ago, when it was called Rocquaine Castle, two young lovers sat on the wall in each other's arms by moonlight and threw themselves together into the sea. 'Whatever did they want to do that for?' I said. 'They was lovers,' she said. 'They was mad,' I said. She said, 'If you was in love with me, wouldn't you want to throw yourself with me into the sea?' I said, 'If I was in love with you, I would want to live as long as I could and have you for my regular girl.' She stopped dead in her tracks and threw her head back and laughed. I didn't know if she was laughing at me, or if it was because she was pleased.

I said, 'Listen here, Liza: be serious for once. I like you and you like me: and I know it.' I did know it. When she had kissed me, her lips was hungry enough to eat me up. I said, 'I don't want you to be going out with Don Guille and every other Tom, Dick and Harry in the town.' She said, 'How is Florrie Brehaut getting on?' I said, 'I don't know how Florrie Brehaut is getting on. She have gone to Southampton and is working in a hospital.' 'I suppose she writes to you every day,' she said. 'She don't write to me any day,' I said, 'and I don't write to her neither.' 'I only wondered,' she said. She had found out what she wanted to know. I was furious.

'If it comes to that, you don't think anything of me really,' she said, 'you think more of that Jim Mahy than you do of me.' I said, 'What have poor old Jim got to do with it? I know where I am with Jim. I don't know where I am with you.' She said, 'I am not going to be chained to you, or to anybody else, like a dog. I wonder who you think you are.' 'I am Ebenezer Le Page from Les Moulins,' I said, 'in case you don't know.' 'I know, I know,' she said. 'Ebenezer Le Page from Les Moulins! Is there anybody can be more Guernsey? He is countrified, he is ignorant, he is small! Why, I am even taller than you are!' 'You are NOT taller than I am,' I said, 'I am an inch taller than you!' 'You are not! You are not!' she said; and she ran up on a rock and stood feet above me. I ran up after her. She was standing on wet vraic and there was a pool of the sea on the other side. 'Aren't I?' she said. 'Say I am! Say I am!' 'It's that thing on your head make you look taller,' I said and grabbed it. 'Give it me back!' she said and started to fight me for it. I couldn't fight fair because I had my Coronation mug in my other hand, and I didn't want to let it fall on the rocks and break it. I gave her a push.

She slipped on the wet vraic and went screaming down into the pool. I jumped off the rock on to the dry sand and went round to see: there she was sitting with the water up to her waist and her golden sandals tangled in the green seaweed and the little fishes swimming round her legs. 'I hate you! I hate you!' she said. 'Here, have your silly hat!' I said and threw it at her and it floated on the water. 'Britannia rules the waves!' I said and went off and left her. When I got back to Jim and the Bichard girls, he said, 'What have you done with Liza?' 'I've drownded her,' I said. 'Well,' he said in his slow drawl, 'perhaps that's the best thing you could have done.' I felt miserable all the way going home.

13

Victor died. He wasn't all that old for a bull-dog and I have always thought he must have got himself hurt inside on his last gallivant. He lost interest and wouldn't move, but lay in his basket all day long and got fat and wheezy. The vet said there was nothing wrong with him: it was his breed and he would get over it; but he began to get shivering fits and had a hot nose. He wanted to drink a lot of water, but went off his feed. Jim's mother said she was sorry but she couldn't have him in the kitchen any longer because he smelt; so Jim put his basket in the stable and gave him plenty of straw. One Saturday afternoon we was all having tea in the kitchen when out comes Victor from the stable and trots across the yard. He was as lively on his bandy legs as when he was a pup, and grinning all over his ugly face. 'Victor's got better!' said Jim. In came Victor and Jim's mother patted him and Wilfred, who was there, said, 'Hullo, Victor!' though he didn't like him much, and I said, 'Well done! Good boy!' and at last he got round to Jim, jumping and licking and wagging his tail; and Jim was nearly in tears, he was so happy. Victor went quiet then and rolled his black eyes at the rest of us and trotted back across the yard to the stable. Jim couldn't wait to finish his tea but must get up from the table at once and make a mash of meat and potatoes to take to him. 'He'll eat this now,' he said, as he went out with it. He hadn't been gone two minutes when he came out of the stable with Victor dead in his arms.

Jim looked terrible. I went outside to meet him, but he turned away from me and went down the meadow. I followed him. He sat on the grass with his big shoulders hunched and laid Victor down in the sun beside him. He spread out Victor's legs so the sun would get to his belly and sat there stroking his back and head. I think in his simple mind he thought the sun might bring Victor back. I was standing behind him, but I couldn't say a word. All of a sudden, he jumped up and said in a rough voice, which was not at all the way Jim spoke to me as a rule, 'Bring a couple of spades, you! What we wasting time here for?' and bundled Victor under his arm as if he was a bundle of rags. I fetched the spades and brought a bit of sacking. Jim chose a tree by the stream and we dug a deep hole between the roots and I wrapped Victor up in the sacking and put him in it. Jim filled the hole and stamped down the ground. When we got indoors his mother said, 'Well, he's had a happy life for a dog. You can always get another.' Jim turned on his mother as if he hated her. 'I don't want another dog!' he said.

Jim began to think about emigrating. He didn't come right out with it at first, but asked me how Horace was getting on. I didn't know. According to Prissy, he was doing wonderful; but you couldn't believe a word she said. La Hetty said if the truth was known, he was begging for his bread from door to door. 'I don't expect he have made his fortune yet,' I said, 'or he would have been back to show us.' Jim said, 'Who wants to make a fortune? All I want is enough to keep myself alive.' It was all very well for Jim to talk. If at any time he wanted a new suit, all he had to do was to have it made to measure by Carré in the Arcade and the bill was sent to his father. When I wanted a new suit I had to save for months, unless I spent some of what I already got put away; but I would never do that.

Though I don't suppose Jim would have been any different, even if he hadn't had money behind him. It was his nature. He worked from morning to night in his slow easy-going way, and didn't think any further. His brothers was different. Gerald, the youngest, was a smart boy and knew it. He was dark and not nearly as tall as Jim; but had a grin made everybody like him. I didn't much. When he was a boy at the Secondary School, Jim and me went to see him act in a play called *Twelfth Night*, which the boys was doing in St Barnabas Hall. He played the part of Maria, who was a wicked little minx; and I couldn't help thinking it was his own nature he was acting. When he left school, he worked in the Old Bank; but the hours was so short you could hardly call it work. He didn't earn much but he knew how to spend it. He was out roller-skating at St George's Hall most nights. Wilfred, the second, was fair like Jim, but had pale hair he kept neatly parted on one side: not like Jim's mop of straw that flopped all over the place. He was slim and wiry; and quicker in the mind than Jim. He was for ever getting ideas for doing things different, and saving time and money. Jim would say, 'Well, if there was better ways of doing things, they would have been found out years ago.' Jim was satisfied to have vraic spread on the ground for manure, but Wilfred had to have patent guano and ordered oat-cakes from Bibby's for the cattle. The cows didn't die of indigestion, as Jim said they would. In fact, they won several first prizes at the Cattle Show that year. 'There, you see!' said Wilfred. Jim said, 'Our cows won the prizes because they come of a good family.' For all that, he did say to me once, 'It's Wilfred, you know, who ought to run this farm when Pop's gone.'

I didn't dream Jim was thinking of going away, until one Sunday afternoon when we went for a ride on our bikes. I said we might as well go by Perelle and call on Tabitha and see how her and Jean was getting on. Jean was home. It was a pleasure going in that house. There was never any quar-

relling, never any black looks. There was no fuss or bother either; and
everything was as clean as a new pin, the way Tabitha always kept things. I
saw how right Tabitha had been to stick to Jean. I don't suppose you could
call him handsome exactly. He had a rough face rather with curly black
hair that grew well down on his forehead; but he had an honest, pleasant
look about him, and you felt at once he was a chap you could trust. He
wasn't tall, but sturdy and strongly built. His face lit up when he saw Jim.
'They haven't burnt you for a boud'lo yet, then,' he said. 'Aw no, not yet,'
said Jim, 'but they will one day.' They sat on the sofa together talking and
laughing, while Tabby and me got the tea ready. 'I know why you've come
today, you,' she said, 'you knew what we've got for tea.' 'I don't know
what you've got for tea,' I said. 'Spider crab,' she said. When Jim and me
got outside, I said, 'I'd like a little home like that, me. I don't know which
of them I envy most.'

I thought we was going to ride back home then; but Jim wanted to go on
to Pleinmont, for some reason. I looked over at Lihou as we passed by
L'Érée, and thought of the two of us on that little island by ourselves all
night. I was wondering if he was remembering too. When we got passed
Fort Grey, I pointed out to him the cottage where old Mère Quéripel
lived. It was a real old witch's cottage. It was built end-on against the side
of a worked-out quarry, and the thatch was so low down you could hardly
see the windows and they seemed to be looking at you sideways; and it had
one crooked chimney coming out of the roof. Jim said, 'I suppose Mère
Quéripel come out of that chimney on her broomstick.' I said, 'I expect
Liza do as well.' 'I wouldn't be surprised,' he said.

He wanted to go right on to the end, so we took the right-hand turning
in front of the Imperial and went along by the Trinity Houses and round
by Fort Pezeries and left our bikes on the grass by the Table des Pions. We
then climbed down between the two big rocks and stood on the edge of the
cliff looking at the Hanois. Jim said, 'This is as far west as we can get, isn't
it?' 'It is,' I said. He said, 'America is over there.' 'I can't see it,' I said.
'Let's go, you and me,' he said. I thought he was joking. 'We'd get on all
right,' he said, 'just two Guernsey boys, eh?' He was bubbling over with
the idea. 'I've been thinking about it for a long time,' he said.

On the way riding back he explained how he had it all arranged. His
father was sending some cattle to the States and somebody had to go with
them. Whoever went with the cattle would have his passage paid; and I
could be the one to go and Jim would pay his own passage. His father was
quite willing. 'I would travel with you, of course,' he said, 'in the same part
of the ship.' I let him talk. I knew it was a wangle for them to pay my
passage and not hurt my pride. He said, 'We'd be sure to get work with the
cows. What d'you think?' I said, 'How can I leave my mother?' He said, 'I
suppose not.'

He didn't say another word for a long time. At last, just as we was turning inland at Gran'-Rock, he said, 'Nothing perfect is ever allowed to happen in this world.' I left him at Les Gigands. He wanted me to go indoors with him, but I didn't feel like it. It was a grey evening and when I got round Sandy Hook the grey sea was coming over the grey stones and the clock of the Vale Church was striking the three-quarters. They was as sad as the bells. My mother was just back from the Brethren when I got in. I told her I had seen Tabitha and Jean and they was well. I didn't tell her Jim had asked me to go to America with him and I had refused for her sake. It wasn't true altogether. I didn't really want to go away from Guernsey. I bet they don't have spider-crabs in America.

Jim didn't go neither. When I went down on the Thursday evening, expecting to hear what I didn't want to hear, the first thing he said was, 'It's going to be all right. Wilfred is going.' His mother said, 'As if we could let Jim go on his own, without you to look after him!' I said, 'I have always had the idea it was him looked after me.' She laughed. Wilfred was gone within a month; and the night before he went I was invited to his farewell party. He was very excited about going. He said, 'When I come back some of you people will have to buck your ideas up.' He was going to stay over there six months, or a year; and study the up-to-date methods. Actually he didn't come back to Guernsey again for ten years; and then it was only on a short visit to his mother after his father died. He had become an American by then and was married to an American girl. I must give Wilfred his due. He had done well for himself. He had gone to an Agricultural College in the States and, so as not to be a drain on his parents, waited on the tables to pay his way. The girl he married was well-to-do and had influence; and he ended up as a judge of cattle at the big shows. His wife was a strapping wench, as I remember her; and I could see she had him well under her thumb.

There was changes at the farm once Wilfred was gone. For one thing, Lydia came more into view. Until then she had hardly done a stroke of work. Once a blue moon she would go in the dairy and stamp a few pounds of butter; but afterwards she was tired and had to rest. Now she began to take charge of everything. She didn't do much herself and still coughed from time to time to let you know she might drop dead at any minute; but she gave the orders and nobody dared to go against the wishes of Miss Mahy. Jim's father was delighted with his Lydia. He was getting very heavy and wheezy like poor old Victor and didn't do much. The brunt of it fell on Jim; but Lydia took on Phoebe Ferbrache to work in the dairy and help with the milking.

I had known Phoebe Ferbrache to say hullo to ever since she could toddle. She was the youngest of the Ferbrache family from Sandy Hook; and there was at least a dozen. From a child she was a wilful little miss with a

pointed chin and a pointed nose and eyes like black marbles. I couldn't
imagine what on earth Lydia was thinking about to have her on the farm;
but when our Phoebe spoke to Miss Mahy, it was as if butter wouldn't melt
in her mouth. She grabbed at every chance she could to be helping Jim. If
I'd had any sense at all, I'd have seen what was going to happen; but it
didn't enter my head that even Jim could be such a fool.

I was nearly struck dumb when he came round one evening and asked
me to be the best man for the wedding. He was sheepish about it, and I
knew there was something wrong. 'Come on, out with it!' I said. 'Yes,' he
said, 'she's going to have a baby.' I said, 'Ten to one it isn't yours.' 'It is,' he
said. 'I was the first.' I lost my temper. 'Damme, your mother was quite
right!' I said. 'What you want is a nurse to look after you!' He said, 'I was
afraid you wouldn't like her.' I said, 'The only thing for you to do is to let
her have you up, and pay her so much a week as the Court decides. It will
come cheaper in the long run.' 'I can't do that,' he said, 'she trusted me.' I
thought I bet she did trust you: she knew just what sort of fool she'd got
hold of. I said, 'How the devil did it happen? Was you drunk?' He said, 'It
was in the barn. She threw herself on my chest and began to cry. I couldn't
do anything else in the circumstances.' I said, 'Well, it's one way of stopping a girl crying: I know that. Myself, I'd have walked out of the barn and
left her there to cry.' He said, 'Yes, but then you haven't got a heart.'
'Thank goodness, I haven't,' I said, 'or I'd be married a dozen times by
now!' He said, 'I wish it hadn't happened.' I said, 'How are your people
taking it?' 'They are not very pleased,' he said, 'but they don't want a lot of
talk. Lydia says she will never speak to her again.' I said, 'All right, I will be
your best man; and I will never say another word against Phoebe. God
help you, Jim!'

She didn't have it all her own way, I'm glad to say. She thought she
would be living at the farm, or at least in one of the cottages; but Lydia put
her foot down. She wouldn't have 'that trollop' living in the house, or near
it, at any price. Mrs Mahy arranged for them to live in a cottage she owned
at Sous L'Église in St Saviour's. The old couple who had been living there
wanted to go and live with a married son. It wasn't a bad little place with
three vergées of ground; but digging and planting and growing wasn't
what Jim had been used to, and he liked plenty of space to move about in.

They was married at St Sampson's Church at eight o'clock in the
morning. They was going to Hastings for a honeymoon and had to catch
the morning boat at ten. The Ferbraches was to the church in force; but,
except for Jim's father and mother and young Gerald, the only Mahy
present was Christine Mahy's sister, Gwen, who was one of the bridesmaids. The other was Phoebe's sister, Eileen, who was as common as she
was. Lydia didn't go. I kept my word and tried to be nice to Phoebe. I told
her the Russel was like a mill-pond and she was going to have a good cross-

ing. She said 'P'raps,' as if she didn't believe me even about that. She didn't trust me from the start.

When the wedding group was taken, I thought I had better make the best of it and so put on a grin like a Cheshire cat; but when I saw the photo in Norman Grut's window in the Pollet, I wished I hadn't. Poor old Jim was smiling sheepishly, but looked like a lamb led to the slaughter. Phoebe had a smirk on her face like the cat who stole the cream. She was wearing a white dress, and it fitted her tight; but I couldn't see no sign of a baby. I wondered. There was a breakfast at the farm; but Lydia didn't show herself. Jim's father and mother and the bridesmaids was going to see the married couple off from the White Rock and I was asked to go with them. I said I must get home and change and go to work. I had been through as much as I could stand. Jim came to the gate with me to say good-bye. He hung on to my hand with both of his. 'I want to see a lot of you when I get back,' he said, 'I'll let you know when.'

14

I didn't see Jim again for months. I knew he was back. I went down to the farm to find out and his mother told me she had been to see him. Gerald had driven her over. He quite liked Phoebe. Jim's mother didn't say much. She wasn't one to let everything out like Hetty; but, reading between the lines, I got the idea Phoebe didn't want Jim to be seeing his parents. Jim's mother said, 'I can't blame the girl really: we don't pretend to be fond of her.' Lydia and Jim's father was dead against her. It was only Gerald who was friendly. Jim's mother said it was nice to have me there, even without Jim, and I must go any time I felt inclined; but it wasn't the same for me.

I went along once more to keep in touch. Jim's mother had been to see him again. She was more outspoken this time and said she wasn't going to be prevented from seeing her son by anybody: not even his wife. He was working very hard. The old couple who had lived there hadn't been able to do much and the garden was a wilderness of couch-grass and dandelion. Jim had done well with the pears and the plums that year, and there was a sunny corner where he would be able to grow outdoor tomatoes the next summer. The house inside was looking quite nice, she said, but, again reading between the lines, I guessed she had provided most of the things. She didn't say if he had mentioned me and I didn't ask. She did say, however, that she hadn't managed to get a word with Jim on his own, without Phoebe being there.

Then one Sunday afternoon I was sitting on the grass in front of Les Moulins, looking down on La Petite Grève and thinking of nothing in particular, when I looked round as you do sometimes if somebody is looking at you, and there was Jim coming round the Chouey, pushing his bike! I jumped up and ran to meet him, and he threw his bike against the hedge and hugged me like a bear. 'Come indoors and see my mother,' I said. 'She'll be as pleased to see you as I am.' She was. She wanted him to stop to tea, but he said he couldn't. He had been to Les Gigands to see his mother and now had to go straight back home because Phoebe didn't like being left on her own. My mother said, 'How is your wife?' 'Flourishing,' he said. I didn't have to ask how he was. I could see. He had the look in his eyes of a hurt dog.

When we got outside, he said, 'All I came for really was to let you know Phoebe says you can come to tea next Sunday.' I said, 'Say to Phoebe thank you very much and I will be delighted to come.' I meant at all costs to try and keep the peace. 'Come early,' he said. I walked to the main road with him and asked him when the baby was coming. I had counted in three months. 'Easter,' he said. That made it seven. 'I hope it's a boy,' he said. 'If it is, there will be another Ebenezer; and you're going to be the godfather.' When I got indoors, I said to my mother, 'They're expecting a baby Easter.' I hadn't told her, of course, Jim had been expecting one before. I saw my mother counting up the months in her old head. 'Ah well,' she said, 'they've taken longer than some people. There's that to be said for them.'

I looked forward to the next Sunday all the week; and went along with all my good resolutions polished up. Jim was waiting by his gate for me, wondering if I was coming. I was a bit late because I couldn't find the place at first. I knew it wasn't far from St Saviour's Church, but I didn't know exactly where. 'Phoebe is upstairs tittivating,' he said, 'come and see the garden.' He showed me round. There was no couch-grass or dandelions now. The ground was freshly hoed and the paths was weeded clean. I knew how much work that meant from our own small patch. There was frames for cucumbers and marrows and pumpkins, and barrels for rhubarb. There was half a vergée or more of fruit garden: red currants and white currants and black currants and gooseberry bushes, and an overhead fig-tree like my little grandmother used to have. The pear-trees and plum-trees was against the gable of the house and against the old stable that was now used as a wash-house. The orchard was at the top end of the garden. 'There's one apple-tree I'd like you to see,' he said. It was the biggest and in the corner, and in the fork of the branches a sprig of mistletoe was growing. 'At Christmas, there will be berries on it,' he said. 'They will be the only living fruit in the garden.'

He led the way to the back door. He had two pigs in the pigsty against the house. They poked their noses over the wall and grunted as we passed. 'Shut up, you swine!' he said, 'you've had your dinner.' They was the only livestock he got. 'I'm getting some fowls,' he said as we went in: 'I want something alive around the place.' The scullery was untidy, and I noticed saucepans and dishes from dinner hadn't been washed up. My mother, or Tabitha, would have never left things in such a mess. Phoebe was in the front room laying the tea. I said, 'Hullo, how are you?' I made my voice as friendly as possible. She said, 'Hullo,' but had her back to me and didn't look round. I said, 'I like your dress.' She turned round then and smiled at me. 'I'm glad you like it,' she said. 'Jim don't.' I didn't neither, as a matter of fact. It was an ugly mauve colour and all pleats and frills and looked common. I said, 'Jim have done a wonderful job in the garden.' She said, 'That's all he thinks about.'

It wasn't a good tea. There was some sort of sausage meat she had bought in Town, and there was peaches out of a tin and a piece of cake; but that was bought too. It looked seasick and had cherries in it. I don't like cake with cherries in it. I thought of the lovely rich gâche Jim's mother made. He must miss it. Phoebe poured out the tea in dainty little cups. It was comic really to see poor old Jim trying to drink his tea like a lady out of a dainty little cup, when I'd never seen him drinking tea out of anything else but a big china mug. There was a fancy lace tea-cloth on the table, but it didn't half cover the wood. It was supposed to be genteel. The table and chairs was good solid stuff; but those I was sure had been given by Jim's mother. The knick-knacks Phoebe got stuck all over the place she had bought from the Sixpenny-halfpenny Bazaar.

I tried to show interest in her. 'How did you like England?' I said. 'Oh lovely!' she said. 'I wish I could live there for good. It was awful having to come back to Guernsey.' 'I don't see why,' said Jim. 'England is all right; but we've got everything they've got, only better.' 'It's not so small,' she said. He agreed. 'Ah yes, it's bigger,' he said, 'and they got nice big fields; and then there's the trains. I liked going in the big train.' 'Well, that's more than I have done,' I said. 'The people are so nice,' she said. 'They don't treat you as if you was dirt.' I must admit she had some excuse for saying this; but it was a nasty thing to say. I couldn't help speaking up on Jim's side. 'Well, you don't know what they're like to each other,' I said. 'Perhaps they're like us and make a fuss of strangers.' I was thinking of Grandma from Alderney. 'That's what I say to her,' said Jim. 'They're nice to you because you got the money in your pocket. Every smile is another sixpence on the bill.' I don't know what Jim would say if he was alive now, when everybody on the island is doing it. Phoebe said, 'Jim is always in a paddy about something. He is never satisfied.' I could have hit her. Jim was the most good-tempered person in the world.

As soon as we had done eating, she began to clear the table. 'Leave the dishes for now, Phoebe,' he said. 'I'll give you a hand with them later on.' 'Oh, I don't mind doing the work while the men talk,' she said. Jim would have got up there and then and helped her, if I hadn't kept him talking. I asked him what Hastings, the town, was like. Was it all that better than St Peter Port? He said it wasn't a patch on St Peter Port. It have miles of front he got tired of walking along, and big ugly hotels; but nothing much of a harbour. The place he liked was Battle. It was more in the country and was where the Battle of Hastings was fought. On the grass a guide was telling a crowd of people he was standing on the identical spot where King Harold was when he got an arrow through his eye. A hundred yards further on another guide was telling a crowd of people he was standing on the identical spot where King Harold was when he got an arrow through his eye. A hundred yards behind another guide was telling a crowd of people he was standing on the identical spot. 'He must have been a slippery sod, that Harold,' said Jim, 'if he could be in three places at once. It's a wonder we ever got him at all!'

Phoebe came back. 'Very funny! Ha, ha!' she said. In his place I'd have flared up, but Jim passed it over. 'You've been quick,' he said. 'I'll have to change my dress first,' she said. I knew Jim would have to do those dishes in the end. I'd had enough of it; and more than enough! I said I had better be going because my mother was on her own. Jim came to the road with me. The front of the cottage looked nice with ivy and a porch. Jim had cleared the front garden of everything, except the feathers in one corner. 'It was a tangle of weeds,' he said. 'I'll get some flowers in when I have the time.' He got my bike for me but hung on to it, as if he didn't want to let me get on. 'Now you know where I live,' he said, 'come and see me whenever you like. This house is your home as much as mine.'

Jim meant it; but when I had said 'Good-bye and thank you' to Phoebe, she hadn't said 'Come again.' I let a month or more slip by before I went again. I went on a Saturday afternoon, so it wouldn't seem I was inviting myself to Sunday tea. I noticed Jim hadn't done anything to the front garden. He was out the back digging. I went round to talk to him. It was in full view of the house and I saw Phoebe's face at the window once. I asked him how he was getting on with the place. He said he was only working on his own land Saturday afternoons now. There wasn't much he could do until the New Year. The rest of the time he was working for Mess Le Sauvage of Les Buttes. He didn't want to have to fall back on the old people for money to keep going, he said. Les Buttes was a fine old farm and Mess Le Sauvage was only too glad to have Jim's help. Mrs Le Sauvage was being very good to Phoebe and had taken her to Town in the trap that Saturday morning. I said I was glad for Phoebe to be having a good friend and neighbour. Jim asked how I was. I said so-so. I had been knocking around with Jim Machon and Jim Le Poidevin; but it was only to have somebody to go with. I didn't like going round on my own. 'Jim!' called out Phoebe from indoors. 'All right, I'm coming,' he said; but he went on asking about the two Jims, who he hadn't seen since he was married. Phoebe opened the back door and stood there with a face as black as night. 'Jim, your tea is ready!' she said. 'How many more times have I got to call you?' 'I'll have to go,' said Jim. He went indoors. I got on my bike and rode into Town. I saw a few to say hullo to and had a drink or two; but I didn't stay long. My mother wasn't in bed yet when I got in.

I hardly went out at all that winter. I decided I would plant potatoes in the greenhouse to have something to do. It wasn't a good idea really. A winter crop tires out the ground and makes the tomatoes late, unless you have heat; and you miss the best price. I saved a bit another way. Poor old Jack was dead, and I sold the trap rather than buy another pony. When it was a horse-bus from L'Islet to the Half-way, my mother wouldn't go in it, she would rather I drive her to Town; but now it was a motor-bus, she liked going in it. I don't know why, because more often than not the old motor-bus broke down. It was the first motor I remember on the island and must have been worn out before it came here. My mother didn't mind if she had to walk from Baubigny, carrying her two heavy net-bags full of groceries. She didn't go Saturdays, because there was too many people, but did all her shopping Wednesdays. I didn't go Saturdays often.

Sunday nights for a few weeks I went out with Ivy Lake from Lowlands. She was quite a pretty girl, but had a silly way of speaking. Everything was a 'dear little' thing, and she would say to me 'Aren't you sweet!' or 'Aren't you mean!' She was very loving and all that; but I soon found out that was as far as she would go, unless she had been to Church first. That didn't suit me. So I changed over to her friend, Mildred Three-in-a-bed. I can't remember what her other name was, but that was the name she was known by. Her mother kept a lodging-house for seamen on the South Side. It may have been true what the boys said about Mildred, for she was a good-natured girl. The last I heard of her she was married to a Gordon Highlander and gone to Bonnie Dundee.

Once on a Saturday night before Christmas I went to Town, and who should I see but Jim? He didn't see me. It happened my bike had a puncture, so I was without it and was getting on the tram by the Town Church to catch the last bus home, when he came out of the Albion with Phoebe and two of her brothers and some chaps I didn't know. The Albion those days was a rough house, especially Saturday nights, and I would never have taken a girl there, or in any public house, for that matter. The brothers, who was rolling drunk, got on the same tram as me, but I was glad that when we changed at the Half-way they went on the top of the bus. I didn't want to have to speak to them. I wondered if they would get their heads knocked off by trees over the road. I always went inside, me.

I thought I had better go down to the farm and wish Mrs Mahy a Happy Christmas. She said she had invited Jim and Phoebe for Christmas Day, in spite of Lydia; but Phoebe was having her mother and father and a crowd of her brothers and sisters for Christmas. So Mrs Mahy had made some puddings and cakes, and Gerald had taken them along. Jim told Gerald that Phoebe's mother and her sister Eileen was going to stay on until the baby was born. Jim was going to have a houseful of women. Mrs Mahy asked me to come on New Year's Day for the party as usual; but I said I would be staying at home with my sister and her husband. I got a

Christmas card from Jim. On the outside was a picture of a robin on a twig with snow. It wasn't very sensible, as I had only seen snow once and that was in April, not at Christmas. Inside he had written 'From Phoebe and Jim.' I didn't like for Jim to write his name as if he was the tail-end of Phoebe. I bet anyway she hadn't sent me any good wishes for Christmas. I hadn't sent a card myself. I'm not one for spending my money on such rubbish.

When February came and spring was on the way, I thought I would take Jim some cuttings for his front garden. I stacked the lot on my carrier and went one Saturday afternoon. He must have got the same idea himself, for he was out in the front garden working. He didn't have much to put in, but there was already some primroses had come out against the house. He was terribly pleased to see me. 'I was afraid you was never coming near me again,' he said. 'You don't ever have to be afraid of that,' I said. I asked him how Phoebe was. He said she was doing all right. She had been having sickness in the morning, but that was over now. I told him I had seen him in Town. 'Who was those you was with?' I said. They was the Sarchets from Hurel. I said, 'Aren't you friendly with the Le Sauvages now?' He said Phoebe didn't get on so well with Mrs Le Sauvage. 'She says those people look down on her,' he said. 'I expect it's only her fancy,' I said. 'It may be,' he said, 'but a girl gets funny ideas when she's carrying. She isn't strong, you know.' I thought poor Jim, she's as strong as an ox, that little thing; but I didn't say so. Jim said it didn't matter about the Le Sauvages, he had plenty of work of his own to do now. Phoebe was happier with the Sarchets. They was more her sort and she enjoyed going to Town with them Saturday nights in the van. Jim thought they wasn't so bad; except that they stopped at every pub on the way. 'It's a good job the old nag know his way home,' he said.

Jim was delighted with what I had brought, especially the roses. He had already made a path down the middle with pebbles each side. He divided the roses and we set to work to put them in. It was like old times. I was thinking to myself how, until that afternoon, I hadn't been really happy since the day he went to England, when the front door opened and there was Phoebe. 'Jim, I want you to go to the shop!' she said. She wasn't standing two feet from my nose, yet she spoke to him as if I wasn't there. She had a basket in her hand and a list of the things she wanted. 'All right, Phoebe,' he said and took the basket and the list. She went back indoors and I heard her speaking to her sister, or her mother. 'Shan't be long,' he said to me and went off down the road. I did a bad thing then. I was mad with Jim. Why the hell didn't he tell her to go herself, or send her mother or sister? I dropped the cutting I was planting and walked out of the garden and got on my bike and went home. I thought when he comes back he'll find me gone. That'll teach him a lesson.

If it taught anybody a lesson, it was me. I kept on telling myself I was in the right; but then Jim hadn't done any wrong. For weeks I couldn't get it out of my mind, until I had to do something about it. I knew now it was no use trying to be friendly with Phoebe, but I couldn't see why that should make any difference between me and Jim. Anyway, the least I could do was to go along and say to him I was sorry for what I had done. I went one evening after tea. When I got to the top of the hill by the church, I could see him out the back getting a bucket of water from the well. I rang my bell, but he didn't look up. I watched him go indoors. He looked absolutely done in. Even his walk was different. He had always walked with his shoulders back and his head up; but now he walked as if he had no heart or pride left in him. I leant my bike against the wall and walked up the path to the front door. I noticed he had finished putting in my rose cuttings. I knocked. Phoebe opened the door. 'Please can I speak to Jim?' I said. 'He's not in,' she said and shut the door in my face. I walked slowly back to my bike. I was too miserable even to go to Town and get drunk. I saw the birth in the Press. MAHY. At Sous L'Église, to Phoebe (née Ferbrache) and James, a son, Stanley.

15

The War came. It came without me knowing it. One day everything was as it always had been, and the next day the War was on. I was to the races on L'Ancresse Common when I heard. I went every year. I didn't bet on the horses, though Jim did and sometimes won a few shillings; but I liked to see the horses running and all the funny sorts of people who was there, who you never saw anywhere else. There was one chap who would sell you a wad of paper full of money for sixpence. You saw him drop the money in, pounds' worth, and roll it up; but when the paper was undone there was nothing in it, not even the sixpence. Those who was fools enough to buy it couldn't say anything, because it wasn't allowed by law to buy and sell money.

I had heard of the Kaiser, of course, and of the murder of somebody or another, and of the scrap of paper that was torn up, and of poor little Belgium; but I hadn't taken much notice. I had other things to think about. Mr Dorey had made me foreman and, what with my own green-house to look after as well, I had plenty to do. I was packing nearly every evening and the tomatoes was making a good price. The weather was wonderful that summer, I remember, and I thought it was mad for anybody to be going to war. I know now I ought to have guessed there was something in the wind, because a lot of big nobs had come over the month before and made speeches about the Entente Cordiale; and St Peter Port was decorated red, white and blue.

Actually, the excuse was they was come over to unveil a statue of Victor Hugo. Victor Hugo was a famous Frenchman who used to live in a big house up Hauteville; but that was before my time. He wrote stories and poetry books in French; but I haven't read any. I used to see his books for sale in Boots' window up Smith Street, but I don't see them about now. The statue was put up in Candie Grounds, and there was a lot of talk about it. Up to the last minute some people was saying it didn't ought to have been allowed. I like the statue myself. He is standing on the edge of a rock with his coat-tails flying in the wind, and looks as if he was alive. The trouble was that at the top of the Gardens there was a statue of Queen Victoria, and all she could see of Victor Hugo was his backside. It seems he had said some very rude things about her when he was alive and it was thought it had been done on purpose by the French as a dig at the English. However, the fuss and bother died down after a lot of writing for and against, and the statue was left where it was put, or perhaps there would have been a war between France and England. It's all right now, because they have built a pavilion between the Queen and Old Victor, so she don't have to look at his behind for the rest of her life.

I didn't like the French, and I think most Guernsey people felt the same. I thought they was dirty. Certainly Fountain Street and Rosemary Steps and round there, where it was mostly French people lived, nobody could say was a clean part of the town. I liked the 'Marseillaise'. It was the only one of the national anthems I liked to listen to during the War. It made you want to go and fight. 'God Save the King' was a funeral march. However, I got friendly with a young Frenchman over the Victor Hugo Fête, and then I thought the French mightn't be so bad after all. I was looking at the statue after it was unveiled and the young Frenchman was standing by me and asked me in English, though from the way he spoke I could tell he was French, what I thought of it. I said I thought it was good, though I didn't know about such things. He said it was good. 'The old man would like to see himself up there,' he said, 'looking out to sea.'

He told me his name was Marcel Duhau and he was French master at the Secondary School. I spent the evening of the Fête with him; and after that went out with him Thursday evenings for several weeks. One of these we was sitting in Candie Grounds listening to the band playing. It was a seat under the trees we was sitting on, and he was wearing a brand-new smart jacket. A bird in the branches up above, who I suppose couldn't get to sleep because of the music, dropped a plop on his shoulder. If I had been wearing a nice new jacket and a bird had done that on it, I would have been very upset. He wasn't. All he said was, 'Dieu merci les vaches ne volent pas!' I have never forgotten it. I only saw him once or twice more. Immediately the War broke out he was called back to France. He had already done his military training and was sent to the Front straight away. He was killed the same year. It was all wrong. A chap who could make a joke like that didn't ought to have been killed.

The War didn't make a lot of difference to Guernsey at first. It wasn't the end of the world, as some people thought it was going to be. A few fellows I knew who had served in the Navy, mostly pilots and fishermen, was called back; and chaps who had served in the regular Army and was on Reserve, mostly fellows from the quarries, had to join their units. Some of the Townies, who wanted to make a show, went off and volunteered; and sons of the gentry who was in the Training Corps of Elizabeth College went for officers, as was only natural for them to do. My boss's son was one and Douglas Blackburn I knew from the top of Sinclair was another. Myself, I was in the Reserve of the Militia, but the Guernsey Militia wasn't the regular Army. I went on raking in the shekels. The tomatoes went up to five bob a basket, and that was good for August, when you only expected three. The boats and trains was more or less as usual. I got a supply of baskets from Munro on the Esplanade and sent my consignment to a Mr J. Winstanley in Weston-super-mare. They seemed to like tomatoes in Weston-super-mare. Then the States passed a law letting the Militia become part of the British Army for the duration, and called it the First Battalion of the Royal Guernsey Light Infantry. I might have to go.

Just about then I ran into La Prissy in Town one Saturday. 'Goodness, aren't you in khaki yet?' she said. 'Ah well, all the men are going to have to go and get killed and the women will be left to do the work!' I shied clear of Prissy when I could. Her tongue was getting more like a needle every day. I wasn't one to say much of what I was thinking those days. I didn't want to get mixed up in arguments and quarrels if I could help it; and then I'm damned if one Saturday night I didn't go and start a fight in the Caves de Bordeaux over the bloody War! I was with Jim Le Poidevin and Jim Machon, and Eddie Le Tissier was there, I remember, and Amos Duquemin and old Wally Budden and Solly Entwistle and a dozen others, I've forgotten now who.

When I walked in all was peace and joy. Mess Fellerah was behind the bar with Jack Bullock from Vauvert serving drinks and said 'Good-evening,' as nice as pie. There was a picture of the King and Queen on the wall, draped in the Union Jack, and another of Monsieur Poincaré, draped in a tricolor, and one of the Tsar of Russia. The Tsar had no bunting, him. That wasn't from lack of respect, I don't think: I don't expect Mess Fellerah knew what colours to put. I'd already had a few drinks before I got there. That was the worst of going out with the two Jims. I said I wouldn't mind a drop of cognac; and that did it! I opened my tatie-trap wider than I had ever done before.

I said I was all for a fight, me; but I didn't see no sense in going to fight somebody I didn't know. 'I don't see why Guernsey have got to go to war because England go to war,' I said. 'Guernsey people go all over the world, but they quarrel at home among themselves: they don't go and quarrel with the people of other countries. They are not the ones who want to paint the map of the world red, white and blue. No! No! No!' I shouted. 'It's for every true-born Guernseyman to stop at home and mind his own business!' The fat was in the fire. There was a hell of a row! Mess Fellerah said, 'That is not the sort of talk I want to have to listen to in here, Mr Le Page!' and pointed to the picture of the King and Queen and to the picture of Monsieur Poincaré and to the picture of the Tsar of Russia with tears in his eyes. Jim Le Poidevin backed me up.

He said the Militia was never meant to go and fight across the water. It was meant to defend the island against Buonaparte, or anyone else who tried to come and take it. Amos Duquemin, who always knew everything, said it wasn't only to defend the island: it was to defend the King's Person. I said the King's Person was quite safe. He was in his big palace in London, eating and drinking. Amos Duquemin said, 'He won't be for long, if the Kaiser gets there!' Old Wally Budden, who was ninety, if a day, and had whiskers on his chin like a fringe of vraic, said, 'I say to you it is the duty of every Guernseyman with red blood in his veins to go and fight for Prince Albert the Good!' I said, 'What on earth have Prince Albert the Good got to do with it? It's George and Mary now.' He didn't know about those. He said Queen Victoria came over and only made bad worse, but when Prince Albert came with her, he made it all right. I said, 'I don't know nothing about what happened those days. What is the use of digging up the past? It's the present we got to live in!' He said, 'His statue is on the Albert Pier.' 'A nuisance of a statue it is too!' I said. 'The birds make their mess in his hat.' 'He'd have liked that, Prince Albert the Good,' said old Wally and started shaking his stick at me. He only wished he was a young man again so he could go and shed the last drop of his red blood for Prince Albert the Good! 'It's not too late, yet, Gran'-père,' said Jim Le Poidevin. 'If the Kaiser saw you coming, he'd run!'

Eddie Le Tissier was trying to calm me down. 'Ebby, be your age!' he said. 'If England didn't look after us we'd starve. Guernsey could never grow everything to feed itself.' He said we had to have tea and sugar and flour sent, and coal as well; and all from England. Besides, it wasn't the Guernsey Militia saved the island from Buonaparte: it was Lord Nelson and the British Navy at the Battle of Trafalgar. Jim Machon said he didn't care a bugger about Lord Nelson and the Battle of Trafalgar, but he wanted to go to the War because it was a chance to get away from Guernsey and have his passage paid. Over here you can't go for a piss without everybody knowing it, but a soldier is here today and gone tomorrow, and can do what he like.

I didn't seem to have many on my side; but Solly Entwistle was wriggling to get a word in. He was over forty, but like a child, and had St Vitus Dance, and was very religious. 'He that taketh the sword shall perish by the sword!' he said in his squeaky voice. 'The Lord is a man of war!' croaked old Wally Budden. 'That's ri'! That's ri'!' said Amos Duquemin. He was drunk. 'If there's any man here who don't want to go and fight, he ought to be tarred and feathered!' he said. 'I'll see you tarred and feathered first, Amos Duquemin!' I said. I don't know if it was me hit him first, or him me; but I do know that the next minute everybody was fighting everybody else. I don't think anybody knew which side they was on. Jack Bullock, who used to take on all comers in a tent at the Fair on the Albert Pier, was around the counter in two shakes and, before we knew what had happened, we was all bundled out. It was cold outside, and we stood shivering on Trinity Square, blindly hitting out, but not hitting anybody. I remember thinking it was a funny sort of square, because it only got three sides.

Jim Le Poidevin had left his van in the Bordage Yard. I had brought my bike, but he said it would be safer in the back of the van than with me on it, and drove me home. Next morning when I woke up I gave myself a good talking-to. 'Who are you, Ebenezer Le Page,' I said to myself, 'to open your big mouth about things you know nothing about? In future, remember you was born one of those who have to do what he is told. If the Bailiff and the States of Guernsey don't know what is the right thing to do, how d'you expect you can?' I thought of what my Uncle Willie said to my father. 'Look after Number One, Alf; and let the world manage its own affairs.' If my father had taken his advice, he might have been alive yet. I wasn't going to volunteer for something I didn't want to do; but I wasn't going to grumble about the War either. If I had to go, I'd go; and obey orders.

At the beginning, there was so many wanted to go the powers-that-be didn't have to call up any; and, later on, they picked on the ones they wanted, but I don't know how. I know some of the fit ones was left behind, and others wangled cushy jobs in the Orderly Room at the Fort and never left the island. Most of the young quarrymen was called up and went to France. The quarries kept on working somehow; but the stone piled up to be sent to England after the War, as there wasn't ships to spare. I never understood about the fishermen. I know Jean Batiste was among the first to be called up; but then he was only one chap on his own, and didn't have nobody to put in a word for him. I was lucky and my number didn't come up.

The price for tomatoes went up and up; and soon they was a pound a basket. That was one-and-eight a pound, and goodness knows how much they sold for. I thought the people who bought them must be mad. I was then sending mine to a Mr Ralph Philips in Covent Garden for sale to the big hotels in London where the officers ate. I changed all the cheques I got into sovereigns. They had stopped making sovereigns in England, but there was plenty in the Old Bank in Guernsey. It was hopeless to try and keep so many in my money-box, because it was already crammed full to the top; so I emptied it into the pied-du-cauche where my mother kept the money she had saved during her lifetime. By the end of the War, there was more than a good many hundreds of sovereigns belonging to my mother and me in the pied-du-cauche up the chimney.

16

La Hetty nearly went mad with worry in case Raymond had to go to the
War. She came round crying to my mother. She didn't get much sympathy, poor Hetty. My mother said it was all written in the Word of God.
She knew the texts by heart. The War was Armageddon and the Kaiser was
the Beast with Seven Horns in the Book of Revelations. It wasn't who
lived or died that mattered. It was who was saved, or otherwise. My
mother didn't worry. She carried on as usual. I can't remember us being
without anything once in those four years. When cards was given out for
meat and other things she took the cards with her when she went shopping,
but she got as much as she wanted of everything. I bought an extra pig and
kept more fowls.

I got into trouble once. It was my mother's doing really; but I ought to
have kept an eye on her. She thought it was nonsense to put brown paper
over the windows when the light was lit. She trusted to the will of God; but
the light showed through the blind. Mr Luxon, who was Connétable of
the Vale, came round and said we was showing lights for the German sub-
marines. I don't think he believed it, but some people from L'Islet, I don't
know who, had told him we was selling petrol to the Germans. They said
they had seen a big black thing in La Petite Grève. It would have been a
good place to do it, as a matter of fact. It was right out of the way. All along
the west coast people was said to be doing it, especially around Pleinmont.
It is certainly strange that not once during the War was a Guernsey Packet
sunk by a torpedo. Mind you, I would believe anything of the people
around Pleinmont; but I am sure it wasn't done in the North.

The Military went so far as to have a Guard on the beach at L'Ancresse
Common. I knew because Amos Duquemin was put on guard there
during his training. He said it was terribly lonely out there at nights; and
once, when he saw somebody come crawling up the beach, he got quite
scared. 'Halt! Who goes there?' he called out. There was no answer. 'Halt!
Who goes there?' No answer. When there was no answer the third time, he
fired. 'Baah!' it went. Amos Duquemin dropped his rifle and ran. He never
got it out of his mind. He was talking about it yet, years after the War.
'That poor old sheep!' he said. It was the only creature he killed during the

War. He was to the Front for years, but didn't set eyes on a German. He was stationed behind the lines looking after the mules. He was luckier than Jim Machon, who got gassed, and when he came back, was spewing up his guts until he died. Jim Le Poidevin lost a leg. Eddie Le Tissier was killed.

Raymond wasn't afraid of going to the War: I'm sure of that. It was other things he was afraid of. I think he was most afraid of doing wrong. He didn't worry much at first, because he was too young to be called up and may have thought the War would be over before he had to make up his mind. He was learning Greek. Miss Mellish, the Headmistress of the Ladies' College, was giving him lessons. I asked him if he was learning Greek because he was going to preach to the Greeks. He said no, but the Greek Testament was more like what Jesus said than the English. He wasn't sure what language Jesus actually preached in: perhaps a dialect of Galilee. 'Patois, if you like,' he said. I had always thought the Bible was word for word what Jesus said. Raymond said, 'It's hard to know what Jesus really did say, sometimes. He says things that don't go together.'

I don't know why Raymond got so taken up with religion. It wasn't as if he'd had it rammed down his throat at home. The Martels was Church, but didn't go. Hetty, of course, was brought up Chapel, and went every Sunday when she was a girl; but she didn't go any more after she was married. Prissy was the same until the War; but when the Bishop of Winchester came over to Guernsey to preach The Mission of Repentance and Hope, she suddenly became very religious. 'God have brought the War upon us for our sins,' she said, 'and He won't see to it we win, if we don't go to church every Sunday and pray for the King and Queen.' She bought herself a new dress for Sundays, and a new hat for every other week. Of a Sunday evening, when the bells of the Vale Church began to ring, you would see her going along the Braye Road with a Prayer Book in her hand and Percy walking two or three steps behind her. Naturally she had to pass in front of Wallaballoo, and Hetty would be sitting out of sight behind the lace curtains of the bow window, as Prissy well knew, watching her pass and reckoning up the price of everything she had on. 'She put everything she got on her back, that one,' said Hetty, 'like a camel!'

One evening La Hetty came round when my mother was out to week-night service and poured her troubles all over me. 'That Prissy only go to church to spite me,' she said. 'She know quite well I can't go, what with Harold and his bald head. He would have to take his hat off and all the people would see I was married to an old man.' Harold wasn't an old man, by any means, but he didn't have much hair. In fact, he didn't have much hair when she married him. Percy had a fine head of hair to his dying day. 'I've ruined my life!' Hetty said and began to cry: 'I can't go anywhere like other people: I can't even go to the Pictures.'

Raymond told me once how, when he was eight or nine, he was taken by his mother and father to Poole's Myrama at St Julien's Hall to see the sinking of the *Titanic*. Jim and me went to see it; and it was wonderful how it was done. It was more like the real thing than the Pictures. Raymond, like other boys, was all excited to go. They sat in good seats near the front. On the wall was a notice LADIES ARE REQUESTED TO REMOVE THEIR HATS. Hetty didn't take hers off because she thought, if she did, it would look funny for Harold to be sitting with his cap on. A lady sitting behind complained to the programme-seller that she wouldn't be able to see because of Hetty's big hat; and the programme-seller came and asked Hetty if she would be so kind as to remove it. Hetty stood up without a word and walked out; and Harold and Raymond had to follow. Raymond didn't see the sinking of the *Titanic* after all.

I said to Hetty, 'Why don't Raymond go with you to the Pictures?' 'Raymond is ashamed to be seen out with his mother,' she said. I didn't believe that for a moment; but then Hetty never did know what Raymond was feeling about anything. He always felt terribly sorry for his mother, but sometimes he was mad with her at the same time. The reason was, if ever he went to Town with her, she would stop and talk to this woman and that woman, and they'd say, 'Who is this then, your young man?' and she'd say, 'Ah but no, it's my boy Raymond, my only boy!' and they'd say, 'Goodness, but haven't he grown? It was only yesterday he was hiding behind your petticoats!' 'I feel about three years old,' said Raymond.

There was one thing he was ashamed of his mother for, and that was the way she spoke English. He was everlastingly teasing her for saying 'tree' for 'three' and 'true' for 'through' and for not sounding her aitches and all the rest of it. I didn't like him for that. It was partly Hetty's own fault, because she had never let him speak in patois, from the days he went to the Misses Cohu's School. She wanted him to grow up to speak English like the gentry. Well, he did speak good English; but he had a gift for words and I think would have spoken well in any language he set his mind to learn. I didn't mind him being particular about the words he used himself; but he was fussy about the way other people spoke. I said, 'It's what a person say that matter. It isn't how he say it.'

I was sorry for Hetty that night she came. 'Well, I'll come with you to the Pictures, if you want to go,' I said. 'I'd like you to,' she said, 'but what will the people say?' 'Bother the people!' I said, 'I'm a relation, aren't I?' 'Yes, there's that,' she said and laughed like a young girl. A Saturday afternoon would be best, she thought. I could meet her in Town outside the Pictures, and we could separate after, and nobody would know. I went with her a few times. When Jim and me used to go to the Pictures, it was to Bartlett's Flea-pit at the bottom of the Rue des Frères. It had been a second-class roller-skating rink before, and was an itchy sort of place.

After you had been sitting for a few minutes you began to notice the people around you was twitching as much as the people on the Pictures. The only Picture I remember seeing there was Pearl White in the *Exploits of Elaine* left hanging by her teeth from a skyscraper, so as you would go and see what happened to her the next week. Hetty didn't like that sort of Picture, but Pictures with Mary Pickford in, or Pauline Frederick; so we went to St Julien's. She would be dolled up to the eyebrows and looked like a jeweller's shop. She had rings on both hands and bracelets on both arms and a gold chain with a locket round her neck and a long gold chain with a watch in her belt and a brooch on her blouse. It was worth while going with her because she enjoyed herself so much. She sat on the edge of the plush seat with her back as stiff as a poker, and her dumpy little legs hardly reaching to the floor; and would be either laughing or crying all the time. She thought the Pictures was real. Pictures was only pictures to me, and half the time I didn't know what they was about; and when I did, I didn't believe it was real: but I liked to sit and listen to the music. The Santangelo's quartet was good.

Once when we came out I said she might just as well have tea with me at Le Noury's; and then who should be sitting at the next table to us but old Mrs Domaille from next door to Les Sablons? 'Why, if it isn't years and years since I have seen you, Henriette Le Page!' she said. 'Is it that you have a new husband now?' 'Ah no, he is the son of my sister Charlotte,' said Hetty. 'I would never have thought it,' said old Mrs Domaille, 'you don't look a day older than he do!' She couldn't have said anything to please Hetty better. When we got out in the Arcade, she said, 'Well, now we're together you might as well come home and have some supper.' I said, 'All right,' thinking nothing of it. I made a mistake there. I ran into Prissy not long after. 'I hear you're going about with my sister that was,' she said. 'Well, I will say this for you, Ebenezer Le Page: you know on which side your bread is buttered. When that Raymond go and get himself killed and Harold is dead, she will leave everything to you in her will.' I didn't tell Hetty.

I got into the way of going to Wallaballoo quite often of a Saturday evening, even if we hadn't been to the Pictures. I had nowhere else to go. I was getting tired of fellows in khaki saying to me in Town 'Ah, so they haven't got you yet!' I always answered, 'If they want me, they know where to find me. I don't hide myself away.' But I felt left out of it. I didn't keep it a secret from my mother that I was going down to see Hetty; but she didn't like me going. She wasn't one for visiting people herself. Anybody could come and see her and was welcome; but I don't think she had ever been inside either of the two houses, and nor had I until then. 'It don't do to come between a husband and wife,' she said. I wasn't coming between a husband and wife, she needn't have been afraid of that; and I would have stopped going sooner, if it hadn't been for Raymond. He said I was an 'old heathen' but for that reason he liked talking to me.

Harold I hardly ever saw. He worked to all hours of the night by electric light in the carpenter's shop in the yard. If he happened to be indoors, he would be sitting by the fire in the back kitchen, with his cap on, reading one of Raymond's books. Raymond used to laugh at the way his father read a book. He began in the middle and read to the end, and then, if he was interested, he read from the beginning to find out how it all started. Raymond would have liked his father to talk with him about the book, say what he thought of the characters and so on; but all he would say was 'A good yarn,' or 'Not a bad yarn,' or 'Not much of a yarn.' Raymond could never have a real talk with his father. Harold knew his job from A to Z, but he hadn't had much education from books. Raymond was too much educated from books, to my way of thinking. Most of his time in the house he spent in the little room over the door reading. There was nine rooms in that house. The back kitchen was the only room downstairs that was used at all, unless they had visitors; and Harold's and Hetty's bedroom and Raymond's upstairs, and his little room over the front door. The other rooms was cleaned and polished and worshipped by Hetty; and always new things was being bought to put in. Hetty did all the housework herself, because she couldn't bear to have strangers touching her things. She did even the heavy washing. She said a paid washerwoman didn't take the trouble to wash the clothes clean because they wasn't her own.

Hetty was always complaining she had nobody to talk to. Raymond was either out, or had his head stuck in a book; and she couldn't talk to Harold. 'If you look at him sideways, he comes like a lion!' she said. He was always all right with me. He would say 'Good-evening!' and 'How are you?' He was never a chap to say much; but the fellows who worked for him swore by him. They said he was as straight as a die and would always see fair play. Hetty herself praised him to me sometimes. 'After all, there are plenty of women who are worse off than me,' she'd say. He didn't drink, he didn't go after other women, and he gave her everything she wanted. When she wanted the house papered, it was done. If she wanted a new suite of furniture for any room, he'd say 'Get it, my ducks!' When she had bought it and wanted him to admire it, he'd say, 'Are you satisfied? If you're satisfied, I am.'

It wasn't until years later Raymond tried to tell me what it had been like for him living in that house. When he was a small boy he would lie in his cot many a night trembling all over, as if he was in the middle of a storm. Harold would be standing out on the landing in only his night-shirt, shouting and swearing; and Hetty would be lying on the stairs, screaming and crying and saying she wouldn't go into his room. Raymond didn't understand then, and thought Harold was going to kill his mother. He would get out of his cot and kneel down on the floor and pray to God that Hetty would run away from Harold and take him with her to England. A storm would be followed by a fine spell, like the weather; but, after a while, he would know another was coming up. For a whole week perhaps, there wouldn't be a word spoken between his mother and father. It was awful at meal-times. When Raymond was at school and a silent spell was on, he dreaded to come home for his tea. He would come in and say 'Hullo, Pa!' and 'Hullo, Ma!' and sit at the table with one on his right and one on his left not saying a word to each other; but they would both speak to him. His father would ask him how he'd got on at school that day, and he would say 'All right'. His mother would ask him who he had seen on the way home, and he would try and think of somebody he had seen. He was careful to answer just the question he was asked. He didn't want to take sides and tell more to one than to the other. 'It was hell!' he said.

When he showed me his little room the first time, he said, 'This is my cell. I ought to be a monk.' I have often thought of that since. If he had lived at the time when there was monks on Lihou Island, I think he would have been happy there and a lot of misery would have been spared to a lot of people. His room was plain enough for a cell. There was a wickerwork armchair with a cushion on it where I used to sit, and a table for his papers and a chair with a leather seat. He used to sit the wrong way round in that chair with his arms over the back, talking to me. He had one picture on the wall: *The Light of the World*. 'Behold I stand at the door and knock.' He had dozens of books on shelves. There was some about religion and some about the history of Guernsey, and stories by Charles Dickens and Sir Walter Scott and others. He didn't like the stories of Sir Walter Scott himself, but had bought them for his father. He liked the stories of John Oxenham and Hall Caine and Florence Barclay. *The Manxman* by Hall Caine was on the Pictures, and for once he took his mother; but she didn't like it because there was an illegitimate baby in it. He also took her to see *The Rosary*, and that one she liked; but he said it wasn't like the book.

He was getting very worried about the War. 'It can't be right for a Christian to go to War,' he said, 'a Christian has to love his enemies, not go and kill them.' 'Well, I don't know,' I said, 'I don't go out of my way to make trouble; but if a chap punches me on the nose, I punch him back. When all is said and done, it was the Germans started it. I don't see how our side can be in the wrong.' He said, 'The Christians in England are praying for victory, and the Christians in Germany are praying for victory. God can't answer both lots of prayers.' I said, 'He can give victory to the best side, surely.' He said, 'Are you saying all the battles in history have been won by the best side? History is a disgrace!' I was getting fed up with the argument. 'I don't know nothing about the battles in history,' I said, 'but I do know when I saw Guernsey beat Jersey in the Muratti, it was the best side won.' He said, 'How about when Jersey beat Guernsey?' 'Oh, that was just luck!' I said. 'There you are, you see!' he said, 'The trouble with you is that you don't take anything seriously.' 'Perhaps I don't,' I said.

17

When Jean Batiste embarked with the First Battalion of the Royal Guernsey Light Infantry, I hoped La Tabby would come home and live with us. My mother asked her to, but she wouldn't. She said she wanted to stop and look after her house, so that it would always be ready for Jean to come back to at any time. She had her Separation Allowance and a little money they had saved; but that was all. She worked the garden, which didn't give much; and worked for neighbours, who wasn't much better off than herself. She earned a little extra that way. My mother did manage to get her to come to Les Moulins Saturdays, though she had to walk all the way; and she would stay until the Sunday night, so that for one day a week, at least, she was well fed. She was a girl who would go to any amount of trouble if somebody else was there, but couldn't be bothered, if she was on her own.

I saw nothing of Jim. I caught sight of Phoebe and Eileen in Town once or twice of a Saturday night with the Sarchets; but no Jim. I was to learn later that he was left at home to mind the baby. I had seen in the *Press* there was a second son, Eric. Actually, Jim was having his happiest times those Saturday nights. The baby was put to sleep, but Stanley, who was then running about, Jim kept up long after his bed-time. It was the only chance he got of being with his son. I think that was the one thing Phoebe did to him that hurt him most. That fool of a girl didn't know that in Jim she'd got hold of a wonderful father for her children. Naturally he wanted young Stanley to go and work with him in the garden, even if he was only being a nuisance. She made every excuse: that he'd get dirty, that he'd eat worms, that he'd fall down and hurt himself; and at last came right out with it. 'Stanley, you are NOT to go out-of-doors with your father!' Jim could only say 'Stanley, I would like you to come in the garden with me, please.' It was the nearest he could get to giving an order. Of course Stanley obeyed his mother.

I got some of it out of Jim in the end, but even then I daren't say a word against Phoebe. He didn't blame her. It was the way she was made. He blamed himself more. He said, 'She made a sad mistake when she married me. I'm not her sort of bloke really.' I should jolly well think he wasn't! Nor was she thinking about what sort of bloke he was when she married him: she was thinking of what she was going to get out of him. There was times when I lost all patience with Jim; yet his faults was good faults. I am glad now I held my peace.

I went down to the farm again pretty often to get what news I could out of Mrs Mahy; but she was too much the lady to say all she thought. She visited them regularly, but I could tell she didn't enjoy her visits very much. Eileen was practically living there; and, often, Mrs Ferbrache as well. Mrs Ferbrache, who drank herself to death before long, had a tongue and didn't care what she said with it. I think Jim's mother was a bit afraid of Mrs Ferbrache. She said Stanley was a lovely little chap, but took more after the Ferbraches. The new one might turn out to be more like Jim. Jim himself did nothing but work. He was working his own place without help and also helping Mess Le Sauvage again. Mess Le Sauvage said he didn't know what he would do without Jim and was going behind doors to try for him to be kept out of the Army. Mrs Mahy smiled. 'Jim takes me aside every time I go and whispers "How is Ebby?" I tell him you always ask after him.'

Tabby had hoped Jean would get leave for Christmas, but he didn't. She spent Christmas with us. She was quiet but happy, and didn't talk about him much; but we drank his health before we sat down to our Christmas dinner. She had brought a bottle of wine and my mother had some. Jean didn't see again the little house she was keeping ready for him. It was a telegram first; and then, later on, a letter from his officer. When she got the telegram she came straight to my mother. I was sent the news to work, and Tabby was in the kitchen helping my mother to get the tea when I got home. Thank God I didn't try to say anything. It was her who came to me and held my head against her breast and said, 'It's all right, Ebby: it's all right.'

The officer in his letter said fine things about Jean: I think more than he need have done. Jean was only a corporal. Miss Penelope Peele, who was sister of the Rector of the Vale and a great one for comforting the bereaved, came to see Tabitha. My mother told her of the letter from Jean's officer, and she asked if she might see it; and she read it. 'Aren't you proud?' she said to Tabitha. She was small, my sister; but she had great dignity. Her eyes blazed. 'I was proud of him before, Miss Peele,' she said. 'Have I any the more reason to be proud of him now?' Miss Peele didn't come to our house again.

Tabitha let her house to Philippe Batiste, Jean's cousin, who had used to help him with the fishing sometimes and now wanted to get married before he was called up. When he came back after the Armistice, she sold it to him outright, furniture and all. She even let him have Jean's clothes and fishing tackle. The only thing she kept was a guernsey she had knitted for him. She said I could wear it, if I wanted to. I didn't like to, while she was alive; but I have worn it since. I still have it and it will last longer than me.

She only stayed with us a few weeks, before she went back to live with the Priaulx. She was well paid and had everything found; but she was more like a young aunt in the family. Jack Priaulx was gone to the War, and it was her really who brought up Annette's two children. Annette Priaulx made a lot of show of loving her children, but was on committees for this and committees for that, and didn't have time to take much notice of them. Tabitha made no show, but was steady and always there. They earned great honour for themselves in the Second World War, but I don't expect anybody will have thought of thanking Tabitha for that. They was a boy and a girl, and she used to bring them along to have tea with us sometimes. I thought then how strange it was that, if Jean hadn't been killed, she might never had the chance of bringing up children; yet when I saw her with Gervase and Louise, I knew she was made for it.

I had the surprise of my life when Jim turned up one Saturday evening. It was when I wasn't going down to Wallaballoo so much, because I was getting fed up having arguments with Raymond. I had been out round the Surtaut and got a few mackerel. It was soon going to be dark and I had turned the boat to come in, when I saw old Jim on the beach. He waved and I waved. I was pleased to see him, but I knew something must be very wrong. The first thing I said was 'Are the nippers all right?' 'Oh yes,' he said, 'they're fine; only I'm going away Monday. Will you come?' I said, 'Where in the name to goodness are you going to?' He said, 'I'm going to England and enlist.' I said, 'Are you off your head?'

I thought he must have had a hell of a row with Phoebe. I said, 'What about Phoebe? You can't just go and leave her like that.' 'She'll be all right,' he said. 'She will have an allowance for herself and for the kids. The Sarchets are going to look after the place. She says she'll get on just as well without me.' I said, 'Have you told your people yet?' He said, 'Yes, I've just come from there.' 'What have they got to say about it?' I said. 'My mother wants me to wait until I'm called up,' he said. 'I told her I was coming to see you. She said you'd soon stop me.' 'I can't stop you,' I said, 'but I'm not coming with you, I'll tell you that from the start!' He said, 'I didn't think you would.' 'What do your father say?' I said. His father was all for it. He said a young man ought to go and fight for his King and Country. I said, 'It's not a question of fighting for your King and Country. When your King and Country want you, they'll jolly well come and get you! It's a different matter putting your head in the lion's mouth.' I didn't know what had come over Jim. There was us standing facing each other, as if we was quarrelling. He said, 'I want to go in the big train again.' It was too much! I sat down on the stones and burst out laughing.

He stood looking down at me, as if it was me who was off my head. I scrambled to my feet. The only sensible thing to do was to get the fish out of the boat and take it indoors. 'Coming in?' I said. 'I've seen your mother,' he said. 'It was her told me you was out fishing.' 'How about something to eat?' I said. 'I promised I'd have supper with Mum and Dad,' he said. He had come on his bike: it was against the hedge. I said, 'Wait a sec then, while I drop these in the wash-house; and I'll walk back with you part of the way.' I thought I would try and knock some sense into his wooden head. It was during that walk he told me how it was with him and Phoebe. I wondered if perhaps she was carrying on with one of the Sarchets. There was three brothers, and only one of them was married, and he wasn't to be trusted. I didn't like to say as much to Jim, but he guessed what I was thinking. He said Phoebe liked going out with the Sarchets for a laugh and a drink; but that was all. It was different with Eileen. She was sort of half engaged to the youngest. On second thoughts I believed him about Phoebe. She was too mean even to give him that excuse. 'I want to be with the boy,' he said. 'Once a chap's married he's alone for the rest of his life.'

I walked with him right as far as the Gigands, and he wanted me to go in and have supper with them; but I said no. I couldn't face his mother. I knew I hadn't done what she hoped. I have blamed myself bitterly since. If only I'd said outright, 'Phoebe may not care if you are killed, or not: but I do! I care more for you to be alive than for anybody else on earth!' he might have listened to me. It's too late now. I didn't. When I said 'Good-bye', he said, 'I'll write to you.' 'Well, don't expect much from me,' I said. I didn't expect he would write often, for he wasn't much more of a fist with a pen than I am; but I got a long letter from him every week. I still have them all: pages and pages in his big clumsy handwriting that went down-hill across the paper. I had to write back somehow and bought a dictionary from old Miss Clarke in the States Arcade who sold prayer-books and Bibles, so as to see how to spell the long words: that is, when I wasn't too lazy to look, or hadn't lost myself in what I was saying. He didn't bother with a dictionary sitting on his bed in the barrack-room, I'm sure; but I have been looking at those letters again and only Jim could have made those big curly G's and E's and those black full-stops like blots, and written the words he always ended with 'From your old friend, Jim.'

He enjoyed going in the big train; though this time it was full of soldiers. He said England was full of soldiers; and he went right across England. He volunteered for a Welsh Regiment; and was glad he did. He liked Wales better than England, he said. It was a more beautiful country. He said there was mountains with roads winding down and around, and valleys with bridges and streams. There was thousands of sheep on the mountains, and miles and miles with very few houses. He didn't think much of the coast, though. He said it was grey rocks, or greenish and not a patch on Guernsey with its red and brown, and the sea wasn't so blue, or so green, as ours; nor purple and pink and mauve and all the other beautiful colours it is in places inshore. I think he was homesick away from Guernsey really, and that's why he wrote so much. He said he liked the Welsh fellows. He liked the Welsh better than the English. They was more natural: they was more like us. They spoke in Welsh to each other, and he could understand some of the words; and they understood some of his, if he spoke in Guernsey French. He said they had no idea where Guernsey was, most of them. Some of them thought it was off Land's End, and others that it was in the Mediterranean Sea. He wrote, 'I wish you was here.'

His letters made me laugh sometimes. Jim wasn't a good soldier. They hadn't made him a lance-jack as he was in the Militia: he was only a private. They had to put up with him in war-time; but in peace-time they'd have turfed him out. He did his best, but he was always doing something wrong, though he didn't get punished for it. I can't imagine any chap being so rotten as to want to punish Jim. The worst thing he did was once in platoon drill, when the whole regiment was on parade. His platoon had to form fours and take two steps backwards and dress by the right. Jim went through the right movements, but he moved in the wrong direction. He landed out in front all by himself. The sergeant walked slowly around him and examined him from every side, while everybody else was standing to attention in dead silence. 'Where have you come from?' he asked Jim friendly like, as if he was surprised to see him there and was just curious to know. 'Guernsey,' said Jim. The sergeant nearly had a stroke. He screeched, 'Have you ever been in a place and left that place and come back and found that it wasn't?' 'Aw no, Sergeant,' said Jim, 'Guernsey is still there.' The sergeant barked like a corgi: 'GET BACK TO YOUR RANKS!' Jim got back safe to where he was supposed to be; but I bet it was in his own slow way.

I went along to tell Mrs Mahy that I was hearing from Jim. She also heard once a week; but he didn't say much. He wrote to Phoebe, she said; but only about the children. Mrs Mahy was disappointed in me because I had let him go. She said she thought I had more influence. I never understood how she got the idea into her head that I had influence over Jim. Anyhow, it was her dear Gerald she was more worried about now. He was mad to go in the Flying Corps. The French had put up a hangar for sea-planes where the Model Yacht Pond was, along the Castle Walk; and I had seen those boxes with wings wobbling over the harbour. I'd have thought they'd have put any chap off ever wanting to fly. I wouldn't have gone up in one of those things to save my life. The only service I would have liked to have gone into was the Navy, but that was the hardest to get into; and I wouldn't have gone down in a submarine for anybody. My idea of getting about was to walk on the ground, or sail on the sea. I have never wanted to go up in the air, or down under the water.

Raymond heard from Horace. I wondered he had the cheek to write, that Horace, after so many years, but he had cheek enough for anything. It happened I went down to Wallaballoo the very day Raymond got the letter. I had seen in the *Press* that Pauline Frederick was in a picture called *Madame X* at the Lyric, and I thought perhaps Hetty would like to go on the Saturday afternoon. Raymond was in by himself. He said his mother had gone to spend the evening with his Aunt Prissy, and his Uncle Percy was with his father in the office. I thought wonders will never cease. Horace was coming back. When Prissy got the news she hadn't been able to keep it to herself, but had run round to tell Hetty. They had cried over each other and kissed and was now more like turtle-doves than ever. Prissy had sent Percy to make it up with Harold and at the same time there had been a letter from America for Raymond. The two families was as thick as thieves. I wondered for how long.

As a matter of fact, it wasn't as Prissy said, because it wasn't at all certain that Horace was coming back. Raymond took me upstairs and showed me Horace's letter. He still wrote in his small handwriting you could hardly read; and he couldn't spell much better, unless it was the way they spell in America. He had become a real Yank. He was in the American Army; and now that America was in the War, he expected to be shipped over to Europe any day. They was coming over to win the War for us. 'America isn't going to let the Kaiser get hold of little Guernsey,' he said. I bet he was the only chap in the American Army who knew there was such a place, let alone where it was. I could read between the lines of Horace's letter all right. He wasn't thinking of fighting the Germans and winning the War: he was thinking of wangling a leave in Guernsey, and coming home to be made a fuss of as the conquering hero. 'Gee, I'll sure be glad to see you, boy!' he ended. Raymond said, 'It's good, isn't it?' Horace had enclosed his photograph. Raymond took it out of the envelope to show me, as if it was pure gold. Horace was in his dough-boy's uniform and I have to give it to him he was a big fine-looking chap; and he didn't look as if he had a care in the world. Raymond sat looking at that photo. 'I wish I was Horace,' he said.

18

My old head is full of tunes. Sometimes of a Sunday evening when I light the lamp and sit down to write my book, for it is mostly Sunday evenings I write my book, not a word of sense will come into my head, but tunes, tunes, tunes. I may remember the words, a few of the words; but they are words I had forgotten, or never knew I'd known. Hymn tunes come back; and I haven't been inside a chapel for fifty years. 'The day Thou gavest, Lord, is ended.' It's a good tune. I hear again, as once I heard, Christine Mahy sing 'O Love, that will not let me go!' and all the angels of heaven sang in her glorious voice that night; and I hear the heavy tramping of soldiers along the roads and rough voices singing:

> Madamemoiselle from Armentières
> Hasn't been fucked for forty years,

and 'Bollicky Bill, the Sailor.'

Tunes, tunes, tunes: I cannot get them out of my head! This island down the years have been a singing rock. When in my father's day the boys went to war, they was singing:

> Good-bye Dolly, I must leave you,
> Though it breaks my heart to go.

and when conscription came in the First World War and the English boys came over to make up the number in our Second Battalion, they was singing:

> Good-bye-ee, don't sigh-ee, don't cry-ee,
> Wipe the tear, baby dear, from your eye-ee;

but those tunes cross and get mixed up with other tunes in my head I don't know the words of, for they was in a language I didn't understand and never learnt. They was sung day in, day out, along our streets and down our lanes by our polite visitors from Germany; but the tramping of feet was not of soldiers singing, but of slave-workers of every nation in rags and half-uniforms and caps and clothes I had never seen before, and treated worse than beasts. Among them was the boy I will see to my dying day: more tired, more hurt, than any of the others; but he was proud and I could see his spirit was not broken.

I have lived too long. I have lived through two world wars and been no hero in neither. Two is one too many for any man. Now I sit and wait for the third. I wonder if I will live to see it. I don't believe, I don't believe, I don't believe in what the Great Powers do. Nurse Cavell said 'Patriotism is not enough'. She was wrong. It is too much! It is enough for us to love and hate our neighbours as ourselves.

When the Germans had to go away after the Occupation and the English boys came over to put us to rights, they was pretty good, the ones I met, anyway; but there was some of the Germans who wasn't so bad, and some of our own people who left a lot to be wished for. I knew people, I had better not write down their names, who only had one complaint against the Germans, and that was that they had houses like the Green Shutters used to be for their soldiers to go to. Well, if you want to have wars, you got to have whores. When it comes to those things, Guernsey is a masterpiece of hypocrisy. After the Liberation, those same people, whose names I have not written down, wanted to shave the heads of all the Guernsey girls who it was known, or thought, had been with German boys. I was against that and let everybody I talked to know it; and I am glad to say they was let alone. They then went out of their way to be as nice as they could to the English boys who had come over; and the game went on as before. I am not sure now they wasn't the only ones who had any sense.

The tunes of nowadays don't come back. In fact, they don't go into my head at all. When I hear the noises from the radios on the beach, or from that abomination of abominations, the T.V., in every house I go to, or from the contraptions in the cafés in Town, I flap my ears over my ear-holes and don't hear. Yet sometimes I say to myself, 'Ebenezer, be fair! The young got to be young; and you was young once.' I used to like to hear the waltz tunes of the old steam-organ of the merry-go-round on the Albert Pier, and that was music out of a machine, if you like; but no, the young people are different these days. The crowd on the Albert Pier was jolly and noisy and sometimes rough; but they was good-natured. There are some of the young fellows around these days who are cold and vicious. They frighten me. I don't mean they frighten me for what they can do to me; but they frighten me for what is coming to Guernsey and in the world.

Three of the St Sampson's gang had a go at me not long back; but they didn't come off so well. Nocq Road, St Sampson's, was always a rough corner: I had my first fight there. Two of them came from Nocq Road but I thought it was become respectable now. It may have done, for I reckon those boys all came from well-to-do families; and I know the father of the other is a Deputy on the States. They have plenty of money, those sort of boys, and spend a fortune on clothes and big motor-bikes. I didn't know any of them before, even by sight, so I can't think what I can have done for them to want to come and hurt me. Anyhow, I was in the kitchen one evening when I heard the noise of motor-bikes coming round the Chouey. It was as if the world was coming to an end. It isn't often they came as far as that; and, if they do, they don't come any further. Les Moulins is right off the map; and the track to it from the corner of the Chouey is of loose stones, and with deep ruts in the bargain. I heard them come right as far as my front gate, and stop there talking and laughing and planning something: then there was a crash of glass, and the brave boys was on their bikes and going down the road hell for leather. I took the lamp and went outside to see what they had done. They had thrown stones and broken half-a-dozen panes of glass of my greenhouse. I thought all right: you wait, my beauties!

I didn't report it to the Police, as I ought to have done. I let people think it was the wind had done it. I thought to myself they have enjoyed their little game, and when they see the old fool haven't got the guts to do anything about it, they will want to play it again. I sat out every night on a box in the greenhouse with the hose-pipe on my lap ready. It wasn't many nights before they came again. They couldn't have arranged it better, if they had tried, for they stood by their bikes with the lights full on them opposite a hole they had made in the glass, and which was just handy for me to point the hose through. I turned the water on. It caught them with the stones in their hands, but they didn't throw them. They was so surprised they didn't even get out of the way. They danced about; and I drenched them. At last, they got their senses back enough to get on their bikes and scoot, shouting threats of what they was going to do to me next time; but I didn't expect what they did do. I had counted without Neville Falla.

I was indoors again by the fire when there was a knock on my front door. I didn't think it could be one of them, for I hadn't heard any sound of a bike; yet I wondered who on earth it could be. Anybody who know me would come round to the back. I opened the door. It was young Constable Le Page. He is a distant cousin of mine, but I don't know him. 'I'm sorry to disturb you, Mr Le Page,' he said, very polite, 'but would you mind coming to the Police Station? There is a matter on which you might help us. I have a car round the corner.' I said, 'I am always willing to help the Police,' and put on my overcoat and hat and took my stick. He was most kind to help me along the rough track, though I could manage it by myself quite well. When I was sitting by him in his nice little black Police car, he said, 'What nonsense have you been up to this time, Ebenezer?' 'I don't know,' I said. 'Why?' 'You'll see,' he said.

At the Police Station he pushed me in front of him into the Inspector's office. 'Mr Le Page has been good enough to come and help us,' he said. Inspector Le Tocq was sitting at his desk; and on three chairs beside him was the three boys, looking like drownded rats. The Inspector stood up and shook hands with me. 'Thank you for coming, Mr Le Page,' he said. 'Will you please take a seat?' Constable Le Page put a chair for me and I sat down, while he remained standing behind me. The Inspector sat down. 'These three gentlemen,' he said, but from the way he said 'gentlemen' he made it clear he didn't have a very high opinion of them as gentlemen, 'want to lay a charge against you.' 'A charge!' I said. 'Whatever for?' 'Assault,' he said. 'Assault?' I said. 'Why, I haven't assaulted them: I only turned the hose on them.' 'Well, in law, you know,' he said, 'that was an action might be considered an assault.' 'I will do it again,' I said, 'if they come and break the glass of my greenhouse!' 'Ah yes, I thought there was something like that about it,' he said, 'but it is not for you, Mr Le Page, to take the law into your own hands.' I said, 'Well, you don't do nothing about it, do you?' He said, 'If you will now lay a charge against them for wilful damage, we might be able to.' 'I won't do that,' I said. 'If they go to prison, when they come out they will be heroes and martyrs for all the rest of their sort on the island. Besides, they have been punished enough.' I knew what I would have felt like when I was their age to have my good clothes spoilt. 'In that case,' he said to the boys, 'I suggest you get out of here, while the going is good.'

I had a good look at the boys then. The two younger ones wouldn't look at me, but looked down at the floor. One was a thick-necked little bully and the other a weed with a loose mouth. They got up and shuffled out. The eldest, who was eighteen or nineteen, was a long lean creature with black hair and very dark-blue deep-set eyes. He didn't look away. He looked at me as straight as I looked at him; and those eyes was as cold as ice. I knew it was him who had thought of coming to the Police. I couldn't help admiring him for his cheek, for it was just what I would have done in his position. He got up slowly to his feet: he was in no hurry to get away. 'Well, thank you for your help, Inspector,' he said with a sarcastic smile on his handsome face; and strolled out. The Inspector shook his head sadly. 'That is Neville Falla, son of Deputy Falla,' he said. 'He is breaking his father's heart.' 'I don't know the boy,' I said. 'I wish we didn't,' he said. Constable Le Page then said he would take me home in the car; and the Inspector said as we went, 'Next time they do it, Mr Le Page, you will report it, won't you?' I said, 'There won't be a next time.' There haven't been yet.

It's the visitors in the summer nearly drive me crazy these days. La Petite Grève used to be a quiet little bay nobody knew of; but now they have discovered it. They lie about on the sand in droves and sprawl on the rocks;

and I have to step over their naked bodies to get to my boat. When they go back to their hotels, or guest-houses, in the evening, they leave behind bottles and paper-bags strewn all over the beach; although there are wire-baskets there all the summer for them to put their rubbish in. I only wish I could stuff them into those wire-baskets. To make matters worse, in the gully is the new prehistorical burial-ground I look after for the States. It was there long before the Germans came; but it is only these last years the States have decided it is an Ancient Monument.

The visitors want to know all about it. It is mentioned in the book they have in their hands and from which they read out what they are supposed to look at. I tell them I don't know nothing about it. How should I? I only keep it clean and tidy. They seem to think I was alive in those times. They look at me as if I was an ancient monument. Yet they can't even say my name right. They call me Mister Lee Page in English; or they go all French and call me Monsieur Le Page. I explain to them patiently that my name is Le Page: Le in French and Page like the page of a book. They don't know nothing, those people!

Mind you, they like talking to me. They say it is nice to meet and talk to a real native. They mean a Guernseyman. Well, I'm not a Jerseyman, am I? Sometimes the Devil get into me and I make out I can't speak a word of English. I speak to them in Guernsey French and tell them exactly what I think of them. They don't understand a word I say; but they know I am not being very polite. Other times I just look at them with my mouth open and make noises, as if I was an imbecile: the same as I used to do with the Germans. They like that. It is what they expect a native to be. Then I think to myself ah well, they can't help it, the poor creatures; and am as nice as pie and tell them funny stories. After all, it's for the good of the island.

The trouble is they can't see a Guernsey joke. For instance, there was two young couples I took quite a fancy to. I could see they wasn't the sort to leave paper on the beach, because they wasn't carrying radios about. I took them out in my boat and invited them back to tea after. The girls was delighted with my old Guernsey kitchen. The fellows wanted to pay me for the tea, but I wouldn't let them. It was me invited them to come in: they hadn't invited themselves. A Guernseyman don't charge to his friends: he want to give to his friends. I suppose they thought I was poor. If the truth was known, I could have bought them all up lock, stock, and barrel twenty times, if I'd wanted to.

One of the girls said, 'Aren't you lonely in the winter, living here all by yourself?' 'I'm used to being on my own,' I said. One of the chaps said, 'Why don't you have a dog to keep you company?' 'It would die,' I said. 'Or a cat,' said one of the girls. 'I don't like cats,' I said. 'They are bad.' I told them about Mirouse, the cat my mother used to have. He was a beautiful big black cat with a white shirt-front; but he was a robber. In the end, in spite of my mother, my father said he would have to go. He would drown him. So one night he tied a brick around his neck and threw him in the Vale Pond. 'Now there will be some food left in the cupboard when I come home from work tomorrow,' said my father; but he was wrong there. The next morning when he looked out of the bedroom window, there was Mirouse! He had drunk all the water and was sitting on the brick.

The fellows sort of smiled in that kind way the English have, as if they was sorry for the poor old man who thought that was funny. One of the girls, who had been getting ready to laugh to please me, laughed before I got to the end of the story; so I knew she hadn't seen the joke. The other stuck out her chest and put on a face like a schoolmistress and said, 'I think your father was a very cruel man, Mister Lee Page. I hope you have not grown up like him.' No: it's no use! It don't do to make jokes with the English. They are serious people. I have learnt my lesson.

I like it better here in the winter when the visitors have gone. It is quiet then. Tonight the sea is pounding away on the rocks of La Petite Grève and the spray is dashing against my windows and the wind is whistling round the chimney and the fire burning blue in the grate. I am in the warm and, as old Jim would say, as snug as a bug in a rug. I could be out visiting this person or that, if I wanted to. They all make a fuss of me when I arrive, and shoo the cat off the armchair for me to sit in; but they are not really interested in anything I have to say. It is not that I want to say much; but I like to sit in a corner and listen to people talking, and put in my spoke now and then. Nowadays people don't talk among themselves around the fire like they used to. As soon as I've sat down and been made comfortable, it's 'Sh! it's Maigret!' or 'It's Eamon Andrews!' and I have to sit in the half-dark and look at the horrible T.V.; and you can't put your spoke in against the T.V.

That is how it is I come to be writing this book. I got to say what I think to somebody: if only to myself. I don't expect anybody will ever read what I have written; but at the back of my mind I always have the hope perhaps some day somebody will. I bought a big thick book from the Press Office in Smith Street, though I didn't think at the time I would ever be able to fill it; but I am already getting near the end and haven't written the half of what I have to say. I'll have to buy another the next time I go to Town. Tonight the tunes have got in the way. I'm looking forward to beginning a new chapter. I like to start on a clean page and forget all the mistakes I have made before.

19

I can't say I was really surprised when Hetty came round and said Raymond was gone in the Army. He was following the example of Horace. Hetty herself was half worried and half proud. 'That Prissy won't be able to say now it is Horace who is winning the War,' she said. Raymond hadn't been called up: he'd volunteered. 'He is not one of those who wait to be fetched,' said Hetty. I was out of favour with Hetty. Raymond himself didn't come and tell me. In his case, I think he was ashamed after all his arguments with me about what a Christian ought not to do. He had been in the Army over a month before he came round to let me see how he looked in his uniform. I didn't bring up the subject of what a Christian ought not to do; but he did say, when he was speaking of Miss Mellish, 'The Reverend Noel Mellish, her brother, has won the V.C., and he is a Christian.'

I was astonished at the change in Raymond. Until then nobody would have noticed he was a well-built boy. Except on Sundays, when he wore a well-made blue serge suit, he used to go around in baggy grey flannel trousers and a loose sports coat that fitted where it touched. Now he began to take a pride in his clothes, and Hetty complained that he was for ever cleaning and pressing his old khaki. The tunic he was issued with he had taken in by Bertie Cox on the Bridge, until it fitted him like a glove; and he bought himself a pair of Fox's puttees for going out and polished his belt until it shone like mahogany, and I bet he was never pulled up for having dirty buttons. It was amazing what a smart soldier he made.

Also he got on well at the Fort: which was the last thing I would have expected. It happened when his lot went down the Soldier's Bay for bathing parade, he turned out to be the best swimmer; and at some sports they held on the Fort Field, he turned out to be the best runner. The P.T. Sergeant spotted him and put him forward to become a P.T. Instructor. I found it hard to imagine Raymond, who had never played a game in his life, becoming a physical training instructor at Fort George; but there it was. He wasn't allowed to finish his training to go to France; but was sent to England on a Physical Training Course and passed out First Class. Hetty was broken-hearted when he had to go, but I said to her, 'He's better off at

Gosport than in the trenches.' He was a lance-jack when he went; and when he came back was made a full corporal. I couldn't help wondering how the quiet Raymond was going to get on when he found himself having to give orders to rough chaps from Birmingham and other big cities in England, of who there was more now in the Battalion than Guernseys.

When he came to see me again, I hardly knew him. The hard grind he had gone through at Gosport had made a man of him. He looked so athletic and trim in a new uniform with his two stripes up, he could easily have been mistaken for a Regular; yet he had none of the swagger some chaps put on. He didn't have much to say for himself. I had to ask him how he was getting on: drilling grown men, many older and bigger than himself. 'Oh fine, thanks,' he said. 'I enjoy it.' 'How about the roughs from Brumma-gen?' I said. 'They're all good chaps,' he said, as if it was a lot of angels he was drilling. I got more out of Archie Mauger, who I used to have a chat with sometimes. He was the son of the Tom Mauger who Harold built a house for and who was the son of old Tom Mauger my father worked for. Archie had been lucky like Raymond and sent away on a course; only in his case it was to Hayling Island for musketry and he came back a Musketry Instructor. He said Raymond was the most popular N.C.O. in the Bat-talion. It began the very first night he joined up. He knelt down by his bed in the barrack-room and said his prayers. According to the Chapel prea-chers, a boy who did that would be laughed at and persecuted, but have his reward in heaven. It wasn't what happened to Raymond: he had his reward on earth. The fellows respected him for it. 'It takes some doing,' Archie Mauger said and laughed. 'I change my religion twice every Sunday morning. At nine o'clock when it's Church of England Parade in the gym, I'm a Wesleyan and stop in the barrack-room and polish up. At half-past ten when the Wesleyans fall in for Ebenezer Chapel, I'm Church of England and get on my bike and go home. They don't have a roll-call for Instructors.' Archie Mauger was a clever boy and went to the University of Bristol after the War and got a B.Sc. and became a Science Master in England; but he didn't have Raymond's guts.

He was fair about him, though. 'Raymond Martel is a chap apart,' he said. 'He ought really to be an officer.' I saw what he meant, but I didn't think being an officer got much to do with it. Raymond was better than the rest of us, I truly believe; and for all that he was a Chapel boy, it wasn't in a way that made you not like him. He didn't smoke, he didn't drink, he didn't swear, he didn't talk smut; but he didn't go about with a long face finding fault with those who did. The dirt didn't touch him: he didn't notice it. He was like a chap lit up. The roughest fellows would fight among themselves as to who would get into his squad to be drilled. It wasn't he let them off light. Archie Mauger didn't understand it. He said, 'If I'm popular at all, it's only because I'm cushy and lose my squads on the ramparts and let them have a smoke.' Raymond put his through their paces as hard as anybody; but he was in sympathy with them, and would never strain a chap further than he could go. He was enjoying himself and they enjoyed themselves with him. They called him 'Corp' to his face, but 'Our Raymond' behind his back. When I think now of Raymond's sad story and of his terrible end, I am glad that for the year or so he spent in the Army he was happy.

He didn't make any special friends, but would bring a couple of chaps home for dinner most Sundays. The English boys had no homes they could go to like the Guernsey boys. They was glad to be given a good meal in a comfortable room; and Hetty who, like my mother, was never without a thing during the War, gave them meals the like of which they had never had before. Raymond invited me down a few times and it seemed a happy home those Sundays. I had to laugh at the way poor Hetty tried to speak the proper English and put in aitches all over the place. She sounded as if she was a horse with the asthma. Harold liked talking to the English boys and getting their opinions on things; and sometimes Percy looked in. By then, Prissy and Hetty wasn't speaking, of course; but, according to Hetty, it was all on Prissy's side. 'Well, she know where I live by now,' she said. 'She can come and see me any time she want to. The back door is never locked.' Percy, for once, was being stubborn and keeping in with Harold. Prissy couldn't say much, because Harold was giving him work to do. There wasn't much doing during the War for a monumental builder; and those who was dying didn't have tombstones in St Sampson's Cemetery.

There was one thing the English boys did do for Guernsey. They spread the pox. The Green Shutters had been closed down; so what else could you expect? I was lucky. The worst I got was the crabs and I got rid of those with blue ointment. I don't remember the girls I went with those years, except for Blanche de Lainé. I don't think that was her real name; she wasn't Guernsey. She sold chocolates and showed the people to their seats in the balcony at St Julien's. I'd noticed her when I was there with Hetty; and she'd noticed me. One week there was a picture showing called *The Birth of a Nation.* Hetty only liked love stories; so that Saturday I went to the matinée by myself. I didn't understand the picture really. I was sitting at the end of the back row by the gangway; and Blanche was standing against the door while the picture was showing. 'You're not with your mother this week,' she said to me. 'That wasn't my mother,' I said, 'that was my aunt.' 'Oh, I thought you were a good boy and brought your mother to the Pictures,' she said. 'I'm not all that good,' I said. 'I wondered,' she said.

When I got outside and was standing on the edge of the pavement in St Julien's Avenue wondering whether to go home, or stop in Town for the evening, I felt somebody nudge me, and looked, and there she was standing beside me. 'Are you lost?' she said. 'No,' I said, 'but I am trying to make up my mind where to go to next.' 'I'm going to have my tea,' she said. I took that as a hint. 'Righto, come along, then,' I said, 'we can go to Le Poidevin's.' Le Poidevin's was a bit cheaper than Le Noury's. She said, 'I'm sorry; but I don't allow a man to stand me treat.' I thought well, she is different from every other girl I have ever met. I looked her over in the light. She was older than I had thought, but looked more of a lady. If I hadn't known, I would never have guessed she was a chocolate girl. 'How about coming to my place and having tea with me?' she said. 'Thank you very much,' I said. 'I'll be pleased to!' I didn't think she could be a whore.

She had a couple of rooms in Pedvin Street. They was very clean and nicely furnished. I saw she was an educated woman. She had a whole shelf-load of books by Marie Corelli. She gave me a good tea of bread and butter and jam and cream cakes; and then got down to what she had brought me there for. It was her made the first move. I wouldn't have, because I didn't know quite what I was letting myself in for. As it was, I had never imagined before that Saturday afternoon that there was so many ways of doing the same thing. At seven o'clock she said she would have to be getting back to St Julien's Hall for the evening performance. I walked with her up High Street and down the Pollet; but my knees was knocking together. She was as fresh as a daisy. At the bottom of St Julien's Avenue she shook hands with me like a man and said, 'Come the same time next Saturday, if you like.' 'I'll see,' I said. The way I was feeling I didn't think I would ever want to do it again.

By the next Saturday, I felt different; and I went to her place every Saturday for two or three months. I learnt a lot. While I was having a spell between goes, she talked to me quite serious. She had a religion I had never heard of. She believed she had lived many times before and was going to live many times more. She had been Cleopatra and Mary, Queen of Scots, and Madame de Pompadour; and goodness knows who she was going to be next. She said that if you had been good in this life, you got a better life next time; but that if you had been bad, you got a worse. She was going to become perfect in the end; but I didn't quite understand what was going to happen to her then. Anyhow, for the present, it didn't matter much, because she wasn't in a hurry. She didn't want to get too good too quick: she wanted to live as many lives as possible. At the same time, she must be careful not to go downhill. There was some things she must not do. I wondered what those things could be. She said she must never go with a man she didn't want to go with, and she must never do it for money. I said I hoped she wasn't losing marks over me. She said far from it. I was making her better because I was good. Well, a chap likes to be told he is good for something; but I have always had the idea in my head I got something more in me than that. I was glad when she went to Jersey. I didn't like her really.

I often saw Liza about in Town; but I tried to keep my eyes off her. She was so beautiful those days it hurt. The way she walked with her long legs and swung her shoulders and threw her head back when she laughed was a poem; but I wasn't going to be the slave of a poem. I saw her round with young Guille a lot, though he was married by then; and after he was killed, I didn't see her for months. Then I saw her going round with a Captain in the Scots Guards. He was a Goliath of a chap and I knew I didn't have a chance in hell against him. I found out his father was a lord in Scotland and that he was staying at Castle Carey while he was getting better from a wound. He went back to the War and the next time I saw Liza she was dressed as a nurse. I have never seen any actress on the Pictures, not even Greta Garbo, to come up to Liza when she was dressed as a nurse. She was nursing the wounded in a hospital in London and was only in Guernsey now and again for a few weeks at a time. I saw her out with one fellow after another, but only officers I noticed; and sometimes she looked sad and haunted, and at others wild and gay.

I ran into Ada Domaille from time to time. Good old Ada was doing good work. She was helping Miss Penelope Peele to send hundreds of parcels of food and socks and warm clothes to the Guernsey boys in the trenches. I asked her about Liza, but Ada got it firmly fixed in her head Liza and me was meant for each other from the start, so she didn't tell me all she knew. It was Jack Domaille, her brother, who let the cat out of the bag. He wasn't in the Army because he had something wrong with one lung; but he had learnt to drive a motor-car and was carrying on as a chauffeur for the Careys. Naturally he knew all about Liza's goings on. She already had two babies. In fact, it was at the Domailles' house at the Marais they was born. Lady Carey knew. Of course, she couldn't very well let them be born at Castle Carey; but she would always have Liza back to live there after. Though she did say to Jack once, 'If my dear Elizabeth must have a baby once a year, I do rather wish she wouldn't always choose to have it over Christmas.' I had no idea what had been done with the babies; but I didn't ask. The truth is I didn't want to know. I didn't want to know they existed.

Jim came home on embarkation leave. The very day he arrived in Guernsey he came round to Les Moulins in the evening. 'We're going to Town Saturday night, the two of us,' he said, 'and you're coming back to the farm for supper and stay the night.' 'Then will you come to dinner and tea with us on Sunday?' I said. 'For sure!' he said. I can't write about that Saturday and Sunday. It was too good. Jim looked magnificent. He was the picture of health, as Liza said, and looked years younger than when he went away, and was upright again and held his head up. When I walked down the High Street with him, I was as proud as if I walked with a king. It wasn't that they had made a smart soldier of him. He was God's own comic soldier. He was Jim. It wasn't three or four, nor five or six, it was dozens who shouted out 'Wharro Jim! Comment s'en va, mon viow?' and up went his big hand and up came his big smile. People wanted to talk to him, people wanted to touch him, and he talked to anybody; but, even then, he dragged me in and kept hold of me by the elbow, as if I might run away. Supper at the farm was like old times, except that Wilfred and Gerald wasn't there. Gerald was then a cadet in a training school for flying in Bristol. Lydia had supper with us and couldn't take her eyes off her brother; and for once I liked her. After supper we went up to his old room and lay and talked in his big bed until I fell asleep against him with his arm around me like when we was kids on Lihou. There have been times in my life when I have thought the Bible is right and it is a curse to be born; but when I remember that stolen day of innocent happiness, how not for one moment was we out of touch, not even when we was asleep, I know it was worth being born for that.

He was up with the lark in the morning and out swearing at the cows. He was good at swearing before, but he was better now and used swear-words even I didn't know. I think they was Welsh; but the cows didn't take a blind bit more notice than when he used to swear at them in their own language. Tabitha came for dinner to our house that Sunday and, in the afternoon, when Jim and me was sitting on the rocks, he said, 'A pity I couldn't have married Tabitha. I would have loved Tabitha.' I too wished he could have married Tabitha; though I liked Jean. He told me about his training. He was a good shot with a rifle, he said; but then he always had been. 'If I can shoot birds, I suppose I can shoot men,' he said; but I knew he didn't like the idea. He didn't like throwing hand-grenades. He said when he pulled the pin out of the Mills bomb, he was always afraid it would go off before he got it out of his hand. He hoped he wouldn't be in a bayonet charge. 'I couldn't do that to a chap,' he said. I said, 'They'll give you rum before you go over the top; and he'll be trying to do the same to you.' 'I can't rip a chap open,' he said, 'it don't matter who he is.'

He spent the rest of his leave with Phoebe and the kids. I got a postcard from him from Southampton, saying he was on his way. At the bottom, he wrote, 'Don't sigh-ee, don't cry-ee!' I got one letter from him from France; but there was black lines through most of it. All I could read was 'Don't think I have forgotten you, if you don't hear from me for a week or two. I'll write again as soon as I can.' I saw the news in the *Press*. I had just come in from work and the *Press* was on the table where the boy had thrown it. My mother was frying some fish for our tea. I opened the *Press* as I always did, hardly thinking of what I was doing. I saw it at once. 'Killed in Action. James Mahy, beloved son of James and Agnes Mahy of Les Grands Gigands, St Sampson's. For God and King and Country.' I went out of doors. I cried.

20

I wondered if I ought to go and see Jim's mother; but I didn't go. There was nothing I could say. My mother didn't say nothing. When I came indoors she had laid out the tea on the table and put the *Press* away. I knew she knew. She did something to me she never did. She touched me. When she put my plate of fish in front for me, she stroked my head and neck with her big rough hand. I looked at her old eyes when she was sitting opposite me. She saw and knew and suffered more than anybody thought, my mother. 'This is good fish,' I said. 'Yes,' she said, 'it was caught this morning.' It was whiting and flakey. I could hardly stuff it down.

I got a letter from Jim's mother. It was in an envelope with a black edge and on paper with a black edge. It was written in her beautiful old-fashioned hand-writing, but I didn't like it. She was the perfect lady, even over the death of her son. I would have had more sympathy for Hetty, who would have gone mad. She began 'I know you will be sharing our grief in our great bereavement'. She went on to say she hoped I would visit them, though she understood why I had not done so. She invited me to tea the next Sunday. I didn't like the idea of going; but I went. It was like going to tea after a funeral. She was in deep mourning and looked very tragic. I thought of Pauline Frederick in *Madame X*. Lydia was in black voile and looked as she had looked when she was going into a decline. Old Mahy wore a black tie and a black band on his arm. I wasn't even wearing a black tie.

They made no to-do, thank goodness. Old Mahy said, 'He was a good lad, our Jim.' I couldn't help thinking how they hadn't seen eye to eye about anything when Jim was alive. Mrs Mahy said she had been to see Phoebe. 'She is taking it remarkably well,' she said. 'She is a brave girl.' At first Mrs Mahy thought of having Phoebe and the kids to live at the farm, and Lydia was now quite willing; but Phoebe's sister, Eileen, was getting married to young Sarchet before he was called up, and they all wanted to live together at Sous L'Église. Mrs Mahy decided, all things considered, it would be best. After tea, she asked me if I would like to have something of Jim's. He had left some books behind in his room when he got married. Perhaps I would like to go up and choose one. I didn't want to go into his empty room. I knew what books he got up there. There was a pile of Bibby's Annuals he kept because he liked looking at the pictures. There was a Bible and a dictionary, but I didn't want those; and there was *David Copperfield* and *The Mill on the Floss* and *Robinson Crusoe*. I said I would like to have *Robinson Crusoe*. She fetched it for me. When I had said good-bye to the others, she came to the gate with me. 'I want you to come and see me often,' she said, 'you meant more to Jim than anybody.' I said I would.

I visited her about once a month until the old man died; and then she left the farm and went to live in her house at St Martin's. It was never known from the Army how Jim was killed; but I know. His officer wrote the usual things, and there was a lot of letters of sympathy from all sort of people his mother showed me: but the best was from a boy in his platoon called David Evans, who had been wounded and was in hospital when he wrote. It wasn't well written and was badly spelt and the paper wasn't very clean; but in it he said 'Jim was the only Guernseyman in our mob. He made us laugh, but we all loved him,' and at the end 'He was the first over the top and at 'em.' Yes, Jim was the one to be ripped open. He couldn't do it. I have dreamt of him many times over the years; but, thank God, it have never been in mud and blood. It have been the happy Jim coming to meet me across the meadow with his big smile and his hand up; and I feel in my sleep that a great happiness is coming to me, but then I wake up.

I have something bad in me. I think it is a devil. I get very angry. I get so angry sometimes I feel I am going to break in two. The worst of it is that it is not for reasons anybody else would get angry; and nobody else would understand. I don't understand why myself half the time. When the fellows at work, and many others, all with the best intentions in the world, said to me 'Hard luck about Jim,' I felt I could have murdered them. Raymond was the only one I opened my heart to. I am sure I would be ashamed now if I could remember all I said to him. I know I kept on saying, 'Jim is not in the world any more! Jim is not in the world any more!' 'He is somewhere,' Raymond said. 'How d'you know?' I said. 'He has to be,' he said. That was all he could say. He didn't know really. When he left, he said, 'I do wish old Horace would hurry up and come home.'

Horace didn't come over and win the War. When the Armistice was signed he was kicking his heels in America; and, soon after, he was demobbed and went back to work for the rich company that could have bought up Guernsey. It wasn't until years later that he came home, and by then a lot had happened to poor Raymond. The last summer of the War Christine Mahy came over for the long holiday from the school where she was teaching in England. I reckon it was then she spotted that Raymond might be a boy like other boys, and not only a boy who read poetry and talked about religion. He didn't chase after her, but she went to Town Saturday nights with her sister, Gwen; and he was usually about Town with one of his chums from the Fort. Christine saw to it he paired off with her, and Gwen was left with the other. There was nothing in the way of courting; but they would go for a stroll, the two pairs, to the end of the White Rock, or along the Castle Walk.

Of course La Hetty got to know. La Prissy was round to the back door full of it. 'Is it true what I hear?' she said, 'that your Raymond is engaged to that Christine Mahy from Ivy Lodge? I couldn't believe my ears! They got nothing but debts, those Mahys. They are less than nobody!' It was true enough. Christine's father, who was a brother to Jim's, was about as good as Jim's at spending money, and quite as bad at making it; and the mother didn't have a penny to bless herself with, and wasn't even of a good family. She was from over the fish-and-chip shop in Fountain Street and you couldn't come from lower down than that. Hetty said, 'If Raymond was to marry that dirty little Mahy, she would never put her foot inside this house!'

I am quite sure Raymond didn't have a thought in his head of marrying Christine Mahy. He was friendly with her, as he was friendly with all fellows and girls alike. Later on, when he was blaming himself for everything, he said to me, 'I made a great mistake when I was a young chap. I used to think girls were human beings like us; but they are not. They are always after something. They are either after your body, or your money, or a father for their children; and, if they are not after your body, or your money, or a father for their children, there is always something they want you to be, or do, that will bring them glory. They are never satisfied to let you be; and be with you.' I said, 'Well, men are after their own ends too, you know.'

Raymond had the sense not to take Christine to his home; but she took him back to her house Saturday nights when he had a weekend pass. He was made welcome. Bill Mahy, her father, was a long, thin, dreamy chap, who didn't say much, as a rule; but he liked talking to Raymond. He was another for reading books and was much more interested in the why's and the wherefores of everything than in making a living growing, which was his business. Emmeline Mahy, the mother, was a scallywag of a woman; but she was easy-going and made anybody who went there feel at home. There was a daughter-in-law, Edna, who practically lived at Ivy Lodge with her little girl, though she had a home of her own, Rosamunda, across the road. The son, Herbert, who was the eldest of the family, was in the trenches. He had always been the big fat jolly boy, and looked like a barrel in his uniform. He would have finished up like old Dredge, if he had lived; but he was killed through some misunderstanding the day of the Armistice.

Raymond didn't get home sometimes until the early hours of Sunday morning; and when he walked in, he would find Hetty sitting up waiting for him with a face like death. She guessed where he had been, but she daren't ask. Instead, she had laid for him a lovely supper of crab, or lobster, which she knew he liked. 'Thank you, Ma,' he would say, 'but I have had something to eat.' He told me how those nights he hated his mother when he came in and found her sitting up waiting for him. If she had gone to bed at her usual time, he would have told her openly in the morning where he had been. As it was, he didn't say a word more; but went to bed and couldn't bring himself even to kiss her good-night.

Hetty breathed again when Christine went back to England. Christine didn't write to Raymond. That ought to have pleased Hetty; but it didn't. 'Fancy that girl not sending Raymond as much as a postcard,' she said to me. 'It only go to show how much she think of him.' Hetty was a woman and ought to have known Christine better. She was sure of herself, that girl. When, alas and alack, she had got what she wanted, she said to me once in her sing-song holy voice, 'I always knew Raymond would be mine in the fullness of time.' She had a way of speaking as if God told her things He didn't tell to other people. The trouble was He didn't tell her everything. However, Hetty soon had another worry. The powers-that-be at the Fort decided the young instructors must do their bit in the trenches, and Raymond was sent back to his platoon to finish his training. 'If he got to go, I'll die!' she said.

He was lucky. A sickness they called the 'flu broke out at the Fort. It wasn't 'flu really, but something worse. A fellow might get it one day and be dead the next. They buried twenty-six in the Military Cemetery at Fort George in a few days. It happened Raymond was at Fort Hommet doing his firing course when the 'flu was at its worst; and so as those who was there wouldn't catch it, they was kept there. Raymond didn't go back to Fort George until a few days before the Armistice; and so he didn't finish his training after all.

He enjoyed his time at Fort Hommet. It was the nearest he ever got to living like a monk. He said Fort Hommet was so cut off from the world, it might well have been a monastery; except that it was built to defend the island against Napoleon. It was built out on the rocks and had a draw-bridge and a moat; and Raymond liked to hear the rough sea beating against the walls outside his window, when he was lying in bed. He was N.C.O. in charge of a barrack-room and had a small corner room to himself. There was an officer supposed to be in charge, but he kept out of the way; and the sergeant had a habit of disappearing and not being seen for days. The fellows was fed like fighting cocks, but wasn't allowed to tire themselves out by doing any work, in case they got bit by the bug. The only parades they had to go on was to line up twice a day and gargle per-manganate. The rest of the day they passed lying on their beds yarning, or reading stories by Victoria Cross, or playing cards or housey-housey.

Raymond passed his time in his little room reading *Les Misérables* in four volumes in French from beginning to end. Evenings nobody was supposed to go down the narrow neck of land that led to the road; but Alice and Allison Le Page, who was twins and third or fourth cousins of mine, kept a little shop along the Vazon Road and entertained soldiers from Fort Hommet in the room at the back every evening. They wasn't whores, but they liked the boys. Raymond didn't go and see my cousins; but often on my way home from work, I'd meet him going to Wallaballoo on his bike to have a good supper. Nobody at Fort Hommet got the 'flu.

Mr Dorey took me aside one day and told me I must expect my calling-up papers early in the New Year. He couldn't hang on to me any longer. Most of the young Guernseymen was killed off and it was now the turn of us older ones to take their place. I didn't care. The sovereigns was mounting up in the pied-du-cauche and my mother would be all right. She could employ an old man and a boy; and Tabitha would keep an eye on her. I began looking at my book of Army Instructions I learnt from when I was a sergeant in the Militia; but the Lee Enfield rifles was different now, and there was Lewis and Hotschiss machine-guns come along since. It didn't seem my training as a soldier was going to be much use. One thing I decided I would do before I went: and that was go and see Phoebe. I wanted to see the kids, if nothing else. I had seen Eileen with her young husband in Town, and sometimes the older Sarchet and his wife; but never Phoebe.

I went one Saturday afternoon. I can't say how I felt when I put my bike against the wall. A lot of mad thoughts was going through my head. I thought I'll take Phoebe in my arms and say, 'Come on, old girl, we both belonged to Jim, let's be friends now; and if I come back from the War, I'll be father to his children.' Yes, I even thought I might marry her. I walked up the path and knocked on the front door. Phoebe opened it. She stood staring at me as if she was seeing a ghost; and then began to laugh. 'He's not in!' she shrieked. 'He's not in! He's not in!' and burst into wild crying and slammed the door in my face.

The Armistice came on me without me knowing: the same as the War had done. I was clearing up inside one of the greenhouses down the Vineries when a chap rushed in and said 'The War is over!' and the sirens and whistles began going like billyo down St Sampson's. The next minute every fellow was out of the Vineries and round the corner into Hutton's pub, though Mr Dorey was temperance himself and didn't like his men drinking. I had a couple and went home. When I got in Hetty was in the kitchen, laughing and crying. 'Raymond won't have to go!' she was saying, all excited, 'it's too good to be true!' My mother wasn't excited. She was sitting quietly with her hands in her lap. 'The end is not yet,' she said.

I think the way the War ended broke my mother's heart. She had expected something different. I don't know quite what; but it wasn't men sitting around a table signing a paper. I never really knew or understood all the funny ideas my mother had in her head. I do know she never had hope of anything much after Armistice Day. Perhaps I am more like my mother than I think; for I had my blackest thoughts that day.

It is easy to say years after the event that at eleven o'clock in the morning on the eleventh of November in the year nineteen hundred and eighteen I knew there was going to be another war; but I did. I was thinking about it all the afternoon while I was working in the garden. The only mistake I made was I didn't think there was going to be as long as twenty years before it came. I was sure, anyway, the rejoicing was in vain. Nobody who was not alive at that time can imagine how senseless everybody was on Armistice Day. It wasn't only relief from anxiety for those who was gone away; or because it was victory for our side. It was the end of the war that was going to end all wars. Never again! Never again! The Kingdom of Heaven was round the corner.

I went to Town in the evening because everybody else was going. I asked my mother to come with me, but she wouldn't. Hetty and Prissy was there, arm-in-arm; and the two husbands together behind. There wasn't room to move properly anywhere; and you just had to go with the crowd and was pushed. I talked to this one and that one in passing; and had a few drinks. The public houses was doing a roaring trade; but what they had left was only slops, and there was more on the floor than in the pint-pot. I saw Raymond with a crowd of fellows from the Fort; and he waved. He looked happy. I tried to look happy too; but I couldn't keep it up. I squeezed my way down the Pollet, where I had left my bike in Grey's cycle-shop at the bottom; and I had a last wet at the Red Lion on the way home. They was singing:

> When the beer ... is on the table,
> When the beer ... is on the table,
> When the beer is on the table I'll be there!

It was only half-past nine when I got indoors. My mother was just getting ready to go to bed, and left me to eat my supper by myself. I didn't go to bed for hours. I sat by the fire thinking. I reckon I thought of everything had happened to me and to all the people I knew until then. I thought well, if that is what being alive in this world is, it don't amount to much. A happy day and dreams of something coming; and then you wake up. A few pleasures you forget the minute they are over; and, for the rest, just go on and on and on like a donkey. That is what I am. A Guernsey donkey. Sometimes I stick my heels in and sometimes I kick out and sometimes I lift up my head to heaven and bray. I don't know if there's anything after, I'm sure. I do know if all the people on Guernsey go to heaven who think they're going, there won't half be some family rows up there. For myself, I've had enough of my relations down here. If I rise from the dead and know who I am, it's Jim I want to meet again.

PART TWO

1

Raymond was among the first to be demobbed. He got a fortnight's leave for Christmas, and then went back to the Fort for two or three days and was out. Most of the Guernsey boys at the Fort was out pretty soon; but those who was in France only trickled back in twos or threes over the months. Amos Duquemin, I remember, didn't come back until the summer; but he was one of those who was with the Army of Occupation in Cologne. He said he had a good time and was made a fuss of by the Germans, who was as glad as he was the War was over. He liked the Germans better than he did the French; but, for all that, if he went down the back streets of a night, it was with three or four British Tommies, in case the Jerries wasn't as friendly as they made out. He would have been surprised if he had known what was going to happen, and so would I, for that matter, even if I did know another war was coming. He lived through two occupations, and died only last year. The second time he was one of those occupied by the sons, perhaps, of those who he had occupied twenty or, to be exact, twenty-one years before. It make you to think.

Raymond came to see me in civvies; but he hadn't gone back to his sloppy clothes. He was in a bluey-grey suit made to measure that fitted him perfectly, and of very good material; and he wasn't wearing a hat, and his hair was blowing in the wind. I hadn't noticed before he had curly hair; but perhaps it only began to curl when he was in the Army. I said, 'Well, how d'you like having to do some work for a change, instead of swinging the lead at Fort Hommet?' He laughed. 'I don't do any work at the Greffe,' he said. 'I sit on a high stool and read the livres de perchage.' 'Goodness, what are those?' I said. He said, 'Didn't you know that every douit and every hedge and every inch and square inch of land on Guernsey is weighed and measured, and has been for centuries?' 'I hope not,' I said. 'There is a flat patch at the top of the gully I don't think belong to anybody. If I was to move my hedge back a few yards, I could save it from going to waste.' 'It belongs to somebody all right,' he said, 'probably to an old lady living in Torteval. There is only one way of getting hold of it.' 'How's that?' I said. 'I'll give you an instance,' he said. 'Monsieur Le Brun from the Hook Chook owns a field that is in the shape of a triangle. It isn't big enough to swing a cat. Monsieur Le Blanc, his next-door neighbour, owns a field that is in the shape of a square, minus the small triangle in one corner. He asks Monsieur Le Brun to sell him the triangle; but, of course, Monsieur Le Brun won't. Ah, but Monsieur Le Brun has a daughter, an only child; and Monsieur Le Blanc has a son, an eldest son. The eldest son is given a hint by his father as to what he must do; and he does it. By the next generation, the triangle has disappeared and the other field is square and belongs to the Le Blanc family in perpetuity.' 'I'd rather remain single,' I said, 'and go without the patch of ground.' Well, I have remained single; but I might have done better if I had left that patch of ground alone. It have landed me into a lot of trouble, one way and another.

'The earth is the Lord's and the fullness thereof,' said Raymond, 'but not in Guernsey. In Guernsey land is worshipped first and money next and the Lord last, if at all.' He was laughing, as if it was a great joke. 'I'm going to be an odd sort of minister,' he said. I said, 'Are you really going to be a minister, Raymond?' He said, 'Of course I am going to be a minister. I can read the New Testament in Greek.' I said, 'Is that all you got to be able to do to be a minister?' He said, 'I will pass an exam in June and go to College in September; and when I come out I will have a certificate saying I can bury, marry, and give birth. As you said to me once, we'll see.'

I thought he had something up his sleeve; but I didn't know what. It was hard to believe this gay, good-looking young chap, laughing and making mock of the very religion he was going into, was the chétif little boy who used to follow the big Horace everywhere and couldn't live without him. I wondered if he had a devil in him, the same as me; but, if so, it wasn't an unclean spirit like mine. His was a clean spirit. I have never seen a cleaner-looking young chap. Nor was he preaching at me to make the Great Decision. He was being something in front of my eyes. He was bubbling over with something. When I remember him as he was those days, I think of what it say in the Bible: 'Blessed are the pure in heart, for they shall see God.'

I think it is true to say that Hetty died from love of Raymond; and, in a way, he killed her. He didn't want that love. It was smothering him. She was never satisfied with anything he did. First, she wanted him to go into a bank; and he went into the Greffe. Once he was in the Greffe, she hoped he would rise to the top, and take Quertier Le Pelley's place as Greffier some day; but instead he treated the whole thing as a joke. Now he was set on going into the Wesleyan Ministry; but when she said she would be able to go and live with him in England, he put her off. He would be sent on Circuit and didn't expect to be more than two years in one place. It seemed she was going to lose him altogether. 'Oh, I'll be back in Guernsey for holidays to see you,' he said, 'as often as I can.' At the back of his mind he was hoping she and Harold would be a comfort to each other once he was gone. He said to me, 'A father and mother ought to mean more to each other than the children do. If they live only for the children, the children don't get a chance to live themselves.' He had a wise head on his young shoulders.

Hetty came round complaining to my mother. 'I don't know why us poor women got to bring children into the world for,' she said. 'They're good while they are small; but when they grow up they are only a trouble and a disappointment.' My mother didn't say nothing about her two. 'Mais ch'est comme chonna,' was all she said. I know Tabitha and me was a disappointment to her, because neither of us was of the household of faith. It is true she would go as far as to say 'La Tabby is not a bad girl.' As for me, she knew I didn't have a very good reputation. It goes without saying she heard from Prissy, or somebody else, of every girl I was supposed to have been with, even if I hadn't. I let her think the worst. In Guernsey, it is just as well to be hung for a sheep as a lamb, since you are going to be hung in any case. She would listen to what people said, but all she'd say was, 'Ebenezer is a good son to me.' She didn't talk in the house about me getting married; but when the time came I picked up with Liza again, she said, 'Now that's a girl will never make a man a good wife.'

I mustn't give the idea Raymond was bad to his father and mother when he came out of the Army. If anything, he was more patient than before. He said to me, 'I'm the one who is the father and the mother in this house. They are just two unhappy children.' He didn't help his father in the yard; but he got him boys' adventure stories from the Library. I remember Harold reading *Coral Island* and *Peter the Whaler* forwards and backwards; and he said they was good yarns. For himself, Raymond was reading a book I looked into, but couldn't make head or tail of. It was called *The Unrealised Logic of Religion*, I don't know by who. There was another book he had I read bits of called *The Beloved Captain* by Donald Hankey; but that book he had bought for his own, because he liked it so much. I liked the bits I read of it, myself. That Captain must have been a nice chap.

Hetty had bought Raymond a piano from Fuzzey's in High Street for him to practise on. She chose it on the advice of Mr Pescott and it was quite a good one. I know it fetched over a hundred pounds at the sale. Harold and Hetty didn't think much of Raymond's playing. They said, after all the money they had spent for him to learn, he couldn't play a piece with a tune in it. That wasn't true. He used to play 'The Death of Nelson' for his father, and 'Home Sweet Home' with Variations for his mother; and then he would play a piece by Beethoven for me. It wasn't I was above liking pieces with tunes. I thought there was tunes in those too; though with lots of twiddly bits. The one I liked best was the slow middle part of a sonata

Raymond said was called The Pathetic. I thought he played that well; but when I told him so, he said, 'I will never really be any good; except as an accompanyist.'

It was after the War that Prissy began to get younger and younger. Her skirts got shorter and shorter and her blouses lower and lower and her hair frizzier and frizzier; and she painted and powdered her face, and wore hats La Hetty said she wouldn't be seen dead in. She laughed at the idea of Raymond being a minister. 'He will never make a minister, that one,' she said. 'All he think about is enjoying himself.' When the spring came he joined the Old Intermedian's Tennis Club at Elm Grove, and learnt to play tennis. Prissy would be watching from her upstairs window and see him go off on his bike in his white flannel trousers and open-neck shirt carrying a tennis racket. 'Why, he don't even go to Chapel!' she said. He did go to Chapel Sunday evenings, and sometimes in the morning; but she would see him in the afternoons with a towel round his neck going to L'Ancresse for a swim. He had given up teaching in the Sunday School when he was in the Army, so as he could be at home with his friends from the Fort.

They had been demobbed and gone back to England; but two or three came over in civvies for a holiday at different times that summer and stayed at Wallaballoo. The one I remember was Clive Holyoak, and I also heard a lot about him from Archie Mauger. If Raymond was the most popular N.C.O. in the Battalion, Clive Holyoak was certainly the most famous Private. When he came over for a holiday, Raymond invited me to go down to Wallaballoo and hear him play his violin, though I had already heard him once at a concert when he was in khaki. He was only a little chap and had silky golden hair and a face, I thought, like a sulky girl. In civvies he was smartly dressed in a loose woolly suit and didn't look too bad; but, as a soldier he was hopeless. Raymond used to let him fall out for most of his P.T., or otherwise he'd faint; and Archie Mauger said that in Ceremonial Drill, when he sprung to attention to present arms, his puttees fell down on his boots.

Archie was in the barrack-room when our Clive arrived with his draft from England. While the other fellows was getting unpacked and laying out their kit for inspection he, if you please, was sitting on his bed with his legs crossed like an Indian snake-charmer, playing his violin. Sergeant Strudwick happened to be crossing the barrack square. I used to see the one-time Sergeant Strudwick the years after the War peddling his barrow of fruit and vegetables from door to door. He was the toughest, ugliest, wickedest-looking scoundrel I have ever seen; except for old Steve Picquet, who lived after the Second World War in a bunker at Pleinmont called Onmeown and died a few years ago. As might be expected, Raymond liked Sergeant Strudwick and said he had a heart of gold. Archie

Mauger said he was the best blasphemer in the Royal Guernsey Light Infantry and, he was willing to bet, in any regiment of the whole of the British Army. He had been Bandmaster of the Manchesters in peace-time and now played a one-stringed banjo he had made himself. When he heard Clive playing his violin, he stopped dead in the middle of the square as if he was struck by lightning, raised his fists to heaven and, in words I dare not write down, called on God the Father Almighty and His bastard Son, Jesus Christ, and Mary, the mother thereof who, according to Sergeant Strudwick, was anything but a virgin, to come down and listen to this! Then he was across the square and up the steps and along the verandah and into the barrack-room like a lion let loose.

The fellows dropped everything they was doing: he looked so fierce. They thought he was going to murder Clive. Clive took no notice whatever, but, lost to the world, went on playing his piece to the end. The Sergeant stood listening with one eye screwed up, and the other swivelling round like a lobster's, in case any fellow dared to move, or make a sound. When Clive had done playing and put his violin back in its case, Strudwick said, 'Report to me in the Orderly Room! At once!' and marched out. 'Poor old Clive!' the fellows said. 'Twenty days C.B.,' said one. 'Twenty years, more likely,' said another.

Raymond was never tired of talking to me about Clive Holyoak; even after he hadn't seen him, or heard from him for years. Raymond was a boy of deep feelings and never forgot anybody he had once admired. Horace remained first in his heart always; but I think Clive had a great influence on his mind. Raymond was the only one who knew what happened between Strud and Clive that morning. When Clive came back to the barrack-room, all he said was, 'The sergeant wants to take charge of my violin for fear you fellows smash it.' Actually, Strudwick had gone for him with all the blasphemous language of which he was a master, and which used to make the toughest fellows on parade quake and tremble in their Army boots. Clive didn't tremble. He listened with a smile. Strud swore at him for joining the Army; when he didn't join it: he was conscripted. Strud swore at him for imagining he could be of any use as a soldier; when he didn't imagine anything of the sort. Strud swore at him for longing to get into the trenches as soon as possible and have his hand smashed by a bullet from a Boche. Well, he wasn't going to be allowed to do it, that was all; and Sergeant Strudwick, with the help of God the Father and His disreputable Family up above, was going to see to it that he wasn't. 'Then I won't, if you say so, Sergeant,' said Clive sweetly.

If the War had lasted twenty years, he would never have finished his training anyhow; for he was always having to do a part again, because he hadn't passed the test. He was pulled up by every N.C.O., except Raymond, and given punishments galore. If he had done all the fatigues he was given, he would have dropped dead; and if he had done all the C.B., he would never have got out of the barracks at all. For some mysterious reason his name was for ever left out on the defaulters' roll. The nearest he came to being punished was over Church Parade. He was like Archie Mauger and objected to going on Church Parade; but he wasn't dishonest enough to change his religion when it suited him. He did go on Church Parade once 'For the experience', as he said; but he refused to go again. He was warned and warned, and almost begged on bended knees to go; until at last, against everybody's wishes except his own, he had to be brought up before Colonel Nason, or the whole business of Military Discipline would have been made ridiculous. When the fellows in his barrack-room said it was rotten luck, he said, 'It will be interesting to experience the luxury of martyrdom.' They gaped. I knew Colonel Nason from when I was in the Militia. He was more of a Colonel than any Colonel on the stage ever was; and I could just see young Clive standing to attention in front of him, rooted to the spot by the Colonel's glass eye. The Colonel's other eye would be searching hopelessly for help, while he was wondering what the hell he could do to get himself out of an awkward corner with flying colours. 'Now tell me, my man,' said the Colonel to Clive, 'on what grounds do you object to attending Divine Service conducted by the Very Reverend Dean Penfold, the Chaplain of our Battalion? I see you have attended once.' 'I was bored,' said Clive. 'BORED!' bawled the Colonel. 'Never in my whole military career has a man dared to stand up and tell me to my face that he was bored by Church Parade! Dismiss!'

Though he wasn't punished by the Colonel, he was marked on his papers as having no religion; and Sunday mornings those who had no religion was put on fatigues, usually cleaning out the latrines. Actually, he was put on scrubbing the floor of the Sergeant's Mess. He was down on his knees just going to begin, when in walked Sergeant Strudwick. The Sergeant's Mess nearly caught fire from his language. Clive didn't scrub the floor. Sundays he spent with various people on the island who was interested in music. He was soon known among the officers and played at Regimental Concerts, and was the first violin of the string quartette used to play for Sir Reginald Hart, the Lieutenant Governor, when he gave one of his dinners. Clive was given what amounted to a permanent pass to go out of the Fort whenever he wanted to. The guard was instructed to let him pass the Barrier Gate any time he was carrying a violin case. The little monkey bought an empty violin case he kept under his bed in the barrack-room and, when he wanted to go out and wasn't going to play anywhere, he walked out with it and dumped it in a hedge along the Fort Road, and picked it up on his way back. Naturally, when the 'flu broke out, he was among the lucky ones to be stranded on Fort Hommet; and Raymond said he used to pass his time sitting on the rocks playing to the gulls.

I heard him play first at a smoking concert for the troops in the canteen of Morley Chapel with Raymond at the piano. I must give it to Clive Holyoak he was a wonderful violin-player. I will never forget the way he used to rise up on his tip-toes on his little short legs to reach the top notes. It wasn't so much as if he was playing the fiddle as if the fiddle was playing him. That night he played good pieces first, and the few officers present in the front rows gave him a loud clap. I don't think the fellows liked those pieces much; but they kept quiet while he was playing, and gave him a few claps at the end. Then he let them have what they liked. He played 'It's a long way to Tipperary' and 'There's a long, long, trail of winding' and 'Way down in Tennessee'; but from the way he slammed his old violin, you could tell he felt nothing but contempt for what he was playing and for the fellows he was playing it to; yet he roused them to singing and roaring and cheering and, when they gave him encore after encore, he just smiled.

I didn't take to him as a fellow when I met him at Raymond's. He was great while he was up in the clouds playing, and he played lovely music Raymond said was by Mozart and was like clear water singing; but when he came down to Wallaballoo, Braye Road, he wasn't so good. I can understand how it was Raymond was for him. He was so much out of it at the Fort, and yet managed to hold his own, though he wasn't given a bad time. By all accounts, the fellows treated him as a pet and was quite proud of him really. I reckon the ordinary run of chaps in the Army was much better natured than he was. He struck me as a mean little sod. He wasn't even very nice to Raymond, considering he was staying in the house for nothing. He said to me, 'Ray is going to be a Bible-puncher. Asinine!' Raymond laughed. 'I'm not going to punch the Bible,' he said, 'it's much too hard!' Clive said, 'Bernard Shaw says "He who can, does: he who cannot, teaches." I say "He who can, lives: he who cannot, preaches."' Raymond said, 'How about if preaching is my way of living?' Clive said when he was sixteen he played at a Revival Meeting in Birmingham and was converted by Gipsy Smith. 'When I recovered,' he said, 'I came to the conclusion there is no God.' I said to Raymond after, 'I don't mind people attacking this religion, or that, but I don't like to hear anybody say there is no God. It's unlucky. It come back on you.' Raymond said, 'Clive has more faith in his little finger than you have in your whole body, you old infidel!' I could never get the better of Raymond in an argument.

2

La Prissy heard the music going on next door and may be it was what put ideas into her head. Anyhow, she made a great friend of her sister-in-law, Lil Stonelake, who was quite a flighty piece and who she had hardly spoken to before. It was a dig at Hetty. Hetty wouldn't have nothing to do with Lil Stonelake because of the famous law case was still going on between Dick Stonelake and Harold over the money from Ronceval. Dick had been over age to go in the Army, but had served as a Special Constable. As far as I know, all he did to win the War was to stop me one night from riding my bike without a rear light, so that I had to walk with it until I was out of his sight. After the War, a sister of his came over from England with her three children, two boys and a girl. They had left school but hadn't started work yet. It seemed it was hard to get work in England with all the fellows coming back from France, and there wasn't all that much work to be had on Guernsey either. I was lucky to be in a sure job.

The sister stayed at Ronceval and came with Lil to visit Prissy; but the children spent most of their time at Timbuctoo from Easter to September, and ate and slept there. 'I like having young people about the place,' said Prissy. 'It's hard when you haven't got none of your own.' She had always been very active, and didn't mind having a houseful of people to look after. The boys got to know girls, and the girl got to know boys, and there was parties galore. Prissy didn't invite me. Although I was like my mother and didn't want to take sides in the Battle of the Martels, I had managed to land myself on the side of Harold and Hetty. I have often found myself doing that and having to take sides, when I really thought it was six of one and half a dozen of the other.

Prissy said to my mother, 'I'm going to spend my money while I'm alive, me: not leave it to other people for them to laugh at me when I'm dead.' My mother said, 'In that case, you got to have the money to spend.' My mother was right, as usual. Prissy was running up bills here, there, and everywhere. If it hadn't been for Harold, Percy wouldn't have been able to pay his taxes, let alone keep the place going. His line of business showed no sign of improving after the War; and the young chap who had been clever with his chisel came back with three fingers blown off his right hand.

Harold's side was doing well, for houses and bungalows was going up everywhere; and he allowed Percy a percentage, as well as paying him a wage. It only meant more parties for young people. Prissy had Percy's work-shop done out and decorated for the young people to have a place to dance in. She bought a gramophone, and night after night you would hear the 'Destiny Waltz' and the young people dancing and laughing: while all around outside, the tombstones that hadn't been sold was standing like ghosts and the cherubs climbing up the crosses.

Raymond passed his exam. He had to go to the Ladies' College to sit for it and got distinctions in French, History and English Literature; as well as passing in Greek and a number of other subjects. It was good because he had only studied on his own in his spare time, and came out better than those who was in the College, or at the Pupil Teacher Centre. When I said to him he had done well, he said, 'I nearly didn't pass in mathematics. For the rest, I happen to have a good memory, that's all.' I said, 'I bet your mother is proud of you.' He said, 'She is proud to see my name in the *Evening Press*.'

It was that summer, I think it was the last week in July, when I was in Town on the Saturday evening and who should I meet coming arm-in-arm down Contrée Mansell but Christine Mahy and Liza Quéripel? They was deep in some very confidential conversation. I didn't even know they knew each other. Christine stopped and said, 'Hullo, how are you?' I said, 'I'm wondering what you two are talking about.' 'Ah, women's secrets!' said Christine. I said, 'Aren't you going to introduce me?' Liza said, 'I think we have met before.' 'Have we?' I said. I wasn't taking no nonsense from Liza. 'He is a terrible little man!' she said to Christine. 'Terrible! You don't know the half!' but she was giving me her loveliest smile. I said, 'Not so much of the little, either!' She said, 'I do know you are an inch taller than I am. I will grant you that. I have a forgiving nature.' 'Thank you very much,' I said.

Jim Le Poidevin passed along the other side of the road with his stump of a leg and his crutches and said 'Wharro!' I made him a sign to come over, but he winked and went on. He had said to me when he came back that no girl would ever want to have anything to do with him again, except from pity; and he didn't want pity. I wished he hadn't had to see me with those two. It wasn't only Liza: there was something about Christine. She wasn't as tall as Liza, and had more sloping shoulders and wider hips and was fuller breasted, and you could see she would be fat when she got older; but she drew the men's eyes. She was in half mourning for her brother, and was wearing a black frock with a tight bodice and a full skirt and a silver peacock embroidered across the front. 'I like your frock, Christine,' I said. It was only to say something to please her. She answered as if she was speaking from heaven. 'I made it myself out of curtain material.' She'd got fuller in the face, and I thought how much she looked like a cat. She looked at you with those big mysterious eyes, as if she was looking into your very soul; but I know damn well it was only her own soul she was seeing, if anything. She didn't know anybody else was there. As she was the only woman Raymond ever went with, I am not surprised he thought women are not human beings.

Liza knew other people was there all right. Perhaps she knew it too well, poor Liza. Those lovely deep-set violet eyes looked at you straight; and she saw who she was looking at. It didn't matter what she said to me that summer evening, it was plain she was glad to be speaking to me. She hadn't made her own dress, and it wasn't made of curtain material. I bet it was made by the best dressmaker in London. It was green with flecks of gold in it, and had a high collar open at the neck; and it fitted over her small breasts and her slim hips without a crease. She wouldn't get fat when she got old. Christine knew she was being left out; and that didn't please her. 'I think we'd better be going, dear,' she said to Liza. 'Well, Ebenezer, I hope I'll see you again soon,' Liza said. 'Same time, same place!' I said. I meant half-past seven Thursday evening by the Weighbridge. She remembered. 'I'm afraid it will have to be eight,' she said. 'I won't be more than half-an-hour late.' I said, 'I will wait for you for five minutes; but not a minute longer!' 'There, you see,' she said to Christine, 'the terrible man he is!' but I noticed she had left out the 'little'; and she looked over her shoulder at me and laughed, as they went on down Mill Street.

I was on my way to Henry's at the bottom of Vauvert to get some gâche for my mother. She didn't have the heart those days to make cakes like she used to. I got the gâche and went straight down to the tram. I know now I was a fool; but I really thought that evening I was going to be happy in this world. When I got home my mother was resting. She gave me a funny look as I came in. 'Well, and what did that Liza Quéripel have to say for herself?' she said. I was flabbergasted. I wondered how on earth she knew. When she was getting ready to go to bed, I said, 'Who come to see you tonight, Mum?' 'Who d'you expect come to see me on a Saturday night?' she said. 'Nobody,' I said. Well, either she was telling me a lie, and I have never known my mother tell me a lie, or it was the second sight like old Mère Quéripel was supposed to have: but my mother thought the second sight was of the Devil. I give up all hope of ever being able to explain how the news travel in Guernsey.

When Thursday came and I was getting ready to go out, she knew all right who I was going to meet, though I didn't tell her. I'd had my hair cut and spent about an hour scrubbing my hands with pumice-stone to get off the black stuff from handling the tomato-plants. I put on my new double-breasted grey flannel suit I had not long since had made to measure, and a cream silk shirt and a green tie; and I went without a hat. ''Bye, Mum!' I said. 'Ah well, fine feathers make fine birds,' she said. I was sorry to have to go and leave my mother feeling vexed with me; but I couldn't help it.

Liza wasn't even a minute late. The Town Church was striking eight when I saw her coming down St Julien's Avenue. I crossed over to meet her. She took both my hands in hers and looked me over. 'Oh, but you do look nice!' she said. I said, 'You don't look so bad yourself.' She said, 'How good it is we can admire ourselves and each other!' She was wearing another dress, white with a belt and covered with sprigs of green leaves and little gold flowers; and she had on a floppy white hat and white stockings and shoes. They was very good shoes, I noticed: of white suède with flat heels, and biggish for a woman. 'Where are we going?' she said. 'Where you like,' I said. 'How about going to the end of the breakwater, eh?' she said, quite Guernsey. 'Righto,' I said. 'I promise you I won't push the boys off the end into the sea,' she said. 'I don't care, if you do!' I said. I was so happy to be with her again she could do no wrong.

She took my arm and we walked along by the new States Offices. The *Courier* was up on the patent slip. She was for ever in trouble, the *Courier*. She had been down I don't know how many times; but she had always come up again. There was a Norwegian vessel in the Old Harbour stacked with timber for Mess Robilliard of La Piette; and Prince Albert was keeping his eye on things. When we passed the gardens on the other side of the Picket House, I was going to say 'The Green Shutters used to be behind there', but I thought I wouldn't. When we turned down by the slaughter-house, she caught hold of my arm tighter and shivered. 'Are you cold?' I said. It was a lovely warm evening and there had been a cloudless sky all day. 'It's what's done in there to those animals,' she said. I said, 'It's done as quick and painless as possible.' 'I know,' she said, 'but they know it's going to happen a long time before.' I said, 'Jim used to say that.' She said, 'That is why I was silly about the boys fishing. If people need the fish to eat, or sell, there's an excuse: but to catch them for fun and then throw them back, if they are small, with their poor throats torn is cruel. However, I've seen too much suffering since to worry so much now.'

There was a fellow on guard by the sentry box across the footbridge to Castle Cornet. I said, 'I wonder what that chap think he is guarding.' 'The Crown Jewels,' she said. I suppose that is what he was guarding really. There was at least half a dozen fellows fishing by the lighthouse but they hadn't caught a fish between them. Young Etor from the Pollet said, 'No luck tonight, Mr Le Page.' I said, 'What else can you expect with the tide going out?' 'Aw, they do bite sometimes,' he said. Well, I have heard hope springs eternal in the human breast. If you give a chap a rod and line, he will sit by a dry well all night and hope for a bite.

Liza wanted to go back and along the Terres. I was wondering why she wanted to go over all the old ground again. On the way she was telling me about when she was a nurse in St Thomas' Hospital in London. I said I thought she must have been a wonderful nurse; and I still think she was, in spite of what she said. 'I hate people who are hurt and in pain!' she said. 'I hate people who are wounded and twisted and ugly!' For a minute I didn't like Liza; and her mouth was cruel. 'It's not their fault,' I said. I thought of poor old Jim Le Poidevin. There was nothing he could ever do so as to have two real legs again. 'They ought to be put out of their misery,' she said. 'It's not fair for the healthy to have to look after the sick.' I must have moved away from her; for she pulled me towards her. 'I don't know why you should worry,' she said, 'there is nothing wrong with you.' I wondered.

She was gay once more and said how much she loved living in London and going to the theatres and music-halls and restaurants at night. She had seen a Zeppelin hanging in the sky like a big black sausage and the search-lights playing on it. 'It was thrilling!' she said. I was beginning not to like her again. 'I am surprised you ever bother to come back to Guernsey at all,' I said. 'I am sure you could find somebody over there to keep you, if you wanted.' It was when we was passing by the bathing places, I remember; and she stopped dead in her tracks and gripped me by both arms and turned me to face her in the wild way she had. She had a grip of steel. She said, 'I swear every day and every hour I am away from Guernsey, my heart is bleeding secretly to be back. When I stand on the deck of the ship coming down the Russel and see Herm and Jethou and Sark behind, and the Brehon Tower, I know I am home!' I liked her then.

She wanted to sit down and we sat on the furthest seat on the grass along Havelet by the tunnel. She said, 'I thought of you when I heard Jim Mahy was gone. He was your friend to the end, then.' 'He was,' I said. She put a hand on my knee, like a fellow. 'You're a faithful soul,' she said. 'There are some wouldn't say that,' I said. 'Ah well, that's different,' she said; and she laughed. She took my hand in hers and examined it. 'You have very good hands,' she said. I had never thought about my hands. They are square with strong fingers and long thumbs; and all I know is I am good at doing things with my hands. 'I always look at a man's hands,' she said. 'They give his real character.' 'What's mine, then?' I said. She said, 'I have never seen you do a clumsy thing, not even when you push your best girl in the water; and you threw the hat straight.' Yes, Liza had a forgiving nature.

There was very few people about, and none came as far as where we was sitting. The sun was setting on the other side of the island, and the sky over our heads was streaks of gold; and there was a purple mist low down. I remember how we sat and watched the lights come up along the Esplanade and round the harbour and on the ships in the Pool. 'It's lovely here,' Liza said in a whisper. 'Yes,' I said. I had to whisper too: everything was so still. The long island of Sark was only a shadow, and a shadow was creeping across the wide meadow on Herm, and Jethou was a dark hump I could only just make out, when the moon began to rise out of the mist. It was only the tip at first; but it grew and grew until it was big and round and copper-coloured, and the light from it upon the sea and upon the islands was a glory I cannot speak. There was no words passed between us, and we wasn't even touching; yet I felt she was near to me, nearer to me than any woman have ever been, before or since. At last she said, 'You'll have to be very patient with me, my dear. I'm one of the ruins Cromwell knocked about a bit.'

She stood up and gave me her hand then, and pulled me to my feet; and we walked hand-in-hand along the front as far as the Salerie Corner. It was surprising how quickly the moon had risen high up in the sky; and by the time we reached the Salerie, it was small and white and looked cold, and the sea was silver. I don't think a word was said all the way. I was thinking she is hurt and she is wounded and she is twisted and in pain; and I am too. We turned up Paris Street and went up Les Côtils Lane to Castle Carey. She didn't go in by the side door, as she used to, for nobody even pretended she was a servant there now. 'Well, good-night,' I said and took her in my arms and kissed her; but it was only her cheek, and her cheek was cold. 'Thank you for a wonderful evening,' she said. 'When again?' I said. She said, 'I'll let Ada know.'

3

One day last week I went to visit young David Livingstone Le Page, who is a great-grand cousin of mine, to be exact. His grandfather was a cousin of my father's, who emigrated to Canada and married a French girl over there. A son, Charles Le Page, came over to Guernsey on a visit, as he thought, but found himself married to Ethel Lenfestey from Les Abreveurs and didn't go back to Canada. Ethel Lenfestey belonged to a lot like my mother's, but with a difference; and my mother would have nothing to do with them. They called themselves Pentecostalists, and held their meetings in a tin tabernacle at Vazon and spoke with tongues; but not one of them could understand what any of the others was saying. My mother said it was vanity. Ethel took it very serious and had to be put away in the Country Hospital for a time, because she got so as she would speak with tongues to anybody she met along the road or on the bus or in Town. However her behaviour was quite harmless among a lot of mad people, and she was let out. Charles Le Page, who was a hefty backwoodsman sort of bloke, married her in his innocence. He didn't know then she was given to speaking with tongues, though I have no doubt people let him know it when it was too late. As a matter of fact, she didn't speak with tongues once she was married, except in Guernsey French.

Her people was well-to-do, and he had every reason to expect she would be pretty well-off; but her brother didn't give her all he ought to have done, when the old people died. Charles managed to make a living here and there; and her brother let them live in the wing of the house. They managed to rub along somehow. They didn't have any children for twenty-five years and then, when she thought she was past having any, David came along. She heard a voice from Heaven when he was born and he was christened David Livingstone and dedicated from birth to 'work in the vineyard'. He was a small boy at school when the Germans came and was one of those who didn't leave the island, because Ethel said it would show lack of trust in God. He got what education he could at a primary school, which wasn't much while the Germans was here; and after the Liberation, was sent to a Bible College in England to be trained as an evangelist. I had heard he was home and was waiting for guidance to enter on his ministry.

I am not as young as I was, and it is high time I made a will; so I am going the round of my relations, those I know of, to see if I can make up my mind who to leave my money to. I thought perhaps young David was being pushed and didn't really want to work in the vineyard. There might be something else he would rather do. When I went to see him, I didn't tell him what I had in mind, of course; but I soon discovered he was quite sincere about being an evangelist. He talked to me with his Bible in his hand. I will say for him he didn't think his church was the only one right. He belonged to the Elim Four-square Gospel Church; but his great friend was the Minister of Trinity Church in Town, which is Church of England. He said, 'The business of every Christian of every denomination is to bring the world to Christ.' I could hardly say anything against that. I asked him where he was going to begin. He said in Darkest Africa. I thought myself he might have begun nearer home. I said it must be going to cost a lot of money surely, to go right out there. Was he going to have to pay, or was the Church? He said the Church was going to pay, but they didn't actually have the money yet. They was praying for it, and the Lord would provide. I thought, in that case, it would never do for me to inter-fere. David Livingstone Le Page is one of my relations I will not leave my money to.

I have said Raymond was religious, and I suppose he was; but, if so, he was religious in quite a different way to David Livingstone Le Page. David proved everything he said was true by chapter and verse from the Bible. Raymond didn't try to prove anything he said by chapter and verse. He made it up as he went along. He said to me once, 'If you ever let yourself believe anything, you by that much cut yourself off from faith in God.' When I look back on his story now, I think he must have been mad to imagine any Church or Chapel of any denomination would put up with him for long. I remember him saying to me, when the Wesleyans had spewed him out of their mouth, and none of the good Chapel people at St Sampson's would be seen as much as talking to him, 'D'you know, Ebene-zer, I doubt every word has ever been written or spoken, I doubt my own mind, I doubt my own existence sometimes; but I do not doubt the exist-ence of God.' I am half-way with him there. I doubt everything I hear, even if I say it myself; and, after the things I have been through and seen happen to other people on this island and known to have happened in the world, I sometimes wonder about the existence of God: but I know I am Ebenezer Le Page.

Raymond went through an experience when he was at the Fort meant a great deal to him. As an Instructor, the only other duty he had to do was

now and then to go on guard. He didn't have to march up and down with
fixed bayonet, but change the guard every two hours. There was a guard on
the Barrier Gate day and night; and another by the wireless mast, over-
looking the Lower Lines, from sunset to dawn. Those was cushy days for
Raymond. There was a fire right up the chimney in the guardroom, and the
best food was sent down from the cook-house. There was beds for the
fellows to lie on between duties; and Raymond himself used to have a nap
after dinner, and a chap would wake him up with a cup of tea. There was
always a big, brown enamel teapot of tea on the boil. When they wasn't
asleep, those who was off duty sat round and yarned. Raymond was glad
just to listen, and be among the others. In his mind, they was all grand
fellows. He said, 'One minute they would be telling smutty stories about
the Royal Family, and the next talking about their mothers and sisters with
tears in their eyes. They were innocent.'

Private Harry Whitehouse was on guard with him that day. From what
he said, I imagine Harry Whitehouse to have been the exact opposite of
Raymond in every way; and it is plain to me he had taken a great fancy to
Raymond. When his platoon went down to the gym, Raymond said Harry
would dodge out of turn to get into his squad. He wasn't one of those
Raymond took home for a meal of a Sunday. For Hetty's sake, he chose the
better educated and well brought-up, who Hetty would think was nice
boys. Harry was a big rough chap and uneducated compared to Raymond,
and only a coal-miner in civvy-street. Raymond hadn't spoken to him off
parade before; but that day Harry chummed up. They talked together
when Harry was off duty the whole day; and, between whiles, Raymond
found himself longing for Harry to come in from his post, so they could go
on where they left off. Harry described the small house in the mining
village of Altofts in Yorkshire where he was brought up with a number of
brothers and sisters and a father who drank and a mother who worked her
fingers to the bone. He went only to the Elementary School, and then
down the mine at fourteen. He was the eldest, and whatever money he
earnt was for the family. He didn't begrudge it. He liked the kids; though it
meant he couldn't knock about with his mates who spent what they earnt
boozing, and he hadn't bothered with girls. Raymond said, 'He gave me
all he had to give. He was as honest, as open as the day; and he spread his
whole life before me. I lived it with him. He was a lovely chap.'

It happened Harry was on the last duty at the wireless mast from four to
six in the morning. During the day Raymond had to change the guard regimental fashion and march the fellow out and put him through his paces;
but at night he didn't bother. The Orderly Officer might pop his head in
the guardroom, but more often than not he stopped in bed. At four o'clock
in the morning Raymond walked up with Harry, letting him carry his rifle
at the trail; and at six o'clock he went up again to bring him back. Harry

was pacing up and down by the wireless mast like a good soldier, and doing a smart right-about turn, but it was only to keep himself warm. 'Time's up!' said Raymond. 'It's cold, be-cripes!' said Harry, and put an arm around Raymond. 'Jesus, I've always wanted to get a feel of you, Corp!' he said. Raymond laughed and pushed him away. 'Go and get a cup of tea inside of you!' he said, 'that'll warm you up.' He let Harry go down to the guardroom on his own. 'I saw the sun rise,' he said to me. He wouldn't say any more. I said, 'It must have been a lovely view of the islands from up there.' He turned on me quite angry. 'It was NOT a view of the islands!' he said. 'Then what?' I said. 'It was the Light upon Gennesaret,' he said, 'and I was in it and it was in me. It was a glimpse of the world as God made it on the first morning of the first day.' I don't know what he meant. Perhaps he was already going funny in the head.

The last time I had a talk with Raymond made any sense, and it didn't make much, he spoke again about that night. When he got back to the guard-room, Harry was sitting by the fire with his tunic off drinking tea. 'Christ, I thought you'd buggered off home!' he said. He said it real nasty. 'It was like a hit in the wind,' Raymond said. On the way down from the wireless mast he had been feeling how he could never hate anybody again, or anybody hate him. He made a bed up for Harry, hoping by doing so to put things right between them. 'Have a couple of hours shut-eye before breakfast, Harry,' he said. 'Might as well,' said Harry, but sulky; and he took off his puttees and boots and lay on the bed. 'Well, you're in the warm now,' said Raymond. Harry lay on his back looking up at Raymond; but he had a hurt look in his eyes. 'You'll never let a chap get near you, will you, kid?' he said. Raymond didn't know what to say, and went and sat by the fire. Harry didn't wangle to be drilled by him again: he wangled not to. It wasn't for long. He went on draft in a fortnight and was killed his first week out. 'I did a great wrong that night,' said Raymond, when he was telling me. 'I don't see how,' I said. 'When I pushed Harry off,' he said. 'I think you did the right thing then,' I said. 'Oh yes,' he said bitterly, for he was being very bitter about himself then: 'I did the right thing! I did the right thing! He asked me for bread and I gave him a stone. I'm no good.'

I have always blamed Christine for what she did to Raymond, and will never forgive her as long as I live; yet perhaps it is Raymond I ought to blame. He did the right thing when he married Christine; and yet perhaps he did her a great wrong. If so, she got her revenge a hundredfold and ought to be satisfied. Myself, I think he was a hero in his way, and Liza thought so too; yet she admired Christine. 'I envy that woman,' she said. 'She goes for what she wants without a thought for anyone else; or what the consequences to herself may be. She has the courage.' Well, I don't know that Liza was lacking in courage herself; but she was human as well as being a woman, and able to appreciate Raymond. 'He was the sweetest-natured, the most understanding person I have ever known,' she said to me, when we had our last big quarrel. 'He was kinder to me, he understood me better than you ever have, or ever could, God rest his soul!' It was funny she should say that; for she didn't have a spark of religion in her.

I didn't hear a word of Liza for weeks after our wonderful evening. I was hoping every day Ada would bring a message; and I knew she would have, if there was one to bring. At last one Saturday afternoon she turned up to ask if my mother wanted anything done, or groceries or meat fetched. She had heard my mother wasn't very well. I said I had done the shopping for her already. She was complaining of feeling tired and always having to sit down, but, as she had been as strong as a horse until then, I didn't think it was anything serious. Ada stopped to tea and, when she was going, said perhaps I would like to walk with her part of the way. I knew then something bad was coming. She said, 'Liza has asked me to let you know she has gone to Scotland.' I hadn't asked Liza who was the father of her children, or where they had gone to. I had thought of it the night I was with her, but hadn't wanted to spoil things. 'For how long?' I managed to say. 'She says perhaps for good,' said Ada.

The Captain in the Scots Guards was the father of the second of Liza's children. Ada didn't tell me who the father of the first was, or if it was a boy or a girl, or what had happened to it. The Captain's was a boy and a fine little fellow, she said. The Captain's mother had come over to Guernsey during the War and taken it back with her to Scotland. Now the Captain had written to Liza and asked her again to marry him. He had asked her before, but she had refused. In the meantime, his father had died, so the Captain was now not only an Honourable, he was a Lord. He was living with his mother and an uncle and servants, I gathered, in a castle, I suppose like Castle Carey, on an island off the west coast of Scotland. Liza was gone to see for herself what it was like.

'Then it's all up with me,' I said. 'I'm going to Town tonight and get blind drunk. I'll paint St Peter Port red, white and blue!' 'Ebenezer, Ebenezer, you mustn't be like that!' said Ada: 'It's all right, it's all right: she won't marry him, she won't, she won't, she won't!' I said, 'How d'you know?' She said, 'There is only one man she can depend on; and she knows it.' 'Who?' I said. 'I don't have to tell you,' she said. I said, 'Well, all I can say is she got an extraordinary way of showing it.' 'She is an extraordinary girl,' said Ada. I looked at Ada with her plain-Jane face and her clumsy body and her buttoned-up boots and her old brown skirt and jacket she would wear until they was worn out, and I said, 'How is it a good girl like you is faithful to that Liza, when she is faithful to nobody? You are worth a dozen of her rolled into one!' 'Perhaps I am and perhaps I am not,' she said, 'but no man will ever ask me to marry him.' When we got to the top of the lane, she said, 'Now you go back home and spend the evening with your mother; since she is not well.' 'All right,' I said; and I did.

I think Raymond was already gone to England when Liza came back to Guernsey, but I am not sure. If so, it was only a matter of weeks. I know Christine was gone; but she always had to go back to her school some weeks before Raymond had to go to his college. They didn't go about together, but sometimes I saw him talking to Christine in Town. Christine would be with Gwen, and Raymond with one of the St Sampson's Chapel crowd. I knew he went occasionally to Christine's house for tea on Sundays. Hetty didn't ask her back, but otherwise didn't make anything of it. She said, 'Well, if my Raymond is going to be a minister, I suppose he got to make himself with everybody: even the lowest of the low.'

I spent a few evenings with Raymond up in his room before he went. It was mostly about the books he was reading he talked to me. He said, 'It does me good to talk to you because you put the famous Ebenezer twist on everything. It's cock-eyed; but it puts me straight.' The books he was reading was a shock to me. They seemed to be all against what he was supposed to be going in for. I blamed Clive Holyoak for that. Raymond had several books from the Library by Bernard Shaw; and others in French by Anatole France. He said Anatole France was an atheist and didn't believe in God, but was very gentle with those who did. He showed me a picture of Bernard Shaw in one of the books. I thought he looked a wicked devil but Raymond said he had a fine face. Bernard Shaw wasn't a Christian, yet thought for people to do what Jesus said was the only way would work. He was a socialist. I said I thought socialism was nonsense. If you give everything to everybody, in the end nobody will have nothing. Raymond said there wasn't much danger of socialism coming to Guernsey, so I needn't worry. I said the book he ought to read is *Robinson Crusoe*. It is a good book. It show how if you go gallivanting all over the world instead of stopping at home where you belong, you only land yourself with a load of trouble. Raymond couldn't stop laughing when I said that. I don't know for why.

He came to say good-bye to my mother before he left. He had been to say good-bye to Prissy. 'Ah well,' she said to him, 'it take all sorts to make a world.' It wasn't at all what I would have expected Prissy to say. I couldn't think what had come over her. I knew she had quarrelled with the Stonelakes and the sister was gone back to England with her children; and my Cousin Mary Ann was often going there. Something must be wrong. As a matter of fact, it was that winter La Prissy took to drink. It may perhaps have made her more forgiving of other people for their foolishness, and was why she was nice to Raymond. He had also received a comic postcard from Horace from America. He got it out of his pocket to show me. It was a picture of a sky-pilot hanging from a balloon by an anchor through the seat of his pants. 'Good old Horace!' said Raymond. 'He is always there to knock the nonsense out of me.' I walked down the road with him and, when we shook hands, he said, 'Perhaps one day I will have a chance of preaching in Guernsey. A prophet is not without honour save in his own country and among his own people. That will be the test.' Raymond, for all his big ideas, was a Guernsey boy first and last.

4

Liza turned up at Les Moulins. It was the last thing I would have expected her to do. After dinner one Saturday afternoon I was out in the wash-house stripped to the waist washing myself down, when I heard a knock on the front door. My mother answered. 'Somebody for you!' she called out. I thought it must be young Ogier from the vineries I had promised some cabbage plants to, though I couldn't make out why he hadn't come round the back. I went out as I was. It was Liza. She had never looked more lovely. She was wearing a tartan plaid skirt and a white silk blouse with frills round the neck and a short brown cape hanging from her shoulders and a round fur hat. She really did look like a princess. 'Goodness, I'm not fit to be seen!' I said. 'I think you look very fit,' she said. 'Come in and talk to my mother,' I said, 'while I go and make myself proper.' I went into my room and left them together. I wondered what on earth was going to happen now.

It was naughty of my mother to call out 'Somebody for you!' when she knew I was washing. She did it on purpose to punish Liza, and put her off me; but it didn't. She came in and sat down in my armchair and, as I went out, I saw my mother sit down in hers with her hands folded in her lap. When I had made myself decent and came back into the kitchen, I expected to find them sitting like two mommets looking at each other; but Liza was talking away in patois about Scotland, and my mother was listening and nodding her old head interested. 'Mais es-che comme chonna là bas, donc?' she said. 'Je n'aurai pas cru.' She had no idea where Scotland was, she thought it was somewhere down south; but she knew where every place in the Holy Land was. I had seen her again and again examining the maps at the back of the big Bible through her magnifying glass.

I said, 'Mum isn't very well these days, I'm sorry to say.' Liza was all sympathy, and wanted to know what was the matter. My mother said her legs was swollen. She hadn't told me that. 'Then you must make that brute of a son help you with the heavy work,' said Liza. 'He do help all he can,' said my mother. Liza said she had come to ask me to have tea with her in Town, as we were old friends; but now she wouldn't think of it. Liza always put the convenience of other women first, before she thought of the man. My mother said I was getting ready to go to Town anyway, and Tabitha was coming any minute. 'Come on, then,' I said, 'let's go!' I went to the cashbox in the drawer of the dresser, where we kept the money for spending. I knew my mother was watching me; but she didn't see how much I took. I had an idea at the back of my head. I was going to strike while the iron was hot.

When we got out of doors, Liza said, 'I've never been as far round this end of the island before. It must be lonely out here.' It was those days. Our neighbour-to-be, Monsieur Le Boutillier, was having his house built, but it wasn't finished yet; and, of course, there wasn't no places to have tea and châlets for visitors then. The Chouey quarry was long since worked out and filled with water; and there was quite a number of windmills around that part with their fans turning in the wind. They was small mills for pumping water only; not old mills with big vanes for grinding corn like the Vale Mill. They turned ever so fast in the wind. 'The windmills are company,' I said. They was, too; but mine is the only one left now. The one thing that haven't changed over the years is the air. It have a tang is fresh and salty as it isn't in Town, or any other part of the island I know. Liza was taking deep breaths of it. 'Ah,' she said, 'it doesn't matter where you go on this island there is a difference.' 'The North is best,' I said. I got her to look down on our little bay. The tide was out and the sand was clean and glistening in the sun. I said, 'Tabitha and me used to pick limpets off those rocks when we was kids.' She said, 'Is that your boat?' 'The *Bijou*, yes,' I said. 'Aren't you a lucky man?' she said. 'You have everything a man can want.' 'Have I?' I said. 'I didn't know.'

I have been telling myself for thirty years I hate Liza, but now when I come to write about her, I begin to wonder if it is true. When she was in a good mood, as she was that afternoon, I doubt if any chap in the world could have hated Liza. She was a wonderful companion for a man. She was gay and warm and friendly, and a lady and not a lady: you could say anything you liked to her. She was so good to be with, I said, 'Sometimes I wonder if you are really a woman at all.' She laughed. 'Sometimes I wonder the same myself,' she said. I wasn't hot for her, as I can be for a girl; but when I blow hot, I blow cold pretty soon. I wanted her; but not under the hedge.

On the bus from L'Islet we sat on the top and nearly got our heads knocked off by the branches of the trees. Another girl would have screamed and been silly; but not Liza. She said, 'I wonder if we'll get to the Half-way alive. I don't care, do you?' 'It's all the same to me,' I said. The tram was waiting at the Half-way. Usually you had to wait ten minutes. 'It always waits for me,' she said. I was sure it did. When we got off by the Town Church, I said we would have tea at Le Poidevin's. I had a purpose in choosing Le Poidevin's, and it wasn't because it was cheaper. 'As my lord and master says,' she said.

The next week several people said to me they had seen me in Town that Saturday, but I had been too proud to look at them. It wasn't that I was too proud. I hadn't seen them. I had no eyes for nobody but Liza. At Le Poidevin's we was lucky again and got a table to ourselves by the window. I could see Bachmann's, the Jeweller's, shop-window opposite; and felt the money in my hip-pocket to make sure it was there. When the tea was brought and Liza had poured it out, I looked straight into her eyes across the table. 'Now, Liza,' I said, 'are you going to marry this Captain?'

She said, 'Am I going to marry this Captain's mother and his uncle who drinks like a fish and old Angus who growls like a bear and the castle in ruins falling into the lake on an island not as big as Jethou?' It wasn't an answer to what I asked her; but I let her go on. She said she could laugh at it now, but she nearly went out of her mind when she was living there. It was the mother who was the worst. 'She sits in a high-backed chair as stiff as a poker,' Liza said, 'and knits, knits, knits.' She didn't even knit like an ordinary human being. She had a bundle of straw stuck in her waistband and a needle stuck in the straw and she worked the other needles on it, on and on and on without ever stopping, while she would be laying down the law. 'Talking to her was like trying to talk to a sewing-machine,' Liza said, 'and whatever she said was right. She has never been contradicted in her life. Besides, I was nearly starved to death: she was so mean.'

I said, 'That's all very well; but what about your small boy?' 'Robert isn't my small boy,' she said. 'He is grandmother's small boy. She only wants me to marry her precious son to make it respectable. That is what I am for. To breed children for the mothers and the wives.' She sounded extraordinary bitter; and there was that twist to her mouth I didn't like. 'Never mind, then,' I said, 'leave that for now.' She hadn't touched her tea. 'You are very understanding,' she said and put her hand on mine. 'Eat up!' I said. I was thinking Don Guille must have been the father of the other child and his widow had taken it. I knew they didn't have any children of their own. After our second cup of tea I lit a cigarette. 'Give me one, please,' Liza said. It wasn't many women who smoked in public places those days. I let her have one, and lit it for her. She smoked as if she was used to smoking. 'I don't really mind not having my children,' she said. 'I like children. I like seeing children about the place, but they don't have to be mine; and they must be clean and well-behaved. I can't stand napkins and snotty noses. I wasn't made to be a mother.'

'That's not being natural,' I said, 'for a woman.' She said, 'Nature isn't fair to women.' I said, 'Nature isn't fair to men, if it come to that. Women have it all their own way.' 'Ho, ho!' she said, 'do they?' 'Yes,' I said. 'A man got to go round on his bended knees begging for a woman to have him.' She said, 'I haven't noticed you going round on your bended knees begging!' I was then, if she had only known it. 'Seriously, though,' she said, 'if you give a girl a baby and clear off, you can forget all about the girl. If a girl is given a baby, she is reminded of the father every time she looks at it. Robert is Ian all over again.' I began to feel sympathy with poor Ian. I said, 'What have Ian done to you that you hate him so much? He looked a fine chap to me.' 'Goodness, I don't hate Ian,' she said. 'He was a nice little piggy wiggy.' It was always the same when I argued with Liza: either I ended up in a rage, or else I had to laugh.

I laughed it off; but I wasn't being beaten, though. I thought then I was right and I still think I was right. Liza could have been happy married to me, if only she'd had the sense to see it. I don't say it would have been perfect, but we would have got on better than most. In some way we was the same underneath. When we got out in the Arcade, I said I would like to look at Bachmann's window. The window giving on the Arcade was full of silver plate and Guernsey milk-cans, and what not. The engagement rings was in the window giving on the High Street and that was where I steered Liza to look. There was some that was marked more than I had on me; but there was a lovely one with a red stone I could have bought. I said, 'I want to buy you a present.' She said, 'I am always willing to receive presents.' I pointed to the rings, and I said, 'I like the third one from the top, do you?' She said, 'That is the one present I will not accept.' I said, 'Why not?' She said, 'Because I do not make promises I will not keep.' I said, 'I suppose you are thinking of going away again.' 'I will not leave Guernsey ever,' she said. 'That is a promise, if you like. I will be where you can always come and see me. I will always be within your reach.'

I must have looked how I felt, for she took my arm, and herself looked sad. 'Thank you for the very great honour you have done me,' she said. 'I am not worth it, I assure you; but now will you buy me a present I would really like?' 'What is it you would really like?' I said. 'A silver Guernsey milk-can,' she said. 'All right, let's go in,' I said. I bought her a silver Guernsey milk-can. She didn't choose the dearest, but it was real silver. It was packed in a box and wrapped in brown paper, and she came out of the shop with the parcel as pleased as if she was a child with a toy. She said, 'This is the one treasure I will never part with, even if I'm starving.' I said, 'You'll never be that.' She said, 'I might be, some day. I have nothing, except what I am given.'

I don't know how I can have been so happy with Liza for the rest of the evening. By rights I ought to have been downright miserable. I remember we walked down the White Rock and saw the *Reindeer* come in from Weymouth and go on to Jersey. A lot of the passengers who came ashore was green from being seasick. They made me laugh. I was too happy to be sorry for other people. I saw Liza back to Castle Carey and kissed her good-night; but it was more like a friend. 'When do I see you again?' I said. 'How about next Saturday?' she said. 'Call for me here.' She couldn't have said anything to please me better, because it meant she was owning me before those grand people; yet now as I write it, I feel the old fury rising in me at the cheek and the conceit of Liza. She had it all her own way with every-body. I must admit she have kept the only promise she ever made to me. She have never left Guernsey. I have always known where she was living: not only before, but after she left Castle Carey. I hear of her now and then from people I meet in Town who live round Pleinmont; and, by all accounts, she is still going strong, though according to her reckoning she must be hundreds of years old. I could visit her tomorrow if I wanted to. I wonder if she ever made a promise to anybody else. I don't think so. I don't believe she have ever said 'I love you' to a single living soul; and she certainly won't say it now.

Christine didn't come home that Christmas, but spent the holiday with a schoolmistress friend in England. Was Hetty pleased? When Raymond came home she had him all to herself. He went to see Christine's people to wish them a happy Christmas, and to Chapel Sunday evenings, but other-wise he hardly left the house. La Prissy and Percy was invited for Christmas Day, and all at Wallaballoo went to Timbuctoo for Boxing Day. There was goodwill in the air. I stayed home with my mother Christmas and Boxing Day; but Tabitha came for the New Year and I went to Hetty's. She really was happy, poor Hetty, that first holiday of Raymond's. He kept on saying how glad he was to be back, and played 'Home Sweet Home with Variations' until I was sick of it.

I didn't think he looked so well, myself, and Hetty thought he'd got thinner. It suited him better being a soldier than studying to be a minister. He said it was awful having to live with a gang of professing Christians. 'I don't want to be a professing Christian,' he said. 'I want to be a Christian who doesn't have to think about it.' He couldn't stand the Holy Willie smile, as he called it; and the voice they put on when they say 'Our Lord'. 'Give me the chaps in the guardroom any day!' said Raymond. I said, 'What the goodness is there you can have to learn for all the years you are going to be in college?' He said, 'Ah, I am being grounded in my theologi-cal position.' His face was wrinkled up with his wicked smile. He was making a joke of something else he didn't ought to have done. 'You don't know any theology, do you, Ebenezer?' he said. 'Not that I know of,' I said. He said, 'There is Catholic Theology and there is Anglican Theology and there is ours. Ours is a hotch-potch of John Wesley, who broke off from the Church of England, and Martin Luther, who broke off from the Catholic Church, and Calvin, who broke off from everybody but himself and who your mother follows, more or less.' I didn't know that, me. He said, 'Before you begin, it has been decided what you have to believe; and, after reading hundreds of pages of closely reasoned argument, you end up by proving what it was decided you have to believe is true. It is like a theorem in geometry at school. It gives me a headache. The others think it is religion.'

I said, 'Well, it's a chance a lot would jump at: to have no work to do and only study.' 'I know, I know,' he said, 'you mustn't take notice of half I say. I use you to let off steam on. They are good fellows, really; but I am a stranger there. When they sing:

> I am but a stranger here:
> Heaven is my home,

I am saying under my breath:

> I am but a stranger here:
> Guernsey is my home.

I will never, never feel at home in England! Never! I look at it; but I don't see it. It isn't real. It's a dream. I wake up when I get back.' Well, I thought, if you let off steam on those in the college the same as you do on me, they will very soon bundle you back to Guernsey.

5

There is a story in the Bible about a man who buried his talent in the ground. I think he came to a bad end. Well, I am that man, I reckon. I don't know what my talent was exactly, but I do know I have done nothing in my life to shout about, except win the leg of mutton off the greasy pole. Otherwise, I have only managed to make a living and pay my way and save a bit and pass for being respectable, even if I haven't always been. At least, I have kept out of jail; but more by good luck than good management. I might easily have landed myself in there once or twice. Nor have they got me put away in the Country Hospital yet, which I suppose is something; but there are some people who think that is where I ought to be. I am not so sure that I don't agree with them. I wasted the best years of my life waiting and hoping to marry that Liza. I must have been mad.

It's true my mother was getting steadily worse; but that wasn't the reason stopped me from marrying Liza. La Tabby was quite willing to leave the Priaulx and come and live at home and look after my mother. I didn't ask her: she offered without me having to ask. She always seemed to know what was going through my mind, my sister. I could have afforded to have a little house built and there was a patch of ground next to ours I could have bought; but I wasn't going to launch out without some encouragement from Liza, and I got none. She said she couldn't leave the old lady. Lady Carey was now getting on in years and wasn't very well; but, as far as I could make out, all she suffered from was the rheumatics. I reminded Liza of what she had said about the healthy looking after the sick. 'Ah, but that was different,' she said, 'men are such babies when they're sick.' What Liza seemed to forget was that she was getting older as well. For ten years or more she didn't look a day older than twenty-six, and people said I looked young for my age. When I got grumpy and quarrelsome, she would laugh me out of it. 'When we are dead and gone, we'll be a legend in Guernsey,' she said. 'Ebenezer Le Page and Liza Quéripel who was lovers to the last day of their lives.' The trouble was we wasn't lovers.

By some miracle, I managed to keep myself from chasing after other girls. It was fat legs made me think of higher things, and now and again I would see a girl with fat legs and lust after her, but it was only with half an

eye, and I would think to myself I'll only be tired and fed-up after, and
didn't bother. I don't think Liza would have cared if I had. She caught me
at it more than once, as I often caught her measuring up any big, tall bloke
she happened to see. Once when we caught each other looking at a couple
going into Gardner's Royal, she burst out laughing. 'My dear, you and me
are tarred with the same brush,' she said. 'Shall we go in and have a drink
and introduce ourselves?' 'Of course not!' I said.

I was being made a fool of. For years I was at Liza's beck and call. It
wasn't she allowed me to see her so often. Sometimes for two or three
weeks she would say she couldn't see me. The old lady always came first.
Sundays she didn't come out with me once. Saturday evenings she came to
Town with me a few times; but Saturdays she preferred for me to have tea
with her in the afternoon at Castle Carey. She had two rooms of her own
there and it was very comfortable and nice; but we was waited on by a
servant and I don't like being waited on by a servant, when I know I am no
better than she is. Those evenings Liza would have dinner with the family
and, if I wanted to go to Town, I had to go on my own. It wasn't one thing,
or the other. To make it worse, she never knew if she was going to be free
the next week. She would let Ada know because Ada had the telephone;
and poor Ada had to come all the way from the Marais to tell me. She made
a servant of Ada, as well as of me. Thursday afternoons was when she liked
going out; and I had to ask Mr Dorey for the half-day off. He let me have it;
but I wasn't paid, as I was having the Saturday afternoon in any case. In
summer what she enjoyed most was going for a picnic to Fermain Bay. It
was the nearest bay to Town and there was plenty smart young Townies
there to admire her. I carried the basket of food. I was the perfect little
gentleman.

Of course, everybody thought we was engaged. When Prissy came to
see my mother, it was always 'Is it that son of yours isn't married yet,
then?' My mother would say, 'Mais ils ne sont pas seulement engagie!'
Prissy would then bring up about this one and that one, who had been
going about together for twenty years and wasn't married yet, and never
would be. 'It don't do to know the one you're going to marry for too long,'
she said, 'or nobody would get married at all. That's why I'm all for boys
and girls marrying young; before they find out their mistake.' She was
hoping Horace would marry a rich American girl and bring her home; but
he said he had too many over there to choose from. He was travelling all
over the States for the company he worked for. They was doing a roaring
business since the War.

La Prissy was one of the first to take regular summer visitors; and, in
fairness to her, I must say she fed them well and didn't charge them much.
Anyhow, they must have been satisfied, because the same ones came again
year after year. Prissy was happy to have the company, and it kept her off

the drink. My Cousin Mary Ann didn't go near Timbuctoo during the summer months. Myself, I was getting so desperate, I was working out mad schemes in my mind to go to America. I wasn't going to tell Liza. One day when Ada would come with a message, I would be gone, and Tabby would be looking after my mother in my place. I thought perhaps Liza would be sorry when she heard. I didn't go, though. Instead, whenever Ada did come with a message, I would start cleaning my hands with pumice-stone and put on my best suit and follow at Liza's heels like a little dog. I could kick myself now.

I went round with the boys on occasion, when Liza didn't want me. It was the same old gang, what was left of it; and when I'd had a few drinks, I'd open my big mouth as I used to about things I knew nothing about and cared less. One night I was in the Caves de Bordeaux with much the same crowd as the night we got chucked out. Eddie Le Tissier wasn't there; and old Wally Budden was gone to be with Prince Albert the Good. Jim Le Poidevin was there with his one leg, and Jim Machon coughing up his guts. He wasn't supposed to drink, according to the doctor, but he said if he couldn't have a wet now and then, what was there to live for? Amos Duquemin was there, knowing the rights and wrongs of everything, as he always did. All the talk that evening was about the money the English wanted the States to pay. The English wanted thousands from us every year to help them to pay for the War. The States was hm-ing and ha-ing in their slow way as usual, but they wasn't paying up. In the end, they agreed to offer a lump sum once and for all; but the English didn't want that, and wouldn't accept it. After a few years they had to, or they wouldn't have got nothing. I was arguing the States didn't ought to pay a penny. I made a nice long speech and everybody agreed with me, except Amos Duquemin. He said the English and the Canadians and the Australians and the New Zealanders and God knows who else was all one big family with us, and we ought to help to pay each other's debts. I don't know where he got that daft idea from. Mess Fellerah said I ought to be on the States.

The King and Queen came over to Guernsey in their yacht, the *Victoria and Albert*. It was a lovely yacht. Liza was invited with the Careys to a Garden Party to meet the King and Queen; but I was grumpy and angry about everything, and swore I would keep out of their way. I said to Liza, 'Those sort of people only come to Guernsey when they want something.' It was a big holiday for everybody on the island, but I worked at home all the morning, and in the afternoon I thought I would go and see Jim Machon. He was getting so much worse he couldn't go out. I knew the King and Queen was going to drive from the Town Church along the Banks and round Bulwer Avenue to St Sampson's. Jim Machon lived at the Grandes Maisons, so I thought I would dodge their Majesties; but I had just come down Delancey Lane and was standing at Luff's Corner, when who should I see coming along the road in a motor-car but the King and Queen. There was two other cars behind with some nobs of the States; but nobody put me in the road. I heard after that they had been held up in Town by the people cheering and therefore had to give Bulwer Avenue the go-by and cut in at Pike's Corner, or they would have been late according to the programme. There was another colossal crowd waiting to cheer them on the Bridge. I was caught. I didn't know what to do. I didn't have a hat on, so I couldn't take it off. I just stood to attention at the edge of the kerb. The Queen was a fine figure of a woman with a bust, and wore a round hat like Liza's. Her face looked as if it was made of enamel and she couldn't smile, or it would crack; but she bowed stiff from the waist up. She didn't look to see who I was. The old King did, him, and put up his hand and smiled. I forgot myself. I waved and shouted, 'Warro, George! Good old George!' He looked back over his shoulder and laughed. God, he was a nice chap, that!

Jim Le Poidevin was the last of the three Jims; and lived for many years after Jim Machon died. He wasn't as big as my Jim, but slim and well-built when he was a young chap; and, before he went to France, used to go to dances a lot. He was engaged to Etienne de la Mare from the Vauquiédor and, when she heard what had happened to him, she said she would marry him if he had lost both legs; but he hadn't been back a week before the engagement was broken off. It was him did it. He was blamed by many people and he let them blame him, but I think he did right. He told me that once, when she was all soft and loving, he said to her brutally 'How are you going to like having a stump in your bed?' and he saw the look of disgust pass across her face, before she could say 'Darling, it don't make any difference.' 'I wouldn't put any girl through that,' he said to me. I don't know what happened to her in the end. I know she went round with Gerald Mahy for a time. Young Gerald came back as cocky as ever and went to work again in the Old Bank. He was waiting for his commission in the Flying Corps when the Armistice came. He was disappointed the War didn't go on longer.

Jim Le Poidevin could have got an artificial leg and pottered about at home. His people was growers and quite well-to-do; but he said he didn't want to be dependent on them for the rest of his life. He made up his mind he would learn a trade and decided to be a cobbler. Clarrie Bellot from by the Tin Church, who was a sapper in France all through the War and came back without a scratch, taught him for nothing: which is just the sort of thing Clarrie would do, though it might mean less business for him. I'm glad to say it didn't, because he was such a steady chap and so much liked he always got more work than he could do. Jim Le Poidevin had a small pension and the Government bought him a machine; and he got a wooden hut built for himself at Port Soif, before you get to Gran'-Rock. It was only two rooms: one where he slept and cooked his food and ate; and the other was his workshop. He lived there on his own for years, winter and summer. I took him all our boots and shoes to mend. He had plenty of friends. It didn't matter when you went in the shop there was some fellow yarning with him, while he was doing his work. As the years passed he got fattish and broad in the beam and a bit of an old woman. He got to know everything there was to know about everybody. When the Germans came and it was every man for himself, he suffered more than most, and the last year of the Occupation, nearly starved. A few weeks after the Liberation he was found dead in his bed.

Monsieur Le Boutillier's house got built at last. Harold and Percy and a couple of chaps was on it for months, on and off. It wasn't a bad little house, come to that, but not to be compared to Les Moulins. They wasn't building solid houses then, like in my grandfather's time; and it cost over a thousand. It was stone under the plaster, but not the good blue granite; and while the gables was left white, the front was daubed a pale yellow colour. I didn't like the colour myself. It was a two-storey house with three windows upstairs and a window each side of the door down. Percy got his way and put on fancy chimney-pots; but the first rough night one blew down and broke some of the slates, as I knew would happen. I watched the goings-on. It was stout chimney-stacks was needed for our windy corner: as those who built Les Moulins knew. The new house was the other side of the gully, thank goodness, and with the gable towards us. That was as it should be. Monsieur Le Boutillier was a Jerseyman. I couldn't imagine what that girl Ozanne from the Friquet, who I had always thought was a sensible girl, could have been thinking about to marry a Jerseyman; but she met him when she went over one year for the Battle of Flowers. They hadn't been married long, and was living with her people at the Friquet while the house was being built.

I made up my mind I would start off as I meant to go on, and let that Jerseyman know we wasn't going to be running in and out of each other's houses. He had to pass our front gate to get to L'Islet, and seemed quite ready to stop and have a chat. I was civil and passed the time of day; but no more. I wasn't going to let him know my business. I didn't want to know his. He got three vergées of ground and was going to grow potatoes and outdoor tomatoes, so he thought; but he soon found out his mistake. His potatoes didn't do too bad, but this wasn't Jersey. There where it faces south it is easier to grow tomatoes out of doors. He was now living facing north and learnt he would have to grow tomatoes under glass, if they was going to be early enough to make any price. He had to have a greenhouse put up.

To crown it all, he was a Roman Catholic. I would see him pass our gate early every Sunday morning on his way to the Catholic Church at

Delancey. It was before breakfast. Those who went to Church or Chapel didn't go at such an ungodly hour. Mind you, it didn't worry me what church he went to. He could go to any church he liked, or none, as far as I was concerned: but it was too much for my mother. She believed the Roman Catholic Church was the Whore of Babylon. I don't think she spoke a single word to Monsieur Le Boutillier all the time she knew him. When she died, he came across and offered his sympathy and I thanked him. I didn't invite him to the funeral.

Mind you, I am not saying I am proud of the way I treated Monsieur Le Boutillier when he came to live at La Corbière. When the time of the testing came and the Germans was all around us, it was Monsieur Le Boutillier who was a better and a truer friend to me than many a Guernseyman I could name. I honour the memory of Jean Le Boutillier. His son and daughter-in-law live at La Corbière now with their family, and there isn't a day passes but one of the young ones come across to see if I am all right. I don't blame my mother so much. She had her religion to consider. I have no such excuse. One live and learn.

6

I was beginning to get really worried about my mother. She had always been a big woman, but now she was having to let out her clothes and her face was getting puffy. It hurt me to see her dragging her great weight about the house. One evening I came in from work and found she hadn't washed up the dishes from dinner; and I knew then there must be something very wrong. I said she ought to see the doctor. She said, 'The doctor can't do nothing.' 'He might,' I said. She said, 'It is the will of God.' Whenever my mother said 'Ch'est la volonté de Dieu,' I knew it was no use me arguing. I have often wondered about my mother's religion: how different it was from Tabitha's. Tabitha went to Church with the Priaulx and to Service with my mother sometimes; but I am not sure she had a religion really. She had faith. I don't know in what, or how. She suffered in her life, yet I doubt if she was ever truly unhappy. She seemed to know that underneath everything was good. I wish I could think the same.

Anyhow, whether it was the will of God, or not the will of God, I went to Dr de Jersey at the Albion Terrace and asked him to come and see my mother. He wanted to know what was the matter with her and, from what I said, he thought it was the dropsy. If so, there wasn't much he could do; but he would come and examine her, he said. When I got back I was wondering if I ought to tell her where I had been, as I knew she would want to wash herself all over before he came; but I was no sooner inside the door than she said, 'The doctor, when is he coming, him?' If my mother wasn't a witch, what was she? I was gone to work when he came; but she looked better for it, I thought. She said he was a kind man. He had told her what she ought to eat and not eat, and was going to get ready some pills and some medicine for her to take. I went to the surgery and got the pills and the medicine, and put them on the dresser; but I didn't see them again. I found them after the funeral at the back of the top shelf on the cupboard, where we kept a bottle of brandy in case of sickness, and they hadn't been unwrapped from the paper. I didn't do no good by going to the doctor.

At last she got it was so hard for her to walk, she couldn't go to Service with the Brethren. It was the one thing she always looked forward to. There was several of the Brethren had motor-cars, but not one of them thought of fetching her from the house and bringing her home. Those people was as hard to each other as the Lord was to them. I was very angry about that. I reckon it is up to us to treat each other better than the Lord do, and teach Him a lesson. I thought the least I could do was to give up my job and work at home, and help my mother all I could. She had been used to dig the potatoes like a man, and fill and carry the bucket from the well, but now it was as much as she could do to stand by the fire and cook.

I explained to Mr Dorey and he understood. He said he was sorry to lose me and would be glad to have me back at any time. Myself, I wasn't altogether sorry to become my own master, though I knew it meant I wasn't going to be so well off. However, I thought I would have a new end built on to my greenhouse and, what with doing more fishing, I would manage to keep going somehow. I gave the work on the greenhouse to Harold, and he made a good job of it. Also I paid him on the dot and he was delighted. He had bills owing to him all over the place. The new end he built was lower than the rest, but of wider span. It was his idea; and I have had some very good crops in it, and ripe early. I cut down the hedge was supposed to be my boundary and let Harold take in a yard or two of the land at the top of the gully. If it belonged to an old lady in Torteval, she must have died without heirs; for nobody have ever said a word.

I didn't know that then, of course; and so as to make it look natural, I had a low wall built where I decided my land was going to end. I left a few feet between the wall and the greenhouse, and dug to the ground so as it would look as if it had always been in use. Harold left the wall for Percy to build. I had already had to stop Percy from painting the gable-end of my greenhouse blue. He built the wall as I wanted it; but while the cement on top was wet, he fished out some stones from among the rubble in the gully, chipped off the edges, and stuck them up all along like spikes. I suppose he thought it was ornamental, but I thought it was a silly idea myself. Anybody could jump over the wall, anyway. It was those blessed stones was my undoing.

By then my poor old mother was on her last legs; or rather, she was hardly on her legs at all. I had to help her even to go to the back, and from her chair by the fire to her bed. Besides, she was very low in spirit. I was glad for Prissy, or anybody else to come and talk to her, and give her an interest, if not cheer her up. Prissy always managed to find out all the private business of her visitors, and she enjoyed spreading it around with her quick tongue, beginning with us. It could do no harm her telling it to my mother, for, in that case, it would go no further. My mother knew what Prissy was and often said 'I don't wonder the people round here call my sister The Guernsey Evening Press.' That year Prissy had two fresh visitors who was staying the whole summer. They was very good class, she said; but she couldn't quite make them out at first. However, she soon got to the bottom of the mystery. They was a mother and a son; but no father. The mother had lost her husband and, without saying so, let it be understood he had been killed in the War; but Prissy managed to screw out the truth of the matter, which was the woman had lost her husband because he had left her before they had been married a month. She was now headmistress of a special school in England for children who was born without fathers. The son was just out of college and very clever, Prissy said. I didn't understand Prissy properly, as my mother told it to me anyhow, and I doubt if Prissy herself knew what she was talking about, but from what I could make out the son was going to be a professor and was only interested in old things. I thought she meant old buildings, or perhaps old furniture. I didn't know then there was people in the world who gave up their whole lives to studying old stones.

Prissy said she would send him for a walk round our way and then I could tell him what I knew of old things in Guernsey. I said he could come if he wanted to and I would tell him anything I knew, so long as he didn't stop me working. He came. He found me working on my new patch of ground between the end of the greenhouse and the wall. 'May I introduce myself?' he said. 'I am Dudley Waine with an "e".' I couldn't see the 'e' mattered all that much, but I said I was Ebenezer Le Page and was glad to meet him, and would shake hands, only my hand was too dirty. I was sorry for him. There was something missing. It was missing from his voice. I could well believe he was born without a father. He was about Raymond's age, perhaps a year or two older, but was plump and had a round baby face and big spectacles; and he seemed always to be looking for something he couldn't find. I said I didn't think I could help him much: but if he was interested in old buildings, he ought to go inside the Vale Church. He said it was only a few centuries old and he wasn't interested. I said, 'St Sampson's Church is old. It was built in A.D. 1111.' It is the only date I know of churches. He wasn't interested in St Sampson's Church either. It was 'comparatively recent'. He was only interested in 'pre-Christian remains'. I said there was a Druid's Altar on L'Ancresse Common; but it was overgrown with brambles, and had railings all round. They was bent in places and you could push your way in; but all the dogs in the parish made their mess in it, as well as human beings on the day of the races. There was another something of the sort I knew of on the way to Birdo at Le Dehus; but you had to ask for the key from next door to go in, and I had never bothered. Also, a few years before the War they uncovered some stones at L'Islet was supposed to be a prehistorical burial-ground or something; but anybody could have arranged those.

I was saying all this to try my best and be helpful, when all of a sudden he clapped his hands to his brow as if he had seen a vision, and was staring through his spectacles at the stones on the top of my wall. 'It is not possible!' he said. 'Where have those come from?' I said the builder got them out of the gully: I didn't think to say Percy had chipped pieces off to make them look ornamental. Dudley Waine was down the gully like a dog after a rabbit: but he couldn't find any more; only the raw material, he said.

Those stones on the top of my wall was prehistorical axe-heads. They had been made thousands and millions of years before 55 B.C. As far as I could understand, they was the first axe-heads ever to have been made in the world, because they was so badly made they couldn't have been made later. He said it was a 'unique discovery' and a red letter day for him, because now he would be able to prove everybody else so far had been wrong. I suppose I ought to have told him then it was Percy who had chipped those stones; but I didn't have the heart. He would have been too disappointed.

He explained. Up to now it had been thought there was people on Jersey before there was people on Guernsey, because once upon a time Jersey was joined to France and Guernsey wasn't; but if my stones really did belong to Guernsey, then there must have been people on Guernsey at the same time as the first people on Jersey. I said there was a Jerseyman living at La Corbière, but I didn't think he had brought over a bag of stones with him. Dudley asked me if I would break the cement and let him have one of the stones to be examined in a museum in London. I thought I had better not. I said I was sorry, but I couldn't do that: it would spoil the look of my wall. He said it didn't matter for the present, because he must have further evidence. There ought to be a midden near at hand, whatever that was; or a burial-place like the one at L'Islet, only older. Anyhow, his holiday was over and he would have to leave it an open question for this year; but, in the meantime, would I please be good enough under no circumstances to mention it to anybody else. I promised I wouldn't, and it was a promise I was only too willing to give. I thought that was the last I would hear of it. It wasn't.

I didn't see much of Raymond the years he was to College. For one reason, I was working harder on my own than ever I had worked as a foreman for Mr Dorey, and I didn't have the time to go to Wallaballoo. He came to see me every holiday at least once; but I thought he had changed somehow, and I didn't like him so much. He didn't let off any steam; and I realised what he did say wasn't what he was thinking, but what he was being taught. I got the idea he was now resigned to trying to fit in, and be a proper minister like the others.

He always brought one fellow or another home with him for the long summer holiday. I have wondered since if the only reason he did so was to keep Christine at arm's length. She reminded me of a big cat sitting by a mouse-hole; and Raymond was the mouse. He had only to be off his guard for one second, and a great paw would come down; after which she would play with him as long as it amused her, and then eat him up. That would be the end of Raymond. I didn't like the sort of chaps he brought over; and I doubt if he liked them himself. He liked big innocent sinners like Horace and Harry Whitehouse. These new friends of his was far from innocent. They was Christian sinners who had been saved. I remember especially one he brought to see me. Donald somebody: Donald Mallison, I think the name was. The Reverend Donald Mallison. He had just passed his final exam and got his license to preach. I took an instant dislike to him. He was a weed of a chap with no chin to speak of and teeth like a rabbit's. He said to me, 'Are you of our persuasion?' Raymond laughed. It was his wicked laugh, so there was hope for him yet. 'He is an old pagan,' Raymond said. 'I don't know what a pagan is,' I said, 'so I don't know if I am one or not; but I don't know what a Christian is either. There are thousands of Christians of all shapes and sizes on this island. They may not all of them go after the flesh-pots, though some of them do on the sly; but they go to war and kill other people, and in peace-time make as much money as they can out of each other, and don't love their neighbours any more than I do.' 'My grumpy uncle is not so far wrong,' said Raymond, 'though he doesn't know all there is to know.' 'Christianity is taking up your cross wherever you are,' said the Reverend Donald Mallison, and showed me his rabbit's teeth in a Holy Willie smile. He may have been right at that; but he wasn't taking up no cross, that one. He was as pleased as punch with himself. When he went, he said to me, 'I will pray for you.' The cheek, I thought.

Well, if being a Christian is taking up your cross, I reckon I took up mine all right when I took up with Liza. I was getting fed up with going out with her. I was feeling like Clive Holyoak when he went to Divine Service. I was bored. I got to the point when, if Ada came along and said Liza wanted me to meet her, I would say I couldn't go because I had to look after my mother. It wasn't always true, as Tabitha came nearly every Saturday and Sunday. The truth was I wanted something a bit less divine. I chased after this one and that one, when I had the time. I expect Liza got to hear of it; but I didn't care.

I saw the old lady's death in the paper; and a few days later there was a lot about the grand funeral she was given. Then on the Saturday morning up comes Ada and says Liza begs me to meet her that afternoon. At three o'clock by the Weighbridge. I cleaned myself up and put on a blue serge suit and a black tie, and prepared to put on a long face and be sympathetic. The bus missed the tram and I was a minute or two late. Liza was already waiting under the clock. She was wearing a beautiful black dress with a long pleated skirt sweeping the ground and a wide black hat that was wider than her shoulders; and she was holding open a ridiculous little fancy black parasol which didn't nearly cover the hat. She didn't look as if she was in mourning: she looked as if she was going to a dance, or on the stage. I said,

'Goodness, you look like the Merry Widow!' She said, 'That's just how I feel. Tra-la-la!'

I don't like crocodile tears, but I did think she might have been sorry. 'She have been very good to you, your mistress,' I said. 'I have never shed a tear in my life,' said Liza, 'and I am certainly not going to begin now. Angela would much rather see me walking down the High Street in this dress than weeping over her grave. Men are soppy!' 'All right, I will take you down High Street,' I said, 'and we'll have tea at Le Noury's, and everybody can see you.' I paraded her up the Pollet and down High Street, though I can't say I walked with her exactly. I walked behind. I couldn't get near her side for the hat. It was nearly touching the shop windows both sides. The extraordinary thing was she gave no sign of knowing anybody was looking at her. Perhaps she didn't know. Perhaps she was only thinking of Angela; but she was being looked at all right. The good country women doing their shopping stood on the edge of the kerb staring at her with their mouths open. The moment she had passed, their heads was together talking nineteen to the dozen; and I don't like to think what they was saying about me.

Over tea I asked her what she was going to do now. She said she was leaving Castle Carey and going to live in her grandmother's old cottage at Pleinmont. I knew her mother was dead and old Mère Quéripel had been dead years, but I thought the brothers, half-brothers, or cousins was living there. 'I'm turning out that dirty lot,' she said. 'They're all born on the wrong side of the blanket. They have no claim.' I didn't know if she had either, for that matter. Anyhow, the old lady had left her some money, and she would have enough to live on from the interest. 'I am going to be an old maid,' she said, 'since no man will marry me.' I could have crowned her with the teapot.

Here was me had been willing to marry her for years; and now she was putting the blame on me. She knew damn well I couldn't marry her just then. I wasn't going to leave my mother, when I knew she wouldn't be with me for long; and, besides, I had spent some of the cash I could have built a house with on my new greenhouse and the wall, and an out-board motor for my boat. It is true I hadn't touched the stockingful of sovereigns; but I couldn't have slept in peace in my bed at nights, if I hadn't known those was up the chimney in the wash-house. 'I am going to become a real old Guernsey woman,' she said, 'and wear a scoop and sabots and feed the chickens out the back, me.' She could speak the Guernsey English when she wanted to. I had to laugh.

I said, 'Aren't you going to be lonely with only the chickens for company?' She said, 'I can take in a lodger.' 'I hope he pay his rent,' I said. She said, 'If he is a nice lodger, I might not ask him to pay rent.' It was no use. I couldn't get under her skin nohow. She patted my hand. 'My dear, you mustn't worry about me,' she said. 'I will get along all right.' 'It is not you I am worried about,' I said. 'It is the poor bloody lodger. You would come out on top, if you was in hell!' 'Now that is the nicest thing I have ever had said to me!' she said.

I paid for the tea, though she tried to snatch the bill. When we got out in the Arcade, I said, 'Well good-bye, then!' 'Is it good-bye?' she said. She sounded surprised. I said, 'I wonder what you take me for?' 'I don't believe he likes me any more,' she said. I said, 'I wonder what you think there is in you to like? Nothing! Nothing! Nothing!

It is only a beautiful picture
In a beautiful golden frame!'

I turned on my heels very dramatic and walked off and left her, but not before I saw her lean against Le Noury's window and throw her head back and burst out laughing; and when I was running down the steps to catch the tram as fast as I could to get away from her, I could hear, or thought I could hear, her laughing.

7

If I had the arranging of things in this world they would be different, I can tell you. I don't mean to say I would go round improving things right and left. I think every improvement ought to be looked in the mouth first: to make sure it isn't an improvement for the worse. Guernsey have been improving so much for the worse these last years, even me, who have lived here all my life, can hardly recognise it. I know things got to change as the years go by; but they ought to change so as you don't notice. The weather, even, isn't what it used to be. When I was a boy, you could rely on a cloudless sky and sunshine from July to September with, perhaps, a thunderstorm or two. Mr Collenette, who used to write up the Probable Future Developments outside the Guille-Allès Library, only had to write 'Fine' or 'Very Fine' for the summer months and he was sure to be right; and in the winter if he wrote 'Fair to Moderate' or 'Rough' he was pretty safe. Nowadays you don't know what it is going to do from one day to the next.

I have another complaint to make about the way things are allowed to go on in this world. I am not one who is all that particular about the letter of the law, but I do think there ought to be some sort of rough and ready order for people to go by. I am now thinking of Raymond. He was either trying to go one better than nature, or, later on, I am afraid, one worse. I got to feel about that boy as if I had a sick child on my hands; though I reckon I knew more about him than most fathers know about their sons. It stands to reason a boy can't very well talk to his parents about what they had to do to bring him into the world. He told me most things about himself in time; and I know for a fact he never got square with the business of man and woman. He never found out how they can live together on earth without killing one another off in some way or another. I can't say I have either.

At least he was right in thinking Harold and Hetty would get on better once he was gone away. It seemed so, at any rate, for a time. I met Hetty one day in Weymouth's shop and she said my Cousin Mary Ann didn't go to see her from one year's end to the other. I took that as a sure sign things wasn't going too bad for Hetty. Hetty was quite worried about it, as a matter of fact. She wondered what she could have said or done to my

Cousin Mary Ann because, as soon as winter came, she would see her passing the house two or three times a week on the way to Timbuctoo. Of course I had no idea then my Cousin Mary Ann was bringing the bottles of whisky from the off-licence Prissy drank in secret for weeks on end, locked up in her room. Percy didn't know either: he just thought she had the shivers. If she came downstairs to eat, it was when he was out to work; and he was put in what had once been Cyril's little room to sleep.

The Easter before Raymond finished College, a Reverend Bingley came over with his daughter and stayed at the Manse at St Sampson's. He was head of the college Raymond was in and high up in the Wesleyan Church. The daughter was a friend of Raymond's, and Raymond brought her home to meet his mother. I would never have believed it possible Hetty could take to any girl who was a friend of Raymond's, but she did to Miss Phyllis Bingley. Hetty had her to the house a number of times, and invited me to tea one Sunday to meet her. She was certainly a lovely girl, or young woman, I should say, for she was a few years older than Raymond. She wasn't mannish, but had a strong-looking face with straight black hair coiled tight around her head, and those clear, clear blue eyes I had only seen in Hetty. She wore a dark costume and spoke very quiet. She was a real lady, you could see, and there was nothing put on about it. She made herself quite at home in the house and helped Hetty to get ready the tea in the front room. Hetty, for her part, didn't bother to try and speak the English properly, so there wasn't aitches flying all over the place. Miss Bingley would have been absolutely the right daughter-in-law for Hetty: all the more so because she was English and nobody knew nothing about her. The trouble with marrying a Guernsey girl is you marry all the scandal in the family for three or four generations, half of it not true. None of the bad things are ever forgotten: rather, a few more are made up.

When Raymond introduced me, he said, 'This is Ebenezer, my wicked uncle.' She shook hands with me and looked at me and smiled. 'He doesn't look very wicked,' she said, 'mischievous, perhaps.' She herself had a twinkle in those blue eyes. After tea, Raymond left us together, while he helped his mother wash up. Harold had been given his tea in the kitchen, where he could keep his cap on. He wasn't allowed to meet Miss Bingley. She began by telling me she had lost a very dear brother during the War, but her mother wouldn't believe he was dead, though the War Office said he was. It was for that reason the mother had not come to Guernsey. She would not leave their house in London, in case he came home while she was away. I said I could understand that.

She said, 'I expect you will have known Raymond a long time.' 'Since before he was born,' I said. 'The night my grandmother died I saw him kicking. It was then I knew the story about being found under a gooseberry bush was a pack of lies.' I had no sooner said it than I could have bitten my tongue off. It wasn't at all the sort of thing to say to a lady; but she only laughed. 'How old were you then?' she said. 'Nine or ten,' I said. 'I am his cousin, not his uncle.' She said, 'My father says he is in grave danger of becoming a heretic.' I didn't know quite what a heretic was, but I didn't think it was anything good. 'Oh, I'm sorry to hear that!' I said. 'It doesn't matter,' she said. 'He also says if I had lived in the Middle Ages I would have been burnt at the stake. My father is a darling!' She then told me she was going on a mission to the women of Turkey. 'Why on earth to the women of Turkey?' I said. 'What have they done?' Oh it wasn't because of anything they had done: it was because they was downtrodden she was going. She had a call to liberate the Turkish women from the tyranny of their men. Well, I ask you? As if any Guernseyman can believe women are downtrodden! 'A man is master in his own house, surely,' I said. 'It say so in the Bible.' I was trying for all I was worth to make her see sense when Raymond came back. 'You were quite right about your wicked uncle,' she said to him. 'He is an old Turk!' 'I am glad you have found him out,' said Raymond. I wish to God she had left the women of Turkey to fight their own battles and married Raymond instead.

The next time he came over he was wearing his collar back to front. It is true most of the time I saw him he was in sports coat and flannels; but the collar made a difference. I felt I had to mind my p's and q's. He didn't like it himself, and kept tugging at it. 'I feel like a dog on a lead,' he said. Then he corrected himself. 'I mustn't be ashamed of it,' he said. It's funny how the boy who wasn't ashamed to kneel down and say his prayers in the barrack-room was ashamed to wear the sign of his profession. It was years later he said to me, 'There shouldn't be any outward sign to separate one person from another; they are separated enough by nature as it is'; but I think he already had some such mad ideas in his head.

He had been found a chapel in England to go to; or rather, a church. The Church people call the Wesleyan's place of worship a chapel; but the Chapel people call their chapel a church. He didn't have to start until October, so he was going to have a nice long holiday. He said he had been to preach a sermon in the chapel he was going to, and they had been satisfied and accepted him. He wasn't happy about it. He had been no good. 'I might just as well have been a gramophone,' he said. He had thought of the right things to say, and it was what they expected to hear; so they decided he would do. He was going to be the youngest of three ministers in charge of that chapel, and was going to live in the same house as the other two. The wife of the one who was married was going to be housekeeper for the three. It wasn't in London, but some way outside, and was the place where Henry Ford made his motor-cars. Raymond said it was nothing but rows and rows of hundreds and hundreds of houses all the same, and like rabbit-hutches. The one where the ministers was going to live was a corner house, and bigger than the others in the row; but it was so badly built you could hear everything that went on next door on either side. I thought I would go mad if I had to live there.

The congregation was made up of people who worked in the Ford factory. Raymond had been over it, and said it was his idea of hell. They had to spend the whole of their working hours doing the same thing over and over again; perhaps fitting a bolt, or turning a screw: click-click, click-click, click-click all day long. They went to chapel in the same spirit; and he couldn't blame them. There was a good organ and a big choir and an orchestra, so they would come to chapel instead of going to the Pictures; but, as far as the religion went, it had to be all cut and dried. The chapel was a barn of a place, bigger than the old Ebenezer Chapel in Town: and he had to shout at the top of his voice, as if he was giving orders on the Fort Field. 'It's a circus,' he said.

I don't expect any young fellow going into the Ministry nowadays would understand how Raymond felt. He would take the circus for granted. I know my cousin, the Reverend David Livingstone Le Page, would be only too glad of the chance of shouting the Gospel of Jesus Christ through a megaphone to a football crowd. Raymond was of another generation. The factory horrified him. He didn't know worse things had happened on Guernsey and was going to happen in the days to come. In my grandfather's day, small boys of ten was made to sit in the corners up the high tower of the cracking machine and pick out any stones with flaws in from the trays as they passed down on the belt. The boys got stone-dust in their lungs, and was most of them dead by fifteen or sixteen. Raymond said Ford's had an ambulance waiting and an operating theatre open and nurses and doctors ready, in case there was an accident; and there was a cemetery out the back to bury those who died. At least, they looked after their work people.

I wish I could write down the story of this island as I have known it and lived through it for the best part of a century. I don't think I have changed much; but I think everybody else have. The young people of today don't know and can't imagine the difference between living on Guernsey as it was and living on Guernsey as it is now. There is a great gulf fixed between the present generation and mine. I wish I could bridge it; but it is too much to hope. The only ones who might feel as I do are either dead, or old people who, like me, are not very clear in the head and don't always remember right.

Mind you, I am not one of those who say living on Guernsey in the good old days was a bed of roses. I think living in this world is hell on earth for most of us most of the time, it don't matter when or where we are born; but the way we used to live over here, I mean in the country parts, was more or less as it had been for many hundreds of years; and it was real. The way

people live over here now is not real: at least, it is not real to me. The people
are not real. When I go out, and that isn't often, I see strange faces everywhere around me and I know at a glance they don't belong; or, if I see a boy
and think goodness, that is young Torode I was at the Vale School with, he
don't know me; and then I realise he must be the grandson, or the great-
grandson of the boy Torode I knew. It is an island of ghosts and strangers.

The best thing for me to do is stop at home. There are so many cars on the
roads, you risk your life every time you put your nose out; and, as for the
boys on motor-bikes, they have no business to be allowed at all. There are
no country parts any more, neither. Guernsey is a factory for the manufac-
ture of tourists now. It is true we still export tomatoes; but that is arranged
for us by a Board with enough rules and regulations to sink a ship. They are
talking about having another Board for flowers and I suppose they will get
it in the end. For years now it haven't been possible to get milk from a cow.
It have to go to the factory at St Martin's and get separated and mixed up
again, but not as the cow gave it. The thin stuff they let you have they got
the cheek to call Guernsey milk. It isn't the Guernsey milk that was two
out of three parts cream I used to fetch from the Roussels of the Grand
Fort. As for Guernsey meat and Guernsey butter, it is so dear it break my
heart to have to buy it; but I won't eat no other. Where are the sheep?
Where are the fowls? Where are the pigs? As far as I know, I am the only
one round here who have pigs in his pigsty. I like to hear them, if nothing
else. They make me feel at home. The cats are coming along; though most
of them was put to sleep or eaten, during the Occupation. I haven't got
one.

The Occupation was the end of Guernsey as our fathers and our forefathers knew it. I don't mean it was the Germans who destroyed it. The
Occupation brought out the best and the worst in all of us; but we was
Guernsey people yet, and our spirit was not broken. It is the English
Occupation since have broken it. I doubt if half the people living on this
island now was born here; or even have relations who was born here. They
are people who think they can live here on the cheap and get out of paying
their higher taxes in their own country. They come over here and live
grand and are made a fuss of because they are English, when they wouldn't
be taken no notice of the other side. Ah well, that is Guernsey now. When I
think what have happened to our island, I could sit down on the ground
and cry.

It wasn't so long ago young Fraser came to see me. He is a reporter for
the *Star* newspaper. It isn't quite so genteel as the *Press* and sometimes
allow a joke to be printed, and even a sly dig at the States. Master Fraser was
very polite. He is only about twenty-four. He wasn't hatched when
Guernsey was alive. He said he hoped I would allow him to interview me
as a 'senior resident' so that he might learn my 'reaction to modern Guern-

sey'. I was interested to learn I was a senior resident. Myself, I thought I
was an old man and a Guernseyman to boot. Anyhow, I let him have my
'reaction to modern Guernsey'. When I had done, he was sitting shrivelled
up in his chair, as if he was on the hot seat. 'Aren't you being rather revol-
utionary, Mr Le Page?' he said. I said, 'God made this island with a good
climate and a good soil, especially suited for the growing of fruit and vegetables and flowers, and for the breeding of two kinds of creatures: Guernsey cows and Guernsey people. I would have thought those was the two
breeds the States would first and foremost want to preserve. As it is, they
are the two breeds there is no room for. Our best boys are going to Australia by the hundred every year, and there is a shortage of pasture for the few
cows are left.' He said, 'I am afraid you ignore the overall economic situation.' I don't know nothing about the overall economic situation! He
didn't print a word I said.

8

It was no wonder poor Raymond came a cropper when he had to preach to his own people. Guernsey people are funny people to have to deal with, if you happen to be a Guernseyman yourself. They know too much about each other. When he was asked to take the service for the Harvest Festival at Birdo Mission, it meant everybody in the congregation would know who he was and where he come from and who his parents and his grandparents and all his relations back to Adam. If he had been an Englishman, they might have listened respectfully and taken what he said for gospel; but they wasn't going to sit mum under Raymond Martel of Wallaballoo. It wasn't they didn't listen. They was spellbound. It was afterwards, when they came to think it over, the trouble began. It was the only sermon he preached on Guernsey; and the last sermon he was to preach anywhere.

When he told me he was going to do it, he laughed and said, 'The Lord hath delivered them into my hands.' I have wondered since whether he didn't engineer the whole thing to get out of what he had let himself in for on the other side. Raymond was deep. When years later he thought he was being persecuted by everybody and lived with me at Les Moulins, he talked of many things over the fire, and I asked him if he was sincere that night. He said, 'A human being is an insincere animal, my boy.' By then he was talking to me as if I was the young one. 'I was sincere in the thoughts of my heart,' he said. 'I was not sincere in the thoughts of my head. I let those people think I believed in things I did not believe in, or they wouldn't have let me say what I felt.'

I had no intention of going to hear him. As I have said before, I don't like people who preach. They put themselves on a pedestal and make out what they say is according to the Will of God and what anybody else think different is of the Devil. I like a chap who say straight out what he think at the moment, and don't care a bugger if he is right or wrong. It was quite by chance I ran into Hetty at her gate when I was passing one evening. She complained she couldn't go and hear Raymond preach because of Harold's bald head; and, if she went by herself, the people would talk. I, like a fool, said I would go with her. Of course, I had no idea Christine Mahy was going to be in the choir and sing the solo. The service was at six and I said I would call at the house for her at a quarter-past five, so as we would have plenty of time to get there. I knew Hetty couldn't walk very fast.

As a matter of fact, I was to the house at five and, judge of my surprise, when I walked in and found my Cousin Mary Ann talking to Harold in the kitchen. Hetty was upstairs dressing and Raymond was already gone to put up the numbers of the hymns and, I rather think, to have a few quiet minutes to himself. My Cousin Mary Ann looked quite bright for her in a flowered frock. Hetty, who was behindhand with everything in the excitement of dressing up to go to Chapel, was delighted to have somebody to get the supper ready for when she got back. When we left, my Cousin Mary Ann had put on an apron and was going to light the fire in the front room.

It was nearly half-past five before I managed to get Hetty out of the house. She had to change out of the hat she was wearing and then, after a lot of examining of herself in the looking-glass, change back into the one she had taken off. I hadn't realised how wheezy she was getting, and heavy on her poor legs; and I only managed to get her to the Mission just as the service was going to begin. The place was packed. They hadn't come to hear Raymond, only because it was the Harvest Festival; but I noticed Mr Dorey, my boss, was there and Mr Fred Johns from the Vale Avenue, both trustees of St Sampson's Chapel; and Albert Nicolle, who was a real old Bible-puncher, and the Minister from Ebenezer Chapel in Town, who was the Superintendent of the Circuit. I thought those must have come to see how their new young minister was shaping out. At first glance, I didn't think we would get a seat; but one of the Noyons, who was showing people to their places, had his pew reserved by the door and said we could sit there, and him and his brother would sit on the steps. The door was being left open for air.

The inside of the little Mission was as good as the Flower Show in the Market Halls. The gas was lit, though it was light outside yet, and there was flowers everywhere of every shape and size and colour beautifully arranged, and ferns hanging from the gas-brackets. There was offerings of fruit and great marrows and pumpkins around the Communion Table, and long loaves of bread on the window-sills and sheaves of corn against the pulpit. I noticed there was tomatoes on the ledge against the pipes of the organ, and was afraid they might roll off from the vibration; but they didn't. Reg Underwood was playing Handel's Largo when we walked in. When we put our heads down for a minute, the way you do when you sit in Chapel, I whispered to Hetty, 'Are you all right now?' 'That girl!' she said. She had seen Christine Mahy in the choir.

Christine was in the Capelles Chapel choir as a rule, unless she was invited to some other chapel to sing; so Raymond must have invited her especially. She was dressed like nobody else. Christine liked to say of

herself 'I am a simple soul.' She was in a plain white dress with a tight
bodice and a full skirt, and wore over it a pale grey silk cloak lined with
blue. She had no hat on, to speak of. For a moment, I thought she had dared
to come in chapel without a hat; but then I saw she had a small, round white
cap on the very top of her pale yellow hair. She was a simple soul. She might
have been the Virgin Mary in person.

Hetty half got to her feet and I thought she was going to walk out, as she
had done from the sinking of the *Titanic*; but just then Raymond came in
from the vestry and she sat down again. He didn't look to me at all nervous.
I know if I had been going to hold forth to all those people, I would have
been shivering in my shoes. He walked up the steps to the pulpit and sat
with his head bent; then he found the place in the hymn-book and stood up
to announce the first hymn. I thought how much he looked the young
minister. He was wearing black, tight for him, I thought; but it made him
look very slim and very young. His white cuffs was showing, and he had a
white handkerchief in his breast pocket. His hair was neatly parted on one
side; and brushed down flat, as far as it could be. There was something
about his face set him apart from the rest of us; and I thought perhaps after
all, up there in the pulpit he was in the right place. The first hymn was 'We
plough the fields and scatter'. It was the right hymn for the occasion, and I
suppose everybody sang it without thinking what it meant. I know I did. I
noticed Raymond didn't sing; but now I come to think of it, I never heard
him sing or whistle. Christine sang, but she was careful not to be heard
above the others. Her turn was coming. She was another who knew what
she was doing.

I hadn't been in Chapel for years: not since I had been with Jim, when
we was doing the rounds. It was the prayers got my goat. In Church you
know what is coming, and for how long; but some of the ministers in
Chapel would pray and pray and pray, and really be preaching God a
sermon while they was praying. Jim and me would look at each other and
wink, and long to be able to sit up and straighten our backs and stretch our
legs. I don't know if Raymond had remembered, but I had probably told
him at some time or another. Anyhow, for the first prayer he only asked us
to say the Lord's Prayer with him, and the second was the shortest I have
ever heard in Chapel. For the Lesson, he read the Parable of the Sower. I
thought what a good speaking voice he had. He spoke the English well; yet
not quite like an Englishman. He was of those who for generations it had
been more natural to speak French. His voice had more in it than an
Englishman's. There was nothing missing. It had all the colours of the
rainbow in it, from dark to light.

I don't remember what the second hymn was. It had something to do
with the Holy Spirit; but I didn't understand it, and I didn't know the
tune. The hymn after the Lesson was a hymn he said was sung by the Manx

fishermen. 'Hear us, O Lord, from heaven Thy dwelling place.' It was one of my favourite tunes; and I can well imagine that hymn being sung by fishermen on just such another shore as Birdo Harbour. I could see through the open doorway some fishermen in guernseys sitting on the grass listening, and a boat was drawn up on the shingle and others moored to the cauchie. The sky was as clear as a pearl, and the tide was out and the butt-end of Herm seemed so near you would have thought you could step on it. It was after that hymn Raymond said his short prayer. 'I ask you to pray with me in silence,' he said, 'for us to be honest in our minds . . . and tender in our hearts . . . and true in our secret places . . . so the love of Christ may dwell in us . . . and unite us one with the other.' There was a long silence; and then he said 'Amen'. It is the only prayer, except the Lord's prayer I learnt at the Vale School, I have never forgotten.

He then came down to earth and read the notices. There was to be a week-night meeting in the Mission Hall on the Wednesday and a meeting of the Y.L.U. in the schoolroom on the Thursday and a jumble sale on the Friday. While the collection was being taken, Reg Underwood played a voluntary. It was the piece by Beethoven I liked so much. I don't know if Raymond had me in mind when he chose it, but I do know he himself arranged every detail of that service as he wanted it. After the collection, he said, 'Christine Mahy will sing the next hymn.' She stood up by herself in the choir. I can see her yet. She let the cloak she was wearing fall off her shoulders on to the chair behind her, and you almost heard the shudder of horror from many in the congregation; for her frock had no sleeves and her arms was bare.

I have pondered and wondered over Christine many times. She was, I think, the most callous and cruel person and the most vain and selfish woman I have ever known. Was she a human being? Or only a female? I don't know. I do know when I think of Christine Mahy, I love old Liza. For all her wickedness and vanity, Liza was human through and through. Dudley Waine choked me off once for criticising Christine. 'Christine is beyond criticism,' he said. 'She is a force of nature.' That may be, but a force of nature can be a great nuisance, if it isn't kept in order; or if you don't find some way of dealing with it. There is nothing holy about a force of nature. Christine seemed to think everything she did was holy because it was Christine Mahy did it. I will go so far as to grant she may have been what she thought she was, when she was singing. It wasn't only every note was pure and every word clear, it was as if she wasn't singing words she had learnt from a book, or to a tune was being played on the organ for her to sing to, but as if she was making up the words and the music for the first time as she went along, and pouring it out of her full heart as she sang:

O Love, that will not let me go,
　　I rest my weary soul in Thee;
I give Thee back the life I owe,
That in Thine ocean depths its flow
　　May richer, fuller be.

O Light, that followest all my way,
　　I yield my flickering torch to Thee;
My heart restores its borrowed ray,
That in Thy sunshine's blaze its day
　　May brighter, fairer be.

O Joy, that seekest me through pain,
　　I cannot close my heart to Thee:
I trace the rainbow through the rain,
And feel the promise is not vain
　　That morn shall tearless be.

O Cross, that liftest up my head,
　　I dare not ask to fly from Thee:
I lay in dust life's glory dead
And from the ground there blossoms red
　　Life that shall endless be.

and as I write down those words I have heard sung so often, but have only heard sung truly once, I know they are the words of Raymond's religion and of the whole of his religion. He came to turn against it and deny it and try and tear it out of himself; but I know he didn't ever quite tear the roots from his heart. When she sat down there was not a sound in the chapel. Raymond stood up and read the text: 'Lo, I am with you always, even unto the end of the world.'

　　Raymond was a clever boy. He was the clever one of the family. I am not clever; and I am glad I am not. It didn't do him much good. I remember he began, 'According to the Scriptures, those were the last words uttered by Jesus Christ before He ascended into heaven.' He didn't say it was so: he said 'according to the Scriptures'; and it was not the Gospel of Jesus Christ Raymond preached that night. I knew the Gospel of Jesus Christ. I couldn't help it. I had heard it all my life. Here was me, or anybody else, alive on earth; and, when we died, we was going either to heaven, or to hell. If we had accepted Jesus Christ as our Saviour, we would go to heaven. It was our only chance. It wasn't going to be the reward for our works; but for our faith. It is true, if you was saved, you didn't smoke, or drink, or fornicate except in the marriage bed; and you didn't rob from your neighbour, unless you could do it by law; but if you didn't believe Jesus Christ died for your sins, none of that would get you into heaven.

Church wasn't so hard and fast; and it suited me better. I didn't bother my head about it much; but I did think if I got what I deserved, I would go to hell for sure.

Raymond's argument was reasonable, I thought. He said it wasn't much use arguing about what may or may not have happened on earth nearly two thousand years ago. Christ was in heaven. That was where we must think of Him as being. He was in Heaven here and now. He is in the heart of God. He is the love in the heart of God. God in the stories of the Old Testament and in the world around us as we see it and in history as we learn it is a bully and a brute; but the heart of the brute God is love. He asked where heaven was. He answered, 'Where Christ reigns.' He quoted two texts from the New Testament to catch the good Christians in his net. The first was 'The Kingdom of Heaven is at hand'; the second was 'The Kingdom of Heaven is within you'. He said Christ is in every creature and every creature is in Christ. 'The whole creation is afloat in Christ,' he said, 'or Christ is not at all!' Reg Underwood, who didn't care tuppence about religion but was mad about music, said to me when I talked it over with him, 'Young Martel blew the fuses and down came the house of cards!'

I don't remember half he said. Once he had cleared the decks, he said whatever came into his head. He made us laugh, I know; and that wasn't often done in Chapel. The Reverend Whetnall of St Sampson's, who was a very popular preacher at the beginning of the War, used to make his congregation laugh, but only at the P.S.A.; and he always made it all right by preaching retribution in the end. There was no spirit of retribution in Raymond. He delighted in the scamps he told us stories of. I remember his story of Jurat Theodore Montpelier, also of the Hook Chook. I knew and everybody else knew there was no such Jurat and no such place; but it was very near the bone. The Jurat came of a good old Guernsey family which, in the Middle Ages, always had the sense to fight on the side paid best; and later on, when they became smugglers, they smuggled both ways, from France to England and from England to France. When smuggling was made illegal in Guernsey and they took to privateering to be respectable, they captured French ships for the English and English ships for the French. The present Montpelier, the Jurat Theodore, who was a very important person on the States and a model of all the virtues, was a staunch Wesleyan; but Raymond wouldn't say which chapel he belonged to.

It was no use looking to the States for the Kingdom of Heaven. If you work on the roads for the States you work from seven in the morning to six at night, and are paid accordingly. If you work only from five in the afternoon, you don't get paid much. In the Kingdom of Heaven you get paid just as much if you start at five in the afternoon, as if you start at seven in the morning. I didn't follow him there. I didn't follow him after. I listened more as if to music, or to the waves of the sea. 'The Kingdom of Heaven is at hand' was the text he really preached from. He spoke of everything being changed. He said, 'In the twinkling of an eye a veil is lifted; and you see with other eyes and hear with other ears and are given another understanding.' I didn't understand then, and I don't understand now; but I know he brought me near to believing in the promise of a happiness I have only known in dreams.

He ended quietly and there was not a movement in the chapel until he announced the last hymn:

> Abide with me; fast falls the eventide;
> The darkness deepens; Lord, with me abide.

and we sang it softly, Christine too, yet her voice was heard over us all. He pronounced the Benediction; but I noticed he said 'keep our hearts and minds in the knowledge of the love of God' and not 'of Jesus Christ, Our Lord.' I was among the first out and asked Hetty if she wanted to wait for Raymond, or go round to the vestry. 'What, and meet that girl?' she said. 'Not me!' The chapel was emptying and I noticed the small groups of people standing around saying little, but smiling kindly at each other. I said to Hetty, 'He was good, you know.' She said, 'I notice he got a lot to say to strangers. He don't have so much to say to his own mother.' She hadn't understood a word.

9

I expected Raymond to catch us up, but he didn't, though I had to stop
several times on the way for Hetty to have a rest. She couldn't get her
breath and complained of her heart. When we got in, my Cousin Mary Ann
had laid the table for supper in the front room, and was cutting bread and
butter. I thought myself there seemed to be a lot of places laid. Hetty said,
'Goodness, is it all the parish is coming then?' My Cousin Mary Ann said
she thought perhaps Raymond would be bringing a friend home. Hetty
said, 'He didn't say nothing about bringing a friend for supper.' She went
upstairs to take off her hat and get out of her tight boots. She always wore
boots a size too small, so as to have small feet like Prissy; but they made
walking for her an agony.

Harold was sitting by the fire without a cap, reading the *News of the
World.* He was allowed to sit in the front room without a cap, if it was only
some of the family was expected. 'The boy remember to say his piece?' he
said. Harold's idea of a sermon was the preacher learnt it by heart out of a
book beforehand and stood up in the pulpit and spouted it. 'I don't think
he forgot much,' I said. 'He got his head screwed on right,' said Harold. It
was the only time I ever heard him say a word in praise of Raymond. 'Was
there many there?' said my Cousin Mary Ann. 'It was full,' I said, 'and
sitting on the steps.' Hetty came down in a blouse and skirt with slippers
on her feet. 'Are your feet easier now, my ducks?' said Harold. She didn't
say nothing but sat on the other side of the fire. 'Tired?' he said. She sighed
and put a hand under her heart. 'Shall I make the tea?' said my Cousin
Mary Ann. 'Might as well,' said Hetty, 'if that Raymond would rather
stop and talk to those I wouldn't be seen dead with than come home for his
supper with his people, he can go without.'

I can remember every look and every word was said that evening. I think
for once I was gifted with the second sight. I would have sworn something
terrible was going to happen. I could feel it coming. I heard the front door
open. 'Ah, here they are!' said my Cousin Mary Ann. It wasn't only
Raymond. He came in leading Christine by the hand and with his clergy-
man's hat in the other. I don't know if souls can love souls without bodies;
but, if so, they looked like two souls in love. I had never thought of

Christine as a beautiful girl; but that night she was beautiful. She was filled with something, as she was when she was singing. As for Raymond, he was thinking all his troubles in this world was over. I didn't like Christine and I did like Raymond; but when I saw them as they was then, I would have done anything, anything, to keep those two together.

It was Hetty who spoke. 'Who is this?' she said. As if she didn't know! 'She is my wife,' said Raymond, as if it was the most ordinary thing to say. For one mad moment I got the wicked thought they had already been together under a boat, or on the Hommet, or somewhere; but one look at Raymond's face and I knew no such thought could have come into his head. In his mind they was married in heaven. The face of Hetty set like a stone; and she stood up on her two dumpy legs and in her carpet slippers. 'I have not asked that girl to my house,' she said. Raymond let go of Christine's hand. 'Ma!' he said; and I have never heard so much pain and so much surprise in one small word; or in any number of words, for that matter. He looked to his father, tried to speak, but couldn't. 'You heard what your mother said, son,' said Harold. Christine showed no sign of being upset. If anything, she looked more heavenly. She held her hand out for Raymond. 'Come, dear heart,' she said, 'we are not wanted here.' He took her hand and followed her out. They hadn't been in the room two minutes.

It would have been better, I think, if Hetty had cried and screamed and made a fuss, as I would have expected her to do; but she sat up to the table as if nothing had happened. Harold tried to jolly it off. 'Eat and keep your pecker up, my ducks!' he said. My Cousin Mary Ann poured out the tea. Never in all my life have I sat through a more miserable meal. Harold said to me, 'How is the good mother these days?' 'She don't get no better,' I said. 'Have you left her by herself, then?' said my Cousin Mary Ann. 'La Tabby is with her,' I said. 'Ah, bon!' said my Cousin Mary Ann. I couldn't think of another word to say. It wasn't about Raymond and Christine I was worried. She would take him to her home and he would be made welcome. It was Hetty I was sorry for. She ate half a slice of bread and butter and pushed her plate away. Again she had done a great wrong; but Raymond must have been mad to walk in and spring it on her the way he did.

My Cousin Mary Ann made a good meal, and Harold and me ate a little; then my Cousin Mary Ann got up to clear away. 'I'll just wash up before I go,' she said and, in the same breath, 'Raymond won't have nothing to sleep in. I had better take him something on my way home, eh?' 'I'll get you his pyjamas,' said Hetty, and went out of the room like an old woman; and I heard her stumbling up the stairs. 'I'll take them along,' I said to my Cousin Mary Ann, 'and save you going the long way round.' I was dying for any excuse to get out of that house. 'Then you had better take him another suit as well,' she said. 'He won't want to be wearing his good black suit on a week-day.' She thought of everything, my Cousin Mary Ann. She went up the stairs after Hetty.

I got up ready to go and Harold sat by the fire with his newspaper. 'That boy have done a bad night's work for himself,' he said. 'Aw, it's nothing to take so much to heart,' I said, 'He's young and he's in love with the girl. He'll come round.' 'He walked out of his home of his own free will,' said Harold. 'He won't come back into it again, if I know it.' It was the first hint I got of how hard Harold could be as a father. My Cousin Mary Ann came down with a suitcase. It weighed half a ton, so they must have put a lot of his things in. Hetty had gone to bed and she hadn't even drunk her tea. I thought of saying I would call back before I went home; but I didn't want to promise anything. I just said good-night.

I had never been inside Ivy Lodge before, though I had seen it often enough when I was passing up the Effards. From the outside, the house didn't look as if it was very well kept. The curtains wasn't too clean and the blinds was all anyhow. It was different from Hetty's where the starched lace curtains was spotless and the venetian blinds always all pulled up to exactly the same level. Christine's mother, Emmeline Vaudoir that was, from Fountain Street, wasn't one to bother. It was her came to the door. She was fat and free and easy and wearing a loose pink dress that looked like a night-gown. She knew me by sight. 'Come in, come in!' she said. 'Raymond was just saying you might bring his things.' They was all sitting round the fire in the front room, drinking coffee out of glasses and eating sandwiches from a table on the side. The room was very untidy with cushions all over the place; but everybody was comfortable. Mahy, the father, looked like a sad, long-faced dog; but he smiled and said hullo when I came in. Being Jim's uncle, he knew me from when I used to go round with Jim. Gwen was there and Edna, the sister-in-law from across the road with her little girl. Raymond still looked as if he was in heaven; but Christine was come down to earth, I thought. She had her cat face on, and I bet was feeling proud of her night's work now she was with her family. Mrs Mahy wanted me to sit down and have coffee and sandwiches, but I said I had only come to bring the suitcase and, if Raymond had a message for his people, I could take it on the way home.

It was Mrs Mahy who did most of the talking. She had her wits about her, that woman, for all her lazy ways. She was delighted she was going to have Raymond for a son-in-law: he was an only son, and would have plenty. She didn't say as much, but I knew that was what she was thinking. What she did say was it was a pity Raymond's mother had turned funny; but she would get over it. They was going to get married at the Capelles Chapel as soon as possible. In the meantime, Edna and the child was going to stay at Ivy Lodge, and Raymond was going to sleep at Rosamunda, so as people wouldn't be able to talk. Christine, of course, would have to give up her job as a teacher in a school; but she could go and help Raymond with his work in England. He was going to write to the chapel he was going to, and say he would be arriving with a wife. They would have to find him a place to live, if there wasn't room with the others. Mrs Mahy had it all thought out and he was letting it happen as if he didn't have a will of his own. He did say he would want some papers from his desk, if they hadn't been packed, but that it was too late for me to go back to Wallaballoo and fetch them that night. I said I would come and see him the next evening when he would know what it was he wanted. He came with me to the door. As I was going, he said, 'Will you be my best man?' 'Yes, with pleasure,' I said, 'and I hope you are going to be very, very happy,' and I meant it. 'Isn't it wonderful?' he said. 'I will never be alone any more!'

When I got home and told my mother what had happened, she shook her head and said, 'It won't turn out well, you'll see.' I was annoyed with my mother. I said, 'Nothing ever do turn out well, according to you.' 'It will for some,' she said. I helped her to the door of her bedroom and remembered she was sick. The next evening, that was the Monday, I went down to Ivy Lodge as I had promised. Christine came to the door and said Raymond was across the road at Rosamunda. I went across and knocked on the front door, but got no answer; so went round the back, and there I found Raymond sitting at the kitchen table writing a long letter to Horace. Pages and pages of it. He said, 'I wonder what old Horace is going to say?' I said, 'Well, it's none of his business anyhow.' I had to remind Raymond what I had come for. I got out of him that all he wanted was a couple of books he had to take back to the Guille-Allès Library and his birth certificate and his bank-book of the Guernsey Savings Bank. It was all the money he had of his own and had been saved for him under his name by his mother. It amounted to about two hundred pounds. As it turned out, that was all the money he was ever to get from his people; and his mother-in-law managed to get hold of most of it.

When I got round to Hetty's, I heard Harold hammering away in his work-shop. Hetty, in her sabots, was getting in the day's washing from the clothes-line, as I suppose she had done every Monday evening since she was married. She didn't seem to have the heart in her to lift her arms, and I got the rest down myself and carried the clothes-basket indoors for her. 'Raymond wants some books and papers from the room where he studies,' I said. 'They are all his,' she said. I went up and found what he had asked me to get. When I came down, I said, 'Why take it so hard, Hetty? Christine will make a good minister's wife.' I doubt if I believed it; but I said it. I wasn't going to be a Job's comforter like my mother. 'Phyllis Bingley was the girl would have made a good minister's wife,' said Hetty, 'and you know it. It's hard when somebody you have always thought was your friend stab you in the back.' 'I am not stabbing you in the back, Hetty,' I said. She said, 'It was on purpose I didn't put his bank-book with his things; and now you are helping him to run away with that girl.' I had the bank-book in my hand. 'Goodness, he is not running away with her!' I said. 'They are going to get married at the Capelles. I will let you know when.' 'All those who call themselves my friends will let me know,' she said, 'you don't have to bother. Go now.' I knew it was no use me talking. I didn't know it was the last time I was to see Hetty alive.

The rest of the story of Hetty I heard from my Cousin Mary Ann; but only many years later. For weeks Hetty wouldn't be seen outside the house: she was so ashamed of meeting anybody. My Cousin Mary Ann had to do all the shopping, or one of her daughters. Also, Hetty was getting funny ideas in her head. She began talking of 'le bon dieu'. Le bon dieu wasn't going to allow it to happen. I don't know if she imagined Christine was going to drop dead before the wedding. There wasn't much chance of that. Myself, I can't imagine Christine ever dying. Unless she was hit by a thunderbolt. Perhaps that is what Hetty hoped le bon dieu would do. Well, there wasn't no thunderstorm; but there was plenty of talk. Prissy came round to ask my mother if it was true Raymond was marrying Christine Mahy because he got to. It was what everyone was saying, she said. My mother said she didn't know, but who was everybody? If I had been there I would jolly soon have told Prissy it wasn't true and given her a piece of my mind! Raymond spent the days he was waiting for the licence in going to the bays with Christine. He brought her to Les Moulins once to ask my mother if she would go to the wedding; but, of course, she couldn't. I thought he was looking worried.

I am the last person on earth fit to write anybody else's love story. I don't know nothing about love. On the Pictures, love is love. The lovers either end up living happy ever after, or die tragic and very beautiful; but love is love. In my experience it is not like that at all. I don't know how far Raymond really loved Christine. I know he wanted to; and perhaps he did. He said to me once, 'When I love Christine, I love the whole world and everybody in it. She is the hardest person in the world for me to love.' I am quite sure Christine didn't love Raymond; or, if she did, it was only in so far as she wanted him to be interested in her, and only in her, and in nobody else, and in nothing else. He made the great mistake of taking her to see places where he had been happy with Horace. She was not interested in how, or where he had been happy with Horace; nor in climbing down over big rocks only to look at little fishes swimming in a pool. Christine wanted to have people, different people, around her all the time, and all of them saying how wonderful she was; and then she swelled out and perhaps she was wonderful. She wasn't a friend: she was a woman. I don't think Raymond realised it.

Even on the wedding morning there was something missing, I thought. It may have been because it was only in a chapel. In chapel they solemnize marriages; but it is not so very solemn. That is why I would never feel properly married, if I wasn't married in a church. It was at eight o'clock and there was no show. Raymond didn't even arrange for the photographer to come. Christine wore a veil, but no train, and only a white silk dress she had made herself. Gwen and Edna was bridesmaids; though I didn't see how Edna could be a bridesmaid, when she was a widow with a girl of five. I thought a bridesmaid was supposed to be a virgin. Raymond wore the same black suit he had preached in. I had a flower in my buttonhole; but Raymond forgot his. Old Mahy gave Christine away. His black clothes hung so loose on him, he looked as if he ought to have been put in a field to frighten the birds. Up to the last minute Raymond kept on looking towards the porch, hoping Harold and Hetty would appear. Prissy was there and made a great fuss of Christine after the service. She made them both promise they would go and see her as soon as they got back from their honeymoon. They was going for a fortnight's honeymoon on Sark. That was Raymond's idea; but Jersey would have suited Christine better. There was a wedding breakfast at Ivy Lodge which had to be eaten in a hurry, because the boat was leaving at half-past ten. I went to the Albert Pier to see them off on the *Alert*. Raymond, I will never forget, caught hold of my arm before he followed Christine down the gangway and said, 'Pray for me.'

I am not the person to pray for anybody; but I said, 'Good luck!' I didn't know then what it was he was afraid of; but I did when he was living with me and said, 'Any chap can do in, out, on guard, once he gets into the habit.' In Raymond's experience, marriage in heaven and marriage on earth didn't go together. For myself, I would have been satisfied with marriage on earth and heaven in sight. He must have suffered on his honeymoon. I know he confessed to Christine every single thing about himself, even his poor little sins of when he was a boy. He was a fool there. A man got to be careful what he say to a woman; or she will turn it upside-down and inside-out and use it as evidence against him. Raymond didn't want to keep anything secret from Christine. He trusted her completely.

I let two or three days pass after I knew they was back before I went down to see them. Raymond had a fortnight yet before he was due to go to his chapel. I thought they both looked very well. Raymond was in white flannels and a white open-necked shirt with a coloured tie for a belt; and Christine was in one of her famous simple frocks. It was all the colours of the rainbow, and I must say she looked nice in it. I said, 'If that frock you got on is made of curtain material, you are a very clever girl.' 'It is,' she said, 'and it cost me seven-and-six.' I asked Raymond how he liked Sark. 'God's Isle,' he said. 'A miracle risen from the sea!' I glanced at her to see if she agreed, but there was no knowing from her face what she was thinking. It was like a big moon.

They seemed quite at home in Rosamunda. Edna had left all the furniture for their use. He was sitting in the armchair like the man of the house, and Christine was sitting on a hassock at his feet, leaning against his knees. He was telling me about Dixcart Hotel where they had stayed, and the wonderful water from the well in the valley. They had been all over the island. He had a swim in Venus' Pool off Little Sark; and the sea in it was so thick with salt, he said, he could hardly keep his body under. He had been along the Hog's Back. He had looked down into the Creux Derrible and seen the sea at the bottom swirling like a witch's cauldron. He said the view from the Pilcher Monument must be the loveliest on earth. Christine, it seemed, had to follow in his footsteps and do plenty of climbing. I wondered if she liked it. She said very little, but smiled at him adoringly from time to time. I don't know to this day how far she was playing the part of the happy young wife. For years she put on that face and didn't complain; and poor Raymond had no idea how much she was scoring up against him. It may be if they had been given a fair start and there hadn't been the trouble with his parents and trouble coming from the chapel people and everything at once, it wouldn't have turned out so bad, in spite of what my mother said.

I felt quite soft about them that night. Raymond was looking fresh and clean, as he always did; and very peaceful. When later I learned his side of the story, I realised he had been through so many feelings in those two weeks, for the time being he had none left. It was as if his whole past was wiped out and he was starting afresh on a clean page. I heard Christine's side as well when the time came; but she was so angry, I don't trust what she said. I am more ready to believe Raymond, because he was more fair to her. I may have made a great mistake that night, though I was full of goodwill towards them both. When Christine had gone out to the kitchen to make some coffee, I asked Raymond if he was going to see his mother. He said they had already been to have tea at Prissy's, but he wasn't going to risk having Christine insulted. I said, 'Go on your own first, and ask your mother if you can bring Christine to see her. I don't see how she can refuse now you are married.' He said he would go.

I knew Hetty had a bad heart, or fancied she had a bad heart; but I didn't know she now got it into her head she was going to die. The whole time Raymond was on his honeymoon she stayed in bed, and my Cousin Mary Ann was there every day. Harold sent for the doctor, who said it was shock, but there was really nothing wrong with her and all she needed was rest and attention. Harold couldn't do enough for her and took her up fruit and chicken and cream cakes from Le Noury and everything she liked; but she wouldn't touch a thing he brought her, and made my Cousin Mary Ann promise she would always make the tea herself, in case he put poison in the pot. She unburdened her heart to my Cousin Mary Ann and cried and raved like a mad-woman. Harold was only waiting for her to die, so he could marry some young girl! He would sell up the house and everything and spend the lot on the new young wife. 'How the people will laugh,' said Hetty, 'when I am gone!'

Then to my Cousin Mary Ann's amazement, one day Hetty get up out of her bed and dresses herself in her best clothes and goes to Town on the bus; though she is so weak on her legs she hardly has the strength to walk to the four-cross to catch it. She was going to see a lawyer, she said, but Harold must on no account be told what she was gone to Town for. My Cousin Mary Ann had no idea then why Hetty wanted to see a lawyer; or what a lawyer could do about it. It do seem as if the fates was against Raymond, for it was on that very day he went to call on his mother on his own. He met his father in the yard. 'What are you doing here?' said Harold. 'I have come to see Ma,' Raymond said. 'You don't live here now,' said Harold. 'Clear out!' Raymond went deadly pale and began to tremble. According to my Cousin Mary Ann, he was going to hit Harold. I don't really believe Raymond was going to hit his father; but my Cousin Mary Ann ran out to separate them. Raymond walked away quietly with his head down. 'If only Hetty had stayed at home that day,' my Cousin Mary Ann said to me often, 'it would all have been different.'

10

I have never known for sure who it was kicked up a shindy over Raymond's sermon. The few people who spoke to me about it praised him. Reg Underwood thought he was grand and Mr Dorey, who always stopped and spoke to me when he saw me, said he had been glad to see me in the chapel and hoped I had enjoyed the service as much as he had. The scandal over Christine may have had something to do with it; but I wouldn't mind betting it was old Albert Nicolle who started the trouble. He was a local preacher and an old fool, who always brought Oliver Cromwell into his sermons, as being the one man who in the past had saved Guernsey from going to perdition. He hated me because I was Church, who he said was back-sliders and nearly as bad as the Roman Catholics, who was worshippers of idols of wood and stone. What made me angry about the whole affair, and it was so like those Chapel people, was it was all done behind Raymond's back. The first he heard of it was the day after he had been to see his mother, when he got a letter from his friend, the Reverend Charles Bingley, the head of his college.

Raymond didn't take it very serious. The Reverend Charles wrote that, not greatly to his surprise, he had received a complaint from the good people of Guernsey that his dear Raymond had preached a sermon of perhaps not quite sound doctrine. Raymond came to let me know he was going to England for a few days. He told me he had been to Wallaballoo and it had done no good; but he didn't tell me what had happened. I wasn't going to worry him about that then, but asked him if going to England meant he was being hauled over the coals. He said old Charles was like a father to him; but he was a fuss-pot. In his letter he had written that he hoped to be able to clear up Raymond's difficulties. 'I haven't got any difficulties,' said Raymond. 'They are the ones who got the difficulties.' He said Christine would miss him, and he wished she was going with him; but she thought it was better for him to go on his own. It would leave his mind free to put the matter right. Anyhow, he was wearing his dog's collar when he went; and when he came back, he wasn't.

He was rather proud of what he had done. I think he expected a pat on the back from me. 'I had to come and let you see I have gone back to nature,' he said, 'I bet you're pleased.' 'I am not at all pleased,' I said, 'and what about Christine? What do she say?' 'She hasn't said anything,' he said. I happen to know now she felt very bitter about it. At least he was sincere in the thoughts of his head with old Charles. The pity was when Raymond was sincere in the thoughts of his head, he left his heart out of count. If you are as sympathetic with people as Raymond was in his heart, you don't go round smashing their idols. It is like taking a toy from a child. I know if somebody was to smash my two china dogs I would feel like murder. He said straight out to a minister and his teacher, if you please, he didn't believe in the Virgin Birth or the Resurrection. Old Charles said they have to be accepted, or Jesus of Nazareth was not the Son of God. The Christian Church of every denomination was founded upon the fact that Jesus of Nazareth was the only begotten Son of God: not that He was a prophet, not even the greatest of the prophets. From what Raymond told me I thought that, for a minister, the Reverend Charles had been very patient and reasonable; and Raymond himself had shown no sense or moderation. He actually said if Jesus was born of a virgin without a natural father, far from being the Son of God, He was a freak. 'Well, I am not surprised the Reverend Charles turfed you out,' I said.

'Oh, he didn't turf me out,' said Raymond, 'He agrees with me really. Those people accept this and accept that; but they don't really think it happened. They decide to believe it.' Raymond got quite excited. 'If he had worked in the Greffe as long as I have,' he said, 'he would know you can't be sure exactly what it was happened fifty years ago, let alone two thousand. God isn't on record in a book! He is in the nature of every creature, and beyond the nature of every creature. He is in the nature of the world, and beyond the nature of the world. If you want to see where God has trod, you can go to Sark: you don't have to go to the Holy Land!' I said, 'Well, what did he do then? Tear your collar off?' 'No,' he said. 'I said I'd withdraw.' 'Is that all?' I said. 'He wanted me to go before a synod and plead my case,' he said. 'Why didn't you?' I said. He shrugged his shoulders. I wouldn't have minded so much if he had stuck up for what he thought and had been turfed out because of it; but just to back out, I had no patience! I didn't want to hear any more.

They had him back to the Greffe; and there he was, after years of studying and going to college, no forrarder than when he left school. It was arranged for Edna and the kid to live with the old people at Ivy Lodge for good; and Raymond and Christine made their home at Rosamunda. He paid his mother-in-law rent and, when the baker or the butcher or the grocer wouldn't let her have any more on tick, he paid the bills. He was soon keeping Christine's whole family. Rosamunda was only a one-storey cottage with two dormer windows and a small garden back and front. Raymond didn't seem to mind; but it was a great come-down for

Christine. For years she had only been a visitor to Guernsey, and thought of herself as a cut above the ordinary run of Guernsey people. Now she was almost one of the poor. To make matters worse, she had no idea how to look after a house. It was a pity, because Rosamunda could have been made into quite a nice little place for the two of them, if she had been the sensible country girl she ought to have been. Instead, she would sit and sew and embroider by the hour and, when she went out, looked as if she had stepped out of a band-box; but in the house she was a slut.

Raymond had to do most of the housework. He didn't grumble at having to do it; but what he didn't like was her untidyness. In his own home, and especially in his own room, everything had a place and everything was in its place. Christine didn't even bother to clear the table, but left the tablecloth and victuals on for the next meal; and there would be wool in the butter and hair-pins on the mantelpiece and dirty underclothes on the sofa. Raymond had to go round picking up after her. 'I'm getting him house-trained,' she said to me. That was one evening when I went down and found her in on her own. He didn't often go out by himself, but that evening he had gone to hear a Miss Margaret Murray lecture at the Ladies' College on 'The Religion of the Witches'. She upset me another way that evening. She was a virgin when she married Raymond; but only just. She had played as near the fire as she could without actually getting burnt since she was the age of twelve, I reckon; and now the fire was lit and burning, it was reaching out in all directions. I don't say she would have done anything, if it had come to the point; but the fluence was on, and she got me hot. I was glad to get out of that house. I vowed if ever I called again when Raymond was out and she said, 'Come in, come in, do! How nice of you to come and see me!' I would be in a hurry and wouldn't be able to come in. I would rather have killed myself than hurt Raymond in that way.

The Chapel people didn't give Raymond a chance. There was nothing said to him openly; but when Christmas came, he wasn't invited to any of the houses where he had been accustomed to go. He was treated as a criminal, or worse; for he was made to feel he had done something so bad it couldn't be talked about. It was partly his fault because he made no excuse, in fact said nothing about it; and all Christine would say was 'There was a disagreement unfortunately.' She still sang in the choir at the Capelles, but he didn't go to any chapel at all. 'It's a chance to get the house in order,' he said. He made no new friends; but she kept all hers as before. She was uppish with Prissy and didn't invite her to the house; but she did allow her to have them both to tea once a week at Timbuctoo. Prissy would then go round and repeat to Hetty everything she had been able to find out. Hetty lived through the winter. She got up, but didn't go out: only dragged herself about the house from morning to night, trying to keep it clean. My

Cousin Mary Ann told me she would listen to every word Prissy had to say about Raymond and Christine, but wouldn't give a message, or say a word could be passed on. Prissy was pretending she was trying to make peace, or perhaps she really was doing her best; but all Hetty would say was 'It is not to be.'

I can't say I treated Raymond any better than the others; for the once I found him on his own I quarrelled with him, and didn't go again. He kept on talking about that Clive Holyoak. He said Clive was quite right when he said 'He who can, lives: he who cannot, preaches.' I said, 'Clive have no right whatever to say any such thing. He play his fiddle.' Raymond laughed at that. He said, 'Luckily you don't have to be examined in doctrine to play the fiddle.' I said, 'If I had your head on my shoulders and could put things into words as you can, I certainly wouldn't be satisfied with going fishing and growing tomatoes. It is all wrong for you only to be working at the Greffe. It is throwing away the gifts of God.' He said, 'I want to be an ordinary chap. I don't want to be one of a peculiar people, as Saint Peter says. If there is anything in me, it will come out anyway.' I said, 'I would have more respect for you if you was to go and stand up in a waggon on the Albert Pier like Sequois used to do, and spout to anybody who would listen to you.' 'I couldn't do that,' he said. 'I know you couldn't,' I said. 'You're soft! It's a waste of breath talking to you! It's all very well to believe in love; but you got to fight for it. Even a cow got horns!' I was angry.

It is impossible for me to say how much Raymond was not an ordinary chap. There was something in his looks and in his voice and in his manner and in the goodness of his heart, I think, drew people to him and made them like him and listen to him, even against their will. I hadn't forgotten what he had done at that service. He hadn't made us feel we was miserable sinners; or, as with most preachers, those outside was miserable sinners and our little lot was bound for heaven. He made us feel there was something good deep in the world, and something good deep in everybody. If he made even me feel that, there must have been something in him; for I am nothing, if not hard-headed.

It was soon after Easter when my Cousin Mary Ann telephoned to Raymond at the Greffe and said to come to Wallaballoo at once because his mother was dangerously ill. Actually Hetty was dead when my Cousin Mary Ann telephoned; but she put it that way to break the news. Hetty had only been in bed a few days and it was thought she would be up and about again, as she was before. It is true she was afraid to eat anything given her and would only drink water; and Harold was being made to sleep in Raymond's old room. She couldn't bear to have him near her. That last afternoon she asked my Cousin Mary Ann to give her something was hidden under some clothes at the bottom of a drawer. It was a long envelope with Raymond's name written on it in Hetty's big childish handwriting. She died holding it tight in her hand. My Cousin Mary Ann telephoned to Raymond before she went to fetch Harold. Raymond told me he felt no grief when his mother died. That came later. When he got the telephone message, he thought at once she might be dead already and, cycling home along the front, he was only hoping she was. He dreaded a death-bed scene. He felt he couldn't stand any more scenes with his mother.

Harold was sitting huddled over the fire when Raymond came in. He was completely broken up. 'She's gone, my Hetty,' he said. All Raymond's sympathies went over immediately to his father and, if it hadn't been for that horrible Mrs Crewe, it might have been all right yet between father and son. They went upstairs together. The doctor had been, but the envelope was still in her hand. Raymond looked at his mother lying dead. Her face when she was alive had always been full of soft feelings. Raymond said in death it was frozen stern and hard as marble. He only felt a great load was lifted from his shoulders. Harold said, 'Aren't you going to read what your mother has written to you?' Raymond had a fear of what it might be from the shape of the envelope. He read it downstairs while my Cousin Mary Ann, saying nothing but all ears, was moving about on tiptoe making tea for the two of them. It was a will. Hetty had managed to get a lawyer to draw it up, whether it was legal or not. As there was a marriage contract, it might have been proved, after a lot of wrangling. It left everything to Raymond with only a life-interest for his father. Raymond gave it to his father to read; but, of course, Harold couldn't understand it. Raymond was used to such things. He explained. Harold said, 'Well, it is your mother's will, son.' Raymond tore it across and across and threw the pieces on the fire. My Cousin Mary Ann was the only one who ever knew; and she didn't tell a soul until she told me years after they was all dead. She went to fetch Prissy; and, once Prissy came, there was no peace in that house until after the funeral.

She came running with the tears streaming down her face. 'Ah, la pauvre Hetty! la pauvre Hetty!' In not a minute the tears was all forgotten. 'I don't suppose she ever even thought of getting a thing ready beforehand. She was always like that, my sister! It was always me who had to get her ready if she was going anywhere, or she would never have got there in time! Ah, la pauvre Hetty! la pauvre Hetty!' Tears! tears! tears! 'Mary Ann, don't you stand there like a mommet doing nothing, you! Is there a big kettle of water on the boil? Have she got a clean night-dress? Or is it in the wash? Ah, la pauvre Hetty! la pauvre Hetty!' Tears! tears! tears! 'Harold, have you written to the *Press* yet? If not, Raymond can telephone and pay when he go to Town. Are you sure, Mary Ann, you have pulled down the blinds of all the front rooms? Is there a white curtain for the window over the door? If not, you better put up a pillowcase. Ah, la pauvre Hetty! la pauvre Hetty!' Tears! tears! tears! 'Raymond, have you got that black suit yet from when you was a minister? It will do for the funeral. After the day, you can wear your sports coat with a black tie and a black band on the arm. People don't go into mourning now like they used to. Harold, you mustn't forget to buy a plot of ground to bury her in. The grave of our mother is full. In any case, this house is in St Sampson's, so it will have to be in the cemetery of St Sampson's. It will do for you as well, when your time comes. Order a small stone with just room for the two names. Raymond will want to be buried with Christine. Ah, la pauvre Hetty! la pauvre Hetty!' Tears! tears! tears!

Raymond had three days off from the Greffe; and with Prissy in charge at Wallaballoo everybody moved at the double and didn't have time to think. The night before the funeral, my Cousin Mary Ann was sitting down to supper with Harold and Prissy. Prissy was saying, 'Ah well, I think everything is done and ready now. If it hadn't been for me, my poor dear dead sister would have been left to rot on her bed,' when there was a knock on the front door. My Cousin Mary Ann went to see who it was. It was Mrs Crewe. 'I think Mr Martel will be wanting a housekeeper,' she said. 'Mr Martel will not be wanting to talk about any such thing now,' said my Cousin Mary Ann. 'He has a dead wife in the house.' 'It is not the dead I am thinking of,' said Mrs Crewe, 'it is the living.' For once in her life my Cousin Mary Ann didn't know what to say or do, and went back in the kitchen to ask. Mrs Crewe followed her in.

Mère Quéripel was a witch; but I don't know if she looked like a witch. Mrs Crewe looked how a witch ought to look, even if she don't. She wasn't as old as Harold quite, but she had scores of wrinkles and looked older, and she had the chin of a witch and the nose of a witch and bright, bright greedy eyes. She spoke as if she wouldn't hurt a fly. 'I saw the white curtain over the door in passing,' she said, 'and I thought there is no time like the present.' It was funny, if she only saw the curtain over the door in passing, she had brought a bag with a night-dress and an apron in it. Prissy said, 'Harold, this is meant! I have the summer visitors coming and can't be over here every day; and you know yourself you can't as much as boil an egg!' My Cousin Mary Ann, who didn't trust Mrs Crewe from the start, said, 'Well, it is rather late to get a bed aired for you to sleep in tonight.' 'I can sleep on the sofa,' said Mrs Crewe, 'or in a chair. I don't want to put anybody to any trouble. I am here to help.' When my Cousin Mary Ann went to close the front door, expecting to find it open as she had left it, she found Mrs Crewe had closed it herself as she came in.

Poor Hetty had a grand funeral. A hearse and the coffin covered with flowers; and a long line of motor-cars. Harold sent a motor-car especially to fetch my mother, and I went with her. It was her last outing. Raymond wore a bowler hat, I remember. Prissy said a bowler hat would do for a son. It wasn't worth while to buy a box hat just to wear once. It looked like a black pudding on his head. Harold and Percy wore box hats. There was tea and bread-and-butter and cheese at the house after; and a lot of cousins of the Martels I had never seen, or heard of, came back. I don't expect Hetty had ever seen or heard of them either; and I dare not think what she would have said if she had known Christine was there. Mrs Crewe waited at the table. Harold asked her to sit down and eat with the others; but she said it wasn't her place to sit down with the family.

After tea, Harold brought down the box in which Hetty had kept her jewels. She had been buried with her wedding ring, but the rest was in the box. He asked Prissy to take anything she fancied for all she had done. She chose the gold necklace and locket. Then he asked Christine if she would choose something. She said, 'That brooch is lovely.' She hadn't said a word until then. It was a gold brooch made like a spider's web and studded with small jewels; and Harold had bought it for Hetty in London on their honeymoon. He pinned it on Christine's simple black dress. She said, 'That is very good of you.' I thought it was too. He was thoughtful of my mother. It was no use offering her jewellery, because she wouldn't wear it; but he made a car wait to take her home. It saved me having to hire one, for she couldn't have walked it. Prissy came to the road to see us off. 'Ah well,' she said, 'my poor dear dead sister will be able to rest in peace now she know she have been properly buried.'

11

I get mixed up as to when it was they changed the money. I can't remember if it was when they called in the sovereigns, or before, or after. I thought it was a lot of nonsense, anyhow. We had managed all right up to then with francs and fippennies and Guernsey pennies; and English money for stamps or a Postal Order. The things in the shops was marked in English and we paid in French or Guernsey, and it was quite simple. When the French money was got rid of and the Guernsey pennies was counted as English, we lost a shilling in the pound because the shops didn't put down their prices. As for doubles, they are not worth anything now; and I have still got an egg-cupful my mother used to keep handy to give the baker change from a farthing. Now, after all these years, they are talking of changing the money back so that you can reckon up in tens again. They can't leave well alone.

It was the same over the daylight saving. I don't see how you can save daylight, when there is only the same number of hours of daylight anyway, whatever you do to the clocks. It was before the War they got that bright idea; and we have had to have our dinner at eleven in the morning all the summer, instead of in the middle of the day, as is natural. It didn't make any difference to the number of hours we worked. In Guernsey everybody work from sunrise to dark and nowadays, they even have electric light in the greenhouses and work half the night. We are not a lazy lot like they are in England.

I know I had my mother with me yet when the sovereigns was called in, because I remember I talked it over with her. There was a notice in the paper that after a certain date sovereigns would no longer be legal tender, but up to that date they could be taken to any bank and changed for pound notes. Gerald Mahy said half the population must have had sovereigns hidden away, because for weeks he did nothing else but count the things. There was one old couple from Albecq, who you would have thought to look at didn't have a penny to bless themselves with, walked into the Old Bank with two tomato-baskets full; and they knew exactly how many there was in each basket too. I didn't have as many as that; but there was well over four figures in the pied-du-cauche. I didn't fancy giving all those to a bank to lose.

I don't believe in banks. I am quite capable of looking after my own money, thank you. Come to that, I can't see what banks are for, except to make money out of other people's money: and then, when they go bust, they don't pay it back. All the same, I asked my mother what she thought, because the sovereigns was hers as much as mine. I explained to her we wouldn't be able to spend them in the shops; but gold is gold and we would have it. She said, 'It says in The Word "Lay not up treasure for yourselves upon earth where moth and rust doth corrupt, and thieves break through and steal; but lay up for yourselves treasure in heaven, where moth and rust doth not corrupt and thieves do not break through and steal." Let us abide by The Word.' I knew then she didn't want a bank to have our sovereigns.

I was by no means pleased when, the summer after Hetty died, Master Dudley Waine with an 'e' turned up again, looking for his old stones. I thought I had seen the last of that nuisance. He came mooching round the garden and round the house and, by chance, his eye fell on my pigsty. 'It is! it is!' he said; and was down on his knees examining the big stone made the trough in the wall I fed the pigs through. The old pig was interested, him: he thought Dudley was something good to eat. Dudley didn't mind. 'Is it possible to get this out?' he said to me. I said, 'It is NOT possible to get it out!' He said it was part of an ancient barrow of the Old Stone Age. I said, 'Well, I don't know nothing about that! I wasn't here then. All I know is it was put there in my grandfather's day when the house was built; and there it is going to stay!' He said it was a crying scandal the way the people of Guernsey made use of the sacred stones of their ancestors for building barns and stables and pigsties. I said, 'Now you listen here, Mr Waine: if you think you are going to start digging up my property, you are making the biggest mistake of your life. There are plenty other places where you can go and dig; and I sincerely hope you will find what you are looking for.' He said he would be over to see me again the next year, by which time he hoped I would have thought better on the matter.

I didn't see any more of him that summer, but he got to know Raymond. They must have met at Prissy's where he was staying. Raymond was never interested in pre-historic Guernsey. He said historic Guernsey was too much for him; but he did show Dudley some papers at the Greffe about old graves and stones which have since disappeared. There was none said there had ever been any such things in the gully of La Petite Grève. Dudley must also have met Christine; but, as far as I know, they didn't become great friends that year.

Raymond went to see his father regular after his mother died. At first

Mrs Crewe was very humble, and called him Mr Martel; but once, when she saw him coming, she came to the door and said, 'Raymond, your father is not very well today. I don't think you ought to bother him. He has had a great shock and is an old man, you know.' Another time, when Mrs Crewe happened to be out and Raymond did get to his father, Harold asked after Christine. She hadn't been to see him since the funeral. 'Why don't she come and see me as well?' Harold said. 'She says she doesn't want to push herself,' Raymond explained. Harold pooh-poohed the idea, and said the next Sunday they must both go to tea. They went. Harold made a great to-do of Christine and, so Raymond said, flirted with her. I have no doubt in my own mind she led him on. Raymond was shocked. 'I had no idea my father could behave in that way,' he said. Mrs Crewe had prepared a good tea for them, for she was a good housekeeper; but when they sat down to table, she came over faint and couldn't touch a mouthful herself. She said she had the palpitations. They didn't eat much, or stay very long. When they said good-bye and thank you, her palpitations miraculously disappeared.

Harold really was poorly in his health for some months after the death of Hetty, and I daresay having Mrs Crewe there livened him up. For one thing, she got him to take her to the Pictures. He hadn't been able to go to the Pictures with Hetty, because he would have had to keep his cap on; but he could sit next to Mrs Crewe without his cap. She didn't care if he had a bald head, so long as he got money in the bank. Then one Sunday, when Raymond and Christine went to tea again, and Mrs Crewe did stuff down a little, Raymond said it would be a good idea if they all went to the Pictures together one night. He didn't go to the Pictures as a rule, but he thought for once he would stand the old couple a treat. He ordered a car to take them all there and back, and booked four seats in the balcony at St Julien's for the Thursday evening. When he and Christine called with the car, Mrs Crewe fainted good and proper. Harold had to lay her out flat on the sofa and give her brandy. When she opened her eyes and saw by the clock there was still time for them to get there, she fainted again. Harold had to stop at home and get her round, and Raymond and Christine go to the Pictures on their own.

It got through even Raymond's thick skull that he and Christine wasn't being made exactly welcome by Mrs Crewe. One night when he saw a light in the work-shop, he sneaked round the house to have a chat with his father by himself. 'It isn't much good Christine and me coming to see you,' he said, 'if every time we enter the house Mrs Crewe falls unconscious.' 'A man can't live alone,' said Harold. Raymond explained he didn't expect his father to live alone, but surely there were enough good motherly old souls on the island for him to get hold of a decent housekeeper, if he advertised. 'Mrs Crewe gives me the creeps,' said Raymond. 'She is used to my ways now; and she is going to stay!' said Harold, 'and since you have made your own bed, I think you had better go and lie on it.' Raymond said, 'Well, you can always come and see us at any time: it isn't a mile away. If you are taken sick, or anything, be sure you send one of your chaps to let us know at once.' It was an unlucky thing to say; but Raymond didn't mean it at all in the way Harold took it. 'I am going to live a long time yet,' said Harold, 'don't you worry about that, my young shaver; and don't you have any hopes either!'

I wasn't seeing Raymond at the time; but I heard from Prissy he had stopped going to see his father. She was all on Raymond's side. She said she would never, never go inside Wallaballoo again, as long as that Mrs Crewe was there. She had been once and it appears the two ladies had 'had words'. I don't know what they said to each other, those two; but I would have given anything to have been there and heard them at it. They was well-matched. La Prissy, of course, found out all there was to find out about Mrs Crewe, and came and told us. She was the widow of a sergeant-major from the Town Arsenal, and had been housekeeper to goodness knows how many old gentlemen, who died and left her money and property. She owned a house in the Rohais and another at the Vrangue; and had a niece she was paying for at the Ladies' College, who she was going to leave all her money to. I listened; but there was nothing I could do. I had my own troubles.

It was a hard winter. I got in tons of coal from the Bird Bros to try and keep my mother warm; but she was always cold. Of an evening after tea, when the lamp was lit, I would sit and read her the Births, Deaths and Marriages to cheer her up. Her poor old eyes was going. She could see to read the big print in the Bible through her magnifying-glass, but she couldn't see to read the *Press*. I would read out 'Elizabeth Le Cras (née Heaume), aged 47, beloved wife of Frederick Le Cras of Le Vaugrat. Gone but not forgotten.' 'Um,' my mother would say. 'Well, now he will be able to marry that young Amelia Robin from La Ramée, and it is high time too!' I don't know about the next world; but about this world she was never far wrong, my mother. Sure enough, in a month or so there was the wedding in the *Press*; and, a few weeks later, the birth.

It was one night after Christmas we had the worst storm I have ever lived through. From the noise on the roof, I thought the rain was coming down solid; and there was a rumbling behind the house made me think Mont Cuet was going to fall on top of us. My mother went to bed as usual. She wasn't afraid if it was the end: she was ready. Myself, I lay awake half the night, afraid of what I would find when I went out in the morning. To my astonishment, I didn't have a pane of glass broken, and Percy's wall had kept my land from being washed away; but what I hadn't taken of what may have been the old lady's land at the top of the gully was gone and, among the mud and rubbage, I noticed a number of rough brown stones like the one the builder for my grandfather had used for the trough of the pigsty. They wasn't arranged in any special way; but a few days later I went down and had a look at those by Sandy Hook and saw how it was done. I thought it would be a pity if, when Dudley Waine came to see me the next summer, he didn't find what he was looking for.

My mother died in the February. It came as a surprise, rather; for she was up, as usual, and seemed better, if anything. I ought to have known when my Cousin Mary Ann turned up that day after dinner to ask if there was anything she could do. She washed up the dishes and said she would scrub out the kitchen. I went out to the greenhouse to transplant some seedlings in boxes. It was the first year I had thought of growing my own tomato plants from seeds, instead of buying young plants big enough to put in the ground from Mr Dorey. When I came in, the kitchen smelt nice and clean and my Cousin Mary Ann had laid the table for tea. I asked her to have it with us, and she laid a place for herself and cleared up after. I gave her a cut off the ham to take home, and she said she would come again next day in case there was anything more I wanted done. The boy had brought the *Press* and I read it to my mother. I got the supper and cleared away and washed up; and, after, she sat up to the table by the light, reading her Bible.

I think the religion of my mother was the most frightful I have ever heard of. I don't know what her idea of heaven was, for she didn't often speak of heaven. In the Bible it say they play harps up there; but that would never have done for my mother. I know what she thought hell was like. The damned was going to be tormented for ever and ever in the presence of the holy angels, and have no rest day or night. The awful part was it was all cut and dried before you was born, which place you was going to. If I had thought that, it would have left me free to be as wicked as I liked in this world, since it wouldn't make any difference in the next; but my mother was a good woman. It is true she didn't go out of her way to help other people; but she didn't interfere either, and make trouble. She was always for peace.

It may be she knew what I was thinking that night, sitting in the arm-chair by the fire, smoking my pipe, while she was reading her Bible; for she often knew what I was thinking, almost before I did. She was reading half aloud in her sad-sing-song voice from the Book of Revelations, and I could hear the terrible words 'and the abominable and murderers and whoremongers and sorcerers and idolaters and all liars shall have their part in the lake which burneth with fire and brimstone' and I was thinking well, I am one of those; when she stopped reading and put down her reading-glass and looked at me in a strange way. 'It is a pity,' she said, 'it is a great pity!' and her old eyes filled with tears and they splashed on to the pages of the Bible.

I went and lit the candle in her room, as I always did; and came back and helped her to get up from her chair. She walked to her room without my help and I followed her in and undid the hooks of her bodice and her waistband, so as she could undress herself. 'Good-night, my mother,' I said; and she said, 'Good-night, my son.' In the morning I had cooked the breakfast and made the tea; but she hadn't come in. Usually she came out of her room when she heard the teapot; and I would hook up her dress for her. I think I knew then she was dead. I called out and knocked on her door; and, when there was no answer, I went in. She was lying on her back with her eyes closed, as if she was asleep, and her arms crossed on her breast. The puffiness of her cheeks and round her eyes was gone, and her straight white hair was drawn back, showing her high forehead. She had a noble face. I went to the Post Office at L'Islet to telephone for the doctor and when I came back my Cousin Mary Ann was there.

I had to let Prissy know. I went down to Timbuctoo and knocked on the front door, but couldn't make anybody hear. I went round the back, but Percy wasn't about; so I walked in and through the kitchen, and called up the stairs. I heard a bedroom door open and Prissy came out on the landing with her hair in curling papers, and wearing only a chemise and a petticoat. 'Whazzit?' she said. She was drunk. I said my mother had died in her sleep. In a split-second she was stone sober. 'Wait a minute while I dress,' she said. 'I will come with you and see to everything!' 'No, no!' I said. 'My Cousin Mary Ann and Ada Domaille and Tabitha will do all that is needful.' I wasn't going to be ordered about in my own house and run off my feet by Prissy. 'She can be buried with your father's Le Pages in the cemetery of the Vale Church,' she said. 'There is plenty of room. They have died all over the world, that family.' I said, 'She is going to be buried Chapel.'

I had to buy a burial plot and decided on a private funeral for mourners only. I wanted her to be buried with dignity. I didn't want the nonsense of a tea-party afterwards, and a lot of cousins who she didn't even know having a good meal for nothing. There was a hearse and two carriages. There was no flowers on the coffin; because she wouldn't ever have a flower, even in the house. Harold came and Percy; and a Mess Tardivel from the Brethren. Mess Tardivel said a few words by the grave. It was a cold, windy day, and grey; but it didn't rain.

I wanted a stone put over her grave, and thought Percy might as well do it. He wanted to know what to put on. I thought IN MEMORY OF CHARLOTTE LE PAGE and her age and the date she died, and, underneath, the words REST IN PEACE would be enough. It was the best I could wish for anybody; but La Prissy said I ought to have as well UNTIL THE RESURRECTION MORN, and I gave in. It was two-and-six a letter; but, after all, she was my mother.

12

Tabitha offered to leave the Priaulx and come and keep house for me; but I wouldn't hear of it. I knew she would have more of everything where she was than she would ever have with me. Besides, she had company. She was quiet, my sister, and while she had Jean she was quite satisfied to be only with him; but, once he was gone, she liked to do things for other people. The Priaulx, from the children who was growing up to the old lady who was now an invalid, depended on her; yet they knew her worth and didn't put upon her. She always found time to knit me socks and do my mending; and she came often to see how I was making out. She sorted out my mother's clothes, and the best I sent to the Brethren for them to sell, or give away. I got Percy to come and do out what had been my mother's room and make it bright. It had always been dark while she was alive, and she would never let me have it done.

Raymond was another who turned up trumps. He came with a message from Christine: at least, he said it was from Christine, but I am sure it was his own idea. It was that I must go there for dinner Sundays, and any evening after work, if I didn't want the trouble of getting myself a meal. I didn't go as often as he said; but I went often enough. I felt uncomfortable about it at first, because I couldn't very well offer to pay him anything; but the garden at the back was in a mess and I said he could easily grow enough fruit and vegetables for themselves and, if he liked, I would give him a hand of an evening. He was quite willing and I brought most of the stuff and started him off. I had thought till then he was only good for books and preaching, and hadn't expected much of him as a gardener; but he had the green fingers, that boy, and I was surprised at the success he made of it.

I enjoyed those evenings and I think he did too. It was nice working together in the cool of the evening and with the smell of burning weeds going up in the air. Those was the only times he talked to me as he used to. When Christine was there he hadn't much to say for himself. She had a way of getting in between him and anybody else he was friendly with. Of course, she made out I was a great friend of hers as well; but I never knew quite what was going on behind those cat's eyes and that moon face and that holy voice. Raymond took her at her face value, and thought every word she said was sincere. She needn't have worried over anything he might say to me about her. He never said a word wasn't in praise of her. He was building up in his mind his dream of a perfect marriage. It wasn't the Kingdom of Heaven he was dreaming about now. Marriage was his religion. He was delighted when I told him I thought Christine was looking very well. She was, as a matter of fact. She never again looked so well as she did those years she was living with Raymond. He said he wished she was going to have a baby. It was the only justification for a man and a woman going together. Every other reason was an excuse. Well, that isn't the opinion of most people nowadays. 'I want a dozen,' he said. I wondered how he was going to keep a dozen on his wages from the Greffe.

Prissy tried to be a help to me too, in her funny way; but she was more of a nuisance than anything else. When Percy and his chap was doing my mother's room, she came to give me advice as to how I must manage in future. The first thing I must do was to get me a wife. To hear her talk, I might have gone to Town and bought one in the French Halls. The girl must be young and strong because, after all, I was getting on. She must be a country girl who wasn't afraid of work; and be able to cook and clean and look after babies. She must on no account be the flighty sort; and it would be all to the good if she had a bit of money of her own. Poor Prissy must have thought I was taking her advice to heart when I said Percy might as well paint the whole house inside and out, while he was about it. I don't think she ever found out what I did do.

I ought to laugh at myself now for what I did. I went to see Liza. I waited until the house was done and my crop was planted and spring was on the way. If I had been eighteen years old I couldn't have behaved more like a young fool. I decided not to go on my bike, because I would get dusty and have my trousers creased from the bicycle-clips. I put on my best suit with a black band round the arm and a black tie; and I went on the bus and tram to Town, and then on the bus to Pleinmont. I was as nervous as a boy with his first girl: far more nervous than I had been with my first, who I wasn't nervous with at all. I didn't know what I would find when I got there. I had asked Ada from time to time how Liza was getting on; and she always said, 'She is keeping very well,' but that was all. I wondered if there would be a lodger; or, if perhaps Liza was married by now and I had missed seeing it in the *Press*. If there was a lodger I could fight him and get him thrown out; but I didn't know what I was going to do if there was a husband.

I got off the bus at the Imperial and walked back along across the grass. The old house was still there and had the same crooked chimney and the wicked windows that looked at you sideways from under the thatch; but there was bright-coloured curtains in the windows now and the wood-work was painted yellow and the door light blue; and, in front, was flowers, flowers, flowers. I walked down the path and knocked on the front door. It opened of itself as I knocked, because it wasn't properly shut. I saw right into the room and the back door was open as well. Nobody was in; but I knew Liza couldn't be far.

I walked round the back; and there was Liza feeding the fowls, as she said she would be. She was wearing a light grey skirt and a white silk blouse and had on a fancy apron she was holding up by the corners, full of corn. She was teasing the fowls and throwing a handful here and a handful there, so they had to run all over the place for it. That was how I wanted to see her in my own back garden. It was as if she knew I was watching her; for she looked my way suddenly. She gave a sort of cry and emptied the apronful of corn all over the poor birds, so they was fighting and jumping on each other to get it. 'Ebenezer!' she cried. 'How lovely of you to come and see me!' and she ran to meet me and was in my arms. She didn't kiss me: just hugged and hugged. 'Where are the sabots and the scoop?' I said. She wasn't wearing nothing on her head, and had on good brown leather shoes. 'Give me a chance!' she said. 'I'll come to that yet.' I bet you won't, if I know anything about it, I thought.

'Come indoors!' she said, 'I want to hear all about you.' I think two rooms had been knocked into one since the days of her grandmother and mother; for it was quite a largish room. It had a low ceiling of oak beams and an open hearth and a terpid, and the green-bed against the bulge of the wall, where the old oven was; but now there was coloured cushions on the armchair and thick rugs on the stone floor, and the green-bed was made comfortable for sleeping on. The other side was a form against the wall, built in with the house, and the table was full length along it. I noticed a number of brass ornaments on a cabinet: boats, a lighthouse, a windmill; and, in the place of honour among them, was the silver Guernsey milk-can I had given her. There was a ladder up to the loft; and I gave it a sideways look. 'That's for the lodger,' she said laughing, 'but I haven't got him yet.'

She made me sit in the big armchair, and curled herself up on the green-bed to talk to me. 'I was sorry to hear about your mother,' she said. I said, 'Well, it was a peaceful end. I wouldn't mind going the same way myself.' 'I have been thinking about you a lot lately,' she said. 'I want you to get married now and have a family. It is the only way you will ever be happy.' I said, 'I quite agree with you.' She said, 'I have given Ada strict instructions to keep an eye on you, because it has to be to a very special girl; and I will have to see her first and approve. I am not having my Ebenezer made miserable.' I didn't like the way the talk was going at all. I was losing my bearings. 'It is too beautiful this weather to be indoors, don't you think?' she said. 'Shall we go for a walk on the cliffs?' I said, 'Yes, let's do that!' I wanted to get her on another tack.

She put on a grey pleated jacket went with the skirt, and we went for our walk up as far as the Old Guard House. It was a lovely afternoon and the sea was like silk. I remember the wild daffodils growing on the hedges and, ever since, when I see wild daffodils I think of Liza. I didn't say anything on the way; and nor did she. I wanted that walk to go on and on and on, for I knew somehow there wouldn't be such another. At last, when we got to the Guard House, I said, 'I have come to see you today with one purpose, Liza, and that is to ask you to marry me.' She said, 'Oh, why must you spoil it? I was feeling so happy to be with you!' I said, 'If you don't want to marry me because you don't like me, say so; but, for goodness sake, give me a reason.' 'I will die a virgin,' she said. 'A funny sort of virgin!' I said. 'I am a virgin, didn't you know?' she said. I said, 'Well, you won't be a virgin for long, if you marry me!' 'That is just what I am afraid of,' she said. 'Now what do you mean?' I said. 'I wouldn't be me any longer,' she said. I said, 'You would be Mrs Ebenezer Le Page of Les Moulins.' That finished it!

'Mrs Ebenezer Le Page of Les Moulins! Mrs Ebenezer Le Page of Les Moulins!' she said, 'and all the people would say "I wonder what in the world that Liza Quéripel, who have lived for years among the English and the gentry, can be thinking about to marry that Ebenezer Le Page from Les Moulins, who is only a rough Guernseyman and a small grower and fisherman and got nothing and is nobody!"' I said, 'I got enough to feed you and keep a roof over your head, anyhow. I know you got money of your own, and I wish you didn't. I don't want it; but you can spend it on your clothes. I like to see you well dressed.' 'Oh my dear, my dear,' she said, 'as if I meant that! I am only saying what the people would say. They would say far worse things about me. "I wonder what on earth that Ebenezer Le Page, who is an honest, decent fellow and work hard and look after his mother until she die, can see in that Liza Quéripel, who for all her grand ways come from the lowest of the low and is a gad-about and a fly-by-night and think of nothing but to make a show of herself. She will never make a good wife for any man, that one!"' I laughed. It was my old trouble with Liza. I felt I wanted to strangle her; and I laughed!

She caught hold of my arm and said, 'Come on, let's go back across the fields, eh? I want to see the three churches.' I let her drag me back across the fields. It was no use me being sulky. I couldn't make her marry me, if she didn't want to. We got to a spot from which we could see the three churches: Torteval Church and St Saviour's Church and the Church of St Peter-in-the-Wood. I wasn't interested in seeing the three churches; and I doubt if she was either. It was just something to look at like most people pass their time doing who come to Guernsey nowadays. She gave me a good tea when we got in; but I didn't know what I was eating. She talked to me about her house and how she'd had it done up inside and out. 'Eva Gallienne comes in to clean,' she said. I didn't know who she was talking about. 'Remember Eva Robilliard?' she said, 'Queen Elizabeth. She is married to a Gallienne now and have five children. The eldest is a hulking

great brute of nineteen who comes and does my digging for me.' I found it
hard to believe it was all those years ago Eva Robilliard was bowing and
throwing kisses to the people at the Coronation Fête. Liza didn't look a
day over thirty, if that.

After tea I said I must be going. 'You're not going yet, surely,' she said. I
said, 'Well, I got to get home some time; and the bus don't go late.' 'Why,
you're your own master,' she said, 'you don't have to be at work at seven in
the morning Go home tomorrow.' 'Liza,' I said, 'I want you open and
above board: before God and all men. Or not at all!' 'As you please,' she
said. I said, 'Well, good-bye, then. I don't expect I will see you again.' I
didn't make to kiss her; or offer to shake hands. She made no movement
either. 'If there is ever anything I can do for you, let me know,' she said, 'I
know it won't be for yourself: you would be too proud to ask; but for
anyone dear to you. I wish I could make you happy.' She was crying when
I left her.

I caught the bus to Town and the tram to the Half-way and walked the
rest. I was too down-hearted even to call in at Hutton's for a drink. It was
dark when I got indoors and I lit the lamp. The house was empty, empty,
empty! I was alone and I knew I would be alone for the rest of my days. I
don't know how I have managed to live since then. I have had friends or, at
least, people I have talked to; and many people have been good to me. I
can't ever say how good Tabitha have been to me; but I took it for granted
while she lived. I have chased after this girl, or that girl, when the spirit
moved me; or, more likely, as Raymond would have said, from force of
habit. I have lived in Raymond's tragic story as if it was my own; but it is a
mystery to me yet, and perhaps I put things wrong when I tried to put
things right. I have held my own against strangers and against enemies
from another country; and against the double-faced behaviour of some of
my own people. I have seen the funny side of things, and made a lot of
people laugh; and I suppose they have thought I am the happy-go-lucky
sort: but since that night I have lived without hope. I have often wondered
what it is I can have done wrong to have to live for so many years without
hope. It is no wonder I think a lot and am a bit funny in the head.

The next night I went down to Raymond's. I couldn't face being in the
house by myself. I didn't altogether like the idea of going, because I didn't
want to get so as I would have to depend on Raymond and Christine; but,
as it happened, it was a good thing I went. Christine was in the kitchen
getting the meal ready. I thought she wasn't looking as pleased with herself
as usual; and I liked her better. 'Will a cold supper do?' she said. 'Yes, of
course!' I said. 'Raymond is in a mood,' she said. 'I can't do anything with
him. I wish you would go in and speak to him.' I found him in the front
room. For the moment I thought he was having a fit. He was sitting on the
floor, pale as a ghost and trembling; and all around him was books I had

seen in his room at Wallaballoo, books from when he was to school, his picture of *The Light of the World*, photos of himself from a baby onwards torn out of the Family Album, baby-clothes and the wickerwork cradle on rockers he had been put in when he was born; and he was touching this thing and that thing, and then pushing it away. 'They are my things,' he kept on saying. 'They are my things! He has sent me all my things!' 'Who?' I said. 'My father,' he said. 'He has sent me everything might remind him of me. He doesn't want anything of me left in the house!' 'Come on, sit up and pull yourself together!' I said. I lifted him up and sat him in the arm-chair, and sat on the arm beside him. 'Now tell me all about it,' I said. He managed to tell me, more or less sensibly.

Harold had sent a chap down with a hand-truck loaded with everything he could find in the house that belonged to Raymond, or had anything to do with him. There wasn't only his toys from when he was a child, but even the letters he had written to his mother when he was in England. The chap said Harold was going to sell up Wallaballoo and buy another house and marry Mrs Crewe. It didn't worry Raymond his father was selling up Wallaballoo. I don't think it even entered his head he wouldn't inherit a penny. Another house Harold could leave to Mrs Crewe. It was being turned out of his father's heart hurt Raymond. 'He needn't have done this to me,' he said. 'He wishes I had never been born! He doesn't want me to be alive! Christine doesn't understand.' 'I understand,' I said, 'but it isn't quite as you say. It is your father's idea of being straight.' It was, in a way. Harold wouldn't keep a thing that had once belonged to Raymond; and then his conscience would be clear. 'He wants to start on a clean sheet,' I said. 'He was the same over his first wife, when he married your mother. All her things was got rid of. She had to be forgotten. It is all, or nothing with your father.' 'I am rather like that myself,' said Raymond. I thought, you are indeed; and you get that, not from Hetty, but from Harold.

I said, 'Now let's get some order in this muddle,' and I put the toys together and the letters together, and helped him sort out the books. He said he would hang the picture over the bed in their room. I said, 'Anyhow, the cradle will come in handy.' He smiled. 'I hope so,' he said. When Christine called us in for supper, he was quite himself again. I saw her give him a quick look; but when she saw he was all right, she carried on as if nothing had happened. I admired her good sense. Nothing was said to upset anybody during the meal; and, afterwards he said he would do the washing-up, and she came to the gate with me. She took my hand in both of hers. 'Thank you, thank you for coming tonight of all nights,' she said. 'I don't know what I would have done. I can manage Raymond on his own; but not when he got his parents round his neck. Mothers and fathers are all right, if you bring them up the way they ought to go. I have.'

13

My Cousin Mary Ann was the only one of the family who managed to keep on speaking terms with Mrs Crewe; or Mrs Martel, as I suppose I ought to call her now, but I have never been able to think of her as anything else than Mrs Crewe. Even during the Occupation, my Cousin Mary Ann went along to see her and Harold, when the old couple was living at Rozel Cottage, the house he bought at the Can'-du-Ré. Mrs Crewe treated my Cousin Mary Ann as everybody else did: that is, gave her the rough work to do and a few things to take home, though it wasn't much she, or anybody, had to give away those days. For the rest, Mrs Crewe didn't notice she was there. My Cousin Mary Ann never interfered, or said anything out of place; though she detested Mrs Crewe. She let be. 'Ah, mais ch'est la misère pour tous partout!' she said. As she only ever went to houses where and when there was misery, what she said was so.

While Harold was yet living at Wallaballoo and Mrs Crewe was only housekeeper, my Cousin Mary Ann heard Mrs Crewe slowly and step by step pulling Raymond to pieces to his father. She was clever, Mrs Crewe; for, while she was pulling Raymond to pieces, she was at the same time buttering up old Harold. He was stupid about women. He didn't know them as well as I do. 'It is a great pity, Mr Martel,' she would say, 'how your son, Raymond, who take after his father and is such a clever boy, haven't done better for himself, isn't it? . . . It is a great shame, Mr Martel, when you come to think of it, after all the money you have spent on his education, he is only a clerk in an office now. . . . It must be a great disappointment to a man like you, Mr Martel, who have worked hard all your life and done well and is respected by everybody, not to have a son who can carry on the business, when it is high time you began to think of taking things easy . . .' and so on and so on and so on. She had another little way, according to my Cousin Mary Ann, of spreading herself out like a cat on Harold's carpenter's bench while he was working, so he could see her legs. Well, Harold was stupid; but he wasn't that stupid. Myself, I don't believe Mrs Crewe would ever have got round him, if Hetty hadn't made that silly will. I am sure it rankled in his mind, as it would have in mine, and killed the love he had felt for Hetty, and any feeling he might have had for

Raymond as his mother's son. To cap it all, Mrs Crewe had the cheek to say, 'Of course, it is only to be expected now Raymond have a wife and a home of his own, he cannot be bothered to come and visit his father, though he ought to know I am only too willing and ready to be a second mother to him.'

A buyer for the house was waiting: a Mrs Dobrée from the Forest, a widow with an only son. She was of the gentry and well off, and gave four thousand for it. The furniture was put up for auction. Mrs Crewe wanted new. It was a great sale, and the advertisement was nearly a column long in the *Press*. I thought I would go along and buy some small thing in memory of Hetty; but the last person I expected to see there was Raymond. I knew the sort of people who go to sales. They go as much to poke their noses into other people's private business and rake up the family scandal as to buy. Harold and Mrs Crewe had the sense to keep out of sight. I found Raymond wandering from room to room upstairs, as if he was walking in a dream. I didn't like the way he looked, and I kept with him. 'She is here! She is here!' he said. The women was quacking like ducks when he came into a room; but they fell silent and watched him without a word while he passed through; and then the quacking began again. 'These are her things,' he was saying. 'These are her things! She touched these things, she chose and bought them one by one, she arranged them lovingly and she thought they were beautiful. Oh my mother, my poor foolish little mother!' The tears was streaming down his face.

Downstairs pictures was being sold, and odd lots. A woman I didn't know was saying, 'I wouldn't want those pictures on my wall, me; and have everybody who come to the house know I got them for nothing with a fashion book!' 'Ah well, one would do all right for on the back of the door of the double-u, eh?' said old Mrs Renouf from L'Islet. The pictures was of a girl in a sun-bonnet standing by a stile, or of a deer in a forest, or of a shipwreck at sea, and such-like; and they had been given free with the Christmas Number of *Weldon's Ladies' Journal*. Hetty had treasured those pictures and got them framed by Gaved in the Arcade in good gilt frames. The auctioneer, young Fuzzey, made a joke of it. 'The frames are good stuff,' he said and everybody laughed. Raymond bought the lot. I bought the china fowl Hetty got from my Uncle Nat. It was sold with a lustre-ware jug for a few shillings, and I have since been offered twenty-five pounds for that lustre-ware jug. I said to Raymond, 'Come on, I've got all I want.' I didn't want him to buy any more rubbage. He came with me, but insisted on bringing the pictures. I wondered what Christine was going to say.

He walked so fast I had nearly to run to keep up with him. When we got to Rosamunda, he said, 'In the back garden! I am having a bonfire.' I let him. He stacked leaves and twigs in a heap and asked me for a match and lit a fire; and then tore the frames apart with his bare hands and smashed down pictures, glass and all, into the flames. I didn't know he was so strong. 'I am not having the people laughing at my mother!' he cried, half in anger, half in tears. 'The people are not going to laugh at my mother!' Christine came to the back porch. 'Whatever is happening?' she said. 'He will be all right presently,' I said. 'I can't stand much more of this!' she said. I felt sorry for her then; and stood by her, watching the sparks go up in the sky. Raymond looked like a devil; and I wondered if perhaps it wasn't only the people he was in a rage with, but his mother as well. He stirred the fire until the flames died down; and then walked past me and indoors as if I wasn't there. 'Up the stairs, girl!' he said to Christine. Christine's eyes opened wide, and they really did look like a cat's eyes do in the dark. He wasn't thinking of a baby then. He grabbed hold of her hand and dragged her up the narrow stairs. I closed the back door quietly behind them and went home.

I didn't like it when Wallaballoo changed hands. I had been in and out of that house for years, as if I lived there. Mrs Dobrée had pine trees planted around to make it more private, and palms in front to make it look grand; and the yard was dug up for a lawn at the back, and a trellis-work summer-house put up. Harold's work-shop was made into a garridge for her car and, later on, another for her son's; and there was a gravel drive laid down from the road. Raoul Dobrée, the son, went to Elizabeth College and then to Oxford University; and afterwards he wrote pieces for the papers in England. They was pieces about books, and he wrote books about books, and made quite a name for himself I believe; but I noticed he didn't lower himself to write for the *Guernsey Evening Press*. Mrs Dobrée didn't mix with people like us; though I heard she did visit the Robins from Coloma and the Le Poidevins from the Grand Fort. I didn't know the son to speak to until the Occupation, and then it would have been better for him if I hadn't.

It wasn't so long before Timbuctoo changed hands as well. That was another blow. I hadn't been in the habit of going there; but it made me feel sad to go along the Braye Road and pass the two houses, and it was strangers living in both. Timbuctoo went down and down, until it was as low as it could go. It was sold first to Harry Snell from the Truchett. I don't know for how much, but I know he got it cheap. He didn't live in it himself; but let it out to three or four separate families. In a few years he sold it at a big profit, I forget to who; and it changed hands a number of times after. It was already in a filthy state when the Germans came; and, after German soldiers had been living in it for three or four years, it looked as if it had died of the D.T.'s like poor Prissy.

For that was what she died of, I am quite sure. My Cousin Mary Ann said she locked herself in her room for days and wouldn't answer; and

when the door was broken open, she was found dead under the bed stark
naked with empty bottles all around her on the floor. At the funeral, Lil
Stonelake said it was brain-fever; and Percy called it cerebral meningitis.
She was buried with the Martels; and hers was the last funeral I went to
until Tabitha's. I haven't been to a funeral since; because, when my
Cousin Mary Ann died, her eldest daughter, Dora, didn't invite me.

However, Prissy was very much alive her last summer, when Dudley
Waine came over again in search of his prehistorical remains. He stayed at
Timbuctoo from May to October; and his mother came over for August. It
was lucky I saw him coming, the first day he came to Les Moulins. It gave
me a chance to get out of the way. I thought it would be better if he made his
great discovery without me having to point it out. He knocked on the front
door and on the back, but I made out I didn't hear; and he looked in the
greenhouse, but I kept out of sight behind a row of tomato-plants. I
watched him go nosing round the garden; and then he noticed what the
rain had done. I expected him to be down the gully like a shot to have a look
at it, but instead he came running back and shouting, 'Mister Le Page!
Mister Le Page!' I thought I had better show myself, and came out and
said, 'Is somebody calling?' He said, 'What's happened down there?' I
said, 'Oh, there was a flood in the winter, and some of the rubbage got
washed away.' He said, 'Haven't you seen?' 'What?' I said. Well, there
wasn't much to see. The stones was half covered with ground and brambles
and looked quite natural. He said, 'Come with me and look, please. I want
you to be able to swear I haven't touched it. It is much too important to
disturb without witnesses. It is without doubt the most perfect specimen
of an Old Stone Age barrow in Europe.' I was glad he was satisfied.

I can't go into all the fuss and bother there was over those old stones. The
next day he brought along a chap from the Lukis Museum and one of the
masters from Elizabeth College; and day after day different people came.
The stones was carefully uncovered, and the earth around raked and sifted.
I must say it looked quite as good as the one on L'Islet. Myself, I thought it
was better made, if anything; though, to my eye it looked newer, rather
than older: but Dudley insisted it was older and more prehistorical.

He didn't get everybody to agree with him, I am sorry to say. In fact, the
argument went on for years. Members of La Société Jersiaise came over
from Jersey to have a look at it, and had the cheek to say it was a fake. They
also had a look at the stones on the top of my wall and said they had been
chipped with a modern chisel. I was furious. I swore they was axe-heads
made by the first people who ever lived in the world. By then, I had taken
sides. The members of La Société Guernesiaise, who came in dozens, all
agreed the barrow was something not to be found in Jersey; but they
wasn't quite satisfied as to what it really was, unless they could find some
bones. I don't remember which year it was; but I know Raymond's boy

was already running about when those bones was found. There was nobody more surprised than me.

That year Dudley was lodging with Christine's mother at Ivy Lodge, where he stayed every summer after Prissy died. Percy had gone bankrupt. It wasn't only the bills Prissy had run up he couldn't pay, but when Harold gave up his business Percy tried to carry on by himself, only to land into more debts. I don't know how well off Horace was in America, but he wrote and offered to put Percy straight. Percy preferred to go bankrupt. Perhaps he remembered how badly he had treated Horace, or had the sense to realise, if he was put straight, he would soon be bankrupt again. He was let off light by the Court; and I think saved a little from the wreck. It was then the house was sold to Harry Snell, and Percy went to live with the Mansell family at the Longstore. I happen to know Horace sent money to Bill Mansell, but on condition he wasn't to say anything about it to Percy; so Horace was helping to keep his father after all. Percy was very bitter over Harold marrying Mrs Crewe and leaving him stranded; and I don't think the brothers met again. Percy died years before Harold.

I went down to Raymond's quite often while the baby was on the way. Raymond was mad with joy one was coming, and almost worshipped Christine for it; but thousands of other women have had babies without being worshipped, or expecting to be. I would come in and find him reading out loud to her. It was usually poetry and I didn't understand. I remember a book of verses called *The Angel in the House* by Coventry Patmore he read her a lot from. She seemed to be listening in a dreamy sort of way; but I doubt if she knew or cared what it was about any more than I did. At the time, however, she would be sitting very big and quiet sewing, or knitting, or embroidering. She was making what looked like a trousseau for the great event.

He couldn't do enough for her those days. He was up at all hours in the morning, working in the garden; then he would get her breakfast ready before he went to the office. He would be home on his bike dinner-time and leave her tidied up for the afternoon; and be home again in time to prepare the tea. If I was there in the evening, it was him got the meal for all of us. Christine's mother could well have come across and helped, if she had wanted to; but she was too lazy to do anything. Raymond had taken to giving lessons in the evening to boys who was backward at school; and he would go to two or three houses some nights. He got two shillings an hour, and it helped; yet he was worried he was cheating the boys. It was for mathematics, most of the lessons he gave; and he said it was the last subject he was fit to teach anybody. His conscience was always troubling him about something or another. Thank goodness I haven't got a conscience is such a nuisance.

He was worrying too if Christine would come through all right; or if perhaps there might be something wrong with the baby when it was born. He had too much imagination. He said one thing I didn't like. He said, 'If it is a girl, I will send it back.' 'That is not a very nice thing to say in front of Christine,' I said to him; but she didn't seem to mind. She put on her Virgin Mary look and said, 'I was born to be the mother of sons.' It made me feel sick the way she said it. I knew she wasn't at all worried about herself, whether she would come through or not; and she had no reason to be. She was as fit and strong as a girl on a farm.

He liked me to go down and spend the evening with her when he was out giving his lessons, because he didn't want her left alone. I wasn't all that keen; but Gwen was in and out, anyhow. Gwen worked for Leale on the Bridge in the desk during the day. I liked Gwen. She was a sensible girl. It was a pity she had a birthmark down one side of her face. One evening when I was alone with Christine, she said, 'I have decided on a name for him.' So it was going to be a him. 'Oh what?' I said. 'Abel,' she said. 'Why, that's a funny name, isn't it?' I said. 'Abel Martel,' she said. I said, 'Well, it don't sound too bad.' I went on about names: how perhaps it would be better if we could choose our own; yet I don't suppose I would be Ebenezer Le Page the same as I am if I hadn't been christened Ebenezer Le Page. She wasn't interested in what I had to say, naturally, but was thinking about herself as usual. 'Abel was the son of Eve,' she said. I ask you?

Towards the end I didn't go so often, as Raymond stopped giving lessons, so he could be home if anything happened. It was tea-time one afternoon and I had just come indoors when I saw him through the window, coming round the Chouey. I knew at a glance it was all right. God, he was up in the air! He burst in. 'Abel it is!' he said, 'and she is doing fine!' I was almost as pleased as he was. 'Come down now and see him!' he said. He wanted me to go as I was; but I made him wait while I got washed and changed. I didn't bother about tea. It had started at eight in the morning, he said: and he had fetched Nurse Wright and rung up the Greffe he wouldn't be going in that day. It was Nurse Wright who had brought Raymond himself into the world, and she had a soft spot for him. She let him stay with Christine until nearly the time, and everything had gone wonderfully well. Gwen and her mother was with her now.

Gwen and the mother was downstairs actually, when we arrived; and Raymond took me straight away upstairs. Christine was sitting up in bed having a tea of fish boiled in milk and thin bread-and-butter on a tray, and wearing an embroidered night-dress I had seen her making. She really did look beautiful and as well as if nothing had happened. I made to take her hand and congratulate her, but she offered her cheek and I kissed her. 'Well done, Christine!' I said. The newly-born was in the low wickerwork cradle on rockers, and Raymond was waiting impatiently to uncover it for me to see. 'He got little nails on his fingers and little nails on his toes,' he said. Well, a baby is a baby, but I must say young Abel was well made; and I liked the way he clenched his little fists. I said I wanted to buy him a present but I didn't know what to buy, so they must get him what they liked; and I put an envelope I got ready in my pocket on the chest-of-drawers. There was twenty pounds in it. I left the three together. I think now perhaps Raymond was too happy. Christine was taking it more in the course of a day's work. Perhaps it is better to live more on a level, even if it is on a lower level, as I do, than be like Raymond, up and down.

14

When I look back, the years between the two big wars seem to have passed in no time. There was nothing much happened to me. I did well, I suppose, for a small grower and fisherman, as Liza said I was. When you got nobody to love and nothing to live for, you can always make money. I employed young Lihou in the greenhouse for the summer months, and a girl Giraud from the Longcamps to help with the packing. I managed my boat by myself. I didn't mind the summer so much. I could get up at daylight and go to bed at dark, and work all day; and the time passed. It was the long winter evenings I didn't like. After I had eaten my tea and cleared up and read the *Press*, there was nothing for me to do except get ready my supper and eat it and, when I had washed up, lay the table for the morning. I got to know Alf Brouard who came to live by the Vale Church with his sister and brother-in-law, and who was an old bachelor like me. He said I ought to join the Oddfellows. He belonged. I didn't want to belong, but I went a few times with him to a Beetle Drive; and twice I won a prize.

I didn't see nothing of Liza. I don't think she ever went to Town. She wasn't the sort to go shopping herself, but would have her things sent. If I ran into Ada, I was careful not to mention her name, but Ada always said, 'Liza asks how you are.' I said to tell her I was all right. It wasn't true; but Liza ought to have known without having to ask. I heard she went to see Christine and the new baby. Raymond was full of praises of her when I went down. I would have thought Christine would have been jealous, but she wasn't: and, for once, she was right. Liza and Raymond was more like brother and sister than anything else. I think she felt about Raymond the same way as I felt about Tabitha. He was somebody who knew her very well and understood her, and yet who was better than her in some way. She brought a big, white woolly beast for Abel. I don't know if it was supposed to be a sheep, or a polar bear. Abel had plenty of toys given to him: even Lydia took him a golliwog; but Liza's beast he wouldn't be parted from. For years it slept with him, even when he was in a cot.

I am always surprised how quick children grow up. Raymond's boy was running about before I had time to turn round. The time Liza saw him, when he was a baby, she said to Raymond, 'Goodness, he is only you all over again! What do you want to go and do that for?' Raymond was as pleased as punch when he told me; but I thought Abel grew to be more like Harold. He had the same black eyes when they got to their proper colour, and thick lips like Harold; but he had fair curly hair. He really was a lovely looking little chap. It was pitiful how proud Raymond was of him. He would come up to Les Moulins of a Saturday afternoon with Abel sitting on his shoulders and hanging on to his neck and nearly choking him. 'How's the nipper?' I'd say. 'That's you, the nipper!' Raymond would say to him. When he started to run about he was a picture; for he was strong and sturdy for his age, and quite the little man already. He was like Raymond in one way: he was very well behaved. I remembered how Raymond used to sit in the boat and say, 'It's nice here, eh Uncle?' Abel didn't say much; but he looked at everything with big eyes. I liked having him in the greenhouse with me. I suppose the tomato-plants must have looked to him like big trees, for he used to catch hold of my hand, and look up at them and say 'Ah! Ah!' very solemn. I will never forget the first time he went in the sea. He was wearing only a little green slip embroidered by Christine, and was as brown as a berry. Christine herself was there that day, and was nervous about him going in; but Raymond said he would be all right. He went in by himself and wasn't a bit afraid; and, when a big wave came, he laughed when it broke over him, and didn't fall down.

He called Raymond 'man' and Christine 'oomie', until she taught him to say 'mother' properly. I was 'Ewwy'. He touched something in me: something I didn't know was there. I am sure he would have done in Harold too, if Harold had been allowed to see him. Raymond had wanted to take him with Christine to see Harold soon after he was born; but she said it wouldn't be wise. She knew the state Raymond got into with his father, and was afraid of what might happen if Harold turned nasty. So, instead, Raymond wrote a letter to his father, asking him to come and see them; and he enclosed a photograph Dudley had taken. They gave me one of those photographs. I still have it and was looking at it only the other day. Christine is looking like the mother of sons; but Abel, who was only seven months old then, is sitting on her arm and grinning all over his face with one tooth. He would have melted a heart of stone. The photo came back in an envelope without a word. It nearly broke up Raymond. When the day came I accused Christine of many things, she defended herself over that; and there was something to be said for her. 'The Martels are a mad lot,' she said, 'and I'm not sure the Le Pages aren't as bad. Raymond is both. Nobody will ever know what I went through with him when he got that photo back. If I hadn't been as strong and as evil as you say I am, I would never have got him round.' The awful part of it was Harold never saw that photo. Raymond didn't know that; and nor did I, until my Cousin Mary Ann told me. She was there in the house when Mrs Crewe opened Raymond's letter to his father; for she always opened Harold's letters before he saw them. 'To save him any worry,' she said. She burnt Raymond's letter and sent the photo back. She was even cunning enough to address the envelope in Harold's carpenter's script.

As soon as Abel could feed himself, Christine took to going out a lot. She went to Chapel mornings and evenings Sundays, and one night in the week for choir practice; and she was in great demand for singing at concerts all over the island. I would see a Grand Concert advertised, and always at the top was CHRISTINE MAHY: SOLOIST. She kept to her maiden name as a singer, I suppose because it was by that name she was known; but it meant people in general thought of Raymond as Christine Mahy's husband, and not Christine Mahy as Raymond Martel's wife. A few times he went with her and played the piano, and Gwen would come in and mind Abel; but Raymond preferred to stay at home with Abel and let Lydia Mahy, who was coming out more and more into the world, go and play for Christine. The winter she was going to sing in a Cantata was being done at Ebenezer Chapel, she was out night after night. I went down to keep Raymond company.

He didn't seem to mind Christine leaving him so much on his own. 'She enjoys singing,' he said, 'and she is good at it. A person with a light mustn't keep it under a bushel.' That was all very well, I thought, but he had a light too, Raymond. It struck me he was putting it out on purpose for her sake. He didn't even play the piano, unless she wanted to try a piece over. When I asked him to play me something of Beethoven, he said the piano they had wasn't good enough. It was only a rickety old piano with a satin front and yellow keys that creaked; not the beautiful smooth instrument he had been used to play on at home. He didn't even read. I would usually find him sitting by the fire thinking. He had been a chap full of hope and faith; but he didn't seem sure of anything now. I asked him why he didn't go to Chapel. He said if he went it would mean he was bearing witness as a believer. It wouldn't be honest. I said, 'Well, damn it, you can't be as honest as all that!'

He said when you are young you are full of trust, but are taught all manner of things which are not true; and then, when you grow up, you have to undo it all, and think different: but you have lost your ability to trust anything taught. The one thing he wanted to make sure of now was that Abel was not taught a lot of lies to start with. I realised he had given up hope for himself and all his hope was in Abel. I was afraid he was going to be disappointed. I wondered where he was going to find a school where Abel wouldn't be taught a lot of lies. The more I got to know educated people, the more it seemed to me that was what schools was for. Oh, he thought it was all right for children to be told stories, he said, so long as they wasn't forced to believe the stories had actually happened.

Tell me the old, old story
Of Jesus and His love

was a wonderful story and the Holy Family was a beautiful picture; but the story was doubtful and it wasn't a true picture. The father in the picture wasn't the real father. Nobody knew who the real father of Jesus was. 'A young Greek, I think,' he said. The early Christians had done untold damage to succeeding generations by preaching God had become incarnate on earth in one human Person. How could He be? He would have to be the perfect child, the perfect boy, the perfect youth, the perfect friend, the perfect husband, the perfect father; and then He would only be half of God Incarnate. He would also have to be the perfect virgin, the perfect bride and the perfect mother as well. I didn't say nothing. I didn't know what to think.

The day came when young Abel was digging in the gully. I had bought him a little spade and kept it solemnly in the shed with my big tools, so that he could help me whenever he came. He liked digging with Ewwy; though by then I was Ebben. That Thursday afternoon Raymond brought him trotting along by his side; but it was Raymond's half-day off and he wanted to go for a swim, so he left Abel with me to look after. Dudley and a couple of his pals was digging among the famous remains, still hoping to find something; and Abel, for some reason, thought he would like to go and dig there too. He wanted me to go with him, but I said it wasn't my business, though he could go by himself, if he wanted to. I knew he would be quite safe. Off he went with his spade on his shoulder like a little man; but he didn't go and dig with the others. He picked out a corner for himself. I kept an eye on him and saw he was making quite a hole.

Another boy, if he had found something, would have shouted out; but not Abel. He went on quietly digging his hole, and made a neat pile on the side of what he found. Myself, I went on working and didn't notice much what he was doing, so long as he was all right. When Raymond came back from swimming and saw only me, he said, 'Hullo, what have you done with the boy?' I said, 'Oh, he is over there digging up a prehistoric monster.' Raymond went over to see. Abel looked up and smiled and showed his father the treasure he had unearthed. 'Tones,' he said. He thought they was stones. 'Ye gods,' shouted Raymond, 'I wouldn't be surprised if he has and all!' Dudley and his two chaps came running to have a look. Abel wouldn't let them touch his 'tones': he said they was for Ebben. I went over and explained the land down there didn't belong to Ebben, so Ebben couldn't have them. He made no fuss, but let Dudley take possession; and that was how Dudley made his great discovery.

More digging was done and more bones, some quite big, was dug up

from the same place. They wasn't bones of human beings. They was bones
of a beast of some breed; but of what breed? According to Dudley, they
was part of the skeleton of a woolly rhinoceros. Others said they couldn't
be. In the first place it couldn't possibly ever have been there. I didn't
understand quite why, but it had something to do with the Third Glacial
Age. Whatever the reason, I was sorry. I liked the idea of a woolly rhinoceros wandering across L'Ancresse Common. I would rather see him
than the golfers any day. In the second place, it was the right shape but the
wrong size. It wasn't big enough. Dudley got over that by saying it was the
calf of a woolly rhinoceros. The mystery deepened when the jaw-bone
was dug up and examined; and it was found there was some marks on it. I
can swear there was marks on it, because I saw them with my own eyes
when it was dug up. They was only lines and bits of circles; but everybody
who knew anything about such things agreed they wasn't there by accident. They was made 'by human agency'. That meant there was people
alive on Guernsey at the same time as the woolly rhinoceros: if he was ever
alive on Guernsey. In that case, there wasn't only people alive on Guernsey at the same time as the first people on Jersey. There was people alive on
Guernsey before there was people on Jersey: in fact, before there was any
Jersey, because in those days it was joined to France and wasn't a place at
all. Dudley was delighted; and so was I. However, the bones had to be
packed up and sent away to England to be examined by the professors, and
compared with other bones with marks on found in different parts of the
world. After nearly a year they was sent back; and you can see them for
yourself to this day in the Museum in what used to be St Barnabas Church
up Cornet Street. They are labelled as the skeleton of a prehistoric red deer.
How the professors knew it was red I don't know.

They also proved the marks on the jaw-bone was made by people of the
New Stone Age, and not of the Old Stone Age; so the burial-place at La
Petite Grève was made by the same people as made the one on L'Islet, and
was not as prehistorical as some of the remains to be found on Jersey. It is a
shame really; but if Science have proved it to be true, who is Ebenezer Le
Page to say it isn't? There was one good thing came out of it. Once the
bones was passed by the professors, nobody could doubt the burial-
ground was the real thing; and even La Société Jersiaise daren't say the
axe-heads on my wall was a fake. I was quite happy the way it turned out;
but Dudley was heart-broken. He vowed he wouldn't have any more to do
with old stones: he couldn't trust the professors to believe the evidence of
their eyes. The next year when he came over he was on the track of the
witches who used to live in Guernsey. He said they worshipped La Gran'-
Mère du Chimquière at La Bellieuse, where is now St Martin's Church;
and their religion was the original religion of the Guernsey people. Would
I please tell him what I knew of the old witches? I would NOT! I said he

wouldn't find any of those at Les Moulins. I'd had enough, and more than enough, of raking up the past! When the Germans came, they respected the prehistoric monuments and left mine alone. It is a pity they didn't respect some of the historic monuments a bit more. The whole time of the Occupation I kept it clear of brambles and furze, because I wanted the stuff to burn; then, after the Liberation, the States, when they was trying to think of something new to show to the tourists, put it on the list of Ancient Monuments and gave me the job of looking after it. So in my old age, I became a worker for the States. I never thought I would sink so low.

I was asked to say how many hours a week it would take me. I was to be paid four shillings an hour. I thought I could do it easy in four hours, or less; but I began to take notice of the fellows who was working for the States on the roads. Mind you, they worked hard leaning on their shovels watching out nobody was coming to see if they was working; but they came in a lorry in the morning, and took an hour or so to put up a canopy and collect wood to light a fire and make tea. I hadn't allowed for that in my four hours. It is true, in the evening they was quicker. The canopy was on the lorry in two shakes and they was gone; and you couldn't see them for dust. Then there was the chap who came round on a motor-bike two or three times a day to tell them what to do, if he could find them; and there was the gentleman in a motor-car who came round to tell the chap on the motor-bike what to do, if he could find him. I was going to save the States all that expense. All things considered, I thought it would be reasonable if I was to put down eight hours.

The trouble was there was so many Committees of the States. I didn't know which to send my bill to. There was the Ancient Monuments Committee. Well, I was doing eight hours a week for them for sure. There was the Cliffs Committee. The ancient monument was on the cliffs, sort of. That would be eight hours for them. There was the Natural Beauties Committee. The ancient monument was a natural beauty. I thought it was only fair they should have to pay as well. It worked out all right. I filled in eight hours on forms I got from the States Offices, and took three in every Friday morning, one to each Committee, for my money. It was a very nice girl in the office. I don't mean I had thoughts about her: I don't have to do those things now; but I took to her on sight, and I think she took to me. She is a real Guernsey girl with a twinkle in her eye. 'All right, Mr Le Page,' she says, 'I will put these through,' and she pays me on the dot. I don't believe for a moment it was her fault the States after a time discovered there was something wrong with their accounts. Ebenezer Le Page was in trouble again. I don't think Ebenezer Le Page and the States see quite eye to eye.

15

Horace came back. If ever a man had a bad angel, Raymond had one in Horace. I tried to make him see it in the end; but it was of no use. When Horace had wrecked his happiness, or at least such happiness as was his, Raymond still couldn't bring himself to turn against him. He said, 'Horace is never sorry for anything he has done. He is sorry it happened, and he suffers for it; but he isn't sorry for what he did. I wouldn't like him, if he was. He is innocent.' It was himself Raymond blamed. He said he had been so full of himself he hadn't seen Christine as she was. 'I disappointed her all ways,' he said: 'She thought I was going to be a famous preacher; and I wasn't. She thought she was going to be a well-known singer in England; and she was stuck in Guernsey. She thought she was going to have a number of lovely children, and be admired by everybody as a mother of sons; and we only had one. She hoped I was going to take her to heaven in bed. I hoped so too: always hoped, always hoped; but never did. A house founded upon the sand cannot stand.'

It might have stood as well as most houses, I reckon. Raymond was a born father. He was better with Abel than Christine was. He was patient yet firm; and knew how to manage him without bullying him, or being unfair. Christine would be making a big loving fuss of him one minute; and the next minute he would be having to do exactly what she said for no reason at all, except it suited the convenience of Christine. She had a lot of other irons in the fire. It may be she would have been satisfied to have a number of men around her she could lean on, but not quite; and keep Raymond for use in the background. She even made a slave of Dudley Waine; though God knows he can have been of no use to her, except to introduce her to other young men he knew. He was a eunuch, that fellow, if ever a chap was. The pity was Raymond had spoken so much to Christine about Horace those weeks while they was waiting to get married. She had a glorified picture of Horace in her mind; and must have guessed he was no eunuch. When he turned up in the flesh, she welcomed him with open arms. Raymond was delighted. 'It is wonderful how Christine has taken to Horace,' he said to me. 'She doesn't mind him at all always in and out of the house. It is like old times.'

Horace had no home to go to. As Dudley was by then gone back to England, he was able to stay with Christine's mother at Ivy Lodge. I didn't even know he was back until Raymond brought him to Les Moulins. I was in the packing-shed when I heard Raymond calling out, 'Ebby, Ebby, where are you? Come and see who is here!' I came out; and there was the big Horace! He hadn't changed much. He was bigger and manlier, if possible; and you could see he had been around the flesh-pots. He had aged more than Raymond, who was boyish yet, but he was still a darn good-looking chap. I liked him better than I had before. He was more forthright. He gave me a real smile and shook hands as old Jim would have done. 'Gee, I'm glad to see you, boy!' he said. He spoke with a twang, but his Guernsey sing-song wasn't altogether gone. 'I guess I must stop speaking American,' he said. 'I am in Guernsey now. I must speak as the Guernseyman I am. I want to forget the United States of America. I want to forget such a country exists. Gee, I'm glad to be home!' I knew something must have happened to him over there put his nose out of joint, but I didn't know what.

As for Raymond, he looked as if he had suddenly come alive again. The last few times I had seen him he had been half dead. He had said to me, of all things to say, 'A man must learn to live crucified. That is what marriage is for.' Well, that was never my idea of marriage; and I bet Christine didn't intend to live crucified. I thought to myself what is sauce for the gander is sauce for the goose; but I didn't say it. He certainly wasn't living crucified when he came up to Les Moulins that day with Horace. He was bubbling over as he used to be, and kept on looking at old Horace and chuckling to himself, as if it was the best joke in the world to have him there. I can't say it was all on one side either. Horace was proud of Raymond, and looking at him in a real warmhearted way. 'Gee, old Ray looks good!' he said. 'He has done the best deal of us all. Abel is a great kid!'

Raymond had come to ask me to be sure to go down to Rosamunda for dinner on the Sunday. Horace and Gwen was going to be there. I went. I stayed the afternoon and evening; and we all seemed to get on well together. I decided that, whatever had happened to Horace in America, he had improved. He played with Abel, and was very gentle with him; and he was jolly with Gwen. He didn't have much to say to Christine and she hardly said a word to him, only smiled her cat's smile and looked at him with her mysterious eyes; but Gwen warmed up and laughed and joked with him, and was gay and happy as I had never seen her before. She wasn't a girl to attract men at a glance; but she had a likeable face and a sincere smile, and you forgot about her birthmark when she was happy and came out of herself. I sat there thinking perhaps Horace and Gwen would make a match of it, if he wanted to settle down. I am always trying to arrange happy lives for other people, when I haven't managed to arrange a happy one for myself. Perhaps I would do better if I was to mind my own business.

When I was leaving, Horace got me on one side and said he would like to know more about what had happened to the old people. He had been to see his father, but hadn't been able to get much out of him; and Christine had warned him off raking up family troubles with Raymond. 'It gives me an uncomfortable feeling,' he said. 'It is almost as if a blight was fallen on our family.' I asked him to come round one evening, and we could have a chat. I thought it would be company for me, anyway. He arrived well supplied with bottles of grog. I don't drink on my own, except for a glass of cider with my dinner; but we sat and talked and drank until midnight. I didn't drink so much; but he fair swilled it down. He said the Yanks were even bigger boozers than the Guernsey boys. It was the result of Prohibition.

I didn't tell him his mother had died of drink. I didn't know it myself for sure at the time. I did tell him she got very nervy and excitable her last years. He said she never recovered from the death of Cyril. He laughed over the speakings and the not-speakings with Hetty. He remembered the famous quarrel over the planchette. He said, 'Good old Ray knew I was pushing it; but he didn't give me away.' He wanted to know how Mrs Crewe had come into the story. I told him what I knew then, which again wasn't much. 'She must have played her cards well to get Uncle Harold to sell the house,' he said. 'It was dastardly to leave Raymond without anything to inherit.' He was worried about Raymond: he thought he must be pretty hard up. He couldn't be earning much at the Greffe; and he had a heavy rent to pay to Mrs Mahy. 'She is a good business-woman, Christine's mother,' he said. He wasn't struck on Christine. In fact, he was already finding fault with her. 'For his own sake, Raymond would have done better if he had married Gwen,' he said. 'She is a girl would look after a man.' He criticised Christine for the way she kept, or rather, didn't keep the house. 'If she was my wife,' he said, 'I would make her do the housework. Helping a woman with the heavy is one thing; but Christine does nothing. She drops everything where she is.' He said he would like to help them with spare cash; but Raymond might be touchy. He didn't want any money business to come between him and Raymond. He would wait and see. He sounded as if he had plenty to throw around.

I asked him what he thought of doing now he was over here. 'Sell,' he said. It was the one thing he had learnt how to do in the States. 'The Yanks are great boys for selling things,' he said. 'They know how to sell what is written on the wrapper.' Dear old Guernsey was fifty years behind the times, and the old fogeys who ran it didn't know they was born yet. He was going to show them! Well, if he was alive today he would see they have caught up, and gone further. They have forgotten a lot of other things they did know: how to give for nothing and be hospitable, for instance; but they have learnt to sell, by God they have, and rake in the shekels like a mechanical rake! They sell their own dear island every year to more and more people for a higher and a higher price. Horace ought to see the crowds in the summer sitting on the beaches in rows, looking at the blessed sea as if they was at the Pictures; and Christ knows how many pounds a week they pay for the privilege of doing it. They could look at the old sea just as well in their own country. England is an island, isn't it?

He came back more full of love for Guernsey than any Guernseyman who have never left it. He may have found a funny way of showing it, but it was a real feeling in old Horace. He described to me coming down the Russel on the boat and seeing first the low, straggly northern end of the island, and then coming in between the other islands and seeing St Peter Port from the sea in the early morning light: houses upon houses rising on the hills and the Town Church down by the quay and the Victoria Tower against the sky. 'They can keep their little old New York,' he said. The truth was America was too big for him. He said on his job he had spent half his time travelling thousands of miles by train. 'It is not from St Sampson's to St Peter Port on the tram,' he said. Well, even the tram have gone now. That was years before the Second World War, though the rails was left; but now they have gone too.

He'd had a good time, as good times go. He said the Yanks was easy fellows to get along with; though he had never quite been able to make out the difference between one and the other. He found friends in every place he went to; but never made a friend. 'A guy will pour his heart out to you over a drink one night,' he said, 'but the next day he doesn't remember who you are, unless you happen to be on his mailing list. They call each other by their nicknames, rich and poor alike. Oh, it's very democratic over there; but they got each other sorted out on a cash basis, equally as much as in Guernsey.' He said he might have fallen for America, if it hadn't been for Raymond's letters. He looked forward to receiving those letters as to nothing else; and they had followed him the length and breadth of the continent.

Raymond had opened his heart to Horace in his letters; and Horace knew full well he had in Raymond a friend who would never change. He had explained to Horace his reasons for becoming a minister, and for giving it up. Horace didn't care much, and didn't understand really; but was glad Raymond had given religion the go-by. 'I believe in what I can see and touch,' he said. Raymond had also written about Christine and his love for her; but what Horace liked Raymond's letters for most was they brought back Guernsey and the comic Guernsey people. They are like people nowhere else; and all different from each other. 'There is no typical

Guernseyman,' Horace said to me. 'They are each a one-man band, and all as cussed as they can be. The Yanks come of every race and nation; but are all alike at rock bottom. They have two gods they worship: dollars and dames; and the dollars are for the dames. The Statue of Liberty is a woman.' He knew the few scrawls he had sent Raymond hadn't been much in return. 'I'm no good at writing,' he said and grinned. 'I can't spell yet!' The fact was he didn't want to write about what he was doing. He was ashamed of it.

He let out what it was when he'd had a few more drinks. He had been a travelling salesman for Bang's Enerjims. 'What on earth are those?' I said. 'I don't have to tell you surely,' he said. 'Christ, is that where they get all their swank from?' I said. 'Out of pills!' 'They don't get much of it out of Bang's Enerjims,' he said. 'It's a name. The salesman is the advertisement; and the bosses know how to pick their man. He got to be the type of guy who will convince the manageress of the drug-store. I swore to those dames I took Bang's Enerjims every night, and more than once I had to prove it!' 'Did you?' I said. 'I mean did you take Bang's Enerjims every night?' 'I never touched the bloody things,' he said, 'but in the States a man got to be a whore to be a good salesman. Yanks are soft; and the tougher, the softer. Raymond is a harder nut to crack than any Yank I ever met.' I wonder how much he remembered next morning of what he said to me that night.

I will say for Horace he had plenty of go in him. There was an old Army hut next to Baubigny Arsenal, and he bought it and had it cleaned out and painted; and there he opened the Arsenal Stores. He set out to build up an honest business in food. At the back of the shop he had a little room with a camp-bed, where he slept; and Gwen gave up her job at Leale's to serve behind the counter. He had enough money to stock it well, and it took on; but the side of the business he did best on was his travelling shop. It is nothing new nowadays with the Co-op van going everywhere; but his was the first. He bought a closed-in motor-van and fitted it out and went with it to a different part of the island each day, while Gwen minded the shop. He also sent to England for more different kinds of food in tins than we had been used to; and he was a good enough salesman to get round the country women to try it out. I let him bring me my groceries, and he even tried his salesman's tricks on me. He wanted me to buy a tin of pilchards in tomato sauce. 'Make your hair curl,' he said. I said I would rather have straight hair and long-nose out of the frying-pan.

I heard rumours, as one do, he had been seen with this or that girl sitting in the van; and the van had been for a long time outside the house of Mrs So-and-so, or Mrs So-and-so. It may have been true, for all I know. He had nearly all his meals at Rosamunda. It was the way he found of helping Raymond. He provided most of the food and, as it was for himself as well, said he couldn't charge for it. I noticed a difference when I went there the next time. The house was spic and span and everything was in its place; and it was Christine who got the meal ready and washed up after. Raymond and Horace dried and put the dishes away. It looked as if at last she was being a sensible girl; and I was glad, for Raymond's sake. I might have known better. She wasn't doing it to please Raymond. She was furious with Raymond. He was always going out with Horace. I was surprised myself when I met him one night in the Channel Islands, having a drink with Horace. I bet he had never been in a hotel bar before; or any pub, for that matter. Thursday afternoons the two of them went out on their bikes; and to the Pictures, or somewhere, in the evening. When they came in, they would sit by the fire yarning until all hours of the morning. Christine had to go to bed on her own.

One night when I went down I found Christine in by herself. I had been feeling particularly lonely up at Les Moulins that night, and was hoping for a chat with Raymond, or Horace, or both. It was a night I thought she went to choir practice. I was disappointed when it was her who opened the door and said, 'Ah, I had a feeling you were thinking about me! Come in, come in, do! I am a grass widow.' She made me sit down in the armchair and arranged cushions at my back and patted me on the knee. Abel was in bed. 'Where are the boys?' I said. 'You may well ask where are the boys,' she said. 'I don't know where they have gone; and I don't expect I will be told.' I came as near to liking Christine that night, as ever I have. She dropped her holy voice, and said what was in her mind. It wasn't a very nice mind; but, at least, she was honest.

She said Raymond had changed completely since Horace was back. She hardly knew him: he was so different. He did as he liked without asking her. He went out with Horace without even bothering to enquire if she had a singing appointment for the evening; and, if she had an argument with Horace, it was always Horace who was in the right. I saw how it struck her. Raymond had been saying 'Yes, Christine' for so long because he thought it was right for him to be crucified, she couldn't understand it now he said 'Yes, Horace' because he meant it. I said, 'Well, they have known each other for a long time, you know. They couldn't be separated when they was kids.' 'They are not kids now,' she said, 'and I don't mind telling you I am going to separate them before long.' The way she said that sent a shiver down my spine. 'Why not have Gwen over here to live with you?' I said. 'There is the little room.' 'That is what Raymond wants,' she said. 'Well, why not?' I said. 'It would be company, and you would have help in the house.' 'Gwen does quite enough for Horace as it is,' she said. 'If he as much as smiles at her, you would think the sun was rising!' Christine wanted to be the only woman in that house.

I did my best to make her see reason. 'After all, you are often out your-self,' I said. 'If I get the chance,' she said, 'and those are the very evenings my lords condescend to stay in! On the pretext of keeping an eye on Abel. Gwen could well come across and do that. When I come back, they have kept him up and are sprawled on the floor playing with his bricks. Raymond will say "They give you an encore, girl?" and he doesn't care two hoots. The Other will say "How about some supper, honey?" That's all he thinks of. Food!' I was getting to feel very uncomfortable. 'Oh, let's forget about them,' she said. 'They are not worth it! What would you like me to get you for your supper?' She patted my knee again. I thought I had been patted on the knee quite enough for one evening, and said I must be going because I got something on the boil at home.

I ought to have guessed what was going to happen; but, more fool me, I didn't. It never occurred to me Horace would do that to Raymond. Anyhow, one afternoon Raymond was at the Greffe and Horace wasn't on his round as he ought to have been. How that came about I don't know. Raymond told me all the afternoon he had been thinking of Christine. He thought of how lovely she had looked when he went up to see her after she had given birth to Abel. He thought of how beautiful she was the Sunday evening they walked home together from Birdo Mission. They hadn't kissed as lovers do, or said sweet nothings; but walked hand in hand. All he had said to her was, 'Will you be my wife, Christine?' and she had answered, 'I am your wife', and he had believed her. Riding home from the Greffe on his bicycle he was thinking how he was going to tell her when he got in that what she had said was true, and would always be true, and she must never doubt it.

She was cutting bread-and-butter in the kitchen when he came in, wearing a stiff white overall: which was Horace's idea of what a woman ought to wear when she was preparing food. She looked very clean: 'bleached', Raymond said. He came bounding in, meaning to take her in his arms and kiss her. He couldn't. She was untouchable. 'Frozen,' he said. He knew in that instant what had happened. The shock was too great for him to feel it then. He felt far, far away and above the earth; and the only feeling he had left for her was pity. She hadn't gone to heaven with Horace either. He saw that from one glance. She spoke to him in a cold, clear voice he had never heard her use before. 'Horace is in the front room,' she said. 'He wants to speak to you.'

Raymond went into the front room. Horace was sitting bent over with his head in his hands. He looked up when Raymond came in. Raymond saw his face. 'It was the face of a man in hell,' Raymond said, when he was telling me. 'So it jolly well ought to have been!' I said. 'How, how could you have brought yourself to forgive him?' 'Forgive?' he said. 'Why, I would willingly have died to get that look off his face!' 'It's all right, Horace,' he said to him. 'It's all right: I don't blame you.' Horace was on his feet and crushed Raymond in his arms. 'Christ, you mean more to me than any woman ever has, or ever will!' he said. 'I was in heaven then,' Raymond said to me. I think it was then something in Raymond's brain cracked.

16

Well, that was how those three people got tangled up together. I heard all sides; but I can't say I am much wiser. Raymond said there was a thin thread between him and Christine, and, though their loving had not been perfect, so long as that thread was not broken there was hope. She broke it for no reason he could see. If she had done it because she loved Horace and preferred Horace to himself, he couldn't have blamed her. He would have done the same in her place. He said you can have goodwill towards everybody; but you cannot choose who, or how you love. That is something you are landed with; as you are landed with your parents, and your body, and the place you are born in. Christine didn't love Horace: she hated Horace. Raymond knew because she didn't want any more to do with him after that once. 'That is what hurt me most,' said Raymond. 'Horace isn't only the lust of the flesh, you know. He is a good man.'

I don't think Raymond got it quite right. I think Christine wanted to master the big Horace, and once was enough for her to know she couldn't ever do it; and that was why she hated him so much. When, during the Occupation, he didn't know where Raymond was living and came and appealed to me to tell him, he said, 'I know you think I am a rotten swine and did the dirty on Raymond; but Christine wasn't Raymond's wife: she was anybody's woman. That woman was the bottomless pit!' The one thing Raymond admitted he didn't know was who made the first move. I knew. I didn't tell Raymond, and perhaps I ought to have done, what Christine had said to me; but he was already getting enough funny ideas in his head, and I didn't want to knock him sideways altogether. As a matter of fact, I don't believe Christine made the move only to separate the two; though it was them being so close made her decide to do it. I think she wanted Horace the moment she set eyes on him. She was quite heartless. She was as cold as the moon and man-hungry. Nor do I think Horace was free of blame. He pushed himself in there, even if he didn't know he was doing it; and when the chance was offered, he took it. It was the lust of the flesh all right.

Raymond was asking for it really. He confessed to me he hadn't 'lain with' Christine since Horace came home. He couldn't. It was the old story. It had to be perfect; or he couldn't face Horace in the morning. He thought, for some reason I don't understand, if a time came when Horace was happily married to Gwen and living near, it would work out perfect between him and Christine. Anyhow, it turned out different from how any of them thought. If Christine imagined she was going to separate Raymond and Horace by having Horace, she made the greatest mistake she ever made. It drew them closer together. She told me she would gladly have killed the pair of them in the days that followed. It had been bad enough when they sat by the fire by the hour talking, and left her out of it; but now they seemed to be able to read each other's thoughts without even having to talk. They would look at each other and laugh, and she didn't have any idea what they were laughing about; and for conversation they would say 'Um, ah, yes, no,' and seem to understand what they meant and agree with each other. They nearly drove her mad. 'They don't even speak like human beings,' she said to me, 'they make animal noises at each other.' I can understand how it was with them myself. They was exactly the same blood, might have been brothers; and both having been with Christine joined them deeper than brothers. Jim and me wasn't of the same blood, nor was there a Christine between us; but we knew what the other was thinking with very few words.

It say something in the Bible about raising up seed to your brother. Well, Christine raised up the seed. It wasn't long before she knew she was going to have a baby. I have no idea what she felt about it. She let it be thought it was Raymond's; but the neighbours knew better. I don't know how. I know she didn't tell her mother who was so loose-tongued she might have let it out. Gwen she told, to show up Horace; but I am certain Gwen never breathed a word. She got a raw deal, that girl. She gave her heart to Horace once and for all, and got nothing for it; yet she was at his beck and call as long as he lived. Christine came off best. When she shook the dust of Guernsey from off her feet and went to England with her two sons, she got everybody's sympathy. She spread abroad she was leaving Raymond because of his unspeakable abominations, what ever that might mean, and she must save the children from his influence. Raymond was left to face a shame from which he never raised his head. The good Chapel people, who already wouldn't speak to or about him, now raised their voices and seemed to know more about 'unspeakable abominations' than Raymond, or even I, did. The truth was he hadn't behaved like on the Pictures. If he had fought Horace, or murdered him, or even Christine, it would have been very wrong, of course; but it would have proved their way of looking at things was right, and they would have been satisfied. As it was, they just didn't understand. It seems to me he behaved rather like a Christian.

The day came when I went down and there could be no doubt about a baby coming. Raymond said, 'Christine is expecting an addition to the family.' I said, 'Fine!' I didn't know then what had happened; but I couldn't help feeling all was not well. Christine was sitting knitting; but being very icy and distant to both Raymond and Horace. She was quite friendly to me, and said she thought I had forgotten she was alive: it was such a long time since I had been to see her. Raymond and Horace was on the floor, helping Abel to build a 'Big house'. When Abel was sent to bed, Horace sat in the armchair as if he was the master of the house. Raymond didn't seem to mind, and sat on a hassock with his arms round his knees. I tackled him about it once. He remembered that night very well, and said the only thing he minded was not being able to tell me the baby coming was Horace's. 'I would have liked to be honest with you,' he said, 'but it wouldn't have been fair to Christine.' God Almighty, as if it ever entered Christine's head to be fair to Raymond! I don't think 'forces of nature' are 'fair'.

It was Raymond got the meal, and Horace helped to clear away after and wash up. They both waited on Christine, and asked her if she had all she needed; and she said 'Thank you', as if they was servants. The washing-up place was small; and I noticed how Raymond and Horace worked in together well, and didn't get in each other's way. I talked to Christine nothing that mattered of people we both knew: gossip really. Raymond admitted he wasn't unhappy those days. Horace was there. He was only wondering how it was going to end. Christine really was living quite on her own. She had the big bedroom with Abel in his cot. Raymond slept in the little room and Horace at the back of the shop. Otherwise, Horace lived at Rosamunda: ate his meals there and was there every evening. Christine gave up singing and choir-practice, and they stayed in together as I found them the evening I went down. I didn't know what to make of it. I knew something was gone wrong; but I didn't really want to know what. I was soon told. I ran into Len Carré from Pleinheaume in the Mariners. 'I hear there's a cuckoo in the nest round your way,' he said. 'I don't know nothing about that,' I said. 'Ah well,' he said, 'it's not the first time that's happened, and it won't be the last.' He went on to tell me about two brothers we both knew who swopped wives; and, after a spell, swopped back again. There was children from all the pairs; and the families now lived next door to each other. The children all played together, and the parents seemed to get on quite well. I didn't say nothing. I didn't want to talk about it. The whole business was upsetting me more than I liked to admit. I thanked my lucky stars I didn't take things as serious as Raymond.

I wish I could leave out the next part of my story; but I don't see how I honestly can. I can't be expected to write the truth about other people, because I don't know it; but at least I can write the truth about some of the stupid things I have done myself. This was the stupidest. It was because I

wanted to forget about Raymond and his serious nonsense I decided I
would go on a gallivant like old Victor. I was more or less on the spree for a
week. It didn't amount to much. I got drunk a few nights and had a couple
of fights, I don't remember who with or what about; and then on the Saturday afternoon I went to Town with the intention of having a last blindo,
but happened to see Gerald Mahy on the other side of the road in Fountain
Street. I thought how young and sprightly he looked, though he can't have
been many years younger than me. He hadn't got into trouble at the Old
Bank yet, and been nearly put in jail. He was talking and laughing with a
couple of girls I didn't know; and I crossed over the road to ask him how
his mother was. He was living with his mother then at St Martin's and I
knew she wasn't very well. He said she was no better; and introduced me to
the two girls. The one he was getting off with I could see at a glance was a
trollop; but I wasn't so sure about the other. The great mistake I made, and
God knows I paid for it, was that in her eyes I was getting on in years. I
thought she was quite taken with me. She smiled and shook hands and said
she was pleased to meet me; and told me her name was Dolly Trouteaud,
and she lived in Doyle Road. I thought it was rather a grand part for a girl of
her sort to live. Anyhow, when Gerald and his piece went off for a stroll
down Havelet, I asked if I might see Miss Trouteaud to her gate. Miss
Trouteaud was delighted. I don't remember what we talked about on the
way; but when we got there, she said, 'Come in and meet my mother. She
will love to meet you.'

I had nothing else to do, so I thought I might as well. I ought to have
known there was something in the wind. As soon as she had introduced me
to her mother, she said she had to go out again, and I was left alone with
Mrs Trouteaud, or Louisa, the name I came to know her by all too well.
She was a woman of my own age, or older; and was stout with a square face,
and had a wooden leg. I felt sorry for her because she had a wooden leg, and
she sat with it stretched out for me to see. I never dared at any time to ask
her how she got it, but from the way she got about on it, I think she was
born with it. It was a big house she lived in; but it came out she and Dolly
only had two rooms on the ground floor. She soon let me know Dolly was
engaged. She was engaged to a young English chap who worked for Le
Riche's, but was taking on a better job as a manager for Sainsbury's somewhere in England, and Dolly was getting married and going with him. I
didn't see the danger. That wicked young puss of a Dolly had jumped at me
as an old man sent by God to palm off on her mother. She and her bloke
didn't want the old woman going to live with them in England, and I was to
be bribed and corrupted into taking her off their hands.

As a matter of fact, I quite enjoyed myself that night. The old woman
was the rough and ready sort, and I felt quite at home with her. She told me
she was a widow and her husband had been a sea-captain; though from

what she said, I gathered he was only skipper of a trawler. When he was alive, she used to go with him to sea, she said: because she didn't trust a man out of her sight. I took that for a joke, and laughed. She got out glasses and a bottle of wine, and buttered some of Guérin's biscuits. I ate and drank, and there was a good fire, and I felt warm and comfortable. She asked me a lot of questions about who I was, and where I came from, and what I did for a living, and so on; and I answered her straight out, without letting her know too much. When I left, she said she hoped I would go and see her again, because she was a lonely old woman. I promised. The next Saturday I went. Dolly opened the door and showed me in, but said she was on the way out. The glasses and the wine and the buttered biscuits was out ready; and Louisa was sitting by a small table, telling herself her fortune from the cards. The moment I came in, she sprang up on her wooden leg and pointed dramatically to the cards spread out on the table. 'It is in the cards!' she said. I was mesmerised like a rabbit. I couldn't move. I couldn't speak. I would like to meet the chap who could have stood up on his hind legs and said to Louisa Trouteaud 'It is NOT in the cards!' I would have to wait a few weeks, she said: the course of true love never did run smooth. She must make sure Dolly got properly hooked up; and then she would be mine! I sort of laughed. I ate and drank, but didn't know what I was eating and drinking; and she talked and I said yes to everything she said. I wasn't listening. I was only thinking of how to get out of the house as soon as possible. I promised faithfully I would go and see her the next Saturday. I had no more intention than the man in the moon of ever going to see her again; or even of ever going along Doyle Road again, as long as I lived. I counted without Louisa.

She came to see me. I was horrified the Monday afternoon, when she turned up and caught me unawares. She said I was a bad boy: I hadn't kept my word; but then she hadn't expected me to: she knew men. I had to ask her in. After all, I had been in her house, but I hadn't gone nosing round. She looked in every cupboard, and in every drawer, and I was in fear and trembling she was going to look up the chimney in the wash-house and find the pied-du-cauche. She went into my bedroom and had a look round; and into what had been my mother's room, and came out looking like a dragon with a night-dress in her hand. She said a woman had been sleeping there. I said yes: it was my sister, when she came sometimes. She didn't believe it was my sister. She said it was high time she was there herself to keep an eye on me. She then began finding fault with everything. Nothing was to her satisfaction. I must have the electricity put in, and the water-works; and she would rather have gas to cook by than my Guernsey range. The pigs would have to go. She said pigs in a pigsty against the house wasn't 'hygienic'. I said I didn't think the place was really good enough for her. She said it was small; but it would do. I saw her to the bus and said,

'Good-bye!' and she said, 'Au revoir!' That is how the persecution of Ebenezer Le Page began.

It went on for years. It was terrible. I never felt safe. It is true, more often than not when she came, I wasn't in. I lived with the front door locked and the back door locked, and I locked myself in the greenhouse or the packing shed; and when I was working out-of-doors, I kept my eyes skinned to see her before she saw me. I would spot her coming round the corner of the Chouey; and, by God, she got along quicker and looked forty times more determined on her wooden leg, than any other woman with two legs of flesh and blood! I looked through my old book of Army Instructions for the drill on how to take cover in the presence of the enemy. She would try the front door, and try the back door, and look in the windows; and once she even looked in the double-u. I would be making myself invisible. I daubed whitewash on the glass of the greenhouse, so as she couldn't look in; and I am ashamed now when I think of myself crawling on all fours on the floor of the packing shed, in case she peeped through the window. Young Lihou was a brick, and did his best to protect me. He would say I had gone to the White Rock, or St Sampson's, or somewhere, and wouldn't be back for hours; and once he told her I was dead in the Cottage Hospital, hadn't she heard? She didn't believe him; and came back in half-an-hour and caught me.

I got into such a state of mind I verily believed the day would come when I would have to stand side by side with Louisa Trouteaud in front of the altar of the Vale Church and say 'till death do us part' as a punishment for my sins. When Raymond was living with me, he didn't have much laugh left in him; but he used to laugh over Louisa Trouteaud. He called her 'Captain Hook'. He was always very sympathetic with her when she came; and he was the only one of us she believed. He would say how sorry I was going to be when I got back and heard I had missed her. I was being tempted to shout out from where I was hiding, 'Oh, you bloody liar!' Raymond found it hard to tell a lie for his own good, but he told dozens for my sake. Well, if there is any justice in heaven, he will have his reward for that!

I saw the birth of Horace's kid in the *Press*. MARTEL. At Rosamunda, Les Effards, St Sampson's, to Christine (née Mahy) and Raymond, a son, Gideon. I heard about it too from old Mrs Renouf I met in Weymouth's shop. 'Ah, I see your cousin, Raymond Martel, got another, then,' she said: 'It is funny they call him Gideon, isn't it? I would have thought, if he was the brother of the other, they would have called him Cain. Cain and Abel, eh?' I didn't feel like giving him much of a present; but I thought I ought to give something. I couldn't think what to give; so I asked Ada Domaille to buy what she thought, and she bought a monkey on a stick. She said it would make him laugh. It didn't. He didn't take any interest in it. He wasn't a bright baby like Abel. He looked like a wizened, shrivelled little monkey himself. Christine thanked me for the present, but said it was too old for him.

She had a bad time having Gideon, and was in bed yet when I went. Raymond told me he and Horace sat together by the fire downstairs the whole day, listening to her screams upstairs in the bedroom. He said he felt very close to Horace that day. They both suffered with her; but there was nothing they could do. Gwen fetched the doctor. She wanted to get them a meal, but they couldn't eat. It wasn't until nine o'clock at night it was over. When Nurse Wright came down with the doctor and said Raymond could go and see his wife and child, Raymond pushed Horace in front of him to go first up the stairs. Christine was sitting up in bed giving Gideon his first feed. Raymond said she was very pale, but had never looked more beautiful. 'Like a spirit,' he said. She didn't look at Horace, but held out the baby for Raymond to see. 'Another for your tribe,' she said. Raymond didn't know what she meant.

I don't know neither. I have often wondered if, perhaps in her heart of hearts, Christine did love Raymond; or, at least, Raymond as he was the night he preached at Birdo Mission. It may be she was jealous of Horace, and wanted to get rid of him by hook or by crook. If so, I am all wrong; and Christine is greatly to be pitied. I can only say again I don't know; for women as they are to themselves are a mystery to me. I do know she couldn't bear to have Horace in the house once Gideon was born. The doctor said it might affect her mind, if she wasn't given way to; and Raymond had to ask Horace not to show himself. Raymond then devoted himself to looking after Christine and the baby. It was him gave Gideon his bath every day. He said he liked doing it. Gideon was Horace's flesh and blood. I said, 'Why on earth didn't you and Christine join up again then, and bring him up as your own?' He just shook his head. 'Why not? Why not?' I said. I couldn't understand it. Liza had been with other men and had children by other men; but it hadn't made any difference to my feeling for Liza. He said:

> 'Humpty Dumpty sat on a wall,
> Humpty Dumpty had a great fall.
> All the King's horses and all the King's men
> Couldn't put Humpty Dumpty together again.'

17

When I saw Christine again she looked anything but a spirit. She was downstairs and blooming. It was Raymond who didn't look so well. I asked her how the infant was. She said I could go upstairs and have a look at him, if I went on tiptoe. He was asleep in Raymond's cradle. He was beginning to look more as if he might be a human being some day; but I would never have thought he would grow up to be the much too good-looking young man he was, when he came over with Christine a year or two ago. I said I thought he was improving. Abel was still up and playing with his toys; but I could see he was crying tired. Raymond said, 'Christine, isn't it time now Abel was put to bed?' Christine said, 'Abel doesn't want to go to bed yet; do you, Abel?' 'I won't!' said Abel, and looked daggers at his father. I saw what Christine was up to. I had seen that game played before. She was going to let Abel have his own way in everything; and then he would be all for her, and not for Raymond. It was for that reason Raymond was willing, and even glad, for Abel to go to England. 'Is marriage only war at close quarters?' he said, when he looked back on it. 'I couldn't fight Christine over Abel's body. I didn't want him brought up on a battlefield, as I was.'

I didn't stay long. I had soon had enough. I was just leaving when Dudley bounced in. 'Hullo, darling!' he said to Christine, and kissed her. 'How is my beautiful tonight?' Raymond said he would see me part of the way home. He couldn't stand being in the same room as Dudley Waine. I didn't have anything against the fellow, myself: I just put him down as English. Well, Christine let him take her to England when he went back in September. It was arranged for Christine to teach in his mother's school; and she and the two children would be able to live there. As it was a special boarding school for the children of separated parents, perhaps they was as well there, in the circumstances, as they would have been anywhere.

I got the news from Horace when he brought the groceries. 'It's a rotten business all round,' he said. He had hoped now he was keeping away, Raymond and Christine would make it up; but he didn't take it as hard as Raymond. As far as I know, he didn't have much feeling for Gideon, if any. He hardly realised it was his. He did offer Christine to help pay for its keep, but she refused. 'Ah well, it's all in a day's work,' he said. He was more concerned about making his mark in Guernsey. He was already getting on the right side of the right people; and by the time the Second World War came, he was a Douzainier. People seemed to forget his part in the story, once Christine and the children was out of the way. It was Raymond who was no good. I did another stupid thing. I got in a rage, when I thought over what Horace had told me, and went down to Rosamunda to let Christine know, before she cleared off to England, what I thought of her. I didn't know the half of what I know now; or I would have let sleeping dogs lie. I didn't do a scrap of good to Raymond, or Christine, or even to myself; except I let off steam.

I chose to go in the afternoon, and it happened I found her in on her own. The children was with their grandmother across the road. It was a battle royal. I let fly and she didn't mince her words either. I don't remember the half of it now. I know she went off about money to begin with. How was Raymond going to keep a family? If he got a rise at the Greffe, it would only be a few shillings. She couldn't earn anything now herself by teaching in an ordinary school, because she was married. How were they to live? If it wasn't for her good English friends, she didn't know what she would do. Ah, so it was Dudley's mother who was backing her, I thought, and that was why she could refuse help from Horace and leave Raymond. 'Raymond is no use to me now!' she said. 'He is your husband,' I said. She laughed. 'In Chapel!' she said. She went on to tell me things about him she had no right to tell anybody. I wouldn't say such things about any woman I had been with, however much I might dislike her. 'I don't want to hear none of that!' I said. I didn't believe half of it, anyway. She said Raymond and Horace was unnatural; and I know damn well they wasn't. She brought up the things Raymond had told her he had done when he was a boy. I said, 'I heard from boys you played about with when you was a girl of things you had done. I bet you never thought to tell those to Raymond!' 'Would to God I had married a man!' she said. 'Well, when you got one, you didn't like it, did you?' I said. 'Pooh!' she said. 'When it was over, he cried because he'd had to betray Raymond. I laughed in his face!' I said, 'I think you are the rottenest Judas of a woman who ever walked the earth!' She said I was a snake in the grass. I said she was a spider! She told me to get out of her house that instant. I said I would get out of her house when I had done saying what I had come to say. I was going to make her see once and for all the sort of creature she really was. All she wanted was for every chap who saw her to be after her, so as she could tie him up and hang him in her web; and, when she was hungry for a man, gobble up the one she fancied most. I thought that would spite her! Instead, she only smiled her mysterious smile. 'Naturally,' she said. 'I am a woman.' 'Well, if that is what being a woman is,' I said, 'God have mercy on every man born!' I couldn't say no more.

The week before she went away, she moved with the children to her mother's house, and left Raymond on his own. She didn't even tell him which day she was going to England. It was Gwen let him know; and he went and asked Horace to go with him and see her off. He hoped she would part friendly enough to let him know in the future how the children was getting on. Horace said all right; but was silent all the way in the van to the White Rock. They got there early, and stood one each side the gangway to be sure not to miss her. She came with Gideon in her arms and Abel walking, holding her hand. Dudley was behind, carrying the luggage, but went ahead up the gangway because he had the tickets; and she passed between Raymond and Horace without looking to the right or to the left. Abel dragged on her hand and was going to speak to Raymond; but she pulled him along. 'Come on, darling,' she said, 'or the big boat will go without us.' Raymond and Horace walked back to the van. They got in and Horace drove as far as the Weighbridge. He was going back to the Arsenal Stores and Raymond to his office in the Greffe. Horace stopped the van and opened the door, looking straight ahead. Raymond got out and Horace drove on. There was not a word said. They didn't speak again until their last meeting.

I didn't see Raymond to speak to myself for, I think, nearly two years; or it may have been nearly three. I saw him in Town now and then and nodded; and I met him in a pub a few times and said 'Hullo', but he was with fellows I didn't know, and didn't want to know. He left Rosamunda the week after Christine went away; and Herbert's widow and child moved back. It was like Raymond to leave behind all his precious books, and the things he had bought for the house, and not ask to be paid for any of it. He found a room in Victoria Road in a house was let in separate rooms to waiters and barmen and such-like, and run by an old woman who drank all the money she got from her lodgers. I never saw the room. Raymond said it was dreary and dingy in the extreme, and he couldn't get it clean; and all he could see through the one dirty window was somebody else's back wall. Those two or three years are the part of his life he told me least about; but I know he lived in hell.

During the day he was a respectable clerk at the Greffe; but at night goodness knows what he was, or who he knew. He seemed to know every chap on the island who was a bit crooked; and most of those I saw him with I wouldn't have trusted as far as I could see them. He said to me once, 'Those who were cast out were the only ones I was fit to mix with: my secret life was the same as theirs.' Len Carré told me he had met Raymond several times in The Beehive. Well, I had been in The Beehive and I knew what he meant. Queenie Brehaut sold very good clothes for men, and cheap, and I would have bought most of my clothes from him, if it hadn't been he always brought the conversation round to the one subject. He was very gentrified and I don't suppose there was much harm in him. It was said he played with the boys. Well, if he did, I bet it was the boys who egged him on, judging from the young ruffians I saw there when I went in. Unless boys have changed a lot since I was to the Vale School, they are dirtier-minded little buggers at fourteen than he was at forty, the poor old sod. His wife was English. She was tall and square-shouldered with a face like a horse, and she wore a tweed jacket like a man and stout brogue shoes. I reckon she knew all there was to know about her Queenie. She used to turn up at the shop regular every evening when it was going to close to make sure he got home safe. She was a good sort, old Flora.

Raymond liked her. He said she was the only person he knew those years who was really decent to him. She had him to the house quite often. They chatted about books, for she was a great reader; and it was through her he got to know the people who had to do with the Little Theatre. The Little Theatre was Bartlett's Flea-pit done up and fumigated; and a company came over from England every summer and did plays there. I didn't go, but I heard some of them was good. Anyhow, I used to see Raymond out with people who I knew could only be actors and actresses. They may have been all right, but they wore showy clothes and as little as possible; and, even so, it wasn't always easy to tell from looking which was the young hero and which the leading lady. Raymond himself was dressed quietly and decently, as he always was, and there was something about him, even in his worst years, made him look a cut above any of those sort I saw him with.

Once I saw him out with a chap I thought was more up to his mark, and that day Raymond looked quite his old self again and waved cheerily. The chap was fair-haired and not unlike Raymond to look at, only younger; and I didn't think he looked English somehow. He was the one friend Raymond did tell me something about. He was a German. He was studying at a University in England, but was mad about islands, and, when he came over to Guernsey for a holiday, used the opportunity to go to the Greffe and look at some ancient documents to do with the history of the Island. It happened it was Raymond who dug out the old papers to show him and they took to each other right away. They arranged to meet, and went for walks along the cliffs and to the bays swimming; and they talked about everything under the sun, and seemed to agree. Raymond said they got on so well, for six months he was only living for his next visit. When he came again at Easter, it began all right; but soon the fellow began to get moody, and then came out with it. Raymond didn't say exactly what. 'I couldn't do it to him,' he said. 'I liked him too much.' The German didn't understand, and turned nasty. He went back to England before his holiday was over, and never wrote. I have always thought it was that friend leaving him gave Raymond his last push. Raymond said to me, 'I thought we would be together for ever: even if we had to live far apart.' The War was on when he was telling me, and he was still worrying about Karl; wondering if he had been put in a prisoners' camp in England. He hoped he got back to his own country.

For the rest, I don't know what Raymond got up to those years. 'I had to try everything,' he said, 'but there is no way out that way. It only makes chaps despise each other and behave worse than women. I was mad to hope. Man is doomed to Woman.' Well, I suppose that is one way of putting it, but I don't know that I altogether like the idea myself. He certainly didn't have any hope left the night I found him huddled up against the sea wall on the South Esplanade. I wasn't in a much better state myself. I had been feeling particularly miserable at home and come to Town on the bus, if only to see people. It was the lovely summer before the War, a Thursday night in August, if I remember right. The War started in September. I went into a few pubs. I had plenty of friends; or, at least, chaps I knew and who knew me. If I was careful not to get to the fighting stage, a few drinks got me jolly and I was good company; but that night, for some reason, the more I drank the more I felt cold sober, until I seemed to be seeing everybody as if I was looking at them down the wrong end of a telescope. They was very far away and very small, and I didn't like them at all, at all! In desperation I thought I would go for a walk down Havelet and sit on the seat where Liza and me had sat that night. I don't know why I got that daft idea into my head, or what good I expected it would do me. I was well past the slaughter-houses, before I realised what a fool I was being. Liza wouldn't be there. That once in our lives we had come close together, but the battle had started again, and we had gone apart. It was no use crying over spilt milk. I turned back and thought I might be in time to catch the Picture bus home. It was getting on for ten.

There wasn't many people about that end, and when I got to the Castle Walk I noticed a chap clinging to the sea wall. It is a thick wall and rounded on top, and he had an arm slung over it, as if he wouldn't let go of it for dear life. He was standing in an awkward position with his legs stuck out, as if he had the rickets; and I thought he must be dead drunk. I was on the other side of the road actually, but crossed over to see if I could help him; before I got to him, I realised it was Raymond. I had never known Raymond be drunk before. He would go into a pub and have a couple perhaps, but only so as to be with other fellows. I said, 'Hullo, Raymond! What you doing round here?' He rolled his eyes at me, but I don't think he knew who I was. 'Uh,' was all he said. 'Where have you been?' I said. He answered me very slow; but he picked his words carefully, and spoke quite clear. He didn't sound drunk, 'I ... have ... been ... to ... the ... end ... of ... the ... breakwater,' he said. I thought it best to make out nothing was wrong. 'Many fishing down there tonight?' I said. He answered me in the same slow, dead voice without any feeling in it whatsoever. 'There was nobody fishing down there,' he said. 'The way was left open for me. I could not do it. I was afraid I would swim.'

I wanted to get him safe home somehow, but I didn't know where he lived. I had asked Horace once, but he had shrugged his shoulders and said, 'How should I know?' I said, 'Where d'you live now?' He came alive at once. 'I am NOT going back to my room!' he said. 'Well, you can't stay here all night,' I said, reasonably enough. 'I am NOT going back to that room! I am NOT! I am NOT! I am NOT!' he said, and clung on tighter to the wall. 'Why d'you hang on to the wall like that?' I said. 'It's company,' he said. I didn't know what to do. I have already said I had been drinking, and was in a strange state of mind myself, and perhaps that can explain what happened. I got a feeling Hetty was there. At the time I would have sworn it wasn't my imagination. She was more real than when she was sitting by me at the Pictures. It was as if she was in me and all around me, and was full of sorrow because this was happening to her boy. I heard myself saying something I would never have thought of saying otherwise. 'Come along now, Raymond,' I said, 'you are coming home with me to Les Moulins; and you won't have to go back to your room, and you will have company.' 'All right, Ebby,' he said. He knew who I was then; but I think he would have gone with anybody. He let go of the wall, and I held him by the arm. 'Can you walk?' I said. 'I think so,' he said. He was wobbly at first, but soon he could get along without me holding him. I said, 'If you can go a little faster, we'll be in time to catch the Picture bus,' and he stepped out. There was nothing wrong with his body. It was his mind.

The people was just coming out of St Julien's when we got there, and the buses was lined up outside. Harold Falla from the Vale was standing by his. 'Going our way?' I said. 'Hop in!' he said, 'but sit at the back: you'll be the last out.' He was a great bus-driver, Harold Falla. He didn't follow any route with his Picture bus, but took everybody as near as he could to their back door. He dropped us at the end of our rough track, where no motor-car can go further; but he had been all round Birdo and nearly to Fort Doyle, and up and down over the grass across L'Ancresse Common to deliver old Mr and Mrs Bell to their bungalow, and back along Les Mielles for the Hamelins, and down L'Ancresse Road and round by the Vale Church. I enjoyed that ride. The bus was full. There was some standing and some sitting on each other; and everybody knew everybody and was talking and laughing and, once we got started, they sang song after song, and the rickety old bus went singing through the night:

> Seven green bottles,
> Six green bottles,
> Five green bottles,
> Four green bottles,
> Three green bottles,
> Two green bottles,
> One green bottle,
> Hanging on the wall!

Raymond and me sat quiet in our back corner. He was leaning against me, and I had an arm around him. He looked up into my face and smiled. 'What's it, Raymond?' I said. 'It's good to be alive,' he said.

18

Raymond didn't go to the Greffe again until the Monday. He meant to go the next morning, but didn't wake up in time; and I didn't wake him. When we got in the night before, I made up the fire and fried him a good meal of bacon and eggs, and brewed a pot of tea. He ate as if he was half starved. He had been having to get ready his own meals, and I don't think he had taken the trouble to feed himself properly. It wasn't because he couldn't. I was never better looked after than the months he looked after me and no trouble was too much for him. He didn't say much that first night. He wanted to thank me, but I said there was nothing to thank me for. I let him have the bed in my mother's room and a suit of my pyjamas. After he had gone to bed, I sat by the fire wondering if I ought to get a doctor for him next day; but when I went in with the candle to see if he was all right, he was curled up sound asleep.

He was asleep yet in the morning when I looked in to give him a cup of tea; and I let him sleep on. I went down to the Post Office at L'Islet and telephoned the Greffe. It was a Mr Ogier spoke to me, and I said Raymond wasn't very well and was at my place. He sounded a nice man, that Mr Ogier, and said he had been thinking for some time Raymond was on the verge of a nervous breakdown. There had been some trouble at home, he said: as if I didn't know! In the office he was much liked and they were all very sorry about it. That is where Raymond was wrong. He thought everybody was against him, but a lot of it was his imagination. Mr Ogier said there was no hurry for him to go back until he was well. It wasn't until five o'clock in the afternoon he woke up; and then I told him what I had done. After tea, he told me about his drunken landlady, and the other lodgers who had women in; and not only women, some of them. I said the only thing for him to do was to pay her off, and bring his things to Les Moulins. On the Monday morning he said he would go to work and settle with Mrs Maloney; and in the evening he came back with a suitcase, which was all he had in the world, except his pay. He wanted to arrange to pay me rent, but I wasn't charging for his company in my empty house.

There can't have been a more pleasant chap to live with. He didn't push himself, and seemed to know without being told how I liked things done.

Living on my own, I had got set in my ways, and any other chap would have rubbed me up the wrong way pretty quick. When Tabitha came for the Saturday and Sunday, I made him sleep on the green-bed; and he didn't mind. He got on well with Tabitha, and she was glad for him to be there. I noticed, however, when he came in from work, he had a haunted look; but once he was indoors and sitting by the fire talking, you wouldn't have thought there was anything wrong with him.

The war with Hitler came, as I expected it would. There had been a lot of silly talk the year before saying there wasn't going to be no war, when Chamberlain went to see the creature; but I didn't see how anybody in their right mind could think anything would come of that. I blamed the English as much as the Germans. After the last war, they had forced the Germans into such a plight, Hitler was the only sort of chap they could turn to. Once he was in power, the English was only too willing to lend him money, provided the interest was paid; but Hitler wasn't going to let the Germans forget what they had gone through the years after 1918 and behave like an English gentleman now. I was too angry to talk about it, or argue. The last time I had been willing to leave it to the big ones to decide; but now the big ones had landed us into it again, who on earth was I to leave it to? I couldn't do nothing myself. It didn't upset Raymond, as much as it did me. 'It is the way of the world,' he said. 'It always has been and always will be, and will get worse and worse as time goes on.' He wasn't exactly cheerful. Anyhow, the War didn't make much difference to Guernsey at first; and we had no idea of what was coming.

I thought Raymond would be staying with me until it was all over; though I was by no means sure this time which side would win. He seemed happy enough at Les Moulins. The weekends he made himself useful in the house, and helped me in the greenhouse to pull up the plants, or came with me out fishing; but when the winter months came he wasn't so well. The long dark evenings he would talk to me by the hour of his misery as a child, and of the half-and-half happiness of his marriage. It was those winter evenings I learnt most of what I have written about him in this book; and a lot I haven't said and won't say. I think his heart was broken because he doubted if God was love. 'Cupboard love isn't love,' he said. 'Is there any other?' I didn't want to have to answer that question. 'Is there, Ebenezer?' he said. 'Have you ever known it?' 'Yes,' I said.

He sat for a long time looking into the fire, saying nothing. At last he said, 'You are thinking of your friend, Jim Mahy.' I said, 'I wasn't think-ing of Jim, as a matter of fact. I was thinking of Jean Batiste and my sister Tabitha.' He said, 'Yes, but Jim and Jean are dead. It is easy to believe in it because it wasn't broken. They didn't break it of themselves.' I said, 'Perhaps it never really is broken, if the truth was known.' I don't know why I said that, because I am not at all sure I believe it. He said, 'I hope to

God you are right!' I didn't know then he was coming home every night along the Route Militaire, because he was afraid he might run into Horace if he came round Baubigny, and Horace not speak to him. Then one night he came in from work white as a sheet and trembling and didn't answer when I spoke to him.

I made him sit down and got out some brandy, but he wouldn't touch it. I said, 'For Christ's sake, tell me what is the matter, Raymond! I don't care what it is; but tell me!' He clung to me and cried. It was as if he was being torn in two. Only once in my life, have I cried like that, and I know it is for something you can't ever tell anybody. 'I understand, Raymond,' I said, 'you don't have to tell me.' He managed to get out a few words. He had run bang into Horace in the narrowest part of the Pollet. They had passed so close their shoulders touched; but Horace had gone on without a word or a look. I said, 'What odds, for God's sake? He is not worth you bothering about!' I was fed up with the big Horace, and the trouble he had brought on Raymond. 'Why the hell couldn't he stop in America where he belong?' I said. As it happened, I couldn't have said anything better, if I had tried. Raymond turned on me as he had never done before, and told me off good and proper; and by the time he had done telling me what he thought of me, he was quite himself again.

I was wonderfully good to anybody I liked, he said, but to those I didn't like I was blind and stupid and unfair. I had liked his mother and his father; but I had always been unfair to his Uncle Percy and his Aunt Prissy. I was unfair to Christine, even when I was being most friendly; and, as for Horace, I had been down on him ever since he was a boy. I thought he was all swank, but I didn't see it was the only way he had of getting along. He was humble really. He wasn't a bully: I was a bully. I didn't realise how different people was made different. I imagined everybody was made the same as me, or ought to be; and if they didn't behave as I thought they ought to behave, it was all up with them as far as I was concerned. That is, except for the few people I took a fancy to, and those, it didn't matter what they did, they could do no wrong. 'Well, you may be right, Raymond,' I said. 'Come on now, son: let's have some grub!' He smiled like an angel.

I let him spend the rest of the evening talking about Horace to his heart's content. I can't say he won me over to Horace's side, or that I agree with him even now; but he did make me see Horace hadn't been too bad to him when he was a kid. Raymond had been a timid little boy when he went to the Secondary School and, until he did a bit of boxing at Gosport, had no idea how to defend himself. The years he was at the Secondary on his own, he had been bullied by the other boys; but once Horace came from the Capelles there wasn't a boy dared to bully his cousin Raymond. It was Horace he had to thank he had blossomed out and got stronger, and done so well his last year at school. Raymond admitted he was better at his school work than Horace, and did his homework for him; but it was a fair exchange. 'It was always a fair exchange between Horace and me,' he said. 'He has something I haven't got and I have something he hasn't got. If we had been born rolled into one, we would have made the perfect husband for Christine.' I had my doubts if Christine would have thought so; but for once I wasn't going to be unfair.

That night I lay on my back in bed thinking of what to do about Hetty's boy. I don't like to be beaten. I had taken him under my wing, meaning and hoping to get him better; but he seemed to be getting worse. I thought perhaps if he gave up going to the Greffe for a while, and pottered round Les Moulins, he wouldn't be reminded of things he would do better to forget. Young Lihou wasn't coming back to work for me in the spring, as he wanted to enlist, so I would have plenty I could give Raymond to do, and he wouldn't feel he was being kept for nothing. Myself, I didn't care if he was. Anyhow, I put it to him next morning when we was having breakfast. His face lit up. He said it would be wonderful; but then began to raise difficulties, as I thought he would, about me keeping him. I said I ought to pay him a wage by rights, but I wouldn't do that. The money in the china fowl was for our present use. He could take what he wanted without asking me, or telling me. He said he wouldn't need it: he had clothes and so on. I said, 'Well, that's settled.'

I offered to go and see Mr Ogier for him; but he said he would go himself and ask for six months leave without pay. I was glad because it gave me a chance to go down to the Arsenal Stores and tell Horace not to bring my groceries to the house any more. Horace was out on his round; but I saw Gwen. I didn't say anything about the meeting in the Pollet; but I did say I thought it would be wiser if Horace didn't come to Les Moulins now Raymond was going to be there during the day. Gwen said she would tell him if I insisted, but she didn't agree. For Horace's sake. According to her, it was only pride on Horace's part. She said he would never have peace of mind again, until he and Raymond were as they used to be. I said that wasn't possible now. She seemed to think it was somehow; but promised to tell Horace not to come with the groceries. I know now it was Gwen, and not me, who was right; though it was not so much a question of pride. It was pride in so far as Horace didn't like being turned out of the house because Christine said so; but he really cut Raymond off because of the dirty things she spread around. It didn't suit Horace to be tarred with the same brush. I was thinking along those lines on the way back to Les Moulins; but it was something I couldn't have explained to Gwen. Raymond came back later in the morning and said Mr Ogier had given him leave and been most sympathetic.

Raymond earned his keep ten times over. I don't know where Harold got the idea from he was no good at doing things. He transplanted all my seedlings, and I got a better crop that year than I have ever had; though most of it had to be given or thrown away because the blessed Germans was here. Also I got some timber, and he built me a fowl-house far better than I could have done it myself. I didn't know the day was to come when I would have to chop down his precious fowl-house, he had put so much work into, for the wood to make a fire to keep Tabitha and me warm. By then, the fowls was all stolen, except for a couple I kept locked up in the wash-house; and Raymond was no more. I look back now on the time he lived with me as the most peaceful I have lived through. He said to me once, 'The monks on Lihou used to live like us.' I said, 'Yes, but I bet they had to pray morning, noon and night, those poor old monks.' He said, 'It is better to do things than to pray.'

He was very quiet. He didn't talk much about his troubles, and I really thought he was beginning to forget. Of an evening after tea, I would sit by the fire with my pipe and read the *Press*; and perhaps have a drink beside me. He would have a drink beside him too; but would be sitting up to the table reading the big Bible. It was funny to see him sitting there reading the big Bible like my mother used to; but having a sip of beer every now and then. 'I wonder why this book is called the Good Book,' he said one night. 'It has been the cause, or the excuse, for more wars and persecutions and tortures and miseries than any other book ever written.' It was the only time he said much about the War. 'Hitler is the Old Testament all over again,' he said. 'It is no wonder he hates the Jews.' I didn't follow him then, and a lot of other things he jerked out from time to time I didn't understand. That time I asked him what he meant.

'Beware of any people who say they are chosen of history, or by God,' he said. 'They choose themselves. There are no Chosen People.' I said, 'Well, my mother didn't think that: she believed in the Elect.' 'So do the Communists,' he said. 'They call them the Proletariat. The Nazis call them the Aryans. It amounts to the same. The Totalitarian State. There is nothing more false. The true total is outside the reach of our human hearts and minds. At most, we only get a glimpse of it.' 'I don't know about that,' I said. 'I have never got a glimpse, even.' 'It is better that way,' he said, 'than to imagine you know it all. Thank God I am an islander; and can never be anything more!' I wonder what he would think if he was alive now. Guernsey become day by day in every way more and more a Totalitarian State. I reckon Hitler won the War.

When he went on about the New Testament, he got me quite frightened. I had always thought in my own mind the Kings in the Old Testament, like the Kings and Queens of England, was a bloodthirsty lot; but I had always thought the New Testament was sort of all right. He said it was worse. 'No man cometh unto the Father but by Me.' Those were the most blasphemous words any man ever uttered. He spoke of Russia. If in Russia you don't think what Comrade Stalin says you are allowed to think, you are liquidated. That is bad enough; but at least the Communists don't believe there is anything after. The Christians do and are totalitarian about the next world as well as this. For centuries they have been consigning countless millions to hell. He said it was Jesus Himself who set the example. On the Cross He promised Paradise to the repentant thief, but not to the unrepentant. 'He was right there, surely,' I said. 'I might bring myself to forgive a chap: but he would have to say first he was sorry. Otherwise, I would have to be forgiving all day long.' 'Yes, but you don't pretend to be God,' said Raymond. He spoke of Judas; and then I really did think he was possessed by a devil. He said Judas was the only one of the Twelve who loved Jesus. The others only followed Him. Judas knew Him through and through for what He was; and died from love of Him and with Him. I said, 'Well, that is not what it say in the Bible, you know; unless it say it in Greek.' 'Where was He those three days?' he said. 'In Hades, begging forgiveness of the damned. It wasn't until the Harlot out of the fullness of her unreciprocated love had raised His spirit from the dead He could ascend into heaven. I tell you, if Jesus of Nazareth does indeed sit upon the Throne of God, judging the quick and the dead; then Mary of Magdala is seated at His right hand, and Judas is the power behind the Throne and stands, holding the bag.' He closed the Bible. 'In this book I will read no more,' he said. I didn't see him open it again; or any other book, for that matter. He glanced at the *Press* occasionally and sat by the fire with his drink and smoked a cigarette and dreamed.

19

It is hard to know what to do for the best in this world; for whatever you do have a way of turning out different from how you thought. When I got Raymond to leave Les Moulins, I honestly thought I was doing the best I could for him. It was the last thing I wanted to do for myself: I didn't want him to leave me ever, and when I got back home from seeing him off on the bus, I felt bereaved. I had my doubts then if I had done wise; yet I had been thinking for some time things couldn't go on as they was. For months I was the only living soul he ever spoke to: except for Tabitha when she came, and Louisa after my blood. At first I had sent him down the Bridge a few times to get things; but he always came back with his haunted look, and said everybody was pointing at him and talking about him. I said, 'Well, perhaps they are, and perhaps they are not. In any case, people point at and talk about other people just so as to have somebody to point at and talk about. If it come down to brass tacks, they are only interested in themselves.'

It was really my fault, or at least through my carelessness, Raymond broke down. It was getting towards the end of May and visitors from England was beginning to come over in spite of the War, thinking they would get away from it. Instead, some of them got caught here by the Germans, and didn't get back until after the War was over: if they got back at all. Anyhow, it occurred to me to weed and rake around the ancient monument, though I wasn't being paid for it then, but just to make it look nice, and I asked Raymond to give me a hand. I just didn't think what I was doing. I was working at one end with my back to him, and he was working the other. I didn't even know anything was wrong until I heard him and looked round. He was sitting on the ground shaking and sobbing; and not able to control himself. I went over and sat by him and succeeded in getting out of him what was the matter. It was Abel. He had been thinking of Abel the day he dug up the bones. He had been so lovely! He was always seeing Abel about the place, he said; and sometimes he couldn't bear it he had lost him. He soon pulled himself together, and said he was sorry. 'It is nothing you have to be sorry for,' I said. 'It is only natural.' He said he had been trying so hard not to give me trouble. 'I know I worry you,' he said.

That evening I talked it over with him quietly. I said first of all he must understand I didn't want him to go away and, whatever happened, he could always come back, if he wanted to; but I did think it would be better for him if he lived where he wasn't known and everybody didn't know his private affairs, and where there was nothing to remind him of the past. I could write to Liza Quéripel at Pleinmont, and I was sure she would do something. I remembered her promise. He could easily find something to do out there, and he would make new friends. It was the lunatic fringe of the island and the people round there was a more free and easy lot, and not nearly as strait-laced as round our way. He brightened up but said, 'Who is going to keep the Captain off you?' I said, 'I can keep the Captain off myself, don't you worry about that!' I was talking braver than I felt. He said it was a pity I didn't think of myself sometimes.

I wrote to Liza and explained as best I could. I didn't let Raymond read the letter because I put in it if she was out of pocket she must let me know and I would pay. I got a very nice letter back. 'My dear,' she began, 'I am happy you have taken me at my word at last.' She said yes, of course, she would take care of Raymond, and be glad to; and he could live in her house, if he didn't mind having the attic up the ladder. She had plenty of jobs herself she could give him to do; or, if he preferred it, he could work for other people. There was a shortage of men and it was going to be worse, as a number of the young fellows were waiting to join up. She said I mustn't think of paying her anything: that would make her really angry. She ended funny, I thought. 'With love, you know. Liza.' Raymond said he would go.

I did one thing I know now was sensible. I might almost have known what was coming. I insisted on fitting him out before he went. I got his shoes mended by Jim Le Poidevin, and bought him a pair of boots with thick soles for working in the ground. I got him a pair of corduroy trousers from Queenie Brehaut, and some strong shirts and a handknitted guernsey. I packed his case for him, and put his old things in the rag-bag. I little thought the time would come when I would be glad to have his old rags to wear myself. He didn't have to go to Town to get the bus, because the summer bus round the coast was running as usual, and I put him on it at L'Ancresse. Before he got on he threw his arms around me and kissed me, as if I was his father. I don't know what the people on the bus thought; but I didn't care. That was how it came about that Raymond was living at Pleinmont when the Germans came. I didn't tell a soul where he had gone, except Tabitha. When people asked me where he was, I said, 'He have gone for a change of air.'

Well, when we saw the clouds of smoke in the sky from the Germans blowing up things across the water in France, and boatloads of French came over with horrible stories of what the Germans was doing to them, I reckon we all knew our turn was coming. There was some fools who thought the Germans wouldn't bother about little Guernsey; but I have never been one to hope for the best when the worst is staring me in the face. The question everybody was asking was whether to stop in Guernsey, or go to England. That is, if they could. One minute it was said everybody would have to go; and the next minute that nobody would be able to. At last it seemed that anybody would be able to go who wanted to. Then nobody could make up their minds if they wanted to or not. I think at least half the inhabitants of the Vale and St Sampson's came to ask Ebenezer Le Page what he thought they ought to do. I knew what I was going to do. I didn't have to think twice. I was stopping. I didn't understand then, and I don't understand now, how any Guernseyman could leave his house and his land and his own people, and go and live without nothing among strangers.

I had some sympathy with those people who wanted to let their children go, or even go with them, because they was thinking for the good of their children; but, for all that, I thought the more Guernsey people there was left on Guernsey, the more trouble we could give to the Germans. As it turned out, we didn't give any trouble to the Germans. There was no English soldiers left on the island to fight for us; and we wasn't left with any guns to fight for ourselves, unless it was a few air-rifles and pea-shooters. I had to put up with a German patrolling regularly along our rough path outside Les Moulins; and wasn't even allowed to go down on the beach and pick limpets, when Tabitha and me was nearly starving. I am glad to say I got the better of him more than once, the nuisance! I couldn't bear to see the German soldiers about in their ugly helmets that looked as if they was put on back to front, and their dirty-looking greenish uniforms that made me feel sick. The nobs of the States had to stop on the island because it was their job; but I reckon most of them would have done so, anyway. I am sure Ambrose Sherwill would have. He was a fine man. His wife also decided to stop; and keep her children with her. She was a brave woman. It was during those days, when nobody knew if they was coming or going, I got friendly with Monsieur Le Boutillier. I met him outside my gate. He said, 'What you doing, brother?' I said, 'Business as usual.' He said, 'Same here.' I said, 'How about the kids?' 'The whole family,' he said. I held out my hand.

I didn't give people advice as to what they ought to do. I said what I was doing myself. What they did was their own business. There was one other at least, besides me, who didn't think twice; and that was Lydia Mahy. I couldn't help laughing when I met her along the Braye Road one day. She was dressed in black voile up to her chin; and walking with her back as stiff as a poker, carrying a little black book in her hand. She looked every inch the old maid and Guernsey lady she was; and Germans or no Germans, was going the round of the houses, collecting her rentes. It was business as usual with Lydia. I said, 'Hullo, so you have not gone then!' She said, 'If they come, every woman, every woman on the island will be raped: every woman!' Her voice was trembling with excitement. They came but the worst that was to happen to poor Lydia was for her to have two German officers billetted at Les Grands Gigands. She said they behaved like perfect gentlemen.

I am not saying I was brave by stopping in Guernsey to face the Germans. There was one thing I was dead scared of: that was gas. I didn't want to end up like Jim Machon. It was perhaps as well I didn't have much chance to think of what the Germans might do to us. I had a more immediate danger on my doorstep. Louisa. She came every day. I didn't have the heart to hide from her, but let her come indoors and talk. She had one idea in her head. She wanted me to go with her to England; and she begged and implored me. I said 'No! No! No!' but I might just as well have talked to her wooden leg, for all the difference it made! She would go home crying; and come back the next day and try again. On the Friday, I heard the explosions from the air-raid on the White Rock. I thought well, here they are: they have come! Louisa was gone home; but in the evening back she came.

She was in a terrible state. She said thousands had been killed on the White Rock. As a matter of fact, it was about thirty, I think. Among them was George Bougourd, who had fifty boxes of my tomatoes in his lorry for the boat. He got under his lorry out of the way; but it was hit and went up in flames, and he was burnt to death. The Germans was gone for now, she said, but was sure to come back: then if we wasn't all bombed and killed, we would be tortured and murdered to death, one by one. She had brought a suitcase and a big black bag. She wasn't going to sleep in her room in Town again on any account. 'Goodness, you can't sleep here!' I said. 'What will the people say?' The people could say what they liked: she didn't care what the people said! She would sleep on the green-bed, in a chair, on the floor, anywhere. I gave in and said she could sleep in my mother's bed. She said we could go on the boat to England in the morning. If I wouldn't go with her, she would never leave me: she would be true to me to death and we would die together! It was a horrible thought.

I played the dirtiest trick on Louisa. I am not going to make excuses. All is fair in love and war. I said I would go with her. I didn't pack a bag, because I didn't have a bag to pack. I have never been nowhere. I put on my best clothes, and wore my thick overcoat; though it was going to be a blazing hot day. I said it would come in handy for the winter. She believed me. I carried her suitcase; and she hopped along beside me to the bus, holding my arm. When we got off at the bottom of St Julien's Avenue, I put down her suitcase. I suddenly remembered I had forgotten to bring any money; except for the few shillings I had in my pocket! I would have to go back home and get some, I said; but she must go and wait for me on the boat. She wouldn't. 'I have plenty for both of us,' she said, and opened her black bag. It was chock block full of five pound notes! I don't know where she got them from: the banks was only letting people have twenty pounds each, I think it was. She must have had them hidden away somewhere, the wicked old thing! I said I couldn't possibly live on her money; but she threw her arms around my neck and began to cry and scream: 'What am I going to do? What am I going to do?'

I didn't know what I was going to do; let alone what she was going to do. I don't know yet what I would have done, if Bill Vaudin hadn't happened to pass down the Avenue; and I verily believe he was sent by the good God to save me. He worked on the White Rock. 'Hi, Bill!' I shouted. 'This lady want to go on the boat. Will you please see she get on safe; and come back and tell me. I will be worried to death until I know.' 'She will have to hurry, then,' he said; and picked up her case, and caught hold of her. I don't think she knew if it was him or me: she was so frightened! The last I saw of her was going along in front of the Fruit Export with a hop and a kick; and Bill Vaudin making her run. In a few minutes, I saw the boat go out past the pier heads. I was praying she was aboard. Soon Bill came back wiping the sweat from his brow, and said she was the last up the gangway. As it happened, it was the last boat to go; so Louisa Trouteaud was the last person to leave Guernsey willingly; except for a few fellows who escaped in small boats later on. I breathed again. I was safe.

When I got home I thought seriously about what I was going to do with my money. I hadn't worked and saved all my life for the Germans to come and have it. I wasn't bothered by people coming to ask for advice that Saturday afternoon, for those who was going was gone, and the others was home in their houses wondering and waiting for what was going to happen next. I made my plans. I decided to leave what was in the china fowl where it was. Besides what I kept in the china fowl for expenses from day to day, there was more than a few hundred pounds locked up in the cash-box. It was a strong iron cash-box I had bought from Leale on the Bridge; and I always carried the key to it on my watch chain. I emptied the cash-box and hid the money in a place where nobody would think of looking. It was easy because it was all notes. It was my golden sovereigns more than all else I didn't want the Germans to find. I got the pied-du-cauche down from up the chimney in the wash-house and I emptied it into the cash-box. The sovereigns filled it right level with the top. I locked it. I waited until it was getting dark, and then went outside and dug a deep hole under the apple-tree. There wasn't a living soul about and nobody saw me. I put the cash-box in the hole and filled it in and raked around. When I was done there wasn't a sign of the crime. My sovereigns are buried there to this day.

Tabitha turned up on the Sunday morning, though I hadn't expected her that week. She said she had come to say she was going to live with me. I didn't argue. I felt a great relief. She had settled it with the Priaulx. Gervase and Louise was gone to England, so she didn't feel under any obligation. Actually, Gervase served in the Air Force during the War, and won a medal like his father. Louise joined the W.R.E.N.S., the Navy for women. Jack Priaulx and Annette was in good health yet; though Annette died during the Occupation, and Jack soon after the War was over. They had both wanted Tabitha to stay with them, but she said, 'My place now is with my brother.' They knew there was no chance of moving Tabitha once she had made up her mind.

She had brought a few things with her, and Jack brought the rest of her belongings in his motor-car on the Monday. The Sunday was a happy day. It was just Tabitha and me again. It might have been the old days when my father was alive. I told her what I had done with the sovereigns and she laughed. I said if the Germans got me and not her, they was for her. She said, 'The Germans won't get either of us.' She sounded so sure I believed it. She cooked me a darn good dinner; and in the afternoon, we sat on La Petite Grève and made stones bounce on the water like when we was kids. The weather was perfect. In the evening, everything was so peaceful I couldn't believe there was a war on in the world anywhere. I didn't know the Germans had already landed on the Airport. It wasn't until the next day when the *Press* came, I knew Guernsey belonged to Germany.

I had heard from Liza that Raymond was happily settled in, and being most helpful. He didn't speak much to people, she said: but everybody around there liked him, only they thought he was a bit simple. She didn't. 'He is hardly of this world,' she wrote. 'I wish I knew the half he knows.' He didn't write to me himself. He said he didn't have the words to say what he wanted to say to me, but made Liza promise to say 'God bless Ebenezer.' After the Germans came, I got a letter from Liza about every six months for two or three years. Raymond was the same, and she wouldn't be without him for anything. He had kept remarkably well; and so was she. He grew quite a lot of stuff in the garden for them to eat; and, for the rest, spent most of his time up in his attic room. Occasionally she heard him talking to himself up there. Otherwise he was quite sensible, though he did stray off sometimes and go where he wasn't allowed to go by the Germans; but they were kind to him. She didn't believe there was a German would do him any harm.

I didn't altogether like her trust in the Germans, but daren't say a word of warning when I wrote back, for I never knew who might get hold of my letter. I wasn't feeling very friendly myself towards the Germans by that time: I was learning what it was like to go hungry. I noticed Horace was looking as prosperous and as well-fed as ever. I also knew he was making a fortune in German marks. He certainly had the knack of getting in with the right people: it didn't matter if they was Guernsey or German. He had a pass to go down to the harbour whenever he wanted to, though nobody knew what for, and he got to know chaps on the barges and ships that came over with provisions from France, and what he got off them on the Q.T. was nobody's business. The Arsenal Stores was never without anything. It is true when you went in, it looked pretty barren, but there was plenty hidden away under the counter. He kept his motor-van longer than practically anybody else on the island was allowed to run a car; and though the Germans requisitioned it eventually, he was well paid for it.

I bought some goods off Horace myself; even though it nearly ruined me. I got pounds of sugar from him, when it was very short: I was tired of seeing Tabitha boiling beetroot. I bought quarter pounds of real tea from him. Tabitha was one who liked a good cup of tea; but she stopped me buying it when she found out where I got it from. She said I was helping the Germans, whose duty it was to allow us enough food; and it wasn't being fair to Gervase and Louise, and so many other Guernsey boys and girls who were in the Forces. I had no argument against that. All the same, I kept on buying tobacco from Horace. I am not sure now what the marks was worth; but I think I paid him round about eighteen bob for half an ounce, or was it an ounce? Anyhow, it was like smoking gold; but dock leaves and rose petals made me feel sick, and I couldn't smoke the tail of a donkey. Horace's argument was there would be more people miserable and starving on the island if it wasn't for him. He was doing the best he could for Guernsey in the circumstances; and keeping up morale. Besides, anything he got on the sly, he had to pay through the nose for himself. The one thing I will give him credit for is he didn't give his customers away. He wasn't the informer sort; and there was plenty of those about. He gave each of us a number, and we had to say our number, if we wanted anything wasn't on the ration. I remember my number was one thousand two hundred and three.

He didn't go round for orders once his van was gone; so I was astonished when one day he turned up at Les Moulins. He looked haggard and in great suffering, as I had never imagined he could look. It was then he begged me to tell him where Raymond was. I said, 'Raymond is well where he is.' He said, 'I am not!' I said, 'That is your own look-out. Why don't you marry Gwen?' He said, 'She is the last woman on earth I would ever marry; or anything else. She loves me.' I thought well, perhaps there is something decent in old Horace after all and I wondered if I was right in not giving him a chance to go and see Raymond. I also thought it might make Raymond very happy. I said, 'He is living in the house of Liza Quéripel at Pleinmont.' He said, 'I know the house. It is far enough away.'

I didn't really think he would go. At that time we was all staying in our own parishes as much as we could; and nobody was going to make the journey to the other end of the island, unless he absolutely had to. He would either have to walk, or go on a broken-down old bike with rope for tyres. Horace must have gone next day. It wasn't a week later when Gwen came to see me. She hadn't seen Horace for days, and he hadn't been back at nights. She wasn't a woman to make a fuss over nothing; but she said she was afraid she might give him away without meaning to. The customers didn't bother to say their numbers half the time, for Horace knew; but she was afraid to ask. How was she to know who had to be given a chicken from under the counter, when they asked for an ounce of fat? If she made one mistake, somebody might talk, and there would be a search.

She brought a book with her she had found under some sacks in the woodshed. In it was the numbers and the names of the people they was for. She asked me if I would keep it until Horace came back. I said I would but, while he was away, she had better give people only what they was allowed. She could make out she didn't understand. I thought it was only fair to let her know he had gone to see Raymond; and, as it was my fault, I said the only thing for me to do was to go myself, and find out what had happened. She said I had taken a great load off her mind. After she had gone, I had a look through that book, and even I was surprised at the people whose names was in it; and there was nearly as many Germans as Guernsey. When I got back from Pleinmont, I burnt it page by page.

20

I didn't know what I had let myself in for when I said I would go to Pleinmont. I wasn't as young as I was; and I was weaker than I thought, from
not having enough to eat. I didn't notice it so much while I was working. If
I felt hungry, I had a smoke; and when I got tired, I sat on a box. Sometimes I got mixed up in the head, and found myself doing stupid things:
like going to the well with a full bucket. I would have to walk all the way to
Pleinmont. My last bike, which was a Humber and a good bike in its time,
was in bits and pieces; and I had given some of the parts to young Le Boutillier, so he could fit up his to ride to work on. He worked at the Airport for
the Germans; though he did as little as he could. Luckily, I had a pair of
good boots with leather soles an inch thick; and those was rare those days,
I can tell you. They was almost too precious to wear.

I had good old Jim Le Poidevin to thank for those soles. When I took
those boots down to him to mend, the uppers was as good as new, but the
soles was all holes, and I didn't expect he would be able to do much to
them. All I had else to wear on my feet was sacking and brown paper. I had
no sooner got inside Jim's cabin and said Hullo, than in walked a smart
young German officer. He was carrying a lovely pair of high boots in his
hand, the same as he was wearing, and the soles might have been thin but,
as far as I could see, wasn't worn out. Jim turned his head away from me, as
if I wasn't there, and said 'Good-morning, mein Herr,' to the officer, and
what could he have the pleasure of doing for him? The officer was as polite
as Jim was, but didn't mind getting in front of me, and being served out of
his turn. He didn't see Jim give me a quick wink. I knew old Jim was up to
something. He examined the officer's boots and tapped the soles and said
they were fit to be mended, and he would do his very best to make a good
job of it: but had the Herr Lieutenant brought a piece of leather for him to
do it with? The Herr Lieutenant had not brought a piece of leather. It was
very sad, said Jim; but he had no leather, and could only mend the beautiful boots with linoleum. There was broken pieces of worn-out linoleum
all over his bench. The officer said it was very sad, it was very bad, ya, but
linoleum would not do and he would have to take the boots elsewhere. Jim
said he could not be more sorry, and thanked the lieutenant for doing him

the honour of coming to him first. The lieutenant bowed stiff from the waist up, and said thank you, and Jim said thank you again, and the lieutenant said thank you again. When he had gone, Jim waited until he was out of sight, and then pulled a thick piece of leather from under his bench. 'This will do for yours,' he said.

I trusted those boots to get me to Pleinmont. I didn't know they was going to weigh ten ton before I got there. I left home straight away after breakfast, which was a turnip and a piece of bread, and something supposed to be coffee. Tabitha wanted me to take the rest of the bread to eat on the way, but I wouldn't hear of it. She said I must try and find somewhere out there to sleep and come back the next day. I said I would do nothing of the sort. I wasn't going to leave Tabitha by herself all night. The only robberies we had suffered so far was from the fowl-house; but you never knew who was about at nights. If for any reason I had to sneak out, I used to creep along by the hedges like a criminal, and was always in before midnight. I promised Tabitha I would be at home by curfew, which was at eight. I had the whole day to go ten miles or so and back.

I decided I would go by Les Rouvets and make for the King's Mills; and then I could cut through St Saviour's and come out on Rocquaine not far from Liza's house. It would be shorter than going round the coast. I don't know how it was I lost my way in broad daylight on roads I had been along dozens of times with Jim. My legs was so weak they was like water, and my head was going round. The traffic terrified me. Great lorries full of Germans was tearing along the roads on the wrong side, if they was on any side at all; and there was one narrow road by St George's with a high wall one side and a thick hedge the other and no footpath, and Jerries on motorbikes coming hell-for-leather round the corner. I thought I was going to be killed.

It was already afternoon by the time I got to the King's Mills: I had to sit down so many times on the way. I went by way of the lanes to Sous L'Église, which wasn't so bad, and there I had to have another rest. There was nobody living in Jim's old house, and some of the windows was broken; but there was heath growing back and front. When I got on my feet again, I really thought I wouldn't be able to go any further; but it wasn't as far to go on as to go back. It wasn't any distance to speak of; but I got into a muddle once more, and lost my way several times. In the end I came out at Les Adams, when I had meant to come down the Coudré, and so I had to walk the whole round of Rocquaine Bay. It was evening when I knocked on Liza's door.

She opened it with a smile on her face. For a moment, I thought almost she was expecting me; but when she saw who it was, she looked as if she was seeing a ghost. She put her hands to her face and gave a scream; and

backed into the room. I was left on the doorstep. I couldn't understand it.
I had never known Liza frightened before, and why should she be frightened of me? I felt I was going to fall, and hung on to the doorpost. 'Can I
come in, please?' I said. 'Yes, come in, come in!' she said. I don't remember quite, but I think I got to a chair. I know when I came round, I was
sitting down and she had shut the door, and was standing by me with a
glass of something. 'Drink this,' she said, 'you are not well.' I took a sip,
and felt better. 'I'll make you some tea,' she said. She lit the lamp and drew
the black curtains. It was getting dark outside. I couldn't for the life of me
think what I was doing there.

I was looking round the room; and it was much the same as I remembered from when I was in it before. The same brass ornaments was on the
top of the cabinet; but then I noticed my Guernsey milk-can wasn't there,
and found myself staring at a radio-set on the dresser. I couldn't believe
my eyes. Anybody who had a radio-set those days kept it well hidden out
of sight, or they might end up in prison, or even in a camp in France or
Germany. Nellie Hamelin from Les Mielles kept theirs hidden in a clothes
basket under a load of filthy washing. She said the Germans would never
find it, because they didn't like to dirty their hands. Liza didn't seem to
care if they saw it. She wasn't afraid of the Germans; or perhaps she had no
reason to be.

She was wearing a very nice black and white frock. It was simple but
good; and looked new. Tabitha was having to do up her old dresses to try
and keep neat, until they was practically nothing but mends. I couldn't
take my eyes off Liza. She was moving about the room, laying the table;
but she wouldn't look at me. I noticed she was wearing good black suède
shoes. Her hair was still the bright colour it had always been, but I didn't
think the colour was quite natural. My hair had a lot of grey in it by then.
Her face was made up, though not much; but she had never made up
before, hadn't needed to: only put on a little powder now and then. She
was getting ready a meal of cold sausages of some sort, and bread and
butter; and the kettle was boiling on the terpid over a log fire. She made the
tea and poured me out a cup; and sat down on the bench facing me, drinking hers. It was real tea, not blackberry leaves; and with real sugar in it. I
was beginning to think awful things about Liza. I said, 'That is a smart
frock you got on. Where d'you get it from?' She said, 'Fritz brought it to
me from Paris.' 'Who is Fritz?' I said. 'My friend over the hill,' she said.

It was a jab, but I let it pass. The tea was making me feel better; and I
knew now what I had come for. 'Where is Raymond?' I said. She said,
'Finish your tea; and then we'll talk.' I sat there and ate her food. I am
ashamed to say it now. I ate very slowly, so as not to upset my tummy, for
the least thing would upset my tummy, if I wasn't careful. The sausages

was good, and I enjoyed them, though I knew damn well they was German; and I had a second cup of tea. When she had cleared the table, we pulled up chairs and sat one on each side of the fire. I couldn't help thinking how anybody coming in would have taken us for a married couple. 'Now I want to know everything,' I said. 'Why isn't Raymond here? Where is he?' 'I don't know where Raymond is,' she said, 'and don't look at me like that, Ebenezer Le Page! I wouldn't have let anyone hurt a hair of his head to save my own life! I am not the one who told that cousin of his where he was.' 'Horace came, then?' I said. 'Horace came,' she said. 'God damn his soul to hell!'

He had come and knocked as I had knocked, but earlier in the afternoon. He had had to walk it as I had; but he hadn't taken all day to get there. He was fit and strong, was Horace. Liza hadn't been expecting Fritz, as when I arrived; so didn't go to the door. Raymond opened it. 'Look, who is here!' he called out. 'Horace! Horace, my cousin!' He pulled him into the room. 'Who let you know where I was?' he asked. 'I asked Ebenezer,' said Horace. 'I thought I'd walk over and see how you are.' 'He asked, he asked!' said Raymond. 'Listen to that, Liza! He asked of his own accord! He has walked all the way from the Effards to see how I am! I was right about God! I was always right about God!' He was mad with joy. 'The big one was as bad,' said Liza. He wouldn't let go of Raymond. They sat close together on the bench against the wall, like two children. 'I was nowhere,' she said. They nudged each other and laughed and made noises. 'They seemed to understand what they meant,' she said. 'I didn't.'

Raymond said, 'Come on now, Liza: get Horace some grub!' He had never spoken to her like that before. He had never given her an order in her own house the whole time he was living there. She got ready a meal for the two of them. It was fried bacon, of all things; and the one precious egg. Raymond made her give it to Horace. Horace put half on Raymond's plate. She was too angry to have anything herself. After they had gorged all the bread and butter, and drunk cups and cups of tea, they let her clear away and didn't even offer to help. 'They sat there like two stuffed pigs!' she said. She was wondering if Horace was ever going to think of going home. At last he got up and said, 'How about a stroll to the end, eh Raymond?' 'Are you mad?' she said. That entire corner of the island was cut off from Guernsey people. It was heavily mined. Besides, it was getting dark, and the patrols was on the go, she said. 'Easy to dodge those boys,' said Horace. 'They go by clockwork.' 'For God's sake, go home at once!' she said, 'or stop the night, if you must; but keep indoors! I can hide you upstairs, if anybody comes.' Horace didn't bother to answer. She mightn't have spoken. 'Let's go as far as the two big rocks,' he said to Raymond, 'I want to see the Hanois light.' 'It isn't lit!' she screamed at them. 'Isn't that just like two fools of men: to go and look for a light that isn't there!' Horace flung the door open, and stood with his fist up, the big fool. 'It will be lit again!' he said. 'Guernsey is our island, not theirs; and we will go where we like on it! Coming, Raymond?' 'Anywhere you say,' said Raymond. They was out and across the road and down the slipway. That was the last she saw of them.

'I was hoping against hope they got back safe to the Effards,' she said, 'until I saw you at the door.' 'Well, what was the end, Liza?' I said. 'I tell you I don't know!' she said. They couldn't have got away in a boat, because there were no fishing boats left at Portelet: they all went out from the Town Harbour. The two hadn't been out of the house five minutes when Fritz came. He liked to listen to Tommy Handley. The first thing he asked was where Raymond was. She said he was up in his room asleep: he was tired. Fritz said he hoped the wireless wouldn't wake him, and turned it on low. They sat and listened to it. There had already been several explosions on the mined parts of the cliffs, and people was getting used to hearing them. Usually it was rabbits who had set the mines off. That night there was an explosion shook the house. Fritz laughed. 'Another rabbit gone to meet his Maker!' he said. Liza hoped Fritz would go early, as he did if he was on duty; but he stayed the night. She had to endure it. She dare not tell him what she was afraid of. When two days later he came again and in the day-time, she could bear the uncertainty no longer. She broke down and told him how she had lied to him about Raymond being upstairs; and what had really happened. He wasn't angry with her, but sympathetic; for he was fond of Raymond. He said he would make enquiries without giving anybody away. The day before I came, he had been in again to see Liza, and said a mine had gone off between the two big rocks. There was no saying what had caused it. If Raymond and Horace had happened to have touched the fuse by standing on it, they would have been blown to pieces in the sea. There was blood on the stones below.

It wasn't Liza to blame, God knows; but I had to blame somebody. I called her by every foul name I could lay my tongue to. I said things can never, never be forgiven. 'I suppose your Nazi friend is ten foot tall!' I said. 'He is no taller than you are,' she said, 'but he is less of a Nazi than you are! He is better-natured, he is kinder than you are, you strutting little bantam cock! Get out of my house, get out! Go back to where you come from, cock of the north!' The last I saw of her face, and the last I will ever see, was with her mouth twisted in such hate I thought she was going to spit at me. I got out. It was pitch-black outside. There wasn't a star in the sky; there wasn't a light from any house. At first I couldn't see my hand in front of my face, or tell where the road was; but then I made out the galley wall, and could hear the sea on the other side. I walked home. I don't know where I got the strength from. I wasn't tired any more. I turned up the

Coudré and could just see the footpath and the hedge, and the shapes of the houses. I kept to the main roads and didn't lose my way. I walked right across the island that dark night: hour after hour, and I didn't meet a soul; yet the place was thick with people.

I don't suppose at any time before, or since, have there been so many people living on this island. There was thousands of German soldiers and workers, and thousands of slaves of all nations; and there was the thousands of us, who was supposed to be shut up for the night in our cold houses, like animals in holes. I passed houses where I knew there was Germans living; for I could hear them shouting and singing, and sometimes saw a torn curtain and a glimmer of light. I passed houses I didn't know if there was anybody living in or not, and some I could see was empty wrecks. I didn't creep and crawl, as if I was on the prowl, but stamped my feet hard on the road. There was not a Guernseyman hearing me would have thought another Guernseyman was passing. I walked as if I owned the island. I wanted to meet a German. I wanted to be met and stopped. There was murder in my heart. I didn't mean to answer any questions. I didn't mean to give any reasons or excuses for why I was out. It would be him, or me; and I didn't care if it was me. Why did they keep out of my way? Why was the way left open? I didn't even meet a thief. I got right to Pleinheaume before my rage cooled down; and then I thought of Tabitha.

I hadn't thought of Tabitha once all day. It was hours after midnight, and she would be by herself in that lonely house. I suddenly felt very tired. I began to wonder if I could possibly make my legs go any further; or if I would drop down on the road where I was. I would have fallen asleep. I mustn't. I felt then as if I was made of air and floating; but I hung on to my wits somehow. I had the sense to remember I mustn't get back to Les Moulins by the front way, in case I met my old friend, the patrol, peddling his bike. When I got to the Chouey, I made my way up round behind the quarry. I knew to an inch without really being able to see it where the edge was. Les Moulins was in darkness. I got over Percy's wall and round the greenhouse and reached the back door. I expected Tabitha to be in bed and the door locked. I had a key, but I tried the handle in case. It was not locked. I went in the wash-house and locked it behind me. I saw a light through the key-hole of the kitchen door. I opened the door quietly, expecting to find Tabitha asleep in her chair. She was sitting by one candle, sewing a patch on the seat of a pair of my old pants from some of the rags Raymond had left behind. 'I thought I would wait up for you,' she said. I saw how grey her hair was, and how thin her face and her body; and she had been a well-made little woman. I was overcome by a feeling of homage for my sister. I knelt in front of her: and she is the only woman I have ever knelt to; and I bowed my head in her lap. She didn't know why I did it; for Tabitha, of all people, would have been the last to imagine anybody could ever pay her homage. She stroked my neck, as once my mother had done. 'Are you hurt?' she said. I said, 'Raymond and Horace are killed, and my lovely Liza is a jerry-bag.'

PART THREE

1

The visitors who come over to Guernsey nowadays know more about the German Occupation than I do. They have read the books. They know exactly what happened and what didn't, and the whys and the wherefores, and who was wrong and who was right. I don't. There are those who say, 'Oh, you poor things! It must have been an awful time,' and I say, 'Well, it was, and it wasn't.' There are those who say, 'After all, you didn't have such a bad time hob-nobbing with the Germans,' and I say, 'Well, some did, and some didn't.' I didn't hob-nob with the Germans. I made one German friend; and I am not ashamed of it. For the rest, I tried to toe the line. I didn't go out of my way to make it easy for the Germans, but I didn't do anything likely to get myself into trouble: except once or twice. Mind you, I didn't like having the creatures here, but that wasn't so much because they was Germans, as because they was the bosses. I don't take to bosses, as a rule, be they German, or English. Or Guernsey.

There was one young chap from England came over for a holiday after the Liberation who got my goat. He was with his girl, so perhaps he was only showing off. The funny thing was he looked like a German himself with his bull neck and his bullet head and his short fair hair; but he said he came from London. He didn't accuse me outright of being a 'collaborator', as he called it, but he said those who was the heads of our government in Guernsey had collaborated with the Germans. I saw red. The head of our government was not the Bailiff of the States when the Germans came, but Ambrose Sherwill who was the President of the Controlling Committee, and I feel about that man the way old Wally Budden felt about Prince Albert the Good: only I think Ambrose Sherwill was better. He was brave outside all reason. He was a major during the First World War, and won an M.C.; and, if when the tables was turned and he treated the German officers as if they was as much gentlemen as he was, it wasn't because he was on their side. He risked his arm time and again for our sake; and he went so far as to give shelter in his own house and steal uniforms for two Guernsey boys, who had been sent over from England like the spies to Jericho. The boys was sent to a camp, but as prisoners of war: so their lives was saved; and Ambrose himself might have been shot. As it was, he was

suspect, and lost his job; and when those who had been officers in the First
World War was sent to a camp in Germany, he was made to go. Gerald
Mahy was in the same camp, and wasn't the sort of chap to have a good
word to say for those in authority. He would have been more likely to be
glad if they fell from their perch; but he couldn't speak well enough of
Ambrose Sherwill. He was the same magnificent chap in the camp as he
was on the island. When he became Bailiff after the War, and was made Sir
Ambrose by the King, he wasn't too proud to put his hand up and smile and
say 'Good-morning, Mr Le Page,' or 'Good-afternoon, Mr Le Page,' any
time he saw me in Town: it didn't matter who he was with.

Young Jack Leale, who took over from him for the last years of the
Occupation, was a different sort of chap altogether, but in his way as good.
He wasn't warm and loveable as Ambrose was, nor as reckless, but he was a
truly honourable man. I write of him as Jack Leale with no disrespect,
though he was made Sir John, for I remember him as a long thin boy, who
used to sit on the rocks in front of the Hawthorns reading a book. He
became a Wesleyan Minister and wasn't a man who liked wars, or wanted
wars; and he didn't want us to hate anybody, not even the Germans: but he
was like steel in his quiet way to get out of them all he thought was fair for
them to let us have. When I think of those who was the heads of Guernsey
during the Occupation, I am proud to be a Guernseyman; but nowadays
when Guernsey is flourishing like the green bay tree, I am not so sure.

The London boy said he was sorry, he hadn't meant to offend me: he
didn't know I felt so strongly about it. I said that was all right: he couldn't
help it. He came from a country where the politicians can back out, when
they make a mess of things, and leave it to another lot to clear up. It wasn't
like that over here: ours couldn't back out, because there was nowhere to
back out to. They had to go on with it, as best they could. He wasn't a bad
boy really and we parted quite good friends. I didn't tell him about the
once when I really did get angry, and that was when Victor Carey, the
Bailiff, put a notice in the paper offering a reward of twenty-five pounds
for information against anybody who put up a V-sign. I may have been
wrong, and perhaps the poor old Bailiff was made to sign on the dotted
line, but I didn't think so at the time. I hadn't taken much notice of the
craze for putting up V-signs until then: I didn't see it did much good; but
when I read that notice in the *Press*, I made up my mind I would put up
some V-signs, and in the enemy camp.

I didn't say a word to Tabitha of what I was going to do, because I knew
she would have tried to stop me, in case I got caught. I slipped out one
night when she was in bed asleep. It was a time when we was going to bed as
soon as it was dark, because we only had a few candles left, and what wood
we had was only for cooking. I happened to have some tar left over from
doing my boat; and I poured it into a paint tin and found a brush and went

down with foul intent to Timbuctoo. There must have been thirty to forty soldiers at least living in Timbuctoo; though I can't think how or where they slept. I suppose in rows on the floors. They was all indoors when I got there; but they had light and heat. They was up yet and I could hear them jabbering. One might come out at any minute, but I knew Percy's yard like the back of my hand; and there was always the tombstones I could hide behind. I was lucky and was not disturbed; and I painted big V's in thick black tar on the backsides of three of the cherubs. I got back safe to Les Moulins and felt better.

There was a lot of laughing around L'Islet over those V-signs, and I was sorry I couldn't say it was me who had done it; but I didn't trust anybody that far. Anyhow, nobody ever won those twenty-five pounds and Guernsey people would have gone on putting up V-signs for ever, if the Germans hadn't got the bright idea of putting up V-signs for themselves; and that stopped Guernsey people doing it, more or less. The Germans left mine on the cherubs, which had already been decorated in front by the soldiers with those parts Percy had left out; and on the big side, I thought, for cherubs. They was still there when the Germans had gone and the two Miss Hocarts from the Hubits bought Timbuctoo and had it done up for a guest-house. They wanted to keep the cherubs as the Germans had left them to show the summer visitors; but the Committee for Natural Beauties stepped in and said they must be cleaned up, and my V-signs was scrubbed off as well.

I was one of the lucky ones during the Occupation. I had a house and a garden and a greenhouse of my own; and the Germans didn't lay a hand on any of it. It is true a lot of what I grew went to feed the Germans; but I couldn't help that. I didn't let the G.U.B. take me over either; though it might have been better for my pocket if I had. I would have got a regular wage, which I didn't always get from working and selling my own; but after a time the growers was all given back the management of their own property, so I was no worse off in the end. I might have been moved out of the house to make room for Germans; seeing as there was only Tabitha and me living in it. It was looked at once by a couple of Germans in civvies; but I think what counted against it most was there was no gas or electricity. As it happened, the last year there was precious little of either for anybody.

Young Lihou worked for me after all. He went to England to enlist, as he wanted to; but was sent back to Guernsey to wait for his calling-up papers in the proper way. He was still waiting for his calling-up papers in the proper way when the Germans came into possession. I took him on full-time for all the year round; and he worked for me the whole five years. He then set up on his own and accepted a little help from me, I am glad to say. I owed him much more. He could have left me at any time and got a much higher rate of pay working for the Germans. He got married and

begat three children before the Occupation was over; so he couldn't have
been too weak in the knees. The Occupation at least cured me of chasing
after the girls. I was getting on in years, I know; but I wasn't by any means
past it yet, and I had some trouble to keep myself in order after the Liberation. It wasn't because I had gone good I lived like a monk during the
Occupation; but I got the feeling if I went on the gallivant, I would be
being disloyal to Tabitha in some way, and land her in danger. The last
year, anyhow, I was too weak and hungry to lust after anything but food.

I depended on Tabitha more than I like to admit. If it hadn't been for
her, I would have done some even madder things than I did do. She was
always steady; and it wasn't so easy to keep your head with all the wild
stories going around. You never knew what to believe, and what not; and
you couldn't believe a word you read in the *Press*. The first year was cushy
actually, and not at all what we had expected. Some people was quite won
over by the Germans: they was so polite and didn't interfere. I remember
old Mrs Renouf from L'Islet saying, 'Ah well, the Germans is not so bad as
they was painted. I always say you got to live with people before you know
what they're like, eh?' There was some more air-raids, but by our own
side: one or two only to drop leaflets, and one broke the windows of the
Town Church and of shops at the bottom end of High Street. Another was
on Fort George, which was full of Germans; but I don't think any Guernseys was killed. When the Americans over-ran the north of France, people
was saying they would come across and free us before they went on
further; and some even thought the Germans might hop it of their own
accord. I was thinking something of the sort myself; but Tabitha said, 'It is
too much to hope.'

Actually, it made it worse for us, not better. Food couldn't be brought
over from France, as it had been, because it would be feeding the Germans
as well as us; and Churchill wouldn't let any food be sent to us from
England for the same reason. If it hadn't been for the Red Cross ship bringing us food the last year, we would have starved; but the Germans took
more of our home-grown food to make up for it, so we wasn't much better
off. At the end, when the War was really won and Hitler was dead, it was
the worst time for Guernsey, and the most terrible stories was going the
rounds. It was said the Germans was going to hang on to the Channel
Islands at all costs; and, if on Guernsey there wasn't enough food for the
Guernsey people, they was going to be herded together at one end of the
island, either to be fetched off by the English, or left there to die. Old Mrs
Renouf, who had changed her tune by then, said the Germans was putting
up barbed wire on L'Ancresse Common; and we was all going to be put in
paddocks like cattle, and guarded by Alsatian dogs like the prisoners on
Alderney. It wasn't true; but I think Tabitha believed it. She said, 'Ah

well, there is only one way of living in this world, and that is to go on from day to day, and see what the next day bring.'

At first there was a certain amount of food and other things you could buy in the shops. I went to Town a few times on the rampage, and came home loaded; but the Germans was buying up everything worth having. I couldn't believe my eyes when I saw those solid lumps of Germans crowding into the shops in St Peter Port. It was like a dream, it wasn't real; and, in a way, those whole five years are like a dream. There is a lot I don't remember, or only remember all mixed up; and some things I want to forget. I don't like people asking me questions about the Occupation, the way the visitors do. I say I don't know. For that matter, when I go to Town nowadays and see all the visitors about, it is as much like a bad dream as when the Germans was here. I feel I got no right to live on the island now; except in the winter.

I am willing to believe the Controlling Committee tried their best to arrange things fair for everybody; but what annoyed me most was having cards for this and cards for that, and everything I got counted. It is a craze have gone on ever since. I must say I think now the Controlling Committee did a bit of juggling with the numbers; but it was honest because it was for our good. I didn't know that then, of course; and I was furious when a young Guernsey chap came round with a book and pencil and wanted to know how many pigs I got, and how many fowls and how many vergées of ground and how many feet of glass and what I was growing inside, and what I was growing outside. I had to tell him all my business; and didn't know him from Adam. The only order I got as a result of that visit was to pull up the flowers in the front garden and plant potatoes, which I was meaning to do in any case.

When the Germans came, I had two pigs; and Monsieur Le Boutillier had two pigs. He said it would be a good idea if he killed one and I had half, then at least we would have some salted pork to eat. When that was eaten, I killed one of mine, and he had half; and nothing was said. The counting hadn't started yet. When that young chap came round with his book and pencil, we still had one pig each; and they was put down in the book. After he had gone, Monsieur Le Boutillier said he was going to kill his, and I could have half again. It would be better than keeping it to feed the Germans. I agreed and said I would kill mine when his was eaten and share it with him. Judge of my horror when Mr Tom Ozanne, who had to do with the Controlling Committee, turned up one fine day with a German Officer and, of course, a book and a pencil. They had come to check the tally of the pigs. Monsieur Le Boutillier's was nearly eaten.

I didn't know the Germans had suddenly got pigs on the brain. They had been struck by a bright idea. They was going to breed thousands of pigs: enough to feed themselves and everybody else on the island. I will say at once they didn't. First of all, because most of their bright ideas came to nothing; and, second, because they never managed to find out how many pigs there was to breed from, or where they was to be found. The numbers was down in the book; but they had the cheek to accuse the Guernsey people of killing and eating the pigs without permission. Anyhow, Mr Ozanne explained the situation to me in Guernsey French; but the German said, 'I speak the English': so Mr Ozanne had to say it all over again in English; only he said it a little different. 'Das ist so!' said the German. He was a nasty German, that one. He had a thin mean face and a moustache like Hitler and an eye-glass in one eye and looked as if he wore stays. I was very polite. I have never been so polite. 'Par il lo, Monsieur, s'il vous plait,' I said. He didn't know what I was saying, but I led the way, and he followed me round the back. 'Le pourchay!' I said; and pointed to the pig in the pigsty. The old pig grunted at him and let go water and made a rude noise. Von Tirpitz looked at it through his eye-glass and said, 'Ein schwein.' Mr Ozanne made a mark in his book. There was one pig in the pigsty, and one in the book. I was all right.

It was for poor Monsieur Le Boutillier I was in fear and trembling. He had no pig in his pigsty as I well knew, for Tabitha and me had eaten most of half of it; and his name was the next on the list. Mr Ozanne said, 'Jean Le Boutillier of La Corbière, it's that house, isn't it?' I said, 'Yes, but the path isn't safe, and the Herr Kommandant cannot go across the gully, or he will get his boots dirty.' Mr Ozanne looked surprised. He couldn't see nothing wrong with the path, and there was no mud in the gully. I said, 'The best way is to go back and along by the Chouey, and round the other side of Mont Cuet: then there is a nice dry path to the front door of Monsieur Le Boutillier's house.' Mr Ozanne said, 'Yes, now I come to think of it, that would be the best way,' and led the Herr Kommandant, who I knew was no more the Herr Kommandant than I was, nearly back to the Vale Church. The next thing for me to do was to get my pig into Monsieur Le Boutillier's pigsty.

It was easier said than done. I have nothing against pigs, I like pigs; but that day I got to hate that pig, he was so pig-headed. I got him out of the sty and out of the gate all right with a big stick; but when I tried to chase him across the ancient monument, he didn't want to go. He wanted to go down on the beach and drown himself; he wanted to go up the hill and fall in the quarry and break his neck; he wanted to go anywhere and everywhere, except up the other side of the gully and into Monsieur Le Boutillier's pigsty. I can't have taken more than ten minutes to do it, but it seemed to me like ten hours; and every minute I expected to see the German pop his head over the wall and look at me. Monsieur Le Boutillier saw me, but I daren't shout to warn him. I made signs for him to go indoors.

Well, I got the pig into the sty and put the plank across; but I thought the poor old pig was going to drop dead. He was in an awful state. He was puffing and blowing, and you could see his heart was going sixty miles an hour; and he kept his mouth open as if he had the gapes. I popped in the double-u and heard Monsieur Le Boutillier answer the front door. He was wonderful. I heard him say, 'Certainly, certainly! Come in, gentlemen: come in!' He only wished he had something he could offer them to drink; but, of course, he didn't have any. He was a liar because he got plenty. The German said, 'Dank you!' and the next thing I heard him say was, 'Ein schwein.' Mr Ozanne said, 'Quite correct.' I then heard Monsieur Le Boutillier showing the German the way to Mr Perchard's house, which was further along; and the German said, 'Dank you!' again. I wasn't worried about Mr Perchard. Old Fred Perchard was a match for any German. His pig had strayed and he had been advertising for it in the *Press* for weeks, offering a big reward to anybody who found it. The fry he gave us had been a real treat.

When Mr Ozanne and the German was out of sight and I showed myself, Monsieur Le Boutillier fell on my neck laughing. 'O boy! O boy!' he said. 'How you bring home the bacon, eh?' I said, 'If we don't kill that poor pig, he will die!' He said, 'It would be a cruel shame for him to live and suffer.' Anyhow, we had plenty of bacon for a time, when the only other meat we could get was a few ounces now and then, if we was lucky. I met Mr Ozanne on the Bridge one day when I was going to get the tiny piece of meat Tabitha and me was allowed. He said, 'Hullo, how are you?' I said, 'Oh, not too bad.' He said, 'How is Monsieur Le Boutillier?' I said, 'He is not too bad either.' He said, 'How is the pig?' I noticed he said 'the pig' and not 'the pigs'. 'He died,' I said. 'I thought he would,' he said. 'Ah well, I will tick him off the Register of Births, Deaths and Marriages.'

2

Little did I think when Monsieur Le Boutillier and me was joking over the pig what was going to happen to poor Jean Le Boutillier. It isn't as if he had done anything wrong. He didn't do harm to a living soul: not even to a German. All he did was listen to a wireless set when he didn't ought to have done; and there was hundreds and thousands on the island who listened to a wireless set when they didn't ought to have done. I did myself. At first, when we was allowed to listen to it if we wanted to, I didn't bother much. I heard it, if I happened to go across to La Corbière in the evening; or, if not, Monsieur Le Boutillier would let me know the news next day. The Germans at that time didn't seem to be able to make up their minds if we was going to be allowed to listen to it or not. Once, to punish us for something, I forget what, all the wireless sets was called in; but they was given back to us for Christmas. Then they was called in for duration, I don't know why, and it was a great crime to have one, or to listen to one.

Monsieur Le Boutillier gave his in the first time, and got it back; but the second time he said it had gone wrong and he had got rid of it. Actually, he had hidden it in the corn-bin. Of an evening when it was dark, he would bring it into the kitchen and listen to it with the door locked; and it was kept very soft, so as nobody could hear it from outside. If anybody knocked, he always asked who it was, before unlocking the door. Mr Perchard from along the road came in pretty regular; and one night Raoul Dobrée from Wallaballoo came when I was there. He was a Roman Catholic like Monsieur Le Boutillier, and they went to the same church. I also met Father Darcy there a number of times. I don't think there was any others; but I reckon I know who it was who tipped the wink to the Germans, though I can't prove it.

It wasn't me, I know that; and it wasn't Mr Perchard. I am as sure of Fred Perchard as I am of myself. He was a real old Guernseyman who had never left the island and lived with his only son, whose wife and children was gone to England. The son didn't come and listen to the radio, because he didn't like to hear about the air-raids on Germany. He said it would only make them come and bomb England, and he was afraid for his wife and children. For a long time he got no news of them; and when he did begin to get messages through the Red Cross saying they was all right, he didn't know in what part of England they was living. He was a worrying sort of chap, and wouldn't have done anything to put himself in the wrong with the Germans; but that is a long way from saying he would have gone and told tales against his father.

It could have been let out by the Le Boutillier children, without them meaning to; but they was old enough to have the sense to keep their mouths shut. It is true young Jean worked for the Germans; but he always made out to be a bit stupid. The Germans was used to Guernsey people being stupid, and it was what they expected and didn't mind: it was in case we was too clever they was afraid. Julia, his sister, was a great girl. She didn't make out to be stupid, and she wasn't. She might have told a German to his face what she thought of him, and got herself into trouble, but she would never have given any Guernseyman away. Actually, she didn't listen to the radio when I was there, because she used to come across to Les Moulins to keep Tabitha company while I was out. As for Tabitha, I think the Germans would have had to tear her tongue out to get anything out of her.

Then there was Father Darcy. Now I must admit I was prepared to dislike that man at the mere mention of his name. He was a Roman Catholic priest and that was enough for me! I had been brought up all my life to believe Roman Catholics was papists and heathen and idolaters, and worse than those who didn't go to any church or chapel at all. It was the greatest shock to me when I met Father Darcy that I should take to him from the moment that I shook hands with him; and I want to say now once and for all, though I don't know what a saint is, I reckon he was nearer to being a saint than any man I have ever known. It wasn't that he was what Raymond used to call a Holy Willie. Far from it. He would often arrive with a bottle under his arm of something for us to share; and I have heard him swear like a trooper, especially on the subject of Hitler and his gang. I can't say how it was, or why it was, he was good; but he was. I began to think if the Catholic religion made men like him, then the Catholic Church was the church to belong to; but now I can't help wondering if, perhaps it wasn't the Catholic Church made him good, but men like him who have made the Catholic Church good.

He have been dead some years now; and I miss him. Up to his last days he used to call in at Les Moulins at least once a week to see how I was, as if I was one of his flock; yet he never preached to me how wicked I was, or tried to persuade me to join his church. I asked him a number of questions, and he answered me straight out what he believed, but that was all. I was interested in his idea of purgatory. I had often wondered how anybody can be good enough when they die to go to heaven; or, for that matter, bad enough to go to hell. He explained to me about saying masses for the dead.

I thought it was a good thing to feel for the dead that way. I know I wouldn't mind somebody saying a mass for me when I am dead. God knows I will need it! I couldn't shift him from his belief in hell. 'Of course God created hell,' he said, 'to frighten the bad boys,' and he looked very stern; but then he smiled his lovely old smile and said, 'Now tell me, Ebenezer, do you really think, as we are in the hands of One who cares if a sparrow falls, there will be anybody there in the end?'

It wasn't Father Darcy who betrayed Monsieur Le Boutillier to the Germans. I don't like to say it was Raoul Dobrée, but from something happened later on, I have a very good reason for thinking it was. The night he came to La Corbière when I was there, he hadn't come to listen to the radio. He knocked on the back door and, when Monsieur Le Boutillier heard who it was he let him in. He didn't even bother to turn the thing off first and put it out of sight. Raoul had come to bring Monsieur Le Boutillier a book about the Jesuits he had written himself; though why he had to bring it at night after curfew, I can't think: unless it was because he wanted to find out something.

Monsieur Le Boutillier was a better educated man than I am, and had been to the Vauxbelets College when he was a boy. He was delighted and proud to be given the book, and showed me what Raoul had written on the inside of the cover. 'For Jean Le Boutillier. From his friend, the Author.' Raoul said he was distressed to find us all listening to the radio. How could we expect the Germans to behave justly towards us, if we ourselves didn't obey the laws they made for us to keep? I couldn't see what justice got to do with the Germans. It wasn't justice for them to be here at all. Father Darcy wasn't there that night, so I don't know what he would have said; but he was Irish and a fighter and said more than once, while it was right for a Christian to turn the other cheek if it was only him concerned, he mustn't hesitate to strike a bully for the sake of other people. I didn't say two words to Master Raoul myself. I was introduced. He shook hands like a limp rag and looked down his nose at me with his big popping eyes and said 'Good-evening' as if he had a plum in his mouth. He didn't stay long; and I was glad when he went. He gave me the creeps.

It wasn't a week before the Germans searched La Corbière and found Monsieur Le Boutillier's radio. He was taken to Town and questioned. I have thought many mean thoughts in my life; but I am glad I am able to say it didn't cross my mind that Monsieur Le Boutillier might give the names of those who had been listening as well as him: which, of course, he didn't. He was asked and asked; but swore he was the only one who had listened to it. Young Jean and Julia was both at work when he was taken away and it was Madame Le Boutillier who came across to tell us what had happened. Olive Le Boutillier was another woman with courage. She knew perfectly well how serious it was and what might happen to her husband, for it had happened to others; but she didn't break down. Her only thought was for what she could do to help him.

The next day she was fetched to Town herself and asked questions. The Germans didn't treat her rough, but spoke to her very polite; and she thought they was being kind. She told them the radio was only ever listened to by her and her husband. She didn't know Jean had said she and the children didn't listen to it, because he only turned it on when they was all in bed and asleep. She made another mistake, for which she never forgave herself. She said she and Jean only used it to listen to the news, but it was the news mostly the Germans didn't want us to listen to. It was the news they made up and got printed in the *Press* we was supposed to believe. Most people only laughed at it. Olive was brought back home; but Jean was sentenced to a year's imprisonment and sent to France. At the end of the year he didn't return to Guernsey as was expected, but was sent on from prison to prison and finished up in Germany. It was only after the Liberation it was known he died the last year; but it was not known how.

Was it before or after the affair of Monsieur Le Boutillier's radio I made a German friend? I can't be sure. I rather think it was after: while we was expecting Monsieur Le Boutillier back at the end of the year. Or it may have been before. It don't make no difference. After all, Monsieur Le Boutillier was a Jerseyman and a nearer enemy of mine than any German could be; yet I loved him and have truly mourned for him. It was over the fishing I met my German. At first I was allowed to go out from La Petite Grève, if I got permission; but some chaps escaped to England in a fishing boat and put an end to that. Then, if you please, I had to go out from the Town Harbour and take a German with me; and give up a fifth of my catch in the bargain. I didn't like that at all. It took the heart out of me; and, say what you like, luck and a good heart got a lot to do with fishing.

However, I went out now and again; and had a different fellow with me each time. I have nothing to say against those fellows, they was only doing their duty, except that they wasn't like human beings. I don't expect you would notice it so much nowadays with all the brief-case boys you see about; and, it don't matter where you go, hear people talking as if they was reciting from a book of rules. The Germans set us the example; and there are enough young Guernseymen now who know how to walk about and look as if they was important, and spout by the yard as if they had something to say. When it came to doing anything themselves, some of the Germans wasn't as good as, from their manner, they led you to expect. Some of those who came out with me had been in a boat before, and some hadn't; and a few knew something about the engine, which was useful because I didn't have a mate; but a bit awkward sometimes, when I had more petrol than I was supposed to have. One night Alf Brouard and me emptied the tank of a big German lorry had got stuck in the mud on

L'Ancresse Common, and been left there for the night; and another night we was lucky with a German officer's car, while he was indoors visiting a certain lady who ought to have known better. Her husband was an officer in the Army in England.

When Otto stepped into my boat I knew he had never stepped into a boat before. I thought the Germans must be mad to send such a boy. He was twenty-three or four and looked as strong as a bull; and surely could have been more use to his great Master than watching out I didn't sail away. It was the last thing in the world I intended to do anyway. He sat stiff as a ramrod right middle of the bànc, looking straight ahead of him as if he was doing eyes front in drill. I thought well, this is an object, if ever there was one! I let go, and when we got out the pier heads I looked at him, and he looked at me. I have to say he wasn't bad to look at. He had a sunburnt skin and short fair hair, and every feature was perfect and strong; but his face looked as if it was carved out of a block of wood. He had big blue eyes and they looked at you wide open. I don't know what he thought of the rough old Guernsey museau he saw in front of him, I am sure. I didn't say a word; and he didn't say a word. I thought, I will have to manage by myself: I can't ask this thing to give me a hand. I didn't expect to catch much fish that day.

It was a fine day with a few clouds and bright sunshine, but quite a high sea running. I thought well, I will make him seasick, if I do nothing else. I wasn't in a hurry: I had all day. I made my way between the Fourquies and the Platte Fougère, where it was real rough; and trailing nothing until we got round the Brayes. There wasn't a sausage; and not a word had been said. I thought if I don't get him to say something soon, I will bust. If only I can get him to say 'Heil Hitler!' it will be something. I said, and I made it as clear word by word as I could, 'The fish go away because you have come.' I didn't know if he understood the English and, if he did, it was certainly taking a long time to go in; but after five minutes I should say, to my great astonishment, he opened his mouth like Balaam's ass in the Bible and gave forth a mighty deep roaring laugh that shook the boat. 'If I on a rock do sit,' he said, 'the fish then will come, yes?' 'Perhaps,' I said. Well, the good God made the rock, and there it was handy; and I drew in alongside and let him step out and sit on it. I think he felt safer sitting on the rock than in the boat.

I got quite a good catch between there and the Silleuse; but all the time I was trying to make up my mind whether I would go back for him or not. The tide was coming in and the rock he was sitting on would not be a rock above water for long. I would try and save him, of course; and even call out for help. There was boats within hail; but it would be too late. That would mean one German mouth the less for us to have to feed. I wouldn't be to blame. I couldn't have put him there by force; for he was armed, and I wasn't. I could see him in the distance, sitting like a fool on that rock; and I laughed. Then I thought to myself no: he trusted me; and I turned the boat round. I only got there just in time. He was standing up and the water was over his feet. I gave him my hand to help him to step in; and he gripped it hard and stood looking at me straight in the eye in the rocking boat. He knew quite well what I had thought of doing. I felt ashamed. When we got back to Town and I left him, he said, 'I with you again come.'

He came out with me many times. He was waiting every time I went down to the Albert Pier, and he would push his way out of his turn to come with me; or make a sign for me to hang back, so as it would be him I would have with me. He soon learned to make himself useful; and I looked forward to the days when I would be going fishing with him. He was simple in the mind; he could only think one thought at a time; but he was as open as the day. He told me his name was Otto Schmidt; and in Germany he lived in a small place which, as far as I could make out, was in, or by, a big forest. What he liked most in the world was to be among a lot of trees; and, before the War, he used to camp out in the forest with his friends; and in the evening, they would sit around a big fire in the open air and play music and sing. That was his greatest happiness. He had never seen the sea until he came to Guernsey; but he said the sea and the rocks made him feel happy like being among the trees. He didn't like cities or any place where there was a lot of houses.

He spoke the English quite well. If it come to that, he spoke it better than me. He had learnt it from books when he was to school; and knew the big words. He spoke every word very exact; but sometimes he put them round in a funny way. I learnt a few German words from him; but not enough to speak with. He told me he had an older brother and a sister. His father was dead, and the sister was living with his mother in Germany. His brother came with him to Guernsey, but got into trouble with the German authorities because he fraternised with a Guernsey girl. Otto said there was nothing wrong in it. They was in love and the girl was willing to marry Hans, and he wanted to marry her; but the German boys wasn't allowed to marry Guernsey girls, though nobody bothered much if it was anything else. So Hans was sent to the Russian Front. Otto didn't expect he would ever see his brother again.

I didn't like to talk to Otto about the War, or how he came to be in the War, for when he was with me in the boat, I couldn't believe we was on opposite sides. It was him brought it up. 'In my country I am for my country,' he said, 'but the countries of other peoples I to have do not wish.' 'It is the same with us,' I said. It was true of Guernsey, anyway. He said, 'I you my country would be happy to show, and the house where I live; now I your so beautiful island have seen.' One day when we was coming back with our catch by the Boue La Grève, I pointed out Les

Moulins to him and said that was where I lived. 'Ach, in a stone house it is you live,' he said, 'in a wood house, I.' I asked him if he would like to come ashore and see it inside. He said, 'Yes, very much, thank you.' It was easy to run into La Petite Grève: there was nobody about. When I had grounded the boat, I picked out some of the best of the fish to take indoors. He didn't say nothing, though he knew I wasn't allowed. I was a little worried as to how Tabitha was going to feel. She had never spoken to a German. I had told her about Otto; but she had listened and said nothing.

She was in the kitchen boiling the everlasting sugarbeet, when I asked Otto to come in. He came in and stood to attention as if he was on parade. 'This is my friend Otto,' I said. She turned round from what she was doing and faced him; but stood as stiff as he was, and didn't make a movement to shake hands, nor say a word. I said to Otto, 'This is my sister Tabitha. She is a widow. Her husband was killed in the First World War.' I trusted him to understand why she was behaving as she was. He said, 'My father was also.' Tabitha held out her hand. He took it in his and bowed his head over it. 'I've brought some fish,' I said; and put it on the table. She said, 'I will cook it now, if Otto can stop and have some.' He said he could. Well, she cooked it and made real tea with some was left over from what I had bought from Horace, which she would never have done otherwise; and there was bread, though it was mousey bread rather, and even a wisp of butter. I taught Otto to say 'orfi'. He said it was good. I know it was the meal I myself enjoyed most of any I ate during the whole of the Occupation. Nowadays, when every year there is a celebration of the Liberation, it isn't so much the cheers and the excitement of when we was freed I think of, though I was as glad and excited as anybody, but of Otto, Tabitha and me sitting round the table eating long-nose. That was Liberation Day.

Otto and me got away and well out, before our pet nuisance was on his round; but we was a bit late back to the Harbour. It was nearly dark, and the patrol boat was out looking for us. I tried to explain to the Jerry in charge we was held up by firing practice off the west coast, which was always a good excuse; but he wouldn't listen to me and yapped at Otto in German like a machine-gun. Otto stood like the wooden block he was when I saw him the first time; but when he saw I had to go, he smiled and shook hands as usual, and said, 'Auf wiedersehen.' I didn't see him again. I went week after week hoping, but it was always some other fellow; and I gave up going. I don't like to think what happened to Otto.

3

I don't know the name of the other. I don't know what nation he belonged to. The only word I heard him say was in German, but it was a word I use myself; for we use it in the patois when we say 'mais non nein dja!' and mean 'no!' very emphatically. He may have used it because he was speaking to a German; or he may have been a German himself, for among the slave-workers who was brought over from being prisoners in Alderney I heard some had been put there for resisting Hitler. He might have belonged to the French Resistance, for the French are not all dark-haired; but he was tall for a French boy. If I had seen him in peace-time down the Harbour, I would have taken him for a Norwegian off one of the timber boats; but I don't know. All I know is he looked like the son of a king.

He was younger than Otto, I thought, though he looked older because he had suffered more; and he wasn't the solid bull Otto was, but quick in the mind, I am sure. He was weak from hunger, but you could see what a fine strong boy he would have been with those broad shoulders and slim body and long legs; and I always remember his proud head. He was in rags with rags on his feet, and sometimes bare feet; and he wasn't very clean, but he tried to keep himself clean, I know, for once I saw him shaved and he was never as dirty as the others. It wasn't I saw him often, for the gang went to work early in the morning and came back late in the evening; and some soup was taken round in a cart to them at dinner-time. I bet it wasn't very good soup. They troubled Tabitha more than they did me at first. She would say when we was eating what little we had to eat, 'I wish I could give some of this to those poor prisoners.' I didn't like to think of them myself. One couldn't help knowing they was there, for they was everywhere building those ugly forts the tourists come and stare at, but they was only animals who we dare not think of as fellow creatures, for at our worst we was living in luxury compared to them. I was mean enough to think they was robbers and murderers, if the truth was known; but I couldn't think that when I saw that boy.

Tabitha had pity for the lot, murderers and all; and she would have had them all in the kitchen and fed them, if she could. She said, 'It is not against those Gervase and Louise are fighting.' Well, it wasn't much we had to throw away those days, but there was a barrel out the back where I threw such scraps as we had: a green crust of bread perhaps, a bone not even good enough for soup, fish-bones and bad fish, or fruit gone rotten; and I emptied it from time to time in the cesspit. One evening when it was nearly time for us to be indoors and Tabitha was getting in the washing off the line while I was in the greenhouse going to lock the end door, I saw the shabby gang of ruffians come shuffling down the hill. They passed rather nearer to Percy's wall than usual; and it was in the corner the barrel was. There was an armed guard behind them and in front, and an armed guard each side, and I wouldn't have thought those prisoners had enough heart left in them to notice anything; but there was a sudden rush and they was over the wall and on to that barrel, fighting each other like wild beasts for those dirty scraps. The guards shouted and I thought was going to shoot; but the prisoners was back in their wobbly lines in half a second. I was watching from in the greenhouse, and noticed the boy was the last back. He hadn't rushed or fought, but managed to get a rotten apple that was left at the bottom. I saw him break it in two and give half to the chap next to him, who looked a double-dyed villain, if ever there was one. I thought, that boy is somebody.

Tabitha said in future it must be food fit for human beings to eat was left in the barrel. I washed it out and filled it nearly to the top with straw; and spread out the few bits we could spare. It wasn't much, but it was clean and could be eaten. The first time, Tabitha and me watched from the greenhouse to see if they would be allowed to take it; but long before they came to the corner of the wall I heard the guards shouting, and it seemed nobody would dare to leave the ranks. I was thinking how with the best of intentions we had wasted our time, when, like a streak of lightning, the boy was over the wall and had scooped everything into a sort of blouse he was wearing and was back in his place. The guard said nothing to him. I thought now for a fight and a scramble, but no: he shared out what he had among those around him, as far as it would go; and they took quietly what he gave them, as though they knew he would by nature share it fair. I saw him going down the hill chawing a raw carrot.

For the few times more they passed there was always something for them, and it was always the boy fetched it and shared it out; and the guard let him. I noticed it was always the same guard his side. There was something about that guard I particularly didn't like; and yet I wasn't sure what. He was as lean as a whippet, but it wasn't because he was underfed: he was full of energy. He had a lean hard face, and was very smart. The boy must have known he was being favoured. I noticed when he broke ranks, the guard smiled; but it wasn't at the boy, it was to himself. I didn't like that smile. The last time we saw them the job must have been finished and they had knocked off early, for they passed in broad daylight and along the path in front of the house; so that day they didn't get what was left for them. I was working in the front garden and when I saw them coming I called to Tabitha, who was indoors, and she came and stood with me by the gate to see them pass. The boy looked our way and I saw his eyes wrinkle and light up and thought of Jim, and he gave a sort of laugh straight to Tabitha, and she put out a hand as if she would have liked to have touched him. I was glad for him to know he had a friend in Guernsey. I only saw him the once more.

Since the day I found out what happened to Raymond and Horace, I wasn't feeling so willing to lie low as I had been. Even before then, I had been going along to the Hamelins from Les Mielles to listen to the radio, after Monsieur Le Boutillier's had been taken away and he was in prison in France. It was a good distance for me to have to go, but I knew every inch of L'Ancresse and would creep along by the hedges and not make a sound. Nellie Hamelin was the jolly sort and Jack, her husband, said she could diddle any German any time. He admitted he couldn't have himself: he would have looked guilty, even if he was innocent. She looked on it as a game, and the house was searched time and again by the Germans; but they never found the radio. I was worried leaving Tabitha for the evening, but she insisted I went as it did me good to go there for a change. Julia Le Boutillier used to come across to keep her company, while young Jean stayed at home with his mother.

Julia worked in the Post Office at St Sampson's; and one evening on the way home from work she came into Les Moulins looking very grim. She had come across a letter in the Post Office which she had stolen, and brought for me to see. It was addressed to the Herr Kommandant at the German Officers' Club at Castle Carey. I knew the writing. I knew that thin, mean, spidery handwriting; and Julia had recognised it too. I said, 'I am opening this.' She said, 'That is what I brought it to you for.' He hadn't written much. I have it yet. He didn't give his address, I noticed; nor his name. 'Dear Herr Kommandant,' he wrote. 'It may interest you to know that radio parties are being held nightly at Beaulieu, Route Militaire, Vale, in contravention of current regulations.' He signed it 'A friend of law and order.' I didn't know the people who lived at Beaulieu, but it might just as well have been the Hamelins, or anybody. I said to Julia, 'I will go and see Mr Dobrée in the near future, and have a few kind words with him.' She said, 'You couldn't do better.'

I went the next afternoon. My luck was in. I walked up the drive and round the back of Wallaballoo and found Master Raoul sitting in a deck-chair on the lawn in the sun, reading a book. He was wearing a clean white open-neck shirt and a new pair of grey flannel trousers. I wondered where he got them from; and how. He said, 'Hullo, Mr Le Page,' and put down the book he was reading. I said, 'Good afternoon, Mr Dobrée. I have come from the German Kommandant in answer to a letter you have written to him about the people who live at Beaulieu.' He looked at me like a frightened rabbit with his popping eyes and didn't know what to say. 'In my humble opinion, Mr Dobrée,' I said, 'a man like you is worse than Hitler. Hitler is mad and bad; but what he is doing he think is for the good of his people. I don't know if you got people somewhere; but I do know you got none on Guernsey.' His mother came to the back door and called out, 'What is it, dear?' 'Nothing, nothing, darling,' he said; and she went indoors again. 'Stand up!' I said. 'I am going to knock you down.' He stood up, the fool! He was years younger than me, and much bigger. 'Be reasonable, Mr Le Page,' he said. 'Try to understand my point of view.' I understood his point of view all right: he wanted the best of both sides. I knocked him down. 'Stand up!' I said. I was going to knock him down three times: that would be enough; but he didn't stand up again. He crawled on his hands and knees across the lawn and up the back steps and indoors. I spat and walked away. I haven't spoken to him from that day to this.

If anything, I went more often to listen to the radio at the Hamelins. For some reason, I wanted to feel there was other people in the world, besides us shut up in Guernsey. One night when I was creeping home along the hedge the other side of the road to Rocque Balan, somebody passed like a ghost on the grass. It was a very dark night, and he couldn't have seen me against the hedge; but I could make out the shape of his head and shoulders against the sky, and knew it was the boy. I had no idea where he was living. I knew a lot of German prisoners lived at Paradise, and it was said terrible things happened there; but it may be he was living in another house that way, perhaps a hundred or more sleeping on the bare boards. My first thought was he had run away, and it was to us he was running. I thought, we will hide him in the packing-shed, and he can come in the house at night; but I don't think now he was coming to us. It was not in his character to make himself a burden on other people, though God knows he would have been welcome! I know now it was not from being a slave-worker he was running away, but from worse.

The next minute I heard the footsteps of somebody else; and it was somebody who was not afraid of being heard. I knew him by his legs and his walk like a jockey, though I couldn't see his face. I know he didn't have a hat on. I have the idea he didn't have a belt either, and the collar of his tunic was unbuttoned; but I don't know how I can have seen. He caught up with the boy just by Rocque Balan, and put a hand on him. I saw the boy lean against the rock. It was from weakness: he was so tired. The guard spoke to him; but I didn't understand what he said. He didn't sound as if he was speaking rough, though, but begging almost. I wondered if he was being kind to the boy after all, and trying to make him see reason and go back quietly. He wasn't armed, I don't think, for I saw both his hands on the boy. 'Nein! Nein! Nein!' I heard the boy cry out. I knew then.

I was across that road. I can't take any credit for it; for it happened without me thinking. The guard was not expecting me, and was taken completely by surprise. My fist caught him sideways on his ear, and he fell. I don't think the boy looked round; or even knew. I think he just thought the guard was finished, and that was that. I saw him pull up his rags of trousers, and drift over the common towards the sea. The guard moved at my feet. It was a miracle I saw a piece of rock was loose: it was a boulder really. It was more of a miracle I had the strength to lift it. I lifted it above my head and crashed it down on his. I heard the bones crack.

I felt nothing. The boy was gone down to the beach. It was no good to follow him: to try and save him now. I knew what he would do. He would walk in his lonely proud way down over the shingle and on to the sand, and on and on until he came to the edge of the sea; and the sea is shallow there and you have to walk a long long way before you are over your height: but he would walk it. The shame was too great for him to live. It is strange he have never come to me in dreams, but only in memory; and I remember him always as he was when he passed our gate, and laughed to Tabitha. The other I have dreamt of often. It is always the same dream of his cracked head and the blood. The strange thing is I always see him with his hair short and sticking up like the bristles of a brush, yet I never saw him by daylight with his hat off to know what sort of hair he got. I have never told a soul, and I heard nothing about it. It is only in dreams it come back, and I feel horror, but I don't feel sorry: even in my dreams.

I committed one other act of violence during the Occupation, and that on an innocent creature; but I cannot say I am sorry for that either. I got into the way of dodging the chap on patrol and going down on La Petite Grève now and then at nights to pick a few limpets, if I could; but the Germans had skinned the rocks and, I heard, lived on limpet soup until they was sick of it. By then, they was nearly as hungry as we was; and one couldn't help feeling sorry for them. In the paper, they blamed our side for the shortage of food: they said ships coming from France with food was bombed by orders of Churchill. I don't know. Anyway, it wasn't to try for limpets, or ormers, I went down on La Petite Grève the night I am thinking of. I don't know what I hoped to find: a few lady crabs crawling about perhaps.

It was half tide and I climbed on to the rock Tabitha and me used to call the flat rock. The sea was half around it, and I knew at the deep end it went in and made a sort of cave. I was hardly thinking of what I was doing, and, more from force of habit than anything, I lowered my arm in the water and began to feel around underneath. I can feel yet the shock I got. There was an enormous creature curled up under there. I grabbed it as best I could, and pulled it out. It was a conger; and a whopper! Now if there is one fighting fish in the sea, it is the conger. He will fight for his life until he is absolutely dead. There wasn't a boulder handy; but I fought with that old conger and he fought with me, until I got him so I could bash his head on the flat rock; and then he stopped wriggling and struggling in my arms. The patrol from round the Chouey passed along the top grinding on his bike, and I was terrified he might hear the noise and stop. That conger was mine! I think I would have killed anybody who tried to take it away from me. I was nearly crying: I was so weak and excited. I wanted to run indoors like a kid and say 'Look! Look what I've caught!' but I held myself back. I knew the chap would go religiously right as far as La Jaonneuse where the barbed wire began, before turning; and, meanwhile I was up and across the road and round the house. Tabitha was in the kitchen doing some mending by one candle, as usual. I went in as if it was nothing out of the ordinary: just something that happened every day. 'I caught this conger, by the way,' I said. It was the only time I saw my sister break down during the Occupation. She came and put a hand round my neck and her head on my shoulder and sobbed; and was stroking the long conger with her other hand.

We put it in the copper for the night, and made sure the back-door was locked, then sat up late planning what we would do with it. She said, and I agreed with her, young Lihou must have a piece; and the next day I gave him a good length of the tail end. The thick part I said we would keep for ourselves; but Tabitha insisted we must invite Olive Le Boutillier and the two children to come and have it with us. It had to be in the evening when Jean and Julia was home from work; so that night we had evening dinner like the gentry. Olive Le Boutillier said it wasn't really right for them to come and eat our food, as young Jean was getting German rations which he shared with his family; but I said, 'This is not on the rations: it is a gift of God.' Tabitha even managed to make some sort of stuffing for it, and we had it stuffed and baked, and with baked potatoes; and two candles on the table to celebrate. There was some left over for us next day, and we had some boiled; and conger soup for a week. In fact, I got sick of conger soup and haven't liked it since.

4

It can't have been many years ago when I was in the States Offices one Friday morning getting my pay, and in walks Steve Picquet and starts shouting to the girl in the desk. He did some work for the States: I don't know what; but I bet, whatever it was, he was diddling them. It was my girl in the desk and she didn't take offence, but smiled and said, 'How goes it, Steve?' and counted out the money in his hand and closed it and patted it. He grinned like an old Tom cat. I knew the famous Steve Picquet to nod to, and had spoken to him a few times; but I hadn't seen him since before the Occupation, though I had read some of his comic pieces in the *Star*, which he wrote under the name of Westerner. In his younger days, he was the greatest boxer I have ever seen. He was only light to middle weight, but quick as lightning on the attack. He wasn't so good on the defence, perhaps, but he could take punishment. The last time I had seen him box was in the Stoneworkers' Hall at St Sampson's, and he had with him a gang of young lads he was training. He was a hero to the boys; and there was some likely young boxers among them. That night he himself took on some tough young quarrymen; but he always got in first, and no chap really had a chance of getting near him. I remember the St John's Ambulance chaps was there to pick up the pieces. He was an amateur only, and didn't make anything out of it; but somehow I always got the feeling he wasn't boxing for fun, but for some reason of his own I couldn't fathom. I don't know yet why he was so fierce.

In those days he was a smart looking chap, and dressed smart; but when I met him in the States Offices that morning, he looked like Robinson Crusoe. I knew he was living with four or five dogs in a German bunker he called Onmeown, built in a hole in the rock under Les Vardes at Pleinmont. He was wearing an airman's helmet he got from a German he found drowned, and a torn jacket and sea-boots and a pair of trousers made from an old Army blanket; and he was carrying a sack on his back to take home his week's provisions. I walked back along the Esplanade with him, and he went into the Picket House to sell some tickets for the Spastic Pools to the bus-drivers. He had a lot of irons in the fire, had Steve. He didn't seem to want me to leave him, for, though he lived on his own in the last place to live in on Guernsey and was called 'the hermit' by the visitors, he was hungry for company: so I hung on and went with him to the shop in Fountain Street where he got his groceries, and to the stall in the market where he got his meat. It was mostly bones for the dogs, I noticed. On the way, he bawled out to this person and that, especially those who he knew would rather he didn't; and he had a voice like a fog-horn. Those properly dressed and important people tried their best to get away with a polite 'Good-morning, Steve', but the children, when they saw him, came running to say 'Hullo!' and his wicked old face would wrinkle up in a smile you couldn't help liking him for, and his wild mad eyes would go quite soft and gentle. He asked me if I would have some grub with him; and I said I would. After Tabitha was gone and I was on my own, I usually got a meal in Town on Fridays; so as not to have the trouble of getting one for myself at home.

We had dinner in that place in the corner of the States Arcade by the meat market, and went upstairs. I noticed he had to go up lop-sided, and had one hand badly broken. I said, 'Is anything wrong, Steve?' He said, 'Those bastards on Alderney!' I didn't know he had been on Alderney during the Occupation; and I don't yet know what for. Steve was a mystery man. He wasn't a Guernseyman. His family was Jersey, though I think he was a distant relation of the Priaulx; but he was born in New Zealand, so he said, and sent to Winchester Public School. He was later a physical training instructor in the Army in India and a schoolmaster, and goodness knows what else. He told me he had been married when he was young and his wife ran off; but I am not sure that was true. He may have only said it to me because he had heard I was one for the women. He admitted he had had little to do with women in his life; and I never heard of him being interested in a woman in Guernsey, though he was friends with a woman now and again who could be of help to him. He was shifty in a way, was Steve; yet he wasn't afraid to let important people know what he knew about them; but when it came down to hard facts about himself, there was no knowing what Steve Picquet had done or hadn't done in his time. He said one thing one day and another another, and you didn't know what to believe; and you couldn't believe a word other people said about him either.

Horace told me Steve ran a Black Market shop in Town during the Occupation, and his customers was people high up in the States: even a magistrate who used to fine him to please the Germans, and then pay him the fine back in return for a rabbit from under the counter. Anyway, he made a mint of money, but it soon went, for he had a bout of heavy drinking after the Liberation. Horace had a down on Steve. He said he was a Nazi in spirit, and was for the Nazis really. I don't believe that for a moment. I don't think Steve was on any side. He was against all sides. He was in with the Police; and made fools of the Police. He had more control over the bad boys than the Police had; and they had to ask him for his help to stop a number from being a nuisance. He never gave the boys away, though. He kept their names to himself, if they obeyed him; if not, he reported them and let the Police do their own dirty work. He was himself in the Town jail a number of times. I never really got to know what for. He said it was for a rest-cure. In my opinion, he thought himself and all grown-up human beings was rotten. He was for children and animals. I am quite, quite sure he never did harm to a child; and he looked after a herd of twenty or more wild goats he kept loose on the cliffs at Pleinmont. He was in everlasting trouble with the States who wanted those goats caught and tied up, because they was eating up respectable people's gardens.

The day I was having with old Steve I had more or less forgotten the last winter of the Occupation, and by then being hungry and desperate was only a bad dream; but something he told me brought it all back again, and I realised that for some people it had been far more of a nightmare than it had been even for me. He said there was a German woman on Alderney, when he was imprisoned there, who was supposed to be a lady doctor; and, among the foreign prisoners was a French boy who had been extraordinarily brave in the Resistance. She cut off his thing with a pair of garden shears and he went screaming mad and died. I made out I hadn't heard. It was too horrible. I was thinking of Raymond in his innocence saying 'God is love. That is true, isn't it?' I was glad he was dead, so he would never know such things could happen, or even be thought of. When we got up to go, I said I would pay for the dinners; but Steve wanted to pay for the dinners, and we nearly came to blows. In the end, for the sake of peace, I gave in and let Steve pay. I walked down to the buses with him; and he got on the Pleinmont bus, and I got on the L'Ancresse. That was the last I saw of him. I read letters by him in the paper from time to time in which he was fighting for the rights of his goats. He won most of his battles with the States, because he knew too much about too many people. There are many who must have given a great 'Ouf!' of relief, when he breathed his last. He was given a grand funeral in Torteval Church. God rest his soul! as Liza said.

What really got my goat the last year of the Occupation was being robbed right and left. Some of it was done by German soldiers, or slave-workers who had escaped and was on the prowl; though most of the slave-workers was gone the last year. The worst was a lot of the stealing was done by Guernseymen. I know Dan Ferbrache, Phoebe's brother, who was a widower and living at Sandy Hook, stole a spade of mine from in my tool-shed; and I believe it was him who took my tomatoes. The spade I have no doubt about, because I saw him digging with it and recognised it as mine: but I couldn't say anything because I hadn't burnt my mark on it. He must have had the cheek to pinch it during the day; for I had long since taken to locking everything up at night. But I was a fool. I locked the door at the far end of the greenhouse, but left the key in the lock on the inside; though the other end I locked from the outside and put the key in my pocket. I had been growing sweet-corn that year; but had a few tomato plants for myself at the far end. It was late in the season but there was still a few tomatoes on them; and I treasured those tomatoes, if only to look at. They was only to be picked one at a time. One morning, when I went out, I found somebody had smashed the glass, turned the key in the door, and gone in and got the lot.

In the house, what food we had was fairly safe. There was a bar across the front door and a bolt on the back; but, even so, every crumb was kept up in the garret where the apples used to be, and the ladder was taken down and locked away in the packing-shed. It was a business going to the cupboard those days. Out of doors, it was hopeless. Turnips, parsnips, carrots went; apples went; beans went; the robbers didn't even give things time to grow. When the tomatoes went, I was so angry I decided I would do a bit of robbing myself. So one afternoon, by accident on purpose, I went for a walk along the lane gives down on the backs of Timbuctoo and Wallaballoo. I kept my eyes open and got the lie of the land. Against the dividing wall between Timbuctoo and Wallaballoo, Harold had built a lean-to in which to grow a few things for themselves. The Dobrées had left it there and was now making use of it. I saw there was quite a nice crop of late tomatoes in it. Ah good, I thought!

It say in the Bible 'Thou shalt not covet thy neighbour's house, thou shalt not covet thy neighbour's wife, nor his man servant, nor his maid servant, nor his ox, nor his ass, nor anything that is thy neighbour's.' Well, I coveted my neighbour's tomatoes and that night, while Tabitha was asleep, I crept out to steal them. It was Providence there was a water-butt handy for me to climb down from the lane into the garden at the back of Wallaballoo; and the lean-to was a good way from the house. I could easily smash a few panes of glass and get in and out before Raoul had time to come out and see what was happening: if he wasn't too frightened to come at all. I was gripping in my hand one of my mother's old net-bags I was going to fill. I didn't hear a voice from heaven saying I mustn't do it; but I had cocked one leg over the wall and was going to cock the other and jump down on the butt, when I was horror-stricken by the picture in my mind of what I had come to. I leapt back into the lane, as if it was from the edge of the bottomless pit: did a smart right-about turn, and marched back home. There are some things a man must not do.

I don't know that starving is such a bad way of dying: at least, so long as you got water to drink. The worst is having just a little to eat, but not enough. If you have nothing for a few days, it hurt at first; but after a while you get weaker and feel like a ghost and don't care about nothing. I know I got so I didn't care if it was the Germans won or us. The whole shoot seemed to me nothing but a lot of nonsense nobody would worry about who wasn't mad; and when you are nearly dying, you stop being mad. That is, while you are awake. It was going to sleep I was afraid of; and I had plenty of time to go to sleep, goodness knows. By three o'clock in the afternoon, even when I had food of a sort, I was so tired I was ready to knock off; and, at that, I had been having to sit down every five minutes. There was only the long evenings to look forward to with no light and no fire; and hours and hours lying on my bed in a sort of half and half state, when I wasn't awake and wasn't asleep and a lot of mixed up nonsense was going through my head; then when at last I did fall asleep properly I would have the most horrible dreams I would wake up from in a sweat. I was never able to remember exactly those dreams; but in some roundabout way they always had to do with food. I never dreamt I was eating anything; and the food didn't have a smell. I wonder if anybody have ever dreamt a smell.

Tabitha said she slept quite well; and I think it was true. She ought to have been more tired than me, for she worked harder than me. She walked miles a day doing the housework; and often it was her went out and got the shopping. I didn't even go out to listen to the radio: I found I couldn't see any more in the dark. Sometimes I worried and thought to myself I wouldn't live to see the end of it. It wasn't the thought of dying worried me: it was the thought perhaps after all I had gone through, it would be for nothing. That thought didn't seem to worry Tabitha. Her mind was at rest. When it was touch and go whether we would be allowed to be brought food by the Red Cross, she didn't get excited, or hope. 'We'll see,' she said. When I heard the Red Cross ship, the *Vega*, was in, I got so excited I had to go and see it. I grabbed a walking-stick had belonged to my grandfather, and off I went to Town on my wobbly legs. There was crowds looking at it; though, of course, none of us was allowed to go down the harbour near it. It was an ugly old boat. When I got back home, hobbling along like an old man of ninety, Tabitha laughed. 'Well, d'you feel you've had a good meal now?' she said. 'As good as,' I said.

Yet it was over those precious Red Cross parcels I quarrelled with Tabitha. I had never quarrelled with her in my life before. I don't know I can say I quarrelled with her even then, for you couldn't quarrel with Tabitha, but I said hard and cutting words to her. I hurt my sister. It hurts me now to think of it; but it is one of those things can never be undone. When we got our parcels, I said, 'Well, they are for you to ration out,' but there was chocolate in mine as well as in hers. 'Except for the chocolate,' I

said. 'I don't want any.' It was true. I had never been one for eating chocolate, even when I was a kid. The only sweets I liked was bull's eyes, twelve
a penny; and I knew how much she liked chocolate. She said, 'I think you
ought to have the chocolate for when you are working: mine as well. It is
you who do the heavy work.' I flashed out at her. 'I am sick and tired of
seeing you sacrificing yourself for me!' I said. She opened her eyes wide in
surprise. 'Ebenezer!' she said. I said, 'What do you take me for? A weak-
ling! It is to show me up, you do it; and make me ashamed!' She said
quietly, 'I don't sacrifice myself for you, Ebenezer. I am with you. I
thought you understood.' Her lips was trembling and there was tears in
her eyes. I said, 'All right: I'll eat a piece of chocolate now and then'; and I
did so to please her. The next time we got parcels, there was tobacco and
cigarettes as well; and she gave me hers, as she didn't smoke. I let her and
didn't say anything: but she hadn't forgotten. She never forgot.

The 9th of May in the year 1945 is the other date in history I will never
forget. I didn't see the first British soldiers come ashore in the morning;
but I heard they had come and some more was expected in the afternoon. I
desperately wanted to see those. Tabitha said she would like to come with
me, but she couldn't walk so far; and I knew she couldn't, for she had been
getting very tired and feeble the last few weeks. She said I must go; but I
wouldn't go without her. How could I be happy celebrating and her by
herself at home? It looked as if we would neither of us go, when Dan Ferbrache turned up and asked us if we would like to go with him in his van.
He had managed to hang on to an old nag for his van. I said it was good of
him to think of us and how about Olive Le Boutillier? He said the more the
merrier. He was already taking old Mrs Renouf from L'Islet. It was a real
old-fashioned lot we was in that van: we must have looked as if we was
going on a picnic from the Town Hospital.

I was full of feeling for the English that day; and was real glad to see the
Tommies, marching from the White Rock, after years of the clock-work
German variety. Of course, they didn't look as smart in their khaki battle-
dress as we used to in our red jackets in the Guernsey Militia: but I cheered
until I was hoarse. There was no getting out of the van: which was just as
well. Tabitha had on her best dress, but it was mended and mended; and we
none of us had anything fit to be seen on our feet. Glatney was black with
people, like the Albert Pier of a Bank Holiday. Tabitha said, 'I wish
Gervase was here. It is him have done this for us; and Louise.' She thought
as much of those two as if they was her own. The last she had heard of them
through the Red Cross, they was all right; but there hadn't been any messages from either of them for some months. I looked at Tabitha. She was
quite the little old woman with her grey hair and her black dress. She was
old before her time.

Perhaps I ought to write more cheerfully about what is supposed to have been our happiest day; but ours was a sad van-load, if the truth is to be told. Old Mother Renouf got a wicked tongue and was a born liar; but she had lost two grandsons she thought the world of, who was killed in North Africa. They was none other than the sons of the very boys who won the first class sailing the day I climbed the greasy pole. Olive Le Boutillier was wondering where her husband was; if he was alive. He wasn't, but she didn't know it for sure yet; though she had said to me several times she felt in her heart he was dead. Dan Ferbrache wasn't much of a chap, perhaps; but there was one person he really loved: that was his daughter. He had let her be evacuated, so as she would be safe, as he thought. He was only living for the happiness of having her home again. She was safe all right; but the people she was put to live with in England didn't have any children of their own and, when the time came for her to come home, they wanted to keep her. In the meantime, she had forgotten Guernsey and her father and got into English ways, and wanted to stay with 'Mum and Dad'. They was well-to-do people and could give her everything of the best. Dan said he wouldn't stand in her way. Our happiness that day was for the moment only; and make-believe.

For myself, I cannot get the idea out of my head that, after the Liberation, Guernsey had a chance of starting afresh it can never have again; but for some reason, it took the wrong turning, even if it didn't go downhill as fast and as willingly as Jersey. It was business as usual: only more so. The dog went back to its vomit and the sow to its wallowing in the mire. There was something else could have been done. I don't know quite what. I haven't the right to criticise. I remember too well how I thought at times when it comes down to rock bottom, I didn't care tuppence about anything, or anybody, except myself; and that everybody else was the same. If that is true, it is something a man should not know. It may be it was the one lesson we learnt from the Occupation; but it was the wrong lesson.

Well, the nobs from England came over and the laws was changed and the States brought up-to-date and the affairs of the island put on a sound business footing; so they said. It was certainly a great chance for some people. I could name more than a few who had hardly a penny to bless themselves with before the War, but by the end of the Occupation was rich men with thousands of German marks they had made by serving the Germans at the expense of the Guernsey people, and which they could now change into good English pounds at a more than fair rate of exchange. There was a rush and a scramble, and those people was the very ones to be made Chairman of this Committee and Chairman of that Committee; while the honest Guernseyman, who was nearly broke, didn't get a look in. Ah well, that is all forgotten now; and perhaps it is just as well. The King and Queen came over. They drove around the island and Tabitha and me went to see them pass on the Bridge. By then Tabitha had a new grey dress, and we both had decent shoes. The Queen was quite different from the other one I saw. She smiled and bowed all around and gave herself to everybody with both arms. The King looked more serious than his father and when I stood on the edge of the kerb and shouted 'Wharro, George!' he didn't look round. He didn't know it was me.

5

Gervase and Louise came over on a visit to their father that summer, and both came to Les Moulins to see Tabitha. By then they had written to her direct to say they was well and was coming over; and for weeks she was making preparations. Jack Priaulx, the father, was a broken man. He hadn't found it easy to knuckle under to the Germans, and when his wife died he lost heart. She didn't die because of hardship under the Occupation, but from some growth in her inside. She was taken to the hospital and operated on by candle-light. It was said the operation was a success; but she died. While she was yet alive they had been allowed to keep on at Le Courtil à Bas, though they had three or four German officers billetted on them most of the time; but once Ann was dead, Jack had to shift out of the farmhouse and live at Le Courtil du Milieu, a small cottage of his he had only used for stores. More Germans moved into Le Courtil à Bas. It is true they was of the better sort, and didn't pull the place to pieces; but he was little more than a labourer, and had a gun emplacement in his front garden. Every time that gun went off against the British aeroplane passing overhead, he thought it might be Gervase in it.

When he moved back into his old house after the Liberation, Tabitha went along to see how he was, and he asked her to go and live there for good as his housekeeper. She refused the offer. She didn't say it was because she didn't want to leave me, and I am glad she didn't; because she did leave me. The reason she refused was because Jack had once asked her to marry him. She said it was all right for her to live there, while his wife was alive; but she didn't think it would be right to live in the same house with him now he was a widower. I didn't know Jack Priaulx, except to nod to and pass the time of day; but I like to think of him waving the Muratti Cup on the boat going out of St Helier's Harbour, and the Jersey crapauds on the quay shouting 'Guernsey donkeys! Guernsey donkeys!'

Louise brought her young man with her. He had been a Petty Officer in the Navy, but wasn't at all the sort of chap you would imagine to be a sailor; yet when the ship he was on was torpedoed by the German submarine, he had done something at great risk to himself, the details of which was not made known, that saved his Commander; and the ship got back to port half sinking, but with no lives lost. He was given the O.B.E. for it; but there was no swank about him. Louise had grown into a big jolly tomboy of a girl, and she was more the one you'd have thought would win the O.B.E.; but she had only worked for the W.R.E.N.S. ashore. They was both out of the Navy now, and going to get married and live in England. His father owned a big drapery business in Wolverhampton, and he was going to manage it. Gervase I didn't take to at all. He had been a squadron-leader and dropped loads of bombs on Germany, and got an arm burnt in a dog-fight over the North Sea. He was going to stay in the Air Force and train others. I had nothing against him: he was one of those who had helped to free us, as Tabitha said; but he had gone very posh and used a lot of words I didn't understand and had a moustache the like of which I had never seen, except on Terence de Freis.

They was very nice to Tabitha in words; but there was something missing. They saw a little old grey-haired Guernseywoman and couldn't know how much she was feeling. If I know my sister, she had prayed si-lently in her heart every night of the War for them to come back home safe and sound. She didn't make a great fuss of them, for she wasn't the sort to do so; and they may have thought she didn't care much. She didn't com-plain to me either, when they was gone; but she did say, 'It is natural for the young to forget.' The one I really liked of the three was Tim Moffatt, the Petty Officer; and I left Gervase and Louise with Tabitha and took him for a stroll to have a look at the fortifications the Germans had put up. I couldn't get him to talk about what he had done in the Navy: he was more interested in how we had managed to live under the Occupation. 'I would rather it had been you than me,' he said. I said, 'Well, I don't know: we wasn't in much danger.' He said, 'Yes, but it is hard to be the same again, if you go through an experience other people don't have.' Gervase didn't have much to say about the Occupation. When Tabitha said for five years we had hardly ever gone more than a mile from Les Moulins, he said, 'Fan-tastic!' She didn't see either of them again. Gervase came over for a few days when his father died; but that was a year after Tabitha. He had written me a letter of sympathy from England, which I answered; but he didn't come to see me.

I couldn't bring myself to believe Tabitha really wasn't well. She had always been like me in that she had never had a day of real illness in her life. When I got more and better food, I soon got my strength back; but Tabitha wouldn't eat much, even when there was plenty. She had never had a big appetite, so I didn't worry at first; but I really did get worried when one day my Cousin Mary Ann turned up and asked if there was anything she could do. It goes to show how little I had gone out I hadn't seen my Cousin Mary Ann once throughout the Occupation and she only lived at the Robergerie and was trudging along the roads and lanes as much as before, if not more. The moment I saw her on my doorstep, I knew it was a bad sign. I sent her for the doctor. He was a new, young doctor, but I think he was clever. Tabitha let him examine her, and I waited to hear what he had to say. He said, 'Mrs Batiste is suffering, like many others on this island, from post-occupationitis. It is nothing a doctor can do much about. I will give her a tonic; and she must rest and eat well.' He sent the bill and I paid it. She didn't take the tonic.

I didn't want my Cousin Mary Ann coming to the house. I thought if I could get her to keep away, perhaps Tabitha would get better; but Tabitha said she liked my Cousin Mary Ann to come and wanted her there to talk to. They became very friendly, those two women. They had at least one thing in common which, I think, is rare among women: they both loved their husbands. I left them to it. I worked hard and had a number of young chaps working for me on and off; but none of them stayed long. They didn't seem to be able to make up their minds what they wanted to stick to. I think I can say I did all I could for Tabitha; but it was another bad sign she let me do things for her. She had never as much as let me cook a meal for myself until then. She didn't stay in bed at first but, in the summer, sat on the rocks in the sun and, when winter came, sat by the fire; but I could see she was getting weaker every day. She wasn't in pain. I tried to make her eat every food I could think of she might fancy. I made her some chicken soup she liked, and I thumped ormers and cooked them my mother's way; but she only nibbled. My Cousin Mary Ann kept on coming two or three times a week, and every Sunday.

One Sunday afternoon Tabitha had gone to lie down in her room and I was left with my Cousin Mary Ann in the kitchen. I was feeling very miserable. I said, 'I am going to get that doctor again for Tabitha.' 'For why, then?' she said. 'She is happy.' I looked at my Cousin Mary Ann; and for the first time I noticed what wonderful knowing eyes she had in her ugly face. I thought to myself she is not ugly really. She said, 'Tabitha is happier now than she have been for a very long time. I wish I could be as happy as she is; but it is not for me.' I began to take an interest in my Cousin Mary Ann for her own sake then; and I asked her how her children was getting on. She said the eldest was married and the second was going to be and the boy was at home. She also told me Harold and Mrs Crewe was fighting it out as to who would live the longer. She hoped Uncle Harold would win. I hadn't given a thought to Harold during the Occupation; except I had seen his name in Horace's book. Now he was alive enough yet to know Mrs Crewe was waiting for him to die and, in his stubborn way he was determined to outlive her. I wondered if he might leave what little he had left to Raymond's boy in England. He knew Raymond was gone because Gwen had been to tell him his son was dead. All he said was, 'I had no son.'

Mrs Crewe got meaner and meaner as she got older. My Cousin Mary

Ann walked all the way to the Can'-du-Ré time and again during the Occupation and, though she didn't say as much, I gathered it was more often her who took things from her garden, than Mrs Crewe who gave her anything. It was to see Harold she went. He was bad with bronchitis every winter; and Mrs Crewe would say 'This time you must say good-bye to your uncle. I don't expect you will see him again. I thought I was going to lose him last winter. I know, I know I will lose him this!' Then she would break down and cry. 'What am I going to do without him? What am I going to do without him? He is such a good old man!' Harold would be sitting by the empty grate looking like a grumpy bear with an empty pipe in his mouth. After Horace was gone, he couldn't get tobacco even on the Black Market.

After the Liberation Mrs Crewe kept on being as mingy as before with the food; and wouldn't let Harold buy any new clothes. 'It is his grave-clothes he must be thinking about now,' she said. He wasn't allowed to get out of his bed, except to do his business in a commode. He had nothing to wear. I don't think he had anything to wear in bed either. He died that winter. My Cousin Mary Ann said there was nothing to bury him in, but Mrs Crewe's niece was married to Phil Randall, who used to play for the Rangers, and he still had an old football shirt; so Harold was put in his coffin in that. Harold would have turned over in his grave if he had known he was buried in a red and white football shirt. He was all for the North.

My Cousin Mary Ann surprised me. She got really upset as I had never seen her before because Mrs Crewe wouldn't have Harold buried with Hetty in the grave he had bought in the cemetery of St Sampson's. I had my doubts what Hetty would have felt about it; and was all for letting sleeping dogs lie: but no, my Cousin Mary Ann insisted it was my duty, as the surviving head of the family of the Le Pages from Les Sablons, to go and lay down the law to Mrs Crewe and see to it Hetty got her rights. I went. I wished to God after I hadn't! When I said what I had come for, Mrs Crewe went for me like a lion. I was only a man: how could I be head of a family? Was I so ignorant I hadn't heard of Women's Rights? 'My second husband is going to be buried with my first husband in the Foulon Cemetery,' she said, 'and when it is God's good will I go to my rest, I will lie in the same grave with my two husbands under me.' Well, she didn't have long to wait. She died in a few months and was buried in the Foulon Cemetery on top of her two husbands. It was her rights, I suppose.

I can't say I felt very sorry for Harold. He had made his bed and, like the rest of us, he had to lie on it. If it comes to that, I reckon Mrs Crewe earnt her few months without him. He was a hard man. My Cousin Mary Ann said he wasn't hard: he was only treated hard; but she always had a soft spot for Uncle Harold. The truth is I was feeling too sorry for myself to feel sorry for anybody else. I saw myself being left alone again. It was impossible to feel sorry for Tabitha. She was weak and tired; but she didn't try and do things she couldn't do, and so make herself miserable. She would get up for a couple of hours a day, but passed a lot of her time lying down. I brought the green-bed from the wash-house into the kitchen, so as she could lie on it by the fire, if she wanted a change from her room. I got the doctor to see her again, in spite of my Cousin Mary Ann; but all he said was she must be kept warm. The days when she stayed in bed all day, I lit a fire in the bedroom.

Olive Le Boutillier came across every day to see if there was anything she could do; and Julia came in most evenings. They both spent Christmas with us, and young Jean Le Boutillier brought his girl. Tabitha got up that day and ate a little of the dinner. It wasn't a very jolly Christmas, considering it was the first for five years we had been able to have what we wanted; but Olive Le Boutillier had just heard for sure her husband was not coming back. She wouldn't have kept Christmas at all, if it hadn't been she wanted to cook a dinner for Tabitha and me. My Cousin Mary Ann had hers with her family, and only came a few times in the New Year. I said to her then I wished she would keep on coming, but she said, 'Tabitha have no need of me now.' She was going to do things for Ada Domaille, who was crippled with arthritis and could only move about her room by holding on to the furniture.

I sat by my sister's side for many hours. Sometimes I held her hand, and she let me; but I knew it was her comforting me, and not me comforting her. She knew exactly what I was feeling, the same as my mother used to. I couldn't deceive her. One day she said, 'Now you mustn't worry about yourself, Ebenezer: you are going to be all right.' I didn't hold her hand again. As time went on, she seemed to get younger. When she lay with her grey hair in pig-tails tied with a ribbon on the pillow, her face looked like a young girl's. I think the last months she had forgotten the Occupation and everything had happened to her since Jean died. She spoke only of Jean. Sometimes she would laugh to herself. I would say 'What are you laughing at now?' She would say 'It is something I can't tell you.' Once she did tell me. 'I was the only girl Jean ever went with,' she said. 'He was shy at first; but he soon got over it.' She remembered things I thought she had forgotten years ago. 'Remember the Sunday you turned up with Jim for tea, and we had spider crab?' she said. 'Of course I remember,' I said. 'Jean liked Jim,' she said, 'I liked Jim too. I had always liked Jim. If it hadn't been for Jean, who knows?'

Well, she lasted the winter. I thought then with the spring coming she might get better after all. I knew she was very weak. She would lie for hours not asleep: just weak. She died on May the first. She had had a little to eat that day; and there was sun on our windows in the evening. She was lying on her back with her eyes closed; when, suddenly, she opened her eyes and held out her arms and smiled. It was not to me. Then her arms fell limp by her side. That was how she left me. I went across for Olive Le Boutillier and everything was done properly. It was a private funeral, like for my mother: a hearse and one motor-car. I invited Alf Brouard, young Lihou and young Jean le Boutillier. She was mourned by two old men and two young ones. She was buried with my mother, in the grave I had bought in the Chapel part of the Vale cemetery. Tabitha was not one to bother where she was buried. All she wanted was to curl up with Jean for eternity.

6

Tabby was alive yet and going on the beach when the Tommies was around clearing up the mess the Germans had left behind. They was certainly a change from the slave-workers. They enjoyed themselves, the Tommies, putting us to rights, and they was nice cheery chaps; though I don't know why the English soldiers are called Tommies. As far as I could make out they was all called Bill. Of course I was asked the everlasting question 'How was it under the Germans?' 'Well, I'm still alive,' I would say; and start talking about the First World War. They looked at me as if I had come out of the Ark. They didn't seem to know there had been a First World War. It is the same with the young chaps nowadays. They don't know there was a Second World War; and the Occupation is a bit of fun they missed.

There is no Guernsey Militia now, and there are no regular soldiers stationed on the island, but that don't mean it is an island for peace. Raymond was for peace; but I doubt if he would get more of a look-in now than when he was alive. The Guernsey people don't want war here naturally, because it might stop them making money; but there are a lot who are for Rhodesia and South Africa, and get a kick out of what the Americans are up to. Lately I got the idea of going to the Pictures sometimes to pass away an evening. I went to the Gaumont, or I went to the Odeon and came home on the bus. I soon gave it up. I hardly ever went but it was shooting and killing. The T.V. is worse. It isn't often I see it, and never if I can help it; but one night I went to visit some Le Pages from the Ramée, who are cousins of a cousin of my mother. They was three families living in one house, and the youngest boy was only fifteen. I thought perhaps I might leave him something. It turned out he was one of those with long hair and tight trousers; but otherwise he seemed a nice lad, only shy. Goodness, he wasn't shy when the T.V. was lit up! It was Americans shooting and killing. A Yank don't think he is a man unless he got a gun in his hand. Young Ernie was watching it trembling with excitement and couldn't keep still, but was bouncing up and down on his seat. All he wanted was to be doing the same thing. I got up and said I wouldn't stop to the end.

I reckon fighting, fornicating and making money are the three easiest things to do in this world; and I have done a bit of all three myself, so I ought to know. I am still making money one way and the other. Once you start, you can't stop. It would be making itself for me if I had put it in the bank, and was having interest paid on it every year. 'Unto him that hath shall be given and from him that hath not shall be taken, even that which he hath.' The trouble is I don't know what to do with what I got now I got it. I won't live for ever. I will have to leave it to somebody. I reckon I have walked a hundred if one mile these last years going to visit relations, or relations by marriage, on the look out for somebody worth leaving it to. I think everybody living on the island must by now be used to seeing old Ebenezer Le Page in his old-fashioned suit and his old-fashioned hat trotting on his bandy legs with his stick along the roads and the lanes; and trying to keep out of the way of being run over. 'Ah, the poor old man!' the people say; but they don't know how much I got hidden in the house, and how much I got buried in the ground. Young Bill Torode, who live in one of the new houses along the Braye, called out after me only the other day, 'Hi, gran'-père, why don't you get a tricycle?' I said, 'What for do I want a tricycle, me? I can get along all right on three legs.'

I don't know what it is about women: but, for some reason, they just cannot bear to see any man, it don't matter how old he is, or of what shape, or of what size, getting along on his own. I think after Tabitha died, all the women living in the parishes of the Vale and of St Sampson's, and a crowd of others, got together on one big committee and decided Ebenezer Le Page of Les Moulins must be married to a wife. The Marriage Marketing Board. It didn't matter when I went out, or where I went, I was stopped and spoken to and given advice by some woman or another. Old Mrs Renouf from L'Islet had her say, of course; and Mrs Duquemin from the Ville Baudu, whose husband drinks like a fish; and Mrs Ogier from the Bassières, whose husband beat her black and blue while he yet had the strength; and Mrs Tardiff from the Tertre who have buried so many husbands nobody knows if she was ever married at all.

It was always the same rigmarole. 'Ah, now your poor sister is gone, it is high time you was looking round for a nice little wife, isn't it?' I would say, 'Goodness, what nice little wife d'you think will want me with all the young chaps coming back?' 'There are dozens who would jump at the chance,' they would say. Well, I didn't see none of those dozens jumping, me; and if there was any, I was quite sure it was for my house and my money they was jumping, not for me. Mind you, I had certain thoughts and feelings sometimes, and my eyes kept straying in the wrong direction when I saw girls about; but I noticed the shorter the skirts got, the thinner the legs. I made myself remember Clara Fallaize, who was a great-grandmother now, and as big as a house. There is no fool like an old fool, and I wasn't going to make a fool of myself, if I could help it.

The summer after Tabitha died, Rita Nicolle from the Bailloterie came to help me with the packing. She was the daughter-in-law of old Nicolle who was such a staunch supporter of Oliver Cromwell, and was a widow with one son. Her husband, Bill Nicolle, was killed in the Commandos and Johnnie, the boy, was about seven. I liked Johnnie. He was a sturdy black-haired little Guernsey boy, and I wouldn't have minded him for a son myself. Rita was forty or so, and a good worker. At first she went home for her dinner, but I said she could have it at Les Moulins, if she would cook mine at the same time. Tea-times Johnnie came from school to fetch his mother; and I gave them both a good tea before they went home. I enjoyed having them in the house; and got quite friendly with Rita. She talked to me about her husband and she had nothing but good to say of him. I liked her for that. I talked to her about Tabitha and Jean, and we got on well together. I am not saying she was ready to jump. She didn't push herself, or play tricks like Mrs Crewe. The only thing she did say was Johnnie had taken a great fancy to me, and was always talking about me at home. All the same, I think if I had asked her to marry me, she would have; and I think she knew I was thinking about it.

It was a reasonable thing to do. Her father-in-law let her live in the wing of his house; but she didn't like the old man, and he was always interfering. She had nothing except her widow's pension and what she earnt. If she married me, she would have a home of her own, and a place to leave to Johnnie; and I would have a companion, and a decent sensible woman at that, as well as the pleasure of watching young Johnnie grow up. I lay on my back in bed many nights thinking it over. I hadn't started yet on my wild-goose chase for somebody to leave my money to; but I was already thinking I didn't want what I got to be wasted. I will say at once I decided against it; but I don't think I can give a good reason. It wouldn't have been a love match. It would have been a business arrangement; but an honest business arrangement. That was just what I was against. I thought of Jim and me: that wasn't business; and of Raymond and me: that wasn't business. I thought of Liza and Tabitha and me: that wasn't business. Raymond said the Kingdom of Heaven have nothing to do with the States. I don't know nothing about the Kingdom of Heaven, but I do know there is something have nothing to do with business. Anyway, I didn't ask her.

I don't know if she was disappointed. If so, she didn't show it. At the end of the season I told her I would be glad if she would come and work for me again the next year, but she said she was going to try and find a job as a housekeeper in a hotel, if they would let her keep the boy. She did find a job, and have been manageress of a big hotel in Town for years. I meet her sometimes and we have a chat. She is a well set up woman now; and Johnnie is grown up and married, and drives a bus for the Guernsey Railway Company. He always shouts out 'Hullo!' when he sees me. Perhaps I was a fool.

It was that winter I started going to see my Cousin Mary Ann. I don't suppose any of the people she had been to help had ever thought of going to see her to her house. She was 'la pauvre Mary Ann' and turned up on your doorstep when there was misery; and at the end of the day disappeared with her bags full, and you thought no more about her. I hadn't been pleased when she turned up at Les Moulins, but Tabitha had been glad to have her there; so I thought I might as well go along and thank her. I went one Thursday evening when the days was closing in, and arranged it so as not to arrive until after tea. I hadn't been along the Robergerie since the day I went to her wedding, and couldn't even remember which was her cottage. I had to ask a chap going home from work. If he hadn't pointed it out I wouldn't have recognised it; for it had been all painted and done up.

I knocked on the front door and I heard her heavy feet coming along the passage. When she opened the door she couldn't see who it was. 'Who is it?' she said. 'Ebenezer,' I said, 'the brother of Tabitha.' 'Oh come in, come in!' she said. 'I am so glad you have come to see me. Nobody ever come to see me.' I felt quite ashamed she was so pleased, for I had gone as much as for any other reason because I had nothing else to do. The cottage inside, as I remembered it, was dark and shabby and crammed full of old furniture; but now everything was new, and looked as if it had come straight out of Fuzzey's window. In what had been the kitchen there was linoleum on the floor and a good rug by the fire; and the walls was papered instead of being varnished boards, and the woodwork of the door and windows painted blue and yellow. It was a modern grate, instead of an open fire and a terpid; and there was cupboards instead of a dresser. The ceiling was done in wreaths of roses. All in all, I didn't think it very homely, myself: but I said, 'It's a nice room you got here.' She said, 'It's my son Eugene who have done it: he is clever at decorating. I'll show you the rest when you're warm.'

She got the electric, the gas, a radio; and I noticed a telephone in the passage. It wasn't a bad little house, come to that; but, when she showed me the front room, I thought there was too many knick-knacks in it. I like having those things I got to have to use; but I don't go in much for ornaments. Eugene liked every sort of useless ornament from a ship in a bottle to a peacock's feather, which I had always thought was unlucky in a house anyway; and there was china birds with long necks flying up the walls. The famous horse-hair sofa where big Clara and me curled up was gone and, in its place was a modern affair on tubes. My Cousin Mary Ann showed me the children's rooms and hers with the double bed. The two for the children, one for the boy and one for the two girls, was small; but done up new and the beds was of light wood. Her own room she had kept as it was with the old-fashioned iron bedstead with brass knobs and a high chest-of-drawers with a bulging front and a mahogany press with a full-length mirror. I expect it was the only room she felt at home in. Over the bed was an enlarged photo of Eugene Le Canu. She said, 'Eugene, my husband.' He looked smart in his coachman's uniform, and quite the lad. It was all she had of him.

She said I must have something to eat before I went home, and gave me a good supper of cold ham. It was from a shop, for her son Eugene had got rid of the rack in his craze for decorating. While she was laying the table she was telling me about her children. I couldn't make out at first which was which of the two girls, for one was called Dora and the other was called Nora; but I worked it out D came before N and therefore Dora was the first and Nora was the second. I realised Dora must be getting on for fifty. She was married to a Domaille from Gran'-Rock, who was a relation of the Domailles who had lived next house to my grandmother of Les Sablons. During the Occupation she had worked in the kitchen of the Royal Hotel, cooking for the German officers; and now she had a guest-house of her own for visitors from England. My Cousin Mary Ann said it was Nora, the second, who had been the pretty one; but on the flighty side. Anyhow, she was at last engaged, it was hoped, but to a chap much younger than her, who had only come to Guernsey since the Liberation. I couldn't make out who, or what he was. He had a funny name: Van-something. Eugene was out courting; but he was always out courting, only not always the same girl. I wondered if perhaps he had turned out to be like his father: but no, it was always the girl who found somebody else she liked better. My Cousin Mary Ann said Eugene was a good boy. I felt sorry for him.

Before I left, she asked me if I would come again, and I said I would. She said next time I must come to tea, and on a Thursday again would be best, because that was the afternoon she was on her own. I got the feeling she didn't want me to meet her children; and I noticed that evening she was anxious to get me out of the house before Nora and Eugene came home. I went often of a Thursday afternoon and got to know my Cousin Mary Ann very well. I don't think she had much love for anybody: not even for her children. She was wise, perhaps. She got no grand ideas about herself either. She didn't think of herself as a good woman going round helping people. She said she only went to help people for what she could get; and they only put up with her for what they could get out of her. 'They give me something to take home because they are too proud to owe to anybody,' she said.

According to her, misery of one sort or another was everybody's lot; and there was nothing you could do about it: except put up with it. Sometimes I thought she was more amused than anything by the way things turned out bad for everybody she knew; and if she had come across anybody who was really happy, she would have been downright miserable. I even wondered if that was perhaps why she hadn't come to see Tabitha towards the end. I could understand her. I was very much the same sort of old prowler as she was; but I am always wondering and asking questions to myself. I am not satisfied to let things be. She remembered the details of everything exactly as it happened: nothing added and nothing left out; and she knew the life-stories of dozens of people. In fact, she was a walking Greffe, my Cousin Mary Ann: only instead of it being written down in the Register of Births, Deaths and Marriages, and in the Livres de Perchage, it was alive and kicking in her head. If it hadn't been for what she told me, I would never have been able to piece together the story of Harold and Hetty and the others, even as badly as I have done.

7

I have noticed mothers don't always get on with their daughters, just as fathers don't always get on with their sons. I don't think my Cousin Mary Ann got on very well with Dora. 'She do what she want, that one,' she said. 'She always have. She ought to have been a man.' She liked Nora better. Nora was a gad-about; and for a time was barmaid in the Crown. I wondered if I had seen her, because I had been in there a few times. My Cousin Mary Ann said when she was earning, she wasn't stingy, and paid for her keep and more. She was at home now while waiting to be married; but he didn't seem to be in a hurry and she ought to have been married long ago. Of course it was Eugene who was the most thought of: he had always looked after his mother. Nora helped in the house, hoping to learn something about how to look after a husband, when the time came. Eugene worked the greenhouse and the garden, and kept the house in trim; and, even when he was courting, it was his mother came first. The girl was given to understand if she married him, she would have to marry his mother as well.

Of the three, it was Dora I was most curious about. I am funny that way. If anybody starts running somebody else down, I at once feel I am on the side of the person who is being run down; or, at least, I have to find out for myself. It wasn't often Dora went to see her mother, but once when she did and heard I had taken to going there, she said, 'You're much too old now, my mother, to have a young man, you know.' 'The cheek!' said my Cousin Mary Ann, when she told me. I asked where it was exactly Dora lived. It was in an old farmhouse at Le Carrefour, and you got to it up a turning off the Portinfer Road. I was quite open with my Cousin Mary Ann and said I would go and see Dora for myself one day. 'I hope you do,' she said, 'and then you will see what I have had to put up with.'

As it happened, I couldn't have chosen a worse day to go. It was the Thursday before Whitsun and she was expecting visitors over the Whitsun holiday. She knew who I was and asked me in. The place was upside-down but she found me a corner to sit. Peter Domaille, the husband, came in for a minute, but there was so many jobs she wanted him to get on with, he only said 'Good-afternoon' and went out again. He looked a very worried man.

My Cousin Mary Ann was right when she said Dora wasn't the pretty one. She had a big plain face and broad shoulders and looked as strong as an ox. She wasn't at all like Eugene Le Canu; or much like my Cousin Mary Ann either. She didn't have my Cousin Mary Ann's nice old ugly face. Having children is a lottery and you never know what you are going to draw out. Perhaps it is as well I got none.

Peter Domaille had been a farmer in a small way when she married him; but it goes without saying the farm didn't pay. That is another thing I have never understood. If you come to think of it, everything you got to have to live on come out of the ground to begin with, or grow on it, or come from the animals who live on it, or from the creatures in the sea: but in Guernsey those are the very things don't pay, and you got to work hardest at to make enough to live on; and, even then, in many cases, only with the help of the States. If you want to rake in easy money, you only got to sell trash to the visitors in Town: Guernsey this and Guernsey that: things got nothing to do with Guernsey except the word 'Guernsey' on, and I wouldn't have in my house at any price.

Peter Domaille gave up farming when Dora got the idea of running a guest-house. The stables was made into little rooms she called 'châlets' and the visitors was going to have to sleep in stalls like the cows. As for themselves, she said Peter and her and the girl, who was to school yet, would have to sleep in the shed for the summer. The rooms in the house was for the married couples. Most of the ground had been sold for building, and such as was left was only to grow vegetables to feed the guests: but most of the food, of course, would have to be brought over from the other side. The visitors are supposed to bring money to the island; but the food they eat have to be brought over by air, or by sea, at goodness knows what expense. It is beyond me. As Eddie Le Tissier said the night I started a fight in the Caves de Bordeaux, there have never been enough of everything on this island to feed the inhabitants. How about now with thousands and thousands extra coming over every year? They talk of the German Occupation!

The house was freshly done up inside, and the furniture was a lot of new stuff didn't look as if it would last anybody's lifetime. Dora said it wasn't paid for yet. 'What I want to meet is a rich uncle,' she said. 'I expect you got thousands in the bank.' I said, 'I haven't got a penny in the bank.' She couldn't get me out of the house quick enough then; but I wasn't in a hurry and kept her talking and, when I wished her good-bye, said I would call and see her again. I went at the end of September. When she came to the door, I invited myself in and sat down. 'Well, how have you been getting on?' I said. Oh, she had had a wonderful season! She could have taken twice as many, if she had had the room; and most of them was coming again the next year. She was now under the doctor for a nervous breakdown, but never mind: she would get over it. She was going for a holiday to Bourne-mouth to look at the shops; and then would come back refreshed and get ready for the next season.

'Tourism' is a holy word these days: though it is a word I didn't learn at school, and have only heard of late years. I know full well to say anything against it on this island is as if you wanted to ruin the island you was born on; but I really and truly believe any place which sell its soul to Tourism is a whore of a place, and put everything on for show and sell it for pleasure, even the gifts God gave it. I met one chap who didn't like Tourism any more than I did, and he worked for it; but he wasn't a Guernseyman. He didn't know how it hurt. It was the tourists themselves he couldn't stand. He said they might be all right at home when they had their noses to the grindstone; but when they was on holiday, they thought the world was made only for them. He came over a number of years running and never missed coming to see me. He said I was the only person he knew on the island who wasn't caught up in the racket. I am talking now of years after the time I was going round visiting my Cousin Mary Ann and her children. By then the disease had really taken hold.

I thought he was a nice chap for an Englishman, he made me laugh; but it turned out he wasn't an Englishman. He was Irish. He said the Irish are like the Guernsey: they all love old Ireland, but will go and live anywhere else in the world, if they get a chance. He liked being in Guernsey himself. He said it was quite like home. Certainly he knew more about the history of the island than I do; and what he didn't know he made up. The first time I saw him, he was coming along by Les Amarreurs with a crowd of tourists following him like a flock of sheep. I listened to his patter. He pointed out the martello tower on our side and the martello tower across the bay on Rousse, and said they was martello towers. I would have thought anybody could see they was martello towers without having to be told. Somebody said the walls was thick, and somebody else said the windows was narrow, and a woman asked what they was built for. He said, 'For shooting bows and arrows.' Well, I could have told him that was wrong. The martello towers was put up for the Guernsey people to get in out of the way of the Grand Saracen. If the poor visitors believe half they are told by the bus-drivers and others, they must go away with some very funny ideas about the history of Guernsey.

He worked for a hotel at St Martin's; and his job was to look after people who came over in parties. He said they was the sort who preferred having a guide, philosopher and friend going round with them, rather than go round and look at things for themselves. He felt like the old woman who lived in a shoe. They came over for a week or a fortnight, and he had to keep them amused every day and all day long. He arranged games for them on the sand; and had to watch out if any went in for a swim they didn't drown themselves. He took them for walks along the cliffs and, as they would insist on going where there was no paths, he had to watch out they didn't get stuck half-way down a precipice and him have to send out an S.O.S. for Mr Blanchford and *The Flying Christine*. I thought of me and Monsieur Le Boutillier's pig. The fellow had all my sympathy. When he took them on coach tours to places of interest, as he had done that day, and let them loose to please themselves, he had to be careful not to lose any, or there would have to be a police search. I was sitting in the sun in my back garden and watched him gather his family around him like a brood of chicks. 'Now you can all go and play with the Druid's Altar,' he said. My ancient monument isn't a Druid's Altar nowadays: it is a Dolmen; but I didn't bother to put him right. 'All be back in the coach in half an hour!' he shouted. 'All of you; and when I say all of you, I mean ALL of you! THE COACH WILL NOT WAIT!' They rambled off in twos and threes. He sat on the low wall of my garden by the path in the shade of the apple-tree and wiped the sweat from his brow. It was a scorching hot day. 'If you want to know human nature at its lowest and its worst,' he said to me, 'get to know it when it is on holiday.' 'Go on, go on, that is lovely!' I said. 'Say some more!'

'I will bet you anything you like one of those won't be back in time,' he said. 'There she goes, the darling! She ought to be kept on a lead.' She was an old woman with rats' tails of hair and a hat like a pancake and holding an umbrella in her clenched fist. It must have been for self-defence because there wasn't a cloud in the sky. He went on talking and when I looked round she had disappeared. I couldn't think where on earth she could have got to. She had vanished into thin air. The others was wandering away; some of them up the hill and some down on the beach. I noticed not one of them had gone to look at the ancient monument, for all the work I had put in keeping it tidy.

Anyhow, he let out his troubles; and could he talk? He said the worst day of his week was the day he took his party to Sark. He really had to keep a close eye on them that day, for there was a number of danger spots and he didn't want a serious accident. Actually, I think he was very patient and very kind, in spite of what he said; and he was a charming fellow with a mop of dark curly hair and blue eyes and a happy laugh: but he swore by the end of a day in Sark, he would willingly have pushed the whole tribe over the Coupée. The only time he really liked them was on the Saturday morning when he went down to the White Rock to wish them good-bye. Unfortunately, it was more than made up for by the awful time in the afternoon when he went to the boat to meet the next week's consignment. He would stand on the new jetty by the sheds and watch the passengers come down the gang-way; and when he saw one who looked a particularly unholy terror, he would say to himself 'I bet she is for me!' and she was. Generally speaking, the men wasn't so bad, he said; but now and again you got one who thought he was a big noise, and he was more obstreperous than all the women put together.

The most to be dreaded was widows on the loose. Once her husband is dead, a woman gets a new lease of life, he said: and she knows all the tricks. Middle-aged married couples was easy: the husband did what he was told, or she had to keep watch on him. In either case, the woman had her hands full. The lonely hearts was a bloody nuisance. Paddy was funny about the lonely hearts. Anything in trousers was in danger of having them pulled off. The hardest part of his job was to remain more or less virtuous, and yet not hurt anybody's feelings. After all, they had paid for their holiday; and he was being paid to see they had a good time. There was lonely hearts male, too, but not so many, perhaps one a week. Paddy found the lonely hearts male came in useful to unload some of his lonely hearts female on; but it was hard lines on the poor chap, as usually he wasn't interested in lonely hearts female: he was more interested in the waiter. Paddy enjoyed himself watching the game.

He said everybody goes up a class when they come over to Guernsey for a holiday. The girl who works in a newspaper shop in England drinks her tea with her little finger crooked like a duchess. It is pathetic really, he said. The class of visitors he had to do with wasn't those who stay at Old Government House. They had saved a whole year for their precious holiday and wanted to feel they was gentry with money to spend for a week. They was willing to blue the lot and have nothing left when they got home except debts on the never-never. Some had spent a week in Jersey before coming to Guernsey; and, from what Paddy had heard, they really do know how to rook the visitors over there. 'It has been reduced to a fine art,' he said. Guernsey wasn't as good at it yet; but they was learning.

When his people began to drift back, he counted them, and there was one missing. Old Mrs Mackintosh. Had anybody seen her? Nobody had seen her. 'If she isn't sitting in the coach, we'll go without her,' he said. I didn't see how she could be sitting in the coach or we would have been sure to see her pass. He said good-bye and hoped he would see me again. I watched him lead his flock back to the coach. I heard it tooting and so knew old Mrs M. wasn't in it. It kept on and on loud enough to wake the dead. At last I heard it start. I was standing outside my back door and worrying rather if she had really gone and done what the old pig had wanted to do: when up she arose from behind the pigsty where she had been sitting in the sun all the time, listening to every word was being said. 'I'm here! I'm here!' she screamed. 'Wait for me, wait for me! Oh don't, don't, don't leave me behind!' and ran full pelt down the path after the coach, and she could run, the old thing, waving her umbrella. The coach was half-way to Grand Havre by then, but the fool of a coach-driver waited; though I expect it was Paddy who was looking round and saw her, and told him to stop. I would like to have heard what the others said when she got in.

I went to see Dora once more: just to keep friendly. She had told me her daughter was leaving school and would be helping with the guests in the summer. I wanted to see what the daughter was like. I wasn't leaving nothing to Dora; but that didn't mean I was cutting the daughter out of my will. I expected to find a house full of visitors, but there didn't seem to be a soul about. When I knocked, a girl of seventeen or so came to the door. She wasn't bad-looking but was wearing skin-tight woollen trousers of a black and white herring-bone pattern, and a skin-tight woollen sweater to match. She would have looked all right in a circus, but I wouldn't have liked to have her around me while I was eating. I thought she was the waitress. I asked if I might speak to Mrs Domaille. She said, 'Mother is having a siesta. She will be awake presently.' I heard Dora's voice calling, 'Who is it, Doris?' 'I don't know,' said Doris; and she sounded as if she didn't care either. I thought you don't get a penny out of me, my girl.

Dora came to see who it was. 'Oh, it's you!' she said. 'What a time to choose! Come in, then: since you're here!' I went in, but she didn't ask me to sit down. I sat myself down in the most comfortable armchair I could see, and looked round. 'Haven't you got any visitors?' I said. 'Three in a room,' she said, 'we're absolutely full up!' 'Where are they all, then?' I said. 'Good gracious, I don't allow them in the house after breakfast,' she said. 'They can have a packed lunch, if they want it; and come back at six for a wash before their evening meal.' I said, 'It's hardly a home from home, is it?' It was a dull blowy afternoon, and big drops of rain was beginning to fall. She said, 'They don't come to Guernsey to sit indoors.' I said, 'Yes, but it rain in Guernsey like it do in other places. Where are they to go when it rains?' 'That is their affair,' she said. 'I can't have them in and out under my feet all day long.' I thought well, if I was a visitor, I wouldn't come and stay in your guest-house a second time.

She wanted to know what I thought of Doris. I got the idea she didn't altogether believe I didn't have a penny in the bank. Doris was in an unsettled state at present, she said: she was helping with the guest-house now she had left school; but of course it was only temporary. She wanted to go to a university and have a career; but that would cost more money, as well as being years without earning. Or she could get married. She already had a number of young men to choose from. 'I am broad-minded,' said Dora, 'and let her have them all here for musical evenings. She is a good girl.' I said, 'Well, she is a well made girl, I can see that; but why don't she put some proper clothes on?' 'She is perfectly decent,' said Dora, 'she likes to feel free.' 'I have no doubt she feel free,' I said. 'She would do fine for a mermaid.' I saw old Dora's face was getting red. 'Fashions have changed since your time,' she said. 'In my time men was men and women was women,' I said, 'and they dressed accordingly. I hate to see a woman in trousers.' She was wearing trousers herself: of brown corduroy. 'How would you have us dress, then?' she said. 'Like our grandmothers?' 'I think a woman ought to look like a flower,' I said. She laughed sort of bitter. 'I am rather past looking like a flower, I am afraid,' she said. 'I can't see that,' I said. 'It is true perhaps it is too late now for you to look like a rose; but you can always look like an everlasting.' I really meant it for a compliment, and to put her in a good mood; but, woman-like, she took it the wrong way. 'Have you come here to insult me?' she said. 'As a matter of fact, I haven't,' I said, 'but, if you want me to be frank, you don't have to go about looking from the back like a Buff Orpington going to lay an egg.' That is why she didn't invite me to my Cousin Mary Ann's funeral.

8

One Thursday the next winter when I went to visit my Cousin Mary Ann, it was Nora who came to the door. I knew at once who she was: I had seen her serving in the Crown, and taken quite a fancy to her across the bar. I ought to have known then she was the daughter of Eugene Le Canu, for she looked so much like him with her red hair, and was slim and quick like he was. She was getting on, of course, and you could see she had knocked about a bit; but she had something yet she would never lose. 'So you're Ebenezer!' she said. 'I wondered. I remember you standing me a drink once.' 'I would do it again!' I said. 'It is my turn tonight,' she said. 'Come on in, do!' Her mother was laid up for a day or two. 'There is nothing really the matter with her,' she said, 'she is only tired of life. Go upstairs and cheer her up; and have something when you come down.'

It was like going back fifty years going into my Cousin Mary Ann's bedroom. She was wearing a pink flannelette night-dress, and there was an old patch-work quilt on the bed. Herself, she looked like an old sheep, lying there with her grey hair all over the pillow. 'What's the matter now?' I said. 'Oh nothing,' she said. 'It must be something,' I said, 'it's not like you to be off your feet. Have the doctor been?' 'I don't want the doctor,' she said. 'What for do I want to be kept alive? Nobody want me now.' 'Well, I would miss coming to see you,' I said. She gave her old laugh like a horse. 'You are not one to miss anybody,' she said. 'You got too much sense.' I don't think my Cousin Mary Ann knew me very well.

There wasn't enough misery about for her: that was the trouble. People was getting on well since the War, and didn't need her help; and her family was settled for. Eugene would have the house when she was gone; so at least he would have a roof over his head. 'He think he is going to be married soon,' she said, 'but that girl won't have him.' 'Who is he going with now?' I said. It was an Eva Tourtel from Prospect Villa, but I didn't know the girl. 'Dora is all right,' she said, 'and Nora have made up her mind to marry that Jan van Raalte.' 'Who is he, for goodness sake,' I said, 'with a name like that?' 'A Dutchman,' she said. 'He have come to Guernsey to grow flowers.' I said, 'Guernsey get more like the League of Nations every day.' 'He is a nice young chap,' she said, 'but he will have plenty of others.' 'Is there anything you don't know?' I said. 'Eugene is the puzzle,' she said. 'He don't speak.' 'Why, is he dumb, then?' I said. 'He do say a few words now and then,' she said. I thought hers was a funny family.

I was looking at the photo of the handsome Eugene over her bed. I didn't know and have never known what happened to him. I expect he ended up an old roué and died of the pox. She caught me looking, for she said, 'He was right to leave me, my poor Eugene. I trapped him.' 'If it come to that, is there any man who isn't trapped?' I said. 'It is the man's look-out.' I had managed not to get trapped; but I couldn't bear the way she was talking. I thought it was better to be dead, than have everything cut and dried and be so hopeless. 'He won't be there to meet me,' she said, and the tears came out of her eyes, and rolled down her cheeks. I wished I could have said something about God, or such-like, to comfort her; but how could I after my gallivanting? 'Cheer up, old girl,' I said, 'never say die!' 'Ah well, I've got what I deserve,' she said. 'It isn't for me to complain.' She dried her tears on her night-dress and smiled her lovely ugly smile. 'I'll come and see you again soon,' I said. That was the last time I saw her.

When I got downstairs Nora had some wine and biscuits on the table. 'How d'you find her?' she said. 'Well, not exactly cheerful,' I said. 'She never was,' she said. 'I don't think I like my mother very much.' 'She have done the best she could for you children,' I said, 'and she had to manage all on her own.' 'She is a kill-joy,' she said. 'I say let the children play; as your cousin Raymond used to say.' 'Why, did you know Raymond, then?' I said. 'I knew Raymond very well,' she said. 'He was a wonderful friend to me: at a time when I had nobody else to turn to, who would even begin to understand.' 'He never told me,' I said. 'There is a lot Raymond never told anybody,' she said. 'He knew how to keep other people's secrets.' I said, 'How is it you didn't step into Christine's shoes, if you liked him so much?' 'I'm a baby-snatcher,' she said, 'to me he was an old man.' 'Then I didn't have a chance when I stood you a drink?' I said. 'Not an earthly!' she said and laughed; but when I left she kissed me good-night.

I saw my Cousin Mary Ann's death in the paper and when I didn't get an invitation to the funeral, I thought of writing a letter of sympathy to somebody; but I couldn't think to who. I couldn't very well write to Dora. Eugene I didn't know; and Nora didn't seem to me as if she would cry much. I left it. I kept my eye open for news of Nora's wedding and when, after some months, I hadn't seen it I wondered if perhaps she hadn't managed to hook the Dutchman after all; but I ran into Albert Le Page, the bone-setter, who is a distant cousin of mine, and he told me Jan van Raalte had broken his thumb climbing a cliff, and put off his marriage until it was mended. I couldn't make out why a chap should put off getting married because he had broken his thumb. I thought the least I could do was to go and see Nora again, and cheer her up while she was waiting; but the day I went to see her at the house at the Robergerie, there was no answer when I knocked on the front door. It wasn't a Thursday, so I wandered round the back in case she was in the garden. Eugene was working in the greenhouse and came out to see what I wanted.

He knew who I was, but I didn't remember having seen him before. He was a big chap with a corporation already, and a flat face rather like Dora's, and he had a thin black moustache. He looked as if he might be a French chef in a hotel. I said I had been very sorry to hear about his mother. He made a noise. It was like a laugh, but it wasn't a laugh. He didn't say anything more. 'It's a nice greenhouse you got here,' I said. He made his noise and signed for me to go inside and see it. He got heat and water from the waterworks and a good early crop ripening; and everything was spic and span to the last degree. I went outside to have a look at the boiler, and had a quiz at the garden. It was the same. There wasn't a weed; and the path was so raked I was afraid to walk on it. I said, 'Well, I congratulate you. I wish my place looked like this.' 'I like everything to look perfect,' he said. Those was his first words to me. I thought he was going to be a hard chap to live with for that Eva from Prospect Villa.

I got the feeling he wanted to be friendly but didn't know how. I liked him myself. When he nodded towards the back door as much as to say 'Will you come in?' I said, 'Yes, I'd like to.' Over the back door was a glass porch of coloured glass with ferns and geraniums in pots on the side and, as we went in, he noticed a few petals was fallen on the floor. He stooped and picked them up one by one. He then took off his boots and left them on the mat. I wondered if he expected me to do the same, but I only wiped mine hard to get the ground off. When he had washed his hands and got into some slippers, he made tea. I noticed he had very small feet for such a heavy man. He was good in the house and laid the table dainty; not rough-and-ready and without a tablecloth, as I do. He turned on the radio. It was the weather. Myself, I don't trust the radio for the weather. I trust my nose; and nine times out of ten I am right. There was music after; and he left the thing on. I asked him where Nora was. From what I could hear him say against the noise, I understood she was at La Passée helping Jan to get ready the house where they was going to live. I noticed a shelf of new books hadn't been in the kitchen when I was there before. I saw they was *The Complete Works of Charles Dickens*. 'Have you read all those?' I said. He said he hadn't bought them to read: he had seen them advertised in a newspaper, and thought they would look nice on his wall.

After tea he washed up the dishes and put everything away in its place; though I can't laugh at him for being fussy, for I am the same about putting things away in their right place. If I didn't, I would never remember where anything was. He made a sign for me to go upstairs with him; and he showed me the bedroom he had done up for when he was married. It was my Cousin Mary Ann's old bedroom and I thought of her lying there dying by herself. He had changed it all. The old furniture was gone and the big bed and the picture of his father. The walls was papered with grey paper like satin; and the wood-work painted white with gold beading. The press for clothes and the dressing-table and the chest-of-drawers was of plain unvarnished wood; and there was two single beds with pink covers, and a pink velvet-pile carpet on the floor. 'If I was married,' I said, 'I would want to sleep in the same bed.' 'I am not getting married for that,' he said. I couldn't make Eugene out at all. I said I hoped he would be happy; but I didn't say I would see him again.

I can't say I was all that delighted when Dudley Waine with an 'e' turned up. He hadn't changed much. He was fatter and rounder and his face fuller; but quite smooth. He hadn't lost his hair, as I was beginning to, but it was iron grey, and he wore it long and brushed right back. He looked very distinguished. He might have been a musician. I said, 'You're looking well,' and asked how he'd got on during the War. 'A strenuous time,' he said. He had worked for the Ministry of Information, and was in London all the years the bombs was falling; but wasn't hit. They say the good die young; and I am sure they are right. He was back in his pre-war university job now, and was come over to go on with his researches. I was scared he would get on to the subject of the ancient monument; but it was our patois he was interested in now. Its roots. He had discovered it was really the language of the religion of the witches of the days of old, and all the dirty words in it was holy words. He said 'Baise mon tchou!' was a royal salute. I had never thought of it that way, me.

He said if I had been alive in those days I would have dressed myself up like a dog with a moon painted on my behind and danced among a crowd of naked women on the sands of Rocquaine Bay. I said the only witch I knew of living round there was Mère Quéripel from Pleinmont; and she was before I was old enough to think of doing any such thing. He agreed there was no witches on the west coast now. They had all moved in from Rocquaine Castle and kept guest-houses along St George's Esplanade. The truth was he had tried place after place along there and been unlucky; but I imagine he was a gentleman who was not all that easy to please. He was now staying at Timbuctoo. He said it was clean and comfortable, and the food was good; but you couldn't come and go as you please, as when it was Prissy who ran it. The Misses Hocart was of the old school. The discipline was 'severe for one who had benefited from a liberal education'.

He wanted to know who lived at Ivy Lodge now. I didn't know; nor who lived at Rosamunda. Old man Mahy was dead and Christine's mother gone to live with her daughter-in-law in England. Edna and her child was among the first to go away before the Occupation; and they hadn't come back since. Gwen was the only one of the family left on the island; but

Dudley had never got on with Gwen. I was glad to be able to let him know
Horace had thought enough of Gwen to make a will in her favour, leaving
her his money and the Arsenal Stores. She had a room built on and lived
there; and carried on the business with a boy to deliver. As a matter of fact,
I got my groceries from her, and used to go down once a month to pay the
bill and have a chat. She didn't hear often from Christine and was bitter
about her; but I at least knew Christine was alive. I thought I might as well
get what news I could out of Dudley.

 'How is Christine getting on?' I said. 'Fine, fine!' he said. 'The spirit of
the woman! Marvellous!' His mother had died during the War. She wasn't
a war casualty in the ordinary way; but even more of a war casualty than
those who were killed by air-raids. She died of a broken heart. The fact of it
being possible for such a war to be broke her heart. She saw all she had
hoped and lived for was in vain. Christine was now headmistress of the
school. It was in the country and, in view of her responsibilities, she had to
mind her step while she was down there. The patron of the school was a
Bishop; but when she came to London, she was able to go the round of her
dozens of friends. 'Among whom I count myself her oldest and dearest,'
he said with a smirk. He was proud it was on him she relied always to take
her to the Opera. 'How many children she got now?' I said. She had only
the two. She had devoted her genius as a mother entirely to Abel and
Gideon; and they both did her great credit. Abel had been to college and
qualified as an electrical engineer and was now doing his National Service
in Germany. 'National Service, what for?' I said. 'In the event of another
war,' he said. 'Oh?' I said. Gideon had been to a School for Business Management and was going in for advertising. 'Advertising what?' I said.
'Anything,' he said. It all sounded very grand, but I wondered what it
amounted to in solid fact.

 'I don't know what young fellows want to go in for those sort of things
for?' I said. 'Wars are a waste of time; and advertising is all lies.' 'I am
afraid, my dear Mister Le Page,' he said, looking very sorry for me, 'you
are an anachronism.' 'Say that word again,' I said. He said it. I said, 'Spell
it.' He spelt it. 'Now what do it mean, please?' I said. 'Out of its due time,'
he said, 'in your case, belonging to a bygone age.' 'I thought you was
interested in old things,' I said. 'So I am, so I am,' he said. 'I find you im-
mensely interesting. As an object of study.' He was looking at me through
his thick round spectacles, as if I was something come out of a hole in the
ground. For a minute, I felt so small I thought it would be better if I was
with my Cousin Mary Ann; but I wasn't going to give in to goggle-eyes,
even if he did know everything. After all, he wasn't so wonderful himself.
'Baise mon tchou!' I said.

 There was quite a bit in the *Press* about Nora's wedding. It was said he was Dutch and his achievements as a horticulturalist much appreciated in Guernsey. The Guernsey and Dutch seem to be hand in glove. It certainly sounded as if he was on the right side of the right people already. I must say in the *Press* photograph he looked a pleasant chap; and she looked so happy, she looked almost as young as he was. They was married at the Greffe; and it said they was going to Holland for their honeymoon. I thought I would give them a few weeks to settle in when they got back, before I went to see them. When I did go, I found Nora in on her own. I hadn't brought a present; really only because I didn't know what to bring: but she gave me such a welcome, I was sorry I hadn't thought of something. However, I thought I might make it up to her another way. She was much more the sort I would rather leave my money to than Dora. I asked her how she liked it in Holland. She said she liked the Dutch people very much. They was free-and-easy and friendly, and not stiff and stand-offish like the English; but she wouldn't like to live there for always. It was too flat. When you come to a town it seem to be floating in the air. She stayed in a place called Zwolle, where Jan's parents was living, and near by was a hill; but that was the only hill she saw, and it wasn't as high as the Vale. For the rest, it was smooth fields and dykes to keep the sea out and canals and thousands and thousands of bicycles. She saw the Queen on a bicycle.

I was more interested to know how she was getting along with Jan; but I didn't like to ask straight out. I had gone latish, expecting him to be in from work. 'Where's Jan?' I said. He had gone to Town that afternoon on some business to do with the Growers' Association; but the meeting must be over hours ago. 'I know I am a fool,' she said, 'but I can't bear it when he is out of my sight. He will most likely only spend the evening in the Channel Islands, talking to commercial travellers; but I can never be sure. He is such a dear simple boy, any woman who sets her mind to it can lead him by the nose.' She laughed, or tried to. 'I have been on and off up to now, as you know, Ebenezer,' she said, 'but this time I am caught good and proper! Life is hell when you're happy!' 'Well, I have never been happy, so I wouldn't know,' I said, 'and I certainly won't be now.'

He came in while I was talking; and she was in his arms and clinging to him, as if he had come back from the grave. I was sorry for her, and yet I envied her; and him too. As my Cousin Mary Ann said: it was not for me. Nora waited on him hand and foot, and he smiled up at her; but he took it as his right. I didn't think he was quite as young as he looked; but I could see he had something about him many a girl would take to. Over tea, we talked growers' talk, and she hung on to his every word, though I am sure she wasn't interested in anything he was saying. He was a go-ahead chap, and was getting ready to grow white chrysanths in pots under glass for the Christmas market, and coloured freesias for the spring, and tulips outside.

I liked him all right and, when I left, wished them both every happiness, and meant it; but on my way home I thought to myself no: I am not going to leave my money to a Dutchman.

One Saturday night I got so fed up with being on my own, I went to Town for a drink; and who should I run into but Eugene? It must have been quite a year since the day I went and saw him. He was leaning against the bar in Moore's Hotel, togged up to the eyebrows in a light blue woolly suit and a fancy pullover and a felt hat with a feather in it. I said, 'Hullo, how is it you are not out with the girl?' He made his noise like a laugh that wasn't a laugh. 'She won't have me,' he said. I noticed he was drinking spirits like water. Well, a chap got to do something. Man cannot live by bread alone. I asked him to have a drink with me; and spent the rest of the evening with him. I was careful to keep behind in drinking, or I wouldn't have been able to get him on the bus. I saw him safe to the end of his road; but I ticked him off my list. I wasn't going to leave my money to another miserable old bachelor like me.

He is dead now. The doctor said he had a weak heart and he got frightened and stopped drinking and dropped dead in a milk-bar down the Pollet. Nora was living with him his last years and died not long after of cancer of the liver. She didn't have much pain and everybody was surprised, even the doctor. He didn't know until they opened her up to see what she had died of. She had been very low in spirit since her marriage broke up. She was among the first, if not the first, to get a divorce on Guernsey. The other woman in the case was a barmaid in the Channel Islands; but Jan didn't marry her. He sold up and went back to Holland, where he joined a firm of bulb merchants. He have been over lately as a commercial traveller; and I have seen him in Town once or twice and had a few words. Naturally I didn't mention the business of Nora. The house at the Robergerie belongs to Dora now; and Doris, who is married to a Hubert with a good job in the Income Tax Office, lives in it. She have two children and with what her husband earns and a chap to do the greenhouse and garden, is getting along nicely. I don't know why it is, but it is always the people I don't like who get on well in this world. Those I do like come to a bad end.

9

I was haunted by Raymond. Until the day Nora said he had been a good friend to her, I had hardly given him a thought since he died. I didn't want to, for some reason. The poor mad mixed-up Raymond was a puzzle to me; as much a puzzle as Eugene. When Dudley Waine turned up on me, he brought back the whole affair. Dudley was nothing: a baby with a big brain; but he looked down on everybody, and always came out on top. Raymond was real and loving and couldn't look down on anybody, if he tried; yet he came to nothing, and threw himself away. I couldn't get him out of my mind. The following winter I often got the feeling he was with me in the house. I don't believe in ghosts. I know a number of people on the island who swear they have seen a ghost. I am willing to believe they have, but what I want to know is if the ghost saw them. I don't think so.

Everybody I had known when I was younger was dead. Alf Brouard was gone, and Jim Le Poidevin; Ada Domaille was gone and Olive Le Boutillier and Father Darcy, bless him; and, before that winter was through, Gwen Mahy died. I felt as if I was a ghost myself, although my strong old body went about its business as usual. I spoke to plenty of people. If I went down the Bridge to get a few things, I would stop and have a chat with a dozen before I got home. 'Comment s'en va?' I'd say. 'Ah, pas trop mal!' they'd say. 'J'sis fier!' I'd say. I didn't care tuppence how they was really; and they didn't care tuppence how I was either. I would have a look round St Sampson's Harbour while I was there, and see what boats was in. They was steamers bringing coal or petrol mostly, but they wasn't the fine old ships I used to see when I went down the harbour with my father. The *Commodore* was up for repairs, but she is not a patch on the old *Courier*. I bet she won't go through half the old *Courier* went through.

I don't think much of the 'Industrial North', as they call it. It don't hum with hope as it did when I was a boy. The young ones of nowadays seem to think the same as me, strange to say, for St Sampson's have the wildest gang of young hooligans on the island. I don't like young hooligans; but they got to do something. They are young. I don't like old men. They make me feel old. Sometimes I sit down for a spell on one of those seats by the Power Station, where there are always old men like me sitting. One will smoke his pipe, and one will chaw, and one will spit; and, if any say a word, it is only about the weather, or how much so-and-so is making, or what the States is or isn't doing that is wrong. I don't think anybody talk about anything else on this island now: except the weather and how much so-and-so is making and what the States is or isn't doing that is wrong. I don't say nothing. I get up and walk away. They don't expect old crack-pot Le Page to take an interest like other people.

It was of an evening when I got indoors and sat by the fire after my tea, Raymond was with me. I had been looking forward to the evening all day. I would think to myself, ah well, when I get on my own I will have company. I don't mean I saw him sitting at the table reading the Bible, or in the chair opposite me warming his toes; but he was there. When he was living with me, we would go for hours sometimes without saying a word, or taking any notice of each other; but if he went out-of-doors for a minute, the room was empty. I don't know I was so much company for him. There was always something he wanted me to understand, and I didn't. He was like a child in many ways; but I often thought of the two of us he was the old one. Well, the evenings of that winter when he was with me without being there, many things he had said came back to me; but I can't say now I got much forrarder. Perhaps a day will come when I won't see through a glass darkly.

He spoke often about when he was a child. His most treasured memories was of the days him and Horace played truant, when they was at the Secondary School. Hetty never found out. Horace was a masterpiece at making up excuses when they turned up at school the next day. It was either Percy had sawed his hand in two, or Harold had fallen off a ladder and broken his leg, or the mothers was laid up with lumbago, or sciatica, or any sickness Horace could think of. It must have seemed there was an awful lot of sickness and accidents around Brayeside; but the master believed what Horace said, and didn't ask for a note. 'He wouldn't have believed a word I said,' said Raymond, 'even if I had told him the truth.'

The two would mooch round the harbour laughing to think how much better it was than being in school. They would sit on a seat over the café at the end of the Albert Pier and eat the sandwiches their mothers had packed for their lunch; then go down in the café underneath and have a mug of tea and fancy they was boys off the boats. They would go down the steps on to the lower landing-stage, and thought it was great fun to run across to the steps at the other end while the sea was sweeping in and out, though they might easily have been caught by the waves and swept out into the Pool. Or they would spend the day at Moulin Huet and go down the water-lanes to the bay; and have sticks for boats on the stream. When the stream changes sides, there are flat stones to walk across; and, if both their boats came out from under the flat stones together, Raymond would see it as a good sign. 'I didn't want those days ever to end,' Raymond said; but they had to leave in time to be back home as if they had been to school.

He liked to talk about Guernsey as it was long before my time: and those was really pleasant evenings for me. He wasn't worrying about religion then; or his troubles with Christine. He knew a lot I didn't know about Guernsey in the old days; and he made it as real as if he had lived in those days. There was sea originally where Wallaballoo and Timbuctoo was built; and the Bridge wasn't a solid quay with shops along one side of it as it is now, but a real bridge over the sea. If you wanted to go to Town from the Vale, you had to go across the Bridge; and the people who lived at Plein-heaume, say, if they wanted to go to the Vale Church, had to go by boat. The Clos-du-Vale was an island to itself; and wasn't built over with houses and greenhouses and bungalows like it is now, but was mostly common with a few scattered farms and no proper roads, only muddy tracks. Raymond thought it must have been a grand place to live in those days. If pirates landed, as they often did, the people got out of their way in the Vale Castle. I don't know I would have liked to live with pirates on my door-step; but Raymond seemed to think it was all right.

I have been told often enough I am an old stick-in-the-mud; but I am positively go-ahead compared to Raymond. He was always looking back over his shoulder, and couldn't see any good at all coming round the corner in front. I would say, 'After all, things have improved in some ways, you know. The world is getting better slowly, we hope.' That was the one idea would get him in a rage. 'Has the world got better in your time?' he would say. 'Well, I don't know,' I'd say, 'perhaps not so as you'd notice.' 'No, nor in anybody else's time either!' he would say. 'What you gain on the swings, you lose on the roundabouts. Progress is the carrot in front of the donkey to make him go round and round.' Once I found him on the beach watching the creatures swimming in a pool. He would sit for hours watching the creatures chasing and eating each other. An aeroplane passed over our heads on the way to the airport. He looked up and said, 'Nature is fallen from God; but it is near God. That thing up there is fallen much further.' I have never understood this 'fallen' business. 'I thought we was going up,' I said. 'Hardly in an aeroplane,' he said.

When I go over in my mind the things Raymond said to me, I think the person he missed the loss of most was Jesus Christ. Jesus was his secret companion when he was a child and kept him pure when he was a young man; but now he was angry with Jesus, as with a friend who had turned out to be not as good as he thought. 'He blessed with one hand and cursed with the other,' he said. I said, 'Well, I suppose He had to, if He was going to make the sinners sorry.' 'Sin is man-made,' said Raymond, 'but suffering isn't. The Christ I stand by bears all the suffering of the world and doesn't care a bugger for sin!' It was the only time I ever heard Raymond swear.

'Jesus cursed the barren fig-tree,' he said, 'AND THE TIME FOR FIGS WAS NOT YET!' He shouted the words at me. 'I expect He was feeling upset at the time,' I said. Raymond looked at me as if he had never seen me before. 'Good old Ebenezer!' he said. 'You are dead right, of course. He has to be forgiven too.' 'There is this to be said for Him,' I said, 'He gave us the best rule to live by. Do unto others as you would they should do unto you.' Raymond shook his head sadly. 'Is it not do unto others as they would you should do unto them?' he said. 'That is how you treat me.' 'I don't pretend to follow the rule,' I said. He was getting me tied up.

He tried and tried again to make me understand, as if I was a child who wouldn't learn his lesson. 'If a man loves a woman,' he said, 'he doesn't do unto her as he would she should do unto him. He does the opposite.' 'Yes, I suppose so,' I said. I didn't want him bringing up those things. 'Well, you ought to know,' he said, 'you have had enough experience!' 'I don't know in my case I would call it love,' I said. 'There is always some love in it,' he said, 'even in the lowest; but it never takes us all the way. God knows I wanted it to; but how, how? How shall Man join together what God hath put asunder?' He raved on. A man is a woman inside out: a woman is a man inside out. It isn't only a few organs tacked on make the difference. They are absolutely different. She may speak the same words, and seem to think the same thoughts, and have feelings she calls by the same name; but they mean something altogether different from to a man. The verb for a man is to do; the verb for a woman is to have. 'When I was thinking of what I was going to do in the world,' said Raymond, 'Christine was thinking of what she was going to have out of it.' 'Yes, but Christine was Christine,' I said, 'you can't judge every woman by Christine.' 'She was quite natural,' he said. 'The natural man is no better. She thinks the whim of woman is the will of God: he thinks the wish of man is the will of God. They are both wrong. God has no will. He lets be. I have no will either now. I am anything; or nothing.' His poor brain was going. He got me scared.

'You are Raymond Martel of Wallaballoo,' I said. 'Would to God I was!' he said. He broke down. He had never done anything right, he had made nothing but mistakes, he wanted to undo, undo, undo!!! He wished he had settled down to be a carpenter and builder like his father. He wished he had never been to a good school, he wished he had never read books. He wished he had never gone to college and trained to be a minister. He wished he had never married Christine because he wanted to love her. 'God!' he cried, 'why didn't I have the sense to marry a girl for bed and board and breeding and live to earn a living and be a local preacher and preach the Gospel of Jesus Christ and know nothing of love, or the meaning of love; and then I wouldn't have been cast out!' I would have given anything to be able to say a word to comfort him; and when he wasn't there and it was only his ghost was with me, I said out loud, 'I am sorry, Raymond: I am sorry!'

10

Christine came over to settle Gwen's affairs. I don't know if she was sharing the money with her sister-in-law, Edna; but I had heard from Gwen the mother, Emmeline Mahy, was gone ga-ga and couldn't feed herself, let alone manage money. Gwen hadn't done badly with the start Horace gave her, and must have had quite a tidy sum put away. I always got on all right with Gwen, but some people didn't like her; and I must say she was a dried up old maid the last years. I didn't know then she got consumption, and was spitting blood. It was old Mrs Renouf told me Christine was on the island and staying with Lydia Mahy at the Gigands. Lydia had sold most of the land, and lived in the big house on her own with a servant to wait on her. She can't have had much left to make all that show. The few vergées she hadn't sold she let to the Le Patourels; and I still used to meet her sometimes going along the lanes as stiff as a poker with her little black book in her hand.

Christine arranged for the sale of the Arsenal Stores to Amelia Renouf, a granddaughter of old Mrs R., and the stock-in-trade was sold by public auction. Amelia was going to open a beauty parlour there; though what Amelia knew about beauty I don't know. She looked like a freak of nature. It is true she had been trained by Monsieur Lafayette in Town; but he was only a Le Sauvage from St Saviour's. I didn't go to the sale. I had come down to eating out of tins sometimes to save myself trouble, and I might have bought a few to put in the cupboard; but I didn't want to run into Christine. When she turned up at Les Moulins, I didn't know who she was at first. I thought she was a visitor. She had a young man with her.

I was working in the front garden, as it happened; and she stopped by the gate and said 'Good-afternoon.' I straightened my back and said 'Good-afternoon,' as I would have to anybody. I saw a well filled-out woman with hanging breasts and popping eyes: so much so I wondered if she drank. She was wearing the same style of clothes as she used to wear, her 'own personal style as a simple soul'; and that was how I guessed who she was. The simple frock was of white dots on black, and the cloak was of black corded-silk lined with red and made her look like Madame Hamon who kept the Green Shutters. She had a small round black cap on the top of her head, and her hair was frizzed and gingerish; though it used to be straight and yellow. Her face had make-up on was supposed to make her look young, but made her look even more of an old hag. I began to feel very sorry for Christine. How was it possible the lovely girl who walked into Wallaballoo with Raymond the Sunday evening he preached was changed in a few years into this awful creature? Raymond had a lot to answer for.

It didn't cross her mind I might not know who she was. 'I am glad you are at home to receive me,' she said. The holy voice was gone; and she spoke as a person accustomed to be important in a deep voice, almost a man's. 'This is my son Gideon,' she said, as if he was the Prince of Wales. He shook hands, but limp. If I hadn't known Horace was his father, I would never have believed it. I couldn't see anything in him of Horace at all. He wasn't very tall, but slim and boyish and much too good-looking; and he had straight fair hair and there was something in his face of Christine when she was his age. I took a dislike to him on sight. He ought to have been on the Pictures; and when he smiled, it was as if he knew he was having his photo taken. I made up my mind there and then he wouldn't get a penny from me. Christine said, 'I have come to see you on the matter of Raymond's property. I assume he left it to you; but he had no right to.' 'Property!' I said. I couldn't believe my ears. 'Raymond didn't leave any property,' I said, 'he didn't have any to leave.' 'It is that we have to discuss,' she said. I said, 'All right, come in; and we'll discuss it!' I was boiling with rage. Did she think I had stolen poor Raymond's things?

'Sit down!' I said, when I got her indoors. She sat. She could see I was angry. I didn't sit, but stood over her like a judge. Gideon was standing behind her, and made a face and winked. I didn't like him for that either: he had no respect for his mother. I gave him a black look. 'Now listen to me, Christine,' I said. 'Raymond when he went away from here left behind a few rags of clothes I wore, or Tabitha used for mending, during the Occupation. His suitcase I suppose Liza Quéripel kept; but there can't have been much in it, perhaps the relics of a few things I got for him. His books and everything else he had he left at Rosamunda.' She was only half listening. 'Oh, of course,' she said, 'he lived with Liza Quéripel at the end. I had forgotten. Gwen did mention it in a letter. Well, well, I didn't think he had it in him!' 'He didn't live with Liza Quéripel in the way you mean,' I said. 'I couldn't care less, if he did,' she said. 'It is not his suitcase I am thinking about: it is the house.' 'What house, for goodness sake?' I said. 'His father owned a house, didn't he?' she said. 'I know he sold one; but he bought another. It is Abel's now.' 'It is not Abel's,' I said. I tried to make her see how Wallaballoo would have been Abel's, if Harold had not sold it; but the house he bought when he married again he was in his legal rights to leave to Mrs Crewe when he died; and she left it to her niece when she died. 'I think you might at least have gone to law about it,' she said, 'seeing you were so fond of Raymond.' I let her think what she liked. It was hopeless.

'How is Abel?' I said. 'Abel bores me!' said Gideon. 'The question was addressed to me,' said Christine. There wasn't much love lost between those two. I reckon they was too much alike. She went on and on about Abel; and though every word was a word of praise, by the time she had done I was sick of the sound of him. There never was anybody so perfect. He was good, he was patient, he was kind; and from a small boy had but one idea in his mind: which was to take care of his mother. He had been the head boy of the school, he had passed all his examinations first class, he had done three years as an officer in the Army in Germany for his National Service; and now he was doing very important work for the Government. 'He is an electrician, isn't he?' I said. 'An electronic engineer,' she said, as if he was the Prime Minister of England. 'Well, what do he do?' I said. 'Ah, that is a secret,' she said, 'even I, his mother, am not allowed to know.' 'Why, is he ashamed of it, then?' I said. 'He lives for his work,' she said. I had been thinking she had lost her holy voice, but it came back when she was speaking of Abel.

I invited them to stop to tea: I couldn't do less; but she said they were expected at Les Gigands. I asked what Gideon was doing, if it wasn't too secret to be told. 'Oh, he has come over to Guernsey to contact the Tourist Committee,' she said. The firm of advertisers he was working for was hoping to take over complete responsibility for the advertising of the island on the other side. 'It is time Guernsey was put on the map,' he said, butting in. 'Good God, isn't it on the map already?' I said. 'It wasn't a bad little place to live in when people didn't know where it was.' Christine got up to go. 'Better have a picture of him on the front page of the brochure,' she said. 'The Immortal Islander!' 'Quite an idea!' said Gideon. He had a camera slung over one shoulder and made a movement as if he was going to take me. 'If you take me, I will smash that camera,' I said, 'and no bones about it either!' I would have too! I wasn't going to have my photo taken to make fun of Guernsey.

Instead he tried to sell Guernsey to me: to ME, of all people! He certainly could talk. He hadn't been on the island three days and knew more about it than the Tourist Committee themselves. 'They are throwing away their chances,' he said. 'They think a few pretty pictures of bays and rocks are going to bring over the crowds. There are hundreds of other holiday resorts with pretty rocks and bays. The one advantage you have over the others is the German Occupation. The Germans made your fortunes for you; if only your people would wake up and realise it. "The only British Territory to be trodden under the heel of the Hun." That is the line to take! That is what the British Tourist wants to see! Photograph every block of concrete the Germans left behind: not try to cover them up, as you are doing! Fence in every fortification and charge for admission, as at least you do for the Underground Hospital. They are lying around empty and disused, when they could be making money: money, man, money! Open them up as casinos, night clubs, pleasure palaces: the bunkers as souvenir shops! Cash in on it: cash in on it!' He was beginning to sweat and had to stop for breath. I managed to get a word in. 'Yes, but where are the souvenirs coming from?' I said. 'Birmingham, Birmingham,' he said, 'where the Sark stone comes from!' Christine had gone down the path and Gideon was following. I ran after him shouting.

'Here, wait a minute, you!' I said, 'I got something to say to you!' I caught hold of his arm. He tried to pull away; but he had no strength. I made him listen to me. 'Have you got any idea what those forts cost to build?' I said. 'The British Government put you on your feet to the tune of three and a half million or so,' he said, 'you have nothing to complain about.' I said, 'Do you know how many boys like you, boys better than you, died building those forts: starved and beaten and dropping dead on the job?' 'C'est la guerre,' he said. 'Oh, I know they wasn't our own people,' I said. 'Our own people was saying, though thank God I didn't say it myself, how good it was of the Germans to let prayers be said in the churches for the King and Queen; but none of us dared to raise a hand to stop the cruelty and the horror and the misery was on our own island all around us. It was the price we had to pay to save ourselves.' I let go of him. 'All right, all right,' I said, 'go back to England and advertise our German fortifications; and let people come over in their thousands and stare at them as the monuments of our shame and our disgrace. I am surprised any Guernseyman have had the cheek to put his nose inside a church since!' I was waving my arms about as if I was preaching for the Salvation Army. 'Oh dear, oh dear,' said Christine, 'you are as bad as Raymond, poor Raymond!' She went away laughing. 'You bore me!' said Gideon.

I was shaking like a leaf when I got indoors. It was the first time it was brought home to me it wasn't good for me to get excited. My old heart was thumping; and I had a pain at the back of my head. I had to sit down until the shaky fit passed over. I couldn't think why I had gone off like a squib. After all, it had nothing to do with me. As for Gideon, I could have wrung his little neck for him. Who and what was he to look down his nose at me? Quite an idea, indeed! What is the world coming to, for goodness sake? It is his sort nowadays who have the say everywhere. All I hoped was I would never set eyes on him again. I am glad to say I haven't.

I did see Christine again. It was almost as if it was meant. I had been to visit Enid Torode who lives at the Vingtaine de l'Épine. She is a cousin on my father's side and a widow; and was on the list I carried about in my head. She was very nice to me that afternoon, and can't have had any idea of what I had gone to see her for; but she was one of those who, as soon as tea was over, had to turn on the T.V. I got up to go. She looked surprised.

'Well, thank you very much for the good tea,' I said, 'I would rather have a chat with you when you haven't got visitors.' I don't think she had the brains to understand. I had no intention of going to see her again, anyway. I walked home by the coast road and, when I got to the Pêquéries, who should I see coming towards me but Christine and another young man? I didn't need telling it was Abel.

I don't think she would have stopped, if I hadn't planted myself in her way. 'Hullo, Christine!' I said, as nice as pie. 'It is being lovely weather for your visit, isn't it?' 'I was hoping we might get to Vazon in time to see the sunset,' she said. 'I am always telling my friends in England how marvellous the sunsets are over here.' 'Is Gideon gone?' I said. 'He only flew over for a few days,' she said. 'He couldn't spare longer. In his profession time is money.' 'How did he get on with the Tourist Committee?' I said. 'Oh very well, very well,' she said, 'they were most impressed. Unfortunately, they are slow to get moving.' I noticed she didn't introduce me to Abel. He was standing quietly by her side, looking at me; and I was looking at him. In spite of all she had said had put me off him, I couldn't help liking him. He was tall and broad-shouldered with dark eyes and thick lips like Harold; but his hair was fairish, and he didn't look such a bully as Harold. I could see what Christine meant when she said he was kind. I thought I am going to get to know this boy.

'Hullo, Abel!' I said, 'we have met before.' 'Have we?' he said, 'I am afraid I don't remember.' 'How d'you like your island?' I said. He smiled; and his smile reminded me of Raymond. 'I haven't seen much of it yet,' he said. 'Well, you come and see me,' I said, 'and I will show you round our corner.' 'I doubt whether he will have the time,' said Christine. 'He is only over on a short leave.' I took no notice. 'My house is easy to find,' I said, 'along the north side of Grand Havre and round the Chouey and you can't miss it. There is a mill and an apple-tree behind.' 'Really, I am getting quite cold standing here,' said Christine, and shivered. 'I will show you where you made your great discovery,' I said. 'It is in the Museum now.' 'I have never heard of this,' he said. I thought I bet there is a lot more you have never heard of. 'I will be in any afternoon,' I said, and waved and walked on. I was pretty sure he would come. I doubted if he was quite as much under Christine's thumb as she thought.

I trusted him to have the sense not to bring her with him; and, sure enough, the very next afternoon, when I was clearing up after dinner, he turned up on his own. The front door was open, but he knocked. 'Who's there?' I shouted out. 'Abel!' he said. 'Good boy!' I said. 'Come on right in!' 'I thought I'd pop round while Mother was having a nap,' he said. 'I'm all arse-over-head,' I said, 'you have to take me as you find me.' I felt quite at home with him already. I thought to myself he is my sort, this one. 'I don't know who you are, though,' he said. 'I am Ebenezer Le Page,' I said, 'the cousin, the first cousin, of your father; and of Gideon's father, of course. Your fathers was first cousins.' I wanted to make sure he knew the truth about himself and Gideon; and hadn't been told lies.

'I know,' he said, 'something went very wrong there. It was tough on Mother. She has always spoken well of my father. She is very forgiving.' I saw how clever Christine had been. I knew just how she would look and the voice she would put on, when she was being 'very forgiving'. Anybody who didn't know beforehand what she was up to would be sure to put all the blame on Raymond, because she was such an angel; and well she knew it! There was a lot more I had on the tip of my tongue to tell Abel about Christine; but then I thought, after all, it isn't for me to turn the boy against his mother. 'Yes, something went very wrong indeed,' I said, 'but whatever your father may have been, or whatever your father may have done, you can take it from me there never was a boy born who was loved by his father more than you. If ever you have a son of your own, you will know what that mean.' He looked down; but didn't say nothing.

I said I would show him round outside. I thought the greenhouse or the garden might remind him; but all he said was, 'It must be pleasant living here.' I said, 'Don't you remember any of it?' 'I can't say I do,' he said. 'Well, you was trotting around here often enough when you was a two-to-three-year-old,' I said. I led the way down the gully and showed him the spot where he had dug up the prehistoric monster. 'That was clever of me,' he said. I think he knew I was disappointed, for he smiled in his kind way. I said we could go for a stroll, if he would wait while I got my hat from indoors. 'I do like this part very much,' he said, when I came out, 'it does seem familiar somehow.' I thought that is good. I chose the path along by La Jaonneuse and took him as far as Fort Pembroke. I wanted him to see across the whole width of L'Ancresse Bay and Fort Le Marchant on the other side. 'Gosh, this is the real thing!' he said and sniffed the air. I brought him back across the Common past La Varde, so as he could have a look at the Druid's Altar. He was interested in it, and went in and examined the big stones which are the roof. 'It's been there a long time,' I said. 'Yes, it has,' he said. He was a big simple chap, and looked at everything in the same slow interested way as Jim might have; and didn't say much. It was a pleasure being out with him.

When we got by the Vale Church, I said, 'Some of your ancestors are buried in that cemetery.' 'Are they?' he said. He didn't sound as if he cared much. 'The church is nice to see inside,' I said. 'Shall we go in?' 'I think not, thank you,' he said. 'I have never been inside a church.' 'It is Chapel you have been brought up, then?' I said. He laughed. 'I have been brought up nothing,' he said. 'I am surprised at that,' I said, 'your mother was Chapel. She used to sing in the choir.' 'She doesn't sing now,' he said. I was going to ask him to come home and have tea with me, but he looked at his wristwatch and said he must be getting along. His mother would be wondering where he was. 'What's this work you're doing?' I said. I wanted to know. 'Atomic research,' he said. 'For to blow up people?' I said. 'In the event of a nuclear war, I am afraid so,' he said.

If he had stuck a knife into me, he couldn't have hurt me more. I had been so happy walking with him across the Common: I had been having a wonderful dream all to myself. I would leave him what I got and make up to him in a small way for what he had lost through his father; and then he would always have a home in Guernsey where he belonged; and, while I was yet alive, perhaps he might come over and stay with me now and again. 'Well, good-bye,' he said, and shook hands, 'I am glad to have met you, Mr Le Page. Thank you for showing me around. I have enjoyed it very much.' He had no idea what I was feeling. He was a kind, polite stranger from England. It was a sad Ebenezer who walked back to Les Moulins. I can understand fighting, man against man; or even going to war, soldiers against soldiers; but to make things to go and kill millions of people you don't know, don't see even, because somebody sitting in a big office say you got to, no: I couldn't leave him what I got to do that! I couldn't.

11

It don't do to get on your high horse in this world, for a man never know when he may come a cropper. I never thought a day would come when I would let a room in my house to summer visitors, but did so for two summers. It is true, it was only to oblige. Miss Eunice Hocart came and asked me if I would sleep out some of her guests, who she didn't have room for at Timbuctoo. She offered to provide the towels and the blankets and sheets; but my mother had left me plenty, and they only had to be taken out and aired. I said I wasn't going to do the washing, because washing and ironing clothes is one woman's job I won't do: but old Mother Tostevin from the Vaugrat comes once a fortnight for a washing day and the next day for the ironing, and I would pay her a bit extra and she could do the lot. Otherwise, I was willing so long as Miss Hocart didn't send me no women in trousers; or any woman on her own, for that matter. I knew how people talk. A man can't be too careful when he live by himself.

It would mean a few pounds extra, and nothing to do for it. Also I thought it might be company; but I can't say I remember much about those visitors now. It wasn't so long ago either. The truth is I was losing interest in the people around me. It was only the winter before, after Abel had been and gone, I had taken to writing my book. I didn't write so much in the summer months; but was looking forward to the winter when I would be able to spend the long dark evenings with those people I had known when I was younger. They was more real to me than any of those I saw and spoke to every day.

Miss Hocart said I needn't give her guests anything to eat or drink, as she was giving them full board; but I got up at six in the morning as usual and, when I'd had my breakfast, made a fresh pot of tea and put it on a tray outside their door with biscuits and cups and saucers and so on, for them to pour their own. Of an evening when they came in, I gave them a bite of supper before they went to bed, if they wanted it; or, at least, a cup of cocoa. They liked to sit and chat to me about what they had been doing and seeing during the day. I learnt a lot about Guernsey I didn't know before. I will say they all liked Guernsey; and they liked my little house. In fact, many of them said they would prefer to stay at Les Moulins all the time: it was more homely. They may have said that only to please me; but I still get cards every Christmas from some of them, though half the time I don't know which they are.

I wondered sometimes if perhaps Miss Hocart was unloading her awkward squad on me; for she certainly sent me some odd objects from time to time. There was James Walker, Esquire; or, as he said when he introduced himself, 'James Walker, not Johnnie, ha, ha!' That was the trouble with James Walker, Esquire. He was always making jokes I didn't think was funny; and if I cracked a Guernsey joke he couldn't see it. The result was whenever one of us made a joke the other was dead serious. He didn't want tea in the morning, but a glass of cold milk put outside his door. It was like putting out milk for the cat. He was rather like a big cat, as a matter of fact. He was the same shape as a pear; and was continually washing himself. He had about a dozen bottles of lotion for shaving and for his hair and for his hands and for all the other parts of him. He wore very good clothes; and I think was pretty well off. He told me he was a dealer in antiques in Chelsea, London; and he liked to rattle off the names of the grand people with titles and plenty of money who came into his shop and bought antiques. I said I wasn't interested in people with money.

I think he was what Paddy would have called a lonely heart, male. He went out during the day, but always by himself; and I had to put up with him most of the evening. He said he didn't like being at Timbuctoo after dinner in the evening: it was only a lot of old biddies sitting round gossiping; but he was as good at gossiping as any old biddy, and he was nosey as well. He had to pick up everything I got and examine it. He said I got some quite good stuff in the house, mixed up with a lot of junk. It was him wanted to buy my lustre-ware jug, and he had his eyes on my china dogs; but I wouldn't have parted with those for the world. He admired my grandfather clock, and was willing to make me an offer; and said he would give me something for my coronation mug. It amused him. I said I didn't want to sell it. He said no doubt it had a sentimental value. I don't know what he meant. Anyhow, he went at the end of the week, and I was glad to see the back of him. I was lucky to have anything left.

The worst nuisances of all was a married couple. They hadn't been married a year, but they fought like cat and dog day and night. I thought by the end of the week they would have murdered each other; and every morning I woke up expecting to have a couple of dead bodies on my hands. Frank and Dorothea. I forget their other names. They are two I never get a Christmas card from. As a matter of fact, I didn't think Frank would have been such a bad chap, if he had been on his own. He was in the Police Force before he married her and was a fine built fellow, if wooden on top, but all right for a policeman; only her family owned a cotton-mill in Bolton, and she made him resign from the Police and take on a job as manager. Goodness knows what he saw in her. She was all skin and bone. She was for ever saying how sensitive and artistic she was; and went about in sandals and wore clothes like Joseph's coat of many colours, and long green ear-rings and a green bandeau round her hair. She looked like something come out of the rag-bag.

I tried my best to make peace between them; but I don't know that I did much good. One morning after a night of battle had woke me up several times, they was carrying on in the kitchen when he made a dash for the bedroom to get a revolver from his trunk and shoot himself. She clung to him then, and cried, 'Oh, don't do it, darling: I love you so much! I can't live without you!' 'Let him do it, you fool,' I said, 'if he want to!' He turned on me and wanted to know what the hell I thought I was up to, coming between husband and wife. He forgot all about the revolver. Another morning he went off in a huff for a swim. He was a powerful swimmer. He swore he couldn't bear to have to sit face to face with her across the breakfast table at Timbuctoo. Whereupon she grabbed my Woolworth's bread-knife and was going to stab herself. 'This will make him sorry!' she said. 'I wouldn't do it with that knife, if I was you,' I said, 'it have a blade like a saw. Try the carving knife: it is sharper. Or better, the skewer: it will go in easy.' She threw the bread-knife on the floor at my feet and said I was a brute and a beast and as insensitive and unfeeling as he was! I thought they might make it up the day they went to Sark, since Raymond said Sark was heaven on earth; but it was rough coming back and she was seasick all over him.

There was two I did like; though perhaps I didn't ought to have done. They was two young chaps, and Miss Hocart said she hoped I didn't mind them sharing a room; but I didn't see nothing wrong in that. Geoffrey and Tony was their proper names, but they called each other Gib and Tib. What I liked about them was they didn't make out to be something they wasn't. Over in England they was only painters and decorators working on their own. They had been working in a factory making match-boxes when they got to know each other, but they didn't like being shut in all day long; so they decided to buy a van and a few things between them, and go round the country parts doing odd jobs. They had done well enough the last year to be able to afford a holiday in Guernsey. Geoffrey was dark and ugly, and reminded me of Jim's Victor; but he was quiet and a chap could be trusted, I thought. Tony was fair and good-looking, and reminded me of the young German Raymond was friendly with. He was the lively one; but was moody sometimes. Geoffrey thought the world of him.

The Friday morning while they was staying with me, I was coming out of the States Offices from getting my pay when I ran into big fat Le Bas. I had been having a heart-to-heart talk with my girl in the pay-desk. She really is a fine girl, that. She reminds me of Tabitha when she was young.

She is neat and small with a round face and a smile for a joke; and is no silly miss by any means, but looks at you with straight honest brown eyes. I said to her that morning, 'It is much too fine for you to be indoors: you ought to be out in the sun.' 'I wish I was,' she said. 'Why on earth do you work in an office?' I said. 'Needs must when the devil drives,' she said. I said, 'What would you really like to be doing?' 'Looking after a husband, and a home and a family,' she said. I wasn't sure I liked the idea of a husband. He would never be good enough. I said, 'Well, that won't be difficult to get for you.' She made a face. 'I don't know about that,' she said. 'It is the husband. He has to be who I want; or nobody.' 'The fellow must be a born fool if he doesn't want you,' I said. 'He is anything but a fool,' she said, 'I can only keep myself available; and hope.' 'I will hope with you,' I said. I thought well, I can leave you a house but I can't leave you a husband, I am afraid; and you don't want an empty house.

I didn't like fat Le Bas: he was like a big slug; but I was feeling so good, I stopped and spoke to him. I asked after his old mother he lived with, who was as cantankerous as the day is long; and it happened while we was talking Geoffrey and Tony passed on the other side and waved. I knew they was going to Herm for the day; so I shouted, 'Got your passports?' They laughed. 'Goodness, you don't know those two, do you?' said fat Le Bas. 'Can't you see what they are?' It is true Tony was happy, and walking along rather as if he was dancing. I said, 'Yes, I know them well. They have been living in my house for a week.' 'Their sort ought to be shot!' he said. God, coming from him, it made me go hot under the collar! I don't say he had been caught doing anything wrong; but everybody knew he had been warned off time and again for hanging round the schools, when the children was coming out, with bags of sweets to offer to the little girls. I said, 'It take all sorts to make a world, my boy; or you, for one, wouldn't be allowed to live in it.' He shuffled off without saying another word. I bet he have been saying plenty about me since.

I did wonder if perhaps he was right about Geoffrey and Tony; and, if so, I was sorry. I have never liked the idea of that sort of thing; yet the way he spoke about them made me want to stick up for them. That evening when they came in, I went out of my way to make it pleasant for them. I don't keep beer in the house, as a rule; but I got in a few bottles from the off-licence on the Bridge, and we stayed up talking and drinking until midnight. They said Herm was absolute paradise. It was funny to think I had never been there, yet had seen it all my life a few miles across the water. I told them some of the things I had learnt from Raymond about Guernsey as it used to be; and Geoffrey was like Raymond, and thought it must have been grand to be living here in those days. 'Turn back the clock and we'll come again!' he said. When they went to bed, they both said they was sorry they was having to leave in the morning.

They was having breakfast at Timbuctoo and going straight from there
to the boat; and when I saw them packing their things, I gave them a couple
of ormer shells to remember Guernsey by. I gave one to each, and I didn't
think I had chosen one better than the other, but Geoffrey gave the one I
had given him to Tony, and Tony gave his to Geoffrey. I said I had a whole
basketful they could choose from, if they didn't like the ones I had picked
out; but Geoffrey laughed and said it wasn't that at all: they exchange
everything they have, and even wear each other's clothes sometimes. I
said, 'That's all right then.' When they shook hands and wished me good-
bye, Geoffrey said I couldn't know how much it had meant to them to have
a friendly face to come back to every evening, and Tony said I had made
their holiday. Ah well, I suppose I could have done worse. I got a nice card
from them the next Christmas, and written on it 'For two ormer shells.
From Gib and Tib.' I was glad to know they was friends yet. I haven't
heard since.

There was one old couple I liked a lot: a Mr and Mrs Jones from Wales;
and I get a letter as well as a card from them every Christmas. They was
another pair who didn't put on airs. I expect Miss Hocart thought they was
not quite the right class, and that's why they was sent to me. He was a coal-
miner until lately; and was now on his old-age pension. I imagined a coal-
miner to be a big and burly chap; but he was short and wiry and spoke in a
high-pitched voice. She was a bustling lively little woman, who talked
very quick, and I didn't always know what she said. They had children and
grandchildren they could have spent their holiday with; but she said the
old people are not really wanted, and quite right too. Instead they decided
to have a second honeymoon. Well, I can say I have never seen any young
honeymoon couple be so happy, or enjoy themselves so much. They went
somewhere different every day; and in their eyes everything was perfect.
They was strict Chapel; and Sundays went to the Capelles for morning and
evening service. When I said I was Church but didn't go, she wagged a
finger at me, as if I was one of her grandchildren. They stayed a fortnight;
and I would have been glad for them to stay longer.

Mr Hungerford Smith was a widower; and I am not surprised. The only
thing his poor wife could have done of her own free will was to die. He had
to have his own way in everything, and he was always right. He was the last
visitor I had to stay with me; and when he had gone, I swore I would never
have another. He gave me to understand he was a very important person;
and he may well have been. I don't know what the Archbishop of Canterbury looks like; but Mr Hungerford Smith looked what the Archbishop of
Canterbury ought to look like, even if he don't. He sat himself down in my
armchair as if he was the Pope and spoke with authority. I didn't understand exactly what he spoke with authority about, but it had something to
do with stocks and shares. He wanted to know all my money business

from the year dot. He asked if the house was mine, if there was anything owing on it, if I had any relations I must leave it to, and if I had any investments or money in the bank. I answered him yes, or no, quite truthfully; but he didn't guess the truth. He thought I was poor. He said he could be of great service to me. He would allow me to sell him my house as it stood, and all ground and outhouses attached thereto; and when he reached the age of retirement, he would have a place in Guernsey to retire to. I said selling wasn't as simple as that over here. He said he knew the law. I am not going to say how much he offered for my small property; but he must have wanted it bad, because it was thousands. He said until the time came for him to come into residence, I could go on living in it; and pay him a nominal rent. He didn't say how much.

I was tempted. It would be a great load off my mind not to have to worry any more about who I was going to leave it to. I could let the greenhouse and the ground; and take things easy for the few years I had left. As it was, I wasn't doing much. I planted and watered and trimmed the tomatoes, and pottered around outside; but it was young Bill Ogier did the heavy work, and his wife the picking and packing. They might just as well do the lot, and make what they could. If his nibs wanted to live in the house before I died, I could move into a guesthouse and be waited on. I would have enough. I had it on the tip of my tongue to say yes; but when it came to the point and I looked at him, I said, 'Thank you, but I am not selling. At any price.' I didn't want his sort settling on Guernsey.

12

I thought of young Lihou. I had kept in the way of going to see how he was
getting on; but I had never thought before of leaving him anything. He
wasn't a relation. It hadn't occurred to me it didn't have to be a relation. I
had cousins; but no next-of-kin. I could go out into the highways and
byways and pick on anybody I liked. He had done well for himself and he
had worked hard for it. He owned his own bungalow and the last time I
had a chat with him he was going to have three hundred feet more of glass
put up. He had been very straight with me and offered to let me have back
what I had let him have to get started. I told him I had given it: I hadn't lent
it. I have always been firm about that. I either give; or I keep for myself.
Lending is having it both ways. I would rather go without than buy a thing
on hire-purchase.

The youngest of his children was just left school. I had seen it in the
Press. She had passed high up in her exams at the school at Beaucamps, and
was going to be an air-hostess. I couldn't see what she wanted all that education for to be an air-hostess. I would have thought all she needed was to
know how to smile. The two boys was working for their father. I don't
think they was bad boys really, but they was mad about motor-bikes. I
had seen the younger one, when he couldn't have been more than fourteen,
riding a big red motor-bike on which he could hardly reach the handle-
bars. It was no use me telling his father the boy would kill himself, for it
was from his father he got the craze. Edith, the wife, said she was sick and
tired of her husband's everlasting motor-bike; and I never went round to
see him but I found him down on his knees worshipping it, like a heathen
down on his knees worshipping his idol of wood and stone.

Anyhow, I thought I would go and see him, and make up my mind. He
was more to my taste than Mr Hungerford Smith. I found him down on his
knees as usual; but this time it was in front of a motor-car. He jumped up
when he saw me and was as delighted as a boy to explain to me all the mira-
cles of his new car. I listened but I didn't understand a word of what he was
talking about. As far as I am concerned, cars are wild animals I do my best
to keep out of the way of; and I don't know the difference between one
breed and another. I asked him how Edith was, and he said, 'Aw, she's all

right,' and went on talking about his car. I don't expect he would have even bothered to take me in to see her, if she hadn't called out tea was ready.

I had never liked Edith much. She was a Keyho from the Vrangue before she married young Lihou and didn't think much of the Le Pages from Les Sablons. She may have been right at that; for my little grandmother's family didn't seem to have come to much. Edith's modern bungalow was very different from Les Sablons. It wasn't a sanded stone floor in the kitchen, and a terpid on the hearth. She had a fridge and an electric stove and an electric iron and a hoover; though I do know the old willow pattern china on my grandmother's dresser was better than the crockery she had bought from Woolworth's. Now that is a shop I don't like. It is supposed to be cheap, but when you work it out, it turns out to be dear. I never go in but I come out with a lot of things I didn't even think of buying. Edith was civil to me, if nothing more; and couldn't very well help inviting me to stay to tea. Over tea he talked about the improved method of packing tomatoes in trays and having them sorted out and sent off by rote from the Depôt in Bulwer Avenue. He thought it was a good idea. I didn't. I like to know the man who my crop is going to.

I chatted and we seemed friendly enough; but it wasn't like it used to be during the Occupation. In those days we was both up against it together; but now he was getting on in the world, and I was getting ready to get out of it. I asked him about the boys, who was both out. He said the second didn't like hard work, but was good at keeping the books. Himself, he wasn't much better at keeping books than I was; and nowadays, if you got a cow or a greenhouse, you got to employ a clerk to keep the books. After tea he said he would take me along to see the new glass houses he had just had put up. It wasn't fifty yards along the road; but, if you please, we had to go in the car. He said, 'What is the use of having a car, if you got to use shanks' ponies?' It wasn't worth the trouble of getting in and out. I said, 'I reckon legs will die out in Guernsey in a few years; and the future generations will be born with big heads on stumps.' After I had seen what there was to see, he had the impudence to say he could run me home. 'I can walk yet, thank you,' I said. That silly business of the car decided me. He won't do.

It was round about the same time I went to see Mrs John Mourant of La Fontenelle. She was Elsie Le Gallez before she married, and a great-niece of my little grandmother; and so, I suppose, a sort of relation of mine. It is true she married so far above us, my mother refused to own her, saying it was not for her to bend the knee to the principalities and powers. Mrs Mourant herself had always known who I was, and would bow and smile when she saw me. She was now a widow and had no children. Her husband, Jurat Mourant, had left her pretty well off; but she had spent a pile of money having the old place at La Fontenelle done up, and now ran it as the Grande Hougue Guest-House. I had heard she gave wonderful food and comfort for what the people paid. In fact, she couldn't have made anything out of it; and it was mostly old or disabled people she had staying there. It was on the edge of the Common and safe for them to wander down to the beach, if they could. She was also on a committee to do with the Red Cross and had something to do with the St John's Ambulance, and with the Town Hospital, I believe. Anyhow, she was altogether a good living and a good doing woman.

I went one afternoon. She made me welcome without asking any questions as to why I had come, and said I ought to have called on her before, and must come again whenever I wanted to. Her guest-house was very different from Dora's. I could see everything was of the best; and I bet it was all paid for. She had a lounge for those who liked the T.V.; and another for those who didn't. She said she didn't care for it herself. The bedrooms was made sound-proof, so the old and sick could sleep in peace. There was a big room downstairs for eating in; and she introduced me to some of the guests who was sitting on the verandah in the sun. I noticed she didn't make them go out during the day; and she spoke to them more as if they was friends than strangers who was paying to live there. In fact, she was so good and kind to everybody, I began to wonder if perhaps she didn't like anybody at all really; but only liked being good and kind. I was looking at the decorations in the dining-room. The walls was washed a pale yellow; and painted straight on was pictures of comic bears and giraffes with long necks and woolly sheep and cheeky rabbits. I said they would do lovely for children; but she said it was a mistake to imagine elderly people didn't like gay things around them.

A servant brought in trays of tea and cakes for the guests, and a tray especially for us. Afterwards it was a bit awkward; because I kept on looking round, and couldn't see the place I wanted. In the end I had to ask her where it was. 'Oh, in the bathroom,' she said; and showed me the way up the stairs, and the door. I had never in my life seen such a bathroom! The bath was pale green, and the walls and the ceiling and the tiles on the floor was the same colour; and even the mats and towels, and the rug to stand on. The windows was of green ground glass and in the green light it was like being under the sea, as it was in Sloan's Circus, only more so; and painted on the ceiling and all the walls was pictures of lobsters with great claws going to get hold of you, and enormous spider-crabs crawling after you, and an octopus with his eight legs going to curl around you, and a huge conger with his mouth open going to swallow you, and long-noses coming straight for you full of teeth. I wouldn't have laid myself down in that bath among those creatures for anything in the world. The nightmares came back to me I used to have when I was hungry during the Occupation and all the creatures I was longing to eat was going to eat me. I couldn't even do my business. I was out of that bathroom and down those stairs and had shouted a good-bye and thank-you to Mrs Mourant and got half-way across the Common before I dared to look round and make sure I wasn't being followed. I had clean forgotten what I had gone to see Mrs Mourant for.

Constable Le Page was another I went to visit. When he came to Les Moulins about those boys, I had thought of him as a possibility, but, for some reason, he had slipped my memory since. The picture of the handsome, sarcastic Neville Falla came into my mind, and so I thought of Constable Le Page again. He was a chap I was surprised was a policeman. When he left school he worked at first for his father, who was a grower at Le Hurel; and I knew he had always been a great boy for Chapel. He taught in the Vale Sunday School, and I had seen his photo in the paper with some other young chaps as having to do with Christian Youth: then I heard he had suddenly married Amy Sebire from Baugy, and joined the Police. It sounded funny to me. As Raymond used to say, a Christian is supposed to forgive the sinner; but surely it is the business of the policeman to catch the criminal and lock him up. I am not saying he is doing wrong, mind you; but I don't understand how a policeman can be a Christian. He have a different Master.

It was one summer evening I went along to his place. I found him in his blue policeman's trousers and shirt-sleeves, washing the outside of the front windows with a syringe and a bucket of water. 'Hullo, is there more trouble your way?' he said, when he saw me. His first thought was the boys had been up to their tricks again. 'I haven't seen hair or hide of the young rascals since,' I said. 'I am surprised at that,' he said; and sounded disappointed. I said, 'Have they been up to mischief elsewhere, then?' 'Well, not as far as I know,' he said. 'Of course, they have lost Neville Falla. He was the real dangerous character.' 'Have he gone away, then?' I said. 'No, but he chucked the gang,' he said. 'He prefers to operate on his own.' 'Why, what have he been up to now?' I said. 'I don't know what he has been up to exactly,' he said, 'but you can bet your bottom dollar he hasn't been up to any good.' Young Falla's father had died recently and, as his mother was already dead, there was nobody now to keep a hold on him. He was an only child and spoilt, and was spending what his father had left him like water; going around shooting his mouth, and making a mock of everybody. It was my guess those he made a mock of most was good honest Christian boys like Constable Le Page.

Anyhow, I hadn't come to see him on police matters; so I asked after his family. He changed his tune at once, and became quite a nice chap. 'Come in and see my tribe,' he said; and we went indoors. He introduced me to Amy, his wife, who I hadn't met before. She just laughed: she couldn't shake hands. She was up to her neck in kids. She was giving suck to one;

and there was three more, who had been got ready to go to bed. The three was all boys: at a guess, about three, five and seven years old, and as much alike as jelly babies, only different sizes; and they was all so exactly like their father they might have come out of the same mould. I said to him, 'Goodness, couldn't you have done something different?' 'The last is a girl,' he said. I could see that for myself from the very way her little fingers was curling round trying to get more drink out of her mother; and when she was put down in the cradle, she was just a round lump like her mother. The three boys kissed their mother and father good-night, and shook hands politely with me; then went in their pyjamas up the stairs to bed one behind the other, the eldest first. They won my heart.

It was a pity supper-time we got into an argument over motor-cars. It was me started it, of course. I said I didn't understand how it was nowadays, when they are making so many laws you can't put your right foot in front of your left without asking a policeman, they don't make a sensible law to keep down the number of motor-cars on the island. There are not roads for so many cars, for one thing; and they are not wide enough in many places; and, if you start widening the roads, it will have to be at the expense of somebody's land: and nobody got enough, as it is. I was quite willing to allow the doctors to have motor-cars; and there have to be ambulances and the fire-brigade; and lorries for hauling, and for carrying the produce to the harbour; but I didn't see why every Tom, Dick and Harry should be allowed to have a car. I know of some who go to Town every day in their blessed cars, and got further to walk to their offices from where they can park, than if they had walked straight from home.

He said, 'What about the people who make a living by selling cars?' I said, 'There are many more honest ways of making a living than selling cars. Half of them aren't paid for, anyway.' He said it was no good me lamming into him: he didn't have a car of his own; but he wished he had, and would have as soon as he was made a sergeant and could afford one. 'You are nobody, if you haven't got a car,' he said. I said, 'Now you have hit the right nail on the head!' It wasn't because all those cars was necessary on the island there was so many, but because if Mrs Domaille happen to have a car, then Mrs Nicolle got to have a car, even if the bus to Town stop outside her gate. Where is there to go to in a car in Guernsey? All they can do is drive round and round, one behind the other; and you can go all round the island in an hour. It is mad.

He said it was no madder than in the days when there was horses and traps. I said it was quite different in the days when there was horses and traps. For one thing, the people was cheerier and more friendly than those who drive about in cars with their noses in the air. 'I will tell you the reason for why,' I said, 'a horse is one of God's creatures, and you can't have it all your own way driving a horse. Our old Jack was an angel from heaven on four legs; but even he got ideas into his head sometimes, and you had to give into him so far. When a man sit at the wheel of a car, he think he is God Almighty, and everything and everybody in creation got to get out of his way.' Constable Le Page said I had gone off on to quite a different tack, and was arguing for the sake of winning the argument, by fair means or foul. I didn't know a thing about cars, if I didn't know every car got ideas of its own. I said, 'Well, all I can say it have come to something, if you got to give in to the ideas of a car!'

Once I get started, there is no stopping me. I went on to say not only was I puzzled as to why there was so many cars on the island, but also as to why there was so many policemen. They are useless objects. There are not less crimes on the island now than there used to be: there are more. I know there was a murder now and again in the past, and a few robberies; but now every week you read of stabbing, and the breaking of shop windows, and stealing, and doing all sort of damage got no rhyme or reason; and nobody dare go out without locking the doors of their houses back and front. 'As far as I am concerned,' I said, 'I don't lock my back door, even when I go to bed. I kept it locked when the Germans was here, it is true; but I am certainly not going to do it now against my own people, or against the English we are supposed to belong to.' He said, 'Well, if you are murdered in your bed one night, it won't do you any good coming to the Police Station in the morning and blame us for it.' 'I'd have more sense than to do that!' I said.

I was right. I know I was right. The more policemen you have, the more criminals you have; and the more criminals you have, the more policeman you got to have to catch them: and so it go on and on, until a time will come when everybody will be either a criminal or a policeman. I am not for stabbing and robbing, goodness knows; but I am not on the side of the police either. There is a mistake in their argument somewhere; but it would take a better brain than mine to find out what that mistake is. I wasn't arguing any more. I said how much I liked the kiddies, and left a present for each of the boys on the mantelpiece; but I went away disgruntled. I won't leave my money to a policeman.

Well, I am more than half-way through number three of my big books; and I could fill up the whole of the rest of it writing about nothing else than the different people, some relations and some not, who I went to visit with a vain hope. I don't know what I was looking for really. All I know is I didn't find it. There was always something to do with the person put me off. I am getting terribly cranky in my old age. Jim said once I didn't have a heart. He was joking then, I know; but I haven't got much of a heart now. It is cold and shrivelled up. I see my fellow creatures as trees walking; and, as Christine said, I couldn't care less. If Father Darcy was alive, I could leave him everything I got; for I would know he would make good use of it. Or I could leave it to Miss Ozanne for her Bird Hospital. I have more sympathy for birds who get hurt than I have for human beings who go to war, for instance. It is not the birds' fault. All the same, I have never been one to go out of my way to do good; and I would die an old humbug, if I made out I was wanting to do good when I am dead.

13

I little thought when I was arguing the toss with Constable Le Page I was myself in danger of getting into the hands of the Police. I could have been brought up before the Royal Court and made to pay, or put in prison; and everybody would have read about it in the *Press*. A man never know what a day may bring forth. I went to the States Offices that Friday morning as innocent as a babe unborn. I had filled in my three pieces of paper for the Cliffs Committee and the Natural Beauties Committee and the Ancient Monuments Committee; and I expected to hand them in at the cash desk, have a few words with my girl, and she would pay me my money as usual.

It was my girl in the desk and she smiled but looked worried, I thought; and when I was going to give her the three papers, she shook her head. 'I am afraid Mr Carey wants to see you,' she said. 'I hope it is to put my pay up,' I said. It was high time too, the way things was going up in the shops. 'I will ring through and find out if he can see you now,' she said. All she said through the telephone was 'Mr Le Page is here.' He said a lot at the other end, because the telephone was rattling; but I couldn't catch what it was he was saying. She said to me, 'Mr Carey says he is very busy, but will make time to see you now.' She looked very serious. I began to wonder if perhaps something was wrong.

She came out of her office and said, 'Come this way, please. I will take you up to his room.' She led the way up the stairs, and I followed her. I took my hat off on the way up; and arranged my few hairs. I wanted to make a good impression. She knocked on the door and a very gentlemanly voice said 'Come in!' She opened the door and let me go in first. 'Here is Mr Le Page,' she said. 'Thank you, Miss de la Rue,' said Mr Carey; then she went out and closed the door, and left me standing in front of him. Well, I knew now she was a de la Rue, though I didn't know where from. I don't know yet which Mr Carey it was: they are all Careys at the States Offices; but you could see he was a very important person, and he sat in a big chair in a big way in front of a big desk.

There was two telephones on the desk. I suppose they was one for each ear; but I wondered how he could speak to and listen to two people at the same time. I know I couldn't. It is as much as I can do to speak to and listen

to one person through the telephone; and I don't do that if I can help it. I
like to be able to see who I am talking to. There was a wire tray on the desk
on one side of Mr Carey with the word IN printed in big letters on it; but
there was nothing in it. There was another wire tray on the other side of
him with the word OUT printed on it; but there was nothing in that one
either. There was a waste-paper basket under the desk by his chair, and
that was empty; but on the desk in front of him was three piles of paper I
recognised all too well: for they was written in my own big wobbly handwriting. They was the accounts I had sent in to the Cliffs Committee and
the Natural Beauties Committee and the Ancient Monuments Committee, ever since I had started look after the ancient monument.

Mr Carey had a pair of spectacles with thick black rims on his nose, and
sat staring at those three piles of paper as if I wasn't in the room. I felt a big
fool standing there and him saying nothing. There was a chair by the desk
on my side, but I thought I had better not sit down on it, unless I was
invited. At last he took off his spectacles and polished them with a big
white silk handkerchief he took from his breast pocket, and then put them
back on his nose again and gave me a long hard look. 'Mr Ebenezer Le
Page, I believe,' he said. 'Quite right!' I said. 'Of course I know you by
sight, who doesn't?' he said, 'and by repute.' I wondered what he had
heard about me. 'Sit down!' he said. It was an order. I sat down and put my
stick between my knees, and my old hat on the crook of my stick. 'Is there
anything I can do for you, Mr Carey?' I said.

He didn't seem to be able to think of anything to say for a minute. He
had trouble with his breath and then said, 'I fear there has been some misunderstanding.' 'Have there?' I said. 'Are you pretending you are not
aware,' he said, 'for over a considerable period of time you have been
guilty of a deliberate duplication of accounts?' 'I don't understand those
long words,' I said. 'I think you understand them perfectly well,' he said,
'but it suits your purpose not to.' He went on and on and on, talking and
talking, as only his sort can talk, and only telling me over and over again
what I knew already as well as he did. I had sent in an account to the Cliffs
Committee every week, and an account to the Natural Beauties Committee, and an account to the Ancient Monuments Committee; and all
three accounts was for the same job of work. What did I have to say for
myself? 'I haven't sent in no account for no work I haven't done,' I said.
'That may, or may not be,' he said, 'but the fact remains you have know-
ingly claimed payment three times over for every scrap of work you have
done for us!' I was beginning to get angry: he was being so unreasonable.
'How can you expect a man like me to know which committee is which:
when there are so many?' I said. 'I only wanted to be sure to do the right
thing.' I thought he was going to have a stroke.

He was red in the face naturally, for he is a man who eats and drinks well;

but now he got so red he looked as if he might explode. He mopped his forehead with his big silk handkerchief. He was sweating. 'The question now is, Mr Le Page,' he said, 'how do you propose to reimburse the States?' 'What do you mean?' I said. This was getting serious. He said, 'How do you propose to pay back the amount you have been overpaid?' 'I can't pay nothing back!' I said. 'I live from hand to mouth.' 'That is no excuse for defrauding the States,' he said. 'Defrauding?' I said. 'Do you mean robbing?' 'Yes, daylight robbery; if you want it in plain English!' he said. I said, 'Why, I have never robbed a penny from a person in my life!' I thought except those pennies from my father; but I couldn't help that. 'A man can rob from Tom, Dick, or Harry,' I said, 'but how can he rob from the States?' Mr Carey lay back in his chair, as if he was going to faint. 'Frankly, I don't know what to do with you,' he said, shaking his head sadly. 'If we go to law and prosecute, it will be like trying to get blood out of a stone.' It was my turn to go red! Goodness, what did he take me for? A beggar? I was in two minds to tell him I could bring him his silly old money that very afternoon, and not miss it; but then I thought perhaps I had better not. 'I am sorry if I have made a mistake,' I said. 'It wouldn't surprise me if you have thousands under the floor-boards,' he said. 'It is stone floors at Les Moulins,' I said. 'A protection against dry-rot, no doubt,' he said. He didn't know what he was saying. He had gone right off the rails.

I thought it was the right moment to bring up the business I had really come about. 'How about my wages for this week?' I said. 'I haven't been paid yet.' I held out to him the three pieces of paper I had brought with me. He reached across the desk and snatched them out of my hand and laid them down on the blotter in front of him as if they was alive and going to bite. 'An ancient monument is NOT the concern of the Cliffs Committee,' he said, 'and since when have there been any cliffs round your way?' He picked up that one of my papers and tore it across and across and threw the pieces in the empty waste-paper basket. My heart was in my mouth when I saw all that good money going to pot. 'An ancient monument is NOT a natural beauty,' he said, 'if ancient monument it be; and it is NOT the concern of the Natural Beauties Committee!' He picked up that paper too and tore it up, and threw the pieces into the waste-paper basket with such force I was lifted a foot off my seat. He gave me back the other. 'The cashier will pay you that,' he said, 'and in future, Mr Le Page, will you please address your account to THE ANCIENT MONUMENTS COM-MITTEE ONLY!' 'I am glad I know now what I got to do,' I said.

I got on to my feet to go out; but I was stiff on my old legs from sitting for so long in one place, and could only walk very slow with my stick towards the door. I had my hand on the door-knob and was going to say 'Good-morning,' when I heard him call 'Ebenezer?' I turned round in surprise. 'You are not as lively on your pins as you used to be, eh?' he said. 'Not quite,' I said. 'Let me have that paper!' he said. I gave it back to him wondering what on earth he was going to do next. 'Let's see, let's see,' he said, and he took out his fountain pen: 'we allow you eight hours a week for that little job, isn't that so? Well, in the circumstances, I think we can allow you twelve.' He made an alteration on my paper and gave it back to me. 'Thank you, sir!' I said. Mr Carey is a gentleman, but he is a Guernseyman as well.

When I got downstairs I noticed there was a young man I didn't know in the office. He was long and thin with long white hands and long pale hair and was wearing a pale grey suit. He seemed to be nosing into all the cupboards and drawers. I wondered if he had been there when I came in, and that was why my girl hadn't said much to me. She came to the opening now and took my paper, but she didn't look at me or speak. I saw her eyebrows go up when she saw Mr Carey had altered the figures. She paid me the money. 'Please check it is correct,' she said. 'Mistakes cannot be rectified after leaving the desk.' She said it like a gramophone. She had never spoken to me in that way before. 'It is quite right, thank you,' I said. 'Good-morning, Mr Le Page,' she said: it wasn't 'Tcheerie!' as it usually was. 'Good-morning, Miss de la Rue,' I said. I went away very worried. I couldn't believe for a moment it was through her I had been caught out; but I was afraid perhaps she had been caught out through me. I would have given anything to know.

The next Monday afternoon, I think it was, a lady I didn't know and who didn't give her name, came to the front door to find out if I was a person fit to be left to live on my own. She didn't put it as blunt as that; but that is what it came to. She was from some Society or another, and I think had been sent by Mrs Mourant, for she mentioned her name. She was very nice about it, but she said she thought it would be better for me if I was to let my house, and go and live in an Old People's Home: either Saumarez Park or, if I couldn't afford it, the Town Hospital. I got a bad fit of trembling. I said I was born in this house and had lived in this house all my life and, God willing, it was where I was going to die. She said I had her every sympathy; but I would be better looked after if I was to go into a Home, and I would have the T.V. and company and every comfort. 'I am well looked after, as it is,' I said. She wanted to know by who. I had to say nobody, because I don't have help in the house: I look after myself. I kept her on the doorstep while she was talking; but she asked if she might come in. I had to let her. She wasn't as nosey as I thought she would be; but she had a good look round. She said she was pleasantly surprised finding the place so clean and well cared-for, and I had every right to be proud of it. I didn't offer her anything to eat or drink: I was feeling too bad-tempered. She went away and left a card with an address on it for me to write to, if I changed my mind. I threw it on the fire when she was gone.

14

The next Friday I went to Town with my paper filled in for the Ancient Monuments Committee, hoping my girl would be in the office by herself, so as I would be able to find out what had happened behind the scenes. She wasn't there, and the pale thin young fellow was in charge. He looked at me as if I had come to steal the Crown Jewels, and examined my paper very carefully; but when he couldn't find nothing wrong with it, he pushed my money across the counter with his long thin fingers. 'Please check it is correct,' he said. I could see it was. 'Thank you,' I said. 'Good-morning,' he said. I couldn't very well ask him what had happened to Miss de la Rue or he might think I was another like big fat Le Bas. He have eyes like a fish and look just the sort who would think such things. I got the awful thought he might be the young man she had in mind. It was too horrible to imagine; but I have known worse things to happen. It is often the nicest girls who are the fools.

The Sunday night I got out my bottle of ink and pen and book and blotting-paper, and sat up to the table to write; but I couldn't think of a word to put down, and not a word more have I written until today. That was months and months ago. It had always been my hope to be able to end my book with my affairs settled; and myself ending my days in complete peace of mind. There didn't seem any chance it would ever be. I would be found dead in my bed one morning; and my house and everything I got would go to some cousins I didn't even know of. I got in such a state of mind I didn't care. I certainly wasn't going to visit any more people. It was a waste of time. I had been looking for a sign. There was no sign.

Altogether this winter have been the most miserable I have ever lived through. It was the long winter nights with nothing to do I couldn't stand. I would bring out the old book in the hope I might write down my thoughts, if nothing else; but not a thought to think would come into my head. I would have to put the book back in the drawer without a word written. I tried to read *Robinson Crusoe* again; but I knew already what was going to happen in the story, and couldn't go on with it. In the day I worked as usual in the greenhouse and outside in my slow way. I thought well, so long as I wake up in the morning, I got to do something; though

God knows what for. I went to even more trouble to keep myself and the house as clean as possible, in case that woman came to see how I was getting along. I thought it was bad enough being on my own; but, if they was to lock me up in a Home and I had to be one of a lot of old people sitting around watching each other die, I would go mad.

She came again just before Christmas; but only to ask if I would like to have a dinner brought to my house Christmas Day. I said thank you very much, it was very kind, but it wasn't necessary, as I always go for dinner Christmas Day to my friends, the Le Boutilliers, who live in the house across the gully. She said she was glad I had friends so near. As a matter of fact, they are not really friends, young Jean and his wife, though I like the kids. It would be different if Julia was there; and I rue the day she ever went to work in a post-office in Essex and met that American airman. She lives in America now, and does not come home, even for Christmas. However, I asked the woman if she would like to come in and have a cup of tea. She said she would love one. I put a cloth on the table for her specially, and laid the tea properly and cut a cake I had in a tin. She was quite a nice woman really; and said no more about me having to be looked after. In fact, she said she thought I was wonderful for my age: I had such bright eyes and was so clear in the head. I felt the better for her visit.

To my surprise, several others came to see me, and brought me presents for Christmas: people I hardly knew. I got three Christmas puddings and a Christmas cake with almond paste and sugar on it, and a tin of cooked ham and enough fancy biscuits to stock a ship; but the greatest surprise of all was when Doris Hubert, Dora's daughter, came. She wanted me to spend Christmas Day with her and Ted Hubert and the children at the Robergerie; and said he could fetch me and bring me back in his car. I explained to her why I couldn't; but I wished I could have gone. She couldn't stay to tea because she was in a hurry to go home and get her husband's ready. I am ashamed to say I had tears in my eyes when I thanked her: I don't want to go soft in my old age. She wasn't as much like a mermaid as the first time I saw her; but she was wearing a very short skirt for the winter, and her legs must have been cold.

There had been a lot of fog before Christmas, and it is fog of all weathers makes me feel miserable; but after Christmas it was very rough, and I don't mind the rough weather so much. On rough days I often wrapped up well and went down on the beach to watch the white horses racing into the bay; or I would go for walks on L'Ancresse Common. I like it much better in the winter than in the summer: it must be more like Raymond said it was when the Clos-du-Valle was an island. I had as much as I could do to keep on my feet and not be blown over; and sometimes I didn't meet a soul. I don't think I went across the Common once without remembering Abel and how I had walked with him that afternoon and been raised up to the skies, only to be knocked down to the ground like the old fool I was.

One afternoon I made the round and came back by the Vale Church. It was sun and cloud and wind and very cold; and yet, for some reason I thought I would go in the churchyard before I went home. It don't make me sad, it cheers me up to see the graves: I feel here at least I am among Guernsey people. I had a look at my grandfather's. The gravestone is old and greenish, and there are others of my father's family buried there; but my grandfather's was the only name I could make out. Ah well, I thought, I will be under there myself before long. I didn't mind; but I got the feeling I wanted to go in the church. I don't go for the services, but that don't mean I wouldn't like to sometimes: only I can't bring myself to stand up and say with everybody I believe this and I believe that, when I am not at all sure in my own mind I do. I pushed open the heavy door and went in; and, as I expected, there wasn't nobody inside. There is something about a church and, for me, the Vale Church in particular, make it different from a Chapel, or a Mission Hall, or any other building. It isn't only a place where people go to sing and pray and listen to the preacher. It is the House of God. For hundreds of years people have gone there to worship and sing praises and say prayers and sleep through the sermon and be hypocrites for the rest of the week; but then, who isn't? My father took me to the Vale Church one Sunday when I was a small boy. I remember the one thing I wanted in the world at that time was a black oil-skin coat like my father wore when he went fishing. It was before I could read and, while the people was bent over praying the proper prayers from the book, I was praying in my own words to have my little oil-skin coat. The funny part of it is my prayer was answered; for my mother bought me one without my asking. I would never have dared to ask her.

It was peaceful inside the church, after being out in the wind. I stood looking at the font where I was christened. I found it hard to believe I had been a baby once and had the water sprinkled on me. I thought how strange it was one is born small to begin with and grow bigger and bigger, only to get old and small and shrivel up. I wonder why that have to be. I know the answer for me is not in the religion they teach you from the books; but it was in the very stones of the church I was standing in. They allow for everything can happen to a man from the rising to the setting of the sun. It is there you are given your name and it is there you are married, if you marry, and outside is the place where you are buried and your name put upon a stone; and in front of you, raised up for you to see, is the altar of God with a Cross upon it, and every man-jack ever born is on that Cross. It is true, it is true; and say what they like, it will be true, if they fly to Jupiter and put a sputnik round the sun!

I knelt down in a pew and said a little prayer. 'Please God,' I said, 'don't let what I got be wasted! Please! Please!' I don't know if He had time to listen to me; but the weather have got better, anyhow. These last weeks it have been a lovely early spring with wild flowers in bloom everywhere, and the gulls having and feeding families and making a hell of a row doing it. The birds outside my window are singing every morning when I wake up; and there is a cheeky blackbird perches on the apple-tree and whistles to me in a rude way every time I go out my back door. I can't help feeling lively in my old bones; and Friday when I went to Town to get my money I was prepared to be jolly even with Fish-eyes behind the desk. 'Spring is in the air, my boy!' I said; but he froze me with a look. 'Please check it is correct,' he said.

When I got out on the Esplanade I felt I didn't want to go home yet. I was thinking of old Steve Picquet, and how he would have wiped the floor with that slob. Steve may have been a wicked old bugger, but he made a hole in the air and sparks flew off him wherever he was. Fish-eyes is more of a ghost than a ghost. I thought I might as well have my dinner in the place at the corner of the States Arcade, where I had it with Steve that day; and I half expected to find the old rascal sitting in the room upstairs waiting for me. When I went in the girl said it was early for dinner, and would I have it downstairs? I said I would rather not and went up the stairs; but the room was empty. Steve wasn't there.

The girl was in no hurry to serve me; and I sat thinking how I had lost my knack with girls. That was brought home to me the day I went to the Press Shop in Smith Street to buy this book I am writing in. When I walked in the shop there was three or four girls who was supposed to be serving, but they was standing in a bunch nattering and took no more notice of me than if I was the Invisible Man. A time was when not one of those girls but wouldn't have noticed me, even if she made out not to. I walked straight through to the other part of the shop to look for my book for myself. There was a thin-faced youngish woman sitting at a desk, but she was busy talking to one of the bosses and had no eyes for me. I went to the shelf and picked out the book I wanted. I don't know if she thought I was going to walk off with it without paying, but she got up and came to me then and said, 'Can I help you?' 'I want this book, please,' I said. 'That will be eighteen-and-six,' she said. 'It is a lot of money for a book with no writing in,' I said. 'The price is inside the cover,' she said. 'Shall I wrap it up?' 'Yes, please,' I said. I gave her a pound note and she gave me the change. There wasn't a smile on her face. I don't expect she would know me again.

The waitress brought me up my dinner; and it wasn't bad. There was some soup and roast pork and a pudding after; and then I wanted a cup of tea; but each time the girl put something in front of me, it was with a heavy sigh. I thought perhaps I had been inconsiderate making her trot up and down the stairs so many times only for me; so I left her a square ten shillings under the plate for herself. Once I got outside I really meant to go down to the quay and get the bus home, for I had nothing to do in Town; but instead I found myself wandering through the meat market in a sort of dream. I was thinking of old Steve going to get bones for his dogs, and how the butcher didn't charge him for the bones, only for the small piece of meat he bought for himself. Well, Steve is dead and buried now; and so are the dogs. He made it known it was his wish for his dogs to be put to sleep when he died. I heard his wish was carried out; but they wasn't buried with him, as they ought to have been.

The meat market isn't anything like as good as it used to be, for most of the meat is either English or foreign; so I cut through to the vegetable, fruit and flower market, and then for a minute I thought I was really back in the old days. It was so lovely it hit you. The only difference was there wasn't the old Guernsey women in scoops and full dresses; but the early flowers and the fresh fruit was there, and the scent and the bright colours. I thought well, here at least is something the visitors won't see nowhere else as good. I thought then I would go through the fish market while I was about it, and perhaps buy a cut of conger, or something, for my supper; but it wasn't a good day. There wasn't much wet fish, and what there was didn't look fresh. The rest was dried or frozen stuff you could buy in a grocer's shop. This is not for me to eat. I was just going to turn out into Fountain Street, and really go home this time, when who should I see come in through the doorway at the far end, of all people in the world, but Master Neville Falla?

I stiffened; and thank God I got a straight back yet! There was no question now of me turning into Fountain Street, and giving his lordship the idea I was afraid to meet him! I couldn't help thinking what a well-grown, fine-looking boy he was. He swung in with his broad shoulders, and his head thrown back, as if he didn't care a bugger for anybody. He was looking to the right, and to the left, at everything around him; and himself looked fifty times more alive than anybody else in the market. He wasn't dressed so fancy as when I saw him before. He was wearing black trousers and a black leather jacket and a red check shirt open at the neck; but he wasn't trying to look like a cowboy on the loose. His black hair wasn't as long as such boys wear it, though long enough: but it is a fine head he got; and where have I seen those eyes?

I was looking straight ahead, as if I hadn't seen him; but summing him up out of the corner of my eye. I was ready for him, and, if he dared to say a word to me, he was going to get as good as he gave. He spotted me from some distance off, and his face broke into a grin; and he got a lovely grin. He was down on me on his long legs, before I had a chance to get out of his way, and had caught hold of me by the arm. I thought I must stand on my dignity against this young rapscallion; but I was helpless in his grip. 'Got yer!' he said. 'The master criminal I've been waiting to catch! Who is it rob the States and get a rise for it?' I was flabbergasted. 'Mind you, I'm not going to lay a charge,' he said. He let me go. I didn't know what to say. 'I don't believe you remember me,' he said, and looked quite put out. 'I remember you all right,' I said, 'but what I want to know is how is it you know my private business?' He laughed. He was happy again. 'Private Eye, Number One: that's me!' he said. 'I'm going to find out all there is to know about you. By the time I've done with you, I'll have shown you up for what you are, you'll see!' 'Well, you're welcome to try,' I said.

'The million dollar question,' he said: 'Who was it planted the ancient monument at the Chouey?' 'Planted?' I said. 'Stones don't grow.' He gave a comic sigh. 'No, but they move,' he said. 'Who was it moved those stones? Was it some neolithic people in something something B.C., or Ebenezer Le Page in A.D. 1930, or thereabouts?' 'All stones are old stones,' I said. He said, 'I wonder if anybody has ever got a straight answer to a straight question out of you?' I said, 'How is it you are so interested in the ancient monument, anyway?' 'I am interested in everything!' he said. He calmed down a little then and got a bit more reasonable. He said he did know part of the skeleton of an animal had been found. He had seen it for himself in the Museum and there are some odd marks on the jaw-bone. It was those marks made Mr McKendrick and other decide the set-up was genuine. I was finding out to my horror he knew more about it than I did. 'Yes, a small boy found that skeleton,' I said. 'I was in my garden watching at the time he found it; and I can tell you without a word of a lie he didn't make those marks on the jaw-bone; and I swear before Almighty God, I didn't!' 'In that case, I will have to take your word for it,' he said; but I could see he wasn't altogether satisfied.

'All right, then,' I said, 'now I will tell you the truth and the whole truth and nothing but the truth about the marks on that jaw-bone. I often heard my father say how his father, my grandfather, had a cow, an old Guernsey cow, called Annabelle. She was buried in that spot. She died of foot-in-mouth disease.' His eyes wrinkled and he opened his mouth and gave a roar; and doubled up laughing. I thought this is the boy I am going to leave my money to. He laugh at a Guernsey joke!

15

I was all shaken up inside: it was so important to me. I saw in a flash what I would have to do. I would have to get hold of a lawyer and make a will; but for that I would have to know more about Neville Falla: who he was and where he come from. I knew nothing about his father, Deputy Falla, except his name; nor where he had lived when he was alive. Nor could I ask the boy point blank. He must never know what I was up to. If ever I saw him again, I wanted him to be as free and easy with me as he had been those five minutes. I would have to think out ways and means. 'Well, I'll be going now,' I said. 'I must get home. I got a lot to do.' 'Hi, wait a minute!' he said. 'Can't I come and see you one day?' 'For sure!' I said. 'Any day you like. Say in the afternoon. If I'm not round the house, I'll be on the beach.' 'Good enough!' he said. 'I'll ask a sea-gull.' He put his hand up and grinned, and strode off through the fruit and flower market; and I turned out into Fountain Street. It was going to work out all right.

He came, but it wasn't until the Thursday afternoon; and every day before, I hoped. I had already written in my book on the Sunday night how I came to meet him; and then, the Tuesday evening, I saw his name in the *Press*. It was a wonder I noticed it, for it was the sort of thing I didn't bother to read, as a rule. There had been some paintings on show in the hall over the Market, and the *Press* had a picture of the four had won prizes. His was the first. It was called *Wildscape*. I looked at it this way, and I looked at it that; but I couldn't make head or tail of it. The third prize was for a painting of the Old Harbour by Rose Guérin. I could see what it was meant to be; and it was her I would have given the first prize to.

The Thursday morning I thought well, if he don't come today, I don't expect he will come this week; and perhaps won't come at all. I couldn't blame him really, for why should he want to come and see an old man? but I knew if he didn't come I would be bitterly disappointed. In the afternoon when I had washed up after dinner, I went down on the beach, so as not to think about him. It was a beautiful sunny afternoon and the sea was far out and very blue, and there was not a ripple. I sat on the flat rock dreaming of the days gone by; when I used to sit there with Tabitha, or Raymond. I can't sit down for five minutes anywhere nowadays, without I float back and dream of the days gone by; yet I was listening for the sound of his motor-bike and longing to hear it, much as I hate the things. I heard somebody coming down over the stones, and wondered who it was; but I didn't bother to look round. The next thing I knew was he had slid down the rock and was sitting quietly beside me. He wears soft shoes and moves like a cat, so I hadn't heard him once he got off the shingle on to the sand. 'Here I am!' he said. 'Aw, it's you,' I said. 'I didn't hear the bike.' 'I walked over,' he said. 'Well, you've chosen a fine day,' I said.

'I suppose you know what I have come for,' he said. 'I haven't the least idea,' I said. 'I owe you something,' he said. 'I don't like being in debt.' 'Well, that is a good way to be,' I said, 'but you don't owe me nothing I know of.' He pulled out a handful of money from his hip pocket. 'I want to pay you for those panes of glass I broke,' he said. That really did take me by surprise. 'There is no need for you to do that,' I said. 'It wasn't a few panes of glass broke hurt me. It was that somebody I didn't even know, and had never done any harm to, hated me enough to come and damage my property.' 'I didn't hate you,' he said, 'I wasn't thinking of you, or your property: you were just another old square.' 'Now what exactly do you mean by that?' I said. 'Don't you know?' he said. 'No,' I said. 'It is hard to explain,' he said. 'The square is why we others are crooked. Anyway, you win. How much is it?' 'For Christ's sake, put that money away!' I said. 'If you want to pay your debt, give up smashing things. Violence never did nobody no good.' He didn't like that very much. His eyes went cold and hard, the way I had seen them at the Police Station; but he was looking at me very straight. 'Have you never been violent in your life, Mr Le Page?' he said. It was me had to look away. 'I am not saying do as I have done,' I said. 'I am not an example for any man to follow.' He stretched himself out on the rock and laughed up at me. 'I like you,' he said.

I like him too; but he isn't going to be all that easy to keep the peace with. He is like some young wild animal, who expect everybody older to trap him; and he is all the time watching out in case. I have to be careful what I say, or he shuts up like a clam. For the time being, he was quite at ease lying beside me in the sun, chatting merrily about his affairs. He had started that week on the line at Bulwer Avenue. Hours and hours doing exactly the same thing; and every movement watched. He hated it. He had done all sorts of jobs, on and off. He had worked on Herm with some other lads for Major Wood one summer, and he had tried Jersey, where he had worked in a hotel; yet he had been to the Grammar School and had a good education. I didn't understand it. I had thought he might be working for the States, since he knew what I had been up to; and I asked him how he knew. He wasn't going to tell me at first; but then he said, 'She won't mind: she likes you. It was Adèle told me.' 'Adèle? Adèle who?' I said. 'Adèle de la Rue,' he said, 'the girl in the desk.' 'You know her, then?' I said. 'I know her very well,' he said. 'She is a darn nice girl,' I said. 'I know she is a nice girl,' he said. 'Mind you I'm not in love with her.' 'Why ever not?' I said, 'I would be, if I was your age.' 'I don't fall in love,' he said; and stuck his chin out, as if it was the biggest insult in the world for me to think he might. Is it a sort of monster he is?

I wanted to know if Adèle got herself into trouble with the boss because of me. He said she had known what I was doing, but it wasn't her responsibility; and she let it pass. All the same, it was her got the blame; and she flared up and left. She needn't have done so, but was glad of the excuse. She was fed up with it there. I said I had wondered if the young chap I had seen in the office with her and who took her place was her fiancé. 'What, that drip!' he said. 'She won't marry anybody, let me tell you, unless I give her the O.K. She looks on me as a father.' I began to wonder if young Neville was as clever as he thought. Her real father was dead, he said; and her mother was married again and gone to Canada. Adèle was living with an aunt who kept a shop at St Andrews; and now she had gone back to serve in the shop. 'I do hope she is going to be all right,' I said. 'It don't sound much of a job.' He said, 'Adèle knows her way around, don't you worry. She will only stay there as long as it suits her.'

I asked him if he could spare the time to come indoors and have a cup of tea. 'As long as you like,' he said. 'Good!' I said. I hadn't found out half I wanted to know about him yet. When I struggled to get to my feet, he jumped up and held out a hand to help me. I said I could manage; but he have nice ways. He hadn't said nothing about his painting, so while we was walking up the beach, I said, 'I saw the picture you painted in the paper; unless there is another Neville Falla.' 'There are a number of other Neville Fallas,' he said, 'but I am the culprit.' 'What is it supposed to be?' I said. 'What it says,' he said. 'I am glad you got the first prize,' I said, 'but I wish I knew why.' 'Of course it has to be looked at in the right way,' he said. 'In any case, it is only a blur in black and white. From how it was printed in the *Press*, nobody could possibly make any sense of it.' Suddenly he caught hold of my arm and stopped, looking up at Les Moulins. 'Now that would make a good picture!' he said. It was a funny view from down there; but with the flowers in front and the path and the edge of the rocks, and the tree and the wind-mill behind, I could see it might look all right. That is, if I would know what it was, when he had done with it. What struck me as funny was here was me going to leave him that house to live in; and all he was thinking about was he wanted to paint a picture of it!

The moment he got in the kitchen, the first thing he noticed was my Uncle Nat's ship on the wall. 'God, did you do that?' he said. I said no: it was done by my uncle years ago. 'Are there any more of his about?' he said. 'I don't expect so,' I said. 'They went to his sisters when he died; and that was the only one my mother had. She didn't want it, and only let me bring it because she didn't want to make bad feeling in the family. The others will long ago have been thrown away as junk.' I knew Hetty hung one in a back bedroom for years where nobody would see it. 'They are only done with wool,' I said. 'It doesn't matter what a picture is made of,' he said. Since he was so interested, I told him how my uncle was making that particular picture while his mother was dying in the next room. 'He didn't know it,' I said. 'He was soft in the head.' 'I bet he did know it,' said Neville. 'It's marvellous!' I said, 'Well, that is one thing you and me agree about, because I have always liked that picture; and have never got tired of seeing it on my wall.'

I gave him a good tea. I'd got something special ready every day in case he came: which I'd had to eat up myself. That day I had a fresh chancre I had cooked in the copper the day before. While I was laying the table, he sprawled full length on the green-bed I had kept in the kitchen since Tabitha died, so as I would myself be able to sleep by the fire. 'Can I do anything to help?' he said. 'No, you're all right where you are,' I said. I liked to see him there. 'Shall I go to Canada, or to Australia, or New Zealand?' he said. 'I would have more room, eh? What do you think?' I felt myself go cold. I didn't want a day ever to come when he wouldn't be coming in and out of the house, as if it was his home; and sprawling on the green-bed and me getting him ready a meal: but he was like a firework going off in all directions at once. I got the feeling he was half asking me to make up his mind for him; but I dare not, or ten to one he would go and do exactly the opposite. 'It is for you to decide where you go to,' I said. 'I can't compare Guernsey to other places, because I have never been to any other places; except for one day to Jersey to see the Muratti.' 'Do you really mean to say you have lived every day of your life in this house?' he said. 'Slept here every night, eaten every meal in this room?' 'Well, I have eaten a few meals elsewhere,' I said, 'and slept at the Huts when I was in the Militia, and usually Saturday nights and always New Year's Eve at Les Grands Gigands when my friend, Jim Mahy, was living there.' 'I never have a friend,' he said; and out came the chin. 'Come on, eat up now!' I said. I wasn't having no more of that nonsense.

The table was laid rough. I poured out the tea in the blue and white mugs without saucers I got from Woolworth's, and the vinegar bottle was on the table: I couldn't be bothered to use the proper cruet. There was a hammer to crack the claws with, and a nut-cracker I use for nuts at Christmas for the legs; and I cut him good thick slices of bread and butter. He tucked in as if he hadn't had a meal for a week. I wondered if the boy was having enough to eat. Suddenly he said, arising out of nothing, 'I think I would do best to make a go of it here: I don't think I could paint anywhere else.' I didn't let my joy show. 'I hear the visitors raving about the scenery,' I said, 'but I don't notice it myself. I like the sea.' 'They don't see the scenery, or the sea, or anything!' he said. 'They only look at it. It is in me from the start. Guernsey it shall be!' I thought it safe to say then, 'Well, I, for one, am very glad to hear it.' 'Unless they push me off,' he said, 'I am not very popular in some quarters.' I thought it best to say nothing. He wasn't to know I knew Constable Le Page.

He wanted to help me clear away; but I said we could leave the things for now and go for a stroll. It was much too fine to stop indoors. 'Your word is law,' he said. I found myself taking him along the very same way I had gone with Abel. Now I look back on it, it seems as if everything was said and done that afternoon might all have been arranged beforehand. I didn't have to think, or make up my mind, only take the next step. Just outside our gate, we met two of the Le Boutillier children, John and Peter. They are seventeen and fifteen, and was coming to see if I was all right. They gave me a funny look, when they saw I was with Neville, and just said 'Hullo!' and walked on. 'They are real good to me, those two kids,' I said. 'They come and see how I am nearly every day.' 'I can't stand kids hanging round me,' he said. 'I don't want anybody hanging round me!' I wondered what had bitten him all of a sudden. 'How is it you are so much like a hedgehog?' I said. 'I am not a teenager!' he said. I said, 'When you are the oldest on the island, as I am, you will only wish you could be a teenager!' 'Who is the oldest on the island?' he said. 'How about old Mrs Renouf from L'Islet, who is a hundred and two? Are you a hundred and three, then?' I said, 'Well, I don't know if I am quite as old as that.' 'Of course you are not as old as that,' he said, 'nor anywhere near it! You are an old sprucer, that is what you are!' Anyhow, it got him into a good temper again.

He is not bad-natured: it is something else. He is good at heart really; that is, so long as you don't let him know it. He kept a kindly eye on me, as if I was a kid he had to look after. He was careful not to walk faster than I could go; and, when we got to Fort Pembroke, he found a comfortable place for me to sit in the sun with my back against a smooth stone. I was being looked after; and I liked it. He threw himself flat on his tummy on the grass in front of me, and grinned up at me. 'Mustn't take any notice of what I say,' he said, 'I am a misfit. I was hatched in the wrong nest.' For the minute, I thought he meant his father wasn't really his father, or his mother not really his mother. He read my thought. 'Lord, no!' he said, and laughed. 'I am not a bastard. It might have been better for me, if I had been. If you had known my mother and my father, you would wonder how it was I ever managed to get born at all!'

His father he had been against as long as he could remember. He was ready to like his mother, but she had always been afraid of him; and that made him angry. In looks he didn't take after either. His mother was fair to gingery and had been beautiful, he thought, when she was young; but she married late, and was pale and delicate after his birth. He didn't remember his grandparents; but knew his grandfather was killed in the First World War. His own father was dark with black hair like himself; but short and stocky. He was a man of good character, who always did the right thing. 'He was the best man I have ever known for keeping his eye on the main chance,' said Neville, 'and he could always think up a good and pious reason for doing so.' He was only a greenhouse hand before the Occupation; but he worked so hard and behaved himself so well, he had made a small fortune in German marks to change into English money after the Liberation. There was a ruined house at Paradise called Sea View, where slave-workers had been living, which was going for next to nothing. He bought it with the land attached, and had it done up; then got married to complete the picture. As a grower on his own account, he did well and was elected one of the new Deputies. He sat on a committee for the growers and Deputy H.J.Le M. Falla of Sea View was a name spoken only in a tone of respect: except by Neville. He was born and brought up at Sea View. 'I came from a good home,' he said, 'a good Christian home. Billy Graham's photo on the piano; and only hymns on Sundays.'

His mother was genteel. She came, or thought she came, of a better family. In the house everything had to be so-so. It was covers on the cushions, d'oyleys on the table, and never a speck of dust anywhere. If she had heard a swear word she would have dropped dead. Neville, in spite of himself, was urged by some devil to do everything he wasn't supposed to do. He finished up by knocking round with the roughest types of St Sampson's and the Vale; only to find himself the leader of a gang of hooligans, who repeated every word he said and copied him in everything he did. 'If there is one thing makes you sick of yourself,' he said, 'it is to see yourself being imitated by a gang of nit-witted hangers-on! It makes you realise there is something very wrong with you, if that can happen.' He had succeeded in shaking them off; but now the good people had no use for him because of his bad reputation, and the wild youngsters didn't trust him and steered clear of him. That was quite to his satisfaction. It was only when he was painting he felt good; even if the painting itself wasn't good. 'Practically everybody is after power,' he said, 'power over other people. Well, I can have it, if I want it; but I don't want it! It isn't worth a tinker's curse! The only power I want is over my paints and brushes.' He was going on painting, and painting what he wanted to paint, and painting it in his own way. For the rest, he didn't care a damn!

He was pretty near broke. His house, Sea View, was let and was going to be sold to the people living in it; but there wouldn't be much left for him to play about with, when the debts on it was paid. For the present, he was living in a room in the attic, and feeding out at cafés as best he could. 'I hope you got a good lawyer to manage your affairs,' I said. 'Yes, I have, as a matter of fact,' he said, 'Eustace de Lisle.' I said, 'I had an uncle who used to work for a de Lisle who lived in the Grange.' 'I don't know where he lives,' he said, 'his office is with the Advocates.' 'Robbers' Row,' I said, 'that is what my father used to call it.' 'Oh, he is not as bad as that,' he said. 'He does his best for me.' 'I don't know him,' I said. I wasn't asking any more. He had let out exactly what I wanted to know. 'It is getting a bit fresh out here now,' I said, 'how about coming back indoors and having a snack before you go home?' 'Rightio!' he said.

I cooked him a good meal of ham and eggs, and he gollopped it down with mugs of tea. I chatted about the visitors I had staying with me, and told him about the old girl who hid behind the pigsty. He roared with laughter. It is his laugh saves him. It warms the world. I was sorry when he had to go. I walked down the road with him as far as the Vale Church. 'I have thoroughly enjoyed myself,' he said, when he wished me good-bye, 'I really and truly have.' 'Then come again whenever you like,' I said. 'Next time I will bring my painting things,' he said, 'and see what I can make of your house.' I trotted back to Les Moulins feeling lively as a cricket. I don't know when I have felt so well. I had no sooner put my head on the pillow than I was sound asleep.

16

The next morning I woke up feeling flat as a pancake. I had as much as I could do to spruce myself up to go to Town and get my money. I knew I ought at the same time to go and see that lawyer, but I had great doubts in my mind if, after all, what I was going to do was for the best. It wasn't because I thought Neville was a young criminal; and, to tell you the truth, I didn't care if he was. He was innocent, as Raymond used to say, and I wondered if it was right for me to interfere, and perhaps change the course of his whole life. I interfered in Raymond's case, and it didn't do much good. I have the excuse Raymond was helpless, and couldn't fight his own way out; but Neville is the fighting sort, and will fight his way out of any trouble, if only to land himself into a worse. Yet I took out the few papers have to do with the house from the drawer in the dresser and put them safely in my inside pocket. If I did it, it might turn out bad; but if I didn't, it might turn out bad too. How was I to know which would be the worse? The truth was the thought of not doing it made me lose heart, and feel I had nothing to live for. I can only say it is something for which Neville will never have to thank me. I am doing it for myself: to keep alive.

I went to Town and after I came out of the States Offices nearly killed myself, by being fool enough to climb up the Pier Steps. I thought it would save time. I got to the top puffing and blowing, and my old heart going like a hammer; and saw myself dropping dead in the middle of the High Street. I must never do that again. When I had recovered more or less, I walked slowly up Smith Street; and, at the top, I stopped to have a look at Jim's name on the War Memorial. I don't expect there is anybody on the island now who remembers what he was like; and yet I could see his old smile as plain as if it was only yesterday I had seen him. I turned to the left and passed in front of the Court; but I don't know my way around there very well. It is a part of the town I have never been to much, and there have been a lot of new big offices built down Robbers' Row. I examined the brass plates on the doorposts, and was lucky, for only the second block along I found one with Eustace de Lisle's name on it. The front door was open and I walked in. On the right, in a small room with a desk and a lot of papers, was a girl with pale yellow hair done up like a beehive on the top of her head, and a skirt up round her neck, and hands that flapped like the fins of a fish. 'Can I help you?' she said.

'Please can I speak to Mr Eustace de Lisle?' I said. 'I am afraid not,' she said. 'He is engaged at present.' 'It is important,' I said. 'If you will give me some idea of what it is about,' she said, 'I can tell you if it is business Mr de Lisle will care to undertake.' I said, 'It is Mr de Lisle himself I want to speak to.' I wasn't going to tell this slip of a girl all my business. 'In that case, you could write,' she said. 'It is not something I can write myself,' I said, 'I want to explain to Mr de Lisle; and it is him who will have to write it down.' 'I could book you an appointment,' she said, 'but there will be a fee.' I could see she thought I didn't have a penny to my name. 'I don't mind about the fee,' I said, 'but I only come to Town Fridays.' She opened a book and turned over the pages. It was a thick book with hard covers like the books I buy for myself. 'Mr de Lisle could see you next Friday morning at eleven,' she said, 'if that will be convenient.' 'I suppose it will have to be,' I said. She asked for my name and address to put down in the book; and I had to tell her. 'Thank you, good-morning,' I said and came out. It was a smack in the eye for me. I had hoped to have it all settled that morning; and imagined myself coming home with the will in my pocket. Now I expect I will have to pay seven-and-six for her writing down my name and address.

I could have kicked myself when I got outside for not saying I could go and see him on the Monday, but it didn't enter my head when I was in the office. The idea of having to wait a whole week was almost more than I could bear.How about if something was to happen to me before the next Friday? All the winter I hadn't cared a button if I woke up from one day to the next; but now there was something I wanted to do, I was worried to death I might pop off any minute. The Sunday evening I got out my book and wrote down about the day Neville came to see me. It brought him back to me with all his sparks and full of life, and I wanted more than ever for him to live in Les Moulins some day, and I didn't care how soon. I knew I would have to wait at least until the Thursday before I could expect to see him again, for the other days he would be working; and for my part I went about my work from day to day as if I was going to live for ever, and tried not to worry or get excited.

The moment I woke up on the Thursday morning I knew it was going to be a good day. I felt as I used to feel Christmas morning when I was a kid, and woke up knowing Santa Claus would have put something in my stocking; though I had been told it was my father really, for my mother said Santa Claus was a heathen superstition. I didn't care if it was superstition, and would have bet anything Neville would come; and, sure enough, I was just finishing my dinner, when in he walked by the back door. 'Hullo!' he said, 'and how is Ebenezer?' I noticed it wasn't Mr Le Page this time.

'Fine!' I said. 'I've brought my gear,' he said. He was carrying an easel and a stool, and had a box slung over his shoulder, and several pictures under one arm. He unloaded the lot on to the green-bed. 'How about something to eat before you begin?' I said. 'No, thanks,' he said. 'I wouldn't mind a cup of tea.' 'Help yourself, then,' I said. He got a mug from the dresser and poured himself a mugfull. He would have made a good picture himself, as he stood there drinking it. He was wearing a blue vest with red rings around it, and blue trousers with sandals; but no socks. For a minute I hated him because he was young and fine-looking, and I was an old crab. He had everything to come, and I had nothing to look forward to; but I couldn't hate him for long. He was far better to look at than I had ever been; and I was glad he would be in the world when I was gone.

'I have brought a few of my great works to show you,' he said. 'I won't understand,' I said, 'I don't know nothing about pictures.' 'There is nothing to understand,' he said, 'and you don't have to know about pictures. All you got to do is look at 'em.' He stood one up on a chair by the window, so as to catch the light. 'Another Wildscape,' he said. It was a picture full of wild and lovely colours, but I was frowning: I couldn't make out what it was meant to be. 'It is too near for you to be able to see it as a whole,' he said, and moved the chair further away. 'Why, that's in Fontenelle Bay!' I said. 'Right first go!' he said. The rough sea was pouring over a lop-sided rock, and there was clouds heavy with rain and rain falling, and rays of sunshine coming from between the clouds and across the rain and shining bright on the sea. It was so real to me I wouldn't have been surprised if I had heard the wind blowing. 'It's good, that!' I said. 'At least it's better than the one got the prize,' he said. That was of the Pea-Stacks in a storm. 'Too obvious,' he said. A gentleman in Town bought it for twenty quid.

I thought that was a lot of money to pay for a picture. 'Well, that's a good beginning, anyway,' I said. 'It will give me a couple of weeks off,' he said, 'but it is a warning.' 'How d'you mean?' I said. 'I mustn't paint with the Market in mind,' he said, 'that would be the end of me.' I said, 'Render unto Caesar the things that are Caesar's, and unto God the things that are God's.' He gave me a quick look. 'Something like that,' he said. He raved on about painting; but most of it I didn't understand. He had no use for this: he had no use for that. He was a modern; and against the moderns. He thought many of the old painters had more to teach the young painter than any modern. As for abstract art, it was long past the time to have grown out of such nonsense. He had more sympathy with the lunatic fringe. It was genuine to the painter: to start with, at least. He must beware. A chap can make a fortune by going fashionably mad. 'I will be post-modern; or nothing,' he said. 'All I want to paint is the real feel of the actual thing in front of me. I will never get to it, I know; but I can try.' I liked him very much when he was talking about his painting. For all his swagger, Neville is humble really.

I couldn't help thinking how, in his place, I would have put that twenty quid away for a rainy day; but I didn't say anything and let him go on showing me the others. There was one of Birdo Harbour at low tide, and Herm quite close. It was evening, and shining peaceful with a few boats quiet on the sea. He thought it was the best he had done so far, and I thought it was good; but the one I liked best myself was of L'Ancresse Common. He had written underneath it *Defences*. It wasn't L'Ancresse Common quite as it is now, for he had left out the bungalows and the new buildings; nor was there any sign of it being a golf links, and Fort Le Marchant with its many windows was not a ruin, but looked as if there might be soldiers living in it yet. There was a grey martello tower quite near, and the others in the distance guarding the full round of the bay. The colours of the sand and of the few rocks, and of the sea and the sky, was really wonderful in that picture; and as different as imaginable from those of the glaring colours of the views of Guernsey they sell in the shops in Town. 'What I like about your pictures,' I said, 'is they are quite different from picture-postcards. They sing.' He said, 'That is the most encouraging remark ever made about my work. I only paint because I am not musical.' I said, 'What I don't understand about your pictures is there are no human beings in them. There is not a living soul on L'Ancresse, or anywhere else.' 'Human beings spoil the picture,' he said. 'I can do with some of the things they have left behind.'

He was in a hurry to get on with it, and picked up his stool and easel and box, and was going. 'Don't wait for me for tea,' he said, 'I won't show up until I got something done.' 'You'll have a meal before you go home, I hope,' I said. 'Thanks very much,' he said. He hadn't given me very much time to look at his pictures properly; and when he was gone I had another look at them. There was some of places on the island I had never been to: rocks and cliffs on the south coast, I think; and one glorious with golden gorse. Those of places I knew I thought even more of the second time I looked at them: there was so much I had missed the first. I couldn't have been more wrong judging from the picture in the *Press*. There was nothing mixed-up or slapdash when you stood away and looked at the whole thing, and all the colours fell together. Afterwards, when I had washed up the dinner things and got the room tidy, I pottered round in the green-house and outside. I can't say how happy I was to think he was down on the beach painting; and would be coming back to have a meal with me when he had done. He wasn't in by five, so I made myself some tea; but didn't eat much. I was wondering what he would like for his supper. I had some fresh whiting I could cook with fried potatoes; or he could have ham and eggs again. It was after seven when he came in. He looked dog-tired, and flopped down on the green-bed. 'God, it does take it out of you!' he said. 'Well, food now!' I said, and asked him which he would like. 'The whiting, if it's not too much trouble,' he said, 'but first have a look at your picture.'

There was enough light yet to see it by, and he stood it on a chair by the window. It was painted on thick card. Well, nobody could have any doubt what it was meant to be. It was Les Moulins and no other house; and even more old-fashioned than it is. It was childish and comic in a way. I had to laugh. The walls got narrower as they went up, and the chimney-stacks smaller; but the windows shone brightly in the sun. The wallflowers in front was really beautiful; and there was the old grey wall of the garden, and the white gate, and the green front door. The apple-tree at the side was skew-jiffy, and the windmill was peeping over the roof. There was no other house in sight, though there are several to be seen now from where he was looking; but those he had left out. He got in some of the rocks and sea, and a patch of beach, and the patch and the hill behind. A lot of it was rough done with thick paint, and the granite of the house looked as if it was really granite; but the sky behind and around was smooth, and in all the lovely colours from pink and pale yellow to a clear, clear blue I could see fading through the window. It made the house stand out real and solid on a foundation of solid earth at the edge of the sea. He was watching my face while I was looking at it. 'Well, what's the verdict?' he said. 'It's lovely,' I said, 'it really is! It is my house; and yet it is not my house. It is something more.' He took it off the chair and had a look at it, as if he was in doubt himself. 'I hope it's as good as you say,' he said. 'Anyhow, it takes two to make a picture: the chap who paints it and the chap who looks at it. It isn't a thing in itself.' 'What's it going to be called?' I said. He gives names to all his pictures. 'I haven't done that yet,' he said, 'but I will now.' He wrote with a thick pencil on the left-hand at the bottom in his beautiful handwriting *The House of Ebenezer Le Page*.

I was going to say he must take great care of it because somebody would be sure to want to buy it, when he said, 'Where are we going to hang it?' I was so surprised I couldn't speak. 'It's for you, you know,' he said. I bustled about getting the supper ready, and didn't even say thank you. I was afraid I might break down. He was looking round the room to find a place for it. 'I think on the mantelpiece will do for now,' he said. It is a high narrow mantelpiece; and he moved aside some of the things on it to make room. 'I hope it won't get dirty up there,' I said. 'It won't for a day or two,' he said. 'I'll make a frame for it, and bring it along: then we can think of the right place for it.' When the supper was ready, I pulled down the blinds and lit the lamp. He drew a chair up to the table, as if he was the son of the house. 'Golly, this is good!' he said. 'It look nice, my picture,' I said, 'even by the light of the lamp.' 'It's not too bad,' he said.

He didn't go until after eleven, and didn't seem to want to go then. I don't think he fancied going back to his lonely room in the attic. After supper he insisted on helping me wash up; and then we sat by the fire talking. He asked me if I had ever been married. I said I hadn't. 'Why not?' he said, 'I thought in your day every chap had to get married.' 'I don't know why not,' I said. I wanted to give him a truthful answer; and it was the only truthful answer I could think of. To this day I don't know how it was Liza and me was always at cross purposes. He said, 'Didn't you want to?' I said, 'Yes, I wanted to; and I am not so sure she didn't want to as well: but never when I wanted to.' 'You could have married somebody else,' he said. 'I couldn't really,' I said. 'Then she must have been a fool,' he said. 'Perhaps it was me who was the fool,' I said.

'I am not walking three paces behind any woman,' he said, 'however wonderful she may think she is; and I don't want a woman walking three paces behind me. I would say for Christ's sake team up with a bloke your own measure. Anyhow, why the hell get married at all, if it is only to be divorced in a few years?' 'Ah well, you can always live in sin,' I said, 'It might last longer. I had a great uncle who lived in sin for donkey's years; and they never got divorced.' 'I don't want to live in sin!' he said; and out came that obstinate chin I was getting to know so well. I said, 'It don't matter what you do in this world, you will find you got to live in sin, one way or the other.' 'You're cheerful, aren't you?' he said. 'That is my experience,' I said. 'It is mine too,' he said. 'The kids think sex ad lib is heaven; but it isn't. It isn't more sex is wanted: it's less and better. Or something else.' I thought goodness, who is it who is the puritan now? I said, 'All I hope is you are luckier than me.'

'Fuck having a woman!' he said, 'I am going to buy a car.' 'Whatever do you want to buy a car for?' I said. 'To get round with my gear,' he said. 'Why else?' 'They cost a lot of money, cars,' I said. 'I will be able to afford it, just,' he said. His motor-bike was going to pay for part of it, and the balance was coming from what little was left over from the sale of the house. 'My last extravagance!' he said. 'Henceforward, hard labour!' I was angry with him for going to throw away his money on a car; and yet, I thought, there is nothing mean about him. He is not one to bury his talent in the ground. All the people I have liked most in my life have been the very opposite to me. Jim, Liza, Raymond, Tabitha, my Uncle Nat: none of them was mean; but, if the truth was known, I have always been a mean little sod myself. I have always held something back, and seen to it I kept on the safe side. It is good to be shown up in your old age for what you are.

He had got up then and was gathering together his things ready to go. I said, 'What is yours is yours, my boy; and it is for you to spend it how you like. I want you to remember I said that: and, if ever it comes to hard labour, I can always find you work to do here for a living.' 'Thanks a lot,' he said. 'It is work I would enjoy; but I am not sure I want to earn my daily bread working for a friend.' He gave me a quick, shy smile, and was gone in a flash. I said, 'Thank you for the picture,' but I don't think he heard me.

17

I didn't sleep a wink that night. I was afraid to. I lay down on the green-bed; but every time I felt myself going off, I sat up with a jerk. I didn't want to wake up and find myself dead. I was up with the sun, and washed and shaved and having my breakfast, before young Ogier turned up for work. I had no doubt in my mind any more about it being good for Neville to have the house. He would always have somewhere to live, and a way of making a living; and he liked the place and felt at home in it already, and was willing to work. I put the papers in my pocket and caught an early bus to Town and got off at the Weighbridge. I collected my money from the States Offices, but wasn't going to risk going up those Pier Steps again. I went back along the front and up the Pollet; and had a cup of coffee in a café on the way. It was stuff out of a bottle, and no good, but it helped to pass the time. When I got to the top of Smith Street, it was only a quarter to eleven by the clock in the Post Office, but I thought I might as well go straight along to Mr de Lisle's office. It didn't matter if I was a few minutes early. I could wait.

I didn't have to. The she-iceberg said, 'Mr de Lisle is expecting you,' and led the way through her office, and out by another door into his. I had expected an untidy room, hanging with cobwebs and stacked with dusty old papers, but it was new and clean with steel cupboards against the walls. There was another room I could see through a glass door where several young chaps was writing, and a girl typing. 'Mr Ebenezer Le Page by appointment,' said Miss Beehive. Mr de Lisle was sitting at his desk. 'Thank you, Miss Fitch,' he said; and she went out and shut the door. He wasn't at all my idea of a lawyer. He looked more like a young doctor. I had imagined a crafty old man with wrinkles and a bald head, but he was quite young, hardly forty I would say, and had a smooth face, and fair silky hair neatly parted on one side. It was a clever face, I thought, but kind too. He got up from his chair, and came round the desk and shook hands with me. 'I am glad to make your acquaintance, Mr Le Page,' he said, 'I have heard of you, of course, but hitherto haven't had the pleasure of meeting you.' I wonder what it is everybody have heard about me. People seem to know more about me than I know myself. He arranged a comfortable chair for me to sit in and then sat down at his desk facing me. I was glad it was him I had come to.

'Now how can I be of service to you?' he said. 'I want to make a will,' I said. 'I am getting on in years.' 'A sensible course of action,' he said, 'at any time of life.' 'At my time of life, at any rate,' I said. 'Have you not previously made a will?' he said. 'No, never,' I said, 'I am not one who believes in going to lawyers.' 'Very wise of you, no doubt,' he said, 'but there are occasions when we have our uses.' 'When my mother was alive,' I said, 'our family affairs was in the hands of Advocate Randall. He is dead now, so I couldn't go to him.' 'Quite so,' he said. 'I saw your name on the pillar of the door,' I said, 'and I thought you would do as good as any.' I wasn't going to tell him I knew he was Neville's lawyer. 'I hope I do,' he said, 'I mustn't let my name down.' 'Aw, it is not going to be much of a will,' I said, 'I am leaving all I got to one person, so it won't cost much to draw up; and you won't make much out of it.' He raised his eyebrows, and opened his eyes wide. It was a way he had for he did it a number of times while I was with him.

He got out his fountain pen, put a clean sheet of paper in front of him, and wrote across the top Ebenezer Le Page, Esquire. 'Have you any other name, or names?' he said. 'No, no other names,' I said. 'Les Moulins, now let me think,' he said, 'is it in St Sampson's, or the Vale?' 'The Vale,' I said. He wrote down my address. 'Have you any near relations, or legal descendants?' he said. 'None,' I said, 'the nearest are third or fourth cousins.' 'Now may I have the name and address of the person you propose to make your sole legatee?' he said. 'Neville Falla of Sea View, Paradise, Vale,' I said. His eyebrows went up again, and he put down his pen. 'Is he a connection by marriage?' he said. 'He is no relation,' I said. He said, 'I want you to understand you are at perfect liberty to dispose of your possessions as you feel inclined, provided they are legally disposed of, but may I ask you, as a matter of interest, why it is you have chosen Mr Neville Falla to benefit?' I didn't mind telling him really, but, after all, he was only a lawyer and there was some things he wouldn't understand. 'He is not a sheep,' I said.

'I happen to be acquainted with Mr Neville Falla,' he said, 'and I concur with you entirely, when you say he is not a sheep. He is in that respect different from a great many, perhaps the majority, of his generation. They make a loud noise and are often a downright nuisance, here as elsewhere; but they blindly follow the trend of the moment and, taken singly, are not much of a menace. Neville Falla, on the other hand, can be a dangerous nuisance, if he sets his mind to it, for he is not a coward, and he is not stupid; but, given his own head, he is not malign. He may well prove a notable credit to our island yet. He has more than talent as a painter.' 'I know,' I said. 'All-in-all,' he said, 'far from saying you are ill-advised, I congratulate you on giving Neville a chance.' I could have hugged him for sticking up for Neville.

'Well, it isn't I got all that much to leave him,' I said. 'I am not a rich man. There is the house and the furniture and the ground and the greenhouse and the out-houses; and some money I have saved. That is all.' I handed him the papers I had brought with me; and explained the house was my grandfather's first, and then my father's and, when my father died, came to me as the eldest and only son. It was for my mother to live in while she lived; and my sister was living with me her last years. She had no children. I had lived in it on my own since. It was in good condition and repair; and there was nothing owing on it. I had included among the papers the last receipt for tax for him to see. He gave the lot a quick glance, and said it all appeared to be straightforward and in order; but he would have to check up at the Greffe, and would like to keep the papers while the will was in preparation. It sounded as if I was going to have to wait another week. 'That will mean me having to wait,' I said, 'I may not be here so long.' He said I looked hale and hearty; and if he looked as fit as I did, and had his wits about him as I have, when he was my age, he would consider himself a very lucky man. However, he would get it done as quickly as possible to put my mind at rest, but I must be patient. He didn't want to draw me up a will about which there could be any dispute later on. 'I notice you haven't included a bank statement,' he said. 'Who are your bankers?' 'Goodness, I don't have no money in the bank!' I said. He said, 'I understood you to say a sum of money was involved.'

'Yes,' I said, 'there is money in the china fowl I use from day to day; and a tin on the mantelpiece marked Sugar full of curly threepenny pieces; and a tin marked Tea full of square ten-shillingses; and bundles of pound notes and bundles of five-pound notes under a board in the bottom of the grandfather clock; and a cash-box full of sovereigns buried under the apple-tree.' Mr de Lisle put down his pen, and gave me a very old-fashioned look. 'Are you by any chance pulling my leg, Mr Le Page?' he said. 'I wouldn't dream of pulling your leg, Mr de Lisle,' I said. I had written down the exact amounts on a piece of paper, and put it in my waistcoat pocket; and now I gave it to him. It added up to a nice few thousand. I said, 'The sovereigns will be worth three or four times now what they was then; so that will be a few thousand more.'

'Has it slipped your memory,' he said, 'sovereigns ceased to be legal tender in Guernsey thirty or forty years ago, I can't say off-hand exactly when?' 'Oh no, I remember quite well,' I said, 'it said in the *Press* they must be taken to a bank, and changed for paper money; but my mother thought it was better to keep them where moth and rust do not corrupt, nor thieves break through and steal: so we kept them in the pied-du-cauche up the chimney in the wash-house. When the Germans came, I buried them under the apple-tree, so as Hitler wouldn't get them.' He said, 'Have you any reason to believe they are still there?' 'I know they are there,' I said. 'The ground where they are buried is as hard as a rock; and have never been disturbed.' I had the key of the cash-box on my watch-chain, and I showed it to him. 'Neville will have to have this key to open the box,' I said. 'Be sure to put it down in the will.'

'I suppose you know, or don't you?' he said, 'you have been breaking the law for a considerable number of years.' 'Have I?' I said. 'Well, if I have been breaking the law, it is for you to mend the break for me, isn't it? That is what a lawyer is for.' 'I fear you have a very exalted view of our profession,' he said. 'I sincerely hope I shall be able to live up to it. At present, I must confess I am completely at a loss.' 'Why, can't you do it, then?' I said. 'If that hoard of yours is dug up at this date,' he said, 'it may well have to be regarded as treasure trove.' 'What do you mean?' I said. He shrugged his shoulders. 'Property of the Crown, possibly,' he said. 'Property of the Crown!' I said. 'If it is going to be given to the Queen, for God's sake find out quick and let me know; and I will dig it up and throw it in the sea!' I was on my feet and was trembling and my old heart was thumping.

Mr de Lisle got up and came round the desk. 'I'm sorry, I'm sorry, Mr Le Page,' he said. 'I ought to have known better than to give voice to the worst possibility. The law may not prove as drastic as I suggest.' 'I want Neville to have those sovereigns,' I said. 'Yes, yes, I understand,' he said, 'but calm yourself now.' 'If you got to pass a little from hand to hand under the table,' I said, 'then do it and I will pay.' He didn't say he would; but I looked at him and he looked at me; and one Guernseyman understand another. He said I must give him a week at least to consult certain people. There had been an amendment to the law in the matter of gold lately, and he wasn't sure himself just how it stood. He said, 'For young Neville's sake, as well as for your own now I know you, I will do my utmost to get as much for you as I can.' 'Thank you: I am sure you will do your best,' I said. He can't help being a crook: he is a lawyer; but at heart he is an honest man.

He put a hand on my shoulder and took me through the outer office where the Fitch girl was sitting, and came with me right to the front door. 'By the way,' he said, 'how does Neville react to the prospect?' 'He don't know,' I said, 'and he must never know while I am about.' 'He won't learn of it through me,' he said, 'or from anyone in my employ.' 'I am glad to know that,' I said. 'He comes to see me because he likes coming. He wouldn't come near me, if he thought he was going to get something out of me. He is the last boy to crawl.' 'I believe you are right there,' he said. 'Nevertheless, he has been singularly fortunate in getting into your good graces.' He shook hands and wished me good-bye. 'Until next Friday the same time,' he said; and waved as I went down the steps.

I was disappointed it wasn't settled, and feeling shaky after the excitement; but it wouldn't do for me to get into a state. I used to laugh at my mother's lot because they put D.V. at the bottom of every notice of a meeting; but, when you come to think of it, they was right really. Even if what you want to do is for the best, it is only D.V. I had done all I could. I wasn't going to worry. I was surprised going down the High Street how many people nodded, or called out to me. Half of them I had forgotten, or never known. I noticed the visitors wandering about already, looking like the lost sheep of the House of Israel. I didn't fancy having my dinner in Town, and went straight down to the bus. I wanted to get home. I feel safer at home. Neville said he would bring a frame for my picture; but I couldn't expect him to bring it until the following Thursday. I was sure he would bring it. He was not one to make promises right and left; but, if he gave his word, he would keep it.

The Saturday afternoon I had just finished having my tea, when in walked young Jean Le Boutillier. I mean the father of John and Peter. He is not so young now, and I wish I could say he is the man his father was: but he isn't; and have changed for the worse, I think, since the Occupation. I liked him well enough in those days, even if he did work for the Germans. These days he is doing well, what with growing and summer visitors, and he is a good-living man and goes to the Catholic Church regularly; but when he speak to you he never have a good word to say for anybody. He said he hoped I didn't mind him butting in, but he felt it was his Christian duty to give me a word of warning. The boys had seen me out walking with young Falla from Paradise; and, another time, he himself had seen him down on the beach painting. Was I having him in the house? I said he came along to see me now and again; and was a very good friend of mine. Jean Le Boutillier said I couldn't know what I was doing.

Somebody's boat had been damaged, somebody's car had been pushed over a cliff, shop windows in Town had been smashed, and a boy had been stabbed at the Salerie and it was only by luck he wasn't killed. It wasn't known who actually was the culprits, but Neville Falla was behind it; for if it wasn't him, it was his gang. Jean Le Boutillier said it was as much as his boys' life was worth to be seen talking to Neville: if he caught them, he would lambast them black and blue. I could have told him Neville had nothing to do with the gang now; but I thought to make excuses would only make Jean more suspicious. It was a case of give a dog a bad name. It stuck. 'He paint nice pictures,' I said. 'That won't keep the wolf from the door,' he said. 'He don't paint pictures to keep the wolf from the door,' I said. 'He paint pictures because he like the island he live on.' I pointed to the one on the mantelpiece; but he didn't look at it. 'D'you keep any money in the house?' he said. 'A few shillings,' I said. 'Then whatever you do, lock your back door when you go to bed,' he said, 'or he'll be in one night and cosh you on the head for it.' 'I hope he don't do that,' I said, 'I don't want him to get himself into trouble over me.' 'It is a waste of time talking to you,' he said. 'You have no moral sense.' I thanked him for coming to warn me. He meant well.

The Sunday night I was sitting up to the table writing in my book, when suddenly there was a loud knocking on the back door, and I heard Neville shouting, 'Hullo there! Are you awake yet?' 'Yes, yes!' I called out: 'Come on in!' I was vexed, though, for him to catch me writing my book; but I didn't have time to put it away before he was standing in the doorway, looking down at me. I had never seen him looking so handsome; and he was wearing a well-cut dark blue suit with a blue silk shirt and a red tie. It wasn't a murderer's look on his face, either, but eyes wrinkled up in a most friendly smile. He had the frame under his arm. 'I have only come to bring this,' he said, 'I was afraid you might think I had forgotten about it.' 'I knew you wouldn't forget,' I said. The frame was of smooth painted wood, and much the same colour as parts of the picture. 'It matches,' I said. He took down the picture from off the mantelpiece and fitted it in. 'Just right,' he said. 'Where shall we hang it? What d'you say to on the wall behind the green-bed? Then it can keep an eye on you while you're asleep.' 'Good,' I said, 'and it won't keep me awake looking at it.' He had brought some cord and a bracket; and I found him a hammer. The job was done in no time. He is very quick with his hands.

I said I would get him ready a bit of supper, and was hoping to get my book out of the way at the same time, without him noticing it; but he said, 'Am I interrupting your accounts?' 'No, it's not accounts,' I said, 'it's only something I am writing.' I didn't say what it was, but I could see he was curious; and then I thought why on earth should I keep secrets from him, anyway? 'I will tell you what it is,' I said, 'but promise you won't tell anybody.' 'Of course I won't!' he said: 'you can trust me for that.' 'This is only one part of it,' I said, 'the last part'; and I showed him the other two books in the drawer. 'I wrote it for company really,' I said. 'I don't expect anybody will ever want to read it. It is my life-story, but have a lot in it about my relations and friends, and people living on Guernsey for the last sixty or seventy years.' 'I bet you haven't written all you have done in your life,' he said. 'I know you wouldn't have.' 'I have tried to put down the worst as well as the best,' I said, 'but you got to read between the lines.'

He launched off into a long harangue about how lucky us old ones had been. I couldn't see that, myself. He said we had the experience of the First World War and the Occupation and the years between; but his age-group had nothing but the years since, and all they had to look forward to was the Big Bang. I said, 'Well, perhaps they will put it off.' 'The threat is always there,' he said. 'I jibe at the kids; but you can't blame them for not caring what they get up to, when the world they live in might be blown to smith-ereens tomorrow. It wasn't the same in your time.' I said, 'Well, no:

because Progress hadn't got so far, and wasn't going so fast. I have tried to write down how it was in my time, though I don't know that I have done it very well.' 'God, I'd like to read that book of yours!' he said. 'Good gracious, no!' I said. I didn't want him reading what I had written about myself; and, now I came to think of it, there was something about him even in the first book. Otherwise I could have let him have that one, as it is the part which is most about Guernsey in the old days. 'Why not?' he said, 'I will take care of it.' 'It isn't finished yet,' I said, 'but I tell you what I will do. I am going to give you my book: the whole three parts; but it will only be yours to read after I am gone.' 'I would rather have you here,' he said. 'I believe you honestly would,' I said, 'but I won't always be; and then you can read my book. I am going to put your name on it now and you can come and claim it when the time comes.' On the front page of the first book I had written the title I had decided on at the start. The next page I hadn't written anything on at all. I thought I might put a text, as they do at the beginning of a book sometimes; only I had never been able to think of any words from the Bible that would suit. I now opened the first book to the blank page, and wrote across the middle in capital letters THE PROP-ERTY OF NEVILLE FALLA.

18

It was like the old days when I used to have supper with Jim at Les Gigands: I had never imagined it could happen again. It wasn't Neville had much to say while we was eating; but then Jim didn't have much to say either. It was just the room was full of something because he was there. He didn't thank me for my book; but I swear he knew I had given him all my secrets for him to read some day. He is very understanding, is Neville. I felt as much at peace with him as if he knew all my secrets already and I had nothing to hide. I was sure nothing he would read he would let turn him against me. Those deep-set eyes of his was warm and friendly every time they looked my way; and he often looked at me and smiled, rather than say anything; and his hand went out to pass me things, and he cut the bread for me and poured my tea. I thought of how it say in the Bible 'they broke bread together.'

While we was drinking our last cups of tea, he said, 'There is somebody else would very much like to come and see you.' 'Who on earth can that be?' I said. I couldn't think. 'Adèle de la Rue,' he said, 'you remember her, don't you? Can I bring her Thursday?' 'Of course I remember her!' I said. 'Bring her, bring her! After you, there is nobody I would like to see more.' He said, 'She says you are not to make any special preparations, if she comes. She will bring stuff for our tea.' 'Goodness, I can get something for our tea,' I said. Then I wondered if perhaps she would enjoy bringing something; so I said, 'All right, if she like, she can bring a cake. I am not all that good at making cake.' He said she had been out with him in his car that day; and he had gone back to her place and had tea with her and her aunt. Her aunt was an old so-and-so. He didn't know how Adèle could put up with her.

It was after midnight before he thought of going. He said he had his car down the road, and it wouldn't take him five minutes to get home. I said, 'Thanks for the frame and everything. Thursday can't come quick enough.' He said I mustn't expect them before three. Adèle had to serve in the shop until one; and he was going to fetch her after her dinner. I said, 'Bring her to the front door, mind! It is a state visit.' As he was going he turned round with a teasing grin on his face. 'Now don't you go getting ideas into your head,' he said. 'It is not you she is coming to see: it is the masterpiece of that promising young painter, Neville Falla!' 'Fiche le can', té!' I said. He don't know the patois, but he knew what that meant all right, and went off laughing.

The days passed quick. It would have been perfect, if I could have thought the will was safe in the drawer; but something might go wrong yet. I kept busy. I gave the house a good spring clean, and left young Ogier and his wife to carry on out of doors. They wanted to know what had come over me, because I was singing hymns all over the house. I said I was expecting visitors. The Wednesday I worked in the front garden. I pulled up the few weeds, and cleared away all the dead flowers. It looked nice when I had done with it. I thought of having a chancre for tea; but changed my mind and got young Ogier to chase round and find me a couple of fresh lobsters. I thought they would be easier for me to cut up and serve. I couldn't very well have a hammer on the table.

Thursday came and they arrived soon after two. I had cleared up the dinner things, but hadn't had time to lay the tea. It was lucky I had decided to change first. It was a lucky day altogether. I hadn't cut myself shaving that morning, and that is always a good sign. I didn't think I looked too bad either. I had put on a clean white shirt and my best black trousers. I don't have to wear braces, only a belt, for, thank the Lord, I don't have a tummy like so many old men. The first I heard was a loud rat-a-tat-tat on the front door, and Neville's voice, 'Hi, open up, there!' I opened the door and there she was: the girl I had thought such a lot of when I saw her on the other side of the counter in the States Offices. I considered I ought to be polite. After all, she was a stranger. 'Come in, Miss de la Rue, if you please,' I said. 'I am delighted to see you.' 'Miss de la Rue, who is she?' she said: 'Adèle to you!' and she gave me both her hands. Neville was grinning all over his face when I pulled her almost in my arms into the kitchen. 'Welcome to my house, Adèle!' I said.

I hadn't made a mistake about Adèle. She is a real Guernsey girl, and could be born nowhere else; and it isn't only her looks and the way she speaks, but she is warm-natured and goes out to people without thinking in a way you never find among the English. They can be polite and kind and all that, but you always get the feeling they are keeping away from you, and looking down on you: even when they are most friendly. 'Ah, le vier Guernèsi!' she said, when she saw my kitchen. 'Mais verre dja, donc!' I said. 'Hey, come off that!' said Neville, 'I want to know what you two are talking about.' 'It is a great pity he don't speak his own language,' she said, 'but otherwise he is of the donkey breed.' She was looking at my uncle's picture. 'Yes, it is wonderful!' she said, 'but it frightens me. It is mad.' 'He was a modern before his time, that boy,' said Neville.

'How about the other?' I said: and turned her round and made her look at Neville's. 'Oh!' she said and burst out laughing: 'that is as sane as houses!' She stood looking at it for a long time: from here and from there, and this way and that way. 'Leave her to it!' said Neville. 'She can't paint for nuts; but I trust her judgment more than anybody's. She knows.' She put on a stern look, as if she was a judge, and was going to pass sentence on a criminal. 'We'll let you off this time,' she said, 'if you promise to do better next.' 'I'll try, teacher,' he said. 'I'm not going to tell him so,' she said to me on the quiet, 'or he'll get conceited; but between you and me, it's damn good! He paints in patois. He is the only painter on the island to do it.' 'I heard the last bit,' he said. 'Where do I dump this stuff?'

He was carrying towels and things under his arm and bagsful of food. 'On the table for now,' I said, 'but goodness, you needn't have bothered to bring all that!' 'I got in a mood,' said Adèle, 'and when I'm in a mood, I must do something. I enjoy cooking.' Neville wasn't interested. His idea was since it was such fine weather, we must all go down on the beach, and they could have a swim before tea; but that wasn't what she wanted. I saw she was a young miss with a will of her own. He must go along and have his swim; and she was going to stay and have a chat with Ebenezer: then we would both come down on the beach when the tea was got ready for his lordship. He said, 'What's going on here? I believe she likes you better than she do me.' 'Of course I like him better than I do you!' she said. 'Who wouldn't?' 'Man not to reason why, his but to do and die!' he said; and picked up his bathing suit and towel and went off.

When he was gone, she wouldn't let me do a thing. She made me sit in the armchair and arranged the cushions in my back; and then sat on the edge of the green-bed opposite me, and looked at me very straight in the face. I knew she had something to say to me, but I was surprised what it was when it did come out. 'Thank you for what you have done for Neville,' she said. 'I haven't done nothing for Neville,' I said. She said, 'He is a different person since he has been seeing you. He is human.' I said, 'Wasn't he human before, then?' 'When he was in front of his easel, yes,' she said, 'but not when he was with people. It was ice where there ought to have been a heart.' 'He likes to make out he is like that,' I said. 'It is all right now,' she said. 'The ice is melted. I only wish I knew how you have done it.' 'I have no idea,' I said. 'I expect just by being you, bless you!' she said, and jumped up and gave me a quick kiss on the forehead, then began to unpack the things on the table.

'If you will tell me where things are, I can cope,' she said; so I stayed in my chair and gave the orders. It was a pleasure watching her moving about the house. She is quick and neat; and never clumsy. I liked her clothes. She was wearing a pleated skirt of mixed yellow-brown and green with black squares, and a black sweater open at the neck. It was just right with her black hair, and her bright, bright brown eyes. I noticed she had on sensible shoes, and not those with high thin heels make a girl look as if she is going to topple over. She got a tablecloth out of the chest-of-drawers in my mother's room, as I told her; and the lobsters from the safe outside the back door. I made her use the best china on the dresser. She knew how to deal with a lobster; and had brought some home-made gâche and cream-cakes. The table looked real nice laid for the three of us. The kettle was on the side and would be boiling by the time we came in.

Neville is a mystery to me, in a way, and will always be, I think. He have something I haven't got, and don't understand; but it is something I like him for. It is what make him able to paint, and be serious about how he paint. Adèle isn't a mystery to me at all. I might have known her all my life. At times I almost forget she is Adèle, and fancy she is Tabitha; though Tabitha would never have said damn, nor worn her skirt up to her knees. At any rate, I was sure she wouldn't mind if I said what I was thinking. I knew without her having to tell me she didn't want Neville only for a friend. He was the boy she had set her heart on; and she wasn't one who would change easy. I said, 'If the ice have melted, as you say, don't you ever let it freeze up again! It is up to you. He won't unfreeze a second time, you know. He is not one who finds it easy to trust people; nor don't you run away with the idea he is going to be satisfied to be only your husband and the father of your children. He have to go on painting his pictures: family, or no family. If not, he will turn nasty and start smashing things again.' She was cutting up the lobsters while I was talking; but she was listening to what I had to say. 'I wonder how it is you know him so well,' she said, 'you are very wise.' I was thinking of Christine who I had never forgiven for putting herself in front of Raymond and knocking him out. 'I like you very much, Adèle,' I said, 'very much indeed; but if, when I am gone, you hurt that boy, I will haunt you, I will!' She laughed. 'He has certainly found a champion in you!' she said.

She wanted to go for a swim now, and got her bathing things; while I put on my hat and jacket, and took my stick. When we got out the front door, she caught hold of my free hand, and we walked down the beach hand-in-hand. It seemed quite natural. Neville was sprawled only in his bathing slip on the flat rock in the sun. He sat up when he heard us coming. 'Now what have you two been hatching?' he said. 'Ah, wouldn't you like to know?' she said; and slipped away behind a rock to get changed. He had already had his swim. I have never been in the sea, except to paddle up to my knees, but how to swim is one of the things I would learn if I had to live my life again. When she ran down the sand, she turned round and waved. I said to Neville, 'Now she don't spoil the picture, do she?' 'Adèle doesn't,' he said. 'If I was a painter,' I said, 'I would only want to paint human beings.' 'I have enough on my plate for the first time being,' he said. 'I am only beginning to see. I might paint Les Moulins a dozen times, and every

time see it different. I wouldn't be surprised if I am painting it yet at the end
of my days: like Cézanne and Mont Sainte Victoire.' 'I hope you will be,'
I said.

I find it next to impossible to write about that happy afternoon and
evening with Neville and Adèle; and happy isn't the word, quite. It was
joy bubbling up inside me. I can't say how much it meant, after being so
many years on my own, to have these two young people being so good to
me. It was a lovely tea. I sat at the head of the table, but it was them looked
after me. Their wet bathing-suits and towels was hanging up in the wash-
house to dry; and the two of them looked fresh and clean in their nice
clothes. I don't remember what was said much. It was silly things mostly:
jokes and laughing. I know I ate a lot. I was made to sit in the grand-pa's
chair after, while they cleared away and washed up. I was altogether spoilt.
It was a golden evening and the sun was shining in at the windows. When it
began to get dark, Neville ran out to put the light on of his car; and then
they pushed the table back and we sat round the fire with the lamp lit and
the blinds down. Les Moulins was a home again.

They made me feel I was one of them. Neville was talking to me, but also
half arguing with Adèle: in fact, near quarrelling at times. He got excited
and started lamming out right and left at everything happening in the
world in general, and Guernsey in particular. He is clothed and in his right
mind when he is talking about painting; but I am not sure when he is
talking about other things. He didn't have a good word to say for his
school; and I thought it was a good school. He said all they taught you was
to pass exams so you could be packaged in the appropriate coloured paper
on the conveyor belt bound for a successful career. It was your selling-
price mattered. The rest was make-weight. 'I will never be able to look
Shakespeare in the face,' he said. 'Say by whom and when spoken "The
quality of mercy is not strained: it droppeth as the gentle rain from heaven
upon the place beneath".' I said, 'A namesake of yours, Mess Henri Falla
from La Moye, used to make us learn that piece by heart at the Vale School.
If we forgot a bit, it was "bend over, touch your toes: whack! whack!
whack!"' 'Oh come,' said Adèle, 'it is not as bad as that now!' She had
been educated by the nuns; and they was wonderful teachers, she said. I
hadn't thought she might be a Roman Catholic, though I had noticed she
wore a cross on a chain round her neck. It was a blow: but at least they
know what is right and wrong.

I was surprised when Neville said, although he was a pagan himself, he
had every respect for the Christian Faith. So long as it wasn't only dead
dogmas. Or just a list of do's and don'ts. Or politics. 'It is when a big noise
stands up in the pulpit of the Town Church and blethers about Christian
Principles in War, I see red!' he said. 'Well, there was the Scribes and
Pharisees and Sadducees, you know,' I said. 'There will always be those

people. They got to live, the poor creatures. The rest of us got to build mansions in heaven.' 'It is the only place you will get one if you are a Guernseyman!' he said. He ranted on about the States. They do nothing for those of their own people who are poor and got nowhere to live; but they will kow-tow to any tax-dodger from the other side who wants to dig in, if only he brings a big enough wad of money to the island. I said, 'Well there was Pontius Pilate and Herod Antipas; but we are lucky to have our own, and not be ruled over by the Romans.' He lay back in his chair and rolled about laughing.

I thought Adèle was looking sad while Neville was talking wild; but she brightened up when it ended with a laugh: yet it was her brought up about the blessed T.V. She said to me, 'I am surprised you don't have the T.V. It would be company for you in the long winter evenings.' I said, 'Goodness, I don't want those sort of people in my house!' That really did set Neville off. He tore the T.V. to shreds; and he had seen more of it than I have. The Big Bang was a threat; but the T.V. was a menace always with us. If you talk to people nowadays, nothing exists unless it has been seen on T.V. It gives people the idea they have seen and know everything, when really they have seen and know nothing. It is the deadliest drug on the market. They go sky-high if the boys smoke pot. It is perpetual pot for the millions of goggle-eyed addicts who watch it nightly. 'Oh, but I like watching the T.V.,' said Adèle, 'for then my aunt isn't nagging at me. She loves watching it herself, and says she doesn't know she ever managed to live without it.' 'I am doing nothing to prevent you watching the T.V.,' said Neville, 'so long as I don't have to see it or hear it myself. I will build you a padded cell where you can watch it day and night.' I thought she was going to flare up, but she answered meekly, 'If I was living with someone who wasn't always finding fault with me, perhaps I wouldn't insist on a padded cell.'

They didn't want much for their supper: only a cup of coffee and a biscuit. I wasn't hungry either. I had some real coffee in the cupboard I had seen ground from the beans; and Adèle made it and we sat with it on our knees. I was sorry they had to go so early; but he had to get her back to St Andrew's by ten. Her aunt was very strict. 'I got to keep on the right side of her aunt,' he said, 'as I may want to take her out on loan again.' 'I should jolly well hope you do!' I said, 'because I want to see her again.' She hugged me when she went. I watched them go down to the car from the front door. 'À bientôt!' she called out.

19

I was afraid that cup of coffee was going to keep me awake; but I slept like a log and woke up late. I cut myself shaving and had to choke down my breakfast. I only just managed to get to Town by eleven. I was hot and cold all over when I got to Mr de Lisle's office. 'I am sorry if I am late,' I said to the girl; but she was as nice as she could be. 'Oh, that's quite all right, Mr Le Page,' she said, 'Mr de Lisle will see you immediately.' She opened the door to his room, and held it open for me to go in. He got up from his desk and smiled and shook hands and said, 'Hullo, Mr Le Page, how are you?' as if I was an old friend. 'I overslept and had to hurry,' I said. 'You shouldn't have done that,' he said. 'Now sit down and relax.' He was more like a young doctor than ever; and when he sat down to his desk, he looked as if he might be going to tell me in as kind a way as possible I would be dead next week.

I noticed the papers I had let him have was spread out in front of him, and a lot of other sheets of paper with writing on. 'I have gone very carefully into your affairs, Mr Le Page,' he said. 'As regards the house, the greenhouse and the land, in fact all your real estate, there will be no difficulty whatever; and the same may be said of the various cash repositories in the house.' I said, 'Yes, but what about the sovereigns?' 'Ah, there's the rub,' he said. 'If there are any of before 1838, those can be freely held and sold.' 'I wasn't born then,' I said. He said there might be some early issues among them for all I knew; but of those of a later date, only four could be held: and even those it would be necessary to get permission to sell. I said, 'Who say all this?' It was the Exchange Control Order relating to Gold Coins Exemption agreed to by the States. 'I don't understand how that can be,' I said, 'gold is gold. The States can't change that, surely.' It seems they could; if they was under pressure from the other side. British currency was no longer on the gold standard, as surely I knew, and any sale of gold in quantity might upset the balance of credit. 'The balance of credit?' I said, 'I haven't the vaguest idea what that mean; but I do know whoever it was made that law are a lot of rogues and vagabonds! I worked for every penny of those sovereigns!' I was real angry.

He said he knew it was hard on me, and he was sorry; but all he could do was advise me which course of action he thought best. If I wished, I could admit now I was in possession of those sovereigns and apply to the Treasury for permission to hold them. It might be granted, or it might not; but it was extremely unlikely I would be given permission to sell any issued after 1837, and certainly not in bulk. He thought the best way out was for me to agree he didn't know I was in possession of those sovereigns. 'I don't see how I can do that,' I said, 'I have told you now.' He said that didn't matter. He might know it personally, but that didn't necessarily mean he knew it in law. 'At that rate,' I said, 'what is so in solid fact and what the law say is so are entirely different.' 'Exactly,' he said, 'Mr Le Page, you would have made quite a good lawyer yourself.' 'God forbid!' I said.

He had drawn up a provisional will, listing my assets, among which was a cash-box, of which I held the key. As it was mentioned in the will, it would naturally be searched for, and he would drop Neville a hint as to where it was to be found. After that it would be Neville's headache. There would be delays and fees and what-not; but at least there might be some compensation. He promised he would advise Neville, according as to how the wind was blowing at the time; and use what outside influence he could bring to bear, so as much as possible would be realisable in terms of ready cash. In the long run, Neville might do quite well out of it. It would be to his advantage he could in no way be held responsible, as I could, for being in illegal possession of the gold, in view of the fact he was ignorant of the legacy. What did I think? 'I leave it to you,' I said. I was too miserable to think. Having those golden sovereigns had kept my head up all my life. 'It seems to me,' I said, 'there is nothing you can be sure of in this world.' 'Strictly speaking, that is true,' he said. 'Money is the measure of our distrust.'

He read the will out loud for me to hear. I could have written it all down on the back of a postcard, but he made pages and pages of it. It sounded all right; and I suppose another lawyer would understand it. 'There remains the appointing of an executor, or executors,' he said. Well, I knew a will had to have an executor, and I had always meant to ask young Jean Le Boutillier to do it; but now I had my doubts as to how he would feel doing it for Neville's benefit. It was going to be bad enough for him to have Neville Falla for a neighbour. 'Is it possible for you to do it yourself, Mr de Lisle?' I said. 'I will pay.' 'I will do it willingly,' he said, 'but in my private capacity; and payment will not be necessary.' 'Thank you very much indeed,' I said. 'Then consider that done,' he said; and wrote down some more.

I thought it was finished now; but he went on to say it was often the custom in a will to give parting advice to the legatee, or set down a condition, or conditions, under which the legacy was to be enjoyed. Had I any

advice, or conditions, I wished to add? 'None,' I said. 'Then it is to be completely without strings,' he said. I said 'Your famous law have tied me up in
enough strings, as it is, without me tying up poor Neville in any more.' He
said, 'That will be all then, I think.' I thought for a minute. 'No, wait,' I
said. 'There is something else. I want you to say I give;' but he stopped me.
'Bequeath,' he said. 'I bequeath,' I said, 'my spirit to my Maker and my
sin-rotten body to be buried with my fathers and my forefathers in the
graveyard of the Church of the Vale, where the bells ring and the wind
blow.' He copied down word for word what I said; and put down his pen
and looked at me. He said, 'I pray to God it will be many a long day yet
before that come to pass.'

We parted good friends. He said if I came in the next Friday morning, it
would be ready for me to sign. I asked him couldn't I sign it before then? I
could come in the next day, if he wanted; or on the Monday. He said he
would rush it through and I could sign it on the Tuesday morning. I asked
him about paying for it, so as to know how much money to bring; but he
said there was no hurry. He would send a bill; and, in any case, the charges
could go against the estate. I would rather have paid. He came with me to
the front door and the girl said 'Good-bye, Mr Le Page,' as we passed
through her office. I don't know what have come over that girl. When we
shook hands, he said it had been a pleasure to do business with me. He only
wished all his clients knew their own minds as well as I do mine.

I had been with him for over an hour. I hadn't had time before to go to
the States Offices; so I went in and got my money. There was nothing for
me to do then but come home. I didn't know how I was going to wait until
the Tuesday. A day is a long time to get through when you get to my age. I
passed the afternoon somehow. The Saturday went quicker than I
thought; but the Sunday was a long day. In the evening I went on with my
book; but I didn't have much heart for writing. It was the real thing I
wanted. I kept on thinking how Neville had barged in the Sunday before
with the frame, and was wishing for it to happen again; but a good thing
never happen a second time. The Monday wasn't so bad. I spent most of
the day in the greenhouse, trimming the plants. I am going to have a wonderful crop of tomatoes this year.

The will was ready on the Tuesday morning, and I signed it. Mr de Lisle
read it to me right through again with the extra bits put on, and then called
in two young chaps from the other room to witness me sign it; and they
wrote their names under mine. There was also a copy. Mr de Lisle asked me
if I wanted to take the original with me, or the copy. I said the original. He
could keep the copy; and I would be pleased if he would keep the papers to
do with the house. They was only in the way in the drawer. He gave me the
will in a long envelope; and I put it in my inside pocket. When I was going,
he said, 'How do you pass your time these days?' I said, 'Working of

course.' He said, 'I take it you draw the Old Age Pension.' 'I haven't come to that yet, thank God!' I said. 'I hope I never will.' 'A challenge to the Welfare State,' he said. 'Now that is something I have never understood,' I said; 'I think a man ought to be allowed to look after himself.' 'Unfortunately welfare does not mean the same as well-being,' he said, 'but Guernsey will fall for it. Guernsey, dear Guernsey, where all the tired platitudes come home to roost!'

Well, I walked down Smith Street with the will in my pocket, and I ought to have been dancing for joy; but, to tell you the truth, I felt flat and empty, because there was nothing more for me to do. I turned to go down High Street: and, to my astonishment, who should come out of Le Riche's Stores but Neville and Adèle? I bumped right into them. 'Good Lord, who let you loose?' said Neville. 'I thought it was Fridays you came in to rook the States.' 'I had some very private business of my own to see to,' I said with dignity. 'More roguery, I bet,' he said. 'It is nice to see you, anyhow,' said Adèle. I said, 'How is it you are not in the shop today?' 'It is Neville's holiday,' she said, 'and he got round my aunt. He would get round anybody, this bad boy!' They was hand in hand, and she looked up into his face. He was smiling down at her. If ever there was two in love, it was those two.

He said they was going to Moulin Huet for a picnic; and showed the hamper under his arm he had just bought at Le Riche's. Where was I going? 'Home,' I said. 'I'll run you back first,' he said. The car was up St Julien's Avenue. It was only a two-seater; but Adèle could look at the shops. 'I can get myself home quite well on my own, thank you,' I said. 'Oh, do let Neville take you!' said Adèle: 'I don't mind waiting, I really don't. I can go to the Library.' 'No!' I said; and in a way showed I meant it: 'you go to your picnic!' 'All right, then,' said Neville, 'be independent! Some people got cussed children.' I wasn't going to take away one minute: no, not one minute, from what they was having. I looked at them standing there, and they was perfect in my eyes. If I could have my way, they would never change. 'I will be round to see you soon,' Neville said, as they was going, 'don't imagine I have done with you yet!' I watched them go down the Pollet; and then went down High Street to the bus.

When I got indoors, I put the envelope with the will in it in the drawer of the dresser. It isn't exactly as I wanted; but it is good to feel it is there. I didn't go out and start work in the afternoon, as I said to Mr de Lisle I would; but went down on the beach. It was lovely weather and there was nobody else on La Petite Grève. A few strangers passed along the top; and some chaps was working in the Chouey quarry, getting out mines the Germans had dumped in it before they went away. I was thinking of my two on the beach at Moulin Huet. I was as worried about them as an old hen; though I was quite sure they wasn't worried about themselves. They was in love, yes: but I know how short and stormy that can be. Will they quarrel? Will they drift apart? Adèle is going to have a full-time job with Neville. He have his eyes on the horizon; but he don't always see the rocks at his feet. It is Adèle who will have to keep the books in that house. What will the big world do to them; and all the millions going to fight? Guernsey got no say in the matter: Guernsey don't count; but oh, what will happen to my darlings, when the big bombs begin to fall?

It was only yesterday I wrote those words, after I had come up from the beach; but so much have happened to me since, I don't know what to think now. Is all one generation can do to set the stage for the comic, sad story of the next? Anyhow, this morning after breakfast, I thought I would put in my twelve hours on the ancient monument until dinner-time. I don't like getting my money from the States for nothing. I raked around. There was the everlasting cigarette packets and ice-cream papers; and two french letters. I thought it was a pill they use nowadays. Anyhow, it is done now for a few weeks. I took my time over my dinner, and had just washed up and got clear, when I heard Neville's voice. 'Come on out, you!' he was outside shouting: 'Come on out!' For the minute I thought I was fancying things. 'Are you about?' he shouted, and came right in. I said, 'Hullo, where's Adèle?' 'I haven't brought her,' he said, 'It's your turn today.' I don't know why, and I was surprised at myself, but I was glad he hadn't brought Adèle.

'I am taking you for a ride,' he said. 'What, in the car?' I said. 'Yes, in the car,' he said. 'Where would you like to go?' 'Anywhere you like,' I said, 'but, if it rests with me, I wouldn't mind going along the west coast.' 'That will do me fine,' he said. 'We can go as far as Pleinmont; and then we'll see.' 'I haven't been to Pleinmont for years and years,' I said. He said I must put on something warmish, as it was an open car, and there was quite a breeze. He was wearing a guernsey and brown corduroy trousers. I went into the little room where I keep my clothes, and changed into a pair of thick blue serge trousers and put on Jean Batiste's guernsey. I was going to wear my hat, but Neville said it would blow off; so I put on an old beret I wear when I go to St Sampson's. 'I look a boud'lo,' I said. 'You look just right,' he said. I stacked the grate with coal, so as the fire wouldn't be out when we got back; and we went out the front way. I locked the front door and put the key under the stone, as I used to in the days of Tabitha and have done ever since.

His is a nice little car. I don't know what make, for I never notice, but it is red and low-built, and comfortable to sit in. He got in his side first and undid the door my side for me to get in. It runs very smooth; but he didn't drive fast to begin with. He went by Sandy Hook and through L'Islet and out to Grand Havre; and then along the coast road. Port Grat and Les Pêquéries have never been much to my idea; and, in any case, I had been

that way not so long ago. From Gran'-Rock on I began to take notice.
Cobo was always ramshackle, but I hardly knew it for all the new houses
have been built. Albecq was much the same as I remembered it; but he let
the car have its head when we got along Vazon. It is no good me saying I
wasn't nervous, because I was; and I was holding tight on to the side. 'Are
you all right?' he said. 'Yes,' I said. I thought well, if I am going to be
killed, I am going to be killed. He slowed up by Perelle; but when we got
passed L'Érée, he went hell for leather round Rocquaine. They have
made such a mess of L'Érée I was trying to think how it was; but he didn't
give me a chance.

He could see I was scared and was laughing at me; but he slowed down
when we got by Fort Grey. I saw the great ugly tower on the top of Pleinmont the Germans built I hadn't seen before. He turned down by the
Imperial, and drove past the Trinity Houses and along Portelet and round
the Vardes and straight on as far as Fort Pezeries. A number of cars was
parked where the road ends, and he stopped the car and said, 'Let's get out
and stretch our legs, shall we?' I hadn't brought my stick, like a fool, and
when I got out nearly fell over. I had to hang on to the car, until he caught
hold of my arm and helped me along. I don't like people helping me; but I
had to let him. 'Let's go across the grass,' he said; and we went along the
path past the Table des Peons and stood in the opening between the two big
rocks. The sea was roughish and sparkling in the sun and great waves was
falling like lace over La Ronde. I saw the Hanois. I thought of Jim and me
standing there. I thought of Raymond and Horace; and the blood on the
stones. I was drowning in memories and was afraid I was going to cry. I
managed to say, 'America is over there.' 'It can stay there,' he said, 'I bet
the Yanks got nothing on this.' I said, 'All the greatest pain and beauty I
have known have had to do with round here.'

He led me gently back to the car, and opened the door for me to get in;
and then went round and got in his side and sat beside me. I said, 'I am
sorry I got upset.' 'It is nothing to be sorry for,' he said. He had himself
had some of his best times wandering on his own along the cliffs between
Pleinmont and La Moye, and had wept at the grandeur of it. He began to
tell me about the pictures he was going to paint. He was full of hope and his
eyes were shining. There was a view of the Hanois from Fort Pezeries he
particularly wanted to do. 'I haven't dared to try it yet,' he said. I thought
how he is like the Hanois himself. He have a light in him. 'Feeling fit now?'
he said. 'Yes, fine!' I said. 'Then we'll get,' he said, 'I'm going to stand you a
slap-up lobster tea at the Imperial.' I said, 'You are going to do nothing of
the sort! I am not having you throwing your money away on no lobster tea
for me at the Imperial. I know where we can get a better tea for nothing.'
'Where is that?' he said. 'It is not far from the Imperial,' I said. 'I will show
you.'

He turned the car round and drove back the way we had come. I noticed the road in one part was further in than it used to be, and the zig-zag was wider, and didn't have ruts in as it had when me and Jim came down it on our bikes. A house or two I seemed to remember being there had disappeared; and where Quertier Le Pelley's used to be was an ugly modern bungalow. When we got to the Imperial, I said, 'Is there somewhere you can leave your car?' 'Here will do,' he said; and found a place the other side of the road from the buses. We got out, and he did something to the car so as no one could go off with it; but I had lost my bearings, and wasn't at all sure which way I had to go. When I used to know it along there, it was open grass with only a house or two and a few cottages; but now it was houses, houses, houses. I said 'Well, we will have to go and look for it: the place I mean.' I don't think he believed there was any such place; but he came with me.

There was quite a lot of people by the buses, and we must have looked a funny pair to any who was watching: him tall and with long straight legs and young, and me old and short and bandy; and I was hanging on to his arm. I wasn't ashamed now. I found a lane behind some new houses I thought might lead to it; and, sure enough, there it was! The gable was against the cliff and the wicked windows was looking at you sideways and there was tall flowers in front and smoke coming out of the crooked chimney. 'Why, this is out of a fairy tale!' he said. I said, 'Liza Quéripel live there.'

20

I let go of him and went ahead up the path and knocked on the front door. There was no answer. I waited and then I said, 'She will be round the back.' I led the way round the back and he followed. I noticed the back garden was doing well; mostly fruit and vegetables, and a fine patch of potatoes. She must have somebody to help her look after it, I thought. In the far corner a little old woman was feeding the fowls. Yes, it was Liza. Her poor old back, which was once so straight, was bent; and she was wearing a scoop and sabots and a grey dress with a full skirt and a black satin apron. I couldn't see her face. She was throwing corn to the fowls, and making them run for it. I stopped. I didn't want to give her a fright; and I made a sign to Neville not to move. She looked our way. She didn't seem at all surprised; but turned her apronful of corn up-side-down over the fowls as she had done was it thirty, forty years ago? She came slowly towards us. She couldn't walk very fast. 'Hullo there!' she said, 'I have been expecting you for a long time.'

Her face was wrinkled and her neck was thin; but her mouth was the same, and her chin as firm as ever it was. Her deep-set violet eyes was bright, and she smiled at me; and it was her angel's smile. She was as beautiful, more beautiful, than the day I saw her first. 'Who is this you have with you?' she said. 'A friend who bring me in his motor-car,' I said. She looked him up and down, as I have seen her look at many a man; and the old mischief came into her eyes. 'Ma fé, mais qu'il est un beau garçon, li!' she said. 'Tout à fait!' I said. She held out her hand to him. 'I am pleased to meet you,' she said. Her voice was deep and strong. He took her hand, and held it gently in his, and smiled. I saw he liked her. 'Your garden is doing well,' I said to her. 'Who do it for you?' 'Paul Gallienne,' she said. I couldn't think for the minute who he might be. 'The grandson of Queen Elizabeth,' she said. 'The grandson?' I said. 'Goodness, how the time fly!' 'Come indoors,' she said.

She stepped out of her sabots on the mat, and put on a pair of black satin slippers, and hung her scoop behind the door. Her hair was white, but thick yet, and she had it cut short and frizzed. I had to take off my beret and was ashamed for her to see my bald head. 'You are looking well,' she said.

'So are you,' I said. 'It is a wonder, then,' she said, 'seeing as I am so many years older than you are.' I wasn't going to quarrel. The kitchen hadn't changed, and was shining and spotless. The first thing I noticed was the silver Guernsey milk-can I had given her was back in the place of honour on the cabinet, among the windmill and the lighthouse and the ships. She saw me look at it. 'I buried it while the Germans was here,' she said. She put a kettle on the terpid. 'Sit down, and I will get you some tea,' she said. For some reason, I sat to the table on the form against the wall, instead of on one of the chairs; and Neville sat beside me. I hadn't thought it might remind her; but it did. 'My ghosts, my two ghosts, will go away now,' she said.

I can only write down the few words was said on my short visit to Liza. I cannot say how deep they went; and Neville had no idea. She was spreading a brightly-coloured table-cloth on the table. 'Would you like some pickled ormers?' she said. 'I have some left.' 'For sure,' I said, 'but I don't know if Neville like them.' 'I have never had any pickled,' he said. 'Then try some,' I said. 'I will,' he said. 'Is his name Neville, then?' she said, 'Neville what?' 'Neville Falla,' I said, 'from Paradise in the Vale.' She set cups and saucers and plates and knives and forks on the table; and the jar of ormers and a loaf and butter, for us to help ourselves. She was thinking. 'Was your mother a Guille?' she said to Neville. 'Yes,' he said, 'why, did you know her?' 'I wonder if it can be she was the daughter of Don Guille,' she said, 'who was the son of Jurat Guille?' 'My great-grandfather was a Jurat Guille,' he said, 'I know, for my mother often spoke of him. She was proud of it.' I knew then who he was. Liza knew I knew.

She poured out the tea, and sat down to eat facing us. 'Est-il marié?' she said to me. I answered her in patois so as he wouldn't know what I was saying. He wasn't yet, but was going to be soon, I hoped. Who was the girl? she wanted to know. Adèle de la Rue, whose aunt kept a shop at St Andrew's, I told her. Liza knew the family. The father, Fred de la Rue, so-called, was not a de la Rue really, didn't I know? Edna de Mouilpied from the Villocq married a de la Rue; but the first boy wasn't his. Nobody knew who the father was. I didn't say a word, or give a sign, but it flashed through my mind, and Liza saw it flash, God knows how! I met Edna de Mouilpied one Sunday evening outside the Câtel Chapel, and took her down Skin's Lane. I saw in the *Press* soon after she had got married, and hadn't given her a thought since. Neville looked up and said, 'I wish to God you people would speak a language a human being can understand!' I said, 'I was only telling Liza about your Adèle.' 'What is she like?' said Liza. Neville looked puzzled. 'I don't know I can say exactly what she is like,' he said. 'As a matter of fact, she is rather like me,' I said, 'only much better looking.' Liza threw her head back and laughed in the old way. 'I should jolly well hope she is better looking,' she said, 'or it is a poor look-out for Neville!' 'Now you come to mention it,' said Neville, 'she is rather like you; and just about as bullet-headed!' 'This rascal hasn't a spark of romance in him!' said Liza. 'I am glad it is not me he is going to marry.'

There wasn't much more said over the meal. Neville was too busy eating and enjoying it; and helped himself a second time. Liza was watching his every look and movement; and it was pitiful to see the pride and joy in her old face. He was flesh of her flesh: and I wished with my whole heart he was of mine; but then Adèle couldn't be. How will I face her the next time I see her? When we had done, Liza asked if we'd had enough; and we both said we'd had plenty. She got up to clear. 'Neville,' she said, 'd'you mind filling the bucket for me with water from the well?' 'With pleasure,' he said; and went out with it. It was only an excuse to get him out of the house. As soon as he was gone, she said, 'How is he off for money, the boy?' 'He will have enough,' I said, 'I have seen to that.' 'I am glad,' she said. 'Paul has been very good to me, and expects what I've got.' I said, 'Neville has been very good to me: and expects nothing. He inherit that from you.'

He came in saying it was going to be a beautiful evening, and it was a shame for us to be indoors. I saw Liza's face flinch with the pain; but he didn't mean to hurt her. He didn't know. 'Yes, you must go now, both of you,' she said, 'and enjoy yourselves.' 'It has been lovely meeting you, Miss Quéripel,' he said, 'and thank you for the grand tea.' He held out his hand; but she went to him and put her arms under his, and her hands round over his shoulders, and lifted up her face. He bent and kissed her on the forehead. He is far from people, as a rule, is Neville; yet when he do come close, he know exactly the right thing to do. She let go of him, and opened the front door for him to go out; and he went down the path. She came to me then, and caught hold of me; and I held her close and kissed her on the mouth. She was small and frail, smaller than me now; but her mouth was hungry yet, and she was soft as a young woman in my arms. 'Je t'aime, Liza,' I said. She said, 'Je t'aime, Ebenezer.'

'Enough canoodlin', you two!' Neville called out; 'or we'll miss the sunset.' I let go of her, and walked down the path and caught him up; but when we got to the end of the lane, I looked back. She was leaning against the gate-post watching us go. She raised a hand, and I raised a hand; and Neville waved cheerily. He was striding along, and I was trotting along-side him like a boy. I had forgotten I was old. He looked down at me, laughing. 'I know now why you didn't marry,' he said. 'There was no one like her.' 'There isn't,' I said. When we got to the car, I was glad to sit down. He spread a rug over my knees, and got in his side. 'Where do you want to go now?' he said. 'Home,' I said. He drove back round Roc-quaine.

There was cars and motor-bikes passing us, and others meeting us; but there mightn't have been any, for all I saw of them. I was looking at Fort

Grey where the two lovers had jumped together in each other's arms into the sea; and I thought how wise they was, and what a big fool this world is. I saw the rocks where I pushed Liza into the water, and knew that when she said 'I hate you! I hate you!' it was love. I looked along the road, and there she was coming in her chariot in a white robe and golden sandals and with the helmet on her head. At L'Érée I was blind to everything they have done there spoil it now; but I saw the trestles on the grass and Jim flirting with the Bichard girls, and me sitting on the form with my Coronation mug in front of me, and Liza saying 'Is there room for me?'

I was wondering why it was I had to be leaving her behind; and was full of loss and sorrow, when the car went round Perelle. I would have told Neville, if I could, to drive back, and looked sideways at his face; but his lean jaw was set firm and merciless. When he drove up past La Catioroc, he kept well in to the left, and was looking more out to sea than at the road. The sun was going down and clouds coming from nowhere, so it seemed, as if they was hurrying for a great event. There was heavy clouds low down, and high mountains of clouds, and fluffy clouds loose in the air, and others like feathers overhead; and all the way round Vazon they was changing from white and grey to red and gold. At Albecq, the rocks was red; and from Cobo, the sun was a huge ball of fire, floating in a cave of fire, and half under the sea. I couldn't bear it. I was going to shout to Neville 'Stop, stop please: you are killing me!' when at Gran'-Rock he drew in to the side of his own accord and switched the engine off. 'This is too good to miss,' he said: and we sat and watched the big sun sink lower and lower, until there was only a tip showing; when suddenly, it dipped under, and was gone! Then it happened. I don't know what. The great rocks was not rocks, nor the sea sea, yet they was real as real; and the clouds was gates of glory, and every way I turned my eyes the view was waves of joy and golden light. 'God, that's magnificent!' said Neville. I had no words but Raymond's. 'It is a glimpse of the world as God made it,' I said, 'on the first evening of the first day.' He gave me a funny look. 'I'd love to paint it!' he said. 'It can never be painted,' I said.

Neville drove on and the glory faded; but not in me. When we got to Grand Havre, it was dull and grey, and there wasn't a soul by the martello tower on Rousse: yet it was alive with gay marquees and boats sailing, and the sun was shining, and all the boys I knew was there; and I could hear their thick Guernsey voices shouting 'Bien fait, Monkey! Bien fait, Monkey Le Page!' and Jim was nursing the leg of mutton as if it was a bunch of flowers, and everybody laughing. I don't know how I looked, but Neville said, 'What you thinking now, Funny-face?' as if I was a child. I didn't want to brag; yet I wanted him to know I had done something once. I said, 'They used to have the Regatta on Grand Havre, and one year I won the leg of mutton off the greasy pole.' His face wrinkled up in a grin;

and his eyes nearly disappeared into his head. 'Gaw, I can just see you doing it!' he said. He looked like a kid himself then; and usually there is something old about his face. I thought it is him who is the old one, and me the young; for the young are born old nowadays, and it is for the old to show them how to be young again.

He drove on through L'Islet and round Sandy Hook, and stopped at the end of our road. He switched on the lights; and came round and opened the door for me. I was stiff and shaky on my legs when I got out, and he was going to take my arm; but I moved away from him. He have given me too much already, I thought: I must not hang on. 'I can manage the rest of the way all right,' I said, 'don't bother to come.' 'I am seeing you safe to your door,' he said; and walked alongside me. I got the key from under the stone, and unlocked the front door; but I didn't ask him in. 'Thank you for taking me for a ride,' I said. 'Bring Adèle to see me soon.' 'We'll be along tomorrow, don't you worry,' he said. I expected him to go; but he stood there looking at me. I don't know what it was about that look, but all the love left in my old heart went out to bless him. He gave a sort of groan, and caught me in his arms and held me close. I don't know why he did that. I hadn't said a word. When he let go of me, he said, 'Are you sure you are going to be all right on your own tonight?' I said, 'I have been all right on my own up to now, haven't I?' He didn't seem to want to go. 'Well, tcheerie, then!' he said. 'Tcheerie!' I said.

I watched him go down the road and swing into his car; and the red light disappear. I came indoors and put the bar across the front door. I was on my own; but was I? I have given away, perhaps thrown away, all I've got; but I am not on my own. There is SOMEBODY HERE. He is like my father was, behind me, on the ladder. He is like my mother was, when she was cooking me ormers. He is not only my father and my mother. He is more. He in Whom we live and move and have our being. Jim is in Him. The Jerry I killed is in Him; and the boy he was buggering. Raymond and Horace are in Him. Neville is in Him; but don't know it yet. I wonder how he will shape out, that boy. He say he is a pagan; and I say he is a puritan. I hope he will not stick his heels in over getting married in a Catholic Church. He is honest in the mind. He must not expect to find what's what in any religion, or any person in this world. I hope he will not let his wild ideas run away with him. As bad as Guernsey is, I hope he will not butt in and try and change it. It will change quick enough without his help; and for the worse and worse. He must endure it. He have Adèle to love and a living to make and his pictures to paint. They are his way of prayer and praise.

I pulled the blinds down and lit the lamp. It was time for my supper; but I didn't want any. I was full of thoughts: more thoughts than I have had in all my days. I don't know how long I passed walking up and down, or resting in my chair, while thoughts came and went. It might have been an hour; for when I went outside for a piddle, it was quite dark. It was a fine clear night and the sky was full of stars. The Casquets light was doing its round: three flashes and down, three flashes and down; and far out to sea ships was passing without a sound. I don't know how many, but I must have seen a dozen, or more. Some was cargo boats with port and masthead lights, and the glow of a cabin or two, but others was great liners lit up like floating palaces on the way to America. I don't want to die, me! I want to stop alive for ever, if only to see the ships pass.

I came indoors. I made up my mind I would write this very night what have happened to me today. I have never written so much at one go. It is near on midnight, and I am writing yet; but now it is death and what come after I am thinking of. There is no after: it will only be now. I don't believe, I don't believe in the harps and the big fire, and the wheat and the tares, and the sheep and the goats; for the Day of Judgment is the Day of Forgiveness, and the repentant and the unrepentant sinner are with Christ in Paradise. I hear Christine singing:

> O Love, that will not let me go,
> I rest my weary soul in Thee!

Sing, Christine: sing! Be not bitter, as Lot's wife was. Forgive them, forgive them; for they have loved much! . . . I wish I could live my life again. I wish I could write my story again. I have judged people. I do not want to judge people. I want to bless. I want to bless every soul who have ever lived and laughed and suffered on this whore of an island, this island in the sun, this island in God's sea!

I am on the last page of the last of my three big books. Who will ever believe I have written these three big books? I want to write another. Next time I go to Town, I will buy another from the *Press*. I want to write down in it all the good thoughts I have left out in this. Now it is high time I thought of going to bed. I mustn't forget to wind the clock; and I will turn the lamp down, but not right out. I don't like it in the dark. I like to be able to see my two china dogs while I am falling asleep. Damme, I am tired, me! I will sleep well tonight, I know. Ah well, that is all for now. À la prochaine!

GUERNSEY ENGLISH

Ebenezer Le Page writes his book in a variant of Guernsey English. It is the language of a man whose unselfconscious, natural speech is the patois of his island. He imbibed it with his mother's milk: but he has never seen it in print, nor seen it spelt in English or French approximate equivalents, or in the International Phonetic Script. In his early years he read *La Gazette*, but that was printed in Standard French; though in his mind, he pronounced the words in Guernsey French. In later years he read the *Guernsey Advertiser* (eventually the *Star*) and the *Guernsey Evening Press*. Both were written in straightforward, grammatical English, but did not wean him from the basic rhythms and syntax of his patois. By the time he is writing his book, he is thinking and speaking in English with a smattering of German words inadvertently acquired, but saying the words he writes to himself with the accent and timbre of his native tongue.

Norman French, descending from the time of the Conqueror, through the Plantagenets to modern times in Guernsey, has assimilated some curious oddities on the way. For instance, 'Mette le byke contre le shed' is good Norman French, as spoken in Guernsey, and the word 'lighthouse' is invariably used in the most patois-speaking parish on the island; while 'garage' is pronounced 'garridge' in both Guernsey French and Guernsey English, though a gentleman in Town, referring to the edifice housing his most precious possession, will pronounce it 'g-ah-r-ah-ge' in French, giving it the benefit of a full blast of English ah's. St Peter Port, the Town, is the only parish to have no characteristic Guernsey speech. It is the centre of government, official, banking and trading circles, and culturally dominated by the most lamentable of the island's institutions, Elizabeth College: an English Public School. It therefore has no native language. It is English.

Elsewhere, the patois varies, if only slightly, from parish to parish. At one time, no doubt, when travel was difficult and rare, each parish had its distinctive way of speaking, and there are still faint but distinct differences between the patois spoken in St Martin's and the Câtel; but the ear-splitting division is between Les Hautes Paroisses (the High Parishes to the south and south-west: Torteval, The Forest, St Saviour's and St Peter-in-the-Wood) and Les Basses Paroisses (the Low Parishes to the north and north-east: the Vale and St Sampson's). The vocabularies vary considerably, and there are two quirks of pronunciation which make High Parish patois sound almost a different language. Les Hautes Paroisses cannot endure an 'r' to begin a word, or occur in the middle of a word with a consonant before it. It must be 'er', and the last 'r' of the word, if there is one, is casually sacrificed. Also they abhor the sound 'ch' as in 'church'. It must be 'tch'; and they will suffer tongue-twisting agonies to insert a 't' in the middle of a word. Both these quirks have to some extent spread to the north and left traces on northern pronunciation.

Ebenezer Le Page is of the north and lives at the Chouet: spelt so according to the map; but Ebenezer has never seen a map. When he writes his book, he spells the places with which he is familiar as he says them. He therefore writes Chouey, which he fondly imagines is how he says it: but it isn't. He says 'Tchouey'. It is an instance where a stray 't' has been blown down from the upper parishes. He is sometimes accidentally correct in his spelling of place-names. He spells Mont Cuet correctly, because that is how he says it; and the Bouet. His inconsistencies are reasonable. He refers to Bordeaux Harbour constantly as Birdo, never having heard it called by any other name; but Les Caves de Bordeaux, the historic wine-cellars in the Town, for which he has due reverence, he both spells and speaks in perfect French.

His few lapses into patois in the telling of his story are mostly in contexts where the meaning is apparent, if the words are incomprehensible; but now and again he may be obscure. 'J'sis fier!' is equivalent to the colloquial English phrase 'Glad to hear it!' Literally 'I am pleased!' (not proud, as French). The transcription of patois would be simpler, if its pronunciation were not so dependent on the temperament of the speaker. A bonne-femme who has a lot to say to another good woman and wants to get it ALL out at once will speak with a velocity that leaves the silent listener staggering in amazement. The pace at which the patois can be spoken by country women has to be heard to be believed. It inevitably tends to a shortening of the vowels. On the other hand, a Calvinist housewife, who gives every word full consideration before uttering it, lest it enshrine a sin, will tend to lengthen the vowels. Ebenezer plonks for a middle course when he reports his mother as saying 'chonna'. From a fast speaker, it would sound more like 'chéna', while in the case of Ebenezer's mother, it probably sounded more like 'chaw-na'.

He is inclined to be misleading as to his own pronunciation. When he writes 'Je t'aime', he hears himself saying 'Je t'oime'; and even when he admits to a Frenchman 'aimé' in his mind rhymes with 'my' and not with 'may', he retains the stem of the spelling he remembers from *La Gazette*. In the same way, he is quite justified when he insists that 'prochaine' rhymes with 'shoine' and not with 'shane'; but he omits to point out that the word he is actually saying is more accurately represented by 'per(o) choine' than 'prochoine'.

On personal names he is only guilty of minor transgressions. Sequah, the famous mesmerist who visits the island, he spells Sequois, assuming him to be French, which he had good evidence for believing. To Steve Picquet, the Hermit of Pleinmont, he grants full French honours; but The Picquet House, spelt exactly the same, he both spells and pronounces as The Picket House: which, indeed, is what its function originally was. English words he spells correctly by the simple expedient of having a dictionary.

The names of the local people he spells as in the paper, having read the Births, Deaths and Marriages since childhood; but an English reader would be surprised if he knew how some of them are being said. Tostevin may be Tos-te-vin (Phonetic), or Tôde-vin (French), or Toad-vin (English). Mr Tostevin will answer to all three. If Mr Domaille lives in the Hautes Paroisses, his name will be pronounced as though the 'll' were a 'y'. If he lives in the Basses Paroisses, the 'll' will be normal. That is, in both cases, if he is addressed in patois. If he is addressed in Guernsey English, he will be called Mr Domoile anywhere. Robin as a surname is not pronounced like the bird, but Ro'-bin; and so on and so on! Remains 'Damme!' It is not said as 'Damn me!' in English; but in one syllable, and is stronger. It derives from the Mediaeval Norman French oath 'Daume!' and, far from invoking the aid of Our Lady, is being sacrilegious.

Guernsey English is spoken in as many different ways (or, at least was in Ebenezer's formative years) as Guernsey French. King's (or Queen's) English emanated from St Peter Port. St Martin's is virtually a suburb of St Peter Port; and as the patois spoken by the country people inclined to Standard French, so the Guernsey English inclined to Good English. The north has always been the most English-speaking part of the island: but of rough English. Ebenezer owes his vocabulary and idiom to quarrymen and seamen; and his vagaries of singular and plural are as much English bad grammar as due to the anomalous features of Norman French. He retains his mannerisms: the resigned beginning 'Ah well,' of a statement from which it is abundantly clear that things are not by any means well; the tendency for a sentence, having made a statement, to turn its tail up at the end and ask the question 'Is it?'; the use of the emphatic: I am going to Town, me. Are you going to Town, you? accompanied by the appropriate gestures indicating who the you and the me are. The Guernseyman of Ebenezer Le Page's day, and before, was a tough bird on a hard, if fertile, rock, and capable and guilty of every wickedness known to man; but he was never cold, never impersonal. He had not become scientific.

The Book of Ebenezer Le Page ends some time in the mid-nineteen-sixties, judging from the people still living, or who have recently died. He is stingy with dates. It is therefore a story of the distant past; for an epoch has transpired since then. It is doubtful whether any Guernseyman alive anywhere on the island today feels and thinks like Ebenezer Le Page. St Peter Port has extended to the remotest purlieus of Rocquaine Bay, where in £30,000 houses nestling in a coign, plastic people display their impeccable selves behind picture windows to the visiting gulls.

The number of cars per mile of road is the peak in Europe. A few cows are allowed to survive for the breed and a few flowers grown for the market. Guernsey Toms maintain their public image on the mainland by being produced under dehumanised pressure of terrifying intensity. The separate villages (villes) into which the island was once divided are now merged into an amorphous mass indistinguishable from the more densely populated districts of Surrey. The cliffs, it is claimed, are unspoiled; but that is for the tourists' benefit, to leave the pests something to look at; though they have to get into a boat to do so. Otherwise, if they are lucky, they can lower their behinds into a vacated hollow of sand. Tourism is an incubus that saps the natural and spiritual vitality of the island. It pays. They say. The Town is paved with gold. It seems. Certainly nowhere else on the earth's crust in a comparable acreage are so many banking companies accommodated, unless it be in the inmost citadel of the City of London. Guernsey people are different from English. When they do a thing, they do it thoroughly. The interlocking system of committees which provides the fodder for the democratically elected and royally appointed States to regurgitate would show up Whitehall. The secret content of the statistical arcana is, of course, unknown; but it may be, like the Holy of Holies in the Temple, if the curtain were rent, it would be revealed as empty and dark. Meanwhile, the great Goddess Smug can reign supreme. The economic future of the island is mortgaged on States authority to the success of a Recreation Centre to be built at colossal expense for the benefit of the coming generation. The irony is, at the rate the island is going, by the time the Recreation Centre comes into existence, there will be no generation left to re-create: only machine-man; and machine-man cannot be re-created. He is the dead end.

I'm glad Ebenezer, who dies alive, doesn't know.*

31st July 1974

---

* Mr Harry Tomlinson, an authority on the patois, asks me to point out that Edwards' account of the difference between the high and low parish dialects is misleading. The transposition of *r* in words and the replacement of soft French *ch* (as in *chercher*) by hard English *ch* (as in *church*) are universal on Guernsey. In fact the most striking difference lies in vowel-sounds, low parish being much nearer to standard French. JF.

GLOSSARY

The French patois of Guernsey is by no means without its own literature, past or present. Its first poet, Georges Métivier (1790–1881), can stand comparison with William Barnes of Dorset and should surely be more widely known. Métivier well symbolizes Guernsey's eternal dilemma, for his master (whose spirit he at times carried brilliantly into French) was Robert Burns. The English are baffled by his language; the French, by his alien mentality. However, a very determined contemporary effort is being made to see that this vigorous tongue of the Cotentin and Channel Islands does not drown under the tide of the standard one. Phrases in that latter are in general not glossed here. I must thank Mr Harry Tomlinson for his very considerable help in compiling this glossary.

baise mon tchou: probably for *baise mon cul*, kiss my arse
boud'lo: a puppet or effigy burnt at year's end (*bout de l'an*)
cauchie: chaussée, causeway, jetty
chancre: cancre, large edible crab
chétif: stunted, puny
chonna: cela, that. *Est-che comme chonna*, Is that how it is?
connétable: in former times an honorary parish policeman
crapaud: toad, a nickname for Jerseymen. Those of Sark were 'crows'; of Guernsey, 'donkeys'.
damme: usually 'cor damme', from *corpus domini mei*, Christ's body
dido: a caper, a fuss
double: obsolete Channel Island coin, eight to the penny
douit: stream or water-course
douzaine: parish council of twelve; *douzenier*, parish councillor
écrivain: scrivener, notary public
fé: foi, faith; *ma fé*, my word
fénion: fainéant, lazy person
fiche le can: fiche le camp, clear out, buzz off
fippennies: perhaps fourpenny pieces, groats
gâche: 'a kind of bread in which yeast and fruit are used with flour, butter, milk and sugar kneaded together'
Grand Saracen: a legendary Guernsey pirate
green-bed: jonquière, a fern-littered couch used by farmers for their midday rest

Greffe: the civil and land registry office of Guernsey

greffier: registrar

grimerai: mais je te grimerai, donc, I'll scratch your eyes out

G.U.B.: the Green-house Utilisation Board, which supervised crop-growing during the German Occupation

j'sis fier: I'm glad

jurat: magistrate and member of the island electoral college

long-nose: the garfish, highly esteemed on Guernsey

mais verre dja, donc: that's very true, yes indeed

mais wai, mais nonnain: of course

Mess: monsieur

mitching: playing truant or hookey

mommet: a lifeless effigy

mon Dou: my God

mon viow: mon vieux, old man, old chap

Muratti: the Muratti Vase, a Channel Island football cup

museau: literally 'snout', in slang face or mug

orfi: another word for the garfish

ormer: the sea-ear, an abalone-like shellfish unique to the islands

par il lo: par là, that way

pied-du-cauche: pied de chausse, stocking-foot for hiding money

planchette: fortune-telling board

Pool: the deep-water part of St Peterport harbour

pourchay: pig

purain: purin, liquid manure

royne: reine, queen, also a kind of frog

Russel: the Little and the Great Russel are respectively the channels between Guernsey and Herm, and Herm and Sark

scoop: a sun-bonnet with a projecting brim over the face

spawls: stone chips or splinters

States: les états de délibération, the Guernsey parliament

té: toi, familiar form of you

terpid: trépied, trivet or gridiron over an open fire

vergée: land measurement, just over one third of an acre

verre: vrai, true

vier: vieux, old

volresse: female thief; *tu fichu petite volresse*, you wretched little thief

vraic: wrack, seaweed used both as manure and as fuel. The island's previous staple industry of stone-quarrying began to give way to the present one of producing early vegetables and flowers in the 1880s. Guernsey soil is not naturally fertile, thence the importance of vraicing, collecting shoreline seaweed. Ancient and complex laws still govern right of vraic.

wharro: a greeting, from 'what ho'